Orphan of Angel Street
&
The Narrowboat Girl

Annie Murray comes originally from Berkshire, where she grew up over an antique shop. She studied at Oxford University and has had a variety of jobs, including in factories, on an Indian railway tour, and as a journalist and a nurse. Above all, she has always written. She lived for many years in Birmingham, where all her four children were born. She now lives with her family in Reading.

Annie Murray

Orphan of Angel Street
&
The Narrowboat Girl

PAN BOOKS

Orphan of Angel Street first published 1999 by Macmillan.
First published in paperback 2001 by Pan Books
The Narrowboat Girl first published 2001 by Macmillan

This omnibus edition published 2004 by Pan Books
an imprint of Pan Macmillan Ltd
Pan Macmillan, 20 New Wharf Road, London N1 9RR
Basingstoke and Oxford
Associated companies throughout the world
www.panmacmillan.com

ISBN 0 330 43262 1

Copyright © Annie Murray 1999, 2001

The right of Annie Murray to be identified as the
author of this work has been asserted by her in accordance
with the Copyright, Designs and Patents Act 1988.

The author and publishers would like to thank Mr Hugh Nayes
for permission to quote from 'The Victorious Dead'
by Alfred Noyes, taken from *The Elfin Artist and Other Poems*
published by William Blackwood & Sons in 1920.

1 3 5 7 9 8 6 4 2

A CIP catalogue record for this book is available from
the British Library.

Printed and bound in Great Britain by
Mackays of Chatham plc, Chatham, Kent

Orphan of Angel Street

For Rachel, in memory of a Mashhad taxi ride

ACKNOWLEDGEMENTS

With special thanks to Mike Price, Jonathan Davidson, and to Birmingham City Council Library Services for their help and support.

Prologue

The woman who called herself Lily was making terrible, high sounds of pain.

''Ere – what's all the racket about? You awright in there?'

Ethel Bartlett stood outside the attic door, her breathing laborious and asthmatic. She wore a threadbare coat wrapped round a yellowed nightshirt with a filthy hem, and handknitted socks through which poked her big toes with their black, overgrown nails.

A helpless whimper of distress came through the door. Ethel knew those cries all right. She'd heard them in slum houses where she'd lived all her life: the noise of birthing women trying not to disgrace themselves or disturb their other children, defeated by the intensity of their pain.

'You can't 'ave a babby in there – not on my mattress. Think of the mess! I'm coming in to 'ave a look at yer.'

'No!' the young woman gasped from the other side of the door. 'I'm quite all right – thank you. I shall sleep now. Please – go back to bed.'

Truth to tell, Ethel was mightily tempted to do as she said. After all, it was none of her business. She'd had more than enough troubles to last one lifetime already, ta very much. It had been as clear as day to her why this well-spoken stranger was here. But that wasn't her business either of course. Push up the rent, no questions asked.

She'd passed the woman two days ago outside the

Barton Arms, and heard her enquiring of someone else in a low voice about lodgings. Ethel butted in.

'I don't take in children, you know,' she said, giving her a sharp look as if she might have a family of six stowed up her sleeves.

The white-faced woman had been wrapped in a sea-blue cloak and was carrying only a small case. She stared steadily back at Ethel. 'No. No children.' There would be no children.

Of course, as soon as she had moved in, the pregnancy had been impossible to hide. It had all happened a bit soon for Ethel, who decided to hang on to her for a while for the rent then move her on. She'd closed her mind to the fact that this stranger calling herself Lily, who barely ever set foot out of the house, would soon have to give birth.

Ethel pulled herself up straight, coughing so that phlegm rattled in her chest. If there was one thing made her feel bad it was women having babbies and all their carrying on.

'It's no good. I can't 'ave yer going on like this in my 'ouse. I'm coming in.'

As she pushed open the rough door a groan, more of mortification than pain, came from the bed. The woman tried to sit up. She had been lying on her side on the stained mattress. Though it was the coldest of nights, she had only a thin blanket for cover, and that one so darned and patched with scraps of cloth that it was impossible to tell what its colour had once been.

The face lifted from the pillow had a sharply defined nose and jaw, white, waxy skin and a head of long white-gold hair darkened by sweat.

Except for a chamber pot, Lily's holdall and a low chair beside the bed on which rested a cup and a stub of candle, the room was completely bare. Even the drip of water which on milder days seeped through the roof of the slum attic was silenced tonight, frozen to a gleaming rind on the tiles under the cold eye of the moon.

'Please go,' Lily implored. 'Leave me . . .'

But in a second she pulled herself up on her knees in an animal posture, seized by the terrible, compressing pain.

'No . . . oh no . . .' Her teeth bit down into the rotten, sawdust filled pillow as the force of it built and built in her, breath hissing through her teeth, nostrils flaring. Her head flung back, hands gripping convulsively now at the edges of the mattress.

'Oh God . . . God . . .' Her mouth stretched open as if to scream, but she let out only a breathy croak as it reached its height, and as the pain seeped away she slumped forward, too exhausted even to sob.

Moments later she found strength to push herself up and take a sip of water from the enamel cup. The hand holding the cup's blue handle was slim and smooth, not calloused by the relentless, lifelong work of the poor. But despite her soft good looks, the pale eyes were full of fear and sorrow.

The landlady stood watching her, lungs sucking in and out loud as old bellows.

'Yer can't carry on like this,' Ethel hissed. 'I mean, I ain't no good to yer. I'll get Queenie Rolf from over the way.' She turned to go, socks catching on the rough wood.

'No – I don't want – ! No one, please . . .!'

But Ethel was off down the stairs. Finally a door slammed making the cracked windows vibrate.

Alone again, Lily listened in despair to her thumping steps. She had never imagined it was possible to sink to a state of such pain and degradation. She screwed her eyes tightly shut. It was coming on again: more and yet more, like an endless road to travel with only more pain waiting at the end.

'Our Father,' her lips moved. 'Who art in Heaven, Hallowed be thy . . .'

The rest of the prayer was taken up into gasping through the next, wrenching agony.

These first days of a new century had brought no special relief to the living conditions in the tightly packed workers' houses of Britain's – in fact the British Empire's – prime industrial city. Mayor Joseph Chamberlain may have razed a great swathe of ramshackle back-to-back dwellings in order to build the grand sweep of Corporation Street in the image of a Parisian boulevard, but there were still plenty of slums left. Their raw edges rubbed almost up against the splendour of the Council House on Victoria Square.

Into these slums were packed the worker bees to staff the great industrial hive of Birmingham which gave of its creativity to the world in metalwork, engineering, jewellery and a whole host of other trades. The children who survived the insanitary conditions were raised knowing no other options but working the factories or in service to the rich until they could hand over the burden of toil to their own children, as had generations of hard-working Brummies before them.

Into one such house on the north side of the city, on an icy night in January 1900, another child was born. Attending the birth were Ethel, yawning frequently to the full stretch of her jaws, and Queenie Rolf, who was built

4

like an all-in wrestler, could drink many a man flat on his back and had tarnished silver hair long enough to sit on, which gave off a rancid smell.

The baby girl came into the world to her mother's silence. The woman's face was pulled into a helpless rictus of pain as she squatted in the candlelight, undergoing the seemingly impossible feat of pushing her child out into life. Then came the catlike cries of the baby, and the blood. Oh heaven, so much blood. Something she'd never known about, such was her innocence.

'It's a little lady!' Queenie cried, hoiking the child up by the legs and giving her backside a robust smack.

Lily lay back on the crinkled sheets of the *Birmingham Despatch* which Ethel had stuffed under her and, not looking at the child, let out a long moan of relief and sorrow.

'Yer awright now, bab,' Queenie said. With skilled hands she dealt with the umbilical cord and, a little later, the afterbirth. She washed the blood and pale waxy rime from the baby's body with water from a cracked pudding basin and was about to wrap her in an old rag when Lily protested in a weak voice.

'No – look! In there . . .'

She pointed to her leather bag. Queenie bent down and her capacious bloomers gave a loud rip.

'Oh Lor' – they'll be round me flamin' ankles in a minute!' She opened the small bag and she and Ethel exclaimed at the sight of a neatly folded and beautifully stitched layette.

'Don't take it all out,' Lily snapped, seeing Queenie's beefy, blood-smeared hands about to reach into the case. 'Please,' she added more politely. 'There are the things she'll need on top.'

5

Queenie drew out a tiny flannel vest and napkin, a strip of muslin for binding the cord and a tiny nightshirt and shawl for swaddling the child.

'She'll want all this on tonight. Proper brass monkey weather.'

Lily herself had begun shaking violently, teeth chattering.

''Ere, Ethel, fetch 'er a cuppa tea, eh? That'll be the shock of it as well as the cold, bab – takes some people that way.' She handed over the tightly wrapped baby into Lily's trembling arms, her foul breath making the young woman shrink from her. 'You'll be able to give 'er a bit o' titty now – that's what she'll be after. Then you can give yerself a good wash over and get yer 'ead down.'

'And we can all do the same,' Ethel added resentfully.

They saw though, that Lily made no attempt to suckle the child. She reached down into the case and pulled out two pound notes. Queenie's and Ethel's jaws nearly hit the floor and their hands whisked out quickly.

'Well!' Ethel's face was all gummy smiles. 'Ooh yer shouldn't really. . .' The money had already vanished into her coat. 'Ever so good of you . . .'

Queenie was stowing the money somewhere deep in the recesses of her cleavage and grinning into Lily's exhausted young face, its blonde hair matted and tumbling on her shoulders. 'You make a picture, the pair of yer. And she's as fine a babby as any I've seen into the world.'

Through chattering teeth, Lily managed to say, 'Thank you. Thank you both for your help.'

An hour later, disregarding her body's crying need for rest, Lily had washed herself as well as she could. She used two of the napkins from the layette to stem her own flow, her hands still shaking as she tried to dress herself. She could hear Ethel's snores, like those of an ancient hound, from down below.

Ethel had cleared away the newspaper from the bed and the room was as bare as it had been before. Lily sat for a few moments on the edge of the mattress in the guttering light of the candle, holding her sleeping baby, looking solemnly into the wrinkled face. The terror had gone from her eyes and now there was only an infinite sadness. She knew the child needed food, but she must resist her own instincts and deny her her mother's milk.

There was not time to sit for long and suddenly her movements were urgent again. Hanging on the back of the door was her blue cloak which she wrapped round her, pulling its velvet hood over her head. She arranged the warmly swaddled child on one arm, and taking the case with her other hand she crept as silently as she could manage down the rough stairs and let herself out into the frozen night.

As morning dawned, winter sunlight seeping through air choked with the effluents of Birmingham's hundreds of factory chimneys, the blue-brick pavements were white with frost which put an illusory shine on the city's grime. Rooftops sparkled as the sun rose, melting the frost into dark, damp patches on the tiles.

The streets gradually came to life: men in broken down boots, collars up on their coats, hurried to early morning shifts, breath swirling from them. Horses' hooves clashed over the cobbles pulling delivery carts and drays, steered by men still red-eyed with sleep as the 'lighter uppers' were extinguishing the last gas lamps street by street. Women were feeding families, sweeping out houses and calling to neighbours in their everyday work clothes: blouse, long skirt, boots, sacking apron and often a cap to top it off. Their day had long begun.

In Kent Road, Aston, the bolts were being drawn open behind the heavy doors of one of two solid, red-brick institutions which faced each other along that street. On one side of the road stood St Philip's Elementary School. Across from it, with its pointed gothic windows and wrought iron railings, Joseph Hanley's Home for Poor Girls, founded 1881, as spelt out by the brass plaque beside the front porch.

One of the heavy doors now opened and a middle-aged woman stepped out, hair caught up in a bun, clothes covered by a white apron and holding a workmanlike broom. She leant the broom against the wall and raised both hands to try and fasten some stray hanks of her hair, then stopped, catching sight of the little bundle in the narrow porch.

'Oh my Lord!' – stooping at once. 'On a night as cold as this. It'll be a miracle if . . .' She lifted the baby close to her, and was satisfied to hear her breathing. The baby woke and began to snuffle, then cry.

The woman, who was called Meg, carried the baby down the steps to the street, instinctively rocking her and saying, 'Ssssh now, will yer.' Seeing no one she could connect with an abandoned baby, in truth hardly expecting to, she turned back, shaking her head.

She didn't see from the steps of the school, a little further along, a young woman in a blue velvet cloak squatting to watch her over the low wall. One of her hands was clenched to her heart, the other pressed tight over her mouth as this stranger holding her child climbed the steps.

Meg looked round one more time and then stepped inside and closed the door. As she did so a great moan of anguish escaped from the young woman at the gates of the school.

'Looks a fine enough child,' the matron said, unwrapping the baby on a table softened only by a piece of sheet. She picked her up for a moment, carefully scrutinizing her face, and went to the window through which poured hard winter light. The baby sneezed twice. 'Doesn't seem blind, at any rate. Pale of skin though, is she not? Could almost be an albino, except the eyes look normal enough.'

'Don't we 'ave to get the doctor in?' Meg suggested nervously.

'Oh, later'll do.' Matron carried on with her inspection at the table, pulling at the naked limbs as the child yawled furiously at the cold and interference by this heavy-handed woman.

'Well, this one's got a pair of lungs and a temper to match!' she bawled over the baby's screams. 'That umbil-ical cord'll need some attention. You can take her up to the infants in a moment or two, Meg.'

Matron's hands felt along the top of the baby's head, fingers burrowing in the fuzz of gold hair for the fonta-nelles. The screaming rose higher. Meg, a softer-hearted woman, winced. This new matron, Miss O'Donnell, fresh over from the west coast of Ireland, seemed more at home with livestock of a farmyard variety than children.

'No deformities that I can see.' She started to close the white garments back over the child. 'Honest to God, leaving a child on the street on a night like the one we've just had. The ways of these people! Shouldn't be allowed to breed – someone ought to have 'em castrated, the whole feckless lot of 'em. Mind you – this one's not of bad stock, I'd say – good strong spine and limbs . . .'

Meg was waiting for Matron to say something about the quality of the child's fetlocks when the woman exclaimed, 'Well now – what's all this then?'

From where they had been tucked between the layers of soft white linen, Miss O'Donnell's thick fingers drew out a wadge of money, and folded neatly with it, a white handkerchief. The matron seized on the notes, counting them eagerly.

Meg picked up the handkerchief and held it out to Miss O'Donnell who was still taken up with the money.

'Five pound – would you believe it! Well, isn't this the fruit of genteel fornication if ever I saw it. Five pound!'

'Look – there's this too.'

Miss O'Donnell took the handkerchief. On one corner of it, embroidered in mauve silk thread, she read one word: MERCY.

'Have mercy,' Meg pondered.

'Ah well.' Miss O'Donnell tossed it back on the table, slipping the folded notes into her apron pocket. 'If she's given her nothing else at least the child has a name. Let her be called Mercy Hanley.'

Part One

Part One

Chapter One

June 1907

'Mercy – come on, 'urry up!'

The second morning bell clanged down in the hall. Even up in the dormitories they could sense Matron's impatience as she rang it. Waiting around for anything was not one of Miss O'Donnell's favoured occupations in life.

'If you're late for breakfast again there's no telling what she'll do!'

Amy, three years older, tugged the worn flannel dress which was really too small, over the younger girl's head. Mercy knew she was quite capable of dressing herself but each of them adored this game of mothering and being mothered.

Amy was kneeling, frantically trying to fasten Mercy's buttons with her bony fingers, her waif-like face puckering with frustration. Playfully, Mercy picked up the two mousey-coloured pigtails from Amy's shoulders and stuck them up above the girl's head like rabbit's ears.

'Oi – pack it in. You don't care, do yer!'

Mercy's solemn little face stared back at Amy as she tugged her plaits back into their normal position, tutting to herself. In spite of herself Amy smiled, and saw a gleam answer her in the little girl's wide grey eyes. Mercy grinned all of a sudden, an expression of complicity and mischief which she reserved for no one else but Amy, and flung her arms round her friend's shoulders, clinging tight like a baby monkey.

'Give us a love, Amy.'

'Mercy!' Amy was pushing her off, laughing. 'Yer 'opeless, yer really are. Come on.'

The last sounds of the other girls' feet were already receding down the stairs. The dormitory held fifteen girls aged between seven and fourteen. The black iron bedsteads were arranged at regimented intervals along the bare floorboards, three rows of five. There was nothing else in the room except a portrait of Queen Victoria at least twenty years before her death, a frozen expression on her face, her eyes focussed on the far distance. At the long windows hung threadbare curtains in a sun-bleached navy.

Amy seized Mercy's hand and the two of them tore along the echoing corridor, feet clattering on brown linoleum, then down the stone stairs. They managed to close the gap between themselves and the last stragglers into the dining room. Miss O'Donnell stood outside glowering.

'You two again – get along now.' She was fingering a bunch of little plaited leather strings she kept tied to her waist in case she felt the need to dole out punishment at short notice.

The dining room smelt of stale wash-cloths, disinfectant and porridge. The girls joined one of the long tables at the far end but there were not two spaces left for them to sit together. Mercy couldn't bear to be separated from Amy.

'Move up,' she hissed at another girl.

The girl shook her head.

'Move up.' Mercy gave her such a sharp ram in the ribs with her elbow that she had to stifle a squeal.

'You're a little cow, Mercy.' Rubbing her side she surrendered the space so that Mercy and Amy could sit together.

The two of them were inseparable in the orphanage, and now that Mercy had started school across the road at St Philips, Amy with her ethereal looks and Mercy, blonde and tiny, were forever together in the playground.

They'd been the closest of friends since they were tiny infants. Amy arrived at the Hanley Home aged two, the year before Mercy. As the two of them grew up they developed an almost miraculous affinity for one another. Since Amy was older she spent much of her days in a different room from the austere nursery where the babies lived out their regimented, white clad existence. But there were frequent cries of, 'Where's that child gone now?' when Amy slipped away into their territory of strained, milky foods and plump hands to find baby Mercy. Miss Eagle, with her assistants, was in charge of the babies. She came back into the nursery one day to find Amy sitting beside Mercy who was then about a year old, a heavy scrubbing brush gripped between both hands, trying to brush Mercy's mop of hair with it. Mercy was crowing with delight, hands waving. The tiny girls' eyes were fixed laughingly on each other's. Miss Eagle slapped Amy hard and sent her away.

'We thank Thee Lord for these Thy gifts . . .' Miss Rowney, the Superintendent of the Home intoned piously over the meagre breakfast. The girls stood motionless. Mercy saw a fly looping round Miss Rowney's head and hoped it would fly up her nose. The live-in staff ate together at a smaller table near the door: Miss Rowney, Miss O'Donnell, Miss Eagle and Mrs Jacobs – Meg, who had first found Mercy. Others, like Dorothy

Finch, the kindest of the staff, only worked there in the daytime.

The tin bowls clattered on the tables and one of the older girls doled out a ladle of watery porridge into Mercy's bowl. Above the fireplace hung two small Union Jacks and a portrait of King Edward's well-fed face after the Coronation in 1901.

They were expected to eat in silence, so the chief sound was the tinny rattle of spoons in the bowls. Mercy wrinkled her nose at Amy. The porridge was lukewarm and slimy on her tongue. She dripped it off her spoon mouthing, 'lumpy' and Amy grimaced back. The food left white tidemark moustaches on their top lips. Even though it was thin, lumpy and tasteless they ate every scrap, for lunch would almost invariably be watery stew and tea a thin soup.

Mercy looked round the table as she ate and Lena, the girl opposite, pulled a face at her. Mercy didn't care, and stuck her tongue out until Amy nudged her to stop although she continued to stare back defiantly. Mercy and Amy's closeness seemed to rile some of the others. Affection was very thin on the ground here, living in a house with sixty other girls with no one to provide real care or attention. Maybe the others were jealous. But Mercy didn't bother about what they thought. She'd got Amy and that was all that mattered. When they'd finished eating she pushed her hand, warm and slightly tacky with porridge, into Amy's under the table.

Miss Rowney stood up, chair scraping the floor.

'Get wiped up now and stay sitting for a few moments. I've got something to say to you all.'

The girl in charge of each table hastily smeared the pale globules away with a sour-smelling cloth. They waited.

Miss Rowney walked to the middle of the dining room and stood looking round at them. She seemed rather excited about something and was massaging the back of her left hand with her right, her expression coy with pride.

'Now girls, today I have a very special announcement.' Her voice echoed slightly. 'I'm going to read out the names of eight girls, and I'd like them to come up here to the front and stand in a neat line.' She pronounced the names rather grandly, as if they were the titles of queens.

'Lisa Maskell, Josie Flanagan, Sarah Smith . . .' The last, and youngest on the list was Amy Laski.

Amy glanced in bewilderment at Mercy, and, pulling her hand away, obediently joined the line of girls with their backs to the staff table.

'I am delighted to tell you that with the help of the John T. Middlemore Homes we have secured places for eight girls to begin a new and rewarding life. So—' She beamed round at them. 'On 9 July, Lisa, Josie, Sarah . . .' she reeled off their names again . . . 'will all be travelling on a big ship across the Atlantic Ocean to *Canada* . . .' this was spoken in fairy tale tones '. . . to a place called New Brunswick where they will all be given homes by some kind and godly Canadian people.'

She put her hands together and everyone saw they were expected to clap, which they did as mechanically as striking clocks, watching the faces of the eight girls, the emotions of wonder, pride, bewilderment, uncertainty, flitting across them like summer clouds.

You could hear her screams from one end of the orphanage to the other.

The other girls were ready, regimented in crocodiles downstairs in the long dayroom where all chairs had been pushed to one side.

'She's gunna get it good and proper now,' a snotty-nosed little girl called Dulcie whispered to to the child she was paired with. 'They'll give 'er a right belting.'

The staff, trying to keep the other children quiet and orderly, listened with tense faces. Mercy again. Today of all days. A couple of the girls started giggling and were given a sharp smack round the back of the head for their cheek. They were all scrubbed clean after last night's toiling with tin baths of tepid water, last minute rough wiping of porridge from faces after breakfast, the starching of pinafores, plaiting of hair and polishing of little boots, so that they were not just Sunday clean, but cleaner than ever the whole year round.

'Now just you remember I want to see smiles on all your faces,' Miss O'Donnell boomed at them after breakfast. 'When Mr Hanley graces us with his presence today he'll not want to see sullen faces round him, but a good example of Christian Cheerfulness. Just you remember – if it wasn't for Mr Hanley, none of youse would have a place to lay your heads or fodder in your bellies. Would you now?' Silence. 'WOULD YOU?'

'NO, MISS O'DONNELL,' they all droned, sitting in lines down the long tables.

But now, here was Mercy, splayed across her bed, clinging to the iron bedstead and screaming as if someone was trying to murder her. The white-blonde hair was slipping out from its shoulder length plaits, her face a livid pink, and she was violently kicking her legs. Miss Eagle, who had been despatched to try and force her back under control, could barely even get near her.

'Will you stop that!' Miss Eagle, a thin, flint-cheeked

18

woman tried to catch hold of Mercy round her waist and was rewarded by a backward sock in the face as the girl loosed one of her hands for a second and flailed it behind her.

'You miserable little bugger! You needn't think I'm going to ruin my best dress just because of you – 'ere, you can 'ave another of these!' She landed a hard slap on one of Mercy's bare legs which produced only more anguished yells and metallic screeching from the bed-springs. The child was not big for her age, but she was a red hot wire of fury and the energy in her was extraordinary.

'Miss O'Donnell'll be up here any minute,' the woman hissed in her ear, trying to prise Mercy's hands away from the bedstead. 'And then you'll be for it. I 'ope she flogs you within an inch of your life, you evil little vermin.'

She managed to yank Mercy off the bed and started slapping her, only to have the child slide through her hands like blancmange and continue raging on the floor, pummelling it with her fists.

The woman landed a violent kick in Mercy's ribs and suddenly everything went quiet. Mercy gasped, then groaned. To Miss Eagle's satisfaction she at last saw tears start to roll down that normally inscrutable little face. The child finally opened her mouth in a roar of pain.

'What in the name of God is going on?' Miss O'Donnell loomed in the doorway of the dormitory, walking stiffly as if she were attired from head to foot in cardboard. Her long black outfit was topped by a black feather-trimmed bonnet and her cheeks, already florid, were plastered with circles of rouge. She was quivering, more with nerves it seemed than anger.

'D'you not know himself will be here on the hour?

Get that child downstairs immediately and stop this horrible commotion she's making!'

Miss Eagle blushed a nasty red. 'I can't. Since Amy Laski went she's been impossible to handle.'

'In God's name she's only – what? – seven years old and a third the size of you!' Miss O'Donnell clearly had no intention of risking the pristine state of her garments either. 'If you can't sort her out go and get Dorothy Finch. She's the only one can knock any sense into that one.'

Mercy was left alone on the cold stone floor. She raised her head and looked up, surrounded by the black bedsteads with their threadbare candlewick covers from which the colours had long been washed out.

Her large grey eyes looked dazed, as if she'd returned from another existence somewhere. She could find no satisfactory way of expressing her need, her sense of being utterly lost. She longed to be held, loved, cared for, yet so alone was she in the world, had seen so little of such care that she scarcely knew for what it was she hungered. Pain speared at her ribs. She lowered her head again and started banging her forehead with a steady rhythm against the floor, muttering to herself, 'Hate you, hate you, hate you . . .' This was how Dorothy Finch found her when she arrived, flustered, upstairs.

'Mercy! Oh Mercy, you silly babby. You've got to stop this!' She swooped down and pulled the girl off the floor hearing her give a squeal of pain. 'Mr Hanley's coming today and the minister's already 'ere. They're all waiting for you. Quick, wipe your face on this.' The woman held out a hanky and brushed the dust from

Mercy's clothes. She avoided looking straight at Mercy, as if unable to face the raw pain in her eyes.

Dorothy had come to work at the Hanley Home when Mercy was still the smallest of infants, about four months old. She had watched her grow into a toddler with a solemn, appraising face and dead straight hair. Dorothy remembered how Mercy had gone everywhere with her hand thrust into Amy's, looking up at her with adoration and absolute trust, trotting along beside her to keep up.

When Amy left, for three days Mercy had spoken barely a word. At first no one noticed, not even Dorothy, for she was always a withdrawn child. But one day when the older ones had gone to school, Dorothy found her lying on Amy's old bed, absolutely silent and still, her face a blank.

'Mercy?' Dorothy had come upon her cheerfully. 'You didn't ought to be 'ere, eh, bab? You'll get it from Miss O'Donnell if she catches you!'

Mercy raised her arm back behind her head and started banging her wrist, hard on the metal bedhead until she cried out and there were tears in her eyes.

'What the 'ell d'you do that for?' Dorothy shouted at her in alarm. 'What you playing at? Go on, get off with you downstairs. I've got quite enough to get on with without you playing me up!'

The rages began and grew wilder. They could strike any time and burn through Mercy with an intensity that no one could control or penetrate. They found her throwing her body about, screaming, biting, banging her arms or legs or head on hard objects.

'She's got the devil in her,' Miss O'Donnell decreed. 'Plenty of hard work, that's what she needs.' She set out to file down Mercy's will and temper by physically exhausting her. As soon as they were big enough to manage it the girls were expected to carry out nearly all the domestic chores. Mercy spent long periods of her days mopping floors, scrubbing floors, polishing floors. But still her unhappy soul flared in outbursts of pain and frustration. Only Dorothy could soothe her, by grasping the little girl's flailing body, holding tight and talking about any old nonsense until the fight suddenly dropped out of her and she surrendered to being quiet, being held.

'Come on, stand proper now,' Dorothy urged. 'Look at the state of you!' With her deft fingers she straightened out Mercy's clothes. There wasn't time to retie Mercy's plaits and the little girl looked quite dishevelled with her rumpled hair and blotchy face. She was small for her age, and with her pale skin and large eyes, very like a delicate, china doll.

'Come on – Violet's waiting,' Dorothy fibbed. 'She wants to walk in with you.'

Silent now, one hand clenched to her burning ribs, Mercy followed her along the corridor to the main stairs. From the dayroom they heard a man's voice in the hall and the eager-to-please twittering of the women, '. . . so nice . . . such an honour . . .' before the nod was given to file into the hall under the Union Jack.

Chapter Two

A visit to the orphanage by its benefactor Joseph Hanley was a rare occasion. His Home for Poor Girls (1881) had been built shortly after the Home for Poor Boys, a mile further out of the city. Joseph Hanley had been in his forties then, and was now a rather corpulent sixty-six-year-old, who had recently passed on his brass foundry on Rea Street to his twin sons and moved to the clearer air of the Staffordshire countryside.

Every so often he made ritual visits to his 'ministries'. He was an intensely religious man, a passionate noncon-formist who had incorporated in the homes a more than average number of washrooms to inculcate Cleanliness and Godliness, and established close ties with the Baptist church on the Witton Road, roughly halfway between his two institutions. On most Sundays the girls and boys – about fifty of each – were frogmarched along to morning worship, swelling the local congregation no end. Every six weeks or so the minister, Mr Ezra Vesey, held a service for them in the orphanage.

Mercy sat cross-legged on the floor which smelt of fresh polish. The staff sat on chairs at the ends of the rows of children. There were windows along one side of the hall and a longer one at the end through which could be seen young horse chestnut trees, the late summer sun-light casting the restless shadows of leaves on the parquet floor. It was on this window that Mercy kept her gaze throughout most of her time spent in the hall, on its shadowland of changing light.

Violet, who was eight, turned and peered at her to see if she was still crying, but the tears were wiped away now, and Mercy's face solemn, eyes raised to the light. Violet elbowed her in the ribs to get her attention.

Mercy's face contorted. 'Ow!' It was almost a yelp. 'Gerroff!'

Immediately Miss Eagle's head snapped round at the end of the row, her face wearing a vindictive scowl. You again, it said. I'm going to get you later on.

Mercy stared hard at the window. When I'm a princess, she thought, I'll show all of them ... I'll have lovely clothes and a hat for every day of the year and my own carriage and Miss Eagle'll be on 'er hands and knees doing my floors all day every day and I'll have a great big horse whip to keep 'er in order. And I'll keep the people I want living there. And the only one who can do nowt is Amy 'cos she'll have her own rooms in my castle, with ...

'Stand up!' Violet was pulling at her pinafore. Everyone else was on their feet and the almost tuneful piano started to thump out, '*What a Friend we have in Jesus ...*'

The younger girls had been placed nearer the back of the hall, no doubt as they were expected to be less well behaved than the older ones. Standing on tiptoe Mercy could just glimpse Mr Hanley, crouched in a special chair at the front. She could see the bald, porridge-coloured circle at the back of his head and his stooped little shoulders. Every now and then he let out a wheezy cough.

Mr Vesey was a very tall man with almost no hair left on his head but lots on his face, as if it had somehow slipped down round his chin, and great big spidery hands. He sang much louder than everyone else except Miss

O'Donnell who almost seemed to be vying with him, loudly and off-key, the feathers on her hat quivering.

'This is the day that the Lord hath made!' Mr Vesey declared in a nasal Rochdale accent. 'We shall rejoice and be glad in it.' His hands traced webs in the air.

Eventually they sang 'All Things Bright and Beautiful' and the piano plinked out the tune until they ran out of verses.

'Now girls.' Miss Rowney moved as if on wheels to the front of the hall. She had a gruff voice, more like a man's. 'Before we go from here you are all going to come to the front and shake Mr Hanley by the hand to show him how ve-ery much you all appreciate all he has done for you. Come on now – from the front!' She beckoned with a beefy finger, directing the older girls to move forwards. Mercy couldn't hear what Mr Hanley was saying to them, only the high, squeaky tone of his voice. Inside she boiled and bubbled. I hate . . . I hate . . .

They filed slowly along the middle, shook hands and dispersed round the sides, some making a little bob, almost a curtsey, all trying to turn their mouths up as hard as they could. Miss Rowney and Miss O'Donnell stood by watching with steam-powered smiles as well.

Mr Hanley sat enthroned on his chair, scrawny legs placed apart to fit his well-rounded belly between, his weskit buttons laced with a gold chain which strained across his front. He had an amiable, ruddy face and, as she drew nearer, Mercy saw that one of his eyes was clear, the other rheumy, and he kept dabbing at it with a large white handkerchief.

A girl called Daisy was in front of her. Shyly she held out her hand.

'Well, my dear,' Mr Hanley said. This didn't seem to

25

be about to lead to anything else so Daisy gave a confused little bob and scuttled off.

'Ah,' Mr Hanley said as Mercy stood before him. 'What a pretty little lass.'

'Yes, now.' Miss Rowney suddenly swooped forward, gushing at Mr Hanley in a voice that suggested he was very sick, very foolish or possibly both. 'We wanted to tell you particularly about Mercy. She's a true foundling. Abandoned at birth – not even a full name. So in your honour, sir, we have taken the liberty of giving her the surname Hanley.' Miss Rowney smiled with great satisfaction at having conferred this extraordinary favour.

Mr Hanley saw two large, and disconcertingly cold grey eyes fix on him, fringed by pale eyelashes.

'Well, my dear,' he said again. 'So you're my kith and kin, so to speak!' He gave a snuffling laugh. 'Won't you shake hands, child?'

A gnarled hand with veins like purple rivers came towards Mercy. She stared at the hand, looked hard for a moment into Mr Hanley's eyes, then caught hold of the end of his fingers. All around the chapel every person's mouth jerked open into a horrified, gasping Oh! as Mercy leant down slowly, almost reverently, and sank her teeth into the loose, fleshy bit between Mr Hanley's finger and thumb. His skin felt stringy between her teeth. The old man let out a yelp of pain and surprise, trying to fling her off.

Mercy's next view of life was of the wooden floor rushing past her eyes, door jambs, alternating shadow and brighter light and the furious swish of black taffeta as Miss O'Donnell seized hold of her and swung her upside down over one shoulder like a newborn calf. The other girls' heads swivelled, some apprehensive, some gloating, as Miss O'Donnell speedily whisked her offensive presence from the hall.

The cellar was almost completely dark. Only the palest lines of light seeped round the upper part of the door.

Mercy sat crouched on the wide top step right next to the door, arms clenched round her knees, rocking back and forth. She was hurting so much, her ribs from Miss Eagle's kicking, her cheeks raw from Miss O'Donnell's violent slaps after she had dumped her down hard on the floor outside the cellar door with a force that jarred right up into her back.

'There – you evil little rat!' she snarled between clenched teeth, her great hands slapping her again and again. 'You don't deserve to live – you're a bloody disgrace. I've half a mind to throw you back on the streets where you came from and good riddance. Now then.' She unlocked the cellar and yanked Mercy up into her arms again, holding her with her head facing down. 'Right down at the bottom, that's where you can go, my girl.' She clumped down bluebrick steps into the dark, cavernous cellar. Inside were ghostly shapes, some long and thin, the shadowy outline of an old mangle against the far wall, then fading to a solid blackness at the back. Miss O'Donnell forced her down on the damp floor against the wall.

'And you can stay in there 'til you rot!'

With heavy tread she hurried back up the steps and slammed the door with such force that the planks reverberated. Mercy heard the bolt rattle across. And then it was dreadfully quiet. All she could hear was her own jagged breathing and a slow dripping sound from somewhere in the blackness.

She stretched her eyes wide, trying to see any speck of light, but there was none at first. After a few moments, at the far end she made out a block of grey, strained light from a grating on the street. Mercy pulled herself up while she still had the courage to move and crawled up the cellar steps where there was a crack of light from under the door. She sat on the top step, hugging herself. From here she couldn't see the ghostly light from the grating. The darkness in front of her was like a gaping well, full of invisible, whispering presences.

She felt a twinge in her belly and realized her bladder was urgently full. Pulling her legs in even closer, she sank her teeth into her forearm, rocking back and forth, making a little moaning noise to herself, needing to hear a sound from somewhere because if she stopped it was so silent and there would be nothing but the dark. She clenched her eyes shut and kept rocking, rocking . . .

'I want—' A whisper escaped from her and became part of the rhythm. 'I want I want I want . . .' as her back banged harder against the rough wall. At first it was angry, hard rocking that jarred the breath in her lungs. 'I want I want . . .' A cry she had never been able to use in her life escaped from her 'Mom!' And then, 'Amy . . . Amy . . .'

But Amy was gone to be a servant in Canada. She'd left weeks ago via Liverpool, with a tin trunk, cloth bag and a label on her coat. In the hall they'd sung 'God Be with You 'til We Meet Again', and after, Amy had hugged her tight and told her she'd always love her and be her friend.

She rocked more gently, tired, her tiny body aching, sobbing at last, so that tears fell on her cotton pinafore and she had to wipe her nose on it, having no hanky. Mixed in with her rage and grief was the thought of the spread of cold meats and salads, of pudding and cakes laid out upstairs, of all the other girls with their hair ribbons, eating plates of this out of the ordinary food, when every other day it was stew, stew, stew. Dorothy had told her there would be jellies: quivering castles of ruby red, royal purple of crushed blackcurrants, the cool sweet smoothness of it down your throat . . .

She cried herself to exhaustion, the sobs making her ribs hurt even more. Her belly was tight and uncomfortable. Putting her hands down on each side of her to shift her weight, her left hand met something long and soft, and she jerked it away, panting with revulsion, breaking out in a sweat. Her palm was coated in a slimy stickiness. She shifted quickly to the other end of the step, wiping the hand frantically on her pinner. All those things, those shapes, down there, that drip, drip, drip . . . things she couldn't see, were they getting closer, were they, were they? And the slimy thing next to her, where was it, what was it doing? Panic swelled right up into her throat until she was gasping with it, and she could hold on no longer. The warm rush of urine, so dreadfully wet, soaked through her bloomers, through the skirt of her dress, fast turning cold on her skin and splashing her ankles, nasty-smelling. She whimpered in distress, holding her knees tightly with her arms, not daring to move to the dryer part of the steps because that slimy thing was there waiting for her.

The door seemed the one solid thing of safety and she thrust her fingers in her ears, and pushed her head down on her knees making herself keep her eyes shut.

If I can't see them they're not there, she said to herself. Nothing's there. Just me, that's all. Nothing can hurt me. Nothing can ever hurt me.

She rocked herself until her arms slid down again and

circled her legs, her head lolled sideways against the door and she fell asleep.

The clatter of the bolt being drawn back came so loud after the long, long silence. Mercy jumped, still half asleep, and immediately tensed, cowering away from the door in dread as to what was out there.

'Mercy?' Dorothy Finch's scared face peered in at her. She spoke in a whisper. 'Oh, you silly, silly girl. What the 'ell did you go and have to bite Mr Hanley for? What's 'e ever done to you, eh? You're your own worst enemy, you are. 'Ere—' She held out a chipped white bowl. 'Get this down you. I'll be skinned alive if Miss O'Donnell catches me giving yer it.'

She saw that the little girl's eyes, screwed up against the light, were fixed on something at the other end of the step. A huge, pale brown slug lay oozing beside the door frame, and Mercy shuddered violently. She was shamefully aware of her wet clothes.

'Ugh!' Dorothy flicked the slug down the steps with the toe of her boot. She held out the bowl and Mercy saw two jewelled scoops of red jelly in the bottom.

Dorothy knelt down, her lithe body dressed in a high-collared white blouse tucked into an ankle-length black skirt. Her long brown hair was pinned up becomingly above an almost pretty face. She took in the little girl's sorrowful expression, her blotchy cheeks.

'Got anything to say then?'

Mercy swallowed a big gulp of jelly and without looking up said, 'Ta.'

'Thank you, you're meant to say.'

'Thank you.'

'You're a proper nib, aren't you? What d'you do it for, Mercy?'

She straightened up suddenly in alarm. Someone was coming.

'Oh my God!' Dorothy stepped inside the cellar, pulled the door closed. 'Ooh – ain't it dark in 'ere?' she whispered. 'Pongs a bit too!' She squatted down next to Mercy who continued, undeterred, to shovel jelly into her mouth.

The tread came closer and stopped outside the door. Whoever it was let out a hearty belch. Mercy snorted with laughter. Dorothy clamped a hand over the child's mouth, praying that whoever it was hadn't heard. There came the sound of metal buckets clanging together and by what seemed a miracle, whoever it was went away again.

Mercy and Dorothy exploded with giggles.

'You don't care, do yer!' Dorothy pushed the door open and ruffled Mercy's hair. 'You just don't give a monkey's you don't. Look, I've got to get out of here. Give us your bowl. You're going to have to stay put in 'ere though, Mercy, 'til Miss O'Donnell comes to get you out. And when she does you'd better start behaving yourself or she's going to have you down on your hands and knees scrubbing floors the rest of your days!'

Before she shut the door again she looked down at Mercy with solemn eyes. Suddenly she swooped forward and kissed her cheek. 'Not long now, eh? Just hold on.'

The door closed again. It was bedtime when Miss O'Donnell came. What she wanted was Mercy penitent, broken. But when Mercy looked up at her the look of brazen defiance was burning there, fuelled by a bowl of red jelly and the knowledge that there was one single person at Hanley's who cared about her.

At least I've got Dorothy, she said to herself as she lay in bed in the dormitory that night. She stroked the spot on her cheek where Dorothy kissed her. Dorothy's got time for me.

Chapter Three

November 1911

'Mercy?' Miss Eagle's voice was shrill with disbelief. 'Mercy Hanley?'

'Do we have any other girl called Mercy in our care?' Miss Rowney asked dryly. She was at the desk in her sitting room-cum-office, her thin hair pulled into a tight knot which made her already large-boned face look even heavier. Miss O'Donnell and Miss Eagle stood before her on a rug so threadbare that patches of the wooden floor could be seen through it. However much they felt obliged to fête Mr Hanley for his generosity, money was nevertheless tight in this establishment.

The sky outside was so thick with cloud that the room was almost dark and there was no fire in the grate, although it was viciously cold.

'But—' Miss Eagle tried to find a way of protesting this madness without sounding thoroughly impertinent. 'Mercy's, well – she's . . .'

'A damn nuisance, so she is,' Miss O'Donnell butted in with no hesitation, hands on her staunch hips. 'She's a flaming little wildcat and now's our chance to get shot of her.'

'We thought boarding out might be the way to settle her down,' Miss Rowney said, attempting to sound a little more professional. 'I mean, heaven knows we're hardly beseiged with requests for foster children. It ought to be a good chance for her. The lady asked for a girl of Mercy's age – well, perhaps what she meant was a little older, but no matter, Mercy's nearly twelve. And she seemed firm enough of character. She has a respectable address in, let's see—' She picked up a sheet of paper and held it at arm's length, squinting through pince-nez. 'Handsworth. Husband employed in a whip factory, I understand. No children. We'll have the place inspected of course . . .'

'We should've packed her off to Canada with the last lot.' Miss O'Donnell strode over to the window and stood looking at the murk outside. It was beginning to rain. 'Heaven knows, I shouldn't mind going to Canada. See a bit of grass and some trees for a change instead of this filth-ridden hole with its strikes and its wife murderers.'

Last year's execution of a Dr Hawley Harvey Crippen who'd deposited his slaughtered wife's body under the floorboards was still playing on Miss O'Donnell's mind as a sign of England's depravity. Even the lavish Coronation of King George V had not persuaded her she was any better off living in the heart of the Empire.

Miss Rowney ignored her. 'We can get this settled as quickly as possible. As for the inspection – I'll have to do it myself. We're not Dr Barnardo's after all – doctors for this and inspectors for that.' She tutted. 'We're short enough this week, with Dorothy Finch taking bad.' Suddenly she waved her hand at the other two women. 'All right, all right, you can go. I'll sort it out.'

The children stood with faces pressed against the railing of St Philip's playground.

'Look!' a little boy shrieked with excitement. 'It's coming – it's getting closer!'

In the road outside a horse clopped slowly past along the cobbles, pulling a dray loaded with barrels. But behind, gaining on the stately pace of the cart, was the object of their excitement.

''Ark at it go!' the boy shouted.

'Look at them wheels!'

'Ain't it beautiful? Oi – give us a ride, mate!'

The Austin motor car bowled past, bodywork gleaming even in the dull light. The wheels were like small cartwheels coated in rubber, and the the two behatted men sat high above the road. They kept their faces turned to the front, not heeding the children's cheers and claps as they leant on the railings straining to get the last views of the automobile before it turned the corner.

'Eh – who's that shovin'? Pack it in!'

There came a jostling and a very forceful pushing from the back of the tangle of children, and one of the smallest girls, all sharp elbows and knees, forced her way to the front, supple as a fish.

'Who d'you think you are, Mercy?' One of the boys pulled her arm, trying to force her back. 'Barging in – we all want to see.'

The boy found the girl's strange, catlike eyes turned on him and a second later received a kick on the shin so hard it brought tears to his eyes and he doubled up to rub his leg. 'Oi, 'er kicked me, 'er did!'

''Ere—' The boy drummed up a group of his pals as the others started to move away. 'That Mercy didn 'alf give me one.'

'She's a vicious little cow!'

'Come on – let's get 'er.'

She saw them coming, circling her. No one stood up for her. The other children watched apprehensively.

Mercy stood quite still, arms crossed tight over her

chest. Her hair was longer now and the bright plaits reached halfway down her back. She was neat-looking as ever, frock straight and clean and hanging below her knees, feet together in her little boots, eyes flaring defiance.

'Come on then, Mercy,' one of the boys goaded as they danced round her. They started to run at her, mocking, then retreating back. 'Gunna shout at us? Gunna scream? Go on – let's see yer, Mercy-Nursie!'

The taunting children circled, faces moving in and out of her view. 'Mercy-Nursie!' they chanted, 'Mercy-Nursie, the Hanley bastard!' Their voices meaner and meaner when they met no satisfying response, no tantrum or any sort of reaction, however much they goaded her about carrying the name of the orphan's patron.

Mercy looked up beyond them towards the red-brick school building. The freezing buffeted her raw cheeks. She felt she was watching everything from the other end of a long, long tube, like looking down through a chimney, the children's faces turned up towards her from several storeys below. She felt nothing for them. She had learned to retreat somewhere deep into herself that no one could touch; nothing they said or did could hurt her. What she could feel, most immediately, was the itch of her rough wrapover vest round the tops of her arms, how her left boot was pinching her burning chilblains, the rough ache of her sore throat. But the other children she let flit around her, distant as summer swallows.

One of the boys shoved Mercy's shoulder hard and she reeled backwards, tumbled on to the hard ground, skinning her elbow.

'Look, she's gunna blart now!' one of them cried triumphantly as tears of pain sprang into Mercy's eyes.

'Come on, let's see yer. 'Er's like a statue – can't move 'er bleedin' face!'

I'm not crying for 'em, Mercy vowed. I'm never doing anything they want – never.

She lay on the ground and curled into a ball on her side, face hidden in her hands. If she couldn't see them they weren't there. She'd killed them. They didn't exist.

The handbell to summon them all inside began ringing, growing louder as one of the teachers, Mr Paget, came out, his arm beating the bell up and down in the icy wind.

'What's all this?' He strode across to the ring of children. 'Get inside the rest of you. Go on – hurry up.' The children fled, giggling with relief at avoiding trouble.

'On your feet, child.' As he bent down Mr Paget saw a dark, creeping line of blood along the girl's wrist. With impatience he pulled her hands from her face and saw her nose was bleeding, huge, plum-coloured drops falling on her school dress. Though she had tears in her eyes she stared up at him with that blank yet insolent look of hers which seldom failed to aggravate.

'What've you done?' Mr Paget fished round irritably in his jacket pocket to find his handkerchief for Mercy to hold against her nose. 'Someone hit you?'

Mercy just looked at him.

'Well did they?'

'No.'

'No, Mr Paget.' He stared at her, tight-lipped. Who could fathom this child?

'We've all had enough of this, Mercy. You cause nothing but trouble. I'm sending you back across the road and I don't want to see you in school for the rest of this week.'

This was Wednesday. A terrible crime, the worst, being

37

sent home from school. It 'besmirched' the good name of the Hanley Homes if they got into any trouble outside.

Mr Paget added grimly, 'We'll let Matron deal with you as she sees fit.'

Miss O'Donnell's footsteps were coming closer.

'Come here, child!' She loomed into view along the corridor, hair wrapped in a starched white cap.

Not the cellar! Mercy's heart seemed about to leap out of her chest. She felt as if she'd fall down if she moved, but she turned and forced herself to walk towards the huge woman who was bearing down on her.

Miss O'Donnell stopped with a swish of skirts and apron and gaped at the girl. Mercy's nose had stopped bleeding, but it felt dry and caked up with blood and she was still dabbing at it with Mr Paget's hanky. She lowered her head and closed her eyes tight, waiting.

'Lord above, we can't have you looking like that – look at all those stains!' Mercy opened her eyes cautiously to find Miss O'Donnell bent over and staring right into her face. She could see the enormous bready pores in the woman's nose. 'Come on, girl, quickly now, off with that frock and we'll find something presentable to put on. It's a blessing they sent you home or we shouldn't stand a chance.'

Matron was hustling her along towards the staircase, prodding her in the back every few steps as if she were a work-shy donkey. Mercy was more astonished than she had ever been before in her life. She'd done the worst thing she could do and Miss O'Donnell not only wasn't punishing her, she was being nice!

'Skin a rabbit!' Matron's bosom veered alarmingly upwards as she pulled Mercy's blood-spattered dress over her head as if she were a five-year-old. 'Now then, let's get you cleaned up.' She looked the girl over, pulled the edge of her vest to see if there were bruises on her torso. Fortunately she seemed clear, although her elbow was scabbed.

'You, Mercy, are going to start a new life today,' she explained, kneeling in front of the child and vigorously washing her face.

'A lady is going to take you away from here to board out with her. She has no children, so she's giving you a great opportunity which you are to make the most of, d'you understand? She has a very respectable house in Handsworth.' Rather bare and sober, Miss Rowney had reported. Perhaps this was some austere religious way of living? But respectable enough, and the woman seemed very keen.

'You'd better behave yourself, Mercy,' Miss O'Donnell threatened suddenly. She was buttoning Mercy into a plain grey tunic several sizes too big for her. Mercy smelt her bitter breath as she hissed, 'If you play this Mrs Gaskin up and make her send you back here, I can promise you, I'll make sure your life isn't worth living.'

'Well, what a pretty little girl!'

After getting cleaned up Mercy had been given a thin piece of bread and butter and a cup of milk which almost made her forget the sore throat. Now she stood feeling very small and bewildered on the holey rug in Miss Rowney's office while the three of them stared at her.

Miss Rowney and Miss O'Donnell were beaming away at her as if their hearts were going to explode with love and pride. And that Mrs Gaskin was smiling for all she was worth too.

'You'll find she's an intelligent child,' Miss Rowney was saying. 'Doing so well at school. Of course, all our children attend St Philip's Elementary School across the way, and Mercy's progressed so very well – learned to read in record time, I gather.'

'Oh well, that's very good,' Mrs Gaskin said, sounding as if her mind was on other things completely. 'She must be a credit to you. Bit small though, ain't – isn't she?'

There was something funny about the way this Mrs Gaskin was talking, Mercy thought. It was like the way Dorothy and Miss Eagle talked but sort of poshified.

'Small perhaps, but very strong and wiry. Come and shake hands, Mercy,' Miss Rowney instructed her. 'Mrs Gaskin has very kindly offered to take you in and she will in effect be your new mother, so you have to be a very good girl for her.'

Mercy stepped forward and shook Mrs Gaskin's cold, fat hand. The woman had black hair which was taken up under a wide, flat hat perched on top of her head, and she was wearing a long, jade green skirt and jacket, which strained across her hips, the buttons of the jacket appearing quite desperate to release themselves. Mercy looked up into a face with dark, rather hooded eyes, round cheeks which protruded more as the woman smiled down at her, and thick lips between which Mercy could see square yellow teeth.

'Well, say something, Mercy!' Miss O'Donnell urged her.

'Where's Dorothy?' Her voice had risen high in panic.

Miss Rowney laughed nervously. 'Dorothy is one of our staff,' she explained to Mrs Gaskin. 'Mercy is rather attached to her. As you know, Mercy, Dorothy's very poorly at the moment – touch of pneumonia, I gather.

She won't be with us for some time. Never mind that dear. Is there anything you want to ask Mrs Gaskin?'

Mercy looked up again into the face of this woman whose relentless yellow smile was beating down on her. She could think of nothing to ask about another life, for until now she had known only the almost unchanging rhythm of the orphanage and school. All she wanted was Dorothy.

Eventually she said, 'Do I 'ave to take my bed?'

More tittering from the women.

'It's awright, bab,' Mrs Gaskin said, her posh accent slipping for a moment. 'I've got a bed for you at home. And you'll have some pretty clothes for yourself and some toys. We'll 'ave a lovely time together, won't we?' She turned to Miss Rowney and asked with sudden abruptness, 'Can I take 'er now then?'

''Er, yes – a few papers to sign of course. Matron, could you make sure Mercy's things are ready?'

'Oh they are,' Miss O'Donnell said fervently. 'Yes, all shipshape.'

Miss Rowney handed Mrs Gaskin her payment for Mercy's first week. 'You'll be sent the rest regularly. It's only a supplement, of course,' she said. 'But then your husband . . .'

'Oh yes.' Mrs Gaskin nodded hard. 'Albert's earning a good wage. But could you give a week or two's in advance – for a few extras for 'er like?' Miss Rowney hesitated, then handed over a ten-shilling note.

'We shall of course be calling on you to see how things are going, Mrs Gaskin,' she said. 'And if there are any problems – which I'm sure there won't be – you can always contact us.'

'Oh I'm sure we'll get on very well, won't we, Mercy? Got a coat, has she?'

Mercy found herself wrapped in an old gaberdine and Mrs Gaskin carried her bag to the door.

'Before you go, Mercy—' Miss Rowney actually had to lay her hand on Mrs Gaskin's arm to stop her rushed progress out of the door. Her tone changed to that of memorized speech. 'We'd like to present you with a little gift, as we do to all children who go forth from here. We know you'll take the good name of the Hanley Homes out into the world with you.'

Mercy found a parcel wrapped in thin brown paper laid in her hands.

'I want Dorothy!' Tears welled in her eyes. How could she go without saying goodbye to the only adult who had ever shown her any kindness?

'Don't be silly, dear, Dorothy's not here.' Miss Rowney pushed her briskly towards the door. 'We'll tell her where you've gone, don't fret.'

None of the other children were summoned to say goodbye as Miss O'Donnell and Miss Rowney saw Mercy off with no embraces, kisses or demonstrations of any kind.

'Be good now, dear!' Miss Rowney called as Mrs Gaskin took the girl's hand and led her down into the road.

'Good luck,' Miss O'Donnell shouted, hissing to Miss Rowney, 'and won't they just darn well need it.'

Still holding the parcel, Mercy turned and looked back at them as they stood, arms raised benevolently, on the very step where she had arrived as a newborn baby. She was too bewildered even to wave.

Part Two

Chapter Four

'Come on, get moving then – we've got a ways to go from 'ere.' Mrs Gaskin said as they set out along the road in the cold, grey afternoon. 'Blimey—' She rubbed one hand vigorously round her jaw. 'Got a proper face ache after all that smiling!'

Mercy looked around her, full of excitement suddenly, despite all the confusion of it. She was going out somewhere new, to a new home! She imagined homes as warm, comfortable places with soft furniture to sit on, flowers in the gardens and kind, benevolent people.

'Give us yer things,' Mrs Gaskin snapped, almost snatching Mercy's woven bag from her which contained her very few possessions. Mercy held on tight to the parcel though. 'Can't stand kids dawdlin' round me. We're going to 'ave ter get on the tram. Will yer come on – I want to get out of 'ere, smartish.' Mercy couldn't help noticing that Mrs Gaskin's smile had dropped away as quickly as had her posh accent.

One hand lifting the green skirt up out of the muck in the gutter, the other carrying Mercy's bag, Mabel Gaskin jerked her head to indicate that they should cross the road, and strode across so fast Mercy had to run to keep up and avoid being hit by a fast trotting horse and carriage.

In her entire life so far the furthest Mercy had ever been was Minister Vesey's church on the Witton Road.

Everything else had revolved round Kent Street. Now they were going to go right across Birmingham to some green and mysterious place Miss O'Donnell had called Handsworth.

''S'Handsworth nice?' she asked, panting a bit.

'Yer what?' They'd reached a main road and Mabel was looking up and down. 'Where's that cowing tram stop?'

'Handsworth,' Mercy persevered. 'What's it like?'

'Ah – there . . .' Mabel dashed off along the road. 'Right in front of me bleedin' nose. And there's one coming – quick!'

The tram trundled towards them. 'Ooh – can we sit on the top?' Mercy pleaded, bold in her excitement. The open top of the tram was edged by ornate iron railings and she thought it must be heaven to sit up there and see everything.

'With sparks coming down on yer, and in this weather – you off yer 'ead?'

The tram swayed to a standstill and Mabel didn't have to prod Mercy to climb up inside. They managed to find two places on the wooden seats downstairs.

'Don't trust them buses,' Mabel murmured, straightening her skirt under her. 'Least with a tram yer know it's got to stay on the tracks.'

Mercy watched, thrilled, out of the window as they lumbered along the cobbled streets past shops, churches, small workshops and dwellings. The walls were painted with signs advertising all manner of things: Birds' Custard, Hudson's Soap, Fred Smith's Ales and Stout, and Mercy tried hungrily to read them all. And it was such a big place! They seemed to have been on the tram for ages already. Mercy kept her eyes fixed on the view through the whole journey, except once when they passed a building which to her looked like a palace. The front of it was all coloured tiles with scrolls and flowers, fruit, and two rounded bay windows with bits of brightly-coloured glass making a pattern at the top.

'What's that?' she asked Mabel urgently. 'Cor – that's beautiful, that is!'

Mabel had taken her hat off and was busy trying to pin it back on top of her twisted skein of black hair. She half looked, seeming agitated. 'What – where?'

'There!'

'That's a pub. Ain't you never seen a pub before?' She stared at Mercy for a moment. What was it about this girl with her peculiar piercing eyes that got on her nerves so much already?

'Right – off 'ere,' Mabel ordered a few stops later. Mercy followed her fat behind along the tram and jumped down behind her.

'Is this Handsworth?'

'No – it's not bloody 'Andsworth!' Mabel was suddenly enraged. 'We ain't going to 'Andsworth so would you shurrup keeping on about it.'

'But I thought . . .'

'Yes, well you know what Thought did . . .' They were walking very fast, jostling passers-by, turning into a wide street with enormous buildings, their walls blackened and the tops of them only hazily visible up there in a soup of damp, gritty air.

'Where then . . .?'

'You'll see. Now shut yer trap for a bit, will yer? We gotta get 'ome quick.' She spoke with such peculiar venom that Mercy decided to do as she was told.

As they turned left out of that street with its grand shop fronts, Mercy saw a sign high in the wall, CORPORATION STREET, and then they were in another road with more huge windows full of clothes, shoes, china and glassware and cloth, the like or quantity of which she had never seen. The street was bustling with people and she gawped at some of the more smartly-dressed ladies with their beautifully fitted gowns in soft colours, after all the grey and black at the Joseph Hanley Home.

Even though she was full of the thrill of being out in all these new places, Mercy began to feel despondent. Her throat was raw in the cold air and she longed to sit down somewhere warm. Mrs Gaskin was walking faster and faster, cursing people who got in her way.

'Come on, yer wretched girl,' she nagged Mercy. 'We gotta get back!'

When they reached the Bull Ring, for a time Mercy forgot she had a sore throat. She forgot her tingling nose and her shivers and this horrible, bad-tempered woman she was with. How exciting it was! From where they came into it, walking down the slope of Spiceal Street, Mercy could see a church at the far end with a tall spire and a big clock with gold numbers marking the face. In between snaked the row of market stalls, most protected by sagging tarpaulins, and a sea of hats: bonnets with little ribbons or posies, cloth caps and Homburgs, even the odd boater here and there.

Everywhere there was movement and a great outcry of sound, with the traders trying to outdo each other shouting out the prices of their fruit and veg.

There were others selling crocks, trinkets and bags and flowers and Mercy's feet were dragging as she stopped to gape. The light was beginning to die and some of the traders were lighting flares at the side of their stalls which burned with a bluish-yellow flame, giving the place a cosy air.

'Keep with me,' Mabel shouted at her over the racket

and seized her arm. 'If I lose yer 'ere I'll never find yer again.'

There were so many smells that were new to Mercy: smoke from cigarettes, and a thick mouthful of it made her cough. But then there came the sweet smell of potatoes baking in a big green and gold handcart which made her mouth water, and other smells, discarded cabbage leaves, crushed onions, bruised apples and oranges left to rot in the street. But not for long. Mercy watched as three ragged children, their clothes caked in filth, slunk round the stalls, darting down now and then to grab some piece of refuse even though the stallholders tried shooing them away.

'Can't we just stay a bit longer?' Mercy begged as Mabel dragged her past a man selling wire toys and a knife-grinder showering sparks.

'No,' Mabel snapped. A woman approached them and tried to push a posy of lavender through Mabel's buttonhole.

'Bugger off, will yer!' She slapped the woman's hand away. They hurried past a big statue behind some railings, and the church. The clock made it well after five.

Soon after they were hurrying up a long, very steep road called Bradford Street. It was dark and the buildings felt high and close together. From every side came the most amazing din Mercy had ever heard. Banging and clanking sounds met them not only from the openings of buildings on the street but from under the ground through the gratings. In some places jets of steam unfurled through holes from down there and drifted raggedly into the air. The hammering and rattling, the sudden scream of metal and tearing crashes of noise met them all the way along.

'What's that?' Mercy yelled, her throat rasping.

Mabel gave her a look which implied the question was almost too stupid to answer. 'Factories. Brass works and that. Don't you know anything?'

'Is this still Birmingham?

'No, it's bloody Timbuctoo.'

Mercy took this to mean yes. Birmingham really was a big place then. They turned off Bradford Street and there were more factories, and then houses too. Now they'd got out of the bustle of the market Mercy's excitement was beginning to wear off. It was fast getting dark, the air felt damp and harsh and when they crossed the road the cobbles were slippery underfoot. She felt the throb of her chilblains in the pinching boots, her raw throat and empty belly, and her head was starting to hurt. She wondered again when she was going to see Dorothy, now she was in this strange, dark place. Her dream of a green paradise was dissolving fast.

'I don't like you,' she said, still clinging to her parcel as the one thing she had left of the home. 'I want you to take me back to Matron. She said you could.'

'Oh no,' Mabel Gaskin sniggered spitefully, 'you won't be seeing them again in a hurry. See, they think we're in my old 'ouse in Winson Green – near enough to 'Andsworth. Me husband's 'ouse, that is – when I had a husband. They ain't going to find you again where we're going, so yer'd better get used to the idea. Least I got that ten bob off of them while I had the chance, 'cos they won't be seeing us no more. I've got plans for you, and you ain't going anywhere without my say-so. Down 'ere—'

She elbowed Mercy down another side street even darker than the last. Soon, pausing by a drunken-looking street lamp she said, 'Up the entry,' and pushed her into one of the pitch black alleys between the houses, which quickly opened up into a court of back houses. As they walked in, the gas lamp in the middle of the court flared into life and Mercy saw a man standing under it with a long pole.

'Bit late, aren't yer?' Mabel said to him in passing.

'And a very good evening to you too,' he quipped.

A gaggle of children was playing up at the far end. There were three houses parallel with the road, and what looked like two smaller cottages to one side of the yard, but Mercy had barely had a look when Mabel swept her at high speed through the door of the house on one side of the entry.

Inside it was completely black.

'Stand still or you'll only go and break summat.'

Mercy stood just inside the door clutching her parcel. Her head throbbed and she felt very small and frightened. There was just her and this nasty woman and she didn't know where she was and it was so dark and smelly in this house. There was a nasty mouldy stench which she didn't recognize as damp, a stale odour of cabbage and onions. And yet another smell which took her with a shudder right back to the dormitory at the home: urine. She really felt like crying again now.

There came the scratch of a match and Mabel lit the gas mantle at one side of the room. She also lit a tiny stub of candle and abruptly disappeared upstairs. Mercy stared round her. The Joseph Hanley Home had been austere and unadorned, but never had she been in a place like this before.

The feeble light from the gas lamp only just reached the walls even though the room was tiny, and all the surfaces gave off a weird yellowish tinge. The ceiling seemed very low and in one corner was a big hole with rough bits of wood sticking out of it and in other parts it sagged and bulged. The room had been distempered long ago but now the paint had flaked away in large bare patches and the dirty plaster showed underneath. With a shudder she saw something scuttle along the wall.

The floor was of rough, uneven bricks, worn down in some parts where there had been the greatest passage over them, and holes where bricks were missing in others. In the middle of the room was a table and two rickety chairs, one with Mabel's coat and hat flung over it, and in one corner stood the range. A broom stood propped against one wall and beside it a couple of old tea chests with a few things sticking out. One looked like a picture frame. Apart from that the place was empty.

Mabel was soon down again. She stooped to stoke the range, saying defensively, 'I've only been in 'ere a few days,' as if sensing Mercy's horrified gaze lighting on the place.

'Oh Lor'!' she exclaimed suddenly, leaping up. To Mercy's astonishment she started unfastening her clothes and stripping them off, first the tight green jacket, then the skirt, wriggled down over her meaty hips. She made grunting sounds of relief.

'That's better. Can't go shovelling coal in this get-up – that's going to Chubb's tomorrow.'

Mrs Chubb, as Mercy would soon know well, ran the local pawnshop round the corner.

'Got 'em off a lady sells second-hand rags in Balsall Heath.' Mabel grinned in satisfaction at her own trickery. 'Got your gaffer believing you're living with a proper lady, din'it?' She laid the skirt over her chair, standing in a grey corset and torn petticoat. 'Shame 'aving to 'ock it, but there we are.'

'You got anything to eat?' Mercy dared ask. The room was so cold she hadn't even taken her coat off yet.

'Eat?' Mabel was struggling into a shapeless brown dress. I've only just got the fire going, what d'you think I am? I'm hungry as well, yer know. Just sit down and shurrup for a bit.'

Mercy sat on the spare chair. She felt overwhelmingly tired, and shivery as if she was getting a fever. All the day's changes had taken it out of her and though she was used to a meagre diet she was starving. Mabel though, did seem to be making an effort to get some dinner ready.

'You going to open that package then?' she said from by the range, giving Mercy a sly look. 'Let's see if it's anything worth 'aving.'

Mercy pulled the loose string away from the parcel and slowly tore off the paper as Mabel breathed heavily over her shoulder.

The first thing to fall out was a small white handkerchief. On the corner Mercy saw that her name had been embroidered neatly in mauve silk. A parting gift from the home? She wondered if Dorothy had sewn it for her. With it was a book with a pale brown cover, designs of black and orange flowers printed on it, the title embossed into a panel of gold. It was by a Dr J.W. Kirton. *Cheerful Homes*, the title read. *How to Get and Keep Them.*

Chapter Five

Mabel heated up a meagre amount of scrag-end. When it was ready, she fished around in the scullery at the back and came out with a new candle which she lit and fixed on a saucer. Taking a plate of stew and a spoon she said, 'Back in a tick,' and climbed the stairs.

A moment later Mercy heard her voice, apparently talking to someone. Mercy frowned. She was sure it was Mabel. But then the walls of these houses were wafer-thin. From next door she could hear plates rattling and people talking. Someone was snoring. Then a woman's voice, 'Get in there. I said get in there, will yer!' very loud and angry. Whoever it was didn't 'get in there' and this was followed up by more yells. A man's voice snapped, 'Oh leave off, yer nagging bitch . . .'

'Who's that up there?' Mercy asked when Mrs Gaskin reappeared, minus the plate and spoon.

'You'll see soon enough.'

They sat at the table together. The sight of the stew was disgusting, the grey meat nearly all fat and bone but it tasted better than it looked and Mercy ate everything she could actually chew, despite her sore throat. She had an uneasy feeling though, about this unseen person upstairs, and strained her ears to hear any sound.

Mrs Gaskin made tea and gave her a cup and she began to feel warmer.

'Where will I sleep?'

'Upstairs, where d'yer think?'

'Have you got a bed?'

'Don't you worry about it, there's beds all right.' The woman seemed a fraction mellower now she was home and fed. Mercy looked up into her blunt-featured face and felt herself shudder.

'You my mom now then?' she asked doubtfully. She had a beautiful fantasy in her mind about what real moms should be like and Mabel didn't fit the bill at all.

Mabel stared across the room and her mouth twisted suddenly, her face taking on an odd, melancholy expression. 'You don't want me as yer mom. You'd better call me Mabel. Can't stand you calling me Mrs Gaskin.' She stood up abruptly. 'Come on – up yer go.'

She picked up Mercy's bag and led the way up the creaking stairs.

'Watch that one!' Half of one of the treads was missing, broken and splintered. 'Proper 'ell 'ole this is,' Mabel muttered to herself.

'I sleep in there,' she nodded to the left when they reached the tiny divide at the top of the stairs. It was a two-up house, with no attic. Two bedrooms upstairs and only the living room and scullery downstairs. 'You'll 'ave to bunk up in there.'

As the door opened, there was already an unsteady circle of candlelight in the room but for a moment Mercy couldn't make out anything. The smell of urine though, was almost overpowering and made her stomach lurch. She saw that most of the space in the tiny room was taken up with a double bed and its dark, heavy bedstead, the footboard so high that from where she was standing she couldn't see over it.

Mabel marched over to the bed and said, 'Finished then, 'ave yer?'

There was no reply that Mercy could hear. Very slowly, even more full of dread, she moved round the end of the bed. For a moment as she looked in the poor light she could see nothing but a jumble of ragged bedding. But as Mabel moved with the candle nearer the head of the bed she saw the light reflect in two dark eyes, and heard herself give a gasp. Could there really be someone under there, in all that mess, making this awful smell?

The head turned and Mercy saw dark hair, and the eyes, set in a small, delicate face, were now fixed on her.

'This is Susan,' Mabel said harshly. 'My daughter. One of my daughters, I should say. This one's the only one I got left and she's a cripple. That's my luck with mother'ood. You'll be sleeping in 'ere with 'er. 'Er's got no feeling in 'er legs so if she needs to go—' – Mabel's gaze rested on the chamber pot down on the floor by the bed – 'you'll have to give 'er a hand. Anyroad, there's ample room for the both of you.'

She picked up the plate from which Susan had evidently managed to eat her tea and went out.

Mercy found her legs were trembling. She went round and sat numbly on the other side of the bed, elbows resting on her knees and hands cupping her cheeks. I won't start blarting in front of her, she thought, I won't! I should have run, when we were in the Bull Ring, while I had the chance! Mrs Gaskin would never have caught up with me . . .

''Ello.' She heard the girl's soft voice.

Mercy didn't answer. She didn't turn round. For a time she just sat there, but she could feel the girl watching her as if her eyes were burning into her back. Eventually she stood up and started to unbutton her frock which she left hanging over the foot of the bed. The room was perishing cold. She knew, despairingly, that she was going to have to get into that foul, stinking bed. The thought made her want to heave but what choice did she have?

The bedclothes, such as they had, were a mixture of old scraps of torn blanket and a couple of old coats. As she pulled them back the smell got worse.

'Oh my God.'

'Sorry – only she's hardly been 'ere for days to help me. Only first thing. I can't move, see.'

The bed was in a terrible state. Where Susan was lying, helpless, it was drenched. Mercy's side was not so absolutely soaked, but definitely damp. There were tears in Susan's eyes and Mercy saw they were tears of shame.

'You cold?'

Susan nodded. Mercy was shivering convulsively now, and when she touched Susan's arm she, too, was icy cold.

'You'd best come over this way a bit,' she said abruptly. 'D'you need to go now?'

'No – she lifted me when she got in.'

Susan was all skin and bone, quite easy even for Mercy to shift a little way across the bed. The two of them didn't speak any more.

Mercy blew out the candle and crawled into her little space at the edge of the bed, careful not to touch Susan who lay silently beside her. The ammonia smell of urine burned in her nostrils. Bugs scurried along the walls. She felt so ill, her head throbbed and she was shivering hard, unable to stop. Finally, in exhaustion, fear and bewilderment, she let the tears come, wretchedly sobbing and shaking. She tried to be quiet but her emotion flooded out.

It was only after she'd begun to quieten a little, snuffling now and gulping, that she felt a little touch on her shoulder and furiously shook it off. But after a few moments the hand was back, stroking her at first, and then a small, bony arm crept round her body, holding her tight. She felt Susan's face against her back and finally the two of them slept, their bodies giving each other warmth.

'Mercy – can you give us a hand?'

The room was still almost dark. A dull light was just attempting to seep through the filthy window. Mercy turned quickly on to her back, completely confused for a moment, thinking it was one of the girls in the home she could hear. Then she took in the sodden coldness of the bed and the crumbling, filthy walls. She was also scratching: there were bugs in the bed.

Susan was trying to sit up. 'You'll 'ave to cop 'olt of me . . .'

'Why should I?' She was rigid with cold and anger.

There was a pause. 'Please 'elp me,' Susan begged wretchedly. 'I'll go in the bed again else.'

Mercy climbed stiffly from the bed, teeth chattering and slid her arms under Susan's and round her chest.

'Skinny, aren't you?'

'Good job, innit?'

Though slightly smaller than her, Mercy had little difficulty in dragging Susan off the bed and positioning her on the pot.

'Ta,' Susan whispered, so humbly that Mercy felt ashamed of herself. She stared at Susan's white legs. She'd never seen such scrawny, wasted limbs before.

'So've you ever been able to walk then?'

'For a bit I could – I can remember walking. I was taken sick years ago. They call it infantile paralysis. My legs 'ave got a bit better lately but they don't think they'll ever be any good.'

Susan looked up at her, her face ghostly in the dim

light, her eyes coal-black like a snowman's and a pudding basin of black hair.

'You come to stop with us then?'

'No!' Mercy snapped, then added helplessly, 'I dunno.' She couldn't even have said at that moment just how much she didn't want to live here with Mabel and her crippled scrap of a daughter. Nothing was real. It was as if she were trapped in a dream and couldn't wake up.

'You don't 'alf bang about in your sleep,' Susan commented. After a moment she indicated that she'd finished and Mercy hoisted her back on to the bed.

'Mom wants you to 'elp look after me like, so I'm not stuck 'ere on my own. She's got to go and find a job or she says we can't pay the rent or eat.'

'Haven't you got a dad?' Mercy pulled the remnants of bed clothing up to cover Susan so just her head was visible.

''E just went. A few months back. Left us.'

She could hear the desolation in Susan's voice, but could only say, 'Oh,' unable to imagine a real dad or real mom, then added, 'Why?'

'Dunno. 'E were a good dad really. Didn't want us any more, I s'pose. And then we had no money so we come to live over 'ere. We 'ad a bit of a nicer 'ouse before but Mom couldn't keep up with the rent.'

Mercy sat down on the edge of the bed, shivering.

'D'you just lie 'ere all day then?'

'I didn't used to before we came 'ere. She'd get me up and that. Miss Pringle – one of our neighbours – she used to come and sit and do things with me. She were a teacher when 'er was younger. It was 'er taught me to sew and knit like. She said if I couldn't use my legs I might as well keep my hands busy. Mom never did nothing with me. Miss Pringle said it was a shame.'

'How old are you? Don't you go to school?'

'No, never. I'm thirteen.'

'Thirteen! Blimey I reckon you're smaller than Amy was!'

'Who's Amy?'

'My best pal. They sent her away to Canada.'

'Miss Pringle was my best pal.' Susan sounded dismal. 'Don't s'pose I'll be seeing 'er now neither.' She swallowed hard. 'How old're you?'

'Twelve – nearly.'

'What's it like in an orphanage then? And school?'

'It's awright.' Mercy couldn't think of anything to say. It was all she knew. What was there to say about it? 'We had much bigger rooms,' she brought out finally, looking round at the bleak space the bed was squeezed into.

It was growing lighter. Mercy went to the window. There was no sign of frost and the glass was running with a mixture of condensation and grime. She wiped one of the lowest panes with the back of her hand and stood wrapping her arms round herself to try to keep warm.

The lamp was still lit outside, reflecting in puddles on the uneven bricks. Mercy could just make out the long stretch of the yard, reaching along to a high building in the far corner. As she watched, a woman came out from one of the houses beside Mabel's and walked briskly across carrying a bundle with one hand and holding her long skirt up out of the wet.

I'm not stopping here, Mercy said to herself. I'll go back to the home and tell 'em. They can't leave me here.

She'd never seen a more desolate place. But she thought of the journey here the day before, and knew she didn't have the first idea where she was or how to go about getting back. She also remembered Miss O'Donnell's warning about what would happen if she did. She swallowed hard. Oh Dorothy, she cried inside. Where are you? If you were here it'd be all right.

'Mercy?'

She didn't want to turn round and let Susan see the tears on her face.

'What?'

'Could yer empty this for me? Mom hates doing it and she'll keep on. She weren't so bad before but she moans all the time since we come 'ere.'

'So she's got me 'ere to be your slave, has she?' Mercy snapped, angrily wiping her eyes on her sleeve. She pulled the rest of her clothes on quickly and went round to Susan's side of the bed to pick up the chamber pot.

'There's a suff out in the yard.'

Mercy straightened up. 'If your Mom thinks I'm staying 'ere she's made a big mistake,' she announced haughtily, and went to march out of the room. But she caught her foot in a trailing loop of blanket and tripped. The chamber pot leapt out of her hands and smashed with a great noise and splash. Mercy fell against the foot of the bed banging her head.

'What the 'ell was that?'

Mabel waddled across the landing like a bloodhound, still attired in the same corset, chemise and bloomers, that Mercy had seen last night.

'Oh yer 'aven't gone and broken the po'?' She stared accusingly at Mercy who was rubbing her cheek. 'Yer clumsy little bitch. Who's going to pay for a new one, eh? You, I suppose?'

'No—' Susan spoke up. 'It weren't 'er fault it were me. I tipped it over – knocked it with me arm. Mercy didn't do nothing.'

Mabel stared from one to the other of them, eyes gluey with sleep, the skin under them wrinkled like rice paper.

Even she could see it was pretty unlikely Susan could create a crash like that, but she wasn't in the mood to keep on about it. She wanted her morning cuppa.

'Pick up the bits,' she ordered Mercy. 'Don't cut yourself or there'll be that to deal with as well. Take 'em down the yard. You'll 'ave to do your business in the bucket from now on, the pair of yer.'

She went off, heavily, down the stairs. They heard her cursing over the broken tread.

Still rubbing her sore head Mercy gaped at Susan in bewilderment. Susan's face broke into a broad, mischievous smile.

Chapter Six

May 1912

'Come and see, Mom – Mr Pepper's nearly finished it!'

Mabel Gaskin sat on a rickety chair outside number two, Nine Court, Angel Street, her face bullish with resentment. Susan's joyous cry as she came rattling towards her along the yard only made her scowl more and pull her arms tight across her pendulous bosom.

Susan's face was alight with hope and laughter as Mercy hurtled along with her, squeezed into the go-kart belonging to the twins, Johnny and Tom Pepper, from number one. Susan was clinging to the sides of the ancient black pram from which it was made, her wasted legs and feet flapping up and down over the end.

'I ain't shifting nowhere,' Mabel snarled.

Her eyes met Mercy's for a second over Susan's shoulder. The girl's hair was a tumbling skein of gold after last night's dunking in the tin bath, and there was so much of it it almost seemed to overwhelm her delicate face. Her prettiness was marred though, by harsh mauve bruising round her left cheekbone, and the expression of loathing in her narrowed eyes directed at Mabel could have melted lead. Mabel glowered back. Every time she looked at that kid nowadays she longed to batter her. And that was often what she did.

''Ere—' Alf Pepper called. He was a huge bloke, a

Black Countryman with a ruddy, bashed up face from boxing and the nickname 'Bummy' on account of his low slung trousers. 'I'm gunna need them wheels off o' there in a minute.'

Eyes smouldering with triumph, Mercy struggled to turn the go-kart and, leaning all her weight on it, rattled back along the blue-brick yard to where a gaggle of the neighbours was gathered round Alf who was building Susan the first wheelchair she had ever had.

Susan turned her head for a moment, eyes pleading, but Mabel stuck her nose in the air and looked away. She wasn't going to stay out here to be shamed any longer. She got up and carried the chair indoors in as stately a manner as possible and slammed the door.

'Old misery,' Elsie Pepper said, bending to pick up little Rosalie who was 'momming' at her skirts. She was a sturdy-looking woman, dressed in her usual attire: a long, rough skirt with a blouse tucked in. Her thick auburn hair was usually taken up under a man's cap when she was working, which was nearly always, but she'd left it off today. 'There's summat wrong with 'er, that there is. That child's right enough given a bit of kindness.'

Elsie was in her mid-forties, had given birth to nine children, eight surviving, and believed implicitly in hard work and family life. She was blessed with more energy than the average person, had a sound idea of how to feed a big family well on Bummy's modest but regular wages as a chippy and, to make means stretch further, took in washing. She always had a house full of it.

There were several things which made Elsie's blood boil and these were dishonesty, men with no sense of responsibility, and cruelty, especially to children.

Cruelty was what she saw in Mabel Gaskin, and Elsie had made it her business, as she did frequently for folk in need, to look out for Mercy and Susan and take them under her wing.

Inside the house Mabel climbed the rotting stairs shaking with rage and humiliation. Going to the girls' room she stood back from the window, peering out at the far end of the yard which was buttressed by the high wall of the wire factory.

They were all out there, laughing and carrying on, all against her as usual. Most of all she loathed the Pepper family with all their kids and their self-righteous ways. Elsie, who everyone seemed to regard as the yard's gaffer, handing out her opinions left, right and centre. 'Course, she'd got Mercy well under her thumb. And all her flaming kids. No one should have that many kids. There were the twins who Mercy adored, and more infuriating still, the Pepper family were so taken with her. And now thanks to that scheming, interfering Mercy, Susan was going to have a wheelchair and she'd be out, for everyone to see her as the cripple she was.

'She's mine!' Mabel's voice came out in a harsh, irrational outburst. 'My baby. I won't let you take her away. She's mine, mine, mine.'

Unable to stand watching any more of this merriment outside she went to her own room. She loathed Mercy for her energy and guile, for her devotion to Susan and for being more than she herself would ever be. Yet now she couldn't do without her. She wanted the very best money could buy for Susan, but she barely had any money and couldn't bear anyone else to be the one to help her. She was above all these slummy people yet had to live among them.

She fell on the bed in a turmoil of self-hatred provoked

by the crowd out there all bunched against her, Susan's glowing hope, the wheelchair – yet another of the things she'd failed to provide. Failed. That's what she was, in every way, and Susan, her one scrap of hope, the one who would always have to stay with her and depend on her, was pulling away now as well.

Mabel Smith was born in 1873 in the workhouse at Winson Green. Her mother, already in poor health, died of TB two years later never having left the workhouse, and Mabel and two older siblings, a boy and a girl, were orphaned. She never knew who her father had been.

At fourteen Mabel was put into service as a kitchen maid to a family in Handsworth. Over the next couple of years her thickset features, which had given her a skulking, toadlike appearance as a child, spread and thinned to an earthy sort of glamour with those gappy teeth, the hooded eyes and long black hair. Her body was generously curved and stayed lithe through housework.

Albert Gaskin – then seventeen, whirling along the streets on a baker's delivery cycle – started shilly-shallying at this particular door in Broughton Road, hoping to catch a glimpse of Mabel's broad hips and supple waist bending over a bucket, the breasts full of promise, strong arms wringing a cloth, sleeves rolled, muscles moving under the skin.

Mabel, whose head had been rammed full of the notion that as a workhouse orphan she'd never be of anything more than heavy domestic use to anyone, suddenly found a more generous slice of hope than she'd been expecting.

Albert, thin, gangly, with high cheekbones, shorn brown hair and a jauntily-angled cap, pursued her with cheerfulness, persistence and a seething eroticism that quite took her by surprise. The sounds of desire he let out even at their first kiss were something she'd never forget.

When eventually Albert said, 'Will yer marry me, Mabel, my true love?' she had long ago made up her mind.

Things started well. Albert moved into factory work and Mabel carried on in service as a 'daily'. They rented a couple of rooms. After all the anticipation the wedding night in 1893 was a sad disappointment (Albert had had several too many pints of Butler's Ale). But things improved on that front and others. Mabel fell pregnant. She bloomed. She had a home, or half a one, a sweet-natured husband in work and she was to be a mother. Workhouse-born she may have been, but look what she was making of herself now!

The baby, a girl who they named Victoria, was born dead. Albert stayed off work for a week and promptly got the sack. After, he came home with two finches in a cage who chirruped mournfully and pecked their ash-coloured breasts until Mabel screamed for him to take them away again.

By the time a second baby was on the way, Albert had long found another job, and the sad darkness haunting the rooms near the canal thinned and blazed into hope again. Dulcie was born on All Hallows Eve, a plump, fair baby. Albert wept again, this time for joy.

At three months Dulcie contracted whooping cough. Mabel rushed for a doctor, uncaring of the expense and cursing the mother with a whooping child she'd spoken to when crumbling crusts for the ducks over in Hands-worth Park. In five days she was dead.

Mabel fell into mourning and depression. They didn't see Albert's scattered family, and with none of her own to mourn with her she took it all on herself. Somewhere in her nature was a dulled, lugubrious space reserved for grief and disaster, perhaps cultured in the workhouse. But this was not the case with Albert. He was sunshine and tears all at the surface, his personality as slim as cardboard, enough to accommodate only the thinnest of shadows.

He didn't start drinking heavily though, until later.

Susan was born in 1899, with Mabel's dark eyes. She smiled from the first week – Mabel was certain of this even though the few people she allowed near the child said it was wind. She was placid and sweet and thrived steadily, if delicately, into a solemn-faced yet mischievous child.

Afterwards Mabel came to think of these as the last years of her marriage. Albert, his frame already shuddering under the terrible weight of responsibility – all these lives, these deaths – was kept steady by Susan. By the light in her eyes when he came into a room, the frantic, joyful kicking of her legs as he lifted her high in the air as a baby, her running to him as she grew into a five-year-old with his own loving nature. Of all his daughters she charmed him the most, softened him as Mabel no longer could, gave him hope.

When she fell ill they thought at first the fever was influenza, unseasonably in July. When the doctor pronounced it something far more serious the first image that blazed through Albert's mind was another small white coffin.

Memories of those days, then weeks were almost impossible to recall, so strange and fragmented were they as to be discounted as a dream. Absolutely sure and certain for Mabel six months later though, was that she had a child who would never run into her father's arms again, a drunk for a husband and that her hopes for an increase in the good things in life had been sadly misplaced.

There were another seven years of something that passed outwardly for marriage. Susan stayed small and loveable. Albert stayed drunk on and off, no longer sweet, sometimes working, sometimes not. He tried to be tender with Susan, wanted to take her out and about.

'But she's a cripple!' Mabel raged. 'Look at 'er legs. She'll 'ave to stop at 'ome. I'll not 'ave 'er wheeled out like a freak show.'

She took over Susan in a perverse, compulsive way. Overprotective, smothering yet ashamed, shutting Albert out. She kept even Susan's existence as secret as possible, only letting very few people see her, like the crusading Miss Pringle with her pince-nez, her bag of coloured sewing threads and offcuts of cotton and felt.

'She has such dextrous fingers,' Miss Pringle said. 'Such a pity to waste a skill like that. She could be marvellous at the piano, you know, or the violin.'

Mabel stared at her as pigs struggled to take wing around the room.

But Miss Pringle did make it possible for Mabel to live with all the contradictions of her feelings towards her remaining daughter. Susan, whom she would have been mortified to take out in the street, Susan, her companion for life who would never leave her because she couldn't walk away and no one would marry a girl with wizened legs. Susan would always be there. Susan, in whom all her guilt, her compassion was invested. Who for so much of the time she couldn't stand to be anywhere near, embodying as she did all the loss, all the failure of a life in which Mabel had once found hope.

Their possessions – not plentiful to begin with – Mabel was pawning piece by piece. They were already poor when Albert left. He had not been getting regular work and the jobs he did get were now unskilled and insecure. He'd had two spells in Winson Green prison for drunkenness. At home he was neither raucous nor violent. Sober, he was gentle with Susan. Drunk he was silent, lost.

And then he was gone. On a beautiful summer day when birds sang in small gardens and there was a breeze to blow the city smoke away, he left and never came back. Mabel who had believed, whatever his state, however distant they grew from one another, that he would always be there, was more shocked than she'd ever thought she could be again. She knew he wasn't coming back – in the summer warmth he had taken his coat and hat.

Her time living as a respectable married woman was over. Now she and Susan were on their own. She was that workhouse nobody again, living in the slums where you had to burn the bugs off the ceiling with a candle before you could get to sleep, and surrounded by slummy people whom she hated almost as much as she hated herself.

'Mom!' Susan's voice rang up the staircase. 'It's finished – come and see.' There was a pause. 'Please?'

'I'll go up,' Mercy said, muttering 'miserable cow' under her breath.

Mabel's hands gripped the cover on her bed, her teeth grating together. She heard the clatter of two pairs of boots on the stairs, an abrupt knock at the bedroom door and to her outrage Mercy and Johnny Pepper appeared.

'Get out!' she shrieked, sitting up in fury. 'What the 'ell d'yer think yer playing at coming pushing your way in 'ere?'

'Susan wants you to come,' Mercy said in a voice of

steel, standing firm in the doorway. She looked in disgust at Mabel whose appearance had deteriorated over the past months. She'd spread and sagged and her clothes were unkempt and often dirty.

'Oh you always know what Susan wants nowadays, don't you? Well, you can tell 'er from me she's gunna 'ave a long wait, 'cos I ain't coming just to see where Mr God-Almighty Pepper's nailed a couple of wheels on to some planks.'

She lay down on the bed again feeling Mercy's piercing look of loathing through her back. Mercy and Johnny went back down again.

Susan was sitting enthroned in her ingenious, very straight-backed chair at the threshold of the house. Her face fell as Mercy reappeared.

'Never mind—' Johnny set out to cheer her up. 'Come on – 'ave a ride!'

He took hold of the metal bar at the back of the chair and careered along the yard so fast that the neighbours had to scatter. Mercy's eyes followed them. It had worked! She laughed with delight. Now she and Susan would be able to get out!

'Johnny!' Elsie bawled at him. 'Go easy!'

'She won't come,' Susan said as they skidded to a halt. 'She ain't feeling too well.'

Everyone saw this for the thin excuse it was.

'Never mind,' Elsie said. 'She'll come round to the idea.'

'Go on then,' said Bummy. 'Take it off up there again – I want to see 'ow well it's going.'

Susan managed to turn the wheels a little on her own, but being unused to any form of exertion was soon exhausted. Mercy completed this next lap of honour for her as everyone clapped, down towards the entry then back up to the factory wall, past the soot-dusted cabbages in the little garden at the front of the two cottages.

'She's evil, that Mabel Gaskin,' Mary Jones spat out in Susan's absence.

'Nah.' Her husband Stan, a taut, stocky bloke with black hair and a thin moustache was smoking, leaning against the brewhouse wall. 'She's all right really, she is.'

'And what would you know?' Mary turned on him. 'You wanna keep yer eyes to yourself, you do.'

'Eh, you two,' Bummy said, then called to Susan. 'D'yer like it then?'

The expression on her face was enough of a reply.

Mabel's fury had been building up all that Sunday, and by the evening she was an unexploded bomb.

Mercy knew she was only biding her time, waiting for an excuse. She knew the signs: the silence, Mabel's clenching of her jaw, the way she averted her eyes from both of them.

Susan was at the table (the wheelchair was to be stowed in the brewhouse at night – Mabel said she wouldn't have it in the house). Mercy was moving round her laying the tin plates and the few eating implements they had, and Mabel was at the range with her back to them, stirring a pot. The room was lit only by the last of the summer evening light.

'What's to eat then?' Susan asked cautiously.

'Wait and see,' Mabel snapped. She looked a dreadful mess from lying round on her bed half the afternoon, hair tumbling everywhere, and she knew it.

Mercy stepped round her, eyes downcast, went to put a fork on the table and dropped it with a tinny clatter on the bricks.

Mabel jumped and struck out savagely with her spare arm, knocking Mercy across the room so she crashed into the wall.

'Yer clumsy little bitch!' Mabel roared. 'You're useless, that's what you are. Dropping things all the time and breaking them!' It was true. Mercy lived in such a state of nerves around Mabel that it made her clumsy and there were frequent breakages. 'What do we want forks for any'ow, when we're 'aving broth? No bloody brains in yer 'ead, that's your trouble!'

Mercy slid down the wall, curling into a ball, head and arms pulled in tight to her knees to protect herself, a position she'd had to take up so many times in her life, it came now by instinct.

Mabel thought she would burst from rage. She grabbed one of Mercy's arms and dragged her with no difficulty to her feet, fingers pressing viciously into her flesh.

'Look at me!'

The child raised her eyes, those glittering grey eyes, which even in her fear were stony with disgust at the woman in front of her and Mabel almost flinched. She squeezed her fingers as tight as claws into the tops of Mercy's arms.

'Mom, don't, please . . .' Susan begged.

'You're nothing,' Mabel went on. 'Filth from the gutter, that's what you are. That's what your own mother thought of you, you know that, don't yer? She didn't want you so she just threw you away. Dumped you on the steps of Hanley's. That's 'ow much she thought of yer.'

Mercy stared at her, stunned. She'd never, never heard this before. As far as she'd understood she'd been spawned in some mysterious way by the Birmingham streets and taken in. In a high voice she said, 'But I never 'ad a mother. I was an orphan.'

Mabel laughed nastily. ''Ark at 'er! "I was an orphan!" Didn't they tell you nothing in that place? We all 'ave a mother, deary – ain't no way of getting into the world without one. But some babbies is wanted and some ain't and you was one of the ones that ain't. Least I never gave none of mine away like your mom did.'

Seeing the genuine shock in Mercy's eyes she loosed her arm and began slapping her face until she'd made her cry.

'Don't, Mom!' Susan was sobbing. 'Stop it, you're hurting 'er!'

Mabel pushed Mercy away in disgust. 'Get out of 'ere. Yer can go up to bed without no tea. I've had enough of yer for one day.'

Later Mabel carried Susan upstairs and plonked her on the bed saying, 'If you need any 'elp you can ask 'er Majesty there.'

Mercy lay with her eyes closed, hugging her badly bruised arms tight to herself. When Mabel had gone she felt Susan's hand tapping her shoulder.

'Brought you this – look.'

From out of her clothes she drew a chunk of bread and held it in front of Mercy's face. 'Don't you want it?'

There was a pause, then Mercy shook her head.

'I wish I could stop her treating you so bad.' Susan leant over her, talking close to her ear.

Mercy shrugged as if to say, who cares?

'Mercy go on, turn over.'

Reluctantly, obviously in pain, Mercy turned on her back. Susan saw that in one hand, close up to her face, she was holding the little handkerchief with her name embroidered on it. Her eyes though, were dry.

'What she said about your mom . . . You never knew?'

Mercy shook her head again. Her face showed her pain as she spoke. 'No one ever said. They never told us much about where we'd come from. They never said I'd had a mom. I always sort of thought that if I'd had one she must be dead, and that's why I was there . . .'

Susan stroked her hair, unable to think what else to do. Mercy caught hold of her hand and gripped it hard. She couldn't explain how Mabel's cruel revelation had made her feel. Shocked, rejected, lost. Her mother wasn't dead, she'd abandoned her, thrown her away! She felt filthy and crumpled like rubbish on the street.

After a long silence Susan said, ' I know 'ow I felt when my dad went.' There was more silence, then she said, 'You won't go away too, will yer?'

Mercy looked up at her. Susan's dark head had a halo of light round it from the candle behind her. She had quickly come to feel even more tenderness and devotion for Susan.

than she had for Amy. Even though the younger of the two, Mercy was the protector, the fighter.

'No – 'course I won't.' She squeezed Susan's hand. 'Where've I got to run away to?'

Chapter Seven

For months Mercy had stayed home with Susan and acted as Mabel's unpaid skivvy. She soon became a familiar figure in the Highgate yard, in her old dress from the home, a piece of sacking round the waistband, labouring back and forth from the tap with buckets of water, kneeling scrubbing the step, her bright hair tied back with a red rag, smudges on her face.

She'd started out determined to make Mabel's house somewhere more fit to live.

'I mean the home wasn't pretty or anything, but at least it was clean. We don't have to have it looking as bad as this.'

'I s'pose not,' Susan said doubtfully.

It was a woefully thankless task. She swept and scrubbed, washed down the windows and rubbed them with newspaper. Some of the window frames were so rotten they had to be stuffed with old rags. She brushed down the walls which sent showers of dusty, yellowed distemper on top of her and Elsie showed her how to stove the house with a sulphur candle to keep the bugs at bay. But however hard she worked she couldn't disguise the fact that they were living in a cluster of jerry-built, mouldering slums and that theirs was one of the worst of the bunch. The paint just flaked more and more, the floor was in a terrible state, and the effluents from the factories coated the windows and step as soon as she'd finished washing them.

They were living in such poverty that they never seemed to have the simplest things they needed, like scissors to cut their nails or a comb that wasn't broken – let alone any new clothes.

But she did like the freedom from Miss Rowney's regime, being able to come and go as she needed, when Mabel wasn't around. And there was Susan.

'You don't 'ave to sit there doing nothing,' she said to her, the very first day, when she'd struggled to help her downstairs, step by step, the two of them sitting squeezed in side by side.

'What can I do?' Susan said, legs dangling from the chair, not even touching the floor. Mercy was hot from her exertions, but Susan was still huddled up, cold.

Mercy caught hold of the chair and inched it over to the black iron range, glad to see it was much smaller than the one in the home. She handed Susan an old rag, and the small amount of polish Mabel had left.

'I'll do the bits you can't reach. No good you sitting there gawping at me all day, is it?'

Susan peered from under her fringe with a grin of delight. 'Mom never lets me do nothing!' She set to work, bony shoulder blades poking in and out as she exerted herself.

The two girls, thrown together, grew close in a short time. Elsie was always popping in to see them, bringing gifts of food: stew, pease pudding, soup – 'I always 'ad to cook for ten before so it won't 'urt me now, will it?' – and asking how they were getting on. The yard was forever strung across with washing, either that of the other neighbours or Elsie, who was in the brewhouse – the shared wash-house in the yard – at all hours, toiling over the copper, maiding tub and mangle.

After school finished was the best time of day, when

the boys came roaring back into the yard. "'Allo Mercy!" they called out every day, and Mercy would feel her heart lift with excitement. 'Come on!' she'd say to Susan, and drag her chair out into the yard to watch. The twins were two years older than her, Jack roughly the same age. The twins were her favourites: freckly, red-haired Johnny, mad as a hatter on boxing, and Tom – kind, brown-haired, quieter. They let Mercy play with them – football with an old pig's bladder tied at the top, tipcat with a ball and a bit of wood, marbles . . .

'Yer not bad, for a wench,' Tom told her now and again as she slammed the football along the yard.

She thought they were wonderful, the whole Pepper family.

They were all out in the yard one freezing winter after-noon, when the sun couldn't break through the clouds and smoke, Susan muffled up on a chair in as many layers as they could find. Tom had carried her out there. Mercy liked the way the twins, wild as they were, were gentle with Susan.

They'd dealt out a few marbles and begun a game when three girls marched in from Angel Street. There was something about them that made Tom and Johnny stand up, hands on waists, elbows out, before they'd even opened their mouths.

They looked like sisters, all with lanky brown hair, the eldest with plaits coiled above her ears, pale faces and narrow, squinty eyes. Mercy felt herself bristle. She didn't like the look of them at all.

'What d'you want?' Tom demanded, defending his territory, chin jutting out.

'Where's that Cathleen?' the eldest said. She wore an old grey skirt, too big, dragging on the ground.

'So who wants her?' Johnny pushed himself forward.

'We do.' The eldest one was left to do the talking again in a harsh, aggressive voice. 'Few things we need to straighten out with 'er. Who're you, any road?'

'We're 'er brothers,' Johnny said, elbows sticking out. 'She ain't 'ere, and I don't reckon she'd want to see you if she was.'

The girl looked brazenly round the yard. 'What's 'er gawping at?' She latched on to Mercy suddenly, who was standing by Susan's chair. 'Ain't you got nothing better to do? Oh my word, what's this then?'

The three girls moved nearer to Susan with jaunty, menacing walks. The second girl pulled the cover off Susan's knees and made a face on seeing her white, scaley legs.

'Urgh, look – she's a cripple. That's 'orrible, that is. Looks like fish skin!'

'Was you born like that then?'

'Can yer walk? Go on, show us, 'ave a go!'

Susan, who had been so hidden away all her life that she'd never been treated anything like this before, shrank down in the chair, eyes filling with tears.

'Ooh, look, she don't like being called a cripple, she's gonna blart now. Go on, cry, cripple – boo-hoo-hoo . . .'

The eldest girl felt her plaits being grasped like handles so her head was yanked backwards and she found herself looking into two grey eyes full of a cold, intense fury.

'That person you're talking to is Susan,' Mercy spat at the girl, tugging on the hair to give emphasis to everything she said. 'And no one talks to 'er like that. No one. Got it?'

The girl scowled, wincing in pain. 'Who d'yer think you are, eh?'

'Me? I'm Mercy. And this 'ere's for you.' She loosed the girl's hair, drew her hand back and gave her a socking great punch on the nose.

'That's from me. And if you come back talking to 'er like that, there's plenty more where that come from.'

The girl was cursing and whimpering with pain.

'Look what you done, you little bitch!' her sister cried. ''Er nose is pouring!'

'Serves 'er right,' Mercy yelled as the boys watched in amazement. 'And so will yours be too if you don't clear off out of 'ere!'

'You vicious cow...!' They shouted over their shoulders as they slunk out of the yard.

'Blimey,' Johnny said.

'What's been going on?' Elsie emerged from the brewhouse.

'Mercy punched that girl in the kisser!' Tom cried enthusiastically.

'She called Susan a cripple,' Mercy said, rubbing her knuckles. 'And I'm not 'aving that.'

'I don't blame you,' Elsie said, gradually getting the picture.

Susan was all blushes. 'You didn't have to hit 'er that hard, did you?'

'Oh yes I did!' Mercy was still flaming. 'What does she know – she's never had bad legs, has she?'

The days were all right until Mabel got home, always foul-tempered. At first she'd found herself a job in a button factory, cutting metal blanks for buttons of different kinds. She complained bitterly about it. 'It's a right bind with my eyesight – I 'ave to practically put me nose in the machine. My 'ead's thumping terrible.' She carried on with it for a few weeks, growing even more demoralized and bad-tempered.

One night she came home and said, 'I've found you two a job an' all.' She emptied out the cloth bag on the table. Inside was a box containing what seemed an endless number of safety pins and a heap of small cards. 'There yer go – yer can earn yer keep. They want one of each size on a card and there's nine sizes. We get tuppence a gross for 'em. Yer might as well get started now.' She pushed the box towards Susan who did as she was told with her dextrous fingers. 'Plenty more where they come from, hooks and eyes, buttons, the lot.'

Every night, in common with many kids in the poor areas of the city, they sat carding, straining their eyes by gas or candlelight until their fingers were raw, while Mabel sat groaning that her head and eyes hurt.

Eventually she got a new job at the Anchor Bedstead Works in the packing department, but her temper didn't improve much and she took all her spite out on Mercy.

'This 'ouse looks like a pigsty,' would be her complaint almost before she was through the door.

'But I've been cleaning all day,' Mercy protested at first, quite tearful after all her efforts.

One day as Mabel came in with her 'This 'ouse looks like a pigsty,' complaint on her lips, Mercy rounded on her.

'That's 'cos it is a pigsty. So what's the use in saying it ain't?'

Mabel loomed before her, breasts heaving with fury. 'You saucy little bitch!'

Mercy saw Mabel's hand coming at her, ingrained with dirt. She gave Mercy a massive slap which knocked her to the floor.

Susan was shouting too, protesting, 'Mom – stop it!'

Mercy lay on her side, rubbing her stinging cheek. There were tears of pain in her eyes but in her fierce pride she wiped them away, determined not to let Mabel see them.

'You've just got me 'ere as your skivvy, and it ain't right,' she snarled. 'Elsie's kids are at school and that's where I should be – and Susan.'

'School?' Mabel narrowed her eyes and gave Mercy such a look of overpowering loathing that many another child would have cowered. 'Oh, you needn't think you're going off anywhere, my girl. What do workhouse brats like us ever need to go to school for, eh? I 'ad a bit of schooling – 'er father 'ad more than I did and look what became of 'im! Whatever yer do you'll end up in the factory so it makes no odds. I didn't bring another mouth to feed in 'ere for you to sit about all day. Yer 'ere to work for me, and work is what you're going to do. You'll do just whatever I say and that's that.'

Chapter Eight

'Quick, she's gone!'

Mercy was peering, terrified, after Mabel who had just disappeared to another day's work. When she was certain Mabel had really gone she tore along to the Peppers'. Tom and Johnny, now in their last year of school, were looking out for her.

'Get the chair from the brew'us!' They ran over, both of them in long trousers too big for them.

It had rained in the night and the yard stank. The twins clattered across with the wheelchair and Elsie came steaming out of her door, already in a state of nerves. She was having misgivings about this school lark. It didn't seem right deceiving Mrs Gherkin or whatever the hell her name was. She was the kids' mom – sort of anyway. And what if she was to find out? But one look at Mercy's set little face and Susan's mix of nerves and excitement as the twins swung her into the wheelchair made her swallow her doubts.

'Careful!' Susan laughed, and clung to their arms as she landed on the old bit of baize padding the seat.

Mercy was so edgy she couldn't keep still.

'It'll be awright, won't it, Mrs Pepper?' Her eyes radiated hope and anxiety. 'They will let us in?'

'Oh, I s'pect so. We'll just 'ave to see.' She wasn't at all sure about Susan. Plenty of children her age had left school already, and she hadn't even started yet! But she couldn't bring herself to say this to Mercy. Give them a chance, she thought, that's all.

She prodded Cathleen who seemed thoroughly clogged up with sleep.

'She don't look too good,' Susan said kindly.

'She always looks like that,' Johnny said, going to push the chair.

'No!' Mercy ran in front. 'I'm pushing Susan.'

Johnny shrugged. 'It'll be hard work.'

Mercy could feel the sun on her face as they got out of the dank yard where the sun only ever shone, if they were lucky, in the late afternoon.

'You awright?' she asked Susan, who nodded hard, too full up with everything to speak. There was the morning street coming to life, a horse snuffing in an empty nosebag at the side of the road, people coming and going. She could smell fresh bread mingled in with the factory smells and horse manure, hear the morning cries, cartwheels on the cobbles.

It was so exciting! And Mercy said that at school she'd learn new things. Find out how to read properly, not just spell out her letters with one finger on the table. Maybe she could be a bit more like the others!

Cathleen said goodbye and went off to work. Johnny and Jack ran back and forth in front of the wheelchair urging Mercy on, Tom walked rather protectively beside Mercy and Elsie came along behind, watching Mercy push on the chair with her slender weight, leg muscles straining. The sight of her wrung Elsie's heart. Her clothes were in a pathetic state: patched and worn, grubby and obviously too small. She'd grown more and more worried about Mercy, heard the shouts coming from Mabel's house, seen Mercy's bruises and cut lips. After all, a quick cuff or a smack when necessary was one thing. No one'd argue with that, but this was different.

'Does she belt you hard?' she'd asked some time ago. Mercy had simply said yes.

She'd tried having a go at the woman and was told to 'Bugger off and keep yer nose to yerself,' and variations on this. What else could she do? She saw now that the child was limping.

'What's up with your foot – boots worrying yer?'

'They're ever so tight,' Mercy said. She'd had no new ones since she'd been with Mabel and they were falling apart. She'd got paper stuffed in the sole to keep the wet out.

Elsie made a mental note to make sure, somehow, that Mercy got new boots. Otherwise the child would be barefoot the winter through. Asking her so-called mother would be a waste of time, the hard-faced bitch.

'Let Jack push Susan for a bit now,' she cajoled. 'You'll wear yourself out.'

'No. I'm doing it.' The reply wasn't rude, just resolute.

When they reached the enormous red-brick school, the boys called out 'Ta-ra!' and vanished into the boys' entrance at the far end, Johnny punching the air as he went.

'Ain't it big?' Susan said in a small voice.

Noisy groups of girls were arriving at the school, all staring at them. Mercy glowered back. What were they gawping at, nosey cows?

'Don't you go losing your temper,' Susan pleaded. 'I don't mind 'em looking. It does no harm.'

Elsie hesitated, even more nervous herself now. 'Wait 'ere. I'll try and get you sorted out.'

After what felt an age she appeared with a flustered

young teacher, austerely dressed in a grey skirt to the floor and a high-necked white blouse. She had a round, plain face.

'Well, that one's all right,' she said sharply, pointing at Mercy. 'But we can't possibly take the other one. This is a school for normal children. We can't have the likes of her here. There are special schools for that sort.'

Susan cringed, visibly flayed by the cruelty of the words.

Mercy gripped the bar of the chair, head held up defiantly. She felt as if someone had their hands tight round her throat.

'I'm not coming in if Susan can't come too,' she managed to say, huskily.

'Well!' The teacher's cheeks flushed a mottled pink. 'What a rude and unpleasant child. You can go somewhere else if that's your attitude. This is not a school for cripples – we couldn't even get that—' – she pointed to the unorthodox-looking chair – 'up the steps. Take it away!'

Although she meant the chair, her whole manner implied that 'it' meant Susan.

Elsie was usually full of respect for authority, but now it was her turn to speak out.

'What kind of a thing's that to say to the poor girl? Call yourself a teacher? You're s'posed to be 'ere to get some learning into their 'eads, not chase 'em away when they come begging for it!'

The teacher spoke in a low, icy voice. 'The fact remains, this is not a school for cripples. Now is this other child going to come in, before you waste my time any further?'

'No,' Mercy said. 'Not without Susan.'

'You don't make decisions at your age!' The teacher seemed set to hoik Mercy bodily up the steps. 'You're supposed to attend school. It doesn't matter about her!'

'You go, Mercy,' Susan said, trying to hide her terrible feelings of hurt. 'You can come 'ome and tell me all about it.'

Elsie Pepper found a lump aching in her throat at this brave show, at the care these kids had found for each other.

'Come on, Susan – we'll go 'ome.' To Mercy she said, 'Go on, bab. She can stop with me in the daytime. We'll be all right.'

'No!' Mercy stood helpless, fists clenched tightly as Susan and Elsie disappeared down the road, Susan craning round, trying to smile.

'Right then,' the teacher prodded her shoulder. 'Hurry up and get in.'

When Mercy and the boys arrived back in Angel Street that afternoon, Mercy was still seething with rage on Susan's behalf. She found her at the table in Elsie's house, chopping onions and carrots. Jack and Johnny grabbed chunks of carrot and ran off outside, and Tom sat down next to Susan.

''Ow d'yer get on then?' she asked Mercy in a bright voice.

'Awright,' Mercy spoke glumly, for she was tired, hungry and emotional. Although she was glad to be at school it had been a miserable day. It was a harsh environ-ment, the rows of little sloping desks, the teacher's cane always there in the corner to remind you of her authority. But it was certainly no worse than life with Mabel, and at least she'd learn a thing or two instead of just being a drudge all day long.

'What've you been doing?' she asked Susan.

'Oh, giving Mrs Pepper a hand. She's been ever so good to me.'

'She patched my other skirt and she's done it beautiful, and now she's 'elping cook our dinner. She's a good pair of extra 'ands round the place.'

Neither of them was going to tell Mercy how Susan had sobbed her heart out when they got back to Angel Street, for so long that Elsie began to wonder how she'd ever console her.

'Now I can see why Mom never wants me to go out,' Susan gulped, cheeks soaked with tears. 'People're that cruel. I can't help how I am, can I?'

Elsie had had to concede that Mabel, while keeping her hidden too much from the world, had at least protected her from the kind of verbal abuse that had so shocked her this morning.

'There's still a lot you can do without school,' she tried to comfort her. 'In any case, it's a bit late to be starting at your age. But you can sew a bit, can't you, and 'ow about I teach you a bit of cooking?'

'Oh Mrs Pepper, you're so kind to us,' Susan sobbed.

She did cheer up and began to enjoy herself with Elsie. She kept little Rosalie occupied while Elsie struggled with yet another load of washing. It was good to be in a proper family, Elsie was in and out, chatting to her, and her married son Frank popped in for a cuppa and a moan about his wife. He was brown-haired like Tom, handsome in his copper's uniform, and he cracked jokes with her. Susan liked him.

'We've been keeping our eye on the neighbours too, 'ain't we, Mrs Pepper?' Susan laughed.

Mr Jones, with his greased back hair and little moustache, had been out in the yard that afternoon in his grubby trousers and singlet, muscles on parade, peering in a not especially subtle manner through the window of number two. He'd sidled back and forth several times, until they heard Mary Jones shouting out of number three amid the bawling of children, in a shrill, end-of-her-tether voice, 'Stan? What're you doing?' And he'd nipped back into his house right quick.

'And Mrs Jones and Mrs White had a fight over the mangle,' Susan chattered on. 'Mercy're you listening?'

'It's not fair!' Mercy exploded, the pent-up emotion of her day gushing out. She burst into tears. 'It's evil and wicked to say those things about Susan. And now she can't even go to school!'

'You know, Mercy,' Elsie consoled her, 'Susan could make a living sewing, she could, she's that nimble at it.'

But another problem was gnawing at Mercy too, now the excitement of getting out was wearing off.

'But 'ow'm I ever going to get anything done when I'm out all day?'

This was a real problem. However was she going to fit all the day's chores into a couple of hours so that Mabel wouldn't notice the difference?

'We'll do it.' Tom spoke up suddenly from where he was sharpening a knife against a whetting stone.

Elsie gaped. 'What – you and Johnny?'

''S'not fair is it?' Tom said. 'Why should she 'ave to do it all?'

He called Johnny and Jack in and after a moment of baffled reluctance they agreed.

Mercy stared from one to the other of them, overcome by such kindness, and started crying all over again.

It worked a treat for a while. Mercy, now easier in her mind about Susan, set off in the mornings with the Pepper boys, laughing and joking on their way. She adored their company.

'More than time that one got to be'ave like a young-ster,' Elsie remarked to Mary Jones as the four left the yard one day, with their usual split-second timing, moments after Mabel. 'Only that one' – she jerked her thumb towards Mabel's house – 'ain't s'posed to know, so don't go letting on, will yer?'

'Oh no,' Mary replied meekly. She was a pale, skinny woman, completely intimidated by the energetic competence with which Elsie greeted every task when she could barely keep her head above water with her own family. ''Course I won't.'

Mercy came home tired, but ready to make up for all the housework. With the boys mucking in, it became a laugh as well as a chore as Tom, Johnny and Mercy darted about with brooms, rags and buckets of water, Jack rubbed ochre on the front step as if in a frenzy and Susan began cooking.

'They'll all make nice little wives for someone by the time you've finished!' Elsie teased Mercy. But in truth she was warmed to see such generous spirits in her sons.

Usually, by a huge effort, they'd completed most jobs before Mabel got in and the boys melted away as if they'd never been near the place. She always found something to criticize though: the floor wasn't dry or the dinner not ready.

'No use to no one, you ain't!' she'd rant at Mercy. 'Can't you get anything right?'

On these warm nights she'd insist on locking the door and Mercy bringing her water so she could half strip off and wash. Mercy felt horribly overfamiliar with Mabel's body, the fleshy upper arms and heavy breasts, the ripe smell of her filling the room. She always tried to look the other way.

*

One evening, Stan Jones, who seemed to be in and out of jobs as fast as a rabbit its burrow, was standing out on Angel Street by the entry to Nine Court, smoking, leaning against the wall in the balmy summer air. Idly, he watched the slow progress of a water cart as it dripped its way along the street.

In fact Stan Jones, who had the body of a bantamweight wrestler and the face of a petty thief, was not loafing about completely without purpose. He had two objectives: one was keeping out of the way of his missis so that she had to deal with the stormiest part of the day with four kids – four too many in his view. The other was running into Mabel.

Stan had had his eye on Mabel Gaskin for some time now. There she was, a woman on her own, with an earthy look and a body that Stan, at least in his mind, couldn't keep his hands off. And there was Mary his wife, scrawnier with each babby she suckled and always scared stiff of catching for another. And Stan had caught a peek of Mabel a week back, stripped to the waist downstairs. Oh, the thought of it! Breasts with enough stuffing in to hang heavy, not like Mary's little pinheads. Stan had worked himself up into a great state of anticipation about the 'widow woman' (Mabel's public version of why she was alone).

Mabel soon turned into the street, scowling to herself, lost in thought, carrying a bag. She'd called into the factory on the way home to fetch a new set of pins for carding.

'Evenin'!' Stan called.

It wasn't the first time Mabel had found him hanging around when she got home. She looked appreciatively at the bulging muscles on his arms. She knew a fine specimen of a man when she saw one. His lean face was smiling appealingly at her and in his eyes – there was no mistaking what she saw in those eyes. For the first time in a very long while, Mabel's mouth curved up in a smile.

'Shall I carry that for yer?' Stan indicated the bag, taking it from her with exaggerated effort as if it contained gold ingots.

'Ta very much,' Mabel tittered.

But then Stan said, 'See you've 'ad your little team on the go again – be awright when my lot're old enough for that!'

Mabel frowned. 'Team?'

'Oh, they'll've finished now.' Stan scratched under one hairy armpit with long, lazy strokes, the bag swinging to and fro. 'You've got 'em well trained doing that, soon as school's out.'

'Mine don't go to school,' Mabel said dismissively, looking full into Stan's eyes. It wasn't kids she wanted to be talking about. She was reluctant to move, was basking in the almost forgotten sensation of being lusted after.

'They do,' Stan corrected her. 'That yeller-haired chit any'ow – gone all day with them, she is.'

Mabel stared at him, the smile wiped from her face, and strode off to her house, slamming the door, leaving Stan holding a huge bag of loose safety pins.

Within minutes Mabel was giving Mercy her most violent beating yet.

She caught them so much by surprise, whipping out with, 'What's this about you going to school?' that they hadn't been prepared for brazening it out.

'So you'd deceive me, would you, you cunning little bitch?' Mercy tried to dodge the slaps that were raining down on her. Mabel caught her hard across the eye and she yelped in pain. 'You'd better not be taking Susan anywhere she shouldn't be or I'll be taking a match to that dustcart of a chair, that I will!'

'No—' Mercy lied feverishly, trying to put the table between herself and Mabel. She had a hand clasped to her watering eye. 'I haven't – honest!'

Mabel strode round and caught hold of the back of Mercy's old cotton frock. They both heard it rip. She yanked the girl round and started punching her, hard, on the chest and face.

'No – no, Mom, no!' Susan was shrieking hysterically, and for the first time ever, Mabel turned and slapped her hard round the head.

'Shut up, you useless little cow. You're just as bloody bad as she is.'

'Don't hit her!' Mercy screamed.

Both Mercy and Susan were crying with pain as Elsie appeared at the door, horrified by the sight in front of her. Mercy's face was bleeding and she was crumpled, weeping in pain, but Mabel was still hammering into her.

Mabel let go of Mercy and shoved Elsie out with the force of her weight and slammed the door so hard that the house rattled.

'Interfering, stuck up bitch!' she yelled, shooting the bolt across. Elsie, along with Stan Jones and the twins, moved to the window. Stan, impervious to Mercy's suffering gazed at Mabel's plump arms and her wide, love-handled hips.

'Bugger off!' Mabel bawled towards the window.

'You—' – she grabbed Mercy again as Susan sat whimpering and sobbing – 'can get down 'ere—' She opened the entrance to the coal-hole and shoved Mercy down on to the filthy slack-covered floor underneath the kitchen. Bolting it shut she shouted, 'Yer can come up when I'm ready and not before!' Mercy sank down on the gritty coal dust, beginning to sob with pain.

'And you lot—' – she heard Mabel shouting out of the window – 'can all mind yer own cowing business.'

'I'll report you,' Elsie shouted. 'Yer not fit to be near children!'

'Oh yes. Report me? Who to?' Mabel bawled. 'Even if there was anyone, who'd listen to you – slummy trollop, breeding like a bloody rabbit!'

Late one afternoon a couple of weeks later a woman appeared, wearing a smart dark uniform, a coat and felt hat with a narrow brim and low-heeled, well polished shoes.

She walked uncertainly across the yard, looking at the house numbers.

Elsie came out of the brewhouse immediately, pointing.

'Who the 'eck's that then?' Mabel peered out of the window. 'Eh – you . . .' Mercy heard the panic in her voice. 'Get upstairs, quick!'

'Why? I'm doing . . .'

'Don't argue with me – get up there, now!'

As she ran upstairs Mercy heard knocking at the front door. She waited, listening, at the top.

The woman was well-spoken, her voice smooth as cream.

'Mrs Gaskell?'

'Gaskin.'

'Oh, I'm sorry. I'm from the NSPCC.' Rather uncomfortably she explained the meaning of the initials to Mabel. 'I wonder if I might see your little girl? I've had a complaint through one of our welfare officers.'

'She's 'ere, as yer can see,' Mabel said unctuously.

'Hello,' Mercy heard the woman say to Susan. 'And how are you, my dear?'

'She's lying.' Elsie was standing at the door. 'There's another girl, she's the one. 'I s'pect she's locked down the coal 'ole or summat. That's one of 'er favourite tricks. She can take 'em off of you, yer know,' she sneered at Mabel.

Hearing this, Mercy's hand went to her mouth. She was so frightened she felt as if her muscles had tied themselves in knots. Who was this woman? Was she from the home, come to take her away again?

'There is another child lodging with me,' Mabel admitted. 'But she ain't 'ere just now.'

'Oh yes she is,' Elsie raised her voice. 'She's 'ere awright.'

'Perhaps you'd like to leave us now, thank you?' The NSPCC woman said. Mercy heard the door closing, then the woman's voice, sharper in tone. 'How old is the child in question?'

'Er – twelve,' Mabel said.

'Oh – I was given to believe she was a lot younger. Still, I'm afraid I've come rather a long way, and if you can't present the girl to me I shall be obliged to search the house to make sure she's really not here.'

Mercy shrank, trembling, into the bedroom. What if this woman saw the bruises, her swollen lip, the half healed graze on her forehead where Mabel had knocked her into the wall? Would they take her to a home, or worse still, the workhouse? She might never see Susan or Elsie again!

'Mercy!' Mabel called up to her in a silken voice. 'Can you come down 'ere a minute, Mercy love?'

She wiped her face frantically on her skirt and walked down on unsteady legs, trying to pull her hair forward to hide her face. Immediately she saw the woman's shrewd eyes appraising her.

'Hello, my dear,' she said again. 'So your name's Mercy?'

Mercy nodded, mute with fear. Susan was at the table, watching her with desperate pleading in her eyes.

'So you live with Mrs Gaskin?'

'Yes.' Mercy turned wide eyes towards Mabel. 'She's my auntie.'

'My sister's child,' Mabel added quickly. 'It were tragic really – she died when Mercy was only a titty-babby so I took 'er in. She's been like me own ever since.'

The NSPCC woman looked sceptically at Mercy's skinny frame, her filthy, threadbare dress, her bare feet, the marks on her face.

'And how are you, Mercy?'

Mabel was looking daggers at her.

'I'm awright, ta – er, thank you.' Her voice was hardly more than a whisper.

'There's no need to be afraid. Are you getting enough to eat?'

'Yes.' This at least was almost true. One thing Mabel was good at was managing with food.

'Come over to the light, child.'

By the window she put her fingers under Mercy's chin and tilted her head back. 'How did you hurt your face like that?'

'I fell over and grazed me 'ead. And there was this girl at school hit me like. We got into a fight.'

The woman released her face. 'And does Mrs Gaskin ever hit you?'

Mercy shook her head. 'No – least, not much. Only, you know, like a mom. She's bin very good to me, taking me in and that.'

For the first time the officer smiled. 'Bright little thing you've got here.'

'Oh yes, she's a good 'un,' Mabel agreed, nodding like a mad horse.

'And where d'you go to school, Mercy?'

Mercy's eyes met Mabel's for a second. Mabel had strictly forbidden Mercy to go to school, out of pure spite since she got the chores done anyway.

'Down Alcester Street.'

'And do you get on well there?'

'Oh yes. It's very nice.'

'It's just a pity about some of the neighbours round 'ere,' Mabel was saying in her poshest voice. 'Where I used to live in Handsworth, you got a better class of person. But 'ere . . .' She rolled her eyes. 'Lord knows what 'er out there's been telling yer, but it's a pack of lies. We're quite 'appy us, aren't we, Mercy? We're a family, and we stick together.'

Mabel showed the woman out at last, all smiles, as if she quite believed the fairy tale she'd been spinning.

'Well, we soon got shot of 'er,' she said. Then turned and saw the granite hard expression on Mercy's face.

'I'm a good little liar, ain't I? D'you know why I lied for you? Because of Susan. I don't care what happens to you. If she took you away and put you in prison I'd be the happiest person alive. But whatever you do I'll never leave Susan. I did tell 'er one true thing though – that I go to school. And if you don't let me go, and if you don't treat us right from now on I'll get her back and tell her what sort of a mom you really are!'

Chapter Nine

November 1913

'You're vile and disgusting – the pair of yer!'

Elsie, sleeves rolled, was gathering in washing from the line slung across the yard, an expression of fury and revulsion in her blue eyes.

Stan Jones, still fastening the last of his fly buttons was swaggering along the yard from the privy at the far end on his way to his Saturday evening rendezvous with Mabel. Cocky as ever, he spat out the cigarette stub from the corner of his mouth and crushed it with his heel, smirking at Elsie.

'Just mind yer own, eh? If you was getting a bit more of it you wouldn't need to stick yer nose in everyone else's business, would yer?'

'What about that wife of yours?' But Elsie was shouting at an empty space. Mabel had left the door unlocked and ready for him.

'Where are yer then, yer great big beautiful hussy?' Stan blared up the stairs in high spirits, not caring who heard. He knew Mabel would be waiting. She always was. She'd undressed, putting on her newest pair of bloomers and a camisole which pulled tightly across her breasts, and was lying on her bed in the dreary room with her hair hanging loose and what she hoped was a seductive smile on her face.

Stan made a loud noise of appreciation on seeing her, hand going straight back to his belt buckle.

He stopped. 'You 'ave got shot of them two?'

Mabel gave a girlish giggle. 'Packed 'em off into town. What about 'er?'

This was ritual, questions they always asked.

'She won't be back from 'er mom's for a good while yet.'

Stan leant over and pulled up Mabel's camisole. She squirmed with pleasure, flexing her back as his hands moved over her breasts. Getting a bit of life for herself she was, at last. Stan's loud and urgent arousal was very gratifying, especially as he got no joy with that miserable scarecrow of a wife of his. And maybe – though she'd never mention this to Stan – maybe she'd catch for a babby. Things could get better. Maybe Albert had been her curse?

Stan ran his hands up and down her flesh, forcing her like sweet dough, eyes narrowing.

'You're a real woman, Mabel. By God you are.'

Now it suited Mabel to have the house to herself she'd relaxed her strictures about Susan going out. Every Saturday, late in the afternoon, Mercy pushed her into town.

'It's the best bit of the week!' Susan said many times. Being out of the gloomy confines of their yard in Mercy's company and going to see all the shops and market stalls – heaven! And Mercy enjoyed it too, hunting for bargains and seeing all the sights. She was canny with money and Mabel, lazy as she was, had long trusted her to do the shopping. It was hard work on the way home though, pushing the chair and the bags back. The middle of

Birmingham was like the dip in the middle of a saucer, hills all around.

'Thank heaven Mr Pepper's put some new wheels on 'ere,' Mercy said as they bowled along the backstreets. 'The other ones was on their last legs.'

'Let me ask for the meat this time,' Susan said. She loved being out, learning to shop, use money, all the things she had never been allowed to do. Mercy felt very sad for her sometimes. She demanded so little of life, Susan did, while Mercy was restless and hungry for it.

She pushed Susan to Jamaica Row first, round the back of Smithfield Market where were sold a great variety of livestock, feed, straw ... At the meat market Susan shouted out for 'a bag of cagmag, please, and proudly held out the coins from Mabel's little pouch of hard-earned money as the red-faced butcher swung over a bag of the cheapest off-cuts of meat.

'We'll get a rabbit later.' Mercy had to yell over all the racket of the carts clattering and shouting voices of this bustling area. 'When they're selling stuff off cheap.'

The Bull Ring was also full of its usual activity.

'Ooh,' Susan called out as Mercy slowly manouevred her through the crowds and past St Martin's Church. 'Can yer smell that?'

There was a delicious aroma of meat roasting in White-heads' cook-shop just opposite the church. Mercy felt saliva gush into her mouth. They were used to the fact that whenever they ate they were left wanting more, but she was ravenous now after the exertion of pushing Susan along.

'Let's 'ave some,' she said. 'A penny dipper – on the way 'ome.'

'We can't – she'll kill us!'

'She won't – you know what she's like Sat'dy nights nowadays.'

Poor Susan had grown used to balancing loyalties between Mercy and her mom, but she knew Mercy was right about this. The girls were completely ignorant about what Mabel got up to with Stan Jones. All they knew was that when they got back on Saturday nights, they found Mabel sated and mellow and not in the mood for a fight.

They meandered along to the market stalls, low sunlight slanting between the tarpaulins, amid the cries of the stallholders.

They bought onions from a lad not much older than them who winked as he tipped them into their bag.

''Aving a nice stew, are yer? You'll want some swede as well – lovely swede, we got today.'

'I can't abide swede,' Mercy said. 'Give us a pound o' carrots instead, eh?'

With Susan holding the meat and veg on her lap they moved along Spiceal Street.

'Oh look!' Mercy cried, stopping outside a shop. 'I wish I could get some of them for Johnny.'

The shop, Green's, sold all sorts of leather goods. There were piles of trunks outside and hanging in the window were footballs, wallets and beautiful, sleek pairs of boxing gloves. 'Wouldn't 'e love them – and those footballs for Jack!'

Johnny and Tom were both out at work now, Tom the more studious of the two, apprenticed to Stern's, the silversmiths, Johnny a delivery boy for a bakery. And Bummy had decided that now he'd come of age he could go along to the boxing with him.

The prices in the shop were way beyond anything they could imagine.

'Someone somewhere must 'ave some money,' Susan said. 'Why do some people 'ave money, Mercy, when the likes of us 'ave hardly any?'

Mercy shrugged, walking on. 'S'pose they own the factories and shops. That's just the way it is.'

Susan was growing despondent. She eyed a shop selling bolts of cloth and sighed, wishing so hard that she could do something better. Really learn to sew properly, make things. She had been doing odd bits of mending for people under Elsie's guidance and word was beginning to spread round the street, but she still had only the most basic needles and threads. She never normally complained, but suddenly she saw their poverty for what it was for the first time.

'Blimey, what a racket!' Mercy stopped again.

This shop sold pets, and outside stood cages with African grey parrots, cockatiels, budgerigars and finches making such a noise that Mercy laughed.

But Susan remained quiet. Mercy stooped and looked into her face. 'What's up with you?'

'I'll never do anything me, will I? I'll always be just an 'opeless cripple.'

Susan hardly ever talked like this. Mercy took her hands and spoke fiercely into her ear.

'You won't, Susan. Not long now and I'll be out at work – we'll 'ave two wages coming in.' Even with Mabel's pay, the carding and the few pennies Susan received for her mending, there was barely enough to pay the rent and eat, let alone keep them even adequately clothed.

'I swear to you, Susan, soon as I get some money of my own you'll 'ave everything you need. I'll set you up so you can always earn a living no matter what happens to the rest of us.' Susan was smiling and starting to cry all at the same time.

'I'll always look after you, Susan. And you know what else? I'll get you one of these birds and you can teach it to talk to you!'

Susan wiped her eyes and, as Mercy straightened up, someone tapped her shoulder and she turned, frowning. For a moment she couldn't think who it was, then the frown melted into an overjoyed smile. 'Dorothy! Dorothy Finch!'

To Mercy's surprise, Dorothy's dark eyes were brimming with emotion. 'Mercy? It is you, isn't it?' Her hand lifted to her mouth for a moment and she stood staring, seeming overwhelmed.

Mercy introduced Susan to Dorothy, but Dorothy, wiping her eyes, barely seemed to hear her.

'Look at you – you've grown!'

Mercy saw Dorothy examining her hungrily, taking in the state of her ragged clothes, the worn-out boots of Jack's that Elsie had handed on to her and her pallid, slum-dweller's skin, and her anger spilled out.

'She 'ad no right to do it, Mercy, that woman, taking you from Hanley's like that and hiding you away so none of us knew where you'd gone. Miss Rowney was – well, she was upset like.' This was a slight exaggeration of the truth and Miss O'Donnell's reaction had been 'Good riddance. She came from the streets and now she's gone back to 'em.'

Mercy's eyes widened with fear. An awful dread seized her.

'I don't want to go back,' she gabbled. 'I can't go back there – I want to stay 'ere, with Susan. I'm never leaving 'er!'

Dorothy smiled, remembering Mercy's devotion to little Amy Laski.

'I don't work at Hanley's no more. I went back after – into service, I mean. Listen Mercy, where're you living?'

'Nine Court, Angel Street. Behind St Joseph's.'

Dorothy nodded. It was a poor, run-down area of the sort she knew well, having grown up on a back yard herself. No wonder the child looked so ragged and pasty-faced.

'And what about that woman? She treat you all right?'

Mercy's expression of utter loathing spoke more than words could have done. 'She's awright,' was all she said. At least the beatings had mostly stopped.

'Look, I've got to get back to the mistress. But I'll come and see you, soon as I can.' Tearful again she held Mercy tight in her arms. She seemed reluctant to let her go.

Feeling choked herself Mercy said, 'It's really lovely to see you again, Dorothy. I never got time to say goodbye to you.'

She watched Dorothy's familiar, straight-backed figure move away into the crowd. Dorothy turned more than once and waved her hanky.

'Ever so good to me, she was,' Mercy said, her throat aching. She remembered the red jelly Dorothy had brought her in the cellar and felt as if she were watching her only family walk away.

'She looks a nice, kind lady,' Susan said, a wistful note still in her voice.

'Come on—' Mercy rallied herself to cheer Susan. 'Let's go and see what's going on up New Street, shall we?'

*

Dorothy Finch returned to her employer's house in an elegant street in Handsworth, in a state of turmoil.

As soon as she'd caught sight of Mercy's bright hair in the Bull Ring she'd been certain this was the child she'd lost sight of two years before. The child she had watched so carefully and fondly from infancy.

She went straight to the large sitting room at the front of the house where she found her mistress, Mrs Neville Weston, sitting with the nanny and the two small Weston boys. Robert, a sturdy dark-haired five-year-old, had the florid complexion of his father and Edward, three, was slender, fair and fragile in looks.

Grace Weston looked up, bewildered to see her maid appearing at this time, for this was her afternoon off.

'Could I have a word with you, ma'am, in private?'

Grace eyed the nanny and children, and there was something about the breathless catch in her maid's voice which hastened her to say, 'Would you please take them up and run a bath now?' The boys began a whining protest at the nanny's attempts to hustle them away. Grace went with them to the hall and stood beside the polished bannister smiling up at them. 'I'll come and see you in just a little while. We'll have a story – as a special treat.'

There was still a smile in her eyes as she came in and closed the door.

As soon as they were alone Dorothy began to sob, the pent-up emotions of relief, guilt and sorrow pouring out.

'Whatever's happened?' Grace moved to her straight away, putting her arms round her, her fair head close to Dorothy's dark one. For these women were much more than employer and servant. They had been a close support and bearer of each other's confidences for some years.

Dorothy turned her head at last and looked fearfully

into Grace's pale eyes. She saw anguish seize her mistress's face as she said, 'I saw her – today, when I was in town. I've found her. I've found Mercy.'

Not many afternoons later, Dorothy arrived in Angel Street bringing with her two dresses, one in yellow lawn, the other in soft blue wool, and a pair of boots that she hoped would fit Mercy.

Seeing both her and her gifts, Mercy blushed with pleasure and danced overjoyed round the room with the yellow dress held against her. 'Oh Dorothy, I've never seen anything so pretty before!'

'And this one will be lovely for Susan – look.' She laid the blue frock against Susan, and Dorothy saw the child beam with delight. She'd been about to protest that both dresses were for Mercy, but she kept quiet. Let the other poor kid have one. The dress she had on now was a terrible grey bag of a thing.

'You didn't buy these did you?' Mercy asked anxiously.

'No – the mistress, my employer – she's got older daughters with lots of lovely clothes . . .' She and Grace had worked on this harmless lie together. They were in fact hand-me-downs from the daughters of friends. 'She said I could hand them on to someone who needed them.'

'She's very kind,' Mercy said, trying to imagine such wealth and benevolence.

'You going to make 'er some tea?' Susan asked timidly. She was rather in awe of Dorothy who, although only a servant, seemed to have appeared from a completely different existence where people still had dresses that looked new when they'd finished with them.

Mercy ran out to the tap to fill the kettle. They

talked all afternoon. Mercy could barely keep still in her excitement at having Dorothy there. She told her cautiously about her life in Angel Street, playing on the positive side for Susan's sake. She talked about school, the Peppers, Elsie's kindness.

'Johnny and Tom, the twins, they're my best pals – well, after Susan! And there's little Rosalie, she's nearly five now . . .'

Dorothy listened, trying to keep all her attention on Mercy's face, but she couldn't help her gaze wandering, taking in the rotten state of the place: furniture supplemented with orange crates, the broken floor, and the mean, loathsome smells of damp and mould which she found unspeakably depressing. The more so because it brought back memories of her own childhood. Going into service at fourteen had been her salvation and she was grateful for it daily.

Preparing to leave after their chat she said, 'Let me know if there's anything you need, Mercy. And you, Susan,' she added kindly.

She was moving to embrace Mercy when Mabel came barging in from work.

'I see no one's bothered scrubbing the step.' She was carrying on before she'd even got in. 'Oi – what's going on?' Mercy heard panic in her voice. 'Who're you?'

Mercy stepped forward and said proudly, 'This is Dorothy.'

'Oh yes – Dorothy who?' Mabel's tone was brazen but wary, her arms crossed defensively. She and Dorothy were eyeing each other up with instant mutual distrust.

'She looked after me in the home.'

'What's that rubbish you're talking?' Mabel blustered. What with the NSPCC turning up on her doorstep and now this, Mabel was beginning to feel quite persecuted.

'You're a born liar, aren't you?' Dorothy said, disgusted. 'It were only two years ago, not a lifetime. D'you think I wouldn't be able to remember what someone looks like? Lucky for you she wants to stay here at the moment or I could make trouble for you. But I'll be keeping an eye on Mercy from now on, and don't you forget it.'

Chapter Ten

February 1914

'I've got it – 'e give me the job!'

Mercy tore into Elsie's house to tell Susan. Thanks to Johnny Pepper she had her first job at the bakery in Digbeth where he was employed as a delivery boy.

'Well there you are,' Elsie smiled. She was fixing up her escaping coils of rusty hair. 'You're a worker. You'll get on, you will.'

''Course you got it,' Susan beamed. 'I said you would, didn' I?'

'I might be in with a chance of the odd loaf or bag of stale cakes, you never know!' Mercy was laughing partly with relief as she went to stand behind Susan. It had been her first shot at getting a job and she'd been nervous. 'Hey,' she said. 'That's beautiful, that is!'

Over Susan's shoulder she could see the neat job she was doing mending the astrakhan collar on an overcoat. She was good at it – and not just hand sewing either. Just after Christmas which had been drab and bleak, a miracle had happened.

Mrs White, the miserable, reclusive woman in the cottage across the yard, had dropped dead, aged fifty-seven. Mr White put it all down to nerves. Shortly after, looking a good deal more cheerful than, as Elsie put it, ''e 'ad a right to,' he started carrying a whole load of stuff out into the yard.

'I could cart it off and flog it,' he said, unshaven but chirpy. 'But I thought if any of yer'd give us a bob for anything . . .'

With an absolute lack of sentiment he laid out Mrs White's small selection of clothes over a couple of battered chairs.

'Oh my word,' Mary Jones exclaimed to Elsie. ''E's even brought 'er drawers out. Well I wouldn't be . . .' She trailed off.

'What? Seen dead in 'em? Don't suppose she 'ad that in mind either. Depends 'ow fussy you can afford to be, don't it?' Elsie looked thoughtful. 'Be different if she'd been the least bit pleasant some'ow, wouldn't it?'

There was a small, oblong mirror, a threadbare old coat and Mrs White's few personal bits and bobs: hairpins, a brush, corset, a doll with a chipped porcelain face, old shoes with bunion-shaped hills in them, spectacles. And – Mercy caught her breath – almost seeming to glow in the knife-edged cold as it sat on its wrought iron base across the yard: an old Singer sewing machine. She galloped across.

''Ow much d'you want for that?' Never mind whether it worked. They'd make it work.

'Well 'ow much can yer give me?' Mr White seemed in a celebratory mood.

''E must be as short as anything – no wage or nothing coming in,' Mercy said to Susan after. ''E just didn't seem to care.'

Susan shrugged. 'Looks as if the only thing 'e really wanted shot of's already gone.'

They gave him five shillings for the machine. Mabel stared at it as if it were about to lay a golden egg. Bummy Pepper gave it a clean up and oiled it, humming to himself.

They bought a new needle and spools and Susan was in business. Well almost.

Gradually, by word of mouth, she was getting odd bits of work. When Dorothy came round Mercy showed her Susan's neat skills.

'I'm sure Mrs Weston – my mistress – will know people who need a seamstress,' Dorothy said. 'I'll see what I can do.'

The jobs had already begun to trickle in. Susan was happier than Mercy had ever seen her. Her usually tiny appetite had picked up, she had a pink tinge in her cheeks and an air of purpose.

'I'm so lucky, aren't I, Mrs Pepper?' she said to Elsie one day. And Elsie's tired face lifted into a smile. If someone in Susan's state felt lucky, she was a lesson to all of them.

'Now you've got two earners in your 'ouse,' she said to Mercy. 'Mabel'll be stopping to put 'er feet up.'

When Mercy had been at work for a few weeks she came home carrying a cage in which there was a grey parrot with lead-shot eyes.

''Ere you are, as promised.' She put the cage on the table. 'It was a lark bringing this 'ome on the bus, I can tell yer!'

Mabel would be outraged with her for squandering money in this way but Mercy didn't care.

Susan gasped at the sight of it.

'He's lovely! Is it a boy one?'

'The bloke said so. What're you going to call 'im?'
Susan put her head on one side. The parrot did the same and Susan, Mercy and Elsie roared with laughter.

'George,' Susan said, wiping her eyes. ''E looks like a George to me.'

One Saturday evening soon after, Mabel was waiting for Stan again. This time she wasn't in bed but sitting downstairs at the stained table sipping strong tea with plenty of sugar and cursing George who was scratching round the bottom of the cage screeching to himself.

'I'd find a recipe for parrot pie if I 'ad my way,' she growled at him. 'Noisy, stinking thing.'

She soon heard the latch go and there was Stan, dressed only in a singlet and braces with his trousers although it was so cold you could see your breath even in the house.

'What's all this?' All these months she'd been upstairs waiting for him, and here she was fully dressed without even a promising bit of breast showing.

'Shut the door, Stan, I've summat to talk to yer about.'

He kicked the door shut and went to stand by the range, slicking his hair back. Not being very observant, he didn't notice Mabel's excited expression.

'What's up – eh? We gunna go and get on with it in a tick?' He jerked his head meaningfully towards the stairs.

Mabel started to smile, showing her big, gappy teeth. 'It's happened, Stan. It had to in the end, didn't it? I'm carrying your babby.'

Stan's face fell into a study of shock.

'But, Mabel, I thought – I mean we've been at it a long time now. I thought you couldn't no longer – not like Mary . . .'

Mabel had in a roundabout way led Stan to believe she couldn't conceive again, and as the months passed she'd come close to convincing herself as well. All this time and nothing. But now . . . Now she had a chance of hooking herself a breadwinner at last and another babby into the bargain! This time she'd have a proper child. Someone to love her. She'd prove she could be a mother like anyone else. She stood up and went to nuzzle her face against Stan's chest, slipping one arm round him, she unfastened her blouse with the other to show her generous cleavage.

'Say you're pleased, Stan?' she wheedled. 'Your babby. You and me. We can 'ave a fresh start now – get away from all our worries. You can get away from her.'

'Are you mad, woman?' Stan pushed her away, agitatedly pulled his fags out. He lit one and stood puffing away, tapping his thigh with his other hand with quick, taut movements.

'I've already got four kids. You told me, Mabel—' He pointed the cigarette like a gun in her crumpling face. 'You lied to me, you did . . .'

Stan's brain never worked quickly at the best of times and it was on overtime shift now. He'd never questioned Mabel's version of her infertility since his only interest was in getting his leg over. Now she was really putting the wind up him and he couldn't think fast enough what to do.

'I don't know why you're laying the blame on me any'ow, you're that easy. 'Ow do I know who else you've been with?'

He used his indignation to propel himself out of the house. Then he stuck his head back through the door.

'And don't you come laying the blame on me and upsetting my missis. She's got enough on 'er plate as it is!'

When Mercy and Susan got home that evening, depositing bags of scrag-end, potatoes and greens on the table with a pound of sausage, bags of broken biscuits and bruised apples, Mabel was upstairs in her room. Good, Mercy thought, that's her out of the way.

'Mom?' Susan called up to her.

No reply. The two of them listened.

'She's blarting,' Susan said, amazed.

'What on earth can've happened?' Mercy was frowning.

Mabel wasn't a weeper, normally speaking, but today she wasn't taking any trouble to hide her sniffles and mewling noises. She'd really and truly believed Stan would drop everything for her. After all, he did nothing but complain about Mary. But now it was she, Mabel, who was being thrown aside like an old piece of scrap. Just when she thought it might be her turn for some luck for once in life! She was carrying another babby with no husband, precious little money and only that little cow Mercy to help her. Let alone what she'd get in the way of clever comments from smug-faced Elsie Pepper. No – she got up hurriedly off the sordid bed. She wasn't having that. There was only one thing for it.

A few moments later she came heavily downstairs, blowsy and dishevelled-looking. The two girls turned wide eyes on her, the blotchy cheeks and swollen eyes obvious even in the gaslight.

'Mom.' Susan looked away, her cheeks turning pink. 'Your blouse . . .'

'Oh, ah—' Mabel fumblingly buttoned herself back into it. 'I've come to a decision. We've got to move.'

'Move?' Susan said, bewildered. Mercy listened in disbelief.

'Yes, move,' Mabel snapped. 'To another 'ouse. Another part of town, away from 'ere. If yer must know,

I'm expecting Stan Jones's babby and I don't want to bring it into the world around the likes of this lot.'

After a couple of days in which Mabel's house was full of nothing but rows on this subject, Stan's brain caught up with his body and he did some (for him) quick thinking. Here he was, still a young man, struggling, with no real skills to get a decent job, a frail and prematurely aged wife and four brats all trapped together in a rotting house. He was drowning in the difficulties of it, could feel his youth and strength being sucked from him. Didn't he deserve another chance?

And Mabel was offering it – a strong woman, older than him, capable of working. One kid – she wasn't bringing that cripple with her, oh no. They could avoid having any more. And she was a bit of all right in bed, Mabel was – that was the main thing about her.

On the third morning, after retching over the scullery sink, Mabel left for work with a bag and never came home in the evening. Susan was worried to death until they discovered that Stan had disappeared too and suddenly it was clear as anything what had happened.

'I knew she was a scheming, worthless liar,' Elsie raged to Bummy that night. 'But I never thought she'd go and desert that kid of 'ers. And as for poor Mary . . .'

The two of them, and Mercy, spent that evening trying to comfort first Susan – 'How could she go and leave us?' she sobbed, hurt to the very core. 'She's my Mom! And to go with that idiot of a bloke . . .' and then Mary Jones, who was almost hysterical with panic.

'How'm I going to manage? We can barely afford to eat as it is! How could 'e? If I ever see 'im again – or 'er

– I'll kill the pair of 'em with my bare hands.' Her youngest child lay suckling at her tiny breast as she sat sobbing and sniffing. 'Oh Elsie, what in heaven am I going to do? I'll have to move back in with me mom in 'er one room – we'll be in the workhouse else!'

'No.' Elsie's jaw was set and determined. 'You won't have to do that, I'll see to it.'

Bummy, stood in the doorway, hoiked his trousers up from behind with one hand and nodded in agreement. 'Terrible that is, the Parish. D'you remember?'

Elsie nodded curtly. Of course she remembered. The time when they had five young ones, Maryann, Frank, Josephine, Cathleen and Lena, the one they'd lost soon after from diphtheria. Bummy had injured his back so badly that for weeks, months, he couldn't work. He'd lain helpless, watching his vibrant, copper-haired wife exhaust herself.

Finally Elsie went to the local Board of Guardians, timidly asking for help. She was given a weekly allowance of bread but she would never forget the terror and humiliation of it, the rude personal questions, the hard, mistrusting eyes of the people on the board. It was such a degrading time in her life, a reminder of the power others could have over her. Even now she felt panic and disgust thinking of it.

As Bummy had recovered with agonizing slowness, Elsie vowed she would never let herself or anyone else she could save from it have to put themselves at the mercy of the Parish again.

She leant over and took Mary's hand.

'Don't fret. I've got Johnny and Tom out at work now as well as the girls. And there's Mercy and Susan, though God knows they've got the rent to keep up on their own now. But we'll all rally round – I'll make sure of that.

If Elsie said they were going to give help to Mary, then Mercy and Susan were going to do as she said.

'We ought to,' Susan said. 'After all, it's my mom who's caused her all this trouble.'

'The one thing she's good at,' Mercy retorted.

Susan was now earning rather well. Mercy had gone round for her putting cards in shop windows, and she found new customers. Sewing for the poor brought in a very small trickle of money, but far more lucrative was the trade from Dorothy. The clothes she bought for Susan to mend were of much higher quality, sometimes they were awed by the sight of them. Dorothy made sure she was handsomely paid. One week Susan made as much as twelve shillings!

Her confidence was growing and her customers were happy too.

'Imagine if they could see where their clothes are going!' Dorothy said to Grace, holding up a cream satin evening gown with lace straps and underskirt. Its owner wanted it taken in over the hips.

Grace was barely listening. They were standing in the small dressing room which extended off Grace and Neville Weston's comfortable bedchamber. Grace seemed to stare through Dorothy, her expression troubled.

'What is it?' Dorothy asked gently.

Grace looked into her eyes. 'I can't bear it, thinking of her there, in that terrible place!'

If her life had proceeded as her stern, fiercely religious father had planned, Grace's only awareness of the conditions of the slum courtyards, the raucous life of the poor, would have been no more than snatched glimpses as she swept past in a carriage to the centre of Birmingham. The life Mercy was leading, the struggles against poverty and squalor, would have been so distant from her as to be unimaginable.

She could hardly bear to think of her desperate time as 'Lily'. It was an abyss in her experience, those days which had denied her her name, her class, her normally comfortable life, her very sense of self. She had for a short time lived and been part of that other alien life in the wilderness. She recalled even now in her dreams the damp, bug-ridden walls, the fetid smells, the awful sense of enforced intimacy with others. And the terror of that lonely birth. Its memory was all the more horrific in its contrast with her other life. As soon as she could stand after the birth she had fled from it, imagining it would then be over, something she could close the door on as soon as she walked away from the Joseph Hanley Home.

Yet she had not forseen its consequences, that she would never escape the hold those memories had on her, or the tiny child she had brought forth.

'It's worse now!' Her voice cracked. 'Now we've found her – knowing where she is again. At least while she was lost to us we knew nothing, and could do nothing, except hope. And she's older now ... I find this present situation ...'

She turned away, gliding into her bedchamber, a lace handkerchief pressed to her face as her shoulders heaved.

'It's unbearable!' Dorothy heard her voice, barely more than a whisper. She saw Grace struggle to compose herself, as she had done so many times over the years, hearing about Mercy when she was at the Hanley Home. She bent her immaculately coiffured head, two golden plaits coiled low behind her ears.

'Dorothy—' She turned, eyes full of tears, appealing to her friend across the white linen of the bed. 'I don't know if I can endure it any more.'

Dorothy went to her quickly, putting her hands on Grace's shoulders. 'Of course you can, Grace, my dear one – you can. You have to be strong for the boys, and you've been so brave until now. The child's a beauty – the image of you. She's fourteen now. If you can just be sure of that position for her ... Just keep yourself together. Good can come of all this, I'm sure of it.'

There was a pause, and both women heard footsteps. Grace pulled her expression into one approaching composure. 'You'd better go. Neville's coming up to change.'

As she spoke, the door opened abruptly.

'Oh – you're here again, are you?' Neville said to Dorothy, pushing past her into the room.

Grace's eyes met Dorothy's, urgently entreating her to leave. Dorothy slipped quietly from the room.

'Forever hanging about, that one, isn't she?' Neville was full of irritation. He sat on the bed pulling his boots off. 'Gets on my nerves.'

'I'm sorry, dear.' Grace spoke in a quiet, even voice, unfastening her hair in front of the mirror. 'I wasn't expecting you up quite so soon. Did you have a pleasant day?' Weston's was Neville's family firm, providing lighting for the railways.

'Pleasant? You think work is pleasant, do you?' He watched his wife from behind, the gentle curve of her hips, that eternal smooth neatness of hers. By God, how he hungered for a woman with hot blood in her veins!

Seeing him watching her in the glass, Grace turned and

attempted a bright smile. Neville ignored her, got up and stumped into the dressing room.

Downstairs, Dorothy thought of the two of them up there, her mouth pulled down in a hard grimace. She had always loathed Neville, had a flesh-creeping distaste for his stocky body, red cheeks and thick brown hair which sat on top of his head with the unsettled look of a wig. Add to that his selfishness and boorishness and Dorothy burned with protective indignation on Grace's behalf, trapped as she was in her life with this ox of a man.

Grace tried to keep up at least the appearance of a civilized marriage, if not a happy one.

'Never mind,' she had said to Dorothy on many occasions. 'I have all I need. I have you and I have my children.

Chapter Eleven

If it hadn't been for Susan's pain over her desertion by her mother, Mercy would have been almost completely happy. She was free of Mabel, could organize the place how she wanted and had kind neighbours. There were Dorothy's visits, every week or two and Mercy had begun to feel she belonged somewhere. No one had set eyes on Mabel or Stan.

Between them, she and Susan were at last making the inside of the house more homely. Mabel, in a perverse way, had refused even to have the rotten stair tread mended, something she and Mercy were constantly having rows about.

'Mr Pepper could fix that soon as winking,' Mercy kept saying. 'I'm fed up with nearly falling through it all the time.'

'We don't need the likes of 'im coming in 'ere,' Mabel would snarl. 'We'll live with it, that's what we'll do.'

'You'd cut off your own nose to spite yer face, wouldn't you?' Mercy snapped, exasperated. She could never get to grips with Mabel's odd combination of self-indulgence and self-punishment.

Now she'd gone, Mercy had had Bummy Pepper in straight away and they had a nice new tread. And bit by bit she was picking up a few bits of furniture: an old settle which Mercy polished until it was a smooth, rich colour, a little cupboard for their few crocks, a comfortable chair for Susan to rest by the fire, and Susan had botched two peg rugs, using old pieces of hessian and scraps of material. They were bright and colourful and covered some of the worst wear on the bricks. Now she was working on some curtains.

The job at Wrigley's Bakery was straightforward enough. Every morning Mercy helped Susan get up. They'd long perfected the art of getting her downstairs. She took Susan in the wheelchair to Elsie's house where she did most of her work.

'I'll bring yer a doughnut!' Mercy sometimes called cheerfully as she set off and Elsie would reply, 'Make it a bagful!'

She walked into town with Tom and Johnny. No longer did she have to hobble along in poorly fitting boots that cramped her feet and chafed her chilblains. Friends of Dorothy's mistress seemed to have a dazzling surplus of clothes discarded by their daughters, and while Mercy didn't wear the prettiest dresses to work, even her plain, serviceable clothes looked quite smart and respectable.

'You're turning into a right toff,' Elsie teased her.

'Well, Rosalie'll be able to have all this lot when she's bigger,' Mercy said.

Yes, life was much better. Elsie noticed Mercy's new softness, a lack of the aggression that had always flared so easily in her before. She was gentle with Susan, tried to comfort her, though knowing there was no true comfort for this kind of loss.

One oppressively grey morning Mercy set off as usual with Johnny and Tom. It was threatening snow and the clouds had already squeezed out a few fat flakes which were drifting down through the biting air. They walked fast to keep warm, Johnny, slightly ahead, impatient as a spring, and Tom beside her, both with their caps pulled down hard and hands pushed into their jacket pockets. Mercy's coat – another offering from Dorothy – was blue with a smooth velvet collar, and she wore a little, old-fashioned bonnet the colour of pigeons' wings. She was beginning to feel small now beside the twins, Johnny especially, who was more than a head taller than her. They walked watching their feet. The pavement was icy.

''Ow's Susan bearing up?' Tom asked 'She don't say much.'

'She misses 'er mom. Cries quite a bit for 'er – nights, you know, when there's time to think about it. But like you say, she don't keep on about it much. She's that busy in the day she's no time to dwell on it.'

'It's rotten when yer come to think of it though,' Tom said, pale face wincing at the cold. 'First 'er dad goes off and leaves 'er, then 'er mom. And that's on top of 'er legs, like.'

Mercy didn't say anything, just walked on, eyes stung by the cold air which seemed to blast up from the hub of the waking city as if from a freezing cauldron. Tom looked round at her with his dark eyes. If Mercy had been looking, she'd have seen the unguarded expression of affection in them.

'I s'pose it weren't any better for you neither,' he said apologetically. They didn't talk like this normally. As a rule it was pranks and gossip on the way to work, the lads sometimes sparring and cuffing each other.

Mercy sighed. 'Never knew my mom and dad in the first place to lose 'em, did I?'

'How d'you get to that home then?' Johnny blurted out.

'Dunno. They never told me. They found me some-where – in the street. That's my mom, the streets of

Brum!' She tried to make a joke of it. 'Any'ow, that's way back now, and your mom's been so good to us . . .'

Tom peeled off to work at Stern's in Bull Street, and once they'd got to Wrigley's in Digbeth Johnny was off on his rounds with the delivery cycle, red-eyed from the cold and warm breath streaming white from his mouth.

Mercy served in the shop. She loved the clean white tiles, the smells of dough, jam, burnt currants and steamy warmth. It was cosy, and sometimes she hugged herself behind the counter relishing the place, its neat rows of tarts and buns in the glass-fronted cabinets, the aroma of crusty bread, speckled gold of cinnamon and nutmeg on custard tarts, rich dabs of chocolate, coconut snow . . .

'I wouldn't swap my job,' she told Susan. 'It's clean and warm, and all the people coming in – it's friendly like.'

Mr Wrigley was a small, anxious man with an almost completely bald head and a pert moustache on his top lip, who toiled, perspiring constantly, in the bakehouse behind the shop. His wife, red-cheeked and stolid, carried in fresh trays of bread or cakes, dressed in a white apron dusted with flour.

''Ere yer go, bab,' she'd say to Mercy. ''Ere's more for yer!' as if it were Mercy's personal task to eat every cake in the shop.

Mercy served the customers, wrapped warm loaves in layers of tissue paper, pushed sticky buns into bags and rang up the purchases on the huge steel till. She also worked to keep the place looking attractive and orderly, sweeping the black and white tiled floor and rearranging the bread and cakes to fill the gaps.

'It's nice for us to 'ave such a pretty lass serving,' Mrs Wrigley told her. ''Specially one who's as presentable as you. Good for business like, ain't it?'

'Well I'm happy in my work, Mrs Wrigley,' Mercy laughed. 'And if it's good for business, all the better.'

At closing time she and Johnny often set off together again, laughing and joking. She always enjoyed Johnny's cheek. Unlike Tom he seemed energized by his day's work, ready for anything, his freckled face pink and weather-beaten. Tom though, usually looked pale and tired after a day at Stern's. His nails were always black with tarnish and silver polish. Mr Stern, a kindly, prematurely aged man with tiny wire spectacles, a grey beard and a large wife, was teaching Tom the art of engraving and burnishing silver. Later he was to learn electroplating. The shop's windows were crammed with candlesticks, cups, medals and jewellery, and it was very dark inside, lit only by a single gas mantle.

'You look like a mouse crawling out of a hole,' Mercy had teased him one day when he appeared squinting into the afternoon.

Sometimes she felt like slipping her arms through Tom's and Johnny's. They were like brothers to her: family. But she knew they'd say, 'Oi, gerroff, will yer! What're yer playing at!'

That snowy day when she reached Elsie's with a bag of day-old Chelsea buns, she found Susan still toiling away on her sewing machine. Cathleen was sitting close to the fire, lips tinged with blue despite the warmth. Jack was at the table with Frank in his uniform, and Josephine, whose usual expression of discontent had quite vanished (she'd found A Man at last). Dorothy, who'd turned down Elsie's offer of tea, was also there waiting for her.

'You're soon back!' Mercy cried, beaming. 'Less than a week, ain't it?' She opened the bag of buns and they were shared out, Dorothy shaking her head when offered a piece of one.

'She giving you some extra time off?' Mercy asked her, chewing.

Dorothy stood up, her face solemn. 'I'd like a word with you, Mercy. In private like.'

Mercy looked uncertainly at Elsie. So far as she was concerned nothing was so private that the Peppers and Susan couldn't hear it.

'Go round to yours,' Elsie said with chilly tact. 'Then you and Miss Finch can talk without all the commotion.' She wasn't sure that 'Miss Finch' didn't think she was a cut above them all, but Mercy seemed to think a lot of her so she wasn't going to make an issue of anything.

'You come to tell me you're getting married?' Mercy joked as they walked into number two.

Dorothy looked astonished. 'No. What in heaven's name made you think that?'

'You look a bit sort of excited. I wondered—'

'Would that be summat to get excited about?' Dorothy retorted, with such venom in her voice that Mercy was taken aback. Dorothy sat, removed her hat and arranged the powder blue folds of her dress carefully on her knees.

'I have got news for you though, and I think you'll find it exciting when I tell you.'

Mercy stood by the table, clearing the plates from their rushed breakfast that morning. She raised one eyebrow curiously at Dorothy.

'We've — I've found you a position, Mercy. A very good one with a respectable family — well off too. They need a maid of all work. It's a great chance for you, Mercy. You'll live in a lovely house — quite different from here. Good conditions, and I know they'll treat you right. You can start as soon as you like.'

She spoke with complete confidence that Mercy would be overjoyed at the offer.

Mercy stared at her, forehead creased as if she hadn't understood.

'It's a job in service, Mercy.' Dorothy stood up again and leant across the table speaking quietly but insistently. 'A good start in life for you now you're old enough. Grab it and take it quick.'

Mercy's sudden burst of laughter took her completely aback.

'But I don't need a job, Dorothy! I've already got one and I'm happy with that. It's nice of you to think of me and go to all this trouble but I don't want another job just now.'

'But you'd be in a beautiful house – carpets on the floor. It's a job many a young girl'd jump at. And it wouldn't end there. You could work your way up – p'raps even get to be cook there one day if you prove yourself.'

Mercy had no idea just how much she exasperated Dorothy by laughing again. 'Oh, I've been cook here for quite a long while already.' She'd begun bustling around, clattering plates, carrying in vegetables. 'No need for me to go anywhere to do that.'

'She won't take it.'

Dorothy stood in front of Grace, her face red. She had felt helpless when she left Mercy, but now she was furious, and ashamed at the failure of her powers of persuasion.

They were in the comfortable parlour, door closed against the rest of the house, a young fire burning smokily in the grate. Grace moved up and down the hearth, agitated, her dress rustling. Her usually smooth voice took on an edge of shrillness.

'You mean . . .?'

'She said she's happy where she is.'

'Those were her words?'

'She seemed to find the offer all rather amusing,' Dorothy confessed bitterly. 'The silly girl.'

'But she can't want to stay there!' Grace burst out. 'Doesn't she know an opportunity when she's presented with it? There she is, living in that terrible . . . slum of a place, and she turns down a position in one of the most prestigious houses in the city! Dorothy—' Grace's eyes filled with tears. 'This is too terrible. It's just her ignorance that's making her react like this. After all, what does my poor child know of fine houses or anything except an orphanage and a workman's house? You've got to go and make her see how much better it would be for her. Go back tomorrow. You've got to make her take that position!'

'Blimey,' Mercy joked when she found Dorothy in Angel Street again the next day. 'You out of a job or summat?'

'Come in here—'

Mercy had been in the yard with Elsie, and Dorothy more or less ordered her into her own house.

'What's the matter?' She wasn't used to Dorothy behaving so sternly. And she saw a hard expression in the woman's eyes which worried her.

'We need to have words, miss.' Dorothy confronted her once more across the table. 'I come here yesterday and brought you an offer of a good job. A flaming good one, the like of which you'll be lucky ever to see again.'

'Oh Dorothy!' Mercy was relieved. 'It's that again, is

it? I told you, I don't need a job. It was kind of you, but—'

'Take the position.' It was an order, almost spat out. The two women stood staring into each other's eyes. A muscle twitched in Mercy's thin face and she clenched her teeth.

'Dorothy, I don't want it. I told you.'

'Take it!' Dorothy slapped her hand hard on the table, nostrils flaring. 'Who d'you think you are, eh? Turning down summat like that as if you could pick and choose? You're an orphan, you've come from the workhouse or near enough, and life ain't about picking and choosing when you're poor – you take what you're given and you're grateful!'

The look that came over Mercy's face as she spoke filled Dorothy with a sudden chill. She had assumed all this time that this child who so resembled Grace, was in fact a minute replica of her mother, would grow into the same woman with the angelic hair, grey eyes, the soft, yielding personality. But there was other blood in Mercy. It was only now, seeing the glint in Mercy's eyes and her jutting chin, Dorothy recognized she was dealing with a far more flint-like character. She experienced a moment of panic, faced with the strength of this temperament.

'I don't know what all this is to you,' Mercy said, her voice polite but steely. 'I'm grateful for the offer but the answer's no and could never be anything else.'

'But why?'

'Because this is my place here.'

'It doesn't have to be!' Dorothy was growing quite distressed. If only she could tell the girl she was the daughter of a wealthy industrialist's wife, have her see that she didn't truly belong here!

'These're my people,' Mercy said. 'They're the only

people who've ever been anything to me – apart from you. Mrs Pepper's been like a mom to me and I'll never, ever leave Susan. She's all I've got and I've promised 'er. So don't ask me. Everyone else's left 'er and I'm not going to do it as well.'

'But she could go to Mrs Pepper,' Dorothy argued desperately. How could she go and face Grace, having failed again?

'No,' Mercy said simply.

'Yer a stupid little fool.' Dorothy's voice was harsh with bitterness.

'Well maybe I am. I'm grateful, more than, for all you've done for us,' Mercy said, turning away. 'But if you think it's bought you the right to come 'ere telling me what to do you can have back every stitch you've brought. I don't want anything from you if that's the arrangement.'

Chapter Twelve

The summer of 1914 was a very hot one. Smoke from factory chimneys hung in the air. It was a struggle to keep food fresh, the yards in Angel Street were full of dust and the dry-pan privies stank and attracted swarms of flies. Dogs panted in patches of shade under carts or beside steps.

Wrigley's Bakery felt like a furnace by day. They propped the door open to the street despite the dust and grime and Mrs Wrigley kept going to stand by the door in her apron, watching trams on the Stratford Road, fanning herself with a newspaper.

'Phew – this is too much, this is!' she'd say, cheeks a burning red. 'We could do with a drop of rain!'

When at the end of June an Austrian Archduke was shot in Sarajevo, most people had their minds on holiday time. Some would get away to the coast or at least the country. In the Angel Street neighbourhood a few visits were planned for the August Bank Holiday, as far as the Lickeys or Clent Hills. As for Mercy and Susan, they were going as far as Highgate Park where they could lie on the sloping grass with straw hats, eat, laugh, and above all, do absolutely nothing for the day except watch white wisps of cloud edge across a Wedgwood blue sky.

'I wonder what Mom's doing,' Susan said sadly as they lay side by side on the freshly cut grass. She always insisted on having her legs covered.

Mercy reached out and squeezed her hand. 'I s'pect

she's all right.' It was the one despondent moment of the day and Mercy felt helpless, and guilty too, as she so preferred life without Mabel. They were managing. She was determined not to be beaten.

Within days of this sunny respite the air was full of war. Shrill newspaper headlines: War Against the Hun! Flags and bunting, excited queues outside the hastily established recruiting offices taking the King's shilling, young men in khaki with tightly bound puttees, and suddenly the city emptied of horses. They were needed more for the War than they were at home! The talk was aggressive and defiant. Old soldiers of the Boer War gathered in pubs and chewed over events. Men were thin on the ground in Nine Court and Bummy went down the pub with Mr White who was streets more amiable nowadays. A picture of the King and Queen went up in the window of the local huckster's shop. In the name of Honour and of Justice, the Hun were going to be taught a lesson they wouldn't forget!

'It's all very well,' Mercy said, arriving back at Elsie's with the twins one afternoon in mid-September. 'But when's summat going to happen?' She pulled off her straw hat and fanned herself with it. 'We tried to get a paper on the way 'ome but they was all gone again.'

'Summat *has* happened,' Elsie said, tight-lipped. 'Our Frank's only gone and joined up hasn't 'e?'

There were gasps from the twins, of envy from Johnny, more of awe from Tom.

Frank had stood in front of Lord Kitchener's recruitment poster, saw the authority of that pointing finger and the handlebar moustache and speedily decided his country needed him. This being a minor incentive compared with getting away from his missis, he'd hurried to the recruiting station in Great Charles Street.

''E's in the First City Battalion – that's the Fourteenth Warwicks, I think 'e said.' Elsie's face was pale under the freckles. 'I don't know whether to be proud of 'im or put 'im across my knee. 'E's off tomorrow, for training in Sutton Park.'

'Cor!' Johnny was ahop with excitement. 'That's bostin'! I wish I could go!'

'You're too young, and it'll all be over before you get a chance,' Bummy said from the sofa. But there was a wistful note in his voice and Mercy sensed he was envious of Frank too in his way. It was the thing to do nowadays, to prove your manhood.

Mary Jones said, 'Well I hope Stan's joining up and they finish 'im off for us.'

She was battling with financial hardship on top of the daily grind of bringing up four young kids on her own: Lisa eight, Molly seven, Percy four and Paul one. Battling, though not sunk. The Peppers were helping her out with the rent and Elsie, who had no real need to take in laundry any more, passed on her dwindling number of customers. The War was biting people in the purse already. So it was Mary toiling in the brewhouse at all hours now, with the dolly, maiding tub and mangle, little Paul round her legs.

Mary seemed to have found in herself a defiant strength, a kind of exhilaration in 'getting by'. She moved more briskly, face tighter, more alert.

'After all, 'e never raised a finger to do nowt when 'e was 'ere,' she said to Elsie. 'So it don't make much odds 'im going. It's thanks to you we're surviving though. I won't forget yer kindness, Elsie. If there's ever anything I can do in return . . .'

133

She'd jumped at the chance of helping with Josephine's wedding in May. When they'd begun to despair of ever getting her married off, Josephine had met Fred Larkin, a widower and publican with two kids. They had a white wedding along at St Joseph's. She was now happily queening it in the Eagle in Balsall Heath and talking babies.

Food prices were shooting up. The price of sugar doubled. People were forever moaning about the cost of bread in Wrigley's.

'Anyone'd think it was my fault there's a war on,' Mercy complained to Susan some evenings. 'They come in all in a panic and buy it all up and then everyone else is left to moan.'

Motley dressed groups of men could be seen drilling in the parks, Belgian flags rippled in the breeze outside houses in Birmingham which had become homes for refugees, and newspapers were producing the casualty lists. Yet the names of the battles – Mons, Tannenberg, the Marne, Ypres – were all strange, foreign, the War far away.

Until one morning Tom Pepper went to work as usual, to find Stern's shop had been set on fire and was a charred, still-smoking husk, many of the silver items lying black among the ash and broken glass where they had fallen.

Tom stood there in shock, cap in his hand, as the fire brigade finished dousing the damaged adjoining buildings.

'What happened to 'im?' Tom asked one of them, jerking his head towards the ruined flat above the shop.

The fireman shook his head. 'Died in their beds – the smoke, see. They've been brought out already.'

Tom nodded, sick at heart. He tried to imagine Mr

Stern lying next to his enormous wife, the smoke furling round them.

Passers-by stared, some silent, perhaps not knowing the shop. But Tom heard one say, 'That'll teach 'em. Hun bastards.'

Tom turned away. This wasn't right, none of it. Mr Stern wasn't his enemy!

Putting his cap back on he trudged off along the road. He'd have to spend the day looking for more work. But after, he wanted to talk to someone, to share his sense of outrage. His mom, of course. But as he turned towards the Jewellery Quarter, he knew the person he wanted to see most was Mercy.

He appeared at their door that evening, white-faced and dejected. Mercy wiped her hands on her apron. 'What's up?'

'Can I come in?'

''Course.' She was baffled. 'I'm brewing a pot now – sit down – you look bad.'

Tom took a chair by the table. There was a smell of stew in the room. Mercy lifted the kettle and mashed the tea. She had no idea how her presence had begun to affect Tom, how a look from her grey eyes made his stomach plunge with excitement. It had made him more shy of her and he stumbled over his words as he told them about the Sterns.

'I know they was Germans like,' Tom said. 'But they've been 'ere years and 'e was ever so good to me. Wouldn't've hurt a fly.'

Susan wheeled herself closer. 'What about the business?'

135

'Well, it's wrecked of course,' Tom said with some impatience. 'Nothing left to speak of.'

'What a terrible thing,' Mercy said thoughtfully. 'It makes all the difference knowing someone, doesn't it? Otherwise you might just say 'e was German and it served 'im right.'

'Can't say I've ever met a German,' Susan said.

'Well you've hardly met anyone, have yer?' Mercy retorted rather sharply. 'Not that that's your fault,' she added quickly. 'So what you going to do, Tom?'

'I've been out all day, over Hockley, trying to get another job in the same line. Either they said they had no vacancies, or when I said I'd worked at Stern's, one of 'em turned quite nasty.' Wearily he pushed his cowlick of brown hair back from his face. 'In the end I gave up on smithing for now. I went over to Dingleys – got a job as a porter.'

Dingleys was a well-to-do hotel in Moor Street.

'Well, there you are then,' Susan said, not quite taking in the disappointment in his voice.

Mercy leant closer and looked into his eyes in a way which made Tom almost overcome with self-consciousness. He was keenly aware of her every move, her small, thin fingers on the back of the chair beside him. Mercy saw him blushing and he couldn't hold her gaze.

'D'you want to stop and have summat to eat with us? We'd be glad of the company, wouldn't we, Susan?'

'Best not.' Tom stood up, stumbling as he tried to push the chair back. He picked up his cap. 'Mom'll 'ave counted me in for tea.'

He paused. 'You managing awright, Mercy? Anything you need you'll come to us, won't you?'

'Yes, ta,' Mercy smiled. When he'd gone she said to

Susan, 'If that'd been Johnny 'e'd just 'ave shrugged it off and that'd be that.'

'I s'pose so,' Susan said. 'Takes things 'eavier, Tom does.'

That night Tom lay awake thinking of Mercy. The very sight of her set his pulse racing. But he was rather in awe of her. She seemed so grown up, so self-contained and untouchable. How could he ever dare tell her how much time he spent dreaming of her!

The War was clearly not going to be over by Christmas. On Christmas Eve Mercy was enjoying the bustle at work, and people coming in asking for space in the bakery oven the next day for roasting their Christmas joints. The oven would be kept working, and Mrs Wrigley did her best to accommodate everyone.

'She's such a kind lady,' Mercy said to Susan that evening. 'Look, she sent me off with this fruit cake, even though things're short.'

Dorothy came briefly that afternoon. Grace longed to send her with gifts, to lavish luxuries on Mercy, but she knew it wasn't fitting, and in any case, such undue expenses would have to be justified to Neville. She had no money of her own.

Mercy greeted Dorothy in the rather more stiff, distant manner which had characterized their meetings ever since the row. Mercy regretted what had happened, but now she'd got a bit of freedom she certainly didn't want anyone organizing her life like that! Dorothy stayed for a cup of tea, admiring the few decorations Mercy had put up to cheer the room. When she stood up to go she stepped forward to put her arms round Mercy, this impulse as much for herself as for Grace. After all, she had watched the child grow up. Mercy felt herself resist for a moment, then told herself she was being silly and hugged Dorothy back.

'Have a Merry Christmas then – see you both soon,' Dorothy said awkwardly.

Mercy waved as Dorothy passed the window. She's nervous of me, she thought. How odd, Dorothy being nervous of me.

While they ate thin mutton stew and spuds, Mercy boiled up water in the kettle and all the pans she could fit on the range. When the plates were cleared she dragged the tin bath over on to the rug in front of the fire, while Susan sat under the gaslight embroidering a little lavender bag and George made whistling noises of interest from his place by the window.

Mercy looked over at him from where she was swirling cold water in with the hot, her sleeves rolled up and steam clouding her face.

'Shush you, or you'll get a dunking in 'ere too.'

George whistled, unrepentant.

'I was thinking,' Mercy said. 'I ought to give this room a coat of whitewash – cover some of the cracks and brighten it up a bit.'

''Ave we got the money?' Susan was always anxious, never confident that they could manage. 'I'm not getting many jobs now. Everyone's cutting back.'

'Oh, I dare say we can manage. Come on then. In yer get.'

She helped Susan undress, pushed the chair right up to the bath and between them, levered her down into the water, Susan supporting herself with her arms and smiling up in triumph as she sank down into the water saying, 'Ah – that's lovely, that is.'

Mercy handed her a sliver of soap, then sat down beside her as she bathed, the two of them chatting idly.

''Ere – let me do that.' Mercy knelt up to wash Susan's back and helped her with her long black hair, supporting her as she lay back in the water as she couldn't steady herself with her feet. Her body, though small for her age, was growing curvaceous, like Mabel's. Mercy watched her with a great rush of fondness as she lay, eyes closed, in the water. Susan's extreme naïveté drove her mad at times, but that kind of innocence was what she also loved most about her.

Soon Susan was beginning to shiver, so Mercy helped her out, drying her on an old, soft piece of sacking. She rubbed oil on her legs.

'Lop a bit off of my hair, will you, after you've had yours?' Susan held up a wet hank of hair. 'It's getting so long I can hardly manage to comb it out!'

Dressed again she watched Mercy tip more hot into the tub and climb in, washing her slight, rosy body in a businesslike way. There was silence, except for the little popping sound of the gas mantle and the light splash of water. Normally Susan was prattling away at such a time, and Mercy looked up enquiringly at her to see her eyes filled with tears.

'What's up with you all of a sudden?'

'You'll get married one day,' Susan said bleakly. It was always there, her morbid fear of being abandoned.

'Nah.' Mercy leant over and squeezed Susan's wrist with her wet hand. ''Course I shan't. Don't talk barmy.'

''Ello, barmy,' George remarked suddenly, and even Susan's stricken face relaxed into laughter.

'Ooh, you're a so-and-so, you are!' she told him.

Mercy was dried and clad in the nightshirt Susan had run up for her, and standing cutting Susan's hair when they heard footsteps outside, the door latch clicked and there was Mabel. She came in, shut the door and stood before them. She had on her old coat and a shapeless green felt hat, was thinner than when she left. She looked both nervous and defiant.

The two girls froze.

Mabel eyed both of them. Mercy's hostility snaked across the room to her.

'Mom,' Susan whispered eventually. She wheeled the chair towards her and Mercy's heart wrung at the sweet hope on her face. 'I thought you'd left us for good.'

Mabel put her bag down. 'It's Christmas,' she said. 'I want to come home.'

Part Three

Chapter Thirteen

August 1916

Mercy pushed past the self-important conductorette, and stepped, heavy-hearted, off the bus into the summer evening. She was dressed in her oldest work clothes, a navy dress with white polka dots, which at work was covered by an overall, her hair taken back under a snood. For she was now a munitions girl, turning out Mills grenades in a factory squeezed between Digbeth and the grey, dripping arches of the railway line.

A few months before Mrs Wrigley had said, 'I'm ever so sorry, Mercy, but what with all the shortages and the price of everything, we haven't the money to keep you on.'

They were crying out for women to go into munitions work then, and the pay! She got a pound a week! But even that didn't go far now, though, and most days she felt she'd more than earned it, standing all those hours in a cramped room lit only by daylight through the windows, bent over a lathe, finishing the opening at the top of the grenades which were piled around her like metal pineapples. The belts on the lathes whirred and slapped round ceaselessly and she breathed in metal dust. Her body was stiff and her feet ached. Still, she told herself, she had some laughs with the other girls. But she couldn't shake off her feelings of worry and dread.

A week ago today it'd been: Jack Pepper rattling at the door after work. 'Mercy – come over ours a minute, will yer?' When she asked why he said, 'Just come!' and ran off.

Mercy got up wearily. At the Peppers' she found Johnny with a grin stretched across his face and Tom, smiling but uncertain.

'We wanted to tell yer—' Johnny was twitchy with excitement. 'We've done it – we've joined up!'

'I like the "we",' Elsie spoke flatly. For once she was doing nothing, just standing. 'I don't have to guess who talked who into it.'

Tom looked solemn.

'You mean they believed the pair of you?' Mercy tried to hide her dismay. 'You're only seventeen!'

'We said we was eighteen,' Johnny bragged. 'No one asked us any different. Any rate, not long now and we will be eighteen!'

Mercy stared silently at them both. Two years ago she'd have been excited for them, proud, but now ... Week after week the toll had mounted: Ypres, Neuve Chapelle, Loos, Gallipolli, Verdun ...

''Aven't you seen the death lists?' Now Frank was at the Front Elsie was never quiet, couldn't sleep of a night.

They were so young, all that energy waiting to be spent. Johnny, tall, wiry with boxer's muscles and impish cheek written in every line of his face. And Tom, dark-eyed, pale, serious. Mercy felt his eyes on her, but saw the longing in them as anxiety about what lay in front of them.

'You think you can just go off and leave me, do you?' Mercy said softly, trying to joke.

'I thought you might talk sense into 'em better than

me,' Elsie said wearily. 'But in any case, it's too late now. I s'pose I should be proud.'

'We'll be back, don't you bother yourselves. Bad pennies us, eh?' Johnny punched Tom's shoulder. At his age he knew he was indestructible. He could hardly wait to get into uniform.

'You just as keen to go, Tom?' Mercy asked.

Tom spoke, looking at the floor. 'I thought I would be. Me and Johnny'll look out for each other.'

Mercy swallowed the lump in her throat. 'You'd flaming well better.'

They left a couple of days later, very early, but most of the yard was up to see them go. Elsie was fighting tears, something Mercy had almost never seen her do before and she was frightened suddenly in a way she couldn't have put into words. The tentacles of events in the outside world, bigger and crueller than any of them could have imagined, reached into Angel Street that morning.

Johnny said his goodbyes to her and Susan with a peck on the cheek. 'Ta-ra, Mercy. Take care of yourself, and look out for our mom, won't yer?'

Tom came to her, obviously full of nerves. He tried to kiss her as Johnny had done, but he knocked his nose accidentally hard against her cheek.

'Ooh, Tom!' Mercy half laughed, half yelped, rubbing her face.

'Sorry – sorry, Mercy.' He couldn't look at her for a moment, and stared at the ground, lick of hair falling forward. But then, forced by the urgency of the occasion he looked up and saw the tears in her eyes.

'Oh Lor' – this is terrible – I've got to say it. If I don't tell you now I might never, and I've waited such a long time . . .' Mercy watched as the young man in front of her almost physically screwed up his courage, and amid the general hubbub of the yard, said, cheeks aflame, 'If I've got to die for anyone, I'll do it for you, Mercy!'

'Oh Tom!' She was very moved by his outburst, by his passion and tenderness. 'Would you really? I didn't know . . .'

He'd always been kind and considerate to her, especially as they'd grown older, but she hadn't seen that his friendliness had developed into something far stronger.

'I've got to tell you, Mercy, the feelings I've got for yer – just in case I . . .' He stepped closer to her, his brown eyes looking close into hers, and took her hands in his. She felt him trembling. She was beginning to shake a little as well. 'You're so lovely, Mercy. I love you. I've wanted to tell you for ages but, I dunno . . . we was just kids and I thought you'd – I've never had the courage . . .'

Mercy was so astonished, touched, grateful, bewildered all at once that she couldn't speak. Johnny, heading down the entry with Elsie and a cluster of others was shouting, 'Come on, Tom!'

'Could you say it to me, to take with me? Whether you feel . . .?'

Mercy looked into his sweet, imploring face and was overcome by fondness for him. Her emotions were a storm of confusion, but somewhere in the middle of it all her heart was singing.

'Of course I love you, Tom!'

In a second his arms were round her, pulling her to him.

'I had to do this – just once, before I go, my . . . love.' He pressed his cheek against hers, then quickly kissed her lips. He looked full into her eyes, then pulled away. 'I've got to go. I'll write . . .'

She followed him down the entry to where Johnny was waiting. Everyone stood on the street, waving them off. Tom's eyes met hers. Mercy smiled, going to stand by Elsie, her heart full to bursting.

'Come back to us, you two, won't yer? For God's sake!' Elsie called to them.

Mercy stood with everyone else until the twins reached the corner and disappeared, still waving. She felt strange and shocked. One moment he had been there, so close, now he was gone. She put her hand to her lips as if to seal his kiss.

Walking home that evening from the bus stop on the Moseley Road, Mercy thought of Tom as she'd done almost every moment since he left. At first she had felt only astonishment. Tom, whom she'd known all these years, in love with her! As she grew used to the idea, recalled again and again his look, his words to her, she bubbled inside with the warm excitement this knowledge aroused in her. All this time and she'd never known – someone other than Susan found it possible to love her! More and more she knew she was in love with him in return, loved him for his gentleness and solidity, his kindness. Above all she loved him for loving her.

She'd felt differently about everything since Tom and Johnny left. The War had moved closer, to her doorstep, her heart. She knew that soon they would be sent to the Front, and then all she could do would be worry and pray.

She also felt an enormous sense of restlessness come

over her, as if between them they had prised open a chink in her mind and let in a view she'd never seen before. There was so much more to life and the world than she ever saw, and the twins had stepped out into it.

Turning into the entry, she felt exhausted and prickly with an unfamiliar kind of irritation. She was sixteen, grown up. Was this grimy yard in a grimy city, living with a woman she loathed all she was ever going to see of life?

Perhaps I was wrong, she thought. I should've taken up Dorothy's offer of that job, and I wouldn't be churning out grenades day after day. But that would have meant leaving Susan . . .

She entered the house rubbing her stiff neck and taking a deep breath, preparing herself to be as civil as she could manage to Mabel. Life felt like one long struggle.

'You all right?' Susan asked her brightly, as George shrieked at the sight of her.

'I'll survive.' She sank on to the settle.

'Mom – give 'er a cup of tea,' Susan instructed Mabel who was on her way downstairs. 'This job's wearing 'er out!'

'Dear oh dear,' Mabel said sarcastically.

'Could be worse,' Mercy said, ignoring her. 'I could be shell-filling like Cathleen. I hate to think what's in them shells. I saw 'er again yesterday and she's yellow as a canary, right down to 'er scalp!'

Mercy drank her tea and tried to smile, trying to shake off her restless feelings. After all, this was home. If it meant living with Mabel still, so be it. She belonged here. She had Susan whatever else. And Tom. Each time she remembered there came a rush of joy. Dear Tom.

*

Things had changed a fair bit in Nine Court over the past year and a half. The two cottages with their scrubby gardens had new tenants: the Ripleys and the McGonegalls. Mary Jones complained that the Ripleys were a 'right rough crew', and the yard was like bedlam with all their children everywhere, but she moaned a bit less when they turned out to be good company for her own.

But there had been one change which had taken everyone's breath away. Christmas Day of 1914 after Mabel first showed herself in the yard again, Mary Jones came roaring out of her house and spat in her face.

'Where is 'e then?' she shrieked at Mabel. 'Where's that bastard now?'

Other choice words followed and the neighbours began to open their doors and enjoy a free show on this frosty morning. But it was all a damp squib so far as neighbourhood entertainment went.

To everyone's astonishment, Mabel stood tall, silently drew her sleeve across her face to wipe off Mary's spit and refused to be riled into fighting back. Mercy watched with everyone else. Blimey, she thought. What's come over her?

'I dunno where 'e is,' Mabel said. 'Not exactly any'ow.'

'Did 'e leave yer to join up?' Mary's face puckered into a vicious sneer. 'Went off to do 'is bit and you couldn't stand being left be'ind?'

'Look, Mary,' Mabel clamped her hands on her hips. 'Stan left me for another woman and I don't know where they've gone. 'E just ran out on me. But I know, and so should you – if 'e hadn't left you for me, it'd've been someone else.'

''E never looked at another woman 'til you come along!' Mary yelled, although the wind was fast disappearing from her sails. It was her right, her role to have a go at Mabel, expected almost. But she didn't want Stan back. She just wanted someone to take it all out on, being left alone, the relentless hardship of her life.

'Think what you like,' Mabel said calmly. 'But I've had a lot of hard thinking to do and I've got a suggestion to make to you – for your own benefit.' She looked round, on her dignity at the people strung across the yard. 'Why don't we go in your 'ouse and discuss it where there ain't so many pairs of ears flapping?'

'You – in my 'ouse! You've got some nerve!' Mary looked meaningfully over at Elsie, waiting to be backed up, but Elsie shrugged in her doorway, keeping out of it.

'Come in mine then.'

Mary wavered, though her face was still taut and defiant. 'No.'

'So – it'll have to be yours—'

Mabel, the older and by far the more forceful of the two, ushered Mary Jones into her own house. The door closed. Outside, everyone looked at one another and Susan whispered to Mercy, 'What's come over 'er?'

Stan had left Mabel a fortnight before and in that time she felt she had scraped the rock bottom of her life. Here she was at forty-one, left alone in two squalid, bug-ridden rooms above an Aston fish shop, the stench of it forever in her nostrils. She'd been deserted by the man she'd run after with such paltry hopes. She'd abandoned her only surviving daughter, and her last hope of having another healthy child had ended in a painful, bloody failure at which Stan had shown not an ounce of sorrow or disappointment.

One terrible, grey day when the clouds sat like a heavy lid on top of the city she'd sat in that dreary room. There was a speckled mirror fixed over a battered vanity table. Mabel leant close, peering short-sightedly at her face. She still didn't feel right after losing the infant. Her face was pale and sagging, hair and eyes lifeless. She reminded herself of a corpse and that was how she felt. The living dead. And at that moment she felt enough shame and hatred for herself to go and finish it all for good in the canal.

Her life had had its low points before, no doubt about that. But none of the other things that had happened had been of her own making. What would she say of any other woman who had run out on her child? And she missed Susan. Deep in her guts she missed her and was overwhelmed with grief and shame.

'Why've you come back?' Mary Jones demanded, holding Paul on her lap and keeping up her expression of bitter hostility.

'I've come back to my daughter.' Mabel didn't sit down, but took a stance stiffly just inside the door, arms folded. 'Did you know I was carrying 'is child?'

Mary's hand moved up to her mouth, eyes widening. 'My God – you never—'

'I lost it. Natural. I never wanted to get rid of it. I've two dead babbies already.' Her voice was hard, defiant almost.

Mary lowered her hand and continued to stare mutely at her. She had never known the first thing about this woman before.

'I've had to take a good look at myself and I haven't liked what I've seen. So I said to myself, "Mabel, you can stay 'ere on yer own like a fallen woman for the rest of your life and die lonely, or you can go back there, ask your daughter's forgiveness, and make amends."' She paused. 'What I think is, we should both try and put it behind us and I'll help you out. I know what it's like bringing up babbies on your own. I'm part of the cause, so I'll do my bit. There.'

Mary allowed herself a bitter laugh. 'Oh – you steal my husband and come in 'ere thinking you can eat humble pie and we're all going to turn round and say "Oh that's awright Mabel, welcome back?"'

'I never stole your 'usband. 'E wasn't a child – 'e chose to go and walked right out and as I said to you, if it hadn't happened now it would've later. 'E's a worthless, selfish good for nothing and you know it.'

'Well if 'e was so bloody terrible, what d'yer take off with 'im for?'

Mabel looked her right in the eyes. 'I wanted someone. It's been a long time.'

There was silence as the two woman stared each other out. Finally, Mary shook her head. 'Both got bloody bad taste, 'aven't we?'

When Mabel arrived home, Mercy felt as if she were being put back in prison.

'We need to make a fresh start,' Mabel said to them that same day, her hair brushing Mercy's little home-made streamers. She was struggling to remain calm. She'd already eaten humble pie for Mary Jones and now she'd have to do it again, but by God this was tougher by half. She could feel all her aversion flooding back towards this mardy little blonde child. No, she saw, not child. Not any more. Two young women were before her, who'd struggled and managed to run their lives almost alone.

'I don't want to live out my life with everyone hating me,' she admitted.

'Well it'd have paid you to think of that a bit sooner!' Mercy blurted out. She'd spent the night sleepless with anguish at Mabel's return, despite her relief on Susan's behalf.

'We don't hate you, Mom!' Susan was overwhelmed that her mother had returned. 'Mercy, I know Mom's treated yer bad in the past, but it won't be like that from now on, will it?' She looked at each of them with huge, spaniel eyes.

'I owe you, Mercy,' Mabel said gruffly. She'd known this was going to be damned humiliating and she wasn't going to back out now. Being left alone had been so much worse. 'You've looked out for Susan when I went off and left her. I had my reasons – I want you to know that—'

'Just don't come back 'ere thinking you can take over and start carrying on how you was before,' Mercy burst out furiously, all aquiver. 'There've been some changes around 'ere and we've all managed perfectly well without you.'

'So I see.' Mabel's gaze travelled over the new furniture.

'The wheelchair's indoors for good,' Mercy decreed, as if everything hung on this.

'It's much better,' Susan backed her up, trying to please Mercy and appeal to Mabel at the same time. 'I can do so much more and the sewing's been going ever so well – before the War it was any'ow.'

'I'm glad for yer,' Mabel said carefully. Mercy watched her through narrowed eyes, arms clasped defensively across her body. However hard Mabel's return was to swallow, she was here, and for Susan's sake she was going to have to learn to put up with her.

It was only a matter of time before things blew up. Mercy didn't believe a word of Mabel's claims of repentance and neighbourliness. She had no understanding of the course Mabel's emotions had taken over the years, did not know anyone might try to change out of need and self-revulsion.

Mabel did everything she could to ingratiate herself with Mercy and Susan and with the neighbours, especially Mary Jones. She started to pay attention to Mary's kids. The two women even had a laugh together. But Mercy watched her, mistrustful.

Mabel didn't have a job at this time and was doing the shopping, something Mercy found hard to make time for, except for bread which back then she could still get from Wrigley's.

She'd asked Mabel to get cheap meat for stewing. Mabel not only came home with fish instead but managed to forget about it and burn it almost to a cinder. It was two women, a kitchen stove and so much more besides.

'So you can't get the shopping right and then you serve us up with cowing charcoal for our tea!' Mercy, already living on her nerves, flew straight off the handle as she came to the table.

'Less of your lip – I was doing my best. I just 'ad to nip out! At least I was getting on with the cooking instead of waiting for you.'

'I don't want you doing it!' Mercy's eyes held an icy loathing. 'We haven't needed you for a long time and we don't need you now!'

Without thinking Mabel whipped out and slapped Mercy hard on the cheek. The girl's hand flew up to her face.

'What're you going to do now?' Mabel sneered. 'Call the welfare people? Don't think they'd be interested at your age, do you?'

'No.' Mercy's voice was clipped, chilling. 'This is what I'm going to do.'

She strode round the table, eyes never leaving Mabel's face, and her fist landed on Mabel's nose with all the force she was capable of.

Mabel reeled, eyes screwed shut in pain, gasping.

Mercy put her face right up close to her. 'Just remember,' she hissed, 'you don't hit me, Mabel. Not ever again.

Chapter Fourteen

Mercy stood aghast in the doorway of the Peppers'. Rosalie was lying on the hearthrug letting out heartbroken sobs as Bummy, Cathleen and Elsie stood or sat round the table, faces bruised with shock. The letter lay on the table.

'Frank?'

Their faces told her it was so, but no words would come.

'D'you want—' Mercy's throat had tightened so much she could barely speak either. 'Shall I go for Josephine?'

'Jack's gone.' Elsie's voice had a far away sound to it and she spoke uncertainly, as if she'd forgotten how to use words.

Mercy went to Rosalie, sat beside her and pulled her across her lap. Rosalie was small for an eight-year-old, and skinny. Her hands were clenched to her face and wet from the tears squeezing out between them. 'I want Frankie!'

Mercy felt her body jerking with sobs. 'I know love,' she said softly, rocking the bony little body. 'I know you do.' Cathleen also had tears running down her sallow face.

Bummy Pepper sat at the table, a stunned expression on his face, rubbing his hand again and again over his stubbly chin. After a time he pushed the chair back and walked out of the house without saying a word.

Mercy's eyes followed him.

''S'awright – 'e'll've gone down the Angel. 'E'll be back

after a couple of pints.' Elsie had turned, within hours, from a woman who looked young for fifty to one who seemed much older. She sank on to her husband's chair by the table.

'Oh Frank. Oh God, my little Frankie. I can't even give 'im a decent burial.'

Soon after, in a corner of the yard up by the brewhouse wall appeared a cross about a foot high made from two pieces of smooth wood nailed together. Above it, a Union Jack was tacked to the wall.

'What's all that?' Mercy asked coming in from work. Under the flag lay a bunch of white lilies.

'It's Elsie's,' Susan said. 'For Frank. She's bin out there 'alf the day. I 'ope she's awright – seems to be acting a bit funny to me.'

Mabel peered out at the little home-made shrine across the yard. 'Nah,' she said with authority. 'It's natural enough. She wants to do summat for 'im.'

There were similar little offerings to be seen out on the streets, rolls of honour, flags and flowers for dead sons, fathers, brothers.

Elsie got into the habit of standing for a few moments in front of hers almost every time she passed it, going about her chores. The day after she'd laid her little memorial to Frank and was standing before it, her body one endless ache of sorrow, she heard someone else come up from behind and stand by her. Then Mabel stepped forward, laid another bunch of flowers close by the others and stood straight again, wiping her hands on her apron. Neither woman spoke, nor did they look at each other.

*

Tom and Johnny came home on leave for the first time in November, striding in large as life one wet midday. Elsie fell on them both, drawing them tight into her arms.

'Mom!' Johnny struggled as she kissed his face. 'Go easy – you'll squeeze all the breath out of us!' He shook her off, embarrassed. Tom kept one hand on his mom's shoulder, silently offering comfort, not knowing what to say about Frank.

'You're both bigger!' Elsie cried, wiping her eyes. 'Oh my God, look at the pair of yer!' They seemed enormous suddenly in her tiny house. 'Wait 'til yer dad sees yer! 'Ere – you hungry?'

'When aren't we?' Tom said. 'We could do with some decent grub, I can tell yer.'

Elsie smiled with a mixture of pride and sorrow as her two strapping, now much more muscular sons swung their kitbags on to the sofa and settled themselves at the table. She scurried around preparing food to hide the tears that kept welling up. Tom looked so like Frank now. Cross with herself she wiped her eyes. Enough of this – she had the twins home for a whole week. There'd be time aplenty to dwell on sorrow.

The two of them tucked in, munching like a couple of bulls, Elsie thought fondly. She'd bought all the food they could possibly afford.

'Rosalie's crazy to see yer,' she told them. 'She's taken it ever so bad over . . .' Everything seemed to lead to it. Frank dead, gone. She was weeping, hadn't meant to . . .

'Eh, Mom!' Tom was up, an arm round her shoulders, struggling to control his own emotion. He'd been close to Frank, looked up to him. Both boys did their best to jolly her out of her crying.

'We'll take you out and about now we're 'ome,' Johnny said. 'Give you a break. Don't you cry, Mom. Us two'll look after each other when we get out there. We'll be all right, we will.'

'I'm awright...' Elsie forced a smile, pushing them down in front of their plates again. 'It'll be cold else. There's more spud.' She scraped round the pan. 'Come on – let's try and be cheerful.'

After a few moments Tom asked, ever so casually, ''Ow's Mercy?'

A twinkle appeared in Elsie eyes. 'Why – who's asking?'

He'd written to her from the training camp three times since he'd been away. Pictured her in his mind coming home, finding his letter ... Reading it with a smile on her face. Every night, lying on the hard ground in his tent it was Mercy who filled his mind. Her often solemn little face breaking into a smile for him, her teeth, small and slightly uneven which made the smile special for him. Made her Mercy. But she was still awesome to him now she was grown up. He thought of her startling pale hair, pale neck curving down into a lace collar. He'd started following that curve further in his mind, imagining how she might look. Smooth, very white, except for those two round ... Tom remembered seeing his mom suckling Rosalie, her breasts huge with milk. He couldn't stop thinking of the tender, swelling shapes under Mercy's blouse. He was certain he was always the last in his tent to get to sleep, dreaming about her.

Trouble was, when it came to writing to her, he couldn't begin to tell her what he was feeling so his letters ended up rather short, just telling her snippets about his training.

'*You should've seen us first time on parade – the sarnt*

said we was like lambs to the slaughter!' – 'Got our uniforms at last – now we feel like proper soldier boys...'

He always told her how Johnny was, asked about Susan and for Mercy to look out for his mom – he said this twice in the letter after Frank was killed. At the very end he'd tried to think how to say what he felt, something soft for his girl. In the third letter he found courage and wrote, '... *thinking of you always, night and day. Love Tom.*'

Mercy read these letters with a complete sense of wonder. She'd never received a letter before.

'Who's it from?' Susan wheeled herself over eagerly when the first one arrived.

''Er – Tom,' Mercy muttered, pushing it into the pocket of her dress.

'Well let's see then!'

'Later – I'm in a rush.'

'Well why can't you leave it?'

'It's addressed to me, that's why.'

She read the letter on the bus to work, so absorbed that she almost missed the stop.

'Got summat worth 'aving there, 'ave yer?' a woman teased as she rushed to leap off at the last moment, holding her hat on against the breeze outside.

The letter was strange, she thought. She had no clue what to expect from a letter. Was this a love letter, this little note telling her about a makeshift army training camp? The one spare word 'love' at the end. Was that it? Yet she was stirred up by it, by its very existence. Her man was writing to her. Her Tom! She was learning to think of him differently, not just as a playmate and the lad next door. And while she was a bit ashamed of wanting to keep her feelings secret, she couldn't share this with Susan. This was hers and hers alone. She wrote him brief, affectionate notes in reply.

The day she knew the twins were coming home she could think of nothing but Tom.

'You with us today, Mercy?' one of the other girls in the factory teased her over the racket of the machines. 'I've asked yer twice already!'

Mercy blushed and there were some 'oohs' and 'aahs' from round her.

'What's on 'er mind, I wonder!'

'Nowt any of your business,' Mercy replied with a mysterious smile which only brought on more catcalls and speculation. She took it all good-naturedly and sank back into her day-dreams. What else was there to think of standing in a factory day after day?

She didn't see him waiting as she walked up the entry in the drizzle, her boots rapping a smart clip-clip on the damp pavement. She was dressed in a calf-length grey coat, the collar turned up, and a navy hat with a narrow brim under which her hair was just visible. Her cheeks were pink from the cold.

She caught sight of him and her step faltered. He was there, waiting! He looked broader, more of a man than before. He smiled, with warmth, but shyly. This was all new. They were no longer just childhood friends. Her heart was beating fast. Suddenly she was all nerves.

'Tom,' she said softly. In those seconds, like Elsie she saw Frank's face in Tom's, felt how terrible this war was. But mixed with this, the delicious, warming sense of knowing he had waited for her, had special feelings just for her.

He walked the last few steps to meet her and they stood in the entry, both with a silver veil of water droplets on their clothes.

'How are you?' she said. Seeing his nervous, solemn face, and out of her own giddiness she started laughing. 'Blimey, you're about twice the size you were three months ago!'

Tom laughed as well and the ice was broken, but Mercy felt she was seeing him for the first time, as if through a new, clear lens: everything about him, his brown eyes, shorn brown hair, the shape of his neck, his jaw.

'You look different too,' he said. 'More grown up.'

'Where's Johnny?' She was about to step into the yard when he caught her arm.

'Mercy – can we spend a bit of time on our own like, this week, without Johnny and—?' He nodded his head towards Mabel's house.

'Susan?' Mercy looked guiltily at him. Susan hadn't seen his letters, was prickly about Mercy's secrecy. But Mercy suddenly, desperately didn't want to spend her life feeling guilty because Susan couldn't walk. She wanted to get out, to get some life of her own.

'Come to the pictures – tomorrow?'

Mercy hesitated. It wasn't going to be easy. 'What'll you tell Johnny?'

'I'll just tell 'im. 'E won't mind.'

'OK.' She smiled, bubbling with excitement. 'I'd love to go.'

Tom swooped forward and kissed her cheek. 'I've missed yer.'

So it was real, she thought, touching her cheek. She'd almost wondered if she'd imagined what he said the morning he left, despite the letters. Heart thudding, and with an enormous sense of wonder she said, 'I missed you too.'

'I'm going to the Electric Cinema with Tom,' Mercy announced defiantly to Mabel and Susan, expecting opposition.

Mabel opened her mouth and closed it again, unable to think of a good enough objection. She knew if she just said, 'You're not,' Mercy would take no notice anyway. She'd done a lot of biting her lip over the past year and it was becoming a habit. It was paying her to keep quiet. Mercy was the main wage earner after all.

Susan looked up from laying crocks for tea. 'What?' she faltered. 'Just you and 'im – on your own?'

'Well – yes.' Mercy, seeing the hurt in Susan's eyes, couldn't keep up her tough act any longer and bent down so she was level with her. 'You don't mind, do you?'

Susan put a plate down, concentrating on it very hard all of a sudden. 'No – you go and 'ave a nice time.' She sounded very subdued, near to tears.

They ate thin stew and beans in silence. Susan kept her eyes on her food. Mercy was all knotted up inside and kept glancing across at her. She was sorry, but she wasn't going to go back on it. She desperately wanted to be with Tom.

'I'm going in to give Mary a hand with Percy and Paul in a bit,' Mabel said, laying down her fork.

'Oh.' Susan's voice was bleak.

'You can come too. Paul'd like to see yer, you know that.'

*

As it turned out Mercy went out with Tom that day and almost every other of his week's leave. Johnny, not to be outdone, was walking out with a girl called Violet up the street and one evening they all went out together.

Watching the twins, Mercy saw that they'd both changed. They were both bolder, more manly. But while with Tom this new found confidence made him less awkward but no less kind, she found her feelings for Johnny changing for the worse.

He's getting to be a right cocky sod, she thought, watching him and Violet walking along in front of Tom. He was bossy with Violet, his arm round her, pulling her here and there as if he owned her.

'Let's just go on our own tomorrow,' she murmured to Tom, and he nodded.

'That's OK with me.'

They saw the new Chaplin film, went to the Bull Ring and ate cockles and roasted chestnuts by the illuminated stalls, stamping their feet and cupping the hot chestnuts in their hands to keep warm. Sometimes they walked the streets between high factory walls, or the closed shops on New Street or Corporation Street, Tom shyly taking Mercy's arm, both laughing a lot, new jokes along with shared laughter from the past.

Mercy was intoxicated with happiness.

'You awright?' Tom asked her. 'You don't want to take cold.'

'Ooh yes! I could stay out all night, I don't care!' she told him. She loved the warm feeling it gave her walking out with Tom. He felt a very solid presence beside her, not wild and skittish as Johnny now seemed. She trusted Tom – more than trusted him. She knew she had learned to love him for his kindness and devotion.

When they'd spent two evenings together he found the

courage to draw her close into his arms and slowly, tentatively at first, they kissed in the foggy darkness, conscious of nothing but each other.

'I love you so much, Mercy. I've always loved you, d'you know that? Ever since you belted that girl one for talking nasty to Susan, d'you remember? You're like a beautiful little tiger, you are.'

Mercy laughed, blushing with pleasure. 'You want to watch it then, don't yer?' She joked, making growling noises.

'D'yer love me, Mercy?'

''Course I do.'

He took her hand and they sauntered down the street, in no hurry to get home.

'I've never had anyone before,' Mercy said suddenly. 'Not to call my own. You've made me so happy, Tom.'

'I know you haven't.' The thought made him feel so protective. 'We'll be together and I'll look after yer. I promise yer that.'

Tom and Johnny had schemed to take Elsie out and about while they were at home but the weather was so wet they were more or less stuck at home.

'Next time we'll go out – up the Lickeys or somewhere,' Johnny said to her. He was full of the joys, had been out to a boxing match with his dad like two pals together.

'I don't mind whether we go out or not so long as you're 'ere and I know you're safe,' Elsie said.

The last evening they were all there in the gaslit room, Josephine heavily pregnant and fat in the face, Cathleen much more lively than she was usually, Jack drinking in all the twins' talk, Rosalie running from one to the other and getting playful cuffs and cuddles. And Mercy and Susan.

Mercy sat next to Tom, feeling self-conscious and trying to make sure Susan was included in everything. Bummy went down the Angel for jugs of ale and they had a very jolly evening.

Everyone tried to think of cheerful things. They reminisced, had a song or two, and Bummy asked the lads questions for the umpteenth time about the training, about soldiering.

After she'd wheeled Susan back home Mercy stepped out again to meet Tom so they could say their goodbyes in private. They stood near the brewhouse close to Elsie's shrine to Frank. Tom was solemn suddenly, the reality of his departure the next day seeming so close now. For Mercy, the thought of being physically parted from him was unbearable.

A light rain was falling and it was so dark they could only just make out each other's outlines. Tom put his hands on Mercy's shoulders.

'You know we're going to France, don't you?'

She nodded, then realizing he couldn't see, whispered, 'Yes.' A lump ached in her throat. The War was so strange to her and far away. Now Italy had joined in well. The reality of it came to them in the form of lists. Closely printed newsheet pages of the injured, missing, dead.

'Poor Frank,' she said. He had died on the Somme.

For a moment Tom rested his forehead on her shoulder.

Mercy put her arms round Tom and held him close. They stood in silence until Tom said, 'You mustn't worry. We'll be awright, me and Johnny.'

'Will you go together?'

'I s'pose so.'

She wanted to believe him, that the two of them would get through. All the life that was in both of them, the life she now held in her arms, it seemed impossible it could ever be wiped out. But the next moment the night air felt colder as Tom said, 'Whatever happens, Mercy, my love, I'll always be thinking of you. I'll always love you.'

They held each other so very tight then, not wanting to let go.

Chapter Fifteen

Christmas was over, and a depressing one it had been. Smoke and fog hung over the city streets, there was a permanently damp feel to everything and nearly everyone was coughing. In Angel Street the yards were permanently mired with a slippery mix of filth and water, however hard the women in the courts worked at them with stiff brooms. Each time Elsie laid new white flowers on her little shrine to Frank they soon looked soiled and bedraggled in the dank, sooty air.

It was New Year's Eve, and Mercy was sitting with Mabel and Susan, listening anxiously to Susan's laboured breathing. She'd had a nasty attack of bronchitis and was still suffering a hacking cough. Her cheeks were unhealthily flushed and she sat with her head lolling back in the chair by the fire, under a colourful patchwork quilt that she'd stitched herself. It was quiet apart from Susan's coughing, the shifting of the fire and George grinding his beak against his perch.

'We'd better get you up to bed,' Mercy said wearily. She was exhausted herself, and not looking forward to another sleepless night lying beside Susan's feverish body.

'Just a bit longer, ' Susan said, staring at the flames. She didn't look round, but Mercy could sense how low she was.

'What's up wi' you?'

Susan turned her head and glanced at Mabel who was

asleep at one end of the settle, head resting on one hand and throaty little snores escaping from her mouth. Mabel had gained the weight she'd lost in her absence, her face had lost its look of bitter aggression, and except for some extra lines, she was ripening once more into a quite handsome woman, more at peace with herself now she'd managed to earn some respect from the neighbours and wasn't at everyone's throats. All the same, Susan knew there were things Mercy wouldn't want said in front of her.

'You had another letter from Tom?' Susan kept her voice barely above a whisper.

Mercy looked down at her lap. She'd had a letter that morning and knew Susan was perfectly aware of the fact. 'I have, yes.' She'd slipped out to read it in the freezing privy, the only place where there was ever any privacy to be had. Tom's letters were so sweet, gave her news of where he was – not yet in France – and always ended with great affection. But they were not so demonstrative or personal that she couldn't have shared them with Susan. The fact was – and Mercy was ashamed of this – she just didn't want to. She wanted something all for herself, something just between her and Tom. She kept the letters in the little chest of drawers in their bedroom with the book and handkerchief she had had from the orphanage. Dorothy had told her how it had been left with her on the steps of Hanley's. She took it out from time to time, looking at its immaculate embroidery as if it were a puzzle, a key to who she was. She ached to know whose fingers had stitched the mauve letters of her name.

Susan's expression had turned sulky. 'You used to tell me everything, Mercy. You're full of secrets now and it ain't very kind, being as I'm just stuck 'ere.'

Mercy felt guilty but impatient. 'I'm not. There's

nothing much to tell. 'E just said they're doing more training and 'e doesn't know what's happening next.'

'And I s'pose you've been grinning away like a Cheshire cat and humming to yourself just because he told you that? D'you think I'm daft or summat? I get more out of 'im—' – she jerked her head at George who was staring gloomily across the room – than I do out of you these days.'

'Oh, think what you like.' Mercy was thoroughly riled by the injustice of this. She stood up. 'I'm going to bed, so if you want to get up there now's your chance. No point in staying up, is there? 1917's not looking to be any different from this year.'

'I don't want to go to bed just on your say-so,' Susan snapped, tearful suddenly. 'You're not in charge of everything around 'ere you know.'

'Susan!' Mercy was really hurt. 'That's not like you!'

Susan burst into tears which quickly broke down into coughs. 'I feel so down and useless,' she sobbed once she could speak. 'You've got Tom, and I'll never 'ave anything like that. And no one's bringing me any sewing any more and that's one thing at least I can do . . .'

'But Dorothy was 'ere only the week before Christmas,' Mercy protested. Dorothy's visits had dwindled since Mabel's return, but she always appeared sometime in a month and usually with clothes for them and a job or two for Susan which she'd collect later.

Susan didn't answer, just kept crying, weak and rundown from her illness. Mercy knelt in front of her and put her arms round Susan's waist.

'Look, I'm sorry. I didn't know what to tell you. Tom and I are . . . well, we have got sort of fond of each other, but that doesn't have to make any difference. I'm always going to be 'ere to look after you, you know that.' She leant down, her hair brushing Susan's fingers, and looked up into her face. Susan tried to smile.

'Come on – I'll take you up.'

Leaving Mabel, she helped Susan, step by step, up to the bedroom, on to the pot and finally into bed as she did every night. When she was ready for bed herself she climbed in, leant over and kissed Susan's burning cheek before blowing out the candle.

'Night, night. Happy New Year.'

She pretended to sleep as Susan fidgeted beside her but her mind was wide awake and active. For the first time she was finding all this care for Susan a burden. Mabel was here, she was the one really responsible for Susan yet it was Mercy doing all the work. And Mercy was restless now, increasingly so as each month passed. She wanted something else from life. But what? she asked herself. More experience, excitement? She barely knew what else there was on offer, yet sensed the close restriction of her existence. Going to work, coming home, housework – and now with the War all the extra 'don'ts' imposed on them. She wanted someone to say 'do' for a change. Do find something more to do with your life. Do get out of this place. Do find out who you really are, where you come from. But all these urgent impulses made her feel guilty too. There was a war on, all these lads getting killed. And how could she ever explain how she felt to Susan?

'Get out of my bloody way, woman!'

Grace heard Neville's arrival, as indeed most of the street must have done in the calm of this spring evening, the door slamming thunderously behind him and the howling of her younger son as he roared, 'And get these brats out of the way as well!' She heard Edward crying as their nanny hurriedly escorted them upstairs. Grace clenched her hands until the nails dug into her palms. Neville had very little time for his sons, spared them no attention or tenderness.

She stepped out of the front parlour into the hall where he was standing, so swollen up with fury she thought his shirt buttons might fly off. She glanced coolly at him.

'Damn it – look!'

'What is it, Neville?' He was so prone to outbursts of temper that she had learned over the years to remain absolutely calm in the face of it. This was effortless nowadays since her feelings towards her childish boor of a husband had passed through pain and loathing to an icy indifference.

'Are you blind, or just dim-witted, woman – look!'

In his hand was a large feather, greyish rather than white, but its meaning as it was thrust at him in the street was clear enough.

'Some damn *woman—*' he spat out the word as if it in itself was an insult, 'had the gall to stick it in the front of my coat!'

Grace tried to summon at least a pretence of indignation as Neville hurled the feather down on a polished side table and poured himself a large whiskey. Grace watched him with distaste. Her Temperance upbringing gave her an inbuilt revulsion for his drinking. He took a large mouthful and she saw his florid cheeks suck in and out as he washed it around his mouth.

You are foul, she thought. You disgust me. He was still young – not yet forty – though a little portly, and dressed in the clothes of a much older man: a thick worsted suit with watch-chain and weskit, and a Homburg for outdoors.

'But where?' Grace asked.

'It was in – I don't know where . . .' He took another gulp from the glass. The fact that he'd been set upon by the woman – one of those suffragette harridans most likely – as he came out of one of the more notorious brothels on the Warwick Road was hardly something he could tell Grace.

'It doesn't matter where, does it? 'Ere I am, working night and day – the factory's never quiet – keeping most of the British Army's Motor Transport in supplies, and I get treated like a shirker and a coward.' He banged the empty glass down on a little rosewood table so hard that Grace jumped.

'But, Neville, you did say just the other day that shirkers ought to be tracked down and arrested.'

'Not me though, for heaven's sake! God knows it's no good trying to talk to your sort. I'm wasting my time.'

He strode out of the room and went crashing up the stairs.

Grace was left standing alone in the middle of the room. 'Oh dear, poor, poor you,' she murmured. The loathing in her eyes and voice was unmistakable.

Two days later he burst into the house again earlier than usual, loud and elated.

'The Master of the house is home!' he bawled from the hall. 'Is no one here to greet him?'

Grace, the nanny, Dorothy and the children dutifully appeared in the hall and stood in a semicircle in front of him. Grace laid her hands on the boys' shoulders.

'Well, I've done it!' Neville let out his bellow of a laugh. 'Come 'ere, boys – your father's got summat to tell you.'

Robert and Edward stepped uncertainly towards him as Grace gave them a little push.

'Well.' Neville squatted down, pulling his sons between his thick thighs. 'Listen to me. I want to tell you summat.'

The two boys fixed their eyes obediently on his face, Robert with his father's thickset looks, Edward fair and slender.

'Your daddy's going away to be a big, brave soldier.'

Grace gasped, hands going to her cheeks. 'What? What're you saying, Neville?'

'It's all fixed. Joe Grable can run the firm – he's too old to enlist and he's worked there since 'e were a lad. Could run the place in his sleep. And I'm off to the Front, to serve my country.' He stood up, shoving his sons away as if they were tiresome puppies.

'But you could get killed, Neville,' Grace said carefully.

'But you could get killed, Neville,' he mocked her in a prattling voice. 'So the little woman has begun to grasp something about warfare these last two years has she?' He strode over and caught hold of her roughly under the chin. 'Concerned for me all of a sudden, are you?'

'You're hurting me, Neville.' She kept her voice even in front of the children, the servants. 'I'm thinking of our – your boys, our sons. You're their father.'

'Oh yes, I'm their father – at least according to you. Well, boys want to grow up with a father they can look up to, and that's what I'm going to give 'em.' He released Grace's chin, jerking her face aside, and as he did so, caught sight of the expression in Dorothy's eyes as she stood at the foot of the stairs.

'Don't look at me like that, woman.' He looked round at them all with a horrible sneer on his face. 'Hell, to think I've got to leave my lads in the hands of all you namby-pamby, coddling women.'

'So, my wench, your husband's off to the Front tomorrow.'

Neville's body thrust against hers, fleshy and bullying in its force as they lay between crisp linen sheets.

'Hardly the Front.' Grace spoke quietly, evenly, though her mind was recoiling with dread. 'You'll surely be training for quite some time yet?' She tried to inch her body surreptitiously away from his, revolted by his hard maleness forcing against her.

'So come on then—' Neville pulled himself up so he was leaning half over her, his breath thick with whiskey. 'Where are the tears, the "Oh Neville, I don't want you to go?" Some wife you are!'

'I don't wish you to go,' Grace lied, struggling to speak as he was forcing the breath out of her. 'But you chose to do it, Neville. You didn't have to, darling.'

'Darling, eh?'

Suddenly he forced his hand up between her legs, rooting against the folds of her nightshirt. 'Let's see how much feeling you've got for me, shall we, you prissy, bloodless creature. All these years I've spent servicing a dead cow. That's what it's like with you – and less rewarding probably. When I want you panting for me you're there with your eyes shut as if I'm serving you poison, you prim neuter, you.'

Grace let out a moan, automatically squeezing her eyes closed.

'Look at me!' He gripped her cheeks between the fingers of one hand, squeezing hard, and Grace couldn't contain her cry of pain, hands clawing at him to release her.

'That's it – if I can't have you moaning with pleasure you'll have to moan without it instead!'

Releasing her face, he wrenched up her nightgown and forced her legs apart. He started to force a thick finger up inside her, cursing.

'Dry as a dusty attic. Well, see 'ow yer like this then!'

He pushed his face into the most private parts of her, so that all she could feel was the hard grip of his hands on her thighs, his tongue licking, intruding, and the painful rasp of his stubbly chin.

'Oh God,' she whimpered. 'No – stop. Please. I beg you, not this . . .' The most degrading, disgusting . . . She felt sick with revulsion at him, at those unseen, awful parts of her body . . . She wanted to lose consciousness rather than feel any more of this gross nuzzling. She put her hands tight over her face, forced her mind right down into the blackness inside herself.

'That's better – I like a nice wet cunt . . .'

He was hugely aroused now, and she knew her own powerlessness was as much a stimulant to him as the feel of her body.

'Now then, my wench.' He pushed up hard inside her, his face, wet with her juices forced against her own cheeks, his thick-lipped mouth on hers making her sick to her stomach.

'Go on,' he pumped urgently. 'Cry out – you've got to cry out . . .'

Grace squeezed out a few distressed, catlike sounds and he climaxed, arms tensed straight, face puce, the veins on his neck sticking out.

Minutes later he was asleep, prone on his belly, breathing heavily.

Grace crept from the bed and poured water from the pitcher on the washstand into the deep, rose-ringed bowl. She washed all that she could of him away from her sore body, still sick with revulsion. She who had, all those years ago, committed this act of union with a man in such rapture! So long ago, the feelings buried by all that had happened since, that it seemed a life belonging to someone else.

She stood looking at Neville before blowing out the lamp.

Die, she prayed. Die an honourable death in France. The stain be on my soul, but God in heaven, please grant it that he die.

Death was to visit Angel Street, one death among so many in 1917, yet one which was as tragic and untimely as any of them.

Early one April morning, returning from the privy down the yard, Mercy heard a woman's high, grief-stricken wail, a shrill keening that no walls would contain.

She hesitated for a moment, unsure where it was coming from, the sound causing the hair to stand up on her neck and her heart to beat like a hammer. Mrs Ripley was also out there, staring down towards the entry, face as hard as a flat-iron.

'My God!' Mercy cried aloud. 'That's Elsie!'

She tore down to number one and as she did so their door opened and Bummy Pepper tore out pulling on his jacket as he ran heavily, lurchingly down the entry.

She heard Elsie's cries coming from upstairs and stepped inside, relieved to see Rosalie looking the picture of health. Jack was with her.

'What's going on?'

'Our Cathleen—' Jack could barely get the words out. 'Summat's 'appened to 'er.'

'Where's your dad . . .?'

'Gone for Dr Manley.'

It had gone quiet upstairs. 'Should I go up?' Mercy asked, full of dread.

'I think yer should,' Rosalie was trembling. 'None of us knows what to do – she's up the top.'

Mercy climbed the narrow stairs which, unlike theirs at number two, had a thin runner of carpet up the middle of them. The second flight was bare and Mercy felt as if her boots were making the most deafening sound.

'Doctor?' Elsie sprang out of the attic room looking like a madwoman. Her red hair was a wild mass round her head and her eyes were stretched wide and full of terror. 'Oh, it's you. Oh my God,' she moaned. 'I thought you was Dr Manley.'

'What's happened? I hope you don't mind me coming up, only . . .'

Elsie grabbed Mercy's hand and pulled her into the room.

'Look – look at 'er! My girl – what the 'ell's 'appened to 'er?'

She broke down again and began sobbing helplessly. 'I don't know what to do for 'er. I just don't know how to help 'er!'

Mercy's legs turned weak and shaky at the sight of Cathleen. A seeping patch of red half covered her pillow and a very straight line of blood led from her mouth down the side of her chin. Her face was sickly yellow against her red hair, lips a strange blue. Her eyes were closed and she seemed lifeless, lying there on her side, except for an occasional shallow, rasping breath.

'I can't rouse 'er!' Elsie cried, going to the bed again.

She picked up her daughter's limp hand. 'Cathleen, Cathleen, chicken, say summat to me! Open your eyes and look at me – it's your mom. Just show me you can hear me for God's sake!'

Cathleen's head gave the faintest movement.

'There – did you see that?' Elsie shook her suddenly, taking her by the shoulders, the girl's head lolling back, and there came a sudden, horrifying gush of blood from Cathleen's mouth. Mercy saw it spurt up in a thick, scarlet jet. Cathleen's back arched and her eyes snapped wildly open for a second as the blood poured out over her chin, spreading darkly across the bed. Elsie screamed in horror, recoiling from her, and Cathleen fell back like a rag doll and lay quite still. Elsie's screams went on and on.

Mercy felt the blood drain from her own face. Blackness come down on her like a shutter. When she came groggily round from her faint she was propped against the wall, head pushed between her knees and Elsie was beside Cathleen sobbing and shouting, imploring her to speak.

By the time Bummy arrived back with Dr Manley, Cathleen was dead.

'I told 'er. I kept telling 'er to get a job somewhere else.'

The doctor told him over and over that there was nothing to suggest Cathleen's munitions work had anything to do with her death, but Bummy needed to blame something and it was all he could think of.

'I've seen 'em,' he said, distraught, to anyone who'd listen. 'Them young girls all fainting and sick outside them shell factories. It killed 'er, that did. It did for our girl.'

The doctor said Cathleen had died of a brain haemorrhage, a ruptured artery in her head. But when he talked to Elsie during the numb days after Cathleen's death he said, 'You know, Mrs Pepper, I've known Cathleen since she was a young child, and I've often suspected that she wasn't long for this world. That bluish complexion, the lack of strength ... The child was almost certainly born with a defective heart. If it hadn't been for this, that would most likely have killed her sooner or later.'

'All this time and we never knew.' Elsie was inconsolable. 'Why didn't 'e tell us?'

''E said 'e couldn't've done nothing except for upset and worry us,' Bummy said, fighting the tears which kept welling up in his eyes. His face was shrunken, the life knocked out of it. After a silence he said, 'I don't know. I don't bloody know, that I don't.'

'At least we've got 'er to bury,' Elsie said. 'Not like Frank. Oh Alf, what's 'appening to our family? We've always looked after our kids, tried to bring 'em up right. Now everything's falling apart. And Tom and Johnny going over there ...' Sobbing, she said, 'I'd cry out before God if I thought there was one, but now I'm not so sure there is.'

Chapter Sixteen

September 1917

They marched into Ypres at evening, along the road from Poperinge, walking in a silence broken only by the clump of boots on the cobbled streets and the thud of guns. It was already almost dark as they crossed the Ypres–Yser Canal, and the silky blue of the sky was lit up ahead by the German counter-attack, shells exploding, flashes of light which quickly evaporated, leaving it seeming a shade darker than before.

Tom marched, half hypnotized by the rhythmic sound of feet around him and heady from drinking rum in the *estaminet* in Poperinge. Johnny was ahead of him along the line, and with them somewhere, two other Midlanders, Billy Cammett from Kidderminster and Fred Donaldson from Erdington. The four of them had been transferred to this company together and were now surrounded by taciturn, undramatic Suffolk men, some of whom had heard the boom of the guns from Flanders across their farmland even before they'd left home. Most were young like himself, no more than lads. In this war you could be a veteran at twenty-one.

The air was rank with smoke and cordite. It was dry tonight. Earlier a hazy sun had shone over the flat Belgian fields as they waited behind the lines, rehearsing campaign strategies, outlining objectives again and again for this push on Zonnebeke, one of the hurdles standing in the way of Passchendaele Ridge. They had eaten well – for here at least – concoctions fashioned from army biscuits, bully beef rissoles, Trench pudding with jam. Johnny had boxed that afternoon against a beefy-faced farm lad from Saxmundham.

And they wrote letters. Tom sent a postcard to his mom and dad. He sat for a long time trying to write to Mercy. Mercy, his girl, his love. He strained to see her face before him, this girl from another existence. He found he had no words. Since August, words to describe anything, to connect in any true way with the life at home, had deserted him. His first experience at the Front, his soldiering baptism, was the Passchendaele salient and even those present were hard pushed to take in the extremity of its horrors. The letter was tucked, barely begun, into the pocket of his tunic, pressed tight to his heart. He kept Mercy's image as a light, a flower in no man's land, a shred of purity to keep him a man.

Tom had known very early on that he was not made for the army: all the noisy camaraderie into which Johnny fitted as if he had been born to the life. Johnny, quickly christened 'Ginger' by the Suffolks, relished the ribbing, the half-friendly brawls, the boxing, drinking, everyone in together.

Almost from the moment he began training Tom had loathed all of it, ashamed though he was to admit it. This was what it was to be a man: soldiering. It had been exciting to get out of Birmingham: Sutton Park, France, Belgium. But he was homesick. Missed his mom and his sisters, even dopey old Cathleen. And with an ache of longing and desire made strong by all the talk of sexual exploits by the other lads, he missed Mercy. He dreamed of her constantly, her face, hair, her bare skin . . . This, all this war was a waste of time for no other reason than it took him away from her.

Tom played football while they were on rest, did his best to join in, but mostly he sat, quiet, on his own. Johnny picked up French or Belgian girls with casual ease, all attracted by his strong muscular frame, his lively cheek, his generosity and jokes. This evening a round-faced blonde had sat on Johnny's lap in the estaminet screaming with laughter, pressing kisses on his cheeks although they shared barely a word of spoken language in common. Tom knew perfectly well that Johnny's relations with women had progressed a hell of a lot further than his ever had.

'You want to get yerself a bird – get cheered up!' Johnny told him. He even thought of it, looked around, sized up a few. But they weren't Mercy.

And tonight, while he put on a show of smiling, cracking jokes as Billy Cammett's chubby face with a little brown moustache grinned back at him, and the little leather-cheeked man played his squeezebox, he had not been able to forget for a single moment what they were being primed for, the place of abomination to which they were being sent back.

'I'll 'ave to go out,' he'd said two or three times as his guts writhed.

'What's up, back door trots again?' Billy guffawed, slapping his leg as Tom nodded grimly, hurrying to the back of the steamy café, face twisted with urgency.

Walking now, he felt weak and nauseous. They'd passed the jagged silhouette of Ypres's ruined Cloth Hall at the centre of this broken, ghostly town and were heading out on the Menin Road. The stench of the salient was already overpowering: of death, of putrefaction, of gas-infused yellow mud. To step into this bulge of land, the foremost tongue of Allied territory held on the Flanders Front, was to walk into hell. It was a place of constant unease and fear.

Since the end of July the fighting had zigzagged back and forth across the ten-mile-stretch of land between Ypres and the ruined village on Passchendaele Ridge. The Allies had speedily taken the first five miles, but had not reckoned on the sophisticated strength of German fortifications further back: iron-reinforced pillboxes defended by hidden gun emplacements. The Allies pushed forwards: were forced back again and again.

It had begun to rain. Then to turn into the wettest August in living memory. This plain of reclaimed Flanders land already existed in a delicate balance, drained by ditches and channels. Bombardment by shells, the constant criss-crossing by carts and horses, gun carriers, thousands of men, and weeks of incessant rain had turned it into a churned-up quagmire, some parts possessing a terrible, active suction which could pull a man down in minutes.

Tom had spent two weeks at the Front, rain falling into his face as he arrived, while he slept on duckboards with the water rising over them, as they fought, moving through knee-deep mud with shells, bullets and water raining down on them. They were never dry. Always rain, rain and stinking mud so that even the rats looked bloated like sponges.

Yet he and Johnny had survived to live with sights that gave Tom no peace in his dreams. And they were going back. He sensed in his guts that he would not come through again. Even now he felt weak and defeated.

He remembered the faces of men he'd seen in the days before marching back from the Front. They had not spoken. Exhaustion weighted their limbs even more heavily than the mud drying heavy and cracked on their uniforms, faces, hands. But it was the eyes. A few, very few, appeared defiantly, almost feverishly cheerful. The rest were vacant, somehow absent in their own bodies as if their spirits had fled in the face of all that had been set before them, the effect of it all the more terrible for being unspoken.

By the time they reached the reserve trenches they were already exhausted. They relieved another company. Tom wasn't sure which, didn't care, but he heard their northern accents, guessed they were Manchesters.

'Good luck, pal,' one said to him. 'You'll bloody need it.' They were desperate to get away to safety, food, to get deloused, to sleep.

There was little in the way of sleep to be had here that night. About a hundred yards behind, the advanced batteries were thundering deafeningly, well before dawn, and the answering bombardment of sound was kept up from behind the ridge. Tom fell in and out of an uneasy sleep, sitting against the side of the trench, head lolling first one side, then the other. He vomited a number of times, too weak and tired even to move, and sat in the smell of it. I ought to report sick, he thought. But even the effort required to do that was beyond him.

They were to wait it out that day. Zero hour would be in the small hours of the next morning. All day, along the line, they waited. Johnny and the others came to see him. The four friends sat drinking tea together, trying to smoke in the damp.

'Marching orders tonight.' Johnny still seemed energetic, while Tom was numb and sullen. 'You awright?'

'I feel fuckin' awful. *This* is fuckin' awful.'

'Shut it,' Fred said with sudden venom, hurling his tea dregs into the sludge. 'None o' that.'

'Everyone got their last will and testament at the ready?' Billy joked, squatting next to Johnny, hands clasped round his cup. He worked in the carpet trade.

'Don't take long, that, do it?' Fred Donaldson was a stonemason, tall and hollow-cheeked. He spoke without humour.

'Got that bit of back pay due to me,' Johnny said. 'What – ten quid? I'll make a note, willing it to our mom.'

Tom's head whipped round, scattering raindrops from the brim of his hat. 'Shut up, will yer? Just shut it. Oh Christ.' He gripped his belly. ''Ere we go again.' He rushed towards the latrines to the raucous laughter of the others.

They spent the day together, watching reinforcement troops arriving, long snakes of them tiny in the distance, bigger at the head. They ate bully beef and bread and Tom managed to keep it down. After a time the rain let up and the sun strained its light through the smoke and cloud. The mud was shiny with water, reflecting the light.

By nightfall a mist had come down. They had the order to move forwards after dark, carrying their full equipment. Tom, as well as his haversack, rifle, gas mask, water bottle, grenades and entrenching tools, was one of the men assigned to carry a shovel strapped to his back for digging in where they were to maintain a position.

They walked, the way illuminated periodically by Verey lights but mostly dark. Tom kept his eyes on Billy in front of him. Johnny was further up ahead. In the mist and darkness, Tom's mind filled with horror at the sea of mud around them and all it contained. He'd seen horses, whole carts with their loads disappear into this foul yellow and grey sludge. He heard frequent shouts of those who had slipped from the walkway and fallen in and his mind almost blanked out at the thought of it. He was still in considerable discomfort, his guts wringing. His equipment felt heavy as lead on him, the shovel making it impossible to bend freely.

'Steady there, Bill,' he muttered as his friend suddenly seemed to make quicker progress in front of him. 'Don't go leaving me be'ind, for God's sake!'

But as he spoke he lost concentration and his feet slid from under him, jerking him off one side of the boards. He fell, rolling in the poisonous, sticky mud, losing control of himself so that diarrhoea squirted from him, warm inside his breeches.

'Fuck!' he cried out, his voice shrill. 'Help me, for Christ's sake!'

'You awright, mate?' He could hear Billy's voice, but see nothing. His feet were in water at the base of a shell hole and he was surrounded by nothing but blackness and slime. Panic engulfed him. They'd go on and leave him in this black stench! He flailed wildly, his legs lifting from the mud with a great squelching noise. He struggled to move up the side, digging his fingers hard and straight down into the ooze, trying to gain a hold. He was making some progress he was sure. A slight change in the intensity of darkness. He must be near the top.

'I can see you!' Billy cried. 'Come on, pal – just a bit further and yer can cop 'olt of my hand.'

Tom frenziedly thrust his hand up again, the fingers jabbing into something tense, inflated, which gave way instantly with a soft belching sound. He smelt the most overpowering, putrid stench. The body must have lain there for many days.

'Jesus! Jesus Christ, get me out of 'ere . . .'

At last he could seize Billy's hand, fingers slipping,

then his wrist and he was up again, plastered in slime outside his clothes, befouled inside.

'I just – fuck. Someone . . . I stuck my 'and in – went right through . . .'

'Come on, come on,' Billy urged him. 'Yer awright, just get going. Just shift yerself. No good thinking about it.'

Only yards later Billy himself tumbled down into one of the drainage channels and Tom had to help him out. They were slipping and cursing all the way along.

By the small hours they had found the tapes marking the starting point east of Frezenberg, and dug into position close to the railway leading to Roulers. A great quiet had come over the place at last. No one spoke. The line of men all waited shoulder to shoulder in position. Tom could just make out the railway embankment to their right, a humped shadow of denser blackness in the dark. Just once he heard the desolate cry of a marsh bird which must have ventured there in the lull.

This is it, he kept thinking. His innards had at last quietened a little. He felt beyond physical concerns now, as if his mind had overridden bodily things and the weakness had left him.

This is it. Oh God, oh God help me, don't let me die . . . He struggled to remember a fragment of a hymn from school:

> All that Thou send'st to me
> In mercy given;
> Angels to beckon me
> Nearer my God to Thee,
> Nearer to Thee!

He couldn't remember any more of it, but that fragment kept going round and round in his head. *Angels to beckon me . . .*

There came a great crashing rent of sound as the barrage of fire started from behind their lines and shells were exploding over towards the ridge.

'Come on, boys!' The whistle blew and Tom, as if dreaming, felt himself move, hauling the burdening weight he was carrying out on to the open ground as the land beyond was lit up by explosions, and flames and smoke rose from the German lines. The men in front of him looked like giants, swollen shadows in the mist and glare, and for a second he thought of Johnny. Johnny's words to him before they parted: 'Keep yer 'ead down, won't you, mate?' Johnny out here somewhere . . . Johnny, someone connected with real life, away from this crashing, screaming nightmare. Then thought left him, and he was an animal surviving.

The German machine-guns were clattering and on all sides he heard the whining of shells, howitzers firing, the hysterical shrieking of horses, the shouts and cries of men. His body felt leaden, the mud not so deep as before, but still clogging every step.

Within moments he was crouching with several other men at the lip of a shell hole. There were no trenches to speak of on the battlefield, just water-filled craters, sometimes so many in a row that they coalesced to form something like a trench, always with a depth of water in them.

'They're fucking miles above us!' one of the others was yelling against the roar of the barrage. 'Got a bird's-eye fucking view – how're we s'pposed to get up there? . . . Where's that bastarding fire coming from?'

The pillbox was their first objective, on a low ridge to

the left of the embankment and the strafing of machine-gun fire seemed to be coming from close to it.

A lull came, seconds only and they decided to break for it, heaving themselves to their feet over the slime. Tom could hear his breath coming in grunts. The fire started again immediately and, as they moved out, one of the Suffolks fell back. Tom, the shovel slung from behind him, was unable to bend or dodge easily. He hovered at the edge as another shouted, 'Come on – leave 'im,' then dived back, following the other man's body. That this was wrong never entered his head. You were never supposed to stop for anyone.

''Ere, I'm coming, it's awright.' Slipping down to the bottom wasn't difficult, borne by his own weight. Tom laboured towards him through the mud which was up to his knees, his hands thick with it. The bloke's face was already under the water. Tom was grabbing him by the shoulders when a shell hit the ground, falling short of their own trenches and he was flung backwards, mud and water raining down on him. As soon as he could he struggled back up, feeling slime creeping down his face, obscenities gushing from his lips, for there was not just mud wherever he placed his hands: sharp slivers of bone, softer bits of flesh or organ. This first section of the battlefield was a churned up morass of human remains. From somewhere near him he could hear moaning.

He seized the feet of his companion and hauled him clear of the water.

'Yer awright – I'll see to it yer awright . . .'

Heaving him up by the shoulders, Tom saw the exploding bullet had blown away nearly all the lad's throat. His head fell back, blood pumping. Aghast, Tom thrust it away from him.

He flung himself out over the top into the murky

expanse of noise and exploding light, instinctively trying to duck, bogged down by his equipment, starting to move in the direction of the railway embankment, looking out the next shell hole for cover. The flash of explosions lit up men running not far ahead through the mist.

Within yards Tom was in the mud up to his waist. An unseen pool of soft, sucking mud. It squelched as he struggled, fast sinking deeper.

'Help! Help me!'

He held his rifle up, trying to throw himself forward but he was in too deep. He could see movement on each side of him, men dodging and weaving, fallen bodies.

'For God's sake, SOMEONE – get me out. Help, I'm going under!' He was roaring with all his strength but his voice was the cry of a small bird against the gunfire. He had to stretch his arms out to the side to keep them clear. The more he tried to move, the greater the appetite of the swampy ground to suck him in. He raised his face, screaming to the sky.

For a few moments looking up towards the smoke-obscured sky, something more chill, more deep and corrosive than panic took hold of him. The possibility of going down into the mud unleashed something in his mind. It was spinning off, already disconnected from its hold on the real world he had known. Here was this black hell of overpowering shocks of noise, of mud and decay, rats, stench, blood and shit, of lice, mutilation, agony. Nothing which linked with what had gone before, the daily reassurance of human life, streets, pubs, washing lines, hearths, mothers, bread, love, life held sacred. Here, he was sinking in this sea of death-filled mud and would be entombed under invisible cold stars.

He was close to blacking out until the sound of rasping, groaning breaths roused him and he knew suddenly that it was his lungs and throat making those sounds. He was a man with a voice, a body, surrounded by other men, and the moment in which he was cut loose, whirling lost, receded.

The butt of a rifle swung towards him. ''Ere – cop 'olt of this, mate, quick!'

Johnny's voice, shrill with terror. In all this, a miracle: *Angels to beckon me . . .*

'Quick – for Christ's sake.'

At first Tom thought it wasn't going to work. Johnny had to keep ducking for although they were in a dip he was still exposed to the enemy fire. Tom could find nothing to push with his feet. Johnny hauled with all his strength until he could reach one of Tom's hands without falling in himself, then both hands. Finally Tom slithered out like a baby from the womb and Johnny flung himself down beside him.

'It's me,' Tom yelled, laughing, drunk.

'Fuck—' Johnny, panting hard, peered into his face. 'So it is! Didn't know . . . We've got to get over there – the railway—'

Their main objective, a spot called Le Moulin, lay ahead of them on this side of the tracks, close to Zonnebeke village which lay on the other.

'Get to the next 'ole, over there—' Instinctively, as ever, Johnny took the lead. Like rats crawling from a riverbank they moved off, stumbling forward through the fire to another shell hole.

'Now!' Johnny cried and they were up and over the edge of the next one and as they did so Tom heard Johnny cry out and clasp his left shoulder. Tom, slightly in front, unable to duck, turned, it seemed to Johnny afterwards, in slow motion, his lips forming the word, 'What . . .?'

Tom fell, mouth still open.

'Tom! Oh Christ, Jesus, no!'

Johnny hauled his brother's body back over the edge of the crater, oblivious to the pain in his own shoulder. Tom's eyes were closed.

'Stay there, brother,' Johnny shouted at him. 'Stay there, mate, awright? I'll be back for yer, I will!'

He rolled Tom on one side and unstrapped the shovel from his back. As he came up over the side of the hole he stuck it into the ground. Rifle clasped under his left arm, and clutching the shoulder with his right hand, he staggered out once more and headed, ducking and lurching, back towards the lines.

Dawn was shrouded in smoke, the sun a blood orange in the sky, guns still firing.

Johnny had made it back behind the lines under cover of the last shreds of darkness. He found makeshift dressing stations along the country road to Zonnebeke, doctors and nurses working in the open. A dark-eyed American nurse wearing gigantic gumboots dressed his shoulder.

'It's a graze,' she said. 'You were lucky – but it's deep – nearly cut through to the bone.'

'Just stick summat on it.' In his feverish state he was ungracious. 'I got to get to me brother – 'e's out there – please, just do it quick.'

'Oh, I don't think you'll be going anywhere,' she said patiently, thinking him delirious. 'We don't want you getting infected, do we?'

But as soon as she'd finished he broke away from her, off along the road, until he met a party of stretcher-bearers lurching exhaustedly towards him, their eyes fixed on the ground, faces shaded by their tin hats. The conditions were so bad in no man's land that it often took a dozen bearers to bring in one of the wounded.

'Steady, steady,' the front one cried. 'Here – get out of the way!'

'My brother,' Johnny ran at them. ''E's out there – get 'im for me, please, pal—'

The men stopped. They were swaying with exhaustion. 'Have you any idea . . .?' another of them said, his voice well-spoken. He pushed his helmet up with a mud-caked hand. 'It'd be like looking for a needle in a bloody haystack.'

'But I know – I can show you, for pity's sake . . .'

'Wait there . . .'

They returned in moments, the stretcher empty.

'Where?' the front man asked.

'Over towards the railway. Look, I'll know when we get there. I'm coming too.'

The sun was paler now, higher, and its rays straining through a sulphurous mist which curled over the surface of the mud and between the blackened stumps of trees. Not a blade of grass, not a hint of any green, living thing remained in this place. For as far as the eye could see was nothing but mud, wounded trees, water reflecting pale sky. The guns had ceased firing except for the occasional report of snipers' bullets. The battlefield was littered with the debris of slaughter.

Johnny walked slightly ahead of the stretcher-bearers, all of them slipping and trying to retain their balance.

They had gone only a short distance when Johnny started to panic, realizing just how difficult it was going to be to find the place. There was nothing to give you a bearing, all landmarks wiped away: woods, farms, villages annihilated in the two years of bombardment. But he wasn't going to show the men that he had scant idea where he was going. Soon he saw the dim shape of the embankment and relief surged through him.

'That way.'

All round them as they waded and hauled themselves so painfully slowly through no man's land, the early morning air was filled with cries and moans. Men lay where they had fallen. Others had taken shelter or tumbled into shell holes, and each hole had its ration of bodies, living and dead, from both armies. As they struggled on, Johnny couldn't look into the eyes of those still alive. They all kept their eyes on their feet. Blood bubbled up from the mud from time to time. The edges of civilization, of decency, of meaning, of the obligation to mercy had simply been blown away. There was nothing here to redeem it, nothing . . . except Tom. Tom's life.

'If you don't find it soon we shall simply have to take someone else.' The stretcher-bearer spoke tersely.

'Sorry – only it was dark. Just a bit further.'

And at last, barely visible, poking up like a tiny matchstick, Johnny caught sight of the shovel. 'There!' he roared. 'See? In there!'

The team of stretcher-bearers, hurrying now, followed him to the edge and stood looking down into the watery morass of the shell hole. They watched as Johnny, with infinite gentleness, hauled the torso of another young soldier into his arms, head bent over him.

There came a small shred of sound from the wounded soldier.

'What's that, mate?' they heard Johnny say.

'Ooom . . . Mo-o-o-m . . .'

Johnny put his head back and turned to them as they stood outlined by the sky where rain clouds were gathering once more.

'Quick,' he said, his voice hoarse. ''E's alive!'

Chapter Seventeen

'Mercy – it's Tom. They've brought 'im home!'

Mercy, only just out of bed with her hair tumbling all over the place, stared at Elsie, unable to make any sense of what she'd said as she burst into their house early one morning.

''E's been wounded – came in on the hospital train . . .'E's up at the university!' Elsie was displaying the first signs of animation that she'd shown for months, and her blue eyes shone with hope. 'That means 'e's out of it. 'E's safe!'

Mercy found herself saying Thank God over and over in her mind. She went out to the privy and had a cry in private, relief and joy flooding through her, overflowing down her cheeks. Only then did she realize how numb with worry she'd been.

Suddenly she felt excited. Tom, home – long before she'd expected to see him! She could visit, help look after him. He was here in Birmingham, only just up the road!

They visited later that day, Mercy with Elsie and Bummy. The bus stopped on the Bristol Road, almost opposite the rather awe-inspiring university building.

'Looks more like a church, don't it?' Elsie said, her worn face upturned as they passed the tall brick campanile in the middle of the university grounds. 'Imagine working here!'

Mercy was trembling with anticipation. In one part of her mind she was preparing herself. Tom was injured: suppose, like a number of the wounded men she'd seen in the streets, he'd lost an arm or leg? Or both? But he'd still be Tom, wouldn't he? She'd still love him whatever, and she couldn't wait to see him, be close to him. As he was wounded he might be home a long time. He might escape the rest of the War altogether!

'They bring 'em in through Selly Oak goods station,' Bummy was saying. He kept clearing his throat with nerves. He and Elsie had put on their Sunday best to come out here and see their son, Bummy in a battered old Homburg which looked too small on his bullish head.

'Ooh!' Elsie took Mercy's arm and squeezed it. 'I feel all of a flutter. I can't believe we're going to see 'im!' She seemed quite light-hearted. Whatever had happened, her boy was home and he was alive.

When they got inside the makeshift hospital, they couldn't find him.

'I'll look on the list for you,' one of the orderlies said, eyebrows puckering as he ran his eyes down the list of names.

'It's a feat of organization, I can tell you. There're a thousand beds here now. Oh – here we are.' He looked up at them solemnly. 'I'm sorry, I hope you haven't come too far . . .' Elsie clutched Mercy's arm as he spoke. 'Tom Pepper? Yes, he's been moved . . .' Elsie let out a shuddering sigh. 'To Highbury Hall – living in style.' He tried to joke, then seeing their bewildered faces added, 'Over in Kings Heath. Joseph Chamberlain's mansion. That's a hospital as well now.'

They thanked him and he said, 'Never mind, just another bus ride.' He watched them walk back towards the entrance. 'Highbury.' He shook his head. 'Poor bastards.'

'When he said "I'm sorry" like that, I thought my heart was going to pack in,' Mercy said as they walked down the road.

'I know, me too.' Elsie was nervy now, tight-faced. The energy had gone from the day and the delay felt ominous. None of them was excited any more, just weary and anxious.

Highbury Hall, though much smaller than the university, felt even more imposing with its long drive and country house splendour, although now there was an ambulance parked outside and the garden was looking unkempt and overgrown.

They walked through an arched doorway into the dark interior of the Hall, the incongruous hospital smell of disinfectant immediately once strong in their nostrils. They could see people bustling about, nurses, orderlies, but the atmosphere was a hushed, careful one.

'Can I help?' A doctor stopped, crossing the hall.

Bummy removed his hat and had to clear his throat twice before he could speak. 'We were told you've got our son.' Mercy felt Elsie take her hand for a moment, gripping it tight.

The doctor was brisk but gentle, obviously aware of the anxiety in their eyes. 'His name?'

He seemed to recognize Tom's name at once.

'Ah.' Mercy saw a tiny movement at the side of his jaw, knew he was clenching his teeth and her stomach tightened further.

'How is 'e?' she asked.

'He's – well, it's very early days.' The doctor seemed uneasy. 'You could go up and see him for a short time, but you should prepare yourselves. He may not recognize you at this stage. He's had a nasty bang on the head.'

They followed the doctor's tall figure up the stairs. He stopped at the entrance to one of the rooms and spoke to a nurse. Even more gently now, he ushered them in.

Crammed in along either side of the room, were rows of black iron bedsteads, and between them, down the middle, two small tables with vases of flowers and a leafy aspidistra resting on lace cloths.

Mercy looked round her, heart hammering. It was very hot in there and she felt overwarm after her walk and suddenly dizzy with heat and nerves. What she saw also began to make her feel sick with dread. In the beds lay young men, or what could be seen of them, so swathed were they in bandages and dressings, and mostly they lay very still and so silent it was impossible to be sure there was life in them. But as they passed, one or two let out chilling cries of anguish. One of them, his face half-covered by a bandage, thrust his arm up above his head, crying in a slurred voice. Mercy didn't know where to look, averting her eyes.

But worst of all, they could hear a loud, inhuman sound, half groan, half gargle, coming from a heavily bandaged figure at the end.

Mercy heard Elsie catch her breath and say, 'Oh Lor,' in a faint voice.

The noise grated on, insistent, nerve-rending. The doctor was steering them towards that bed.

'No!' Elsie stopped, adamant. 'That ain't Tom. That's never my son making that noise.'

There was nothing Mercy could associate with Tom.

So little of the face could be seen. There was no smile, no voice or welcoming embrace. Was this him, this creature lying there, the man she loved? The one in whom she'd invested all her affection, her future hopes? She stood beside Elsie, the two of them paralysed at the end of the bed, as white lights began to flash at the edges of her eyes. She couldn't get her breath: it was stifling in here.

It was Bummy who moved slowly round and bent his red, scrubbed face close to the wounded lad.

'Son?' He spoke softly. 'Son. It's yer dad.'

As he spoke, Mercy felt the heat and flashing lights swell until the lights clicked off and there was only blackness. She slumped to the ground at the end of Tom's bed.

Tom had been taken from the Ypres salient to no. 46 Casualty Clearing Station at Proven (otherwise known as Mendinghem), with a bullet embedded deeply in his skull. After an operation to remove it he was sent home as a cot case on the ambulance train and finally reached Highbury Hall, which had begun to specialize in neurological cases and in a new technique still in its infancy – brain surgery.

'Will he be all right? Will he learn to speak again? Will he walk?' They kept on and on asking the doctors, wanting answers to the main question 'Will he be our son again – our Tom?' No one could give them straight-forward reassurance. They were to operate again and see what progress could be made. But it was only right to warn them: damage to Tom's brain appeared to be very severe, perhaps irreversible.

Coming home from that first visit, Mercy still sick and groggy, they were all sunk in shock. They had seen this 'thing' on the bed, hearing the sounds he made, but could barely recognize him as Tom. Mercy felt she was in a waking nightmare.

The next week when they visited she had a few moments with him on her own. Elsie and Bummy had already seen him together and said they'd wait outside. They had operated on Tom on the Tuesday and he was now in a different room. His head was still dressed thickly in bandages but this time they left both his eyes free.

As Mercy walked with weak legs towards the bed he was staring at the ceiling, lying absolutely still. She found herself tiptoeing, afraid to disturb this stranger for whom she'd dressed in her newest, prettiest frock decorated with rust-coloured autumn leaves which set off her hair beautifully.

There was a wooden chair squeezed between his bed and the next, and Mercy sat down, out of range of his view, watching him. His hands lay outside the covers of the bed and the one nearest her was never at rest, the fingers plucking at the turning on the sheet. She knew at last that it was truly him. She knew those hands, had known them for years so that they were now almost as familiar as her own. The hand beside her had gently held hers as they walked in the winter dark together.

She wanted to touch him then, but held back, sitting up very straight to look at his face. His cheeks were thin and pale against the yellowed bandages, and he lay as if he was in a trance.

Mercy could bear it no longer. She leant closer. 'Tom. Tom—' she half whispered, unsure whether any of the other prone figures around her could hear. 'It's me, Mercy. It's me, my love.'

Slowly, he turned his head a fraction towards her and

her spirits leapt with hope. She jumped to her feet and looked down into his eyes.

'Tom, sweetheart – Tom?' She picked up the twitching hand and pressed it to her cheek, her lips. 'Say summat to me – just say you can hear me!'

She saw him watching her, his gaze focussing gradually on her face. But in his eyes she saw nothing of the affection that had been there before when his expression had softened at the sight of her. Now he glared at her, and at the heart of that look she saw a total blankness, a complete lack of engagement with her.

'Oh my God.' She dropped his hand, afraid, stepping back from this terrible coldness. 'Tom? Tom, don't look at me like that – don't!'

She turned her head away, but each time she looked back at him the iron gaze was still fixed on her.

Unable to stand it any longer, she rushed from the ward. Those eyes followed her all evening and into her sleep. Nowhere in them could she see the soul of the man she loved. Wherever it was Tom had been, he had left there the key part of his very self.

Elsie, with a mother's eternal optimism, was certain he would recover.

''E was looking at us, I know 'e was!' she 'd say after their first few visits. ''E knew us awright!'

Whatever Mercy had seen or failed to see in Tom's eyes, Elsie clung to her conviction. 'By Christmas 'e'll be right as rain – the doctor said 'e'd improve, didn't 'e?'

They visited week after week, feet swishing through fallen leaves on the pavements outside Highbury Hall, then the leaves were frosted white, then coated in snow.

As the winter took hold, Elsie's hopes slowly began to dissolve. Mercy went with her each time, dread hard in her as stone.

Elsie would sit at Tom's side, her now fast-greying hair fixed up under her best hat, ankles neatly crossed, chatting to him, holding one of his clammy hands.

'We've had a note from Johnny,' she told him just before Christmas. ''E's in Italy now. Says 'e's awright. You comfy there, love? Anything I can get yer? Just say, won't yer? Your Mercy's 'ere to see you again – look, there she is, over there. Never misses a visit, she don't. You got to get better for 'er, you know that, bab – and for me and your dad. Can't 'ave you carrying on like this, can we?'

Bummy, when he came, would sit silently beside her, hat in hand. Mercy sometimes had to leave the room, choking back her tears on hearing Elsie talk, what remained of her bright hope still fluttering round her son.

By Christmas Elsie had withdrawn from life on the yard in Angel Street. She was thinner, more stooped, and between her grief for her dead children and her concern for those still hanging on to life she had no energy to give to anyone else.

It was to Mabel that everyone was gradually turning for help and advice. Mabel who was seen as the strong one, who had 'come through' and was always there to help Mary Jones and, increasingly, everyone else. Even Josie Ripley, a hard case of a woman who was hardly ever heard to say anything to her six kids unless it was, 'Ger'over 'ere or I'll belt yer one!' had been known to turn to Mabel. Mabel made sure everyone took their turn to clean out the dry pan lavs down the yard, and had their go at washday in the brewhouse. She'd organized the yard women into a 'didlum club', taking pennies from them week by week as savings for Christmas. She'd gained in dignity, walked stately and handsome in her tartan shawl. She had people's respect. She was Someone nowadays.

She even showed sympathy to Mercy over Tom.

'It's a terrible thing, that,' she said to Susan. 'Like a living death. Be better if 'e'd – well, you know – altogether, wouldn'it?'

Mercy didn't want her sympathy. She still couldn't talk about Tom, even to Susan who seemed to feel that now Mercy was in effect 'alone' again, the two of them should be as close as ever. But Mercy didn't feel released from Tom. She had come to dread this helpless wreck of a man who had come home to her, yet she was still tied to him by his suffering, by the past, by guilt.

One afternoon, freezing outside, she sat by his bed looking at him. Once again, he was staring up at the ceiling, hands twitching, an occasional disconnected sound coming out of his mouth. He could do nothing for himself: not feed or walk or clean himself in any way. He had, in all ways that meant anything to her, ceased to be a person, certainly a lover. Yet here he was, this troubling, physical presence that was undeniably in the shape of Tom.

'Are you there?' she asked him over and over. 'Are you still in there? Can you hear me?' She leant over so that her face was level with his eyes. 'Please, Tom – if you can understand me, show me somehow. I can't stand this.' He seemed to be looking straight through her.

'You was everything to me . . .' She began to cry, the first time she had allowed herself to in front of him, though she had many times after leaving the hospital. The old Tom would have been distraught at the sight of her tears, would have done anything he could to comfort her.

This Tom shifted slightly in the bed and let out a low groaning sound, but Mercy knew instinctively that this had no connection with her words. She sank back on to her chair, taking his hand and kissing it, wetting it with her tears.

'I want you back,' she cried. 'I can't bear it. Don't leave me. Come back to me, Tom, my love, please!'

In the end, the only person Mercy could confide in fully was Dorothy. She hadn't told Dorothy about her feelings for Tom, but now she had to talk to someone. She waited until Dorothy was leaving one afternoon and said, 'I'll walk a bit of the way with you.'

'Oh, there's no need,' Dorothy said, gathering up her coat. 'It's ever so cold out.'

'No – I want to.' Mercy eyed Susan, but she was eagerly looking over a dress Dorothy had brought to be altered.

Dorothy saw the desperate look in Mercy's eyes and said, 'Come on then, if you like.'

The two women, both warmly wrapped, walked out along the slushy street in the dusk. Mercy poured out her troubles.

'His mom thinks 'e's going to get better, keeps telling me to hang on. But it just ain't going to happen, Dorothy. He don't even know me now, and I loved 'im, I really did love 'im . . .' She broke off, unable to speak any more.

Dorothy stopped, saying, 'Oh bab, oh Mercy,' and drew the girl into her arms, overcome at seeing her so sad and vulnerable.

'I thought I'd found someone,' Mercy sobbed into her shoulder. 'Someone who could really be mine and be family. And now it's just like talking to a stone. He can't do nothing for hisself, and the way he looks at me. It's as though he's staring right through me, as if he hates me.'

'Oh Mercy, poor babby...' Dorothy sounded near to tears herself. 'We – I had no idea all this was on your mind. Why didn't you tell me before?'

Mercy shrugged, head resting on Dorothy's shoulder, still crying, relieved at being able to let out her feelings to someone.

'I know I ought to want to be with him – say I'll stay with him even if he is injured. It ain't his fault, is it? His life's ruined. But...'

'There, there – it's a terrible thing's happened to you, and to 'im.' Dorothy's heart was heavy. 'I'm sure no one expects you to stay with 'im forever, course they don't.'

Mercy raised her head, wiping her eyes. Dorothy thought how pretty she looked in the dim light, even in her misery.

'We would've got married, I'm sure of it. I wanted to stay with him for ever, and now I feel I still ought to—'

'Don't!' Dorothy broke in fiercely. She took Mercy by the shoulders, her dark eyes stern. 'Don't ever marry someone unless you want it with all your heart. It'll only lead to misery for both of you. Remember that. I've seen it at close hand and believe me, you're better off without it.'

Mercy frowned, calmer now. 'Where've you seen it?'

Dorothy hesitated, her expression bitter under the rim of her hat. 'If you'd known my mother and father you'd've thought marriage was summat invented by the devil himself. Come on – keep moving or we'll catch cold.'

Mercy walked beside her suddenly seeing how little she knew Dorothy.

'No one's going to expect you to have a married life with a man who can't even speak to you, let alone anything else. Don't be a fool, Mercy.' Dorothy spoke with fierce authority. 'For God's sake don't throw your life away.'

The Weston household had enjoyed a harmonious few months with the master of the house absent. Neville had been sent into a Motor Transport Division behind the lines in France, and wrote home very occasionally.

With him gone, Dorothy lived alongside Grace almost as her equal. The boys were far more relaxed, especially Edward, the younger one, whose sensitive temperament, similar to Grace's, grated on his father who tried to insist that he behave 'like a proper boy'.

When Dorothy returned rather later than expected that evening, Grace was sitting at her little writing-desk looking through the household bills and she turned, smiling, although the smile was, as ever, tinged with anxiety.

Dorothy sat down opposite her. Seeing her sombre expression, Grace's face fell.

'Whatever's the matter, dear? How is she?'

'If only we had more control of the situation,' Dorothy burst out. 'If only you could see her, tell her . . .'

Grace looked down at her lap. 'I can't. I just can't risk it.'

'But while he's away . . .'

Grace gave a wan smile. 'My darling Dorothy, how fierce you are on my behalf . . .'

'Not just yours, Grace.'

'No, I know what Mercy is to you too. But I'm so

afraid. I simply daren't risk such an overturning of all our lives, even with Neville away. There are the boys to think of. If Neville were to find out – and we don't know what Mercy might do, do we? While she is my daughter by birth, I can't be certain of her loyalty and her affections, can I?' Grace stood up. 'Look, dearest, what's happened?'

Wearily, Dorothy rubbed her temples. Grace went to stand behind her, circling her fingers gently along the older woman's forehead. 'Please tell me what's the matter.'

As Dorothy talked Grace stopped her massage and sat down beside her, her expression increasingly troubled.

'She said she thought she'd found someone – real family at last. Not just the young feller – of course, she's close with Elsie, his mother as well. But now . . .'

Grace's eyes filled with tears. 'Now she's been abandoned all over again.

Chapter Eighteen

February 1918

The day they brought Tom home the remains of snow lay on the ground, rounded, filthy cushions of it still bunched in untrodden corners. Mrs Ripley's snotty-nosed kids picked it up to chew mouthfuls as the ambulance pulled up, melting it to metallic soot in their mouths.

Elsie, the only one at home, walked beside the stretcher as they carried him in, clinging to one of his hands, her back ramrod straight. He still had a light dressing on his head and round it his hair was growing back as a brown stubble.

The two men who accompanied him were quiet but gentle.

'There yer go,' one spoke at last as they lowered him on to the bed Elsie had ready downstairs. 'Home sweet home.'

Elsie propped Tom up on what she had in the way of pillows and he lay staring across the room.

'There y'are, love. You can be at home with yer mom now. See – you can watch me while I'm cooking and cleaning up, and whenever you want anything all yer 'ave to do is say. I'll look after you. Now – will yer 'ave summat to eat?'

*

When Mercy came in from work that night Mabel was frying onions in a pan on the range, trying to spin out the meagre amount of food available. Her hair was greying but still more pepper than salt, and was fastened in a thick coil behind her head. When she saw Mercy she pulled her shawl tighter round her.

'I've seen 'im,' she said. 'Bad, ain't it?'

Mercy's face was very pale in the gaslight, her eyes glassy with exhaustion. Even Mabel took in the pinched expression of despair. 'He's home then?'

Mabel nodded. 'I looked in earlier. She's got 'im sat up downstairs like Patience on a monument . . . Be better up out of the way to my mind.'

'What – the way you kept me?' Susan retorted sharply. 'Some people ain't ashamed of their family whatever state they're in, you know.'

Mercy turned to the door again and said in a tone of heartbreaking flatness, 'I'll go and see them.'

''Ave yer tea first – it's ready.'

'No – I'll not be long.' She knew if she went now, she'd have an excuse to leave.

Mercy had not been in to see Elsie and Alf for some time. She'd been unable to face the house, empty of children except Jack who was out at work now, and Rosalie. And Elsie's grief, a black depression she'd slip into for days at a time alternating with a determined, brittle optimism about Tom.

When she walked in there that night, the living room was transformed. Gone was the horsehair sofa, and instead there was only just space to open the door without colliding with the foot of Tom's bed. The table was almost up against the fire and Elsie, Alf, Rosalie and Jack were

211

squeezed round three sides of it. The room smelt dismally of the damp washing which was hanging everywhere.

'Come to see 'im, 'ave yer?' Elsie said brightly. ''E's been waiting for you, 'ain't yer, Tom?'

Mercy's eyes moved from Elsie's thin, exhausted face to Tom's expressionless features. She could feel all of them watching her expectantly. What did they want – that she should run over and embrace Tom as if he were still the same? Would that make them feel better? She knew she couldn't do it – just couldn't. She tried to force a smile to her lips.

'Nice to see 'im back.' She was unable to lift her voice out of the sadness which encompassed not just her own feelings for Tom, but for all of them. They were all so changed, Elsie like an old woman at fifty-two, her face framed by dusty-coloured hair in which almost none of the former copper remained, Alf – for he was always Alf now, his nickname somehow buried with his children – had a redder, coarser face. Jack was the least altered visibly, red-haired and very like Johnny, but he was quiet, had lost his spark. And Rosalie, now ten, who'd always been a rounded, rosy child, was so terribly thin, her face pinched and sad. Mercy, pulling herself together inside, stepped over to Rosalie and put her hands on her shoulders, kissing the top of her head before she went over to Tom. She sat down, hands in her lap. Though she was close to Tom she just couldn't touch him. She felt somehow afraid of him.

'So how's 'e been?'

'Not so bad,' Elsie said as Tom let out a long groan which sounded like water disappearing down a drain. ''E's 'ad 'is dinner. Nothing much wrong with 'is appetite any'ow.'

Tom could eat once the food was in his mouth, but he no longer had the coordination to put it there himself.

Mercy asked a few more questions, tried to be warming and cheerful with this family who had, over the years, lifted her own spirits so many times. But after a few minutes she could think of nothing else to say and she could feel her own distress mounting. Tom seemed to take up so much of the room, filling the place with a sense of all that was broken in their lives. If he had looked very different it might have been easier to accept, but his disfigurement was mostly internal. Added to that, all the empty chairs ... Cathleen's, Frank's, no Johnny either ... Mercy suddenly felt she could bear it no longer.

'Mabel's got my tea ready—' She stood up. 'I said I'd only be a minute.'

'Come whenever you like, won't you?' Elsie pleaded. 'After all, you're more or less one of the family.'

That night, when she had blown out the candle in their bedroom, Mercy turned and cried for a long time in Susan's arms.

'Oh Mercy,' Susan said as her friend's sobs finally calmed a little. 'I'm so, so sad for you. But I'm so glad you've come back to me.'

The world was convulsing round them. The end of 1917 had seen more fighting: the remainder of the long battle of Ypres, and at Cambrai. The Tsar had been overthrown in Russia and now the United States was also in the War. At home, they were told the German civilians, their ports blockaded by the Allies, were starving.

'We'll be bloody starving soon too at this rate,' Mabel complained. She'd finally taken on proper responsibility for the house. 'There's hardly any meat to be had, and that stuff they're passing off as bread – like eating chaff, that is.'

For Mercy, the limits of life had shrunk more than ever, so that it was comprised of the grenade factory and numbers one and two, Nine Court, Angel Street. She'd got into the habit of paying a visit to the Peppers every night after tea. They seemed desperate for her to come. Mabel and Mary Jones sometimes popped in during the day, but Elsie, utterly tied to Tom's needs, was isolated and very down. Whenever Mercy walked through their door, their eyes fastened on her hungrily as if she represented normality and hope, things they couldn't keep hold of when left alone together.

Elsie was enormously protective of Tom. She couldn't bear to feel people pitying either him or herself.

''E's awright – 'e'll get better. The doctors said it'd take a bit of time after what 'e's been through.' She toiled day after day to keep him clean as a whistle, fed him, talked to him endlessly.

But to Mercy she complained. No one was doing enough.

'Alf's out all the time, and Jack. I'm left to do it all. And Josephine hardly ever comes over now. It ain't right, keeping a littl'un from seeing his nan. It ain't fair. She ought to come.'

'She's got 'er hands full,' Mercy tried to reason with her. 'What with the pub and that flat and little Janey to look after . . .'

Josephine had come sometimes when Tom first arrived home. She'd turned to Mercy on more than one occasion with a look of desperation in her eyes when Elsie wasn't looking. One day, when Elsie had popped outside she said, 'I can't stand seeing 'im like this.' Looking across at

Tom her eyes filled with tears. 'Look at 'im – 'e's just not 'ere, is 'e? Where's 'e gone? It ain't right, none of it. Would've been better to my mind if 'e'd . . .' She bit her lip, suddenly busying herself picking Janey up and wiping her hands. 'I shouldn't talk like that, I know. Mom'd 'ave a fit . . .'

Her words sent a great wave of relief through Mercy. Josephine was the only one who'd expressed what she herself was thinking. This wasn't hopeful, all this. Tom wasn't a hero. It was a dreadful, heartbreaking hell seeing him in this state day after day, this man whom she'd loved, whose hand she had wanted to hold into the future.

Josephine appeared on rare occasions now, but ever since then Mercy had felt some release. She could begin to let go of Tom, to acknowledge that he really was lost to her. She could visit and try to support Elsie without feeling she had to catch hold of a dream and hang on, for her dream had already dissolved. The man she loved was dead.

It was a long, sad winter. The fighting on the Western Front was held up. No moves could be made before spring, and morale among the troops was low. The casualties at Ypres had been vast and there was a shortage of troops. Johnny Pepper had spent much of the winter up on the freezing *altipiani*, the 'high plains' between Italy and Austria, among the divisions sent to reinforce the Italians. As the snow began to melt, however, and spring came, they were being despatched back to the Western Front. First though, Johnny was sent home on leave.

He arrived in Birmingham at the end of March. A tall, stringy-looking figure now, his shorn hair merely a red haze round the edge of his cap, he strode back into Angel

Street, feeling he was in a dream. This was home, but now it seemed so strange, so alien. It was as if the army, for all the degradation and horror it entailed, had become his true home, the only true way of life.

Elsie would never forget her son's face as he walked into the house that day and saw his twin. Johnny's eyes, already red from lack of sleep, fastened on Tom's face, and Elsie saw burning in them horror, pain and disgust. That sight of hope dying in Johnny's face broke her heart more than she had allowed Tom's condition to do so far.

'Tom?' Johnny swung his kitbag to the floor and went to him. Elsie watched, pulling her old cardigan tight round her.

'Tom – it's me, Johnny. ''Ow are yer, mate?'

Tom was in his usual position, staring intently upwards as if the flaking ceiling was a puzzle which held all the secrets of the universe. When Johnny spoke to him he moved his head a little.

'Tom!' Johnny took him by the shoulders and started to shake him violently. 'Say summat – speak to me, for God's sake. Stop playing about!'

'Johnny, stop it – you'll hurt 'im!' Elsie tried to pull him off. ''E can 'ear yer – I'm sure 'e can. But 'e can't say anything to you – not yet.'

'Not yet!' Johnny stepped back, eyes stretched in horror. He slammed his fist on the table with such force that one of the cups flew off and smashed on the floor. ''E's been home nigh on six month! You wrote and said 'e was doing all right. D'you mean 'e's been like this all the time?'

'Oh, 'e was much worse to begin with—'

'They said to me that day—' Johnny was shouting, completely distraught. 'They said 'e'd be awright – that's what they said. And all this time I thought, well whatever else, Tom's awright . . .'

'But 'e is—'

'You call that awright? 'E's nowt but a vegetable!'

He strode out of the house again leaving the door swinging. He didn't come back until evening.

'Hello Johnny,' Mercy said softly.

Johnny looked up from his tea and saw her in the doorway. She was dressed in her work clothes, thinner, more grown up. But God she was lovely, he thought. Those little white teeth, the deep, inscrutable eyes.

'Mercy—' He put his fork down, wanted to say more but couldn't think of anything. In that moment though, for the first time, he really felt he'd arrived home. She was still Mercy, while otherwise at home nothing else was the same. His mom and dad had turned into old people, and in this short time he'd had to take in Tom's condition, Cathleen's death and the extent of the grief they still all shared for Frank . . . No one and nothing was as it had been. But Mercy . . . Johnny watched as she took off her coat, the smooth way she moved. His mind was skipping on fast. She wasn't Tom's any more – she couldn't be, could she? So why shouldn't he have her?

Mercy said hello to Tom, then sat down at the table between Johnny and Alf.

'You've seen 'im, then?' she said.

'Yeah.' He was looking down at his plate.

'So how are you?'

He looked at her out of the sides of his eyes. 'Awright.' She was so close to him, and he found himself sizing up her breasts as if she were a Belgian whore.

217

'Good to be home, eh?'

'Yeah. I s'pose.' He didn't know what to say to her, could only think of the excitement rising in him, shaming him. But he wanted her. Sex was his customary way of briefly finding warmth and humanity. He wanted Mercy under him, the hot clutch of her round him so he could come in her and forget.

'Johnny—' Mercy was disturbed by his manner, his short, savage answers to her questions. 'It's – it's been very hard with Tom. We all hoped he was going to get better than this. They operated on his head and that, but – well, it must be a shock to you.'

'I've seen worse.'

'I dare say.' Mercy found she was furious. 'But this is your brother. He's had a bullet in his head and it's done a lot of damage – he was really badly injured—'

'I know 'e was bloody badly injured!' Johnny stood up, yelling with all his force so that Tom made a whimpering noise and Alf protested, 'Eh, son, son—'

'I know what happened to 'im, I was there, wasn' I? It was me brought 'im up out of the mud, and now I wish I'd fucking well left 'im there!'

Mercy went out with Johnny the next evening. He came round and asked and she didn't feel she could refuse.

'Just give me a tick to get changed,' she told him.

'Least he seems more cheerful than yesterday,' she said to Mabel and Susan. ''E was ever so funny with me last night. Must've been the shock.'

'They've all had more than their fair share, that's for sure.' Mabel was clattering plates in the scullery. 'He's come home to a basinful.'

It was a mild evening, and not yet dark. Johnny waited

out in the yard. As Mercy came out he eyed her up, suddenly afraid. She was dressed in matching brown: a calf-length skirt, a white blouse with a little tie at the neck over which her coat was hanging open, button up boots and a little felt hat with a feather in it.

'Posh nowadays, aren't yer?' he said, unable to keep the aggression from his voice.

'Only because of Dorothy. She gives me hand-me-downs.'

She knew his eyes were on her and felt as if her skin was tingling. It was somehow a threatening feeling.

'Where d'you want to go then? Pictures or summat?'

They sat in the picture house together. Mercy had always loved it before, the excitement of going out, a gripping picture to take your mind off things. But now it only reminded her agonizingly of Tom. She kept glancing sideways at Johnny, his profile in the flickering light from the screen. She could not have mistaken the two of them. Johnny's face was thinner, longer, the nose more snub.

Seeing her looking at him, Johnny suddenly reached over and caught hold of her hand. She sat stiffly, keeping her hand in his, their palms going sticky. Once he let go and smoothed his hand along her thigh and she froze. He took her hand again. At the end of the picture he let go. She wiped her palm on her skirt, and knew he had seen her doing it.

It was dark outside. Both of them were subdued, each feeling less and less at ease. Mercy wanted to talk to him, ask him things, but what was there to say?

Johnny was used to women who spoke little English. There were lots of hand signals, giggles from them as he clowned it, he could touch them, each of them knowing how it would end up. But here he felt expected just to walk and talk in the darkness. And Mercy was so grown up now, so pure and beautiful, so well dressed. He felt at sea, and then angry and frustrated.

'So what d'yer wanna do now then?' he asked in a harsh voice.

Mercy was just as much at a loss. With Tom she could walk anywhere, close and comfortable, holding hands, not needing anything outside themselves for entertainment. But Johnny seemed a complete stranger to her now, and one who was smouldering and unpredictable.

'Shall we just go home?'

Each of them looked at the other, desolate for a moment, then in an offhand voice, yet burning with fury inside, Johnny said, 'Oh awright then, if that's all yer want.'

He was used to being courted, women eager for him, his cheeky good looks, the meagre pay he gave them which, close to the front line, they needed to fill their bellies. But now this superior little bitch wanted to get away from him as fast as she could. He felt deeply, terrifyingly lonely.

They were walking quite briskly now, towards the bottom of Bradford Street. There was silence until Mercy could bear it no longer.

'Johnny—'

'What?' His tone was savage again.

'Was it really you – saved Tom's life?'

'Yes.'

There was a long silence.

'Will yer tell me 'ow it 'appened?'

'No.'

'Why?'

'Because yer don't want to know.' He was walking so fast she could barely keep up. 'None of you want to know.'

'I do.'

Even if he had wanted to he couldn't have described Ypres for her. And why should she know, just by hearing of it? Why should she have it so cheap?

'I want to know what happened to 'im, Johnny.'

''E got shot in the head. There's nowt else to say about it.'

She was pleading, desperate to break through his cruel harshness. 'I need some way to feel close to 'im.'

I'll show you, he thought. I'll show you how to feel close to Tom.

'Come 'ere.' He took her hand, pulling her round the corner into Rea Street, walking between steelworks and dark warehouses.

'Where're we going?'

Johnny turned on her, filled again with angry desire. He shoved her up against the warehouse wall.

'Johnny for God's sake—' Her voice was high and frightened. But his need was driving him too strongly to hear her, his body taut. He didn't speak. His hands were in her clothes, pulling, lifting, forcing. Mercy felt the air cold on her legs as he drew her skirt up and she clutched uselessly at it trying to keep it down.

'What're you doing? Don't – oh Johnny, don't!'

She could just see his eyes in the darkness and they were looking, but not seeing her. She was present but somehow cancelled out and this silenced her. Her head was grinding against the wall. Johnny was pushing his body against hers, his breaths sharp and urgent, hands tearing at her bloomers and she fought him, shouting, 'No, Johnny – no!'

Frustrated he pulled at her, unable to reach, to get in. This was no good. Why didn't the silly cow get in the right position?

'Move!' he ordered her.

'What d'you mean? Oh my God, Johnny, what're you doing to me?' She didn't know what he meant, what he wanted.

When she felt him naked, thrusting against her, panic overcame her. What was this . . .? Oh my God, no . . .

He was more than ready, felt himself begin to come, yet thwarted and he clutched her tight, groaning in surrender.

'Johnny – stop it – you're horrible!' She shoved him away from her with every fibre of herself, running, sobbing, towards Bradford Street.

'Bitch!' His cry came after her, distraught. 'Horrible, am I? You don't know nothing, yer stuck up little bitch! . . .' The sound of her running footsteps faded along the street. 'Don't go . . . Mercy . . . don't leave me!'

Chapter Nineteen

When they heard that Johnny had been invalided home, Elsie took the news very quietly, as if she had no spark of hope left in her. The dead or the living dead – what other fates lay in store for her young ones?

Mercy's feelings were very mixed. Johnny had gone back to the Front in March without saying goodbye and with no apology for what had happened that night. She had kept out of his way for the rest of that week, only seeing him with the others, and then they'd barely spoken to each other or exchanged a glance. None of them had heard from him since he'd gone back. Mercy didn't exactly blame him. He'd been like a complete stranger to her, one whose presence would have been disquieting had he really been a stranger, but as an old childhood friend, almost a brother, she had found him frightening and sad.

She felt weighed down by exhaustion and grief. Tom sat there day after day. There seemed to be no future to look to, only the ashes left of her hopes. Her old childhood feelings of uncertainty, of not seeming to fit or belong anywhere, had come back very strongly now Tom had been taken from her. She'd grown into a woman, but the roots of her being, who she really was, were hidden from her. Sometimes she looked at Mabel and Susan and thought, I don't know who these people are, not really. I don't belong to them, or have blood ties with them. I just ended up here somehow.

The spring of 1918 had passed into summer with its own slow, tragic rhythm. Any shred of glory there had been at the beginning of the War was gone and it was now a long, heartbreaking struggle.

'What's the point of all this?' Mercy complained to one of the other girls in the factory. 'Here we are turning out all these grenades day after day just so's it'll all go on and on. The whole thing's just a waste of everybody's life.'

The other girl stared back at her, worried. 'Ooh, you'd better not go talking like that, Mercy. No good, that ain't. You'll get us all into trouble.'

But Mercy found herself thinking: everything's lost. I'm lost.

Johnny was in hospital in London for a time, then they sent him to Birmingham.

'Mercy—' Elsie's eyes were watery, like those of an old woman. 'Will yer go – with Alf. Just this time, and tell me . . .?'

Mercy nodded, heavy-hearted. She knew Elsie couldn't stand any more, was afraid Johnny might be in the same state as Tom.

She and Alf travelled to Dudley Road together, to the Poor Law Infirmary which had also been turned over to nursing war casualties. Alf had no jokes now, to speed them along. He seemed lost too, cut loose from the moorings of his own life.

As the two of them walked the long, scruffy corridors to Johnny's ward, Mercy found she was praying, her lips actually moving. 'Please, please don't let it be bad, not like Tom—' When they reached the door her legs were shaking so much she could barely stand.

Tears of relief poured down her face when they spotted Johnny sitting up, his hair a fraction longer than the last time they saw him, his eyes immediately registering who they were. As she and Alf walked along to him, there came a low whistle from a couple of beds away.

'Hey, mate,' a voice called. 'Yer a lucky fella!'

Blushing, Mercy realized the lad was talking about her. She gave him a half smile.

''Allo, son.'

'Awright, Dad?' Johnny said. He smiled as Mercy said hello as well.

They moved to the side of his bed, conscious of being watched. The long Nightingale ward was packed with rows of beds down both sides, each one occupied by a young man, many of them with dressings and bandages, but the atmosphere was completely different from Highbury. These men had 'caught a Blighty' while fighting and were now fortunately 'out of it' for the forseeable future, more a cause for celebration than anything.

'What happened to you?' Alf asked. Mercy saw his hands were shaking.

The lower part of Johnny's body was hidden by a tent of bedclothes, the covers raised away from contact with his legs by a wire frame.

'Bloke bayoneted me by mistake.' Johnny suddenly let out a gleeful chuckle. 'Before we'd even got started. Stuck it right deep in the back of my leg, 'e did. Reckon 'e saved my life.'

'Thank goodness you're awright.' Mercy was shaking. 'Your mom'll be in – only she just couldn't . . .'

Johnny understood, she could see. She watched him, her embarrassment and anger over what had happened between them almost forgotten now. None of that seemed important, not compared with life and death.

*

Just when life seemed set on a downward spiral into despair, the course of the War changed. Through August and September the headlines were full of uplifting Allied progress, of victories at Amiens, and, at the end of September, against the previously impregnable Hindenburg Line south of Cambrai.

During those weeks Mercy visited Johnny as often as she could, at first out of a sense of obligation and later because, hard as she found him to be with, she could see the acute loneliness in his eyes. She kept her visits brief. She took anything she could get hold of in the way of flowers or fruit. He was always civil enough to her, if distant, and seemed pleased to see her. He was less harsh now he knew he would be home for some time. His mates on the ward interpreted her presence as part of a devoted courtship, and he hadn't apparently contradicted them.

So much of what war had left behind in all these young men was hidden to Mercy, until one day in October when she was visiting Johnny. It was chilly with a cold wind blowing, and Mercy's head was pounding as she walked into the hospital. When she had almost reached the ward she found lights dancing in front of her eyes and knew that if she didn't stop she was going to faint. She leant against the wall and bent over, holding her hat on, until the blood roared in her ears and her vision returned to normal.

'You all right, miss?' a voice said.

Mercy righted herself groggily to see one of the nurses eyeing her anxiously.

''Er, yes. Thanks. Just come over a bit faint for a moment.'

'Oh – I know you, don't I?' the young woman said.

She was blue-eyed and kind. 'You've come to see Mr er...'

'Pepper.'

'That's it. He's doing well. One of the lucky ones, I'd say. 'Course, it's not healing quite as fast as it might because of him forever trying to get out of bed, but there we are – same for a lot of them.'

Mercy was puzzled. Perhaps the nurse had mistaken him for someone else. Johnny always sat quite still in bed whenever she saw him. 'What d'you mean?'

'Oh – the nights...' The nurse rolled her eyes tactlessly to the ceiling. 'Completely different place. You wouldn't recognize it here at night. Dreams, you see – nearly all of them. It's like a madhouse with them jumping about. Wouldn't think so to see them all joking and card sharping now, would you?'

After this conversation Mercy went to Johnny's side feeling a new tenderness for him. She sat by his bed, still feeling groggy and shaky but trying not to let it show. They talked about the family, how Rosalie was, and then Mercy said, 'Johnny – d'you have bad dreams of a night?'

'No.' He frowned. 'Why?'

'Oh.' She was confused. 'Just summat the nurse said. It doesn't matter.'

There was always a tantalizing feeling that he was holding back a huge reservoir of thought and feeling, and Mercy, still nervous of him, was not sure whether to press him to talk.

Mostly they avoided mention of Tom. His state was a subject too painful for both of them. But that day Mercy told Johnny that Elsie had taken down her little shrine to Frank.

'She said she's got to think about the living,' Mercy

said. 'Mabel says she thinks she's done 'er grieving that way and ... Johnny, you listening?' She was finding it hard enough to concentrate herself today. The ward seemed stiflingly hot and her head was thumping.

Johnny was staring ahead of him. His hair had grown a lot in the past two months and now almost covered his ears. It made his face look softer, less gaunt than before.

'D'you hear what I said?' Mercy repeated.

'I can't go back there.'

'They say the War's nearly over,' she assured him. 'You won't be in any state to go back for months yet—'

'No!' he said fiercely. 'To Mom. Home. Or what's left of it. I can't go back there and live with 'em. Tom sat there all day. It's no good for you either, Mercy. You ought to get out. Get away.'

She tried to joke with him, though she was having to concentrate harder and harder to talk at all. She was burning hot and the walls seemed to be rippling strangely. 'Oh yes – where d'you think I'm going to go, Johnny, little orphan girl? All alone in the world, me.'

'You'd find your way.' He looked at her with sudden intensity. 'Clever girl like you. It's not that difficult. But—' – he shook his head – 'as for going 'ome – I feel as if I've lived years longer than them already. And walking back in there ... It's like living in a grave. I'm getting out. Soon as I can walk.'

It took her two buses to get home and as she went, Johnny's words hammered in her mind. Her cheeks and forehead were feverishly hot, her legs unsteady, and as she waited at the first stop on Dudley Road, she longed just to lie down, curl up and not have to move for a very long time. When the bus came it felt horrifyingly hot and stuffy and she had to go upstairs to find a seat. Her throat was very sore, she was dizzy, and sickened by the stench of cigarettes and stale old clothes.

'Get out while you can,' Johnny's voice boomed in her head, riding on the hard throb of her blood.

By the time she had crossed town, caught the second bus to the Moseley Road and was walking home, she was shivering violently and her hands and feet felt like thick chunks of ice, while her head was still overheated and felt heavy enough to snap her neck.

'I feel ever so bad,' she said as she got to number two and almost fell through the door. George let out a shriek at the sight of her from his perch and she thought it might split her head.

'Oh ah, well feel bad when yer've given me a hand,' Mabel said, disgruntled.

'I can't.' Mercy sat leaning her head against the back of the settle. Now she'd sat down she felt she'd never be able to get up. 'I just can't.' She was swaying, floating.

Susan wheeled herself over and peered at her. 'She looks bad, Mom. Like you said about Mrs Ripley. I reckon it's that influenza.'

'Oh well, that's marvellous bringing it in 'ere,' Mabel grumbled unreasonably. 'Best get yerself to bed then – you ain't going to be any use down 'ere, are yer?'

'I can't.' Mercy slumped to one side, her body on fire. 'Can't.'

They had to look after her downstairs. Mabel wasn't prepared to get her upstairs, Susan couldn't help and Elsie insisted that they had the thin old mattress off Cathleen's bed. Mercy was sweating and shivering, burning up with fever, her head pounding and limbs hurting. She had terrifying, shapeless dreams and often cried out in her sleep, too ill even when awake to know how worried they were about her.

She was aware of different impressions of the room: light or dark, the sharp smell of slack as Mabel stoked the fire with their meagre supplies, cooking smells, voices. In the daytime the fever let up a little and her head was clearer but she was so weak she could barely move. The mattress felt punishingly hard under her. Come the evening, the fever raged through her again. Susan laid wet rags on her head and body.

'Can I have water?' Mercy kept begging her. 'More water?' Often she didn't know where she was. Her head felt as if it might burst.

'We should get the doctor, Mom,' Susan begged.

'There's nowt 'e can do. When 'e saw Josie Ripley with it 'e just said to keep 'er comfortable, plenty of water . . .' But even Mabel was getting worried. 'She do look bad though . . .'

One evening Mercy half opened her eyes, aware of Susan sitting close by.

'I'm dying,' she whispered.

'No—' Susan's voice rose in panic. 'No, Mercy, you're not – you just feel bad but you'll get better!'

Mercy fell back into her half-sleeping state, her mind full of odd, buckled images.

When she was alert to what was going on around her she almost always opened her eyes to see Susan beside her, her sweet face, dark hair swept back, fastened now in a bun rather similar to Mabel's. Susan's eyes watched every twitch Mercy made, every shallow breath she took with a caressing devotion. Mercy saw the love in her eyes, felt it wrap round her, holding her.

'She's getting ever so thin,' she heard Susan say

anxiously one night, speaking into a silence which had been punctuated only by the little popping sounds from the gas mantle. 'Look at 'er wrist – like a matchstick. She's wasting away.'

Mercy didn't hear Mabel's reply. But as Susan sat leaning over her, holding and stroking her hand, the one thing she knew was that she was being cared for. She tried to find the strength to squeeze Susan's hand.

'Thank you,' she murmured, before sliding into sleep.

As the fever died in her and she began to recover, Susan brought her thin broth.

'Try, Mercy,' she begged. 'It'll 'elp get yer strength back.'

Mercy attempted to find the energy and will to make her arms push her body up from the mattress. In the end Mabel had to support her as Susan put the spoonful of salty broth into her mouth.

'Johnny's just come home,' Susan said to her. 'Bet you didn't know that, did yer? 'E's on crutches and that, but they say 'e'll be right as rain in a few weeks. Seems awright in 'imself. There's ever such a lot of others down with this influenza now though, all along the street. There's people out there with hankies pressed up to their noses in fear of catching it.'

Mercy looked up at her. She hadn't the energy to reply. She felt very strange and light, purged in some way, as if she were floating. Johnny, all the Peppers, seemed miles away, like strangers.

Johnny came in to see her. His leg was bandaged but he'd managed to get his trousers on over the top, so that except for the crutches and the stiff way he was holding his leg, there wasn't much left to see.

'You feeling better?'

'I'll soon be up and about,' Mercy whispered bravely. 'Feel as if I've been hit by a tram.' She looked him in the eyes. 'You're home then?'

Johnny looked down, tapping the foot of his good leg on the floor. 'Ah. For now.'

As Mercy recovered, moving slowly about the house, Susan started to complain of her head hurting and shivering, and soon she was in Mercy's place on the mattress.

'Getting like the Peppers, we are,' Mabel grumbled, still fit as a flea herself. 'Beds downstairs.'

Now Mercy was having to take a turn nursing Susan, although she was still only just strong enough to move. If she didn't go back to work soon there'd be no money for food, but she barely had the strength as yet to get across the yard. She often lay exhausted on the settle beside Susan in the dying light from the fire, not having the energy to go to bed upstairs. Seeing the frightening severity of Susan's illness she knew just how sick she'd been herself.

When she thought Susan could hear she talked to her, tried to find things to cheer her.

'When you get better, when the War's all over, we'll go somewhere,' she promised her. 'I'll go out and earn some more money and you'll be able to do your sewing again, and we'll go somewhere. We'll go to the sea, shall we? Wouldn't you like to see the sea, Susan?'

She waited, listening for a murmur in reply, but nothing came except Susan's quick, feverish breaths.

Chapter Twenty

For days Mercy's waking existence revolved around Susan. She took turns with Mabel, washing her, giving her sips of water, holding and talking to her. She sang odd scraps of songs or hymns she could remember from the Hanley Home. Remembering the enveloping feeling of love Susan's presence had given her when she was sick, she hoped she could do the same in return.

But by the fifth day Susan was showing no sign of getting better. The fever was raging through her, her face, already thin, was hollow, had taken on a bluish tinge, and she could barely gather the strength to speak. Mercy watched helplessly as she struggled for every breath.

One afternoon she opened her eyes and was obviously trying to say something. Mabel was out looking for work to keep them going and Mercy, who had been half dozing on the chair beside her, immediately leant forward.

'What's that, Susan?'

Susan's eyes opened wide suddenly as if she'd been startled by something. 'I'm going to die.'

Mercy knelt down, heart aching, and took one of her bony hands between her own. She pressed it to her cheek. It felt so cold and fragile. 'No, yer not. That's what I said, wasn'it, when I was that bad? You just wait a bit and you'll soon feel better.'

Susan closed her eyes again. There was something in her face after she'd spoken, such a look of exhaustion and defeat. Her skin looked sallow against her black hair. All that afternoon she seemed to be fading away from them, her breathing more and more laboured. Mercy held her, crying silently, as if she might physically drag her back to health.

'Oh Susan, hold on – for God's sake hold on!'

By the time Mabel got home Mercy was frantic at the door waiting for her.

'She's not gaining – she's getting worse if anything.'

Mabel saw Mercy's frightened eyes and rushed to kneel beside her daughter. She listened, frantic, to Susan's breathing.

'Susan. Susan – love?' Mercy could hear the panic in Mabel's voice.

Susan's eyelids fluttered. 'Mom . . .'

Mabel let out a long, tremulous sigh. 'We're 'ere Susan. Yer going to be awright. Just try for us, won't yer, pet . . .'

As Mabel struggled to her feet again, Mercy saw tears in her eyes, the first tears of sorrow she had ever seen her shed.

'I don't know what to do,' Mabel said, wringing her hands. 'Should I go for the doctor?'

'Yes!' Mercy looked at Susan again. 'And be quick!'

She knelt waiting beside Susan, holding her hand, kissing her, humming softly, her own tears falling into her lap and on to Susan's hand. She willed all her own meagre strength to her, her sweet, placid Susan who'd been her home, her anchor all these years.

'Oh please,' she sobbed, thinking of all the two of them had done together, all the ordinary days they'd struggled and worked and laughed together. She was choked with remorse for the times when she'd found looking after her a burden. 'Hold on. Just hold on. Get better for Mercy, please, Susan. You're my sister – you're all I've got.'

Susan's eyes struggled half open again, seeing only Mercy's face, the grey eyes filled with desperate, loving tears.

'Don't leave me, Mercy.' Her voice was a rasping whisper. 'Don't ever . . .'

Mercy began to cry even harder. It was unbearable. 'Oh Susan, Susan . . .' She lay down beside her, drawing Susan's frail body into her arms. 'You know I won't. I'll always stay and look after you. I'll never leave you, Susan.'

'Mercy . . .' Susan murmered. 'Mercy . . .'

When Mabel returned, panting, with Dr Manley, the two girls were lying there, raven black and golden hair mingled together, their arms wrapped round each other, Mercy's tensed tight as if she would never let go. There was a slight smile on Susan's lips, but when Dr Manley knelt to examine her, she was no longer breathing.

They buried Susan in Lodge Hill Cemetery, under a louring November sky. Alf Pepper came with them bringing Johnny, Jack and Rosalie, and Mary Jones was there too. Everyone was silent, stony-faced as Mabel's daughter was laid to rest, the earth rattling down on Susan's pitifully small coffin, Mercy's posy of flowers fluttering down after it, then the sound of Mabel weeping.

'She's all I had,' Mabel sobbed as they moved away from the grave. 'Three children, all taken from me . . .'

Rosalie crept up beside Mercy and shyly took her hand. Mercy gave a little smile through her tears. Mary Jones walked with Mabel and took her arm as they walked between the quiet trees. To her surprise, Mercy also saw

Alf catch up with them and take Mabel's other arm to support her.

Johnny hung behind to walk with Mercy, swinging along beside her on his crutches as her tears fell. She found his presence a comfort.

'I can't bear it,' she said to him. 'She shouldn't've died. She'd hardly had any life. And she was lovely, she was – I loved 'er . . .'

''Ere—' Johnny stopped, awkward on one leg, and leant his crutches against a tree. 'Come 'ere.'

Mercy loosed Rosalie's hand and felt herself drawn into Johnny's arms like a child. Gently removing her hat, he kissed the top of her golden head.

Less than a week later the Kaiser was forced to abdicate, and in another two days the War was over. The celebrations began, the parties and songs and cheering. Angel Street came alive with flags and bunting, singing and drinking. But in every court along the street there was also so much raw emotion: as much numbness, grief and sorrow as joy and relief. And the need simply to get used to the idea that the War, which had become a way of life for so many, was over.

On Armistice night Mercy was left alone in the house. Mabel had spent most of the time since Susan's death with Mary Jones. She couldn't stand her own home.

Mercy looked round the room, a place so full of memories of Susan there was hardly anything she could rest her gaze on without wanting to weep. Everything I've ever cared about is gone. Susan, Tom . . . She could hear cheers from the street. Despite her grief, she put on her hat and coat, feeling drawn to go outside, to be with other people. Staying here alone with her thoughts was too much to bear.

I s'pose I could go to the Peppers', she thought. But the idea of piling more grief on to her already aching heart was too much for her. She stood in the yard, taking in breaths of the dark, smoky air. The celebrations were growing louder. There were shouts and shrieks of laughter, singing. She stood feeling more alone than she had ever felt in her life before. She nearly went back inside, but then came the desolate thought: inside, outside, what does it matter? There's no one for me wherever I go.

The door of the Peppers' house opened and she saw Johnny outlined in the door frame. He came out, awkward on the crutches, and closed the door. She saw a quick snatch of flame as he lit a cigarette.

'Johnny?'

'That you, Mercy?'

She walked over to him. 'Lot of carry-on out there, eh?'

The two of them walked down the entry and stood looking out into the street. A bonfire had been lit in the middle of the road, sparks flying up to the dark sky and a ragged circle of people carousing round it. A woman stood near them, swigging from a bottle. Further down was a piano they must have dragged out of the pub, and the street was full of people milling about in the flickering light.

Mercy glanced at Johnny, propped against the wall. She knew she was never going to hear much from him, of the memories that haunted his mind. But as they stood there she sensed an understanding between them, of the sheer burden of sadness they carried, so at odds with the party going on in front of them.

After a time Johnny stubbed his cigarette out on the wall and threw the butt aside.

'It's no good. I've got to get away from 'ere. There ain't nothing for me. Not any more.'

There was a long silence, then Mercy said, 'Me too.'

Part Four

Part Four

Chapter Twenty-One

March 1919

'Oh Dorothy, is this where they live? These houses are ever so big!'

Mercy eyed the enormous mansions along the Wake Green Road from under the brim of her hat. She'd never been as far as Moseley before, or seen so many prosperous middle-class dwellings clustered close together. She was churned up inside with nerves.

'This is it. We're nearly there.' Dorothy's hand landed on her shoulder. 'Let's have a look at yer.'

Mercy stood still as Dorothy brushed down her coat for the third time. The two of them were just about the same height now, though Dorothy was ageing to look rather matronly, her face careworn and a little severe. She cast away some imaginary specks from the navy-blue shoulders and straightened Mercy's hat, also navy, but brightened round the brim by a strip of spotted fabric, black on white.

'That'll stop you looking like a war widow,' Dorothy had said, trimming it for her earlier that morning.

But I am a war widow, Mercy thought as she slid the hat on, seeing her own, wan expression in the mirror.

Dorothy finished her inspection by stepping back to look down at Mercy's boots, still bright with much polishing below her calf-length skirt.

'You're making me nervous,' Mercy said. 'Will you stop looking at me like that? You're in more of a dither than I am.'

She leant to kiss Dorothy's dry cheek. 'Look – your hands are trembling! It's me going for the job, not you!'

Dorothy gave her a stiff smile. 'I just want the best for you, Mercy. You know I do. Now remember, try and put your aitches on if you can, and call 'er "Ma'am". It's a companion this Mrs Adair's after, not a maid. And don't go telling 'er exactly where you've come from. Not yet any'ow. No one'd think to look at you you was living there . . .' She gripped Mercy's arm and led her on.

'The woman's rather down in 'erself, I gather, so be a bit cheerful like. Come on – here goes.'

They turned into the gateway of a rambling, gabled house. There was a tall conifer in the front garden. Was she to live in this house? Mercy wondered. Start a new life? She looked up at the brick facade, tilting her head. For a dizzy moment she felt as if the house were swaying towards her, and she stumbled.

'Eh – watch it!' Dorothy caught her arm. 'For goodness sake watch where you're going. We don't need you breaking a leg now, do we?'

She took the brass knocker in two hands and lifted it for two loud bangs.

A skinny maid with freckles and a long nose asked their names and led them into the rear of the house. The hall floor was a mosaic of vivid blues and whites, orange and black, and there was a wide runner of red carpet on the stairs and a well-polished bannister. At the far end of the hall a glass door led out to the garden and Mercy could see trees and a white wrought-iron bench. The whole impression was of colour, light and cleanliness. Mercy looked round in delight, in disbelief. So some people really lived like this – she had never seen a house with anything like such beauty, such comfort!

Her heart was beating very fast, and she took in a deep breath, trying to calm herself. What could the woman be like who was mistress of a house such as this? Dorothy squeezed her arm and she let out a ragged breath.

'Mrs Adair?' she heard the maid say. 'A Miss Finch and a Miss 'Anley to see yer.'

'Ah – oh yes.' They heard a soft voice from behind the door, well modulated but unmistakeably flustered. 'Just one moment . . . Oh goodness.' There was a small sound, obviously from a baby.

'One moment,' the maid said to them unnecessarily. Soon she added, 'You can go in now.'

The room was light and pretty, comfortable chairs covered in a chintz fabric, winter sun casting thin shadows on the richly coloured rug. In front of them, a plump woman with pink cheeks and baby-fine fair hair was holding an infant on one arm and evidently still struggling to fasten the top button of her blouse. On the chair behind her lay a tangle of white linen and a thin, crocheted blanket.

''Er – Emmie—' She called the maid back. 'Please call Nanny to come and fetch Stevie. I must apologize—' She turned to Mercy and Dorothy. 'I must admit, I'd completely forgotten our appointment. In fact I don't know quite what's happening to me lately.'

Mercy eyed her round pink cheeks and generally rumpled air and was relieved. She'd pictured someone stiff and chilly. Immediately she warmed to the flustered, vulnerable woman in front of her.

''Er – do take a seat.' Sounding slightly breathless,

Margaret Adair gestured towards the sofa. Mercy and Dorothy perched side by side on the edge of it. Mercy looked over at the window, entranced by the sight of a ruby glass jug on the sill, glowing in the light.

'No – please sit back and be comfortable,' Mrs Adair urged them. 'We shall have to wait just a moment or two. I'm afraid you've caught me a little bit on the hop . . .'

She jiggled the baby on her hip and he stared fixedly at the two of them with his brown eyes. He had a fuzz of brown hair and a solid, healthy look to him. Not like Mary Jones's babbies, Mercy thought. Scrawny little mites, they were. The only thing marring little Stevie Adair's looks was a wound on his left cheekbone, still pink and not quite healed. He suddenly let out a little belch and Mercy giggled, which made him show his gums in a big smile and kick his legs in excitement. He tried to throw himself forward.

'Stevie . . . Stevie . . .' his mother reproached him. 'Gently now. He's forever bumping himself,' she apologized.

'He's a real bonny babby,' Mercy said. The woman turned to her and smiled, though it was a smile which did not for a moment leave behind the look of anxiety which seemed to haunt her face.

'Thank you, Miss . . . er, oh dear, I'm so sorry. I'm Margaret Adair. You must be . . .?'

'Dorothy Finch.' Mercy felt Dorothy pulling her to her feet. 'And this is Miss Hanley. Mercy Hanley.'

'Mercy – how pretty a name. Do sit down again. I'm so sorry—' She went and peered out into the hall. 'Oh where is – ah, here she comes.'

A moment later, the nanny appeared. Mercy saw a very thin woman, Mrs Adair's senior by about fifteen years, clothed in a black dress topped by a starched white apron.

She stood in the doorway, feet neatly together. She had remarkably thin ankles, even for a woman of her slender build, and wore flat, very pointed black shoes. She was small featured, and could almost have been pretty, had she not pulled her black hair back into such a severe knot behind her head, leaving only a fringe, dead straight across her forehead.

'You wanted me?' Her voice was rather high and nasal, with only a trace of a Birmingham accent. Her eyes took in Mercy and Dorothy across the room. Mercy felt herself being closely, coldly examined. Something about the woman, correct in every way as she was, filled her with an instinctive unease.

'If you could just take him for a time?' Margaret Adair was as apologetic with the nanny as with her visitors. 'I haven't quite finished the feed, but as you see, I have company.'

'As you like ma'am,' the woman said. She moved briskly forward, holding out her arms. Her hands, poking out of the stiff cuffs, were very small, Mercy noticed, like a doll's.

At the sight of her, Stevie Adair's face crumpled with dismay and he let out a roar.

'Oh dear,' his mother said. 'He was so cheerful just now. Perhaps his face is still bothering him. It still doesn't seem to be healing very well, does it?'

'I'll see to it,' the nanny said. She spoke in an even tone, yet managed to imply the younger woman's inexperience, stupidity even. 'As for the state of him now, that'll be colic. Look at the way he's pulling his legs up. Of course, overfeeding a child brings it on. Come along now, Steven,' she commanded, forcing him from his mother's grasp. 'Time for your nap.'

'Oh – do you think he really needs to sleep again?'

Mrs Adair's voice was tremulous. 'He does seem so lively.'

The sounds of distress turned into screams, his face turning blotched and sweaty.

'Now, now, now – tired out, that's his trouble.' Stevie writhed, perched on her angular hip. 'We'll just get you back into a routine, Stevie boy, and you'll be right as rain. That's all he needs. You mustn't be tempted to give in to him.' She gave Margaret Adair a smile which did not warm the frozen depths of her eyes.

'Perhaps if I were just to hold him again, to calm him?' Margaret Adair pleaded, as her son arched his back and screamed in the other woman's arms.

'No need. You have quite enough to do. Leave him to me.'

They heard the screams recede up the staircase, growing ever more hysterical. Mercy saw that Margaret Adair was digging her nails into her palms, her breath shallow and uneven. A door closed, muffling the noise, and she unclenched her hands and tried to compose herself.

Mercy was bewildered. Didn't people have servants so they could order them about instead of the other way round?

'Nanny Radcliffe is very experienced,' she said tremulously, sitting down opposite the two of them. Mercy saw it was herself she was trying to convince of this fact.

'Now, er . . .' She looked dazed, as if she was still trying to hear the sounds from upstairs.

'We've come about the position,' Dorothy said. 'You was looking for a companion, and Mrs Weston suggested I bring her to you.'

'Ah, Grace – Mrs Weston. Yes, of course!' Mrs Adair managed to rouse herself, and for the first time, her round face broke into a smile. 'Dear Grace, how is she? And those lovely boys?'

'She's well.' Dorothy spoke abruptly, and added with apparent reluctance, 'And of course she sends her warmest regards.' Mercy listened with interest. Dorothy seldom said much about her employer. They had concocted an almost true story. 'She wanted to recommend Mercy to you. We've known her for a good while. She's an orphan child who we've taken some interest in . . . although she's young Mercy's already acted as a companion to another girl.'

'Oh?' Mercy found Margaret Adair was addressing her directly. 'Why was that?'

'She was paralysed, ma'am.' Mercy spoke as correctly as she could manage. 'She stayed at home – didn't go to school. So I was there to keep her company, teach her a bit . . .'

'But you attended school yourself?'

'For some of the time I did, yes.'

'And she no longer requires your company?'

'She died last year, ma'am. Of the Spanish influenza.'

To her great mortification Mercy felt tears filling her eyes and she looked down into her lap, clenching her jaw. For heaven's sake don't start blarting now! she ticked herself off.

'How very sad,' she heard Margaret Adair say. 'So you have spent all your working life with, er . . .'

'Susan.' Mercy quickly wiped her eyes and looked up. 'No – I worked in munitions . . .' She looked uncertainly at Dorothy. Was she supposed to tell her prospective employer this? 'I made Mills Bombs in the War.'

'Goodness – you look so young.' Mrs Adair sounded slightly awestruck. 'I've never met anyone who . . . What was that like?'

What on earth did she want to know that for? Mercy glanced at Dorothy again, but Dorothy could give her no advice about what to say. 'It was tiring. Long hours standing up.'

'But you thought it worth it – for the war effort?' The woman questioned her intensely, seemed hungry to know.

Mercy hesitated. She could think of nothing else to say except the truth.

'I did. To start. And the money was good. But then the lads were coming home with no legs – or worse – or not coming back at all. And then I started to think, was we wasting our time? Was it all wrong? But I suppose I was wrong to think like that—'

'Anyway, that's all over now,' Dorothy interrupted.

'Yes, of course – thank heaven.' Mrs Adair pulled her attention back to the matter in hand. 'Now, this position. It's really my husband's idea and of course he's not here. He feels I need a companion in the house, though I do feel a little foolish about it.'

'What are the duties?' Dorothy asked.

'Well . . .' Margaret Adair looked down, a thick roll of flesh appearing under her chin as she did so. 'I hadn't really thought. I suppose I want someone . . . to be a friend.' She looked up into Mercy's eyes.

She looks frightened, Mercy thought. What's she frightened of? She felt bewildered, but drawn to this plump, somehow helpless woman.

'Do you think we can be friends, Mercy?'

'I, er . . .'

'Oh, I'm so stupid, how can you possibly answer a question like that? I should try to explain your duties. Audrey Radcliffe has an afternoon off every week so I shall need some help then. I shall need a few errands done, though of course we do have our maids. Otherwise your main task really is to keep me company, and Stevie, when he's allowed to be with me. To keep me from becoming too glum, that's what James says anyway!' She tried to sound light and self-mocking, but instead sounded sad. 'Perhaps you think me very weak and foolish. Only since Stevie was born, I've been finding life rather a strain.'

Mercy felt she was expected to respond, and fell back on something she had heard Elsie say. 'When you have a babby everyone forgets to ask about the mother, don't they – even if you're tired out. As if it's only the babby that matters.'

To her horror, the fleshy, ungainly woman in front of them burst into tears. Dorothy looked at Mercy as if to say, for heaven's sakes now look what you've done!

'Oh – I'm ever so sorry for upsetting you – oh dear . . .' Mercy stood up, but could think of nothing else to do.

Margaret Adair let out several loud, unstoppable sobs, the emotion seeming to rush out of her like compressed air. Then she wiped her eyes.

'I'm so sorry. Oh dear. This is so undignified of me.' Her face was blotchy. 'But at least you can see, I really don't feel quite myself. James – my husband – thinks that if there was someone here to take my mind off things . . . She tried to collect herself. 'How old are you, Mercy?'

'Nineteen, ma'am.'

'And you have no mother or father – no family?'

'None I've ever heard of.'

'You must be so strong to live so alone in the world, dear. Would you like to come and live here with me?'

Live here! Was she offering her the job? It was like another existence from Angel Street. Almost unimaginable.

'You mean sleep here? Where'd I sleep?'

Margaret Adair smiled gently. 'How solemn you are my dear girl. Don't worry, there's a nice little room on the top floor. Simple, but clean. With a window overlooking the garden. And our maids Emmie and Rose have a room together up there, so you wouldn't be all alone. If you feel you could live here, I'd like to give you the job, from tomorrow, if you can manage that. I feel we'll get on. Do you agree?'

For a moment Mercy was too amazed to speak. She felt Dorothy prod her ankle with the tip of her boot.

'Oh yes.' The smile poured across her face. 'Yes, please.'

That evening, James Adair travelled home as he did in all but the foulest of weather, on one of the cycles manufactured at his own works in Greet, nearly three miles from the centre of Birmingham. In heavy rain or snow he drove his motor car. But he not only designed and built cycles, he loved to ride them, test their metal, the wind rushing past his ears. He reached his own house, dismounted, and paused outside, bending over the cycle and turning a pedal fast backwards and carefully examining the chain.

James was thirty-three years old, a tall man, solid though not weighty, with light brown hair which curled and frizzed a little and was already fast receding from his forehead. His face, if not exactly handsome, had a kind, if slightly austere look to it. His hands, as he made a show of adjusting the bicycle chain, were not built to force or damage: he handled objects with respect and precision.

At this moment though, the cycle needed no adjustment. It was in fact the newest Adair Safety Bicycle for Gentlemen. The mechanics and balance of it were almost flawless, and James had ridden it with excitement, knowing its chances in the fiercely competitive market, even against the big firms – the BSA, Rudge-Whitworth – were excellent.

What he was doing now though, was putting off the moment when he had to walk through his own front door. Family life had come as a shock to him. He had grown up as an only child in a respectable, orderly household, a self-contained boy with a passionate interest in anything mechanical. He had been easy for his parents to entertain and control.

The birth of his own son, Steven, had brought him a sense of joy and renewal he could never have put into words. Even now the child was six months old he watched him with an astonishment which almost touched on unbelief. Every single day of those months, returning from the works, he had felt his heart speed up at the thought of seeing him, of simply being able to look at him, to say to himself, My son. This is my son Steven.

But it was not all pleasurable. What disquieted him, the reason for his hanging about out here with his bicycle, was the abrupt slide into chaos which had accompanied Stevie's birth. He found the irrationality, the unpredictability of family life disturbing. Even in his household with its requisite number of staff – maids, a cook, a nanny, a gardener – James felt his home ensnaring him as he walked in.

There was the child's crying for a start. Surely Stevie shouldn't howl as much as he did? Delightful though he was when cheerful, he did cry for long, grating periods and the noise was almost impossible to escape in any part of the house.

Thank goodness for Nanny Radcliffe! James thought, stowing his cycle in the alley between the house and the garden wall. That woman at least was reassuring. She was strict about order and routine, because without that Margaret would let everything slide into shapeless mayhem.

He went round to the front of the house and rang to be let in, feeling the now familiar sensation of dread.

Let her be all right today. None of that foolish emotion. Just back to normal.

There were times since Stevie's birth when he could scarcely recognize the woman he married. For those five years (it had taken them a long, sometimes despairing time to conceive a child) Margaret had always been well rounded, sensual, with her peaches and cream complexion and pale, girlish hair. During the pregnancy she had bloated and the fat was still piled on her even now, unflatteringly so. It wasn't her size in itself. He found that inviting, sensuous. Yet he was shut out: her lactating breasts which by their swollen tautness seemed to invite his caresses, seeped at his touch, and his wife wrapped herself defensively in her layers of nightclothes and turned away from him. Her emotions were the worst. The agitation the baby seemed to cause her, the weeping, especially at night when they heard Stevie crying.

'He needs me,' she'd sobbed during the early weeks. 'My little one needs me. I must feed him!'

She knew perfectly well that Nanny Radcliffe's regime didn't permit night feeding. That it weakened the constitution and gave him irregular habits.

At times James felt he would try anything to get his old wife back, cheerful and yielding.

'Margaret?' He pushed open the door of the front parlour, his eye gladdened by his beautiful array of green glass in the remaining light through the window. The grandfather clock ticked steadily. But there was no fire and the room was empty.

Then her voice, 'I'm here...' came from the back room. She sounded light and cheerful and he felt encouraged.

She was sitting with Stevie on her lap.

'Hello dearest.' She smiled. Stevie turned and beamed at him too.

'Hello there, my two.' Suddenly outrageously happy, he bent and kissed Margaret's cheek, then knelt and played with his son as he lay in Margaret's lap, offering him a knuckle to suck.

'Shall Rose bring in a tray of tea?' Her voice was sweet.

'Oh, I'm all right – dinner will be ready soon, won't it?' He laughed as Stevie sucked hard on his hand. 'What power in that little mouth!'

'I hope your hands are clean – think what Nanny would say!'

He was even encouraged by her scolding. This was the first animated greeting he'd had in weeks.

'And how are you?' He looked up into her eyes, puzzled to see excitement in them.

'I've found someone.'

'Found someone?'

'A companion. As you suggested.'

'You mean – you've already made a decision? Without my seeing her?' He stood up, hands on his waist, frowning in concern.

'Well, darling it's me she'll be keeping company. She was recommended by Grace Weston – you know the Westons, in Handsworth? One of her maids brought her here. She's very sweet, a real breath of fresh air. She's nineteen, and—'

'*Nineteen*?'

'Yes, but ever so sensible.'

James was appalled. He'd pictured Margaret in the company of some staid matron who would bring her to her senses.

'Oh James, don't tell me I've been stupid. I feel sure she'll be all right, and that you'll feel the same about her when you meet her.'

'Well, I hope so.' He went coldly to the door. Honestly, just when he thought she was beginning to see sense! 'I do wish you wouldn't rush into things in this irrational manner, Margaret. We'll give the girl a month's trial, and then see whether or not I think she's suitable!'

Chapter Twenty-Two

'So you're going then – with nowt more to say?'

Mabel stood huddled in her shawl in the doorway of the dank bedroom. Her face was further hardened by grief, hair turning grey. She watched Mercy gathering together her clothes and her few other possessions.

'What else is there to say?' Mercy was folding her grey work dress. 'You mean, no fond farewells? Oh, there'll be fond farewells all right – to Elsie and Alf. They're the ones who've been a mom and dad to me.' She turned to face Mabel. The woman was truly on her own now, but Mercy could find very little pity for her.

'I don't owe you a thing. Eight years you've had me 'ere to act as your skivvy. You stole me, you did. And the only reason I ever stayed in this pigsty of a place is because of Susan and Elsie and the lads. They're my people and they always will be. They looked out for me and took care of me while all you could ever think of was yourself. So don't go telling me I owe yer summat. I don't.'

She laid her book *Cheerful Homes*, and the embroidered handkerchief on top of the little pile of clothes.

'When I came 'ere these're all I had in the world. And there's not much more to show now, is there? Anything else I've ever had's been down to Dorothy Finch or Elsie.'

'But Mercy – you've been like a daughter to me . . .'

Mercy listened to the self-pity in Mabel's voice and felt her temper spilling over.

'No!' She turned on her. 'You never once treated me like a mom should treat a daughter, and in your case it's a good job or I might not be alive to tell the tale, like the rest of your kids!'

Mabel gasped as if she'd been punched and her face took on a terrible, twisted expression.

'You wicked little bitch, saying a thing like that . . .'

Mercy gathered up her bundle and pushed past her. 'And where did I learn to be cruel, eh? I'm going now. I'll be up Moseley, living in a better house than you'll ever set foot in. And I'll be back – to see Elsie. You've got the parrot if you want some company.'

It was far sadder saying her goodbyes to George that afternoon, than to Mabel. Mercy bent and looked into his cage, smelling the sharp odour of him. He was busy burrowing his beak into his chest, cleaning himself.

'Ta-ra, Georgie boy. Make sure she takes care of yer.'

She thought of the hours Susan had spent with him, talking to him. The house felt so desolate now.

She went to take her leave of the Peppers. Time seemed frozen in their house: Tom forever lying there, Elsie with him, shrunken and pinched in the face. She couldn't say goodbye to Alf or Jack as they were out at work, Rosalie was at school and Johnny was gone. He'd joined the police, was in lodgings somewhere across town.

'I'm not really saying goodbye, not for good.' Elsie and Tom looked like ghosts in the dark little slum room.

Elsie came over, opened her arms and drew Mercy into them. Mercy put her arms round Elsie's waist, feeling her thinness, breathing in the greasy smell of Elsie's old green woolly. For the first time Mercy could ever remember, Elsie, once strong, vibrant Elsie, sobbed her heart out there in her arms.

'Oh Elsie, don't, please...' Mercy's own tears were falling. She stroked her hands along Elsie's back. 'I'm not really going. I'll come back all I can to see you, and Tom. I'm sorry for leaving you...'

'Can't yer stay?' Elsie drew back, wiping her bony hand across her eyes. 'No, I know it's wrong of me to ask you. But you could come and stop with us, away from Mabel. And you'd be near Tom...'

'Elsie—' Mercy steered her to the table and gently sat her down. 'You know I can't always stop with Tom, don't you? That we can't be anything to each other now, not as 'e is? I did love 'im, you know I did, with all my heart. But 'e's gone, and I can't – my Tom's not here any more.'

Elsie's watery eyes looked up at her. 'I know, bab. And my Tom too. 'Course I know that. It's bad of me. At your age I was marrying Alf and having Maryann soon after. Never see her from one year to the next, now do I? Not as if Coventry's very far off.' She looked round at Tom. He seemed to be sleeping, his mouth hanging open.

'Sometimes I think about finishing 'im off, d'you know that? My own son.' She started crying again. 'Who's ever going to look after 'im but me?'

Mercy couldn't answer her. She was weighed down by the truth of her words.

'Elsie, can I have a cuppa tea with yer before I go?'

''Course you can. Look at me, wallowing in self-pity. Some send-off for yer.' She went to stand up.

'No – let me do it, you sit there.' Mercy saw Elsie sink back on the chair with relief.

She got out two of Elsie's willow-patterned cups and

laid them on saucers. The two of them sat sipping a strong brew of tea together. It was like old times, yet Mercy could already feel she was slipping away, that her life was elsewhere. She could come and visit, but it would never be the same again. Tears stung her eyes, but she fought them back. No more of that.

Before she left she went to Tom's bed. With a pang she saw that asleep, he looked more like his old self, the accusing blankness of his eyes hidden behind quivering eyelids.

'Goodbye, love,' she whispered. And leant over to kiss him. His face smelt of coal tar soap.

Elsie looked her over at the door, smiling bravely.

'You've grown up to be a right stunner, Mercy. And God knows you deserve a bit of happiness.' She took Mercy's arm for a moment. 'If you run into Johnny, ask 'im to come and see me. I'm not going over there begging.'

Mercy nodded. ''Course I will.'

'Come on.' Elsie summoned all her energy. 'You can't go without seeing everyone.'

She went round the yard, digging them all out of their houses: Mary Jones in her apron, Josie Ripley, the Mc-Gonegalls, everyone except Mabel.

'Don't forget us, Mercy!'

'Ta-ra bab – come back and see us—'

''Cos we ain't going nowhere!'

'Give us a kiss . . .'

'Ta-ra – God bless, love – bye!'

They walked down the entry out of the yard as if in triumph, and after all the hugs, pats and kisses, they waved her off down Angel Street. Everyone turned to stare at the beautiful, golden girl after whom the street might have been named, carrying her bundle, a flower in her hat, as she turned to wave a last time, then was gone.

Her room in the Adair house was simple, as Margaret Adair had told her it would be, but she loved it immediately. It was small, squeezed in at the top of the stairs, with just enough room for a bed, a chair and a small white chest of drawers. Resting on it were a pewter candlestick and a bowl and pitcher decorated with honeysuckle. There was a little tasselled rug laid beside the bed on the bare boards, and a high window through which she could only see sky, unless she stood on the chair and looked down across the garden. A small rectangular mirror hung on the wall beside the door, in a white frame.

That evening, as she was stowing her few belongings in the chest of drawers and feeling strange and lonely, she heard a knock at the door, accompanied by giggles.

'Come in?'

More giggles as the door opened and Mercy saw Emmie, the freckly maid, followed by a younger girl with wavy brown hair and enormous brown eyes who Mercy knew must be Rose. Both of them were dressed in plain grey frocks and both had the titters and couldn't seem to stop.

Mercy watched as they sat down on her bed, feeling the infection of their laughter until a grin broke over her face and she was giggling too. The three of them ended up prostrate with laughter on the bed before anyone had spoken a word.

'Ssshh!' Rose sat up after a time, trying to sober them. 'Or she'll be after us.'

'Mrs Adair?' Mercy asked, surprised.

'No.' Rose was scathing. 'The old tartar – Radcliffe, the nanny. You want to watch 'er, she's a right mardy cow.'

Rose jumped off the bed suddenly and strutted about, face like a po'. 'What this child needs is a regular routine . . .'

Mercy laughed with recognition. She already liked Rose a great deal. 'I saw her – when she was here yesterday.'

'We reckon she's a witch,' Rose said, plonking herself down again. 'Don't we, Em?'

Emmie, taller, older, had a lot less to say.

'We just couldn't believe it when she took you on,' Rose said. 'You going to be a companion or summat? We thought 'e'd make 'er 'ave another Radcliffe. Someone all starchy with a face like the back of a tram. 'Ow old're you?'

When Mercy told them they gasped in amazement.

'You're only a year older than me!' Emmie said.

Rose was seventeen, and in charge of cleaning the upper floor, and Emmie worked downstairs. They both helped out in the kitchen. The cook, Mrs Parslow, was apparently all right once she got to know you.

Mercy could see Rose was busy having a good look round at what little Mercy had brought with her. 'You been in service before?'

'Not like this, no.'

'You got a nerve!'

'They awright then – to work for?'

'Not so bad. Mrs Adair's scared of 'er own shadow, 'er is. 'E's awright, when 'e's in a good mood . . .'

'Which ain't been very often lately,' Emmie commented.

Mercy felt thoroughly cheered up by their company. It

was a long time since she'd had a laugh with anyone her own age. The two of them took her to see the room they shared. Rose led them along the landing. On the way she leant close to Mercy, pointing to a third door and whispering, 'That one across there is Radcliffe's – when she's not down there scaring the wits out of that poor babby.'

They sat for a few moments in Rose and Emmie's room where there were two beds and a small window facing the road.

'I think I'd better go down,' Mercy said.

'Eh – if you're 'er companion,' Emmie said as Mercy stood up, 'does this mean we 'ave to wait on you?'

Mercy grinned. 'Oh, I blooming well hope so!'

'I want you to know,' James Adair told her, 'that I am at first only employing you for a trial period of one month.'

Mercy stood before him in the front parlour. Mr Adair turned away and addressed her reflection in the gilt-framed mirror over the mantelpiece. Mercy thought how tall he was. She could see where Stevie got his looks, the shape of the face, brown eyes. He stood there with his legs apart, swaying backwards and forwards a little, one hand stroking his moustache. Mercy did not know how to speak to him. She saw Margaret Adair smile at her across the room, trying to be reassuring, but only managing instead to look more anxious.

'Any trouble,' Mr Adair went on, 'anything missing from the house—'

'James!' his wife protested miserably.

'Any upset in the household routine for which I consider you responsible, and you will have to go before the month is up.' He turned round again and looked at her sternly. 'Is that clear?'

'Yes, sir.' Mercy looked at the rich swirls of crimson, fawn, green, on the rug under her feet. He didn't want her here, that was as plain as anything. At that moment she felt like running back home to Elsie.

'I'll be direct with you.' Mr Adair spoke as if he were addressing a clutch of businessmen. 'I should not have employed you myself. My wife acted rather hastily. I should have looked for someone more mature to be a decent and respectable support to her.'

Mercy felt very deflated and cold inside. Perhaps after all her defiant words to Mabel, she didn't have a future in this house.

Seeing her dismayed expression, Margaret Adair spoke gently to her.

'Mercy – perhaps this is not a good moment to discuss too many things. Come down to me tomorrow morning and we shall talk about your duties properly.' She looked apprehensively at her husband. 'You've finished with Mercy, haven't you, dear?'

He nodded curtly.

'You can go and ask Mrs Parslow for a plate of food, and then if I were you I should have an early night.'

Mercy slunk out of the room. After she'd eaten some cold beef and potato, she slowly made her way upstairs. She didn't know what else to do but shut herself in her room. It felt too early to go to sleep.

The attic stairs were next to Stevie's nursery. Pausing by the door, Mercy heard the sound of splashing water. It must be his bathtime. She pressed her ear to the door, suddenly full of longing. He was such a nice babby. It would have been fun to go in and play with him if he hadn't had such a off-putting keeper! She smiled, hearing Stevie gurgling behind the door. Oh well, perhaps she'd get a chance to play with him when he was down with Mrs Adair.

As she moved her head away from the door, a high shriek came from the room, a sound so sudden and tormented it could only have been of pain. It was followed by a few seconds' silence, in which she heard the nanny's voice say, sweetly, 'There, oh dear, there we are,' before Stevie gathered his breath and began to scream and scream.

The sounds followed Mercy up to the attic. She sat on her bed. His crying went on for a long time. Eventually it went quiet.

Mercy didn't know what to do. It was growing dark and cold. She lit the candle and put it on the chair by the bed. Then she undressed. She got in under the soft, worn covers, reached for her *Cheerful Homes* by Dr J. W. Kirton and began slowly to read,

'*It is the most natural thing*,' the book began, '*for young people to indulge in the hope that some fine day they will fall in love with someone, and someone will do the same thing in return.*'

She turned the book over, lying with it on her stomach, looking up at the candlelight shadows on the white, bugless ceiling. She thought of Tom, of Elsie and the others waving her goodbye that afternoon. This house felt so big and quiet and strange, and it was obvious Mr Adair didn't want her there. Full of sadness and uncertainty, she wanted to run back to all the familiar things of Angel Street. She closed the book and turned over, hugging her pillow. She cried quietly to herself.

The next morning she found Margaret Adair giving Stevie his morning feed in the cheerful back sitting room.

'Do come and sit by me, Mercy,' Margaret said, smiling.

Mercy went and sat tentatively at the other end of the couch. She hadn't been sure what to wear, and had put her black skirt on again. She was also warm inside from eating the nicest breakfast she could ever remember having. It had been slops, it was true, but with all milk and crunchy grains of sugar on top. With her stomach comfortingly full she was ready to take on anything.

'Sit back, dear,' Margaret encouraged her. 'I so want you to feel this is your home. I do have such a feeling we're going to get on. I'm so sorry for James talking to you in that harsh way last night. I'm afraid he does get into a panic when anything the least bit different happens and then he can get rather stiff and starchy . . .'

Mercy watched her carefully, not having any idea that her big eyes and intent stare were making her employer feel quite nervous.

'I really do want you here, Mercy.' To Mercy's astonishment the woman reached across and took her hand for a moment. Hers felt warm and soft.

'I suppose Mr Adair was expecting someone a bit more . . . well, posh?'

'Oh, I don't know.' Margaret sighed. 'Older certainly. He thinks such a lot of our nanny, Audrey Radcliffe. I think she reminds him of the nanny he had as a boy.'

'Poor him then.' Mercy clapped a hand over her mouth in horror, eyes stretched wide. What was she saying! 'Ooh, I'm sorry – I shouldn't've said that.'

But Margaret Adair had hold of her again, was squeezing her wrist, face full of concern. 'Is that what you think? D'you think she's wrong, and unkind?'

Mercy felt out of her depth here. What a strange

household. Why on earth should this woman be consulting her?

'I've only seen 'er the once,' Mercy said. 'I don't know whether she is or not – I'm sure she's very good . . .'

The white hand was still grasping her wrist. Margaret Adair's eyes were pleading.

'I just . . .'

'Yes – what? Please speak frankly, Mercy. I think I shall go completely mad if I can't find someone to speak honestly with.'

Mercy kept looking into her eyes. 'When I was in the home, the orphanage, that is, there were women working there who shouldn't've been within a mile of children. I suppose she just reminds me . . . there's summat about her – but that's just me . . .'

'Oh Mercy, thank you.' Margaret Adair gave her wrist another squeeze and then released her. She seemed triumphant, and carried on speaking in a rush. 'You have no idea what it means to me hearing you say that. She's so harsh and rigid and Stevie's so obviously unhappy with her. But James can't see it. Anything that goes wrong, if Stevie cries or the routine gets upset, he blames me. Routine is his god. Everything Audrey Radcliffe does is right. She knows. That's his way of looking at it. Babies have to be taken in hand and trained. I'm only allowed to feed him when she says, however much he cries. She barely allows me to play with him. You'll see, she'll be down any moment. Some days I feel as if I'll just explode and shout and scream, I feel so helpless and frustrated.'

Her tears started to fall as she finished speaking. She held up a handkerchief to her mouth. Feeling the quivering of his mother's body, Stevie came off the breast and poked his head curiously from under the shawl.

'Oh, and he's such a darling!' Margaret lifted him upright and he kicked his sturdy legs. 'And your nanny isn't such a perfect archangel either, is she, letting you bang your head again. Look – show Mercy.'

The place above his eye where Mercy had noticed the scar before was raw and inflamed, the skin pink around the wound. Mercy thought about the noises she'd heard.

'When he was having a bath?'

'Yes. She said he caught his head. On the corner of the table.'

Mercy frowned. 'Couldn't you get another nanny? I mean, not that it's any of my business.'

'Oh, but I want it to be your business.' Margeret's voice was pleading. 'You must think me a very strange person, but when you came here, even by little things you said, I knew you had courage. Far more than I have. That you'd question things. I need someone to tell me I'm not wrong and foolish. I need you to be on my side, Mercy. Please don't be afraid. Say what you think to me . . .'

Mercy's bewilderment increased. Why was this woman not in charge of her own household? Surely that was how it was supposed to be when you had money? It all seemed very strange to her. She did know though, that she liked her and that she didn't like the look of Nanny Radcliffe at all.

'Well, I'll do my best,' was all she could say.

When Stevie had finished his feed his mother sat him up and he beamed milkily at them both.

'He's beautiful,' Mercy said, drawing closer. She held out a finger to him and he clamped it in his strong fist. Mercy shook her finger and he let out a gurgling laugh.

''Ello there Stevie – you're a fine fella, aren't you? I must say, Mrs Adair, he's one of the bonniest babbies I've ever seen.'

'D'you want to hold him for a moment?'

'Ooh yes!'

Mercy took Stevie on to her lap, holding him upright.

'He'd almost sit by hisself – look how strong his back is!' She jiggled him up and down, playing horsey and making clicking sounds with her tongue and Stevie chortled, his beaming face only marred by the harsh red wound above his eye.

They were so busy playing with him, they didn't hear the footsteps outside. The door opened and Radcliffe stood in the doorway. Stevie, his back to her, carried on chuckling. Mercy, still with Stevie's hands in her own, saw Margaret Adair's face tense up, the smile dying from it.

'Time for a nap now,' Radcliffe commanded. She stared hard at Mercy.

Mercy stared back. I know you, she thought, her flesh creeping. I know your sort.

'I'm sorry – I should introduce you both,' Margaret said. 'This is Mercy who is to act as my companion.' Mercy thought she'd better stand up.

'Pleased to meet you,' she said, forcing a smile.

Audrey Radcliffe smiled, showing small, uneven teeth. 'I'm glad to see you're getting to know Steven.'

'He's a lovely little lad, isn't he?' Mercy said.

'Oh yes, he is indeed.'

What was it about this woman? Mercy thought. She had an air of command, of coldness even when she was pretending to be nice as pie.

'Come along now, Steven, dear,' she said.

'Oh, couldn't he just stay a little bit longer?' Margaret appealed. 'He and Mercy were just getting acquainted.'

There was no reply. The woman just stood there waiting to be obeyed, her disapproval seeping across the room.

Margaret quailed and gave in, reaching over to take her son. 'I suppose time is getting on.'

As she tried to hand Stevie over he clung to her blouse, face crumpling. He'd already begun crying as, without a word, Radcliffe took him away.

Chapter Twenty-Three

Over that first month Mercy settled into the big house on the Wake Green Road. She spent her evenings with Rose and Emmie in the little sitting room at the far end of the kitchen, talking and laughing. She started to feel young again and more energetic, especially as even the servants' food in the Adairs' house was better and more plentiful than anything she'd ever been used to. Mrs Parslow went home in the evenings to a little house in Kings Heath. But she was kind enough when she was there, once she'd decided Mercy wasn't going to get above herself.

But Mercy knew she was still on trial.

'He might send me packing come the end of the month,' she complained to the maids one evening.

'Well, I 'ope you don't go,' Emmie said, huddling close to the tiny fire in the grate. 'It's been a good laugh since you've been 'ere.'

'I hardly ever see 'im, so I don't know how he thinks he's going to know what's going on.' Mercy only ever saw Mr Adair in passing and he never seemed to take any notice of her. This wouldn't have worried her – she didn't expect him to – except that he was the one who would decide whether she could stay or not. And it was growing more and more important to her that she did stay. The thought of going back to Angel Street would come over her like a rainstorm on a sunny day. She liked Margaret

Adair, and her job was easy. She could scarcely believe what a comfortable life she had suddenly found. No more poverty, no more scraping for every penny in that damp, jerry-built house, having to see Mabel's horrible face! It seemed like a miracle. If only she knew for sure she could stay!

But there was one other thing that made her ache for this certainty and that was Stevie. She adored him almost as if he were her own. She looked forward every day to seeing his wide, brown-eyed face and when she heard him crying she had to stop herself running to give him comfort. If only she could get closer to him. She found it hard to understand Margaret letting herself become so cut off from her child.

If I had a babby, Mercy thought, I'd never let it out of my sight.

'I'd love to see Stevie more,' she said to Rose and Emmie. 'He's so beautiful. I wish I could just take 'im off and play whenever I like.'

'You'll be lucky!' Rose guffawed with scorn at the very idea. 'Not with that guard dog 'e's got looking after 'im!'

One day she was passing through the hall when Nanny Radcliffe pushed Stevie's black perambulator in through the front door. It was a windy day and Mercy ran forward and helped her shut the door.

''Er, thank you,' Audrey Radcliffe said, sounding surprised but not hostile. She smiled. Mercy felt encouraged, and bent over Stevie. 'Hello there!' She reached out and tickled him under the chin. 'How's the beautiful lad then?' She looked up at Audrey Radcliffe who was standing, watching. Mercy was taken aback. She had expected the woman to stiffen and tell her to leave off but instead she saw an odd, wistful expression on her face.

Mercy smiled at her again, her heart thudding. What was it about this little woman that made her so uncomfortable to be with? All her childhood nerves around Miss O'Donnell and the others rushed back through her. But this was a chance, and she decided to risk it.

'I, er – I like babbies. I was wondering if I could come up and see him like – I could give 'im a bath or summat for you?'

The woman seemed to tighten up. 'Oh, I don't think so.' She started to push the pram on down the hall. 'No. That's my job. You leave all that to me.'

Soon after, when Margaret had gone out for an hour and the sun was winter bright, Mercy looked out and saw the pram in the garden. Through the glass she could hear Stevie crying. There was no sign of anyone else. Nanny Radcliffe must have put him out for his sleep. She was rigorous about him getting enough fresh air.

Mercy had a great rush of longing. If only she could just go and take a peep at him! She was alone: Rose and Emmie were busy, and she would have loved to play with him or walk him round the park. Perhaps she could just go and rock him to get him to sleep . . .

She went to the back door, unlocked it, and went out into the garden, hugging herself. She had no coat on and it was freezing cold! She could hear Stevie's cries, loud now, and wretched.

When she reached the pram, she gasped, horrified. Stevie had been put outside with no covers on. Not one! He was clad simply in a vest and napkin, his arms and legs bare. He was crying wretchedly, his nose was running and his fingers and lips had a blue tinge.

'Oh my Lord, the stupid bitch!' Mercy reached in without giving it a thought, gathered him up into her arms and carried him back into the house. Sitting by the fire in the back sitting room, she held him wrapped in a shawl and rocked him, warming him until eventually he grew drowsy and slept in her lap. She still carried on humming, looking down into his chubby face, the scar over his eye at last beginning to heal properly. She laid him softly to rest on the couch and sat watching him, mesmerized. Imagine if he were hers. Belonging to someone! Really belonging. Being able to call him family. She pretended to herself that Stevie was hers, imagined trying to build a life for him. How she would work to see he had everything better than her! And she would never, never leave him . . .

'What are you doing?'

The voice at the door made her jump violently. In that split second she had to decide what to say. She wanted to shout, but knew she must be polite.

'He was crying. I just thought I'd give 'im a bit of a love, that's all. He was cold,' she pointed out, trying to speak humbly. She had to keep on the right side of this woman.

Audrey Radcliffe stared at her for an uncomfortably long time. Mercy saw that she, too, was struggling, having to decide how to play this one. To Mercy's astonishment she walked across the room and sat down. She put her feet in their pointed shoes neatly together.

'You shouldn't go against what I say, you know.' Her voice was oddly childlike, wheedling almost.

'Sorry,' Mercy said, controlling her anger. 'Only it is cold—'

'I'm the child's nanny, not you.'

'I know, only—'

'Me. Not you.' She smiled suddenly, eyes fixed on Mercy's face, then stood up again. Mercy noticed to her astonishment that her hands were trembling. In a desperate voice she said. 'Don't tell her.'

'Tell who?'

'Mrs Adair. About this afternoon. It won't happen again, really it won't.'

'Awright. No, 'course I won't.' Mercy smiled up at her. So she was human after all. She was worried about losing her place here! But looking at her Mercy could still only feel the same sense of disquiet. There was something oddly wooden about her. Something not right . . .

'Shall I bring him up when he wakes?'

'All right. Straight away though.' She was on her dignity again now, and went out of the room without another word.

'Well,' Mercy murmured to the sleeping baby, 'she's a rum'un all right, that one.'

'You surely have no objection to her staying with us now?' Margaret Adair pleaded with her husband. 'She's been here a month and she's been marvellous.'

James Adair had arrived home from the works and the two of them were in their bedchamber, changing for the evening. James was sitting on the edge of the bed unfastening his shoes. He hesitated before answering.

Margaret assumed this thoughtful pause was his way of justifying his initial doubts about Mercy, of asserting his control of the household.

'James – darling . . .' Margaret came round the bed. 'Perhaps we could invite Mercy to share our dinner with us tonight? You complain that you don't know what she's like because you scarcely ever see her!'

She turned her back to him, inviting him to button her up. She was dressed in a rather matronly frock, blue, with a maroon paisley pattern, which accentuated her already considerable curves. She had tried to pin up her hair, though wisps of it were already escaping down her back.

'You look nice,' James offered, even though he didn't quite feel it was true. Surely a woman should have more instinct about what clothes would suit her?

'Oh, thank you!' She turned her head, startled. It was a long time since he'd paid her a compliment.

James smiled. Things are getting better, he thought. It was days – no, more than that – since he'd come home and found her weeping and incapable, her clothes all anyhow, some of the buttons left unfastened. And she was definitely smiling more. He stood up and before doing up the dress he slipped his hands inside. Feeling her soft, curving form he wanted her with such a reconciliatory stab of desire that for a moment he felt like weeping. Perhaps all could be well again. He pulled her closer to him.

'James,' she murmured, reassured by his sudden affection. She turned and faced him. James smiled, the skin crinkling round his eyes.

'My love – You seem more . . . yourself.'

'I am! I do feel better. Except . . .' She stopped, chewing her lip.

'What?'

I want her out, she felt like shouting. Get rid of that wretched Radcliffe woman who rules my life and all will be well. But she didn't want to sour the moment.

'Nothing.' She brushed her hands down the lapels of

his jacket, her expression sweet. 'You didn't answer my question about Mercy.'

James laughed. 'You're a strange one, aren't you? Why eat with us? She's a servant! Still, I suppose she's not so much younger than Lizzie. A replacement sister for you, eh?'

'Yes.' Margaret's face was bright. 'Just like that.'

Her beloved sister Lizzie had left her father's Warwickshire farm as she had done, to marry another farmer and settle outside Carlisle. Margaret missed her sorely. 'So may she?'

James's spirits were high, and he could feel the pleasant sensation of wanting her increasing in him. 'Oh, all right, if it keeps you happy. How's our boy today?'

Margaret's face fell. 'He's all right. From what I've seen of him. That woman took him out in a terrible rainstorm. She's obsessed with this fresh air business. I hope he didn't catch his death.'

''Course not. Toughen him up. She knows what she's doing.'

Margaret tried to demur, but she could see James was barely listening. Such close proximity to his wife after the deprivation of months of union with her was overcoming him. Cautiously he ran his hands over her enlarged breasts. The feel of them was extraordinary.

'Oh, my love,' he whispered, leaning to kiss her soft mouth. He was overcome with need for her.

'James, we must go down – they'll be waiting for us.'

'Let them wait.'

Gently, she moved away from him. 'Let us think about – that . . .' A blush spread over her face as she appealed to him. They never spoke of the physical things which happened between them. 'Later – please?'

'Very well.' He struggled for composure, unsatisfied desire bringing him for a moment to the edge of violence. But he must control himself. Self-control was vital, was the mark of civilized behaviour. He turned from her, clearing his throat hard.

'They want me?' Mercy was in the kitchen with Emmie and Rose. She often gave a hand in the evening while Mrs Parslow was plodding round on her big flat feet amid the steaming saucepans.

Rose was grinning. 'Ooh,' she teased. 'Miss La-di-dah. We are going up in the world!'

'Better go and put a clean frock on,' Mrs Parslow commented, testing the potatoes to see if they were boiled. 'You can't sit in there with them unless you're clean.'

'But I haven't got another clean frock!' Mercy was all nerves at the thought of eating a meal in the presence of Mr Adair.

'Ah well,' Mrs Parslow said dryly. 'You'll 'ave to do then won't you? Go on – best get on in there.'

Mercy rushed to wash her hands and then went timidly to the dining room. Why have they asked me? she wondered. Was it to tell her whether she was going to be allowed to stay or not? If they were going to turn her out, would they have asked her to eat dinner with them?

The light was on over the dining table and three places had been set. Mercy thought Mr Adair didn't seem in a very good mood and Margaret Adair was flustered and apologetic in her too-tight dress.

'Come in and sit down, dear,' she said as Mercy slid into the room.

The three of them settled at the well-polished table, Mr Adair at the end with Mercy to his left and his wife to his right. A few moments later Emmie and Rose carried in the food, both smirking at Mercy behind the Adairs' backs and Mercy had to look down at the hunting scene on her place mat to stop herself grinning back. What was she doing sitting here when she should be out in the kitchen with those two clowns as normal!

'So how are you getting along?' Mr Adair asked her once the three of them were alone.

'Oh—' Mercy was startled. 'Er – very well thank you,' she said, unsure how to respond. 'Very nice.' She was watching intently to see what the Adairs did with all the implements on the table. There was a generous slice of belly pork on her plate which smelt delicious.

'Here we are, Mercy.' Margaret passed her the potatoes. Mercy could feel her mouth watering at the sight but the dish was so heavy that in taking it in one hand she almost dropped it.

'Sorry,' she murmured, blushing as James Adair's hand reached out and caught it.

'Steady,' he said. He smiled suddenly, a kind smile. Mercy smiled back, relieved, and for a moment his eyes dwelt on her face as if puzzled, before reaching for the other dish.

'Swede?'

'Oh, no, thank you.'

'Do you not care for swede, Mercy?' Margaret asked. 'I must say I never liked it as a child . . .'

'No, I don't.' Mercy felt her voice coming out very quietly.

She accepted greens, and they all began to eat. The food was delicious, and she was grateful when Mr Adair began to talk to his wife.

'I had a letter today from that Kesler chap – the one in New York.'

'Oh?' Margaret frowned with her fork poised in the air. 'Kestler? Isn't he German?'

'He's an American by birth.' James's tone silenced any argument. 'This is business, darling.' There was a moment's silence.

'And what did he have to say?'

'Well . . .' James laid down his knife and fork, speaking with the kind of animation which only work could bring out in him. 'He's thinking and planning very much along the same lines as we are. That for smaller companies to survive we'll have to get into one of the specialist niches in the market – and fast. And develop that as hard as we can. Kesler's company is on about the same scale as ours.'

'How marvellous,' Margaret said.

James chewed on a mouthful of meat, then chuckled. 'Oddly enough – in fact it seems like fate, almost – he's also putting together a new model of racing cycle. It's rather different from the approach Silkin and I have been working on, but Kesler's full of all sorts of ideas about all these new aluminium alloys – lighter, you see, and . . .'

'That sounds very exciting,' Margaret enthused, just a little too much.

James smiled and looked at Mercy. 'I don't suppose all this kind of business talk is of any interest to you?'

'It is,' she said truthfully. 'What is the name of your company, Mr Adair?' She knew, actually, but thought she'd ask again.

Mr Adair looked a little taken aback at her interest. 'Well, it's Adair and Dunne actually. Dunne's made the parts for the cycles, or a lot of them any rate. So my company bought them up just before the War. We still have to go out to Dunlop for the tyres, and of course your best lamp is a Lucas lamp, but there're local firms too. Of course, during the War—' – he was really getting into his stride now – 'we went over to making spares for military vehicles, which wasn't unprofitable, I must say.' He gave a self-satisfied chuckle. 'But now's our big chance to develop.'

Mercy frowned. 'I always thought the BSA made all the cycles.'

'Oh no.' He laughed again, expansively. He was relaxing, flattered by Mercy's interest. Margaret was visibly relieved. 'The BSA are big of course. But there are quite a few firms. Some of the smaller ones have combined – take Weldless Steel Tubes, for instance. Now twenty-five years ago, they were—'

'James, I can't see that Mercy really needs to know all this,' Margaret interrupted gently.

Her husband looked a little rueful, and sat back in his seat, stroking his slightly gingery moustache with one hand, his fine crystal glass in the other.

'Factory life. There we are. You ever been in a factory?'

'Yes,' Mercy said simply. 'I made grenades – Mills Bombs – for two years. Up Deritend.'

'Did you now?' He glanced at his wife, eyes reproachful. No one had told him he'd employed a factory hand in his house.

Shyly, Mercy began to question him. One question led to another. She was interested, and she also saw her attention pleased him. Margaret was bored by his work. She didn't know anything much, of course. How did he know what people wanted? she asked. How did they know how many cycles to make? And if there were all these other cycle manufacturers in Birmingham, why did he need an American gentleman?

He answered indulgently at first and she was just relieved he didn't laugh at her or become impatient.

'There are nigh on 1,500 employed in the firm altogether . . .'

'Is that big?' Mercy's eyes were wide. As Mr Adair answered she felt Margaret watching her.

'Big enough.' James Adair sat back as Rose and Emmie cleared away the plates and brought in dishes of stewed pears and junket, and pretty ivy-patterned bowls. 'Not big by BSA standards though. 'Course, they can design and produce a whole range. But our route will be through specialized models – racers, leisure bicycles. Now the War's over there's huge demand. And it happens that the most like-minded designer I've come across is over the water.'

For the first time Mercy eased herself back in her chair and sat comfortably, more relaxed. She was not without anxiety though, nervous in case her manners should be found wanting. And were they going to tell her whether she could keep her job or not?

As they finished their sweet, James Adair pushed his chair back, crossed one leg comfortably over the other and lit a cigar, his soft worsted jacket unbuttoned. The room was dark round them, the table a pool of light in the middle.

'So Mercy, are you going to tell us a bit more about yourself?'

Mercy's heart started to pound. Was this it now? Was he going to find out all about her and then decide she wasn't suitable to remain in his wife's company? What in heaven did he want to know? She reddened in confusion, feeling her mouth turn dry.

'Oh James, not tonight!' Margaret intervened.

Mercy looked gratefully at her, knowing she was being protected. 'I'm sure we've tired the poor girl quite enough—'

'Nonsense!' James laughed. 'She's been lively as a cricket – full of questions. Haven't you, Mercy?'

'Well I—'

'Would you like to go to your room now, dear?' Margaret said.

''Er, yes – please.' Mercy couldn't meet Mr Adair's eye. She stood up, gracefully smoothing her skirts.

'You'll join us again, won't you?' James Adair had stood up and was holding out his hand. Confused, Mercy took it, looking up into his eyes.

'Thank you,' she said.

'Goodnight,' Margaret called to her.

Mercy closed the dining-room door behind her and let out an enormous sigh of relief. Well, they hadn't said she couldn't stay yet!

'Good God,' James Adair said as Mercy left the room. He spoke in irritation at himself. What did he think he was doing, shaking hands with a servant like that? He sat down, stiffly continuing to smoke his cigar.

'That was very gallant, dear,' Margaret teased him. 'I see you approve after all.'

'Perhaps,' he said gruffly, 'In fact, yes, she's a great deal better than I'd feared.'

He was left with an unsettled, almost itchy feeling, the image of those large, striking eyes watching him as he'd talked.

'So what do we know about the girl?'

Margaret thought quickly. She wanted to please James, knew that later, in private, she would have to. But in the matter of Mercy she also wanted his approval. Mercy had told her very few things, and those inadvertently, about her past life.

'I only know for sure that she was an orphan – abandoned at birth from what she said.' She watched her husband's face. 'Poor little waif. What a thing to do to a child.'

'Poverty.' James shook his head, leaning forward to knock ash from his cigar. 'The desperation of poverty.' Margaret was surprised and touched by this insight of his.

That night, after they had retired, she didn't instantly turn away from him as they lay together, though she was quiet, listening, he knew, for sounds from Stevie's room.

James caressed her belly through the soft organza nightdress. Felt her sigh, very slightly.

'You, er ...' He felt he must ask, embarrassing as it was. 'You don't mind?'

'No,' she replied dreamily. 'I don't mind.'

Carefully he moved her nightdress up, at last allowing himself desire, and uncovered her breasts in the soft light.

Chapter Twenty-Four

That Saturday Mr Adair called Mercy into the parlour. Speaking very formally he said that her presence in the house and her behaviour had been satisfactory and beneficial to everyone, and that she could consider herself now employed for the forseeable future.

However serious she tried to look, Mercy could feel a beaming smile breaking out across her face.

'Oh thank you!' she cried when Mr Adair had finished speaking. 'Thank you so much!'

'There's just one thing . . .' Mr Adair looked rather stern. 'Audrey Radcliffe tells me you have taken issue with her on a few matters concerning our son. I won't have that. So far as I'm concerned she's making a marvellous job of caring for Steven. I believe her to be very sound and I don't wish to hear any more about you causing her trouble.'

'But she—' Mercy looked stricken, but closed her mouth again. This was no time to start arguing. 'Sorry,' she mumbled. 'It won't happen again.'

When she was alone with Margaret she said, 'I'm ever so glad. I was afraid you wouldn't be satisfied with me – especially your husband.'

'Oh Mercy, not at all,' Margaret laughed. 'James can see how much you've cheered me up. It's been such fun since you've been here. I do hope you feel happy and settled with us?'

'Oh yes.' Mercy was beaming again. 'I've got used to it here with you and Stevie. I don't think I could stand going back now.'

She had been back to Angel Street though, on her two afternoons off. The first time it was hard. It had only been two weeks after all. In one way she felt as if she'd never left, yet in another, that she'd been away months, years even.

She went straight to Elsie.

'Eh, bab, you're back!' Elsie's face glowed at the sight of her. She was already putting the kettle on.

Mercy went and sat by Tom.

''Ello love.' He was propped upright, awake, but she didn't kiss him. He made a sound, and a sudden movement with his head.

'See – 'e's glad to see you.'

Mercy sighed softly. 'So how've you been?'

'Oh – you know.' Elsie spoke with her back to her, spooning tea from her battered tin with the green lid.

'And Alf?'

'Oh, 'e's not so bad. 'E saw Johnny last week, in town. Said the lad were awright. 'E said 'e'd come over and visit but 'e 'ain't turned up yet.'

She turned round to lay out the cups on the bare, scrubbed table, and Mercy was shocked by the grim, unguarded expression on her face. Was she imagining that Elsie looked a lot worse or was it just that she was now used to Margaret Adair's robust appearance?

'Elsie, are you awright? You don't look well to me.'

Elsie tried to smile but succeeded in something more like a wince. 'Oh, I'll do. Now – ' she spooned condensed milk into the cups – ''ow're they treating you?'

Mercy chattered on to her as they drank their sweet tea, telling her about her first fortnight, how Dorothy had popped in to see her, about Stevie, and Nanny Radcliffe – Elsie tutted as Mercy described her – and about the Adairs. She told her about the house and all the beautiful things in it, Mr Adair's glass collection and the soft chairs and the pretty painted firescreen in the parlour.

'And they've got a great big grandfather clock which ticks ever so loud, and antimacassars on all the parlour chairs . . .'

Elsie was smiling and listening, glad for her, Mercy could see, but a couple of times she saw her close her eyes tight for a moment.

'What's up?' Mercy felt her stomach churn in fright. 'You got a pain, Elsie?'

'What? Oh, no, love. I'm just a bit tired, that's all.' She jerked her head at Tom. ''E were a bit restless in the night so I was up and down.'

Mercy ached for her. She felt as if the walls were closing in round them. Back here. This endless, futile struggle.

'How's she?' She nodded her head towards Mabel's.

'Oh – doing odd bits of work. Mary's 'elping 'er out.'

'Ah – I bet she is.'

'You been in to see 'er?'

'No.'

Elsie gave a long sigh. 'Well, I can't say I blame yer.'

Mercy stayed late enough to see the others come in. Alf greeted her like a long lost daughter which made her happy, and she sat chatting to Jack and Rosalie for a bit.

'Don't forget us, will yer?' Elsie joked as she left.

'I'll see you in a fortnight.' She turned to wave, going

to the entry. As she did so she caught sight of Mabel peering out from the window of number two and turned away. Mabel didn't come out.

Stevie was crying. The sound of it wormed its way into Mercy's sleep until she opened her eyes in the dark. He didn't wake every night now, but on occasion there came a roar from the nursery and then his anguished howling, as if he'd wakened from a terrible dream.

After a time, if it didn't stop, Mercy would hear Audrey Radcliffe's bedroom door squeak open and her abrupt tread going down the stairs.

But that night, though Stevie carried on crying for many minutes, there came no sound from the room opposite. Mercy turned on her back, wide awake now. The baby's cries were pained, or frightened. Those helpless shrieks into the darkness touched something in her, setting her nerves on edge. She felt almost like crying herself. She couldn't lie in bed listening to him.

Moving silently across the floorboards in her bedsocks, she pulled on a cardigan and lit the candle and went down to him. Audrey Radcliffe's door was still shut.

Stevie quieted for a second when she entered the nursery, the light from her candle thinning out the dark. Mercy had to look round to see where the cot was, for Radcliffe kept the room so much as her personal fortress that Mercy had barely even glimpsed inside until now. Then Stevie let out another high whimper.

'It's awright, little'un.' She put the candle on the table by the wall and went to pick him up.

'There – Mercy's 'ere to see you. No need for all that racket now, is there?'

As she held him, Stevie cuddled in close to her, one

hand grasping the sleeve of her cardigan, tangling in her long hair, the other tucked up close to his face, thumb in mouth. He was still gulping and sniffing, but Mercy felt that he was calmer, reassured.

For a few moments she walked round the room holding him, then sat on the rush-seated chair and rocked him, humming, starting to pat his back. Suddenly he stiffened in her arms and let out another great howl.

'Now . . . now . . . there,' she was saying, then looked up startled as the light from another candle appeared at the door.

'Oh Mercy – thank goodness it's you.' Margaret Adair was clad in a long, pale gown. 'What're you doing down here? Do you often come to him at night? I thought it was . . .?'

'No, I don't,' Mercy whispered back. 'Only she didn't seem to hear him.'

'I've not heard him cry like that in a long time.' Margaret looked worried.

'He was awright – I don't know what set him off again.'

'May I?' Margaret held her arms out. Mercy handed the warm, distraught child to her.

'I've wanted to get up to him so often and had to restrain myself,' Margaret said softly. 'I should have just followed my instincts.'

Mercy watched the look of tenderness on Margaret's face as she cradled her son. It suddenly made her feel very sad. This was what a mother was supposed to be, wasn't it? She was supposed to love and cherish her baby and hold it close. The reality of her own mother went through her like a chill. She had left her almost as soon as she was born, dumped her like a parcel on a doorstep. What sort of mother was that?

'She says I'll spoil him,' Margaret was murmuring. 'How could I spoil him? It seems so unkind.'

'What does she know anyway?' Mercy hissed, with a viciousness in her voice that made Margaret look at her, startled. 'Has she ever had a babby?'

''Er – well, I assume not!' Margaret reached out and touched Mercy's shoulder, felt her trembling, whether from cold or emotion, she couldn't tell. 'Poor dear Mercy. You're so sweet with him. With all of us.'

Another light appeared in the doorway.

'What's all this then?'

Radcliffe's tone was frigid. She was wrapped in a heavy wool gown, her hair hanging in a plait down her back. The candle she was holding hollowed out her already gaunt face with shadows. The sight of her set Mercy's heart pounding.

'It's all right,' Margaret said hastily, bending to replace her son in his cot. 'He's going off by himself now.' But as she lay him down, Stevie started to cry again.

'But why do I come down and find people meddling with him?'

Mercy, rage swelling in her, took a step forward. She must control herself, or Mr Adair would send her away, but . . .

'You didn't seem to've heard him. So I came down. What's the harm in that?'

Nanny Radcliffe stared back in disdain at the angelic picture Mercy made standing before her, her pale hair tumbling over her shoulders. The expression on Mercy's face was anything but angelic though. Her chin was jutting forward and her eyes narrowed, arms folded tight.

'It's not your place to interfere.' Radcliffe spoke with exaggerated patience as if they were all terminally foolish, she the only one with any insight into Stevie's requirements. 'Children should not be pandered to. There's nothing he needs for his welfare in the middle of the night. He has to learn not to go attracting attention unnecessarily and inconveniencing other people. You don't want him to grow up into a weak, demanding character, do you?'

''Er, no, I suppose not—' Margaret began doubtfully, when a louder voice said, 'Hear! hear!'

James Adair came into the room, a silky, red dressing gown over his night clothes.

'Margaret – get back to bed,' he ordered, tight-lipped. Margaret scuttled from the room.

'Radcliffe – see to the child,' he said curtly. 'I apologize for this interference. It won't happen again.'

He came and stood before Mercy. With the light of the candle behind her, her face was in shadow so he could not see the defiance written on it.

'I've warned you. You do not interfere with Radcliffe's responsibilities. I don't know why a slip of a girl your age thinks she can come into my house and start transgressing all the established rules. The presumptuousness of it quite astounds me! Now – it'd better not happen again . . .'

Between her teeth, Mercy said, 'Why shouldn't he have what he needs? Making people suffer doesn't make them stronger and better it makes them cruel and nasty.'

James Adair stared at her, stunned, scarcely able to take in that she'd challenged him like that.

'Just leave it to someone who knows,' he demanded. Irritably he turned to the nanny. 'Can't you get that child to stop squawking like that?'

A couple of mornings later, when Stevie was downstairs with Mercy and Margaret for the short period he was allowed with them, he seemed fretful, and even all their smiles and jigglings on knees couldn't seem to cheer him. He cried when they picked him up and he cried when they put him down.

'Perhaps he's feverish?' Margaret said, worried. 'He does feel rather hot, don't you think? She's got him rather well wrapped considering the worst of the winter's over. 'Let's take this off.'

She peeled Stevie's white matinée coat off, but this didn't seem to make him any happier. He grizzled even harder and seemed thoroughly out of sorts.

'He really seems rather unwell,' Margaret told Audrey Radcliffe when she came to take him upstairs again.

'Oh dear,' the nanny said in the sugary voice she sometimes put on to talk to Stevie. Mercy stared at her. You're a nasty cow, her eyes said, however much you act all sweet.

'Let's go and sort you out.' Audrey Radcliffe went to where Stevie was sitting on the floor, surrounded by wooden building blocks. Ignoring his protests, she bent over and briskly removed him. Stevie's face screwed up and he began crying again.

'Oh heavens.' Margaret had tears in her eyes. 'What's the matter with him? He doesn't seem well at all. I've never heard him make a noise like that before.' She saw the taut look of fury on Mercy's face, her fists clenched, arms straight by her side. 'What is it?'

'There's summat not right about her,' Mercy burst out. She had to say it. Her instinct that there was something horribly wrong about that nanny was growing on her by the week. 'She's doing summat to him. I know she is. She's a cruel, scheming bitch.'

'Mercy! I've never heard you talk that way before.'

Mercy's eyes were burning with emotion. 'She made me promise not to tell you . . .'

'What on earth?'

'Back when it was cold, really cold, she left him out there—' – Mercy pointed at the daffodil filled garden – 'with almost nothing on. No covers, nothing. He was going blue when I went out there to get him. And that mark on his head. He never hit it on the table – she did it. I know she did . . .'

Margaret Adair's hand went up to her mouth in shock.

'Let me go up, now . . .' Mercy marched to the door. She was desperate not to lose this job, but if it was a choice between Stevie suffering and her keeping quiet, what sort of choice was that?

'But—' Margaret said.

Mercy was already on the stairs. She went speedily to the nursery door and opened it without knocking.

Audrey Radcliffe was standing by the table with Stevie in her arms. She seemed just on the point of changing his nappy, and while fretful, he was no longer screaming. There was nothing out of the ordinary to be seen.

'What d'you think you're doing?' Audrey Radcliffe spoke in a very flat, quiet voice.

Mercy stepped towards her. 'You think you can do just what you like round here and get away with it, don't you?' Her temper was up, ready to spill out everywhere but she tried to keep a hold on it. 'You may have Mr Adair and her down there dancing to your tune – but not me. I ain't scared of you or of what Mr Adair thinks. I'm worried about that babby and why he cries every time he claps eyes on you. I'm watching you, missis. You don't fool me, so don't you forget it.'

The woman's eyes flickered for a moment with some

odd, disturbed emotion and her top lip curled up in contempt. But she took control of her face, bringing it back to her flat, professional expression.

'Watch away, dear. I'm an experienced nanny and Mr Adair has every faith in me, so I wouldn't speak like that to me if I were you.'

'I've told her you nearly froze him to death in the garden!'

Radcliffe stared at her for a second. 'I don't remember anything of that nature happening.' She turned back to Stevie. 'You should watch me. You might learn a thing or two. Now get out of this room so I can do my job.'

That evening when Margaret Adair went in to say good-night to her son, he was clearly very unwell.

'He's so hot!' she exclaimed, bending to kiss his flushed cheek. 'He looks so poorly, the lamb. Feel him – he's burning up.'

Stevie was moving restlessly from side to side in the cot, never at peace, making distressed whimpering sounds as if he'd even lost the will to cry.

Audrey Radcliffe came to stand beside Margaret. She was wearing her stiff, white apron. Margaret felt as if the woman's eyes were boring into the back of her head.

'It's just a touch of cold,' Radcliffe assured her patiently. 'I've got it well in hand. He'll be as right as rain in the morning.'

'And how did he get a cold?' Margaret turned, eyes full of hostile anger. 'It wouldn't be from being left out to freeze in the garden again with no bedcovers, would it?'

Audrey Radcliffe looked shocked and scandalized. 'Of

course not, ma'am! Who would think of doing such a thing to a child? I'm afraid you may be imagining things again . . .'

Margaret turned abruptly and went to fetch her husband. Standing by his son's cot in his shirtsleeves and braces, James Adair had to admit Stevie was looking very unwell.

'I'll take him down for a while, with us,' Margaret said, leaning over the cot. 'And if he doesn't improve we'll call a doctor.'

'I'd strongly recommend you leave him where he is.' Nanny Radcliffe, as ever when Mr Adair was there, spoke in tones of courtesy and reason.

'Oh?' James turned to her. 'You think . . .?'

'Well, it's only a cold, and you don't want him to start thinking he can just try that one whenever he feels like it, do you?'

'Margaret, perhaps—'

'No, James.' She scooped Stevie up in her arms and he immediately let out a cry. She turned to the nanny. 'If you don't mind, he's my son, not yours. You are simply paid to look after him. You don't own him, nor do you have the right to control our household.'

'Margaret!' James, outraged, followed her down the stairs. 'For heaven's sake, what sort of behaviour is this? She's worth her weight in gold – we don't want to lose her . . .'

'Worth her weight in manure, more like!' Margaret turned, boiling over with long repressed anger and frustration. 'Don't we want to lose her? Don't we? Who doesn't?' She lowered her voice. 'Mercy is convinced she's doing harm to Stevie.'

James Adair's eyes widened, then he roared with laughter. 'Mercy? What in heaven does Mercy know about anything? This is absolutely ridiculous foolishness. What on earth has come over you? You really are getting things out of proportion, darling.'

'I'll tell you what's come over me, what this behaviour is! It's that of someone who has been tyrannized in her own house for far too long, by you and that, that woman up there. She's made my life a misery. Mercy's quite right. I should be able to look after him how I think fit.'

'Mercy?' James said again in angry bewilderment.

'Yes, Mercy. Now be so good as to open the kitchen door for me please – Mrs Parslow?' Margaret called through the open door. 'Could you fetch Mercy through for me, please?'

Mercy appeared, her face still pink and full of mirth, until she saw them. Oh Lord, her expression said, sobering immediately. What've I done?

'Mercy.' Margaret sounded stern. 'Come through here with us, please.'

They went into the back sitting room.

'Light the lamp please, James.'

'I'll do it.' Mercy proceeded to do so, while Mr Adair was still recovering from being ordered around in this peremptory fashion. Margaret knelt down and laid her feverish son on a blanket on the floor and he let out a sound of anguish. Margaret looked up at her husband.

'Mercy has said to me more than once that she believes Radcliffe is not a fit person to look after our child, that she is neglectful, even wilfully cruel—'

'Oh really – look, enough of this,' James snorted. 'Did you really come out with all this tripe, Mercy? I really thought you had more sense. I mean on what grounds are you making all these accusations?'

Mercy blushed, heavily. She had very little proof. But she knew. She just knew. She couldn't speak.

But in any case Margaret held up her hand to stop her as if holding up a train.

'It suddenly came to me this afternoon, after Stevie had gone up, and he was so distraught ... I took his little jacket off this morning when he was hot. And d'you know, that's about the most I've done for my child since the week he was born? I never dress him, undress him, bath him ... I'm never allowed to, even if I want to. I barely even know his dear little body. And all those bumps and bruises ... he's not crawling or walking. How could he hurt himself so?'

As she spoke she started to peel off Stevie's clothes, untying the silky ribbons which fastened at his neck and removing his nightgown.

'Margaret, really.' James stood harumphing beside Mercy. 'This is so silly. But have it your own way.'

'I shall, James,' Margaret looked up at him. 'Whether you like it or not, I'm afraid.'

As she moved Stevie, he whimpered, and when she sat him up to remove his little vest he began to scream frantically. The vest would not come away from his back. It was stuck to him with dried pus.

'Oh my!' Mercy whispered. She had a horrible feeling in the pit of her stomach. James Adair stood, silent now, beside her.

By the time Margaret finally managed to ease the vest off Stevie's skin, his screaming had become hysterical.

Mercy gasped. Her eyes filled with tears. 'No wonder he screamed every time I touched him.'

The three of them stared in appalled silence at his back. There were two huge round welts, the centre of each dark with blood and pus, the flesh around them swollen and angry with inflammation. It was obvious the wounds were sorely infected.

Margaret was shaking and crying, Stevie's head pressed against her. 'Oh Lord. Oh my little boy, what has she done to you?'

'Good God!' James Adair had gone white to the lips. He bent closer, peering at the wounds. 'She must've . . . with a candle! She must be quite . . . insane . . .'

He ran from the room.

Margaret's eyes met Mercy's, her face distraught. 'He's been suffering, all this time and I didn't see it. All those bumps and cuts – she made it look as if . . . Mercy, next time you give me advice, make sure I take notice of it a great deal more quickly.'

They heard James climbing the stairs to the servants' quarters.

Chapter Twenty-Five

The police took Audrey Radcliffe away. So far as they knew she was carted off to one of the city asylums.

Mercy had thought James Adair was going to explode with fury that night. He marched the nanny downstairs, barely even giving her time to pack her bag while he stood over her. Mercy never knew what was said upstairs in her spartan room, but when he came down with her he was shaking.

He made her stand in the hall, and James was still wringing his hands, pacing, unable to stand still.

'Why did you do it?' Margaret asked her, weeping. 'What could have possessed you to do such a thing?'

The woman stared at her. Her expression was impenetrable. In a queer, childish voice Mercy felt she would never forget, she said, 'Well no one ever looks after me, do they?'

'I'll make sure,' James said wagging a rigid finger at her, 'that you never go near another child again in your life.'

The doctor came and dressed Stevie's wounds, shaking his head. By the time they were left alone again, Margaret Adair had seemed to grow in stature and courage. Her instincts had been right all along! They all stood in the hall. James seemed stunned, stood wiping his forehead with his handkerchief.

'She broke all the rules. She just flagrantly . . .' He turned away with an anguished sound, unable to finish.

Margaret was still holding Stevie. No one was going to tell her to put him down now.

'James – now she's gone I'd like Mercy to be Stevie's nanny.'

'But . . .' He turned, catching sight of Mercy by the bannister, blushing with astonishment. 'She's so young, so—'

'Sensible? Trustworthy? A good judge of character? Better than either of us, perhaps?'

'Well . . .'

'Please, James, this makes complete sense. Why employ someone else when we have the perfect person here already? Mercy adores Stevie – don't you?' Mercy nodded, fervently, hardly daring to let herself hope. 'She risked her own position here to make us see what was going on with that evil woman . . .'

James looked at his wife, then at Mercy, standing there so quietly, and as if overcome by the presence of them both, sat down on the stairs.

'I owe you an apology, Mercy. I really believed that that woman was doing the best thing. That she had standards . . .' He looked up into Mercy's eyes. 'Very well. We'll try it.'

Over the next three months, Mercy was the happiest she could ever remember being. She was comfortable, well fed, she had the company of Rose and Emmie to giggle and joke, and the sisterly affection of Margaret Adair. Margaret had taken Mercy on as a project for improvement: correcting her speech, forever telling her things – the names of flowers, birds, capitals of the world (Mercy was proud to show she was good at those already).

Best of all there was Stevie, who grew more delightful each week. His back healed quickly until there were just two little scars. Mercy oiled his skin after she'd bathed him, tickling him and kissing his bare tummy so that he let out his wonderful, free-flowing chuckle which made her laugh too. She played with him, fed him, rocked him to sleep. She adored him and Stevie thrived. No more the pained grizzling, he was a robust, happy boy, pulling himself to stand up now on the nursery chair. The Adairs could hardly get over the change in him.

'Where's my lad?' James Adair often called when he came in from the works. Mercy would see an expression of boyish affection come over his face when he caught sight of Stevie. James would come and pick him up, swinging him into the air as if now free to play himself, until Stevie was breathless with giggles.

Life was much smoother and more contented than it had ever been. The only thing that troubled her was her increasing reluctance to go back to Angel Street. As the fortnightly free afternoon came round, she dreaded it. She'd returned faithfully all spring, found Elsie worn and low, Tom the same, always the same . . . If only there was something I could do for them, she thought. Going there was like walking into a living death which made her own happiness feel selfish and wrong. Gradually, full of guilt, she'd stopped going, and it became easier to stay away.

Margaret Adair, through a mixture of timidity and lack of organization, did not much seek out the society of other women of her class. Nor did she seem disturbed in any way by the fact that most women did not walk out with their nannies and treat them as friends. In her vague way she simply did what came instinctively to her: her need for a true confidante who she could be comfortable with outweighed considerations of class or age.

She and Mercy often went for walks together, each taking it in turn to push the pram.

As they wandered back through Moseley Village one beautiful afternoon in June, Margaret stopped and bought a newspaper. Mercy waited for her with the pram.

'Look—' Margaret opened it out to show her. *Daily Mail* – Golden Peace Number.

'Oh!' Mercy gasped. 'It's gold!'

The burnished ink caught the afternoon sunlight and seemed to glow. A picture of the King and Queen stared glassily at them.

'Look at her necklace!' Mercy smoothed her finger over the choker of pearls fastened high round Queen Mary's neck. 'Ain't they something?'

'Aren't,' Margaret murmured absent-mindedly.

'Aren't. Aren't, aren't, aren't!' Mercy did want to learn to speak better. She wanted to do everything better!

'We'll look at it properly at home,' Margaret said.

They settled in the sitting room with Stevie playing at their feet and a pot of tea. Mercy couldn't stop stroking the pages of the newspaper. 'It's lovely ain't – isn't – it?'

'It's to commemorate the signing of the peace treaty.' Margaret sipped Earl Grey from her delicate, ivy-patterned cup. There was a picture of the crowded Hall of Mirrors at Versailles, of the signed treaty.

Mercy squinted at them. 'They don't write any too clear, do they?'

Margaret laughed, replacing her cup on the polished tray. 'I think once you become really important you can write as poorly as you please. Listen – I'll read you this poem.'

Across the front page was a long poem, 'The Victorious Dead' by Alfred Noyes.

> Now, for their sake, our lands grow lovelier,
> There's not one grey cliff shouldering back the sea,
> Nor one forsaken hill that does not wear
> The visible radiance of their memory . . .

It was a long, sweeping poem, and as Mercy heard Margaret's soft voice reading it, the emotions she was trying so hard to keep down swelled up in her. She took a deep breath, trying to calm herself. But the beauty of the words, the hopes and ideals of the poem for a happier time, a more virtuous nation, crashed again and again in her mind against the thought of Tom, eternally broken, lying in that sunless little room. Of Elsie's old offering to Frank, her shrivelled, sooty flowers, of the fact that she couldn't bear to go there any more. The words hit her like knives releasing her grief for Elsie and Tom, the deep ache in her for all that might have been.

> They have made their land one living shrine. Their words
> Are breathed in dew and whiteness from the bough
> And where the may-tree shakes with song of birds,
> Their young unwhispered joys are singing now . . .

Her heartbroken weeping stopped Margaret before she'd even reached the end.

'Oh, my dear girl – what is it?'

For a time Mercy was unable to speak. She felt Margaret's arm round her, pulling her close.

'What's troubling you, Mercy? This is so unlike you.'

After a few moments Mercy wiped her eyes and looked into her friend's round, kind face. She drew away a little, watched her fingers fiddling in her lap and told Margaret about Tom.

'If he'd died I could've grieved for him, for losing him, then put it away. Started afresh. I know my Tom died in Flanders, the Tom I loved.' Her tears started coming again. 'But his body's still there, day after day. Like a child – no, not even a child. Stevie's got far more life in him. I can't forget him. And I can't stand to see it.'

'Oh my poor, poor girl.' Margaret's eyes were also full of tears. 'Why ever didn't you tell me this before?'

Mercy just shook her head, still weeping.

'Sometimes I feel you've lived a great many more years than I!'

'There's people like the Peppers—' Mercy struggled to speak, gulping. 'Who're so stuck in their lives and nothing ever changes – or if it does it's for the worse. I'm so scared of going back to that. Of getting stuck too . . .'

Margaret squeezed her shoulder. 'There's no reason why that should happen. We'll help you Mercy. And think how strong you are – I don't think you'd ever allow yourself to be trapped by circumstances. Take heart, dear. You're like my little sister now. I'll take care of you.'

As they talked, the sun was going down, the sky glowing pink, and soon they heard James's voice at the front door.

'Hell-o? Margaret?'

Margaret looked at Mercy in amusement. 'Goodness he sounds excited – yes, we're here, dear!'

'Come out here, both of you – I've something to show you!'

They hurried to the front door, Mercy with Stevie in her arms. James Adair was standing in the front garden holding by the handlebar a brand new bicycle. His face was ashine almost as much as the cycle's black paintwork.

'Look – the finished model. The Adair Safety Bicycle for Gentleman, ready for action. This is the first one!'

He moved it closer so they could admire it, childlike with glee. He'd ridden it home and it had gone like a stallion. It was smooth, fast, marvellous!

'Darling, it looks very good!' Margaret smiled at his enthusiasm. She went out and walked round it.

'What d'you think, Mercy?'

Mercy blushed. She was still shy of Mr Adair, kind as he was to her. 'It's beautiful.'

'Goes like anything. I've never been on such a good ride. Here,' he cajoled his wife. 'Give her a try?'

'But it's a man's cycle – I'll never get on!'

'No matter.' He took off his jacket and draped it on the garden wall. 'I'll lift you.'

'Lift me?' Margaret laughed wholeheartedly. 'You'll do yourself a mischief! No, dear – I'm not up to that, I'm afraid. What about Mercy?'

'Splendid – come on, Mercy. Give it a try!'

'But—'

'Oh, go on, put him out of his misery. Here, give Stevie to me and I'll take him in. It's getting cool out here.'

Mercy wished Margaret would stay, but she'd already disappeared into the house. Her stomach started fluttering with nerves. She'd never ridden a large bicycle before, and she was shy, alone with Mr Adair.

'I don't know how,' she said timidly, moving closer to him.

'I'll soon show you – easy as winking. Just keep your

feet on the pedals and push. This is rather high for you, of course. I shan't let go. Look, I'll lean it against the wall to start with.'

Mercy felt James Adair's large hands grasp her round the waist from behind, and lift her high on to the saddle.

'Light as a feather!'

Mercy felt very high up and not especially safe. To her mortification the bar of the cycle was forcing up her skirt, making it ride high in her legs and showing her white bloomers. Thank goodness she had quite new ones on!

'Now, hold still. You put your hands on these.' He directed her to the grips on the handlebars, but it was a long way for her to lean. She felt his arm encircle her waist, his warmth through her thin frock.

As he moved the cycle forwards, Mercy's heart was beating faster and faster. She was wobbling, she was going to fall! The bicycle lurched to one side and his arm tightened round her.

'Steady!' he laughed. 'That's it – now we can have a proper go.'

'Out here?' Mercy protested. She'd expected a quick turn in the garden and he was heading out along the pavement!

'There's hardly anyone about. Don't worry, we shan't knock anyone over.'

Mercy didn't feel she could say she was more worried about whether anyone could see her bloomers! She thanked heaven it was nearly dusk.

The saddle felt hard and uncomfortable between her legs, and the pedals, at their lowest point, were too far down for her to reach. She found she kept losing them on the way round. She was suspended, rather painfully, eyes fixed on James Adair's white sleeve, the hairs on the backs of his strong hand as he guided the handlebars for her.

Yet the feel of the air rushing past her face, blowing her hair back, was invigorating. Once James Adair broke into a trot, leading her along the quiet road away from Moseley Village, the sadness of the afternoon was blown away and she let out her full-hearted, gurgling laugh.

'Nothing like it, is there?' As he spoke, Mercy felt how close he was, his breath on her ear, the foreign, manly smell of him, his arm close round her. She had hardly ever been so close to any man apart from Tom, and was uneasy and embarrassed, but she could do nothing but cling on as he held and steered her.

'Phew!' He slowed down after a time, panting. 'I'm not up to all this – have to turn round – walk a bit.'

'I've – had ...' Mercy wanted to say, 'quite enough' but she continued, '... a good go on it – thanks.'

She turned her head a little to speak to him and he looked round at her, into her eyes. He was so close, smiling at her and she could see perspiration on his forehead. She turned to face the front again with a sudden sense of unease. She liked James Adair and enjoyed being treated almost like his little sister as well as Margaret's. But this closeness, him holding her like that, didn't feel quite right.

'There now.' As they turned in through the gate the cycle gave another big wobble and Mercy shrieked, grasping James's arm with one hand.

'It's all right.' His voice was soothing, almost caressing. 'I've got you, Mercy.'

Carefully he propped the bicycle back against the wall and lifted her once more into his arms with a lingering lack of haste. He held her high for a moment, almost as he did with Stevie, and Mercy laughed, exhilarated.

James looked up into her face, smiling broadly, eyes crinkling at the corners, then lowered her to the ground.

'Little scrap of a thing, aren't you? So – what d'you think?'

He laid his hands on her shoulders and she could feel their damp heat. She couldn't look him in the eyes.

'It's lovely. Thank you.'

'She is, isn't she? A little beauty. I'm glad someone was game to give her a try.'

He released her with sudden abruptness and turned to the machine.

'I'd better go in,' she said, relieved. 'Thank you again.'

Chapter Twenty-Six

How had this come about? James Adair mused to himself as he walked behind Margaret and Mercy, who was pushing Stevie in his pram, down the hill to the park.

'Mercy's never been boating,' Margaret had implored him. 'And it's such a beautiful day.'

It was indeed, a burnished August day. Holiday season: an atmosphere of Sunday afternoon languor pervaded. They had attended church at St Mary's in Moseley, eaten a good lunch of tender lamb and mint sauce, and now James felt a great sensation of wellbeing surge through him.

After all, what could be the harm? He was going out in public with his wife and his son's nanny. He would not be alone with Mercy: he could enjoy the afternoon in a pure attitude of companionship with a clear conscience. He knew, as he had known for some time, had had confirmed that evening when he held her in his arms during her cycle ride, that he must not be alone with her. She was a temptation, a thorn in his conscience, a tune which played insistently through his head. The memory of touching her made him ache with desire. This went against all the rules of the code by which he lived. He wanted to believe that he was upright, scrupulous, faithful. Since then he had gone out of his way to minimize his contact with her.

He watched the figures of the two women – my

women, he found himself thinking – swaying gently in front of him. Margaret was in a fussy dress of sky-blue and white candy stripes, looked plump and overdressed. She had on a wide-brimmed, white hat with a cascade of blue flowers tumbling from it. James found himself wincing at the acid colour of them. She was still a country girl by instinct. In contrast, Mercy was all slim simplicity in her white dress with the sailor-suit collar, white button shoes and a simple straw hat. Her hair was gathered up loosely in a plait which swung between her shoulder blades.

By heaven she was lovely! He found his eyes hungrily following her every movement, the twitch of her plait as she turned her head to talk to Margaret, the lean curve of her as she leant over Stevie, the light, eager walk. He imagined peeling off the dress, slowly, over her head, unveiling her, the wondrous, magical shape of her . . .

For heaven's sake, he railed at himself, pull yourself together, man! What sort of thoughts were these for a married man to be indulging in?

But fantasies of her had gradually begun to bombard him: at home, at the works, even when she was nowhere near, until he was thinking of her a great many times a day.

He stopped for a moment to remove his blazer and fell a few paces behind, freeing his arms, flinging it boyishly over his shoulder by the collar.

These feelings had crept up on him so gradually he had barely known it was happening. Mercy's wide, serious eyes turning on him when he spoke, her interest in him, her untutored intelligence. The way, Margaret had told him, she'd confronted that Radcliffe woman. Margaret would never have had the guts to do that! And further still, he had learnt from his wife of the girl's tragic past, of her maimed lover. The thought of her sadness and devotion moved him unutterably.

Margaret and Mercy stopped at the gates of the park and turned, both still laughing at something.

'Come on, James!' Margaret called. 'You're dawdling!'

'Coming!' He beamed at them both: at Margaret's new serenity, at his son's happy, tanned face, at Mercy, fresh and sweet as a spring flower. What a blessed life he had!

As they neared the lake they could hear excited voices, shrieks of laughter, the plash of oars and their creak in the rowlocks and occasional indignant quacking of a duck hurriedly taking flight. The small expanse of water was crowded with rowing boats and paddle boats, their passengers clad in bright summer clothes.

James paid for the hire of a rowing boat. 'We'll have to wait our turn. They're all taken at the moment.'

They stood contentedly in the shade. Margaret poured lemonade for them to sip. They helped Stevie to throw some crusts to the ducks and watched the other pleasure-seekers until a boat was ready for them.

'I think I'll feel safest if I hold Stevie,' Margaret said, lifting him from the pram. She handed him to Mercy. 'I'll get in and you can pass him to me – and then you can relax for a bit.'

James helped his wife climb in in a rather ungainly fashion, waiting until she'd sat down in the stern and readjusted her hat.

Mercy carefully handed Stevie to her and Margaret settled him on her lap.

'Take my hand,' James said.

Mercy gave her uncertain smile. 'I've never been in one of these before.'

'It's quite safe – Here—' Gallantly he took her little hand, melting inwardly at her inexperience. 'There's a first time for everything.'

She settled on her seat in the bow while James moved to the rowing seat, sitting with his back to her.

'Off we go!' The oars were ready and they pulled away, in and out of the shade of trees, James leaning forward and back, forward and back with an easy, rhythmic stroke.

'All right?' He turned his head, conscious that his back was sweating from his exertions.

'Yes, thank you,' Mercy said dreamily. The sunshine seemed to make her glow.

James tried to concentrate on watching Stevie who, wide-eyed, was letting out shrieks of excitement and struggling to get down from Margaret's lap and throw himself over the side.

'Dear, oh dear!' Margaret laughed. 'I'd never have believed a small child could be so strong – my arms are aching!'

After a time James stopped and turned round. Mercy was sitting sideways, the brim of her hat pulled low to shield her eyes from the bright, sunlit ripples.

'Have a try?' James invited softly.

'What? Rowing the boat!'

'Of course, why not? Come on.' He spoke more briskly than he meant to and cursed himself inwardly for sounding like a sergeant major.

She came to him, hand over hand, instinctively adjusting her weight with the tilt of the boat until she reached him.

'You sit here.' He patted the space beside him. 'We'll try one each to begin with.'

He gave her the right hand oar and showed her how to

manoeuvre it, up, back, down, then spooning the water away. His right leg and her left touched, side by side. Mercy frowned with concentration, and James kept watching her, smiling. He longed to lean round and kiss the furrowed brow, to smooth it with his fingers. He found his mind shaping extravagant words of adoration to her.

All he said was, 'That's good. You must come from a seafaring family.'

'Well...' Mercy smiled without irony. 'I s'pose I could've done.'

'Oh – yes, of course.' He was uncomfortable at having highlighted her uncertain origins. 'Anyway – how about trying both now?'

He stepped behind the seat and gently urged her to move to the middle, kneeling behind her.

'Now – take both and do the same.'

She dipped the oars in and pulled with her wiry arms. The boat made a promising surge of progress.

'Good!' he cried. Then she forgot to lift the oars and pulled so the blades stumbled in the water, ruffling it up, slowing them right down. The left oar flung out of her hand and James lurched over to catch it for her.

'Never mind. Here, let me help, just 'til you've got it.'

Reaching round her he laid his hands over hers and as he did so, breathed in her smell, a mixture of soap and warm flesh and hair, a warm animal smell which caught him by surprise.

'That's better.'

She half-turned her head, animated. 'I think I can do it now.' He released her, desire raw in him.

'Perhaps she'll row all afternoon!' he joked, turning to Margaret, afraid that his feelings were plain in his face. But she was taken up with Stevie's antics.

'Here – please, darling.' She handed him over. 'He's exhausting!'

James busied himself with his son, gladly sitting him in his lap in order to conceal the gross outward sign of his desire, distracting both Stevie and himself, talking to him, showing him the ducks, letting him wet his hands.

All the time though, he was conscious of Mercy's every move, her legs stretched out in front of her so that sometimes his ankle brushed against her as he moved, her lithe frame bending back and forth, her dazzling smile of happiness as he caught her eye.

Oh God, James thought. God help me. He would have to put a stop to it. He couldn't live like this, with this constant longing gnawing at him. He didn't know how long he could control himself in her presence. He couldn't get rid of her – however could that be explained to Margaret? He must struggle for self-control – bury himself in his work. What sort of man was he otherwise?

'Do take over again,' Margaret urged him eventually, as he sat staring ahead. 'Mercy must be quite exhausted by now!'

That night James Adair made love to his wife with an energy and urgency that startled both of them. He was more passionately aroused than she could ever remember, and at the height of it he cried out loudly as if the release of it was painful to him. Afterwards, still startled, she held him, caressing him as he lay in her arms, his eyes tightly closed.

'I had a wire from Kesler today,' James announced a few weeks later, as the three of them sat round at dinner one evening. Margaret insisted that Mercy ate with them still at least once a week and couldn't understand why her husband was being so awkward about it recently, trying to insist that as Mercy was an employee she should be treated as such and kept in her place.

It was a mellow evening in early autumn, the light dying over the now tarnished leaves in the front garden.

'D'you mean the American?' Mercy asked, passing Mr Adair a well-filled gravy boat.

Margaret looked at Mercy in some gratitude that at least she had remembered who her husband was talking about as her own mind had a tendency to flit on to something else as soon as he began to talk about work. James also smiled appreciatively at her.

'That's the one.' He nodded to Emmie to indicate they had everything they needed. She left the room with her usual smirk at Mercy. She and Rose were always cross-questioning Mercy – 'What did they say? What do they talk about?' – but were habitually disappointed by the information.

'Didn't they talk about anything else?' was usually Rose's complaint when Mercy reported conversations about the health of the cycle market or Stevie's daily doings. 'Don't they ever 'ave a good fight?'

But the Adairs didn't. Most of what passed between them was a low current, under the surface. To Mercy they seemed calm, which she took to mean contented. Tonight, by their standards, James was animated.

He accepted the gravy, then picked up the delicate glass beside Margaret's plate to pour water into it, then Mercy's. Mercy was still nervous of drinking from the long-stemmed glassware, but James disdained drinking out of anything of lesser quality, even though he was abstemious and seldom drank alcohol.

'Kesler's planning a new works outside New York – in Rochester. They should be moving out early next year, and he suggests—' – James sat back, holding his glass with an air of triumph – 'that when things have progressed a bit further, I visit him in New York!'

Margaret, who had been eating with a hungry sense of purpose, looked up startled.

'You – go to America!'

James laughed youthfully. His moustache shifted when he smiled, making the smile appear broader. 'And why not? It's not the moon, you know. It's only a few days' voyage, and I gather Cunard will be taking passenger bookings again before too long. I think it's a splendid idea. Kesler and I will have a hugely productive relationship, I'm certain of it. He has all that New World drive and enthusiasm, and with all our technical know-how put together ... Ideally I'd go sooner, of course, but if we're to travel on the best ship in the world, we shall have to wait until she's ready for us.'

Margaret was frowning at him.

'The *Mauretania*, of course – she's undergoing a complete overhaul. They had to convert her for War service—'

'Yes, yes,' Margaret said. 'But you said "we"?'

'Of course you must come with me! You're forever saying you never go anywhere or do anything.'

'But James – Stevie.'

'Oh, Stevie will be perfectly all right with Mercy here. My mother can come and stay for a few weeks. She'd love it – we'll be gone a month at most. What harm could come to him?'

'James,' Margaret spoke with unusual resolve, 'I am not going to travel to the other side of the world and leave my son. Least of all with your mother. He barely knows her and she's as cold as a dead herring. I'm just not. I'm sorry. You'll have to go alone. After all, it is business.' She popped a piece of potato in her mouth as if to emphasize that she wasn't going to say anything else.

Mercy listened expectantly. Was she now going to have something approaching a row to report to Rose? After all, she did just call his mother a dead herring . . .

'But, darling—' – James was stroking his moustache with his left hand as he tended to do when irritated – 'Kesler has a very nice wife – and children. And he's requested that you come.' (The final phrase of Kesler's telegram had read 'Bring wife.')

Margaret looked defiantly at him, swallowing the potato. 'How on earth do you know she's nice? Whatever this American has requested, I am not leaving my son. He's had quite enough to contend with in his short life already. And that's that.'

'Oh to hell with it. Let Stevie come as well then.'

'And Mercy.'

'Mercy?' A momentary look of alarm swept over James Adair's face. But of course, the child could hardly travel without his nanny. She could travel second class, somewhere well away from him . . .

'Very well,' he said with dignity. 'Mercy too.'

'D'you hear Mercy?' Margaret was overjoyed. The thought of being alone with James and a collection of strangers for weeks at a time had filled her with panic. She was maladroit socially, and what on earth would she and James have to say to each other all that time? She thought it a sad but inevitable truth that husbands and wives had very little conversation beyond the common interest of their children. At least in normal circumstances there were other people. But now, if Mercy was coming, and Stevie, she would have familiar companions.

'We're going across the sea to America, the first chance we get!' James said.

Mercy was so astonished she couldn't take it in. 'I've never even seen the sea!'

'Well, you'll be seeing plenty of it soon!' James laughed. Suddenly he seemed full of joy.

Part Five

Part Five

Chapter Twenty-Seven

March 1920

'Mercy – Mercy dear. You'd better wake up!'

Margaret Adair was leaning across from the opposite seat of the train. Feeling the warmth of the hand on her knee through her dress, Mercy slowly opened her eyes. Stevie was asleep on top of her, crunched up like a crab, his damp head resting under her chin, making her hot and sweaty inside her clothes. She had a dry mouth and a bar of dull pain stretched between her temples. The seat was rocking gently, the train chugging, der dum der dum ... Wherever was she?

'We're coming into Southampton.' James Adair was sitting up very straight, peering with boyish enthusiasm out through the sooty window. 'Soon get a look at her!'

The ship – of course! She was on a train going to the sea and they were travelling to America! Mercy was wide awake suddenly, gently sitting up and trying not to wake Stevie.

'Bless him.' Margaret Adair looked fondly at her son. She had seen James smiling at the two of them as they slept and was moved by the tender expression in her husband's eyes. What she had achieved in giving him a son!

Stevie, eighteen months old, was very active once

awake, but now, oblivious of her adoration, let out a shuddering little sigh in his sleep.

'I don't suppose he'll remember any of this,' Margaret said. She stopped speaking rather abruptly and Mercy saw her close her eyes and rest her head back as if in discomfort.

Mercy looked out as the train snaked between warehouses and factories. She saw rows of dwellings, church spires, occasional faces topped by workmen's caps turned up to watch the boat train hurtle past. She was surprised to see these familiar things, as if, having left Birmingham for the first time, she was expecting a completely different world.

'We must be about the last train.' James's watch hung on a gold chain from his weskit. 'She sails at noon.' He was trying to sound like an old sea dog.

When the train came to a halt with a groaning of brakes, Mercy eased herself and Stevie out of the comfortable first-class seat. She wrapped a blanket round him carefully as he stirred and carried him out into the chill spring air.

The platform was full of excited crowds. From first class spilled gentlemen in expensive suits, trilbys, bowlers, even the odd top hat, and their womenfolk, stylish gowns covered by fur-trimmed coats and stoles and a dazzling variety of hats, feathered and flowered, some outrageous with wide brims and decorations of fruit, others pared down, elegant skullcaps trimmed with a single gorgeous feather. Mercy felt small and poor and bewildered amid the loud ring of upper-class voices, some with foreign accents, all so ripe and confident. They found a porter, and negotiated their way through the heaving mass of people shuffling along, slowly, to the dock.

'Smell that!' James cried, leaning close to her ear.

She breathed in, and through the thinning smoke from the trains, smelt for the first time the salt of the sea. As they moved out, the bracing air hit her face. She felt an odd sensation go through her suddenly, tingling, excitement and wonder making her breathless. Such beginnings she had come from, she who was nobody to anyone in the world – and now this!

James Adair looked as if he might burst with pride when they saw the *Mauretania*. Over and over again during the past weeks he'd told them, as if for the first time, 'D'you know, she's held the Blue Riband since 1907 – fastest passenger ship across the Atlantic – never beaten in all that time!'

'He seems to think it's one of his bicycles!' Margaret murmured to Mercy with a wry smile.

But Mercy barely heard her. Her head was back, her eyes, at least as awed as James Adair's, taking in the massive bulk of the ship. The huge black hull stretched way above them like an endless wall, topped with white which was interspersed by the hundreds of windows of the ship's prime living quarters. Crowning it all were the four enormous red funnels. Everyone was looking up, exclaiming.

'Look, Stevie,' she said, leaning him back in her arms and pointing. 'Look at the big boat – and up there, red chimneys. Chimneys, Stevie!'

The little boy's eyes were wide and solemn.

The place was swarming. Mercy felt herself jostled at times and held tight to Stevie. James stood protectively close to her. Once she found herself looking into his eyes. He smiled at her. She heard people exclaiming, laughing, some weeping, many hugging each other farewell for a short time or a long, perhaps even for ever. Mercy started to notice many other sorts of people, the poor as well as the rich, some dressed in odd, foreign-looking clothes and shawls. Smoke from cigarettes and cigars was quickly blown away by the brisk breeze.

'Come along.' James guided her arm, speaking over all the commotion. 'We'll take you to second class and we'll come and find you after. Stay close to me . . .'

They made their way gradually to the second-class embarkation point, amid a more soberly-dressed, respectable gaggle of people, many businessmen in Homburgs, some with anxious-looking wives beside them. High above them, the rails were lined by passengers who had boarded earlier and now had the leisure to watch the proceedings below, calling down and whistling to friends or relatives on shore.

There was a smell of tar. Mercy felt her face buffeted by moist air and thought for a moment it was raining, but it was a damp, brackish gust from over the water and it subsided. As they drew near the gangway and the clatter of feet grew louder, she felt her stomach tighten. The dark, deep gap between the ship and the dockside, with its gurgling strip of water, appalled her. She wanted it to be over now, to be on board.

'Go to the steward at the top,' James instructed. 'He'll give you directions to your quarters. We'll find you . . .' He smiled reassuringly as she stepped up, tightly clutching Stevie, then he turned back to join his wife.

Halfway up the gangway, as she slowly followed an elderly couple, the man leaning on a stick, a gust of wind lifted the front of her hat and carried it over the back of her head where it hung, flapping from its pin. She was flustered and afraid of it flying right off, but didn't dare loose Stevie to fix it. She'd see to it when she reached the top.

But suddenly the hat settled back on her head, the pressure of a hand on top of it. She turned, startled.

'Allow me.'

She found herself looking into a young man's face, long and pale, with deep grey eyes, a wide mouth and striking, dark eyebrows which were pulled into a slight frown of concentration as he straightened the hat. Briefly Mercy also took in details of a baggy tweed suit on a tall, but thin body.

'Thank you.' She was taken aback. 'Trouble is,' she said timidly, 'I've got my hands full.'

'So I see. That's quite all right.' He smiled, the rather mournful face brightening for a second. 'I often forget how windy it is on the coast as well.'

'Two pins from now on,' she agreed.

'Go on – get a move on!' someone called grumpily from behind, and it was only then Mercy realized they'd stopped and turned to scurry on upwards.

A smartly-dressed ship's officer stood at the top to welcome them all aboard. James had booked her a fine room – a second-class state room on C-deck just for Stevie and herself so she would not have to share with a stranger. It was close to the Nursery and Children's Dining Room.

'Oh look, Stevie! All for us!' she gasped with delight when she saw it.

It was like a little house all in itself: two beds, one on each side of the room, a table and two chairs, a little cupboard, a basin and her own WC ... Her luggage, which they'd sent in advance, was already waiting for her in the middle of the floor. She put Stevie down and the two of them scurried round, looking at everything. Soon after there was a knock at the door.

'Ah – this looks very good,' James said. Margaret

followed him into the room. She steadied herself against the wall for a second, then sank down abruptly on one of the beds, her face nearly as white as the paintwork.

'Whatever's the matter, dear?' James peered at her, concerned by the pallor of her face. He sat down beside her and took her hand. Mercy went and knelt on the floor beside her.

'You feeling poorly? Must be all the travelling. Takes it out of you, doesn't it?'

Margaret leant dizzily against her husband, who removed her hat and helped her loosen the neck of her blouse.

'It's been getting worse all morning – I feel so faint and hot . . .'

'Put your head down.' James and Mercy helped her lower her head between her knees, Mercy fending off Stevie who was all for tugging at her hair. Eventually she sat up, her complexion a little pinker.

'Oh dear,' she smiled weakly. 'Perhaps I'd better go back to our room and have a little lie-down. I keep feeling so strange.'

James helped her to her feet. 'I'll take her to rest,' he told Mercy, 'and then come back here. We'll be off fairly soon. It'd be a great pity not to be up to see it.'

James Adair pulled back the silky eiderdown in their sumptuous first-class stateroom and helped his wife ease herself on to the bed. She looked very pale and shaky still. The brass bedstead creaked gently as she settled herself down and closed her eyes.

'Shall you be ill, Margaret, d'you think?'

James stood over her, eyes on her plump face, concerned but not without a little exasperation. He didn't want anything to mar this precious journey – Cunard's very first passenger voyage with the *Mauretania* since the War!

Margaret opened her eyes, a half smile on her lips. 'Darling, it's early days – I'm not sure, but I think we might soon be giving Stevie a little companion.'

'Oh, my dear!' A glow came into James's eyes and he knelt down beside her. 'You think – it's possible – again?' They had taken so terribly long to conceive Stevie.

'It seems very like it to me – I feel even more ill than last time.'

He leant over, overjoyed, newly powerful, and kissed her cheek.

'Then we must take the very, very best care of you. Should you like something to eat or drink?'

'Just a little water . . .' Margaret seemed mown down by exhaustion. 'Food . . . perhaps later . . .'

'You'll miss the departure,' he said, standing up. But she was already lost to sleep.

He would go and fetch Mercy and Stevie. Who better to share this experience with than his son – and Mercy with her naive enthusiasm for life? She mustn't miss it. He went to the little bathroom and looked in the mirror, ran damp hands over his hair and straightened his tie. He could feel that illicit, eager excitement rising in him at the thought of being with her, standing close to her, giving her a new experience in life. How he had worked to avoid the lure of her presence through the winter months! There had of course been moments of temptation, of huge intensity of feeling. But he had plunged into his work. He had been strong and controlled, even averting his eyes at times when coming upon her so as not to disturb his thoughts.

But now he would be alone with her. His pulse quickened. He could feel himself beginning to slide, surrender to the force of it. Of course though, he wouldn't be alone with her, he reassured himself. There would be crowds up there . . . His behaviour was perfectly within bounds.

Mercy took Stevie up to the first-class promenade deck, where James said they should join him as they'd have a good view. Stevie was bright and frisky after his long sleep on the train and toddled along, wanting to run off here, there and everywhere.

'Here – let me take him!' James picked him up and strode off, his unbuttoned camel coat sweeping behind him.

Mercy was glad of a few moments' respite from Stevie. There were already a lot of people waiting out on the deck, and Mercy felt overwhelmed by the opulence of the furs and jewels she could see displayed around her. Once again she was humbly aware of the simplicity of her blue wool coat and little cloche hat – she'd taken off the one with the brim. Her clothes were respectable enough and new, the hat even rather fashionable, but she still felt drab.

'Am I allowed up 'ere?' she asked.

James turned, looked tenderly at her. 'Of course. You're with me.' As if reading her thoughts he lowered his voice and said, 'Don't you worry – you look lovely. Not like some of these overdressed peacocks.'

Mercy blushed at this personal remark. She had been confused by his behaviour towards her of late. In front of the other servants he addressed her as one of them, which was of course what she was. When she was alone with the Adairs he had previously been more relaxed, brotherly almost and teasing. But recently he had been home so little, forever working, only appearing for dinner, and then he had often seemed remote, if not actually cold. When Margaret insisted she join them for dinner, which she soon realized made things easier for Margaret – it made the two of them make an effort together – he confined his conversation with her to questions about Stevie. Mercy had almost forgotten his former friendliness, the cycle ride. But it had relieved rather than troubled her. He was her employer after all and she knew where she stood.

But now the light-hearted, friendly Mr Adair of last summer was resurfacing, now he was not so preoccupied with work. He seemed younger, a spring in his step.

'Come – let's find a space where we can see.'

Still carrying Stevie, he led Mercy to the rail. They were so high up! As they nudged into a space there came the brisk sound of a bugle, though it was hard to tell from which direction.

'Ah look.' James freed an arm and pointed. She saw an orderly flurry of activity as a group of men hurried down the last remaining gangway. 'Those'll be the chaps who work on shore.'

Mercy knew he loved all this, relished telling her about it. He leant over, supporting his little son between his chest and the rail, and pushed his brown trilby on harder. 'Don't want to lose it,' he smiled at her.

The last gangway was being pulled into the ship.

'Bang on.' Once more James pulled out the well-polished gold watch. The two hands were exactly on the twelve. A few moments later they heard the bugle again. The tugs had already cast off. There came a great, soulful burst of sound from one of the funnels and James laughed as Stevie's head shot round, his eyes peering upwards, astonished.

'That gave you a shock, didn't it?'

The ship eased itself away from the dock, girded by its

tugs. There was much waving and calling out to the crowd below.

Mercy looked down at the dark water. It was astonishing to think that all the way to America, for days and days, would be water. She thought of little Amy Laski, so small she would barely have been able to see over the rail as their ship bound for Canada slid out of Liverpool harbour. Where was her sweet friend Amy now?

The people, then buildings, wharfs, cranes, docks, began to fade, blur and lose colour until even squinting Mercy couldn't make out their shape. As the view faded a quiet fell over the passengers. With majestic lack of haste the *Mauretania* nosed along Southampton Water and they began to feel the wind quicken on their cheeks. She was bound for the short call in at Cherbourg before turning west across the Atlantic.

There came a sudden release of tension, of anticlimax, as if separation from the land was a trauma now passed through and they were free to get on with everything else.

James straightened up, taking in deep breaths of air. Stevie kicked his legs against his father's stomach. 'Marvellous, the sea – gives you an appetite. Time for lunch, I'd say. How would you like to join me?' he asked her recklessly.

'I don't think – not with him,' she said, uncertain, holding out her arms for Stevie.

James's face fell. 'Ah no, perhaps not. Silly of me. Look, I'll accompany you down.'

'How's Mrs Adair? Will she want anything to eat?'

'She said all she wanted was sleep, thank you,' James said. They went down the first-class staircase to B-deck where he drew her aside. 'Look – you'll have to know soon enough. The fact is—' – He seemed hugely embarrassed suddenly, covered in blushes – 'Margaret is, in fact . . .' What on earth? Mercy was thinking. Surely he wasn't going to tell her that Mrs Adair had her monthly at the moment? She wouldn't know where to put herself.

Mr Adair seemed to be struggling for words. 'She – well, soon, quite soon, you, er – you'll have more than one little one on your hands.' He was red to the ears.

'Oh! She's having another babby?'

'Ssh!' He looked round as if he were imparting state secrets.

'Sorry,' Mercy whispered, beaming at him. 'That's wonderful news, Mr Adair! I'm ever so happy for you both. And it'll be lovely for Stevie to have a brother or sister.' She shifted Stevie on to her left hip, balancing him with one arm. 'Won't it, pet?'

James smiled bashfully, thrusting his hands into his pockets. 'There's something about this kind of news. Makes you want to tell someone. I know some women are superstitious about it – in case, you know, but I can't think of anyone better to tell than you, Mercy.'

'No – well I'll be the babby's nanny, I mean—' – it was her turn to blush – 'that's if you think . . .?'

He looked deep into her eyes. 'Of course I think.'

On impulse he took up her spare hand and pressed it to his lips. She felt them, warm on the back of her hand, and the slight prickle of his moustache. She was touched, but very embarrassed. What was he doing! She had no idea what to say.

He was also overcome by confusion again, dropped her hand and became abrupt all of a sudden. 'Come this way,' he said, striding off along the corridor. 'I'll show you where Stevie can be fed.'

*

He knew when he left Mercy that he should go and see how Margaret was, but he was too agitated, full of a restless desire to walk, to be out on the promenade deck in the fresh air. He returned to A-deck, nodding to a few other passengers on the way, but walking briskly to avoid any attempts at conversation. A coastline was still visible, the green and chalk white of the Isle of Wight, like a hazy mirage in the distance.

'Help me, oh Lord, to do what's right.' He leant looking out, his lips moving in a childlike chant. 'Help, oh Lord . . .'

What in heaven had he kissed her hand for like that? She must have thought him so peculiar, unbalanced even. Yet he wanted so much more of her! And hadn't he seen an answering warmth in her eyes – surely that was what it was?

At home his feelings had seemed monstrous. It was unthinkable that he should harbour such intentions, such a force of desire for anyone but his wife, and towards a servant at that . . . Away from home, even now so freshly cut loose from the coast, he felt altered, freer. As if, even with his wife and son on board he was – could be – a different man. Images he had for so long tried to keep at bay flooded through him. Mercy's parted lips moving to meet his, her eyes languid with need of him, his hands removing her clothes, peeling open to reveal what he had until now only imagined, her shy, eager, wanting . . . His fancy drove him on to caress her white thighs, the wet, silky opening between them parting for him . . .

He put his hands over his face, afraid that anyone passing should read in his expression the content of his thoughts.

I will ask her, he resolved, to dine with me tonight.

The boy would be asleep by then and could be left. With us – quickly he corrected himself – with us. For surely Margaret would be recovered by then? This fact came to him like a chill shower of rain.

Chapter Twenty-Eight

'Hello again.'

Mercy turned, closing the door of her room very quietly. She had finally lulled Stevie to sleep. The ship had left Cherbourg and was picking up speed, and she had to brace her legs so as not to lurch across the corridor.

For a moment she didn't recognize him. A tall man stood in front of her in working-man's overalls smeared with grease, and his hands and face were blacked with it too. But the smile was familiar, and the voice.

'I – er – your hat, on the gangway. Remember?'

'Oh yes!' Mercy laughed. 'I didn't know you for a minute. Whatever's happened to you?'

He joined in her laughter, ruefully. She saw him keep looking over his shoulder to see if anyone was coming. Most people were already at dinner.

'I shouldn't be seen up here in this state, of course. We're supposed to clean up down there but I forgot to take a set of clothes to change into. I haven't got into the swing of it all yet.' He held his hand out. 'Paul Louth – oh!' He withdrew the hand. 'You can't really shake that, can you?'

'I'm Mercy Hanley.' The ship rolled and she found herself lurching towards him. Paul instinctively put a hand out to steady her, catching her by the wrist and leaving a black oil smudge on her sleeve.

'Oh my goodness, I am sorry!' He looked perturbed. 'How ridiculous of me.'

'No – you're awright.' Mercy smiled. 'It ain't – isn't – the end of the world, is it? The pattern hides it and it'll wash out.' She held her hands behind her back as if to give him permission to stop worrying about it. 'How did you get in that state then?'

'I'm a student, in London – Imperial College. Well, I've nearly finished there actually. Engineering. I was lucky enough to get the position – experience the working of a real ship. So I'm spending a lot of the time seeing her in action, learning on the job.' As he spoke his eyes flickered towards her and away repeatedly, his expression serious, earnest. He rubbed nervously at the oil on his hands.

'There's another student – from Cambridge.' Paul's expression suddenly became wry and he lowered his voice. 'He's travelling first class. Not really my scene. The silly thing is, I actually come from Cambridge and his people live in London. Quite daft when you think of it.' He looked nervously up and down the corridor. 'Look, someone's bound to come along. I shouldn't really stick around here.'

But he still didn't move away, and stood bracing his legs in a relaxed way against the sea's motion. Mercy was learning to do the same. She was flattered that he seemed to want to talk to her.

'Was that your little boy I saw you with?'

'Oh, no, I'm not married! I just look after him for Mr and Mrs Adair. They're upstairs.'

'In first? Now, where're you from? No – let me guess. Birmingham, by any chance?'

She smiled. 'Right first time. Am I that broad?'

'No more than anyone else. That's what a stint in the

army does for you – you learn to pick out all sorts of accents. Great city, Birmingham. An engineer's paradise. Is this your first voyage?'

'Never been out of Brum before.'

'Oh well, in that case I could show you around,' he said enthusiastically. 'She's a great vessel. I could show you parts of her that no one else would...' He looked stricken all of a sudden. 'I'm sorry, Mercy – I mean only if you'd like, and you're able?'

'I'd love it. Would you really – are you allowed?'

Paul looked surprised at this notion. 'I've really no idea! Don't see why not. Would you like to tomorrow – if it's convenient?' He seemed reluctant to let her go. 'In fact I'll be dining soon, alone, unless you'd like to join me?'

'Oh, no, I can't. I've got to go up and have my – and dine – with Mr and Mrs Adair.' Mercy rolled her eyes comically as if it was all a bit of a trial eating in first class. At that moment it did rather feel so. It was nice to talk to someone of her own age. 'But I'll see you tomorrow?'

'That'd be very nice. ' He sounded surprised she'd agreed. 'I should be free soon after five-thirty tomorrow. Where shall I find you?'

'Oh, I don't know...' She had no routine yet, barely knew where anything was. 'Shall I meet you here? Quarter to six?'

'I'll look forward to it.' Paul slowly backed away. 'Better go down and make myself look respectable now!'

Margaret Adair was sufficiently well by the evening to dress for dinner. She wore an elaborate gown stitched in panels of eggshell blue and café creme silk with a low waist and floating panels of the same materials falling from waist to ankle. Her feet were squeezed into elegant blue shoes. James had refrained from mentioning that the subtle pastel colours made her already pale skin look even more washed out.

'You look delightful, my dear,' he told her, adjusting his collar. 'I'm so glad you're well enough to come down. I've invited Mercy to eat with us – just for tonight.'

'Oh good,' Margaret said, dabbing a last-minute touch of powder on her nose and cheeks.

'Yes – I thought it'd be an experience for her, first class.'

Mercy felt quite overpowered walking into the first-class dining room. It was the most sumptuous, luxurious room she had ever seen. She followed the Adairs as they walked with extra sedateness between the comfortable swivel chairs to their table, past a glittering array of evening clothes.

Thanks to the grease mark on her best dress she had changed into a soft woollen frock patterned with pretty blue flowers which she liked very much normally but in here it felt very plain and run of the mill. She had twisted her hair into a rather elegant knot, but even that felt rough and childish now. She sank down thankfully into the chair James Adair indicated for her. He looked very smart in a new, crisply pressed evening suit. At the far end of the room a group of musicians was playing soft, but cheerful music.

'Well this is something, isn't it?' James looked round the room, lined from floor to ceiling with beautifully carved wooden panels. 'They say it's in the style of Francois I – King of France in the sixteenth century.'

'No two panels the same,' Margaret said. She sounded rather weak and quiet.

Mercy looked about her at all the wood and the

beautiful ceiling, elegant furniture. She felt all lumps and bumps, awkward under the eyes of the stewards in their starched jackets and very conscious of the posh voices and extravagantly dressed people around her. Talk about fish out of water! Many of them in their jewels and lace and fur made James and Margaret Adair look very staid.

'Don't worry, Mercy,' Margaret leant closer, seeing her alarm at the amount of cutlery. 'Just start outside and work inwards. Then you can't go wrong.' Mercy saw she was nervous as well.

A steward handed them menus printed on thick, good quality paper. Seeing him eyeing Mercy a little askance, James Adair said rather sternly, 'Miss Hanley is our guest for this evening.'

'Yes, sir, of course. Quite so.' The steward seemed offended that he felt it necessary to justify himself. James smiled across at her reassuringly, but Mercy rather began to wish he'd thrown her out so she could go back to second class, third even, where she'd be far more comfortable. It was too hot and she wished she could roll her sleeves up.

James Adair selected from the menu for her.

'No swede here, don't worry!' he joked. He seemed to take delight in choosing for her a bewildering array of food. She sat nodding solemnly, clenching and unclenching her sticky hands on her lap. He kept looking at her and smiling. Even when she was talking to Margaret she could feel his eyes on her, so intensely that his gaze almost seemed to burn her skin. She wondered if he was watching to see if she behaved properly. It made her even more uncomfortable.

They ate oysters, poached sole, capons, a delicate selection of vegetables: asparagus (what's this? she wondered), glazed carrots shining with butter, parsley potatoes, slim green beans dressed with lemon which squeaked a little against her teeth.

'Let's order some wine,' James said, and a bottle of chilled white wine was brought to their table in a starched white cloth.

'Not for me, thank you,' Margaret said. She was struggling with the food.

'You'll try some, Mercy?' He filled her glass.

Mercy sipped the wine curiously. It was strong and fruity. She thought it tasted like cough medicine and decided a few mouthfuls would be enough. But she smiled back dutifully at James Adair as he raised his glass to her, beaming. If only he'd stop watching her all the time she might be able to relax a bit.

'Good health to you both. We're in for a marvellous voyage and a great adventure!'

Drinking more than he was accustomed to, James Adair grew red in the face, his forehead beaded with perspiration, and he was very talkative. He went on and on about the ship as if it were necessary to fill every second with words, despite the violins playing softly in the background.

'She was at Gallipolli you know,' he said rather loudly. 'Hospital ship – picking up the wounded. Quite a thought, Mercy, isn't it, that this very room was probably full of hammocks containing injured fighting men. Imagine that!'

Mercy felt she'd rather not imagine it. The thought made her stomach turn. Long before they reached the cheeses and the orange and lemon soufflé she was already full and longing for the second-class dining room where she could enjoy something like a chop with spuds and carrots and have done with it.

'I'm sorry about this afternoon,' Margaret Adair said

when she could get a word in. She was only picking at her food and had refused the roasted capon altogether. 'I gather James has told you . . .?'

'Yes, he did.' Mercy touched Margaret's hand for a moment. 'I'm so pleased for you. And Stevie'll love having a babby to play with.'

'I feel so foolish,' Margaret said. As usual, strands of her soft hair were coming down and she kept trying to press them up with her fingers. 'I'd begun to wonder – but I was showing no sign and I couldn't be sure. But it was like this with Stevie, only rather less extreme. Perfectly well one day, and the next, bang! Sick as anything. But what a catastrophic time for it to happen!'

'Maybe you'll be all right tomorrow,' Mercy said. 'You never know.'

'Never mind, darling.' James was in a very genial mood tonight. 'You'll still be able to experience the voyage and we'll take good care of you, won't we, Mercy?'

''Course we will. Oh!' Mercy remembered suddenly. 'I met someone ever so interesting tonight. He's a student, working down with the ship's engines and that. He said he'd show me round the ship and all sorts.'

James frowned. 'Well, who is he? We can't have you – and Stevie for that matter – just knocking about with any old person.'

'He's not just any old person, by the sound of it,' Margaret pointed out gently. 'Mercy said he's a student and I expect he's far too busy to be thinking about a small child.'

'He's from Cambridge,' Mercy said, eager to prove Paul's respectability. 'And some college in London – I forget now. He talks ever so nice.'

'Which is more than can be said for some people,' James retorted. 'Sure he's not a bit above you?'

'James!' Margaret was incensed. 'What on earth has got into you?'

'Well, we don't know the first thing about him, do we? We can't have her going off with just anyone.' He put his dessert spoon down petulantly.

'Honestly, darling, I've never heard you talk such nonsense,' Margaret said quietly, but with the firmness she occasionally mustered. 'It's not as if he can actually take her anywhere far, is it? We're on a ship. And I'd say it'd be nice for Mercy to make a friend – he sounds very kind. In case you've forgotten, James, Mercy is really rather a good judge of character . . .'

Mercy watched the two of them in alarm. Mr Adair seemed to be getting so angry all of a sudden and she didn't understand why. How had she offended him?

He took another mouthful of wine and looked across at her. After a moment, more calmly, he said, 'Just be careful. It's Stevie I'm concerned for. Don't want him associating with the wrong people.'

'I wouldn't dream of letting him come to any harm.' Her feelings of hurt were plain in her voice.

'Of course you wouldn't,' Margaret said. 'Now don't you worry. When I was expecting Stevie I wasn't much company for a few weeks and it may well be the same this time. So if you meet a nice friend your own age, dear, then I'm pleased for you and so will James be when he stops this old fuddy-duddy mood he's got into. You spend far too much time with us old things as it is. Well it's true, James,' she added, seeing her husband's disgruntled expression. 'Mercy may be in our employ but that doesn't mean she doesn't deserve to have some life of her own.'

The steward loomed over James's shoulder. 'Shall you require the cheeseboard, sir?'

James looked round the table. Both women shook their heads emphatically.

'I feel like a stuffed chicken,' Mercy said, before realizing that the first-class dining room was probably not the place to admit such a thing.

But Margaret laughed. 'Quite a meal, wasn't it? We shall all have more flesh on us when we reach New York.'

As the diners finished their meal the musicians struck up dance tunes and the stewards began to shift the empty chairs and tables back, creating a dance floor.

'It's no good,' Margaret said. 'I'm sorry, darling, I'm not up to any more tonight. I must retire to bed.' She looked pale still, unusually fragile. James stood up courteously when his wife did. Mercy stood up as well.

'There's no need to come,' Margaret said. 'I know my way. Goodnight, Mercy.' Suddenly she leant over and her soft lips touched Mercy's cheek. 'See you in a little while, darling,' she said to James. Then she was gone.

Mercy felt James's hand on her back, its heat. She stiffened, wanting to step away. She was already too hot, and could see how he was sweating.

'How would you like to dance, Mercy?'

'Me? I can't dance!' She tried to laugh off the suggestion.

'Oh, you'd pick it up in no time.' He caught her hand. 'Let me teach you, my dear.'

No, she thought. Please. She was even more uncertain of him after his harshness earlier. But she sensed he was trying to make it up. His eyes were pleading.

'I should go and see if Stevie's all right.'

'He'll be perfectly all right.' He still clasped her hand. 'Sleeps like a log once he's off, the little fellow, doesn't he? Just one dance – for me. Please?'

A few couples were already on the floor, their feet moving expertly to a waltz.

James took her in his arms, his right hand pressing her close at the waist. She could only shuffle and stumble after him when she knew he longed for her to whirl, to match his expertise. All the time she had to look down at her feet.

'One, two, three; one, two three,' he counted. If she glanced up his eyes were always fixed on her face. It made her feel uncomfortable. She felt he wanted something from her and she didn't know what it was.

When the music finished she left him with enormous relief, after he had kissed her hand and said, 'Goodnight, my dear.' She wanted to be back in her stateroom with the little light on and Stevie's little breaths coming to her across the room.

On the promenade deck, moist air rushing past his flushed face, James Adair stared, unseeing, over the dark ocean. After a time he raised a clenched fist to his mouth and bit on it so hard that his eyes started with tears.

Chapter Twenty-Nine

Mercy padded round the stateroom in her bare feet. Her oil-stained dress was drying over the back of the chair. She had rubbed the smudge with soap and done her best to scrub it out.

She undressed and slipped on her white cotton nightdress, still able to marvel that she possessed such a garment. The little electric light was burning on the table, shedding a soft glow round which the rest of the room was a circle of shadow. It was not bright enough to disturb Stevie. It had been decided that he should sleep in one of the beds with pillows tucked along the side. If conditions grew rough they could ask for a cot for him.

Mercy was still like a child with a new doll's house. She went and stood by the basin, turned the taps on and off, drank from the tooth mug and leant forward to look closely in the mirror. She brushed her hair out and plaited it into one thick braid. Even in the subdued light she could see her colour was high. Her cheeks looked quite swarthy, though she had drunk only a little of the wine, heady after a few sips. She'd left the rest.

'You'll have to watch it, eating and drinking wine with all them toffs!' She grinned cheekily in the mirror. 'Bet some of 'em wouldn't've wanted me up there if they knew . . .'

She washed herself then sat on her bed, pulled her knees up and hugged them, full of wonder. Everything felt so soft, so comfortable. She'd sleep like a princess tonight.

But her happiness never came unmixed with guilt and sorrow. Every time she'd been to see Elsie she'd looked worse and worse. More drawn in the face, more exhausted. When she had begun visiting regularly again in the autumn she was terribly shocked. She found Elsie in a chair, weak and shrunken, barely able to move.

'Elsie—' With a tight feeling in her chest Mercy rushed to her side.

'Oh – oh Lor' – Mercy—' She tried to raise herself in her chair, giving a whimper of pain.

Mercy was really frightened. She felt as if the breath had been knocked out of her. Elsie's face was so pinched and thin, barely recognizable. Her hands clutching at the arms of the chair were bony as twigs.

'What's the matter, you look terrible! Oh Elsie, I'm sorry. I meant to come more often. I didn't know things were this bad.'

'You're awright.' Elsie's voice had changed. It sounded high and reedy. 'I know yer busy, bab. I just ain't been too bright lately.' She tried, unsuccessfully to laugh. 'As you can see, I've got a bit be'ind with myself.' She jerked her head in Tom's direction. 'With 'im and that. Rosalie does 'er best to 'elp like, but you know . . . 'Ere, let's 'ave a cuppa tea.' The range had all but gone out and the room was dank and cold.

'Don't move, Elsie.' Mercy was fighting back tears. The sight of the two of them, mother and son, stranded in this room together was so pitiful she could hardly bear it. She wished she could knock the rotten house down and rebuild it, warm and clean and comfortable for them.

'I'll make tea. I'll cook for you. And let me sort Tom out . . .'

She fetched a bucket of slack and stoked the range, noticing as she moved round the small room the dirty state of the place, the grimy floor, bugs in the crevices, running up the walls.

'I was going to stove the place today,' Elsie said, seeing Mercy looking round. 'Only I just never got round to it some'ow.'

'What's wrong with you, Elsie?' Mercy asked gently, but the only reply she got was, 'Oh, nowt worth wasting breath on, bab.'

It took a long time for the kettle to boil. Mercy got the broom out and briskly swept the room, swishing bugs from the corners.

'And I'll come and sort you out in a tick when I've got some hot water,' she said to Tom.

She handed Elsie a cup of tea and prepared a pail of water, soap and a rag.

The bed was in a filthy state, the smell of it overpowering. Tom had been settled on a collection of rags to try and preserve the sheet, but they were badly soiled and the stained sheet was wet from edge to edge.

'There's a spare.' Elsie pointed to a sheet hanging over the chair beside the dead fire. 'Might still be a bit damp.'

Mercy moved the chair next to the warm range and stood the bowl on another chair near the bed. By the time she'd made all her preparations, Elsie was dozing again, the cup of tea forgotten on the table. Her clothes were holed and stained, stockings crinkled down her thin legs.

Using all her wiry strength, Mercy rolled Tom over. He let out a groan. His body was so much thinner now, the limbs pale and wasted. She turned him on his side. Even in his soiled state she could see the sores at the base of his back, the skin chaffed away from pressure on the bed to form two deep wounds.

'Oh my God.' She stood holding him, aghast. For a few moments she was overwhelmed, felt as if her sorrow would drown her. Tears coursed down her cheeks. 'My poor, poor boy,' she whispered. 'Oh Tom, what's happened to you, my love?' For those moments, soiled and vulnerable as he was, he was once again the quiet, kind lad she could still remember with great tenderness.

She wiped her eyes with the back of one hand. In a fury she pulled all the filthy rags out from underneath him and bundled them up by the door to be thrown out. The mattress was so wet and foul. If only she could get him on to another bed! But there was nothing, and even if there had been she had the strength only to roll him over and pull the sheet out from underneath him as she'd seen Elsie do so many times.

She wrung the cloth out over the pail, pushing wisps of hair away from her face with her wrists. She set about washing him with a bar of carbolic. With great gentleness and care she soaped his body, massaging his stick-thin arms, the pale, almost hairless chest. He made no sound, though when she turned him on his back he was watching her with a puzzled look on his face. His belly was soft, sunk inwards. Very gently she washed the small shrunken part of him that should have fathered her children and felt in it not a flicker of life. She dried him, put the other, still damp sheet on the bed and tucked a bottle between his legs. Of course he'd move and it would spill, but it might help preserve the sheet. Mercy kissed his soap-smelling cheek, emptied the bucket, and sat spooning tea into his mouth. All the while he looked sternly at her.

'Mercy?' Elsie looked round at her with the dazed eyes of a much older woman. 'Oh, you're still 'ere. I must've dozed off.'

She reached for the tea and Mercy rushed to help. 'It's gone cold – I'll get you some more.'

'Rosalie'll be in soon.' This was an important moment of the day, Rosalie's return from school.

'There must be a place, you know,' Mercy said very gently, moving her chair closer to Elsie's. 'Somewhere you could get Tom looked after.'

Elsie ignored her. She seemed far away, as if nothing anyone said fully sank in. Her face puckered in pain. Hissing through her teeth she reached under her left arm, moaned, eyes streaming.

'What's the matter, love? Let me look.'

She didn't protest as Mercy, hands trembling, unbuttoned her blouse. The skin under Elsie's arm and round her breast was taut and blackened.

'Radiation.' Elsie stared down at herself as if at a stranger. 'That's what it does to yer.' Covering herself again she looked into Mercy's eyes. 'I want Johnny. Can yer find 'im for me?'

She tried Johnny's address in Aston. He'd moved on. His second landlady was not many streets away.

'Johnny Pepper? Ar – 'e were 'ere. Ain't no more though. Went more'n a month ago. 'E couldn't afford the rent like, after the strike.' The police strike had ground on through the summer. Mercy had hardly given it more than a passing thought. ''E were one of the ones they let go. Quite a few of 'em with no job at the end of it. S'pose it serves 'em right really,' she said complacently. 'Any'ow, 'e couldn't pay the rent no more.'

'D'you know where he went?'

'Can't say I do, bab, no. 'E said summat about the country at one time. Moody lad, 'e was. Nights 'e'd be up moving about, in and out all hours. Used to walk the streets. I don't know. Sorry not to be more 'elp though. 'E yer brother?'

'No, just a friend.' Mercy tried to smile, despite her sinking heart. 'Ta any road.'

She told Elsie. 'The woman said 'e'd gone to the country. I s'pect he'll be in touch. She said 'e'd got himself a really good job on a farm somewhere.'

'Ah well,' Elsie said. She seemed cheered. 'That'll be nice for 'im. 'E always liked to be out and about.'

Elsie died in the December. With Margaret's permission Mercy had visited every week and helped as much as she could. She knew Elsie was not going to get better. She was in bed through November and they watched her sink until she could no longer speak and didn't know anyone. They took her to hospital where they gave her morphine, and after two days she was gone.

Rosalie gave up school and stayed at home to look after Tom. The funeral was at St Joseph's and Margaret gladly granted Mercy time off to go.

'She was like a Mom to me,' Mercy told Margaret. She felt clenched up inside with sadness.

The sun shone in weakly through the long church windows, panels of light dancing with dust. They sang 'Abide With Me' and 'Safely, Safely Gathered In'. Rosalie leant on Mercy and sobbed and Mercy stroked her auburn head. Poor kid, only twelve and the woman of the house now. She was a brave little thing. Maryann had come from Coventry, and Jack was there, but they hadn't found Johnny. Josephine was there, pale and tired-looking. Things were strained with her husband. Alf's hair was almost white but he still looked strong, upstanding. At his side, Mabel, in her smartest dress, hair piled high under her hat.

Mercy shyly kissed Alf as the organ played at the end of it.

''Allo, wench.' He seemed stunned. 'You're looking very nice. Thanks for coming to see 'er like. It meant a lot to 'er.'

Mabel, who seemed to be a fixture beside him said, 'I 'ear you're doing very well for yourself, Mercy. That Dorothy Finch still looking out for you?'

'Yes thanks. I see Dorothy from time to time.' She was very taken aback. She expected to hear rancour or sarcasm in Mabel's voice, but there was none. She even felt a little ashamed for harbouring so much bitterness towards her when she'd helped Elsie. This was Elsie's funeral and she must behave nicely.

'How're you, Mabel?'

'Oh, I'm awright.' She smiled a fond, gap-toothed smile at Alf. 'You know – going along.'

The neighbours were all there: the Ripleys, Mc-Gonegalls, Mary Jones and her kids. Everyone acted pleased to see her, was kind. She'd seen them in snatches on her visits to Elsie. But Mercy had felt strange, known their distance from her in their exclamations about how well she was looking.

The sadness of the funeral was deepened by her own sense of being an outsider. Thinking back on it now in this seaborne room so far from Angel Street, she knew it had been Elsie who had tied her to the neighbourhood. She'd changed, moved on from them. She couldn't share their day-to-day concerns. The realization was one of melancholy and loss mixed with excitement. Her life was opening out, it had possibilities which she could never have dreamed of in Angel Street. It seemed her future lay with the Adairs.

Chapter Thirty

Chilly now, and feeling sleepy, Mercy slipped out of bed to switch off the light.

She heard a low knocking at the door. She stood still holding her breath. Had she imagined it? The knock came again, still restrained but a little louder. Without stopping to think she went and opened the door a crack.

'Oh goodness, I didn't think you'd have gone to bed this early!' Mr Adair sounded very flustered. 'Margaret's feeling very queasy again, so I said I'd come down and see Stevie instead. But I suppose', he added lamely, 'he's asleep and peaceful?'

Mercy was confused. Margaret usually came to see Stevie much earlier when he was awake. James never usually came at all.

'Well, yes. He's sound asleep.' She was speaking very softly. 'Seems happy enough on the bed for tonight.' She didn't know whether she should open the door wider. She was acutely aware that all she had on was her nightdress. 'D'you want to see him?'

James looked agitatedly up and down the corridor. He was holding his hat, circling the brim round between his fingers. 'Perhaps, as I'm here. If you don't mind.'

She stood back to let him in, his coat brushing her arm. Immediately she'd shut the door she pulled a cardigan on over her nightdress, for the sake of both warmth and modesty.

He stood in front of her. The fiddling with his hat went on. He stared at his hands, looked as if he was about to speak, closed his mouth again, sighed.

Mercy felt terribly awkward. His presence was so large and imposing in the small room and she, despite the wool garment she was pulling tight round herself, felt naked and foolish. She clenched her jaw to stop her teeth chattering. Why on earth didn't he look at Stevie and then go away again?

'He's there.' She pointed.

James stepped over and looked down at his son. Stevie was flat on his back, arms stretched out, his cheeks pink, mouth a little open. He looked adorable with his long eyelashes and dark curly hair. Mercy smiled. She stood with her arms tightly folded.

'He looks perfectly comfortable.' James spoke in a forced, jovial tone, which softened as he turned to her and said, 'And you, Mercy? Is everything all right for you?'

'Oh yes, thank you, Mr Adair. It's lovely.'

'Good. Good. Very well.' There was a note of appeal in his voice as he said, 'Is there nothing you'd like?'

''Er, no, thank you,' she said, bewildered.

'Right then. Good. I may come another night. Margaret's still poorly.'

In that case, Mercy thought, she'd make sure she remained dressed until he'd been. It was all very strange. Perhaps as he was on holiday he thought he should see as much of Stevie as possible?

He put his hat on and went to the door. 'Goodnight,' he said tenderly.

'Goodnight, Mr Adair.'

*

As Mercy closed the stateroom door behind him James Adair had to resist an impulse to lean against the wall of the rolling ship and bang his head on it at his own folly. But there were people coming, a respectable-looking couple in modest evening clothes earnestly reading the numbers on the doors.

He couldn't bear the thought of the smoking room, or reading room. He didn't want other people, nor could he possibly be still. He stormed along the passage and climbed one staircase, then another. The promenade deck: blast it, he was in second class still, of course, but the deck was more or less empty so no matter. It was too late, too bracingly cold out there for most people.

He went to the side and looked out. From inside he could hear the sound of a piano. It struck him how odd it was to hear a piano in the middle of the ocean. The ship's lights dimmed quickly into the far greater darkness beyond for it was cloudy, moonless. He could sense the sea rather than see it, except for occasional riffles of white foam which appeared and vanished so quickly, he felt he might have imagined them. The wind was scouringly cold against his cheeks, but he welcomed it. He raged at himself.

Stupid, deluded imbecile. What the hell has got into you? What must she have thought of him turning up like that when she'd already retired to bed? It was asinine, it was insane!

He leant his elbows on the side and rested his head on his upturned hands, letting out a groan. The expression on her face! She must have thought him deranged! But no, damn it, he justified himself. He could call in and see his own son if it suited him, couldn't he, for heaven's sake?

He ought to be thinking of his plans and projects, of Kesler, of how they would work together. That was the entire purpose of the voyage – the business; his life's work. Instead of which he knew he would not sleep for the ceaseless longing in him which ached for relief. Never in his life had he experienced such helplessness. He knew, whatever his rational mind told him, that he would go to Mercy again. Somewhere in him the battle was already lost.

'Oh Mercy – oh, help me . . .' he groaned into the buffeting Atlantic wind.

'Good evening.'

A young man approached, smoking a cigarette. The glowing tip of it moved in his hand. James jumped, heart pounding. How long had he been there? Had he heard?

'Evening,' he replied brusquely. Under the low lights he could make out a long face, deep-set eyes, a baggy suit. He was about to turn away when the young man spoke.

'Queen of all ships, isn't she?'

James relaxed. Perhaps he hadn't heard. The wind was strong. And even if he had, civility would prevent him from commenting.

'Yes, indeed,' he replied, attempting geniality. 'A real privilege to travel on her.' He held his hand out. 'I'm an interloper along here. Really should be in first class. James Adair.'

The young man seemed unmoved by the information but he returned the handshake. 'Paul Louth.' He frowned. 'Adair? I believe I met your – would she be nanny? – earlier on. I offered to show her around. I hope that's acceptable?'

James bristled inside. This must be the student! He felt a violent rush of resentment.

'Mercy? Oh yes – she looks after our son. So you're

the student? She said she'd met you.' It stuck in his throat to mention this, but he wanted to find out more about him.

'Yes, I am,' Paul said, brightening. 'I just had the opportunity to work this round trip. Fascinating to see her in action, though of course the work's filthy and rather repetitive. I did see round the *Olympic*'s engine room once. Marvellous – 'course she's a triple screw, whereas they put the quadruple screw propellers in this one . . .'

They spent a good half hour sharing engineers' talk. They discussed the workings of the ship, its construction, the intricacies of the Parson's turbine engine. James told Paul about his business with Kesler. He relaxed. Watching the young man's pale profile, his serious expression as he spoke, he could not harbour dislike for him. He had intelligence, expertise. There was a sadness about him, as of so many of the remaining young men of his generation. It was when he talked of his trade, of the ship, that he became animated.

When they parted for the night James strolled back to first class feeling calmer, mellowed, ashamed of his earlier jealousy. Mercy had only spoken to him once after all. What did that signify? He was a pleasant young man. An odd mixture of charm and melancholy. And hard to place somehow – well-spoken, clearly educated, but travelling second class and without the kind of well-heeled assumptions of superiority James would have expected, which would have made him bridle. Bit of an oddball perhaps, he thought, but certainly a well-informed one. He mustn't mind Mercy seeing the boy or whatever would she think of him? His display of temper at dinner had been bad enough. He was being a fool.

The door of his stateroom creaked as he opened it.

Margaret was moving restlessly in the bed, her face white. Once in bed, against his expectation, he slept immediately.

The next day was one of cloud broken by occasional bursts of sunshine. Mercy spent the day chiefly with Stevie. They went to see Margaret but she was so sick they left her in peace. She took Stevie out on deck, well wrapped up, letting him run up and down on his sturdy legs, pointing and babbling. His red muffler streamed in the wind like a flag. He could say few words clearly as yet but compensated with a great many inquisitive and expressive sounds. He was very intrigued by a stack of folding deckchairs, not in use as it was too cold to sit out. Mercy had to put one up and down several times to show him, and herself for that matter, how it worked.

'Come on, my lad,' she said eventually. 'That's enough of that. Let's go and see if we can find some toys, eh?'

She picked him up, both their cheeks cold and glowing.

He was on a rocking horse in the nursery, crowing with delight, when James Adair appeared. He stood at the door in his coat and hat, smiling.

'Dadada!' Stevie yelled, pointing. The nurse in charge smiled indulgently.

'Just thought I'd have a look in.' James came over to them. 'Everything all right, Mercy?'

'Yes, thank you.' She smiled shyly. 'Is Margaret any better?'

'Not much, I'm afraid. And the motion of the ship's not helping. She said she'd like to see you both later – just for a few minutes. She's very fed up of course.'

'I know.' Margaret had been tearful when she went in earlier. 'Poor thing – what a time to feel bad.'

'I, er—' – James pushed his hands into his pockets – 'I met your friend last night.'

Mercy lurched over to support Stevie as he began to slide off the horse. 'Who?'

'Paul Louth.'

'Oh – yes!' she smiled. 'He's going to show me round later on!'

'Good. That'll be interesting.' He spoke with determined enthusiasm. 'You'll have to tell me about it. He seems very nice. Quite put my foolish fears at ease!' And he laughed, long and loud so that Mercy felt obliged to laugh a little with him.

She met Paul at a quarter to six. He had already washed and changed back into his too-large suit.

'I'll have him with me—' – she indicated Stevie – 'at least for another hour or so. Will it matter?'

'Course not!' Paul squatted down. 'Hello, Stevie. Are you going to come and have a look round with us?' Looking up at Mercy he said, 'Tell you what. If we take him down with us now we can have a quick look in the engine room. He won't be frightened by the noise, will he?' Mercy shook her head. 'Then perhaps after dinner we could look at some of the less dramatic bits?'

'That sounds lovely!'

'Come on then.' He stood up. 'The tour begins here.'

She picked Stevie up and they moved down through the ship, through a warren of narrower, much more rudimentary corridors the passengers never normally saw. The throb of the ship grew louder each time they moved down a deck.

'Are you s'posed to bring me down here?' she asked, following Paul's eager stride.

'Don't know really.' He turned to her, looking quite unconcerned. 'They can hardly throw us off the ship, can they? I shan't keep you down long. It's pretty filthy lower down, and noisy. But it'll give you a sense of what goes on below decks, what keeps it all ticking over . . . Would you like me to carry him for a while?'

'No – I'm awright for now. He might not go to you anyway, as he doesn't know you.' But she was touched by his protectiveness.

The powerful, vibrating hum grew more insistent. She could feel it through her feet. The floors were metal now, clanked as they walked on them. There was no natural light down here. All the work was done under electric lamps. Stevie sat quite still in her arms now, head turning this way and that, a finger in his mouth.

'Now – look in here,' Paul said.

They stood at the threshold of the main engine room. Mercy looked up, up at the working puzzle of steel girders and plates, levers and tanks, dials and chains. So enormous and complicated, so much weight in all that throbbing, churning metal. She gave a gasp of awe and amazement.

Stevie's eyes were like giant marbles. Mercy felt his tight grip on her shoulder.

'It's enormous!' Mercy shouted. 'Don't know why – it reminds me of a church!'

She saw, rather than heard Paul laugh. 'Quite right too!' he shouted back. Suddenly he took her arm. She was warmed by the familiarity of it, as if they'd been friends for years.

'You must see down here . . .' He had to put his mouth close to her ear for her to hear him. 'I'm afraid it's pretty filthy . . . Coal gets in everything.'

'Well I'm learning not to wear my best clothes when I see you!' she yelled.

'Oh dear – didn't the oil come out?'

'Yes,' she replied, hoping it would eventually.

Holding her elbow he led her down another staircase, then stopped.

The floor was black with coal dust, the air stiflingly hot. All around she could hear the clang and rattle of metal, shovelling sounds, bangs and shouts and the trundle of wheels as the trimmers shifted loads of coal from the bunkers ready to be shovelled into the furnaces. There came the sound of a gong banging loudly amid all the other noise. From the stairs Mercy caught glimpses of men clad only in singlets above their trousers, their faces and muscular bodies black and shiny with coal and sweat so that they looked as if they were made of iron.

Mercy and Paul stood poised on the stairs. Mercy could feel the heat beating against her cheeks. She pressed Stevie's head protectively close to her. The air smelt evil and was full of ash and dust, and within seconds the three of them were all coughing. It was like hell down here, Mercy thought, holding her hand as a shield to Stevie's face. Those people in first class ought to see this, to make them realize what kept their luxurious saloons and dining rooms churning across the sea! The inside of her throat was burning.

'Come away,' Paul said, taking her arm.

They retreated very gratefully upstairs, longing for a drink of water.

'D'you know,' Paul said – there was no need to shout now – 'each of those men shifts about five tons of coal a day.'

'I couldn't stand it even for five minutes,' Mercy said. 'How the hell do they put up with it?'

'Beats me,' Paul said. 'But they do. Do it well too.'

They reached C-deck and stopped between his room and hers.

'I'll get this little'un to bed now,' she said.

'He's been very good, hasn't he? Not a murmur.'

'Thanks ever such a lot, Paul.' She hesitated, not sure if he'd still want to see her later.

'Pleasure's all mine.' He hesitated. 'Would you like to join me for dinner? Not quite like first class, I'm afraid, but it'd be good to have some company.'

'I'll eat with you,' she said happily. 'I'll turn up your sleeves for you too if you want!'

Paul held his arms down straight at his sides. The cuffs dangled halfway down his hands. 'I think I'm still supposed to be growing into it,' he said ruefully. 'If you would . . .'

'Give it 'ere. No – wait. Let me get the door open first.' Paul took her key and unlocked the door for her. She put Stevie down inside.

'See you then?' Paul handed her the jacket. 'At seven?'

'Better say seven-fifteen,' she said. 'What with the sewing.'

Chapter Thirty-One

She saw him outside the dining room before he saw her. He was standing sideways on to her, his thinness more obvious without the jacket. He was looking into the dining room as if watching the diners there, but she sensed that his mind was far away, his expression one of deep melancholy. The sadness she saw in him almost stopped her in her tracks. Before, with her, he had appeared cheerful.

'Oh hello!' He saw her and the smile blazed across his face.

'Here you go.' She had speedily unpicked his cuffs while waiting for Stevie to fall asleep, and sewn them up almost an inch shorter. 'I damped them down a bit, but they need pressing – I couldn't do that in time as well.'

He slipped on the jacket and tried the length. 'That's marvellous – thank you! I'll press them myself. I'm so grateful. So – are you ready for food? I'm absolutely ravenous.'

They settled themselves at a table beside the wall.

'You look – very nice,' Paul said stumblingly.

She smiled. 'Thanks.' She'd put on the dress with the blue flowers, plaited her hair simply. She'd wanted to look nice.

'Sorry – I'm not used to much conversation. I don't see many people who aren't engineering students!'

They turned their minds to food.

'Ooh, lovely – roast beef!' Mercy brightened further. 'They have all sorts of odd stuff up in first class, I can tell you.'

'Yes – it'd be too rich for my palette, I must say. Especially several days in a row. Stanley – he's the other student – has been full of praise for it all.' Paul grimaced. It was obvious he was none too keen on Stanley.

They ordered food and then fell silent as if something in the air had shifted that prevented them talking. They each looked down at the table, looked up smiling, fiddled with the simple provision of cutlery. For a moment, in this silent, face-to-face awkwardness, Mercy was acutely aware of the difference in their class. He was obviously educated, better off, superior. What on earth were they going to talk about?

Paul, who seemed for the moment equally at a loss peered into his cuffs and said, 'Thank you again. It's a very neat job.'

'Oh – not really. I'm not much good at sewing. It was . . .' She was about to say Susan. Susan's the one who can sew. But that was the past now. She didn't feel like explaining. 'Doesn't your mom do that sort of thing for you?'

'Oh no – my mother's dead. She died before the War.'

'Oh dear,' Mercy said.

'Yes. We miss her.'

'Are you a big family?'

'Only myself and my brother Peter. Two little dickie birds, we were, growing up together. He was three years older than me.'

He paused, sitting back and opening his napkin, spreading it on his lap. 'He joined up as soon as he was old enough. Desperate to go. He was killed at Loos.' Paul looked across the room. Mercy kept her eyes fixed on his face, willing him to keep talking.

'My father stayed in Cambridge throughout the War – at the university. He's a linguist – French and German. We were never close. Certainly aren't now. The War somehow put paid to any sort of communication – it was precarious enough before. It was another life over there...' He paused as if looking for words. 'You brought it all home in your mind but you couldn't talk about it.'

Paul stopped, obviously feeling he'd said too much, unsure what was right, to talk or not talk. He lit a cigarette, smoked in nervous little puffs. Once more he looked away across the room and Mercy could feel his unease. She thought of Tom and Johnny. Both of them before the War. Just ordinary lads. The sadness that bled eternally from those years of war.

'So you left home?' she asked hesitantly.

Her question seemed to put him at ease, to show him his talking wasn't a burden and he was able to look at her again, if shyly, drawing on the cigarette.

'I can't abide being in the same house as my father. Don't seem to fit in the way he wants me to. He'd have liked me to be an academic, a man of letters ... He just has a housekeeper now.' Paul shrugged. 'Still, all you can do is go on.'

'Yes.' His simple statement hit home. Her own life: her mother, Tom, Susan ... but she had to go on. 'I s'pose so.'

'Are you close to your family?'

'Me?' Mercy gave a bitter laugh. 'I ain't – haven't got a family.' It was always a difficult admission.

'What, no one?' He sounded startled, and sorry.

She shook her head, took a sip of water from her tumbler, not like the elegant cut glass upstairs, then looked up into his eyes.

'My mom, whoever she was, left me on the steps of the workhouse – well, orphanage – when I was just a few hours old. All she left with me was a little hanky with my name embroidered on it – least, that's the name they gave me. Hanley came from the name of the home – the benefactor was a Joseph Hanley. But I've looked at that hanky so many times and wondered whose fingers stitched my name; why she couldn't keep me . . .'

'Poor woman,' Paul said. 'How terrible.'

'Yes, I know, but . . .' Mercy felt her emotion boiling to the surface, the hurt and anger. 'But to just throw away your own child as if she were a bag of rubbish!' Tears stung her eyes and she wiped them away furiously, hanging her head.

'Oh dear,' Paul said wretchedly. 'I'm sorry. The last thing I want is to upset you.'

When she looked up his eyes were full of concern. She tried to smile.

'No – it's all right. I'm glad I told you. I don't know why it is, it always feels like summat to be ashamed of. I've tried so many times to think what it must've been like for her. I don't know whether she was too poor to keep me. She might've had a whole host of other kids. She might be dead . . . I just wish I knew who she was, that's all.'

The soup arrived, leek and potato, plentiful and tasty. Paul put out his cigarette. For a time they chatted more lightly, about the ship, the voyage.

'We're not up to speed, you know,' Paul told her. 'Barely managing twenty knots. She used to be able to average twenty-six before the War – more sometimes.'

'Does that mean the journey'll take longer?' She'd been told they'd be five days on board.

'A few extra hours at least.'

'Oh well – I won't complain about that,' she smiled. 'I'm enjoying it all too much to want to hurry.'

The dishes were cleared, and plates arrived arranged with slices of well-cooked meat and generous servings of potato, carrots and greens.

'This is the nicest beef I've ever had,' Mercy said.

'It is good.' Paul spooned horseradish. 'Makes you appreciate good food when you've done without it, doesn't it? In the army we were all obsessed with the food – well, when nothing much was happening. Food and dry boots!'

'Where were you, Paul?'

'The Somme area. I joined up towards the end. I was there five months – not that long really but it felt like a whole lifetime. Ended up near le Cateau. I went in with two friends – with the Lincolns.'

She waited, seeing he had more to say.

'Neither of them came back. John went first, early on. Eric and I – well, he said I had a charmed life and I suppose it turned out to be true. He was shot. I don't know how exactly, or where. I found out afterwards. And I—'

'You got through without a scratch?'

'Well, no, I didn't as a matter of fact. That was the extraordinary thing. I was hit twice. The first time it came from a long way away – the bullet caught the rim of my helmet. Must have been that far from my eyes.' He held out his finger and thumb. 'The second time I was holding my rifle, like this, elbows out. A bullet zipped straight through here, under my left arm and out the other side. Burned a lump out of my arm as it went. I remember looking down and my uniform was smoking – there was a whopping hole in it. The arm bled like anything, but in fact there was no serious damage. Again, a few inches further across and it would have killed me.'

'What fantastic good luck!'

'Yes, but the worst of it is, it makes you feel responsible. I don't know what for exactly. But hundreds, thousands of men had the same luck in reverse. It didn't miss. And you start thinking, why me? What's so bloody special about me? Oh, look – I'd better not get going on this.'

'I don't mind. I'd like to know.'

He couldn't look at her and she could sense in him a shame which matched her own.

'What about other friends?' she asked.

'I don't seem to have too many now. Everything's different . . .' He gave a hugely weary sigh. 'Look, let's not go into that. Go forward from every day, that's my motto. Tell me some more about yourself.'

'I can't think of anything much. I'm not very educated or anything. Just ordinary, you know. I mean I'm not . . .' She stumbled to a halt.

Paul picked his knife and fork up again. He leant towards her. 'Not what?'

Mercy felt herself blushing. 'Just that I'm not your class of person, am I?'

'And what class of person am I? Do tell me, because I'm damned if I know any more.'

She stared back at him. In Paul's eyes she could see a sad, hungry expression which moved her deeply.

'People are just people, Mercy. That's all. If there was one single thing the War taught me it was that. So please . . .'

So she talked. About the home. About Mabel and

Susan, Elsie, Tom, Johnny. And Paul listened, intently. The waiter brought a steamed marmalade pudding with custard and they ate, barely tasting it.

'Johnny said the same as you when he got back, that he couldn't stop at home. I don't know where he's gone now.'

Paul looked sorrowfully at her. 'You've had so many losses.'

'I've been so lucky working for the Adairs though. Dorothy found 'em for me. They're ever so good to me.'

'You were lucky in Dorothy too.'

'Oh yes – she's awright, Dorothy is. She's a good sort.'

'You don't think ... Perhaps I shouldn't say this ...' Paul eyed her sideways on, hesitating.

'What?'

'Well, that Dorothy might actually be your mother?'

Mercy stared at him in speechless astonishment. She started to laugh. She laughed so hard that people stared and her bubbling mirth eventually made Paul join in as well.

'Dorothy? You mean – oh no. No!'

'I'm sorry. I didn't realize the idea was that absurd!'

'She's just not. No ... Oh dear no. She's just Dorothy.'

'I'm sorry. Shouldn't have even said it.'

'D'you know, it'd never even crossed my mind.' Mercy wiped her eyes. She looked thoughtful for a moment, then shook her head. 'No. No, she just isn't.'

'Ready to explore now?' Paul asked impishly when they'd finished.

'Let me just look in on Stevie. He's a very good sleeper but I must make sure.'

Paul waited as Mercy tiptoed in and replaced Stevie's

covers which he was forever kicking off. She leant over and kissed him.

'He's so beautiful when he's asleep,' she smiled, re-locking the door. 'All warm and peaceful. Where're we going then?'

'Let's just follow our feet, shall we? Hmm.' He stopped as they reached the third-class staircase. 'I suppose just meandering round inside might get a bit dull. Shall we go and get our coats?'

'OK.' Mercy didn't mind in the least where they went. It was all fun. More than fun. She surprised herself with the thought: this is the best night of my life!

They were just turning back when someone came running up the stairs behind them, three at a time.

'Eh – eh!' There came a loud burst of a language Mercy had never heard before.

A man, swarthy-faced with a black moustache, a cap, and black workaday clothes seized Paul's arm, talking urgently: 'Daktar – daktar . . .'

'No, I'm not a doctor!' Paul said. 'I'm sorry . . .'

The desperation on the man's face was unmistakable. He made dramatic gestures, sweeping his calloused hand over his stomach and talking frantically.

'What the hell's this language?' Paul said exasperated. 'Is it, are you . . . Polska? Polska?'

The man nodded emphatically and flooded them with more incomprehensible language.

Mercy watched his hands. 'Someone's 'aving a babby,' she said suddenly. 'That's what. Down in third class.'

'Wait – I know who can help. Stay there – DOCTOR,' Paul said to the Polish man, and ran off.

A few moments later he returned with a dour-faced young man dressed in white with almost painfully prominent cheekbones.

'He's the kosher cook,' Paul panted as the two other men spoke. 'Speaks bits of all sorts – English, German, Yiddish – Polish too, thank heavens.' Mercy's eyes were intent on the Polish man's face.

'He says', the cook informed them disdainfully, 'that his wife is with baby and he needs a doctor.'

'See!' Mercy said. The cook disappeared, shaking his head.

'Get him to show you where and meet me back here.' Paul was already moving away. 'I'll find the ship's surgeon.'

The man beckoned her down the stairs, then down again until they were on F-deck. Their feet clattered on the steps.

In one part of the corridor a small crowd of people, mostly women, were huddled anxiously near one of the doors. Mercy could see they were poor, their skirts made of thick, workaday cloth, clutching shawls round their shoulders. They reminded her of a cluster of starlings. The man spoke to them, pushing past to the cabin door. 114F. Mercy memorized the number. She could already hear the sounds of the birthing woman.

To her great surprise the man indicated for her to enter. She pointed back down the corridor. She had to meet Paul. But he insisted, taking her arm, motioned her inside. The other women outside all stood round the doorway. Mercy began to wonder if they thought she was a nurse but since she had no way of explaining she followed the man in.

The room was lit by one small bulb and was stuffy, full of cloying, intimate smells, especially sweat. Two narrow berths were squeezed in down either side, and Mercy saw that the young woman, barely more than a girl, was lying, panting, on the one to the right. At her head, on the edge of the bed an older woman was perched, talking endlessly in a low voice, a string of beads dangling from her fingers. It took Mercy a moment to see she was praying.

For the moment the young woman was quiet and the man beckoned Mercy forward. Mercy felt timid, confused. What did the man want? She couldn't speak any Polish. She knew nothing about having babies.

The young woman turned her head and Mercy saw that her black hair was drenched in sweat. Such a sweet face, but so exhausted and frightened. She put her hand out and muttered something. Mercy took the hot hand and squeezed it.

'The doctor's coming,' she said. 'You'll be all right. You'll 'ave your babby soon.'

Pain gripped the young woman again and she began to writhe and groan horribly, her body lifting from the bed. She loosed Mercy's hand and clawed at the thin bedcover, her cries becoming a long, sobbing wail. Mercy felt her knees turn weak. She motioned to the man that she was going up to meet the doctor. She saw in his eyes, then, that he loved his wife and how afraid he was. He had needed her to see. She spoke English: she would be able to speak to the doctor when he was unable to.

Paul and the doctor were coming down the stairs as she reached them.

'This way.' She ran ahead of them.

'What's the trouble?' The surgeon was a middle-aged man with a bushy moustache and a brisk air. He smelt of whisky.

'She's pretty far on by the sound of it,' Mercy panted as they clattered along F-deck. 'I think summat might be wrong but I'm no expert, doctor.'

'I hardly supposed you were,' he replied dryly.

'Here.' The crowd stood back respectfully to let him through. The door opened, letting out the woman's distressed cries.

'Poor thing.' Mercy leant weakly against the wall on the other side of the corridor. The sound of such suffering made her feel faint. The other spectators were eyeing her and Paul curiously.

'Well, we've done our good deed,' Paul said. 'Would you like to go up on deck now?'

Mercy looked at him as if he were a madman. 'Of course not! I'm not going anywhere 'til I see how she gets on. I want to know if she's awright and if she has a boy or a girl.' She folded her arms adamantly.

It took another two gruelling hours. Mercy ran back up twice to check Stevie was still asleep. Several times Paul suggested tentatively that they go up and have a cup of tea before resuming the vigil.

'You go if you want. I'm staying.'

The young woman was clearly having a very difficult time. At every agonized outburst Mercy tensed, folding and unfolding her arms across her chest, hands clenched, listening. 'God, I hope she'll be OK. Oh my ... oh dear ...' she kept saying over and over. She felt as if her own innards were being torn out. The sounds of pain were terrible to hear. Paul paced helplessly up and down, seeming just as bothered by Mercy's distress as the Polish woman's. Towards the end it seemed everyone in the corridor was willing her on with every fibre of themselves. They all stopped talking. Almost stopped breathing. There came a final, terrible bout of screams which had Mercy bent double and almost tearing out her own hair. Everything went quiet. After a moment they heard the wild, outraged scream of a newborn child. There was a collective gasp from all the other women, relieved talk and laughter and embraces. Mercy found herself sobbing.

'Hey, hey . . .' Paul felt in his pockets for a hanky but failed to find one. After a moment's flustered hesitation he put his arm round her shoulders. 'You don't even know her!'

'No . . .' Mercy found her own hanky and wiped her eyes. 'But she looked at me and took my hand.' She tried to smile. 'Daft, ain't it?'

After a moment the doctor put his head round the door. 'Could someone—' – he spoke tersely, looking at Paul – 'go up to the galley and fetch some hot water?'

'Is she all right?' Mercy cried.

'Yes, yes . . .'

There was toing and froing with water. The stooped, elderly woman carried a bundle of bloodstained bedding from the room. Eventually the doctor left.

Soon after, the dark-haired man came out of the room, a smile under his moustache. His face looked more youthful with relief. He beckoned to them. Mercy and Paul looked at each other and stepped inside. The crowd of Poles followed until the room was full.

The young woman was sitting up, hair plastered back on her head. Her eyes were like dark pools in her exhausted face, but there was a gentle smile now on her lips. The baby lay wrapped in her arms.

'Oh!' Mercy cried, tears filling her eyes again. So much pain, she thought, for such a miracle!

The woman gently held out the little one for her to see. Mercy looked into a crinkled but perfect face with a tiny shading of barely formed eyebrows. Its eyes were closed as if to cling on to the secrets of life before birth.

'I wonder if it's a girl or a boy,' she said to Paul.

As if the woman had understood, she unwrapped the baby for a moment. Mercy saw where the umbilical cord had been cut and bound.

'A girl! Oh Paul, she's a real picture!'

She saw his eyes appraising the new child, seriously and with complete attention, and was filled with tenderness for him. Everything was full of wonder tonight.

She felt her hand being grasped and the young mother raised it to her lips, kissing it again and again. Mercy was startled, but then pulled the linked hands back towards her and kissed her new friend in return.

The father presented Paul and another man with a tiny glass, hardly bigger than a large thimble, full of liquid. He handed another to Mercy. They must have brought these glasses with them, among what looked like pitifully few possessions. The man threw his head back and gulped his liquor down. Paul did the same and gagged and spluttered until tears ran down his cheeks. Everyone else laughed heartily, slapping Paul between the shoulder blades. Mercy took a cautious sip. The stuff tasted explosive. Even that small amount was like a fire in her throat! Paul was still recovering, wiping his eyes.

The man held his hand out and Paul took it.

'Petrowski,' he said. 'Tomek Petrowski.' He pointed at his wife. 'Yola Petrowski.'

Mercy and Paul told them their names, and then felt the time had come to leave this new family in peace. With a great deal more nodding and smiling they departed.

It was only when they began to climb the stairs that Mercy noticed a long, oval stain on her dress.

'Oh no – look, blood!' The mark was nearly the size of a hand. 'Must have been off the side of the bed.' She turned to Paul. 'Honestly – next time I go anywhere with you I'm going to wrap myself in an old sack!'

'Oh Mercy,' he laughed. And she heard a wealth of fondness in his voice.

'Where on earth have you been?'

James Adair was pacing the corridor, his expression livid. 'I've looked all over the place for you!'

He was full of pent-up emotion, a mixture of jealousy, frustration and self-righteous anger. He'd known Mercy was with Paul. She should be here, damn it, looking after his son! But then he noticed her dress.

'What's happened? Are you all right?'

Mercy explained. 'I kept coming up to see Stevie was asleep though – every hour or so. He's been perfectly all right!'

'Yes, yes.' James felt his ire melting away. His besotted imagination had tortured him with images of her and Paul alone together . . . but this had clearly not been the case.

'Well—' – he tried to speak lightly – 'how very exciting. I'd better get back to Margaret. She's not at all well tonight. I'll see you tomorrow. Will you be dining with us, or with Paul here? Up to you of course.' He forced himself to sound jovial, an old fuddy-duddy joking about the fact that she might choose to spend time with him.

Mercy looked at Paul.

'It'd be my pleasure,' he said.

'Paul, I think, Mr Adair.' He didn't fail to notice the flush in her cheeks.

'Right you are then.'

He turned away in an agony of contradictory shame and longing.

Chapter Thirty-Two

Mercy tried to spend a short time with Margaret each day, taking Stevie to see her. She called in mid-morning the next day. Margaret seemed no better. She tried to sit up and play with Stevie who wanted to crawl all over her and roll on the bed. Her face was very pale, and her soft, peach-coloured nightgown only seemed to make her complexion look more sickly. Her hair hung down limply and she was weak and lethargic.

Mercy chatted to her, telling her about the Petrowskis' baby and she tried to smile.

'You went down to third class? How brave!'

Mercy refrained from saying she had felt far more at home down there than in first class.

'I'm sorry,' Margaret murmured after a short time, her head lolling back on the pillows. 'You'll have to take him away. This terrible nausea ... If only I could be somewhere calm and still.' She lay down, grimacing as she moved, and closed her eyes.

'Come on, Stevie.' Mercy lifted him from the bed and he protested for a moment, wrapping himself round her like a monkey. She noticed his nose was running. Perhaps she'd kept him out in the air too long yesterday?

'Could you pass me a little more water?' Margaret barely had enough energy to speak.

Stevie on one arm, Mercy poured a glass of water and passed it to Margaret's outstretched hand. She took a few sips, then whispered, 'James should be back soon. Poor chap – I'm really cramping his style. He'd like to be staying up, dancing, out and about. Perhaps you could dance with him tonight, Mercy? I just can't . . .' She slumped down again.

'It's not your fault, is it?' Mercy said, trying to cheer her. 'Nobody asks to be poorly. I s'pect he's enjoying himself anyway – the ship and that.'

'But he's been so grumpy and out of sorts . . . oh dear . . .' She was slipping into sleep.

Mercy could scarcely wait for Paul to finish his day's stint down in the bowels of the ship. Now it was the third day of the voyage, the ship and the constant circle round them where dark sea met pale sky were losing their novelty and everyone was beginning to need a little more stimulation.

She whiled away the day with Stevie, passing time with some of the other nannies who visited the nursery. Scarcely any were as young as herself, but there was one not much older who was friendly. Ruby was a thin, bright-eyed young woman from Leeds who'd moved south to work for a London family and the two of them chatted idly.

James Adair called in twice to the nursery and Mercy noticed throughout the day that no other fathers did this. Both times he saw she was busy and left again looking ill at ease.

'Funny bloke,' Ruby said the second time. 'You'd never find 'er dad—' – she jerked her head at Charlotte, her two-year-old charge – 'coming down to see if she's all right. Or still alive for that matter.'

'Oh, Mr Adair's very fond of Stevie.'

'Oh yes – is that all 'e's fond of?' Ruby gave a chesty laugh.

'What're you on about?'

'Don't act all innocent. You know what I mean full well.' Ruby rushed off to rescue Charlotte who had fallen bang on her face.

Mercy frowned. Did Ruby mean ... was she saying ...? Uncomfortable thoughts came to her mind of the look in James Adair's eyes when he held her on the bicycle those months ago, of occasions when she'd seen the same look in his eyes since ... But no. What did she know about how men should might look at you? She actually shook her head to dismiss these thoughts. What was she? A servant, that was all. It was just ridiculous.

That night James Adair dined alone again, despite Margaret telling him that she was sure Mercy would come and join him.

Mercy met Paul for dinner and they talked and talked, and laughed together.

After dinner he said, 'Shall we go and see how the Petrowskis are getting on?'

'Ooh yes – I want to see that babby again. But first—'

'You need to look in on Stevie?'

She smiled. Happiness gave her face an extra glow. 'I ought to. That is what I'm here for! And I'll get my coat.'

They found the Petrowskis in the third-class sitting room. The place was furnished for very basic comfort, with slatted wooden seats round the walls. The air was full of smoke, tumblers of ale stood on the tables, round which there was a loud buzz of conversation in different languages, games of cards and dice and in one corner there was a sing-song going on, someone playing a fiddle. Mercy stood on the doorway with Paul looking round at the mass of people with their mix of nationalities and felt rather intimidated. It was if she'd just walked into another country altogether.

But Tomek Petrowski noticed them almost immediately and strode across, talking fast, shaking Paul's hand over and over. He motioned them to come and join his friends. They were a group of Poles, mostly men but a few women also. They all smiled and made welcoming gestures. Work-roughened hands were held out to them. Mercy saw Yola sitting watching her.

She stepped over to sit beside her and everyone made room. Tonight Yola's face was still tired, but relaxed. She welcomed Mercy happily. The baby was lying asleep in her lap, only her tiny face visible.

'Hello,' Mercy smiled. She felt such affection for this woman, strange as it was. 'You look better.' And Yola smiled and nodded back.

Mercy leant round to look at the baby and for a time she and Yola communicated in a universal language of smiles and coos and baby conversation. They sat with their heads close together, Mercy as fair as Yola was dark. When Mercy told her how beautiful the baby was, Mercy knew she understood her meaning.

Yola pointed at the sleeping child and said, 'Peschka.'

'Peschka? Is that her name – Peschka?'

Yola nodded.

'It's very pretty. She's very pretty.' Once more lots of nodding and smiling and appreciating. Yola lifted Mercy's hand and kissed it until Mercy felt quite tearful at receiving so much unbidden affection.

Paul found himself plied with more of the fiery liquor by the men and this time he took miniscule sips. Mercy saw Tomek hand him a slip of paper and a photograph. Paul looked at them and nodded before handing them back. After a time he stood up, looking across at her, asking with raised eyebrows if she was ready to leave. She said goodbye to Yola and joined him.

'I think I'd better go before they get me too tight to move!' he said.

They took their leave, smiling until Mercy felt her face might crack.

'Let's get some fresh air,' Paul said. 'Goodness – I don't know what that stuff is, but it's like drinking lava.'

'What was it they were showing you?' she asked, pulling her coat round her.

'Well—' – He stood back for her to go ahead of him up the stairs –'it seems they've got some relative in New York already – the chap in the picture. A brother or cousin maybe? His is the address Tomek showed me and they're hoping to join him.'

'What d'you mean, hoping?'

'They don't just let everyone in, you know. They have to have all sorts of checks – health and suchlike. They look robust enough to me though. They're from a village near Katowice – at least, I think that's what he meant.'

'They're a lively lot, aren't they?' Mercy said. She found herself feeling anxious for them. 'Imagine travelling all that way, starting a new life somewhere you don't speak a word of the language. I s'pose she hoped they'd reach America before the baby came. I think they're ever so brave.'

'Yes.' They stepped out into the dim light of the promenade deck. 'Sobering thought, isn't it?' He chuckled. 'Maybe that's why they're not keen to stay sober very much of the time!'

They strolled along, passing a few other couples out to

take the air. When they'd walked the length of the second-class promenade deck they stopped, as if of one mind and leant on the side to look out. Mercy breathed in the salt air, the wind buffeting her cheeks. Ever since she'd been aboard the ship her cheeks had taken on a healthy glow. They stood close together, hearing dance music drifting to them from inside, soft, then louder, according to the shifting wind.

Mercy looked at Paul beside her, his pale profile, a lock of his hair moving in the wind, dark against his forehead, the long, slightly crooked nose, wide mouth. At the end of this, she thought, I'll never see him again. And the thought was suddenly unbearable.

'D'you think you could do it?' she asked eventually.

Paul turned to look at her. 'What?'

'Just up sticks and go, like the Poles. Leave everything – your house, family, country – everything you know.'

Paul thought, staring out over the sea, biting his top lip.

'Yes. I really think I could. It's a peculiar thing. Before the War I felt British. English, let's say. It seemed unthinkable that anywhere but England could be home. It was the centre of my world – *the* world come to that, so far as we were concerned. Now though, I feel I could live almost anywhere. It wouldn't make that much difference.'

He snorted. 'We British are so self-important. I suppose instead of feeling English now I just feel human. Like one tiny dot in the human race.'

Mercy listened to him with a strange mixture of emotions. Often when he talked she felt his sadness, the sense that through the War so much had been lost forever. Yet now there also rose in her a pounding sensation of euphoria. That was the other thing he made her feel – he gave her freedom, a heady feeling of excitement! Here, on this ship, she was not trapped by her past, her class, her circumstances. The ship was as class-ridden as anywhere else, but with Paul she could be anyone. She could simply be herself and that was all he required her to be. She moved a little closer to him.

'How long will it take now?'

'A couple of days.' He spoke rather absently. 'As I say, she's not doing her best, nothing like, the poor old girl.'

'I don't really want to get there.'

Paul remained silent. He continued to stare out into the blackness. She felt he had slipped away from her into the world of his own thoughts, leaving her bereft. They had so little time left and she wanted to talk and talk, but he suddenly seemed so distant from her.

'Shall we go in?' she asked eventually, in a flat voice. He agreed with a sigh, and as he followed her downstairs she was acutely aware of his presence behind her. She longed to know why he had gone quiet so suddenly.

They stopped outside Mercy's room. She had been afraid of finding Mr Adair pacing up and down again but there was no sign of him. She looked round at Paul.

'What's up?' she said gently.

His hands were thrust into the pocket of his greatcoat which was, like his suit, too capacious for his build. He stared at her, seemed to be looking deeply into her.

'Paul?' She moved closer, stricken by the look of him. 'What on earth's the matter?'

He shook his head and looked down at his shoes. 'Nothing. Nothing that I can explain anyway.' Looking up again he forced a wan smile. 'Sorry – I can be a moody so-and-so. I don't mean to be.'

'No, you're not,' she said, not quite truthfully.

They stood apart, paralysed by the intensity of feeling in each other's eyes.

'Can I – I mean, shall we eat together tomorrow?' Mercy asked uncertainly.

'If you're sure you'd like to.'

'Paul . . .' Lost for words to describe quite how sure she was, she said, 'I'd like to. Yes. Please.'

'Goodnight then.' He turned away, towards his room. Then he looked back and said softly, 'Sweet dreams.'

Mercy's hands trembled as she unfastened her dress. She felt churned up. She knew how strong her feelings were for Paul with far more certainty than she ever had with Tom. She had wanted to go to him out on the landing and take him in her arms.

But she was very anxious and unsure. His melancholy eyes seemed to look at her from every corner of her mind. She didn't know if he returned her love. Life had given her so little love, and she didn't dare to expect it from anyone. Why should he feel the same? she thought. It had felt as if Paul was drawing away from her tonight and it all made her unsettled, full of longing, and afraid.

She tucked Stevie in and lay down in her own bed, her cheeks burning. The pillow was not sufficient to cool them. She turned on her back, the light still on, casting a soft circle on the ceiling. All she could think of was Paul, his thin body wrapped somehow pitifully in that enormous coat, the way he looked at her, how tender his eyes had been at the sight of little Peschka, how she could speak about anything to him and feel safe, how kind he was. But maybe that was all it was – kindness? Even though he seemed to look at her with such feeling.

She tossed from side to side. Time I turned the light off, she thought. But how ever am I going to get to sleep in this state?

Eventually she got up, went to the mirror and unfastened her hair to brush it out. Her face was glowing with health, the reflection of her large eyes seeming to burn back at her. She brushed her hair forward over one shoulder.

'I love you, Paul,' she dared to whisper. 'I really, really love you.'

She put the brush down and brought her hands together, close to her face as if praying, giggling quietly at herself for her silliness. Then her face sobered. 'Goodness only knows what he thinks of me though.' She longed to feel certain, for the strength that would bring.

A knock on the door made her jump. She listened, heart thumping hard. Could it be Paul? She flung her hair back and went to the door, not thinking of anything but that he wanted to see her again.

'Please. Let me in. Just for a moment.'

James Adair's tone was so urgent, distraught, that she stood back immediately and he stepped into the middle of the room. He had no coat or hat on and his tie was pulled askew. Mercy closed the door and stood with her arms folded.

'Whatever's the matter? Is it Mrs Adair? If you're worried about Stevie, he's perfectly all right. I know he's got a bit of a cold but look – he's not even feverish or—'

'No.' He turned away from her. 'No – none of that. Margaret's asleep.'

He sank down on the edge of her bed as if his legs had given way. 'I was just getting ready to retire for the night and I . . .'

He looked across at her and Mercy was startled by

the anguish in his face. She stood before him, completely unaware of her effect on him, how in his eyes she looked like an angel in her white nightdress, the curves of her breasts, the mass of gold hair tossed down her back.

'Mercy – oh God, God,' he groaned, burying his head in his hands. She was appalled to see him begin to weep, dry, desperate sobs shaking his whole frame.

'Oh goodness – whatever's the matter? Please don't, Mr Adair.' She paced up and down in front of him, clasping and unclasping her hands, completely unable to think what to do.

He raised his face and she saw tears in his eyes. He held out his arms.

'Save me.' He was past holding back now. Whatever was moral, seemly, correct, he was quite beyond all of it. 'Please say you'll come to me. I can't stand it any more. I love you, Mercy. I can't sleep. I can't rest or work for thinking of you. Look at me! Before you came, I was a man asleep. I didn't know it was possible to feel like this. All I can see is you until sometimes I think I'm making myself ill with it.' He covered his face with his hands again.

Mercy stood in front of him quite still, eyes wide and frightened. Her mind was in complete confusion. What Ruby had said ... No, she had fallen asleep and this was a dream. James Adair sitting on her bed saying these things, crying over her, it wasn't real.

'If I can't touch you I'm going to go out of my mind.' He looked up again. 'The very sight of you ... I can't go on like this, Mercy. You've got to save me.'

Her mouth had gone dry. 'Save you?' She could barely get the words out. 'What d'you mean?'

'Margaret wouldn't mind, if that's what you're thinking.' He stood up, words flooding from his lips which he'd said over and over to himself in justification. 'She doesn't really like – any of it. And she's ill. You'll be helping her, though of course she mustn't know. It's not wrong, Mercy, believe me . . .' She was shrinking away from him, holding herself very tight. Blood pounded in her ears.

'Wrong?' she whispered. 'I don't know what you mean.'

He seemed to loom over her and she felt tiny beside him. He put his hands on her shoulders. She saw his face twitch with emotion, his forehead perspiring.

'It's the best thing in the world, a beautiful thing. Oh, whatever it is, I can't be obedient any longer. This has to be right!'

Her mind seemed to have stopped working. She felt completely paralysed, unable to speak or think, she was so afraid. Surely he didn't mean . . . She remembered Johnny pushing her up against the wall that night . . . Mr Adair wouldn't . . . No, he couldn't mean . . .?

He turned her round to face the mirror. Her stunned face stared back at her. She felt it was someone else, a stranger.

'Look at yourself. You're the most lovely, perfect thing I've ever seen.' He leant down and put his face beside hers. 'Look at us, my loved one.' She felt his breath hot on her neck. He pushed her hair gently aside and his lips brushed the flesh just behind her right ear. She could feel the prickle of his moustache. Somewhere in her mind a voice – not even a voice, an impulse – hammered, stop him . . . This is wrong. Wrong! But she felt hypnotized by the strength and authority of his desire. How could

383

she argue? How could she go against Mr Adair? She should do something, say something, but she couldn't speak or move.

His hands moved round her, enormous and dark against the white nightdress. Trembling, hardly daring at first, then feverishly, he began to fondle her breasts. She heard his breath catch behind her and he gave a groan of surrender. She was mortified by his touch. It started to hurt and she gave a whimper – 'Please!' – which made him grasp her even more firmly. Her cheeks were burning. She felt dirty. This was wrong, all wrong, horrible . . .

Help me – please, God Almighty, help me, she prayed. Help me tell him to get off . . .

'Mr Adair!' Tearful, she tried to turn and face him. 'This ain't right—'

'Oh it is . . .' He held her tightly. His body was strong, taut with need. 'It's the rightest thing that's ever happened. I love you, Mercy. I adore you. This was ordained by the gods . . .'

He released her and began to fling off his clothes.

I should run . . . She eyed the door. But where to? To Margaret? Paul? How could she go out there, half dressed, and admit this to either of them? It was impossible. And still she couldn't scream, shout. Not to Mr Adair. She was trapped by his desire, his power over her.

'I want to see you,' he was saying. 'To be naked with you. Adam and Eve in the garden . . .' He was feverish with impatience, flinging his shoes across the room.

Naked, he presented himself to her, walking towards her, proud, his body as a gift. Tears poured down Mercy's face. She was shivering, wretched, afraid of him with his acrid, foreign smell, that cloud of hair at his groin, his . . . his . . . she couldn't even say the word to herself . . . standing up like that . . .

'Oh no – no!' Her voice cracked. 'I don't like this. Please, Mr Adair, get dressed again. This is all a mistake. I don't know how I've given you wrong ideas, but this isn't right! You can't mean to . . .'

James came to her, arms outstretched and she shrank away, sobbing. 'My dear, sweet, Mercy.' He was a fraction calmer, and spoke soothingly. 'Don't be afraid, my lovely, my darling one. Don't you see how much I feel for you? I'm going to help you. I want to be the first to teach you, to give you all the pleasure in the world.' He bent to lift the hem of her nightdress.

Pleasure? She found herself looking down at the back of his head where his hair was thinning. What did this have to do with pleasure?

'Raise your arms,' he instructed firmly.

She resisted for a moment, but then half raised them. He pulled the garment roughly over her elbows. Mercy gasped as the cool air brought her body up in gooseflesh.

'There we are, my love.' He took one of her hands and held her away from him to admire her slim, curvaceous body. 'How could anything so beautiful be wrong? You must believe that.'

'What're you going to do to me?' she said in a small voice.

'Come here.' He pulled her into his arms, letting out a sound of pleasure as he felt her against him.

'Please, just let me go . . .' she sobbed. 'I don't want to have a babby!'

'No, no – you won't, my dear one. It doesn't happen just straight away, you know, it takes some time. Believe me.'

Her view of him was level with his collarbones and the sprinkling of sandy, curling hairs on his flushed chest. She turned her head up to look into his face, her eyes wide and welling with tears. Perhaps if she looked into his eyes, she thought, he'd see how much she wanted him to stop.

But his hands were moving on her buttocks, pressing his body, jerking, against her, hard into her stomach. His eyes closed. He wasn't seeing her any more. She cried out, horrified at the feel of his fingers between her legs.

Abruptly he made her lie down. The bedcover felt cold against her back. She knew she couldn't fight him. She must do as she was told and it might be over quickly.

'That's it – I need . . .' He forced his way up hard inside her, instinct driving him. Mercy screwed her eyes shut at the tearing, burning pain. She whimpered, then it eased a little and he was thrusting, panting, groaning, anguish and relief at once flooding his face. His climax was intense, silent. Then he fell into her arms, half laughing, half weeping, twitching faintly inside her. Her tears trickled back into her hair. Every trace of her freedom and euphoria with Paul was wiped away. For those moments she was Mercy Hanley, rubbish off the street, something to be taken and used by everyone. She had never felt such despair.

He kissed her wet face again and again. 'You see? I told you, didn't I? You angel. Oh, my little angel.'

After he'd dressed himself and gone she lay, damp and burning between her legs. Her body felt very cold. She couldn't stop shaking and weeping.

Eventually, teeth chattering, she got up and washed herself, tears still rolling down her cheeks. She couldn't bear the thought of ever lying in her own bed again. Climbing in beside Stevie, she wrapped her arms round him, curled up tight beside his innocent, oblivious warmth.

Chapter Thirty-Three

Stevie woke her the next morning, poking his fingers experimentally in her ears and nose, trying to prise open her eyelids, enchanted at the novelty of finding her in his bed.

Light filtered through the curtains. The soreness between her legs was a reminder of what otherwise would have seemed a crazed dream. That she had seen James Adair in that state, what he had done – what she had allowed him to do – seemed impossible in the morning light. Thinking only of himself he had taken from her the innocence a woman was supposed to prize.

But her body had taken in the enormity of what had happened. Her head ached and her limbs were like lead. She felt numb and shrunken inside.

'Stevie – don't,' she pleaded as he kneaded at her face. She rolled over, shielding her head with a moan. If only she could just lie here all day, bury herself and hide from everyone. Most terrible was the thought of facing Margaret Adair. Their friendship now could never be as it was: she could never confide this to her. If only she could just disappear and never see either of them again! But she knew that somehow she had to rally herself, act as if nothing had happened, look after Stevie.

Once she left her room, the night before did seem to fade into unreality, especially when James Adair came to find her in the nursery. He drew her out of the door so they could still see Stevie pushing a little wooden trolley. He was his usual reserved, courteous self.

'I came to invite you to dine with me tonight,' he said politely. She saw he was nervous, left hand smoothing his moustache, which increased her feeling of bewilderment. 'If you would like to join me?'

'I . . .' She felt like weeping and couldn't meet his eyes. Was he completely barmy? Even his look seemed to contaminate her. She spoke very quietly. 'No – no, thank you.'

'I see.' He became curt. 'Are you dining with Paul Louth?'

Mercy nodded. She knew Ruby was watching them.

There was a pause, then he said, 'I could order you.'

She couldn't look up. She just stared at the floor in silence.

'Very well then,' he said savagely. 'I'm glad to know you've made such a fine friend.'

Mercy watched him stride away. What have I done? she wondered. Everything felt desolate, as if nothing good could come of anything now.

She moved over quickly and picked up Stevie's little coat to go outside. She didn't want to be with anyone today.

James Adair found himself pacing the promenade deck alone for the umpteenth time of the voyage.

When he thought of the night before, need stirred in him again, the relentless, imprisoning gnaw of it. Yet that piercing mixture of agony and shame he had seen in Mercy! She who had always been so clear-eyed, sunny-faced, looked so drained this morning, was unable even to meet his eyes.

He slammed his fist down on the side. Damn her! She'd wanted him all right last night, hadn't she? It had been – he smiled grimly – extraordinary. Not just the satisfying of his desire but the fulfilment so longed for by his hungering soul. So what the hell was the matter with the girl, giving him those hangdog, hostile looks?

He turned, touching his hat to a couple walking towards him. Very queer fish, women, that was the truth of it. All he knew was that it was right, what had happened. Intended. It was an experience that had burnt through his life, brief, illuminated. And it had had to happen here. At home it could never be. Not in his real, morally confined life. This period on the water was his special gift from life, his epiphany . . .

A surge of panic interrupted this lofty thought. He hadn't made her promise not to say anything to Margaret! Of course she wouldn't, surely – how could she? It would cost her her living, she must see that! But he knew he must say it. 'You mustn't say a word to Margaret, you know, Mercy. You do know what would happen, don't you?'

He felt euphoric again suddenly. The supple loveliness of her moved in his mind's eye, still his, for a short time yet, left to enjoy.

'Are you all right?'

Paul looked closely at her across the table, dishes of tomato soup and crumbled bread on plates between them. Mercy could barely eat.

'Yes. 'Course I am,' she said dully.

'You look tired,' he said, so kindly that her eyes filled with tears which had waited all day to be shed.

'Oh dear.' Paul sounded really concerned. 'Mercy what is it?'

'Nothing – honest.' She wiped her eyes and forced a smile. 'It's just tiredness. Stevie was restless last night, sorry. Look.' She tried to divert him, holding out her arm. 'The oil all came out.'

It was almost true. The mark was hard to detect now amid the soft-edged pattern of leaves.

As they ate she tried to pull herself together. Nervously she asked Paul questions about his day, trying to be jolly, joking about Stanley who was of course dining in first class.

'And did Mr Adair want you to dine first class tonight?' Paul teased.

Mercy felt herself freeze. 'Yes.' She kept her eyes on her plate. 'I said I'd rather be with you.' She spoke so fiercely that Paul frowned for a moment.

'He's tolerant.'

'Yes.' She was only just short of snapping at him.

'I thought you liked him.'

'What d'you mean?' She cursed herself for sounding so alarmed.

'I don't mean anything! I just thought he was a kind employer. Mercy, what is the matter tonight?'

'Nothing.' Nothing, except that everything, everything was spoilt and dirty.

They didn't find the Petrowkis that evening. Mercy was disappointed. She was longing to be alone with Paul yet dreading it at the same time, afraid. There may be only one night left after this, she thought, as they went up on deck. And then he'll be gone.

'Let's stay out all night,' she said. Nothing would induce her to return to that terrible room early tonight.

Paul gave his chuckle. 'What, and have them find us frozen to death in the morning?'

I shouldn't mind if I was with you, she thought.

The future, the idea of going on without him, returning with the Adairs, was utterly desolate. She found herself unable to joke any longer and fell silent.

They walked along the boat deck, the lifeboats lined up between them and the sea. It was blowing hard tonight and Mercy and Paul both took their hats off for fear of losing them.

'Let's sit here!' Paul said. A bench facing the stern of the ship offered a small respite from the buffeting. They had to sit close to hear each other speak.

'Reminds me, when I come up here, of going to France.'

Mercy looked round at him. Their faces were in the shadows. She was relieved to hear him talk. She desperately wanted things to be right between them. Here, in the darkness, she willed herself to think of nothing but Paul, so that these moments were the only ones that mattered, unspoilt by James Adair.

'D'you think about the War a lot?'

'Yes – even though I try not to. It never leaves you.'

'Paul,' she said, suddenly, 'please don't ever leave me.'

For a second he was still. Then with a fierce motion he pulled her to him, almost knocking the breath out of her, and she was pressed into his arms, her head resting under his chin. She felt his trembling, the hard beat of his heart.

'I love you.' She knew somehow she must speak first. 'I love you, Paul.'

Afraid, she looked up. But everything she needed to see was there. The emotion in his face overwhelmed her.

'Mercy—' – his eyes were serious – 'I was afraid that—'

'What?'

'That I felt too much, that you couldn't possibly feel the same, not so soon. I've become so used to being alone – I mean, deeply alone, within myself. I had begun to think this was how it would always be. But you just came and . . . you make me feel complete – more human. As if with you is the only place I fit.'

'Yes,' she said, hearing him describe her own feeling. 'Sort of coming home. I've never had a home before – not a proper one.' She began to cry suddenly, brokenly. Paul rocked her, stroking her.

'Perhaps with each other is the only way we can fit. I don't know how – we'll work out a way somehow.'

When she had calmed a little, his face moved down to hers and their lips met, warm, searching, arms holding each other with such tender force. Mercy could hear a pounding in her ears as if her blood and the sea were one. She felt Paul's frail frame in her arms, his eyes closed, face intent. She wanted to stay in this moment for ever, where no other thoughts and feelings, no other person could intervene.

He rested his cheek against the top of her head and gave a huge sigh of joy and relief. She reached up and stroked his face.

'You're too gentle to fight, Paul. Too kind.'

'No.' His voice was profoundly sad. 'No – I'm not. That's the worst of it. It'd be good if we were all too gentle to fight. Mercy—'

She turned her face up to him.

'That's better.' He cupped her cheeks in his hands, wiping her tears away with his thumbs. 'You're so, so lovely . . . every time I see you I feel weak just looking at you.'

She smiled. 'Do you? I couldn't tell.'

For a few seconds their lips met in quick, playful kisses, then at length, urgent, passionate, the strength of their feeling expressed wordlessly.

Later they walked together again, arms wrapped round each other. They strolled back and forth, along the gently rolling deck, amid all the noises of the ship. There was a half moon tonight, as if it had been rubbed away as in a child's drawing. Nothing else mattered to Mercy, not the coldness of her hands and feet, nor James Adair or even Stevie. The only important things were Paul and what the two of them felt for each other.

He stopped her in the middle of the deserted promenade and took her in his arms again, smiling joyfully into her face.

'You look happy,' she said.

'Happy isn't even an adequate word.'

'Paul.' Her face became painfully anxious. 'Am I good enough for you? I don't feel ... you know, I've done things I'm ashamed of. I'm not ...' The reality of last night crashed back in on her. It was so raw, recent. I'm not what you think, I'm spoilt, she wanted to tell him. I'm not worthy of you.

'A good enough person?' His tone verged on anger. 'How can you ask me that? You're the only person. You've made me feel whole again – I can't get near anyone else. Nobody. But with you everything's different, I love you Mercy, more than I thought I'd ever be capable of loving anyone again.'

'But I'm not good,' she insisted. She couldn't look at him. However much she wanted to put it out of her mind, the stain of James Adair was on her. Her face burned with shame.

Paul shook her lightly to make her look up. 'Mercy,' he said gently. 'Don't think like this, please. Whatever could you have done that's so bad? Isn't it that things have been done to you? And perhaps you should think about whether I'm good enough for you. I've killed other men. Not perhaps, but certainly. I've seen men fall under my fire and that's the truth. Think of that and ask yourself if I'm worthy of you.'

'But—' She was glad he couldn't see the red in her cheeks. She had had her innocence taken from her.

'What is it?'

She looked into his kind, loving eyes. 'Nothing.'

'Look, what difference does anything make here – where we've come from, what we've done or been? I told you, we're all just people. All the same fundamentally. That's all that matters.'

She gave in, falling into his arms. 'I love you so, so much. This is the happiest I can remember being ever!'

'Yes.' He kissed her eyelids, nose, lips. 'Me too.'

They stayed out very late, as late as Mercy could possibly waylay him, though that took very little effort. Neither of them wanted to let the other go. When they finally returned inside their hands were stiff with cold, cheeks raw from the wind. They talked and touched, kissed, warmed each other for hours. Time fled past.

Mercy felt her insides turn with apprehension. Stevie! She had completely forgotten about him! But when she reached the door of her room all was quiet.

'It's nearly twelve fifteen!' Paul said.

'Marvellous nanny, I am.' Mercy rolled her eyes. 'Still, it sounds as if there's been nothing wrong.'

'I should have reminded you.' He rested his hands on her shoulders. 'On a night like tonight though, it's hardly surprising we forgot.' Mercy looked up, loving his smile, his wide mouth, loved every atom of him. She reached up to kiss him and they held each other again.

'Goodnight,' she said. 'I'm so happy, Paul.'

'And me. I can't believe how much.' He squeezed her tight, then released her. 'Tomorrow night?'

'How can you even ask!' She poked him, teasing. 'I wish it was now.'

He went to his door and she watched him. They blew each other a kiss. He waved before he closed his door.

Mercy turned to go inside and saw James Adair moving fast down the corridor towards her room.

In panic she rushed inside and shut the door, locked it, and stood inside, panting loudly, her heart racing.

In a moment she heard his knock.

No! She was trembling. It was so late – surely he hadn't been waiting, watching them even? She stood with a fist clenched to her lips. A terrible helplessness washed over her. What could she do? He was her employer. If she didn't do as he asked could he refuse to let her back on the ship for the return voyage? Leave her stranded? She could run out and shout for help, but then everyone would know – Paul would know. She was trapped. Unless she just ignored him – perhaps he would be shamed into going away.

Another, sharper knock followed.

'I need to see my son,' he said, with icy politeness. 'Open the door, please, Mercy.'

Eventually she opened it a crack, starting violently at the sight of him even though she had known he was there.

'What's the matter?' He sounded livid, pushed his way in straight away. 'Expecting a knock from someone else?'

'No.' She could barely speak. She was shaking all over. At least she was fully clothed. She couldn't be said to be offering temptation . . . If only she'd told Paul, if only – but how could she have done? James pushed her out of the way and closed the door, standing against it.

'Please – no,' she implored him. 'Stevie's not really asleep. Not in front of your son. It's so late, and . . .'

'And?' The chillness of his voice gave her no clue to the reservoir of pent-up emotion which had built in him all evening, as the night grew later, knowing she was with Paul. 'What's the matter, my dear? I thought we'd come to an agreement?'

'What? What agreement?' What was he saying?

He went and stood over Stevie, half-whispering so as not to disturb him.

'Just for the voyage, we shall enjoy this little arrangement together. You won't say a word to Margaret because if you do, when we reach England you'll be without employment or references. When we get home, we shall resume life as it was and I shall not come to you again.'

She could see his high colour, knew he'd been drinking and in some quantity.

'Does that sound fair?'

'Fair?' she asked faintly. 'How can it be fair when you ain't – aren't – giving me any choice?'

'Oh, I think you have a choice, Mercy. You could just go now, out of here. Go on – go.'

She looked desperately at the door. 'Should I spend the night outside then?'

'If you consider being with me a worse option, then yes.' He stepped towards her as she was still wildly eyeing the door, and gave a heavy sigh. 'It's a torment to me, seeing you look at me like that, knowing you've been with him all evening.'

'Mr Adair—'

'James, for heaven's sake!'

'I'm in love with Paul Louth!' she gabbled. 'And he loves me. I don't want this. You're spoiling everything. It's wrong of you—'

James actually flung his head back and laughed loudly. Mercy looked across at Stevie, praying he would wake, but there was no sound from him.

'Paul Louth – you can be sure – wants just the same from you as I do, my dear. That's students for you. Anyhow – if that's what he wants at least I can give you some practice!'

He put his hands on her shoulders with a kind of confidence which said he owned her. Hatred and fury surged inside her. She collected saliva in her mouth and spat it into his face, her eyes narrowed with loathing.

'You don't deserve your wife. She's kind and sweet and a lady. But you – you may be a gentleman on the outside, but underneath you're just filth, worse than filth.'

Slowly, as if in a daze, James wiped her spittle from his nose and cheek.

'I see.' His voice was so cold with fury, Mercy felt herself go rigid with fear. 'So it's going to be different today is it, angel?'

He was on to her before she stood a chance of moving, tearing at her, hurling her back on the bed, half winding her. His face was a grotesque mixture of lust and fury. He pulled her legs in the air and stripped her as she tried to kick at him.

'Stevie – Stevie, wake up!' she shrieked. 'Look what your daddy's doing. This'll make you proud of him, won't it?'

'Shut up.' James's red face loomed close to her. He was holding her down with one hand, unbuttoning himself frantically with the other. 'Just shut your mouth.'

He lunged into her, face straining. 'That's it – now I'll have you . . .'

Mercy lay under him, squeezing her eyes closed. She was dry-eyed with loathing and disgust. Hold tight until he's finished, she thought. Just hold on and it'll be over and he's never, ever going to do this again ... Over and over she repeated it in her mind to his lunging rhythm: never, never, never ...

He rolled off her, leaving her curled up, wet with his sweat and juices and, at last, with her own tears pouring from her in a torrent of shame. He enclosed his sticky body in his clothes, disgust and horror settling on him like extra garments. He looked down at the pitiful little body on the bed.

What had happened to his glorious ideals of their love, his fantasy of her gratitude and devotion? She was lying there, naked and vulnerable, curled up with her hands over her eyes, unable even to bear looking at him.

He let himself out of her room without a word and walked disconsolately back to his own. What a fool he was! A naive, ridiculous idiot, seeking paradise between the thighs of a servant like many another boorish master! That his behaviour fell into the realms of such a run-of-the-mill cliché only increased his despair.

All of it was finished, he knew. He would avoid her from now on – in America, once he was busy with Kesler this would be easy. And once they were back in England she would have to be moved on. He couldn't have her there, knowing, reminding. And Margaret – the thought of her knowing how he had behaved, he who always saw himself as superior to her! Oh, the humiliation! The thought was too appalling to contemplate.

He did not think though, that she would tell Margaret. He tried to rally himself. Why should he let her have this power over him? Who was she, anyway? A servant, dross from the workhouse, a nobody! He should just forget it.

But his last sight of her would not leave his mind, her utter dejection as she lay there on her bed. He burned now with contempt, with remorse for his grotesque behaviour. And he was weighed down by sadness – for his loss of innocence: for her bitter tears.

Chapter Thirty-Four

'This is our last night,' she said to Paul the next evening with a heavy sigh. She was longing to leave the ship: her room now filled her with abhorrence. What had happened in there with James Adair could not be undone. He had shamed and abused her, and while she was on the ship she could never get away from the fact. Once off the ship it would be over. Finished. James Adair's madness was something conjured by the sea.

But she was also afraid that with the landfall something else would evaporate: the magic wonder of Paul loving her. She was afraid he would see her with new, more critical eyes. She knew she would love him whatever.

They sat after dinner in the second-class saloon. First class and James Adair felt like another existence. Raw and fresh as his forced visits to her were, Mercy had grown used to pushing things she couldn't bear to think about into the darkest pockets of her mind. She didn't want any sadness or pain to colour her time with Paul.

They talked of what Paul was to do next.

'I'll be on the return voyage of course. The next main thing will be to look for a job.'

'On a ship?'

'Oh no – not actually on a ship. I'm best at design, I think, so it could be marine engineering – I'll have to see what opportunities there are. So – the future's rather uncertain. Shall you mind that?'

Mercy's heart stepped up its pace. He was including her in his future!

'No! All I'd mind is not being able to be with you.'

Paul laid his hand gently on hers. 'You're so sweet and trusting. But it may take a little time before I have a living.'

Mercy looked up earnestly at him. 'Paul – knowing that I've got you – somewhere – that we love one another . . . They're the things that matter most. The only things.'

Eventually, as usual, they went outside, where a quietness overcame them both. It was a clearer night than the three before, the wind gentler, and they kept their hats on, Paul's misshapen trilby, Mercy's hat with the brim. Paul smoked a cigarette.

After a while, Paul said, 'I wonder where we'll be in a year.'

'Don't!' Mercy shuddered.

'What's the matter?'

'I don't like talking like that.'

He stamped the cigarette out and put his arm round her shoulders, pulling her close, then gently removed her hat, freeing the pin and pushing it carefully through the brim to keep it safe. He kissed her hair. Mercy closed her eyes and leant against him.

'All I want', Paul said softly, 'is to look after you. Care for you. It's all that matters. Both of us seem to be so alone in the world.'

She opened her eyes and wrapped her arms round his neck, felt his round her. He was still holding her hat.

'Do you really love me?' she asked urgently. 'Really?'

'Of course. More than I can say.' He went to kiss her but she held back.

'You could forgive me – anything?'

'Mercy.' He stroked her face. 'Why do you feel so bad and unworthy? Of course, my love, anything.'

She held him tight, kissed him, overwhelmed by his care and trust.

'Listen,' he said after a time. 'You can hear the music even better tonight. Can you dance?'

'Me? No!'

He laughed. 'No, nor me. But let's do it anyway!'

He laid her hat on a chair and, oblivious of two men pacing the deck, they grasped each other awkwardly. Mercy couldn't forget being hauled around the dance floor by James Adair. Paul held out his left hand and Mercy placed her right hand in it, looking uncertainly into his eyes.

They started off swaying and shuffling, each trying to move in different directions and stumbling over the other's feet. By trial and error they made up their own half-galloping, half-twirling dance up and down the deck until Mercy was panting and whooping with joy. Ignoring the music, they linked hands and spun round and round, counterbalancing each other, until the windows, cables, funnels, sky, became a spinning circle of lines and blurred light.

'Stop – my head's gone all funny!' she begged.

Laughing like children, they held and steadied each other, Paul's back resting against the side of one of the lifeboats. When their laughter faded it was replaced in his face by a solemn, hungry expression. He took her cheeks between his warm palms, gently stroking her face and looking at her with such a longing intensity that she felt awed.

'I love you,' she said, afraid for a second.

'I never thought . . .' He paused for a second. 'I never thought I should ever feel anything this strongly.'

She looked into his face and saw her whole world in front of her. For a long time they stood in each other's arms on the deck of the *Mauretania*, a tiny island of love and hopefulness in a dark, hurtful world.

Much later, dizzy with happiness from Paul's embraces, she lay in her room.

'I don't want to go back in,' she'd said. 'I want to stay out all night.'

Paul squeezed her shoulders. 'Anyone'd think that room was haunted.'

Mercy gave a pained frown in the darkness. 'It is.'

If James Adair came tonight, he could knock the door down before she opened it. He could do no worse to her than he had already done.

But the night was undisturbed. He didn't come. She slept.

She was woken by knocking, gentle, then louder and more insistent.

She could tell by the sound that it wasn't James Adair.

'Mercy?' Paul hissed as she opened the door a crack. 'We're coming in. You can see land. Come up on deck!'

'What time is it?' She felt disorientated.

'Only seven – will you come?'

She wouldn't miss it for anything. 'But I'll have to bring Stevie . . .'

She dressed herself hurriedly, then the sleepy boy, wrapping him warmly. Paul waited for them outside.

'Let me take him,' Paul offered. 'He's such a weight for you.'

Stevie went to Paul without protest, and sat quiet and

wide-eyed as they went up on deck. Mercy followed, smiling at the sight of Stevie's little hand draped over Paul's shoulder.

It was chilly and damp, the early morning sky rubbed with smudges of darker cloud. Mercy felt the air stinging her nose. There were already a number of people up on deck, all looking in the same direction, some raising a hand to their brows as if better to focus their vision.

Paul led Mercy to a space where they could see. And there it was, already closer than she had expected, there, with sea all around her, the statue on her plinth in the mouth of New York harbour. From here she still looked grey and indistinct. Beyond her they could just see little puffs of steam from boats further into the harbour.

'Lady Liberty,' Paul said.

'Is that what it is?'

'The Statue of Liberty. She's holding up a torch for freedom.'

The end of his sentence was lost in a massive blast of sound from the *Mauretania*, as if in salute, as she rode majestically into the harbour.

'Look,' Mercy said. 'Look at that.'

It was as if they'd entered a fairy tale. A magical, unpredictable land was rising out of the sea to greet her. Her stomach fluttered with expectation. Between the shifting water and pale sky, the uneven line of buildings, high, pointed towers, square, blockish constructions, too distant as yet to see their detail, some tall, some squat, seemed flat and melded together from here as if in a painting, with its unique proportion and beauty. Mercy narrowed her eyes, trying to see it more clearly.

'It's hard to imagine there are streets and people behind there, isn't it?' Paul said.

'It looks lovely.' Mercy leant her head against his

shoulder. His old coat felt soft and worn. 'Let's stay here, shall we? Just live in America and never come back.'

Everything felt different now land was in sight. There was a new purposefulness in the air after the languor of the crossing. She and Paul would soon have to part: he was wanted at work downstairs.

'But we shall see each other,' he said as they climbed down from the deck. 'I'll make sure of that. You're staying with this Mr Kesler, aren't you?'

Mercy could not hide the dread his words aroused in her. She would have to live in the same house as Mr Adair. She wouldn't be able to avoid him as easily as she had done on the ship. A wave of terrible emotion passed through her as land drew closer.

'I don't know where. I'll ask Mrs Adair to write the address for you and put it under your door,' she said, subdued.

'Cheer up.' Paul squeezed her hand. 'Things'll work out. Have faith.'

'Oh,' Mercy said wanly. 'Yes. I s'pose.'

'You know,' we ought to go and say goodbye to the Petrowskis! They won't be going the same way as us.'

'Won't they? Why not?'

'They take all the steerage immigrants over to Ellis Island to be processed, I gather. To see if they're going to be allowed in.'

'You don't really think they won't be allowed to stay?'

'It's possible. They do turn people away. But they must have a good chance.'

They went down to third class, Mercy carrying Stevie. The Petrowskis were, as ever, pleased to see them, but enormous anxiety now showed in their faces. They looked as if they'd been too worried to sleep. Yola was tearful. She was sitting in the overcrowded, smoky third-class saloon holding Peschka, a pitiful little bundle of belongings tied in a shawl, resting at her feet. She grasped Mercy's hand and pulled her down beside her, with Stevie on her lap. Mercy could see the mingled hope and desperation in her eyes. She squeezed Yola's hand, kissed it. Tomek and Paul were shaking hands, hugging. Tomek showed Paul his precious slip of paper again.

Yola started talking in agitation, the Polish words cascading from her lips.

'Oh Yola, I wish I understood you better,' Mercy said, trying to show with her own eyes all she hoped and prayed for this new little family. She reached over and stroked Peschka's forehead. Yola looked down at the baby, pride, love, fear all clear in her eyes.

'Yola,' Mercy said, 'I wish you and Tomek and Peschka all the luck in the world. I hope you find your family and everything goes well for you.'

She suddenly knew a way to make Yola understand all she hoped for them. Awkwardly, touching her fingers first to her forehead, she made the sign of the cross. Yola flung her arms round her and they held each other in a tight embrace.

On the way upstairs, Mercy burst into tears in earnest, all her gathered emotions coming to the surface.

Paul gently touched her shoulder. 'Don't worry, my love. They have a good chance, and so do we.'

They had to part. Even though she hoped it would not be for long, Mercy felt her heart was being torn out. She looked up at him with huge, sad eyes.

'I love you, Paul.'

'I love you,' he said, kissing her. 'Don't worry.'

*

Margaret Adair was still very weak and groggy.

'I'm sure I shall feel better just for being off this ship,' she said. Mercy helped her wash and clothe herself.

They all sat in silence together in the first-class saloon, waiting to disembark. James Adair was very distant, businesslike. Just once, Mercy felt his gaze on her, but when she looked at him he immediately turned away. In that second, Mercy was chilled by the disgust she saw in his expression. The same emotion, and more, had showed itself in her own.

She wanted passionately at that moment to be away from them both. Now she had met Paul she could only feel diminished by them. To them she was a servant – Margaret was exceptionally kind, it was true, but he had shown what he thought of her. She was something to be used, like an old rag, then thrown away. And both of them were deceiving Margaret. Mercy sat full of shame and revulsion. But here, now, thousands of miles from home, she could do nothing. Margaret needed her to care for Stevie more than ever before.

'I don't think I'm going to be able to walk far, I'm afraid.' Margaret's voice was thin and feeble. She had visibly lost weight during the voyage, eating very little and then not keeping it down.

'You won't need to walk. Kesler said he'd send a car.' James spoke so abruptly he almost snapped at her. He picked Stevie up and went to stand by the window, making a show of talking to his son. Showing what a marvellous father he is, Mercy thought savagely.

'Oh dear,' Margaret put her hand to her head in distress. 'I do feel so ill. And I feel such a fool letting James down like this, but really I can't help it. And he's so angry and tense – look at him. I know it's my fault.'

No, Mercy wanted to assure her. You haven't let him down. It's the two of us who have let you down, and far, far more badly than you know.

'Stay with me, Mercy,' Margaret implored. 'I'll be able to bear it all if you're with me.'

'' Course I will.' Mercy squeezed her arm. 'Where else would I be going?'

'But you must see him while he's here, my dear.' Mercy had asked her earlier for Kesler's address. 'That young Mr Louth. I insist. I want you to have a happy time, Mercy. Some freedom. You'll only be young once.'

Kesler's driver was a talkative fellow with a stocky body, a jauntily angled Homburg and a thick accent Mercy couldn't at first identify.

'A warm welcome to the United States of America,' he said, after James had spotted him among the throng outside the Battery, holding a piece of card which had, ADAIRS FROM ENGLAND printed on it. He introduced himself as Tommy O'Sullivan, shaking their hands with his huge, brawny one.

James said curtly, 'Do we have far to go?'

Margaret had only just endured the formalities of arrival.

'No, sir,' Tommy O'Sullivan said, not seeming to notice James's rudeness. 'Not far at all. Well, hello there little fella!' His stubbly cheeks shifted into a wide smile at Stevie. 'We'll have to find you some candy when we get on home.'

The road was busy, but Tommy had managed to park the car remarkably close.

'Nice machine Kesler's got there,' James said, thawing a little at the sight of the stylish black motor car.

'Yes, sir,' Tommy said. 'Ford T – nothing but the best for Mr Kesler.'

Between them they helped Margaret into the back seat and she sank into it gratefully, closing her eyes. Tommy stowed their bags. Mercy sat Stevie between herself and Margaret, and James removed his hat and took his seat at the front. He did not turn round.

Mercy stared at the back of his head. He sat very stiff and upright. Beside Tommy O'Sullivan's easy lounge at the wheel he looked rather foolish. Mercy could see his pink flesh glistening through his sandy-coloured hair. The thought came to her of his head close to hers, the rasping cheeks, his heaviness on top of her as he strained into her. A horrible blush spread all over her body.

I wish you didn't exist, she thought. That I'd never met you. She sensed he was feeling the same.

As they left the Battery at New York's tip, Tommy O'Sullivan nudged the Ford through the cars, carriages and streetcars of Manhattan with some aplomb.

'Mr Kesler says I'm to show you a thing or two on the way up,' he said, his hairy hands expertly manoeuvring the wheel.

He gave a running commentary on the journey, turning his head as if he was addressing Mercy, had picked her out. She felt easy with him, as if there was a bond between them. They were both servants of a sort. She listened, craning her neck to see the things he was talking about.

'We got the tallest buildings in the world here in New York. Space, you see – saves space. Beautiful, aren't they?'

And they were, dizzily tall, stately skyscrapers crammed in between the other buildings, dwarfing the bustle of life on the streets below.

'This your first time here?' Tommy jerked his head round to look at her.

Mercy was so excited, so busy trying to take in all the new impressions, she almost didn't reply.

'Yes,' she said, and at the same time James replied, 'It is, yes,' sounding as if he didn't like to admit it.

'If you look out this side—' – he jerked his head to the right – 'that's the East River. This here's Manhattan Bridge.'

He stopped at a junction with the second bridge. Traffic wormed across its gigantic, metal span. The car turned into a busy mesh of streets and Mercy was already beginning to feel drunk on all these new sights and sounds. She found herself wondering what Paul was doing. The thought of him sent an excited rush of feeling through her.

Paul, I love you, she thought. She missed him, ached to see him. Would he find her? Would he come?

Names spilled from Tommy O'Sullivan's lips: Park Avenue, Grand Central Terminal, and then the park moved past their windows to the right. They were still passing it when they turned into a side street and Tommy drew the car up outside a gracious brown-stone dwelling.

'So – here's home,' he said cheerfully, opening the car door. 'Mr Kesler's waiting for you.'

As he spoke the front door opened and a rather short, stout man with ruddy cheeks and spectacles, wearing a tight brown suit, bounced down the steps, beaming.

'James, my dear friend!' He was shaking James's hand through the window before he had even had a chance to get out. Mercy saw James Adair relax visibly, and felt herself do the same, for how could you not in the cheerful face of William Kesler?

'My wife Margaret ...' James managed to extricate himself from the car and step round to her door. 'I'm afraid she is feeling rather unwell.'

Margaret roused herself, managing to sit up and give a strained smile. Mercy climbed out, lifting Stevie into her arms.

'Oh – and your beautiful son!' Kesler enthused. 'My children will be so pleased. You must come and meet Gerder, my wife – ah, here she is! Gerder, come on down!'

Gerder Kesler was a slight, dignified woman, also not grand in height. She came shyly towards them and Mercy felt immediate liking for her. She was relieved. The personality of the woman of the house always seemed to be what made it homely and welcoming or not. Mrs Kesler wore simple, rather old-fashioned clothes – a grey skirt which reached almost to her ankles and a white blouse embroidered with small blue flowers. Her voice was soft and sweet, the American accent gentle and very different from Tommy O'Sullivan's.

'We'd like to welcome you most warmly to our home,' she said smiling.

'Mrs Adair needs some assistance.' Kesler nodded meaningfully at his wife, who peered into the car.

'Oh my dear,' she said. 'What a terrible ordeal for you. We must take you indoors and make sure you are made very, very comfortable.'

At hearing the wonderful kindness in her tone, Margaret Adair covered her face with her hands and began to sob.

Chapter Thirty-Five

The Keslers' was an elegant, orderly home, every well-upholstered chair in its exact place, Kesler's collection of china all perfectly dusted on shelves and in a glass cabinet, shining mirrors, and a smell of polish as soon as they walked through the door. Gerder Kesler was its deceptively soft-spoken, efficient organizer.

They had four children: Konrad, fifteen, Lise, twelve and Karl, eight, who were all at school, and little Andreas who was five and was looked after by Helga, a pale, plain woman in her twenties. She barely raised a smile at Mercy, but as soon as she saw Stevie, her face shone with happiness.

'A baby!' she cried, in a strange, guttural voice. 'Oh – let him come to me, won't you? Andreas is getting such a big boy now – he'll soon be away to school!'

To Mercy's surprise, as personally she thought Helga a wee bit odd, Stevie went to her straight away with absolute trust.

Margaret Adair wept even more at the sight of the immaculately made bed in her room, the piles of pillows encased in stiff, white linen. Gerder Kesler was all concern, and Margaret immediately confided in her the nature of the problem.

'I shall feel better later, I feel sure of it,' she said, once she was lying down. 'I just need some time to recover . . . Mercy—' – She reached her hand out and Mercy took it

– 'Paul Louth asked my permission to see you during the days the ship is in port . . .'

Mercy waited, nervously.

'Is that what you'd like?'

'Oh yes,' she replied fervently. 'Yes please, if that's . . .'

Margaret looked at Gerder. 'Mercy is my very special friend as well as Steven's nanny. Owing to my illness on the voyage she has been working very hard. I wonder if Helga would mind . . . ? For a day or two?'

Gerder smiled at Mercy. 'You could see, I think, how delighted Helga would be! She's a simple girl, but you'll find she is nothing but kindness and she has a rare gift with small children. So please, Mercy, feel relaxed here. I can see—' – she sat down on the end of the bed with a graceful movement – 'that Margaret and I are going to be firm friends. And I don't suppose we'll be seeing very much of the men, do you?' She laughed softly.

Margaret squeezed Mercy's hand and then let go. A spasm of nausea passed across her face. 'There you are – and you deserve some time to yourself.'

'Oh, thank you!' Mercy went to find Helga, her heart singing.

As soon as James Adair stepped into the Keslers' house a huge tide of relief swept through him. His emotions during the voyage had reached such extremes of agony, desire, relief and shame that his life had felt like a shattered glass, the pieces distressingly scattered and misplaced. Quite apart from what had taken place with Mercy, Margaret's sickness had confined him. He had been reduced, on the ship, to a kind of passive, semi-domestic situation. But he could reassemble himself here with Kesler, step back into the comforting, manly world of work.

413

He dined with the Keslers that night at an oval, rose-wood table, a silver candelabra unlit at the centre. To his relief he found that Mercy was expected to eat with Helga and the other servants. He enjoyed the simple but flavour-some meal of soup and beef and fruit tart, and questioned Kesler about the ornate pieces of china he saw arranged round the room.

Once Gerder had excused herself, he and Kesler spent the evening discussing business. Kesler, ruddy-cheeked, offered him brandy and a cigar, and the two of them sat back into slippery leather chairs so large they looked as if they might swallow them up.

'What I propose', Kesler said, resting one plump leg on the other and blowing smoke towards the ceiling, 'is that we take a few days here in New York City. After that we can go on down to Rochester and I'll show you the new place. It's coming on. Another couple of months and I'd say we'll be on the move. But I'm glad for you to visit now. Of course, New York City has far more to offer a visitor.'

James appreciated Kesler's directness and enthusiasm. He gave off an air of anything being possible. 'That all sounds very satisfactory to me.'

'So—' – Kesler leant forward – 'while you're here – let's sit down and design the greatest damn racing cycle the world has ever seen. Agreed?'

James blew out the smoke from his cigar and grinned, suddenly boyish. 'Agreed.'

Retiring to bed that night, James was full of drive and excitement from his conversation with Kesler. After the afternoon's rest and all this enthusiastic talk the last thing he wanted was sleep. He'd like to have been out on the town, dancing, laughing, throwing off the constraints of his life again. He was restless, amorous.

Very quietly he opened the door of his room. Margaret was awake, to his surprise, watching him as he stepped close to the bed.

She wrinkled her nose. 'Goodness, you smell of cigars.'

'Kesler's a generous man.'

'You had a good evening then, darling?'

'I did!' He spoke with rather overdone enthusiasm. 'He really is rather marvellous. And are you feeling better?'

She thought about it. 'I'm not sure how permanently, but yes, at this moment I don't feel too bad.'

He could feel her eyes on his as he undressed for bed. Then they lay together, in a rare, companionable position, each on the left side, he wrapped round the back of her.

'I've given Mercy permission to spend some time with Paul Louth,' Margaret murmured.

His jealous, at odds feeling returned. 'What, go gadding off? But she's a servant for goodness sake. And you need her more than ever . . .'

'Nonsense. Helga, that pale creature downstairs, will take over Stevie. Mercy's in love. Haven't you noticed? But then no, I don't suppose you have!'

He was silent. Of course he had noticed. He felt relieved, in some way vindicated. He nuzzled Margaret's neck. Her rounded, soft body pressed against him made him harden with desire.

'Won't she need a chaperone?' he murmured.

Margaret elbowed him playfully. 'Don't be such an old fuddy-duddy. And anyway, Paul seems very nice and responsible to me. She arched herself against him, surprising him with her sudden, slightly wanton energy.

He reached round for her lolling breasts, sculpting

them into peaks while she squirmed. He let out a groan of relief and pleasure. Kissing her hair he slid up into her, feeling her, moist, taut, enclosing him. In a fraction of a moment, before thought ceased his mind said: at last, something proper, something right.

The next morning Mercy was sitting restlessly with Helga, Stevie and young Andreas Kesler in the nursery when the doorbell rang. Helga, oblivious to the effect this was having on Mercy, continued to chatter on.

Mercy found she was holding her breath and wishing Helga would do the same. She strained to hear the voices downstairs. Her heart was racing. Surely – she just caught the sound of it – that was Paul? A moment later she heard footsteps in the passage and Gerder Kesler appeared smiling at the door, her spectacles catching the light from the window.

'Your friend is here, Mercy dear.'

'Oh – thank you!' Mercy scrambled to her feet in confusion. Gerder Kesler was even more informal than Margaret and barely treated her like a servant at all. 'You shouldn't have had to come . . .'

'Not at all.' She smiled at the obvious elation on Mercy's face. 'I'm only sorry the weather's so inclement for you.'

'Oh . . . well,' Mercy said. Weather? What did weather matter! 'Never mind.' She hesitated, awaiting permission of some sort.

'It's all right, dear, you may go. Helga is perfectly fine looking after little Steven.'

Mercy kissed Stevie's cheek hurriedly with a 'Be a good boy now, won't you?' smiled gratefully at Helga and dashed for her hat and coat.

He was waiting for her in the hall and the sight of him, slightly dishevelled-looking as ever, filled her with immense tenderness and joy. He was real! He had come for her!

'Hello,' he said, with a shyness that suggested he, too, might be afraid she'd changed her mind.

'They're letting me off – the days you're here. Isn't it marvellous?' she whispered.

Paul's face fell a fraction as he picked up his sodden umbrella from the stand behind the door. They went out into the rain and he opened it and held it over her. 'The thing is – I'm afraid I've only got two days.' He sounded apologetic. 'They want me back on board the day after tomorrow.'

Mercy took his arm and squeezed it. 'Two whole days though!'

He looked down at her fondly, relieved. 'Yes! Let's make the most of it.'

'How about saying hello properly then?'

'What – here?' He looked round the respectable Upper West Side street.

'No one knows who we are, do they? And anyway, I thought you didn't care about what people think.' She felt euphoric in the rain in this great, exciting city.

Laughing, he scooped her closer to him and their lips met, finding each other hungrily.

Paul rested his forehead against hers for a moment and gave a loud sigh of happiness. 'Everything feels right again as soon as I see you. I can somehow make sense of things. See a point to it all.'

Mercy took his face in her hands. 'I've missed you' – kiss – 'missed you' – kiss – 'missed you!'

They set off with more purpose, arms linked, elated at simply being together, and further intoxicated at the thought of this place to explore freely.

The rain fell steadily, the sound of it all round them. They walked the distance of a few blocks through Riverside Park, smelling the pungent scent of wet spring flowers and hearing the doleful blast from the hooters of steam boats chugging along the brown water of the Hudson. Then they turned east again. Paul had a plan of the city which he opened while Mercy held the umbrella.

'Let's come back through Central Park later, shall we? It'll be interesting to look at more of the streets.' He glanced down at her. 'Are you all right? We're going to get soaking wet.'

Her pigeon grey eyes beamed back at him from under her blue hat. 'I don't care!'

They walked on, stopping to admire grand buildings, talking, exclaiming, swerving round the puddles which were forming everywhere.

'I tell you what though.' He stopped abruptly as they made their way towards Fifth Avenue. 'I think I can remember the address – shall we go and see if we can find the Petrowskis?'

Chapter Thirty-Six

Paul was certain that Tomek's scrap of paper had said Broome Street. When they reached the Lower East Side, they found themselves in streets edged by high, dingy tenements between which streetcars rattled and cars hooted. The buildings were astonishingly shabby with shutters hanging off and ancient, peeling paint. From the windows spilled hanks of bedding, and laundry festooned every possible spare hanging place. Racks of clothes for sale splayed across the sidewalks. And there were people everywhere, teeming through the streets, sitting on steps, standing in doorways, yelling from windows. Mercy looked round in fascination at the men in shabby black clothes like dishevelled crows with their hats and beards and ringlets, and the shawls and embroidered blouses, the stiff, old-fashioned dresses and assortments of garments and materials worn side by side that she'd never seen in her life before, on people of a kind she'd barely ever seen either, with their high cheekbones and raven hair. And a pandemonium of different languages, guttural sounds shouted along the milling streets where you had to shout simply to be heard at all.

Broome Street was as crowded with activity as anywhere else. Paul remembered that Tomek's number had been forty-three. They walked slowly along the row of poor tenement houses, amid a curious gaggle of ragged children, and found a house with forty-three chalked on the door. They looked uncertainly at each other. A man sitting on the step of a house two doors away stared at them, then hawked and spat into the gutter.

'I think this is right,' Paul said. 'Can you hold this a minute?' They had bought bread and spiced meat in the Italian Quarter on their way, and Paul handed the bag of food to her.

Going to knock, he found that the door shifted a little and he nudged it with his shoulder. When it opened he turned and grimaced comically at Mercy.

'Well, here goes.' He led her inside.

When the door swung shut again they found themselves in almost total darkness. The air was thick with smoke and there was an overpowering stench of lavatories mixed with stale smells of cooking and a general frowstiness.

'Ugh,' Mercy said. She was afraid to move. But then she said, 'Listen, Paul – that's a babby crying upstairs! Could be little Peschka.'

'It could.' Paul went and opened the front door again to let in some light. It was then they noticed that the walls and ceiling of the hallway were also very dark and seemed to be covered with some sort of pattern.

'Good Lord!' Paul tapped his hand on the wall. 'I do believe it's lined with – tin, it feels like. Embossed tin! How strange. Bit wasted in here, isn't it? It's like the Black Hole of Calcutta. I tell you what – let's see if there's anyone in here.'

He went to an inner door off the hallway and knocked softly. After a moment it opened a crack and a woman's face, very pale and gaunt, peered out at them. Mercy could just make out an arc of frizzy red hair round her forehead which was wrinkled with suspicion.

'Er, Petrowski?' Paul said to her. 'Petrowski? Polska?'

Without altering her expression she opened the door a little wider, pulling the ends of her shawl round her. Mercy heard a clicking sound behind her, comfortingly familiar, and realized it was a sewing machine. The woman pointed silently up the stairs.

It was Tomek who opened the door. His face remained blank for a moment as he peered at them in the gloom. It was then transformed with joy as he recognized them and he pulled Paul into his arms, chattering madly.

Two young children also peeped out through the door at them.

'Yola – Yola!' Tomek shouted.

Yola came to them from what appeared to be a second room behind the first. As she walked across the bare boards of the dingy room and saw them, emotion immediately welled in her dark eyes. She clung to Mercy, weeping, kissing her and clutching her hands, as if she were a true sister who'd come all the way from Poland to find her.

The Petrowskis' living quarters, which they shared with Tomek's brother and his wife and children, consisted of two rooms, where they had to cook, wash, live and sleep, amid the smoke from the range. Yola showed Mercy the little back room in which a bed was curtained off from the small amount of space remaining. She indicated that she and Tomek slept on the floor in the other room.

Yola's sister-in-law Zanya, who spoke some broken English, explained haltingly to Mercy that her husband was finding Tomek a job at the docks, that soon he and Yola might be able to find a place of their own. She was taller than Yola, with a lighter complexion and more pointed face, her hair fastened back in a green scarf. When Yola told her who Mercy was she smiled and kissed her.

Yola looked exhausted, Mercy thought, but did not seem downhearted. The four of them and Zanya's children shared the food that Mercy and Paul had brought and Zanya brewed coffee on the stove. Tomek insisted that Mercy sit on one of the chairs and Yola, suckling Peschka, had the other, while the others sat round on the floor. The Poles exclaimed to each other over the Italian meat, which was as strange to them as to Mercy.

They communicated in the usual way of nods and gestures, and with a little help this time from Zanya.

'Is Yola happy to be here?' Mercy asked her.

Zanya asked the question of Yola and the two women laughed.

'She is happy,' Zanya said. 'She is . . .' She struggled for the words. 'We have help here – she not alone. Not to be hungry now . . .'

Mercy nodded, understanding.

'She will be sewing,' Zanya said.

Yola suddenly got up and went into the other room for a moment. She returned holding a brass candlestick which she unwrapped from a piece of soft cloth, and a photograph. The woman who stared back from it had a face as lined as bark on a tree. Mercy looked up and saw that Yola's eyes were once again full of emotion.

'Her mother,' Zanya said.

She didn't need to explain that they would never see each other again. The candlestick was evidently also one of the few precious possessions she had brought from Poland.

They sat for some time. Mercy held Peschka and fussed

over her, and then they left, promising to visit again the next day.

Mercy's two days with Paul passed with terrible speed. That first night she lay in bed across the room from Helga, praying that the woman would soon cease her continual chatter, fall asleep and leave her alone with her thoughts.

When Helga did eventually sleep, Mercy turned on her back, the bed creaking as she moved. It had been wonderful to see the Petrowskis had fared well on Ellis Island and now had hope of a new life. Their bravery, the risk they had taken, filled her with burning determination. She, like them, would leave her past behind and look forward. Whatever James Adair had done, she would leave it behind. She would not let it mar her future. Like the Petrowskis she was going to begin again.

When we get back to England, she thought, I'll look round for something else. I'll get away from him. She would be sad to leave Margaret after all her kindness, but her presence in the house could only mean trouble for Margaret. She would wait for the right time, for something suitable. Then she would go. She would wait for Paul.

The day she had just spent with him seemed the most perfect she had ever had. When they parted that night they had held each other for a long time in a shadowy spot round the corner from the Keslers' house. They touched and kissed and he spoke such loving words to her. Her body filled with desire for him, seemed to have a will of its own. For a moment she couldn't forget the revulsion she had felt with James Adair, but she forced him out of her mind again.

I loved Tom, she thought, I can love. I feel even more for Paul, love him with all my heart, mind, body ... His words of affection, of passion, were still fresh in her mind and she was full of wonder.

'I want to be with you always, Mercy. I want to spend my life with you. Life would be nothing without you now.'

She was almost too thrilled and excited to lie still.

I must be, she thought, the happiest person in the world.

The next evening they had to part. When they met in the morning this still seemed far off – they had a whole day in front of them! But it rushed past.

Once more they walked, talking and laughing all day. They watched the almost imperceptible movement of the East River from Manhattan Bridge, bent their heads back to look up at New York's most soaring buildings, and once more visited the Petrowskis to say, for the time being, their goodbyes. Amid the hugs and blessings and tears, she and Paul promised that they would keep in touch, and they left them in their cramped little rooms which held so much hope for the future.

Late that afternoon, Mercy and Paul walked back, with painful reluctance, towards the Keslers' house.

'Now's our chance to see more of the park,' Paul said.

'Slowly,' Mercy added wretchedly. 'Oh Paul, I wish we could just stay here. Forget about everything else and start a new life ourselves.'

'I know. I wish too.'

The closer the time to part was approaching, the more difficult they both found it to speak. Mercy's heart was weighed down by the thought of not seeing him. They were to be in New York another two and a half weeks and even when they got home Paul would be in London and there was no telling when they might meet.

'You will write to me, won't you?' he said. 'Letters from you would keep me going.'

'I'll try. Only I've hardly ever written letters before!'

'Just write the way you talk to me. I'm not up to much at it either, but at least it's something.'

They passed along the winding paths of Central Park, eyes full of green grass and spring leaves. Paul's arm was round her shoulder, hers at his waist, now it was dusk and they were away from the streets, and few people were in the park.

They stopped at the lake and stood together, looking across the wrinkled water, at the black, spindly trees beyond.

The lake seemed to hold secrets, Mercy thought, the unknown spread out in front of them, like their future.

She was acutely aware of Paul close to her, could feel his heart. The city was beating distantly around them, but here it was quiet, serene, a breeze riffling the water.

Paul took a deep, nervous breath.

'Mercy?'

She turned to him. He looked tense, eyes full of longing.

'I know things are very uncertain. I can't offer you much, not with any guarantees . . .' He trailed off, watching for her reaction. 'Could you – will you marry me?'

Mercy's hand shot to her mouth.

'O-o-o-h!' She reached out for the support of his shoulders, lest her legs give way. 'D'you really mean it?' But she could see that he did. 'Yes,' she said softly. 'I'll marry you, and cherish you with every bit of my heart.'

With a cry of joy he held her tight to him. 'Thank you – oh God, thank you. My beautiful, beloved Mercy!'

Too happy then, for words, they stared across the water in each other's arms. Mercy took off her hat and rested her head against Paul's shoulder.

How lovely everything is, she thought. The New World. A new life, new tomorrow. With this man whom I love. New beginnings are possible, and I'll make this one the best of my life.

Part Six

Chapter Thirty-Seven

May 1920

Mercy knelt on the linoleum in the Adairs' bathroom, resting her forehead against the cold rim of the bath and closed her eyes.

'He said it couldn't happen!' The words escaped as a desperate whisper from her lips. She was too sick and exhausted even to cry.

Screwing her eyes even more tightly shut she prayed, 'God in heaven help me! What am I going to do?'

It had begun gradually, with a slight feeling of queasiness which she put down to something she'd eaten. But it had got worse and for three weeks now she'd been bad in the mornings, and all day long was plagued by exhaustion of an intensity she'd never experienced before. She felt as if she'd turned into an old woman, barely able to get through the day, and it was frightening. Whatever was the matter with her?

The truth was too terrible to think about. If it wasn't for the way she felt she would have shut it right out of her mind. But she couldn't pretend to herself any longer. She'd seen the state of Margaret, and while she wasn't anything like as bad as that, she grew more and more certain that she, too, was carrying a child by James Adair.

She turned slowly and sat on the floor, resting against

the bath, shivering, arms hugging her knees. Her head ached, and the small amount of breakfast she'd managed to eat didn't feel at all safely stowed in her stomach. Nausea rose in her like water filling a bucket.

'Mercy – are you there?' Margaret called through the door.

'Just coming,' she managed to reply.

'That's all right, dear, no hurry. Stevie's ready whenever you are. You might take him out this morning as it's such a fine day.'

'Yes—' Mercy lurched forward on to her hands and knees, trying to stand up and catching her foot in her pale blue frock – 'I'll do that.'

She heard Margaret move away, and got up, feeling dreadfully sick. Her innards clenched and she retched miserably over the basin until her eyes and nose ran and she was panting. But she felt better after and washed the basin thoroughly.

She met Rose on the landing, carrying an armful of dry linen.

'Blimey – you look bad.'

'No.' Mercy pulled her foul-tasting lips into a smile. 'I'm awright. 'Course I am.'

Rose frowned, watching her as she walked determinedly towards Stevie's room. Whatever she said, Mercy looked terrible. It was obvious she was putting on a brave face.

'You're such a help to me,' Margaret told her all the time. She was at last beginning to feel better. She had been unwell, in patches, through most of their visit to the United States. For a day or two she might be all right, and then the sickness would return and she was laid up.

Mrs Kesler had been kindness itself and the two women grew very close. On days when Margaret was weak and sick, Gerder and Mercy took it in turns to keep her company. When she had the strength to venture out they had taken gentle walks in the city, strolling the avenues and the park. When James and Kesler were there at the weekend they had motored out to Long Island, to a place called Westhampton. It was a long drive, but when they arrived they picnicked by the ocean, the sand piled in heaps behind them and stuck with sharp, papery grass. James Adair did not speak a word to Mercy all day, did not even meet her eyes.

But she was full of excitement and euphoria at the sight of the sea. She and Stevie frolicked on the sand and watched the Atlantic swoosh up on to the beach, hearing the pound of it against the shore, feeling it rush cold over her feet. *Paul, Paul*, the breakers seemed to whisper, and through their roar and mutter she heard his voice, 'my beautiful, beautiful Mercy', and she smiled and laughed, running in and out of its lacy edge.

'Another letter for you,' Margaret said when Mercy eventually carried Stevie downstairs. 'Mercy – are you still feeling unwell? Perhaps we should call a doctor?'

'Oh – no!' Mercy forced a smile and pretended to be surprised. 'I'm on the mend, thanks.' She took the letter and put it in her pocket. The sight of Paul's sloping, untidy handwriting sent an agonizing pang through her, and she tried to hide her tears, busying herself with Stevie. 'We'll go straight away. Get the best of the day.'

She was glad to be out in the fresh air. Stevie sat in his pushchair, left thumb comfortingly in his mouth and his little grey rabbit snuggled up to his face. Mercy pushed him down the hill to the park. She felt weak and light-headed, but her thoughts seemed to hammer in her mind. Not for one second would they leave her in peace. A babby . . . a babby . . . inside her, and it was going to get bigger and bigger. Margaret Adair was four months gone with child and her belly was already growing. When she grew like that she wouldn't be able to hide it any more, and then what would become of her? Everything she'd hoped for, a new job, new life, would be lost to her. James Adair had torn into her, made her dirty, a disgrace. Now she was home again, where everything felt different and she could no longer block out what had happened, her shame and regret were enough to overwhelm her. She hated herself. She should have run out of that state room, screamed for help from Paul, suffered disgrace then, instead of being left to live with the consequences for ever.

As for Paul . . . the letter in her pocket nudged against her leg insistently with every step . . . The very thought of him filled her with anguish. She couldn't help it, couldn't stop herself weeping even as she walked down the road, keeping her head down to hide her face under the brim of her straw hat. She felt as if her very soul were pouring out, flooding the street.

She'd been such a ninny, thinking she could start afresh, that she could lift the curse of her beginnings and put the bad things of the past behind her. Everything had seemed possible when she was with Paul, but how could she have forgotten who she really was? That all her fresh hopes had always ended in suffering and loss?

She passed through the park gates with trembling legs and a leaden heart. The beds of bright spring flowers seemed to mock her. She began to sob so hard that Stevie craned round to look at her.

'Here—' – She bent over him, trying to sound normal – 'you can have a little run round now, can't you?'

He was still at an age when he wanted to keep her in sight. Mercy sank down on a bench and, steeling herself for fresh pain, took out Paul's letter. Once again it was from Cambridge. Paul had returned to London after his post on the *Mauretania*, but shortly after, Mr Louth had been taken seriously ill and he had been forced to go home. Mercy's heart had gone out to him. She knew how hard it would be for him to be with his father.

My dearest Mercy,
  Another week and I'm still in Cambridge. Father has been out of hospital for several days now, but is still very weak and incapable. His right leg is not making the progress they hoped and as yet he can barely utter a word that anyone can understand. The doctor came to see him this morning and said he should be sent back to hospital, that they had allowed him home far too soon. I agree really, but the agony in his eyes when he heard those words! It's terrible to see him. The horror for a man like my father – a teacher, a linguist – of not being able to make himself understood, is almost beyond imagining. I can imagine enough though, and feel in a constant state of unrest, impatience and sadness seeing it. I looked after men in France in far worse condition, but there's something impossible about it when it's your own father. If only you were here. I miss you. Perhaps it would all make sense if I could see you . . .

Mercy broke off as Stevie ran to her carrying a flower.

'Oh dear.' She managed a watery smile. 'Thank you,

darling – but you mustn't pick any more flowers, Stevie love. No more.'

He ran off, wide-eyed. She saw him stop, eyes following the looping flight of a yellow butterfly.

> . . . I have had some time to think, Mercy, and I wonder whether, when this is over, the best thing would be for me to come to Birmingham and find work. Not ships of course, but I haven't gone far down that path yet. Birmingham couldn't be a better place for an engineer. The more I think of it, it seems the very best thing. As soon as I can safely leave Father.
>
> What I know is that life is very short and fragile and the best things in it have to be carefully cherished. All that matters is that we can be together, and I long for that. Apologies: today finds me in a rather mournful, philosophical mood. Do write soon, my love . . .

He finished the letter with more loving greetings that started Mercy's tears afresh. She put her hands over her face. 'Oh Paul, Paul . . .' If only he were here! If she could only weep in his arms and tell him all her pain and troubles. But he was the very last person she could be with now or confide in. She was racked by a multitude of emotions. Everything was wrong. It should have been his child that she carried, he who should have touched her and bound their lives together. But no. It could be no more. He'd said he could forgive her anything that had gone before. But this wasn't before – it was now and for the future. No one could forgive her that.

'Oh,' she sobbed. 'I can't have a child! I haven't the strength to do it all on my own.' For she would have no help from James Adair. He and Margaret must never, ever know. His knowing would only compound her shame and humiliation, and Margaret would find out that she had been betrayed by both husband and friend. She knew that from now on, she was alone.

Stevie toddled up to her and patted her knee when he saw her crying. The sight of his sorrowful brown eyes made her sob even harder. For he, dear, lovely little boy, would be lost to her too. She would have to leave him as completely as she left his parents and the thought broke her heart.

'It's awright, bab.' She scooped him up into her lap and held him tight, resting her wet cheek against the top of his sun-warmed curls. 'Mercy's awright, don't you worry.'

She clung to the soft, warm flesh in her arms, kissing him. For a moment she was overcome by utter astonishment. Inside her, another child was growing. It was part of her and she was its mother. Joy passed through her, just for a second, like a fork of lightning. She was going to have to survive, to struggle alone, and at this moment she had no idea how. But however hard it was, she was going to do right by this child. With burning determination she thought of her own mother.

I will never desert you, she pledged. I'll never abandon you as my mother abandoned me. You'll be mine and I yours, and whatever it takes, come hell or high water, we'll stay together.

Every day, for the rest of that blossom-filled week in May, she did her jobs for Margaret Adair, and hid her sickness. At night she tossed and turned in her attic room, rigid with fear and worry. Her mind spun round and round. How much longer can I stay here? Where can I go?

On Saturday evening she made a bundle of clothes. She lay on her bed fully dressed, knowing she was never going to sleep. Late on in the night she slipped down into Stevie's room, her heart hammering so loudly she felt it might wake the household. It was still very dark and she had to feel her way across the room towards the sound of his breathing. She couldn't reach far enough over the side of the cot to kiss his face, so she kissed her palm and stroked it against his warm cheek, held his curled hand for a moment. She had cuddled and kissed him that night for a long time before he slept. Now the time had come she had to be quick.

'Goodbye, darling Stevie. Mercy will always love you, wherever you are. Have a happy and blessed life.' With one more kiss, she left him.

The clock downstairs chimed four thirty. Almost dawn. With great care she drew back the bolt and turned the key of the door. She took a last look into the hall, just able to make out the shadowy shapes of its furnishings. Already, with the leaving of it, the place felt distant from her.

'Goodbye, Margaret,' she whispered. Her throat ached with unshed tears.

Carrying her bundle, she stepped out into the misty garden.

Light began to finger the edges of the city as she walked down the Moseley Road and the mist slowly cleared. She didn't hurry. No one was awake, she wouldn't be missed, and besides, she hadn't the strength. She pulled her coat round her in the cool air. She hadn't been able to bring all the clothes Margaret had generously supplied her with, but she kept the blue overcoat.

Down the hill she walked, into Balsall Heath, and how much it felt as if she was sinking down! As the light grew firmer it highlighted the grime and delapidation of the place, the filthy cobbled road, the smoking chimneys which coated everything in muck. The buildings shrank to small, menial dwellings, shops and workshops, houses with yards squeezed in behind. She had left her temporary dream life of the big, well-appointed house, and as her feet trod the road towards Birmingham, she felt as if the streets were closing in on her, claiming her. A slum child, returning to her rightful place in the slums. She found herself thinking of Yola Petrowski, the kinship she felt as if they were sisters, even though they hadn't a single word of language in common. They were two of a kind: poor and needy. She remembered baby Peschka and felt a moment of exaltation – she too was going to have a child! – followed by a sinking desolation. She had no Tomek. There was no one for her.

She stopped for a moment, slipping her hand inside the bundle. A car backfired, breaking the silence and she jumped violently, heart pounding. Its engine chugged off down a side street. From the bundle she pulled out a letter and walked on. At the next posting box she would send it, and that would be that. The future cut away from the past.

Dear Paul,

I'm going to say this quick, because I don't know how else to. I can't marry you or ever see you again.

I'm sorry. Don't come to Birmingham, there's nothing
for you here.

Forgive me. Forget about me now.

Love,

Mercy

She hadn't been able to sign off without the word
'love'. Anything less seemed so callous and abrupt. And
she did love him. She ached with love and longing for
him.

Fifty yards further along she saw a pillar box. She
stopped, the envelope resting against her lips and closed
her eyes for a second. Taking a deep breath, she quickly
pushed it through the slot.

Angel Street looked just the same: the sloping, cobbled
street, huckster's shop on the corner, that tilted street
lamp just along from their entry. Mercy paused. She had
to face Mabel. Whatever the humiliation it might mean
putting herself through, instinct and common sense had
driven her back to the one place she might find a roof
over her head. She pulled her shoulders back and went
into the yard.

She saw Josie Ripley's eldest son John coming out of
their house. He stopped, putting his cap on, and stared at
her as she went to Mabel's door.

'Awright?' he said, coming over. He had a thin face
and narrow, squinting eyes. 'Mercy, int it? You're 'ere
early.'

'Well, you're up early too.' She felt horribly conscious
of what a pathetic waif she must look standing there with
her little bundle of all she possessed in the world.

'If you're after Mabel, yer won't find 'er there – there's

a new bloke in now. She's over there.' He pointed at the Peppers' house.

'Oh, she is, is she?' Mabel hadn't wasted any time.

John was still hanging about, kicking at an uneven corner of brick.

'All right then, ta,' Mercy said tartly. 'I think I can manage to knock on a door by myself. Ta-ra!' She waited until he'd gone off down the entry.

'Who's that?'

Mabel's voice was the first she heard through the window as she knocked loudly several times. From upstairs, eventually, came the sound of someone yanking at the sash but it would only open a crack. 'Who's making all that racket? What d'yer want?'

But the door opened a second later and Alf stood there, bare chested except for his braces, looking blearily out at her. His eyes were red, cheeks covered in pale stubble, but he still looked a strong man.

'What the – Mercy? Is that you, wench?'

'Can I come in?'

''Course yer can, course yer can . . .' He stood back. She could hear his chesty breathing, smelt the sweat on him as she squeezed past.

'What's up?'

'Alf, I need somewhere to go. I'm in trouble.' She put her bundle down on the table, speaking very fast in the hope that she could talk to him before Mabel got down and stuck her oar in, tell her where she could get off. Her heart was beating very fast. 'Can I stay here – for a while, anyhow?'

But Mabel was down by then, without her blouse properly fastened up and Mercy could see her wide, flaccid chest and her cleavage above the top button. Her hair was all hanging round her face and she looked like a witch.

'My God.' There was already a note of triumph in her voice. 'What the 'ell d'you want then?'

'Mabel,' Alf commanded her sternly. 'Don't start on the kid. 'Er says 'er's in trouble. 'Ere, have a seat, Mercy.' He pulled out one of the chairs by the table.

Mercy sat, chin stuck out as she looked up at the two of them. They'd have to know soon enough. Best to get it over with. 'I'm 'aving a babby. And I've nowhere to go.'

She expected Mabel to rant and shout, laugh even. Instead, she sank down on one of the chairs by the table, pulling the neck of her blouse together.

'I'd've thought you'd've had more sense. What happened?'

'What d'you think happened?' Mercy retorted fiercely. To her fury she felt tears welling in her eyes. Mabel hadn't immediately cast her out. There was hope. It was such a relief to be back in this familiar place among her own people, even George there by the window, on his perch.

'But who's the father?'

'I don't want him to know. Never! It wasn't my fault. It was all a mistake.'

Alf stood by, at a loss, breathing heavily.

Mabel leant forward, eyes narrowed. 'Was it that Mr . . . what's his name?'

Mercy nodded, looking down on her lap, her cheeks burning red. Oh, the shame of having to admit such a thing to Mabel of all people!

'Did 'e take advantage of you?'

Mercy hesitated.

'Well did you want it too?'

'No! Never!'

'So 'e took advantage.'

He did. Yes, he did. Mercy nodded again.

'Ought to be ashamed of hisself – young kid like you. You could be 'is daughter . . .'

Alf suddenly laid a warm hand on her shoulder for a second. ''Course yer can stay. You've always been like one of the family. Can't she, love?'

Mercy slowly raised her head and looked at Mabel. Instead of the mean exhaltation, the crowing she'd expected, she looked up and saw tears in Mabel's eyes.

'You can stay,' she said gruffly. I know I never treated yer right as a kid. It were a rotten time of my life that, and I want to put it behind me. But I'll try and do right by yer. You were always good as gold with Susan. You're my daughter, sort of, even though it were never regular like. And nothing's regular about this child that's coming, is it?' She wiped her eyes. 'But I've always loved having a babby in the 'ouse, that I have.'

Mercy rested her head on her arms on the table and burst into tears.

Chapter Thirty-Eight

'Where's Tom?'

Mabel had brewed tea and they sat sipping it from the chipped willow-pattern cups that reminded Mercy so much of Elsie. The room looked the same, although George was there, pecking at his feathers, but now there was so much more space in it. Mercy had only just fully taken in this fact.

'Have you moved him upstairs then?'

Alf looked shamefaced. 'No, we, er—' – he glanced at Mabel –'Tom's not 'ere, love. 'E's being looked after over at Hollymoor. 'E was in a terrible state, what with Elsie being bad and ... and that ...' For a moment he seemed unable to speak. 'They took 'im up the 'ospital and they said 'e should be looked after proper like, somewhere where there's nurses to see to 'im.' He took a big breath. 'Any'ow – it's for the best.'

'We don't know if 'e knows any different,' Mabel said.

'Thing is – we'd best tell 'er Mabel.' They looked at one another for a second. Suddenly Mabel smiled. Mercy saw, like a revelation, that she was happy. 'Mabel and I are getting wed.' Alf rubbed a beefy hand over his stubble. He spoke the words like a confession. 'Next month like ...'

'Oh,' Mercy said. It stood to reason – they'd already set up house together, and Tom would've been in their way. She wanted to be angry with them. Didn't she owe it to Tom to stick up for him, with them having him put away to suit them? But if all the doctors said it was the right thing ... And she, too, could feel the relief of his not being there. Guilt too, but yes, relief. She had to believe he was all right, being well looked after.

'Well,' she said, 'I hope you'll be happy.'

'Oh, we will,' Mabel said.

Rosalie and Jack came down after a while.

'Mercy!' Rosalie ran straight to her for a cuddle, even though when Mercy stood up she saw Rosalie was almost the same height as her now.

'You're like a beanpole, you are,' she said. Rosalie was thin and gaunt, auburn hair scraped back, cheeks pale, wrists like sticks. 'Barely an ounce of flesh on your bones!'

'Yer back at school now any rate,' Alf said to Rosalie.

'You stopping?' Rosalie asked.

Mercy blushed. 'Yes. I'm stopping for a bit.'

Rosalie beamed. 'Oh good – ain't that lovely. You not working up Moseley no more?'

'No,' Mercy said quietly. 'I'm not.'

Jack, twenty now, was tall, his hair still a bright ginger and for a moment Mercy almost thought he was Johnny, except he was broader, more stocky, like Alf.

He nodded to her and they exchanged a few friendly enough words, but she could tell immediately that he and Mabel didn't get on. He acted as if she wasn't there. He'll be leaving home soon, Mercy thought, and they'll be lucky if they see much of him again. She was surprised to note that Rosalie seemed all right with Mabel.

Mabel stood cutting bread with the loaf under her arm. They ate a bit of breakfast before Alf and Jack went off to work, Jack with barely a word, and Rosalie to school.

'Take the ticket for Chubb's,' Mabel said to her as she

443

left. 'And don't go and lose it. I want yer to get yer dad's suit out for Sunday on yer way 'ome.'

'Awright.' Rosalie tucked the pawn ticket in her pocket. 'You will still be 'ere when I get back, won't you, Mercy?'

''Course I will. See you later, love.'

Rosalie departed, smiling.

'There's no need to breathe a word to anyone – not yet,' Mabel told her once they were alone. She stood riddling ash out of the range. Mercy watched her. Mabel's body had thickened and spread, but had kept its curves. She now had a rather stately figure, and was a handsome woman, despite her sluttish ways. Mercy could smell her, that ripe, sweaty odour which always hung about her.

'Why're you being so nice to me?' Best to get it over, know where she stood.

Mabel straightened up, brushing ash off her sacking apron.

'Look – I'm not all bad, yer know. You used to rile me as a kid. Always looking at me as if I were the devil's mother or summat. And I didn't always treat yer kindly, but can't we let bygones be bygones?'

'Awright.' Mercy still felt wary. Old feelings, years of cruelty, weren't so quickly overcome. But she also felt queasy again, and absolutely exhausted. She rested her head on her hand, elbow on the table.

'Alf's a good man and 'e's giving me a chance, even if I don't deserve it . . .'

'You helped Elsie,' Mercy said grudgingly.

'I did what I could.'

Mercy was silent for a moment. Stevie would be awake now. They would know she was gone.

'Mabel – I need to go to sleep.'

Mabel pushed a chair in under the table. 'Yer look all in. Go up on Rosalie's bed – sleep all day if yer want.'

Mercy passed an odd, restless few days of sleep and sickness. She kept dreaming of Stevie, of the daily routine at the Adairs', and she'd wake, bewildered to find herself in Rosalie's bed in the bare little back bedroom with its cracked ceiling.

The first day she slept almost all the time, prostrate with exhaustion. Mabel brought her up water and tea and she was too far gone even to be surprised. In the evening Rosalie made herself up a bed on the floor.

'No,' Mercy protested weakly. 'You must have your bed!'

'Don't be daft,' Rosalie said. 'You're poorly. I can sleep down 'ere easy. It's the best thing having yer back, Mercy.'

'Is Mabel awright to you?'

'She ain't so bad.' Rosalie sat on her bedding on the floor, unplaiting her hair. 'It felt a bit funny at first – 'er and Dad like, yer know. As if it was wrong some'ow. She was really good to our mom when she was bad and that. Sometimes I don't like 'er being 'ere, as if she thinks she's taken Mom's place, but Dad'd be lonely without someone. It's for the best really and she's awright to me. It's Jack can't stand having 'er 'ere – not that quick.'

'I could see.'

'But even Mom said, life has to go on. Mabel'll never be my mom but it's nice to have someone 'ere. I was all on my own with Tom before, see.'

'You've been a real good kid, you have.' Mercy was

drifting off again. She didn't even seem to have the strength to move an arm or leg.

It was such a relief to be able to lie down for a time, and not pretend any more. She wouldn't be turned out on the streets, she was safe for the moment. But now these immediate needs were met she kept thinking of Paul. She dreamed of him too, kept seeing herself in New York with him, everything happy and undisturbed. She felt that enormous warmth and joy in the knowledge of his love and woke with tears streaming down her cheeks into her hair. Once she woke like this to find Mabel standing over her.

'What's all that about?'

'Don't know.' Mercy wiped her eyes, trying to sit up. 'Just everything.'

'You'll be all right.' Mabel handed her a cup of tea. Mercy still felt she was dreaming this, Mabel being kind. At that moment it was all too much and she burst into tears again.

A week passed. She got up, had to get out and face the neighbours.

'I'm looking for a new job,' she told them. She simply couldn't bear to tell the truth. Not yet. But each time she saw anyone, Mary Jones, Josie Ripley, Mrs McGonegall, blushes flamed in her cheeks. She wasn't going to be able to keep this up for long. But after their initial surprise they all treated her as if she'd never been away. There was a new man called Samuel Formby living in number two, the old house, but he was out at work all day and in the pub most of the rest of the time.

'I shall look for a job,' Mercy told Mabel. As soon as she felt a bit stronger she helped out round the yard, maiding and mangling on wash days, cooking, scrubbing. But she was still being sick a bit, on and off.

'Wait till you've got over that,' Mabel said. 'We'll manage.'

Mercy watched Mabel's new happiness and wondered at how much of a person's nature was built on circumstances.

Of course everyone soon found out about her. One morning Mercy was out in the yard and felt nausea rushing up in her. She dashed down to the lav, just making it, and stood heaving in the foul-smelling privy. Josie Ripley was in the one next door. As soon as they both stepped out, Mercy walked off trying to pretend nothing had happened, but Josie strode up behind her and tapped her on the shoulder.

'Mercy!' She looked round into Josie's crooked face. Even Josie couldn't fail to see the agony and shame in the girl's eyes.

'You in trouble?'

'Trouble?'

'Yer know what I'm saying. In the family way?'

Mercy nodded, looking miserably at her dirty work pinner.

'Thought so!' Josie was triumphant, hands on hips. 'Coming back 'ere sudden like, I knew there had to be more to it. Bit of a comedown eh, after what you're used to miss?'

Mercy didn't answer her.

'Does Mabel know? 'Cos if she don't yer'd better tell 'er right quick.'

'She knows.'

'So—' Josie was always one to get things straight. 'You're no better than the rest of us then are yer?'

Mercy shook her head and looked up indignantly.

''Course I'm not!' She'd never thought she was – had she?

'Any'ow—' – Josie softened suddenly, backing away – 'if yer need anything . . .'

Mercy folded her arms over the pinner and walked slowly back to the Peppers' house. She could see her future spread out in front of her. Angel Street, work, the babby. She'd grow old like Josie, Mary, Mabel, among all these people she'd known almost all her life. It was good enough for them, she told herself. And it would have to be good enough for her. But as she looked up at the drab, mean-sized little dwelling, she felt as if her very soul was dying inside her.

She got a job at the Futurist Cinema in John Bright Street, sitting in the little wooden booth selling tickets.

'Your pretty face'll bring the punters in,' the manager said. Not that people needed bringing in. They came in droves, especially Saturday afternoon. The job was easy. Tickets 3d, 6d, 1/6d, 2/6d. She could sit down and do it. She smiled as sweetly as she could at everyone. No one would have guessed at the shattered, lonely heart inside her.

On the second Sunday she caught a bus down the Bristol Road to Hollymoor Hospital. Her sickness was easing a little now, leaving room for her enormous loss and loneliness. Rosalie was good company, of course, and the neighbours were all right. But she hungered for someone she could really talk to.

Hollymoor seemed like a world of its own, shut away

behind its high walls like a self-contained village, the forbidding hospital buildings clustered together.

Eventually she was directed to where Tom was, out in the grounds. He and several others were sitting in an oval-shaped ring of chairs, round which two nurses in starched uniforms came and went, fetching, carrying, cajoling. The men mostly sat still, some with their heads lolling, some just staring, one with bandages across his eyes. Mercy's heart contracted with pity.

There were a couple of other visitors here, sitting patiently beside their sons, brothers or lovers in half-concealed desperation. Mercy picked up one of the spare seats and placed it beside Tom's bath chair, facing into the sun. He didn't register her presence and she reached for his nearer hand and held it in hers so that he stirred slightly. His eyes were watering in the bright light.

'Hello, Tom.' She spoke quietly, feeling self-conscious. 'It's me, Mercy. You're looking well, love.' He was, compared with the last time she saw him. He was clean, shaved and groomed and his cheeks and nose were turning a faint pink in the sun.

'I've moved back home now.' She wondered if anything she said ever reached him. 'Living with Alf and Mabel and Rosalie. They're all going to come and see you again very soon. Everyone else is much as usual . . .' She watched a woman across the circle from them clinging to what must have been her son's hand, staring at him with tormented eyes. A moment later she got up suddenly, as if overcome by emotion, and left.

Mercy sat in silence with Tom as he made odd sounds and fidgeted. She needed him so badly that day, needed to believe he could hear her and offer friendship and comfort as he had in the past.

'We've both got a life sentence, haven't we?' She didn't look at him as she spoke. 'There's you here and me back where I started when you and me was kids. Shame we can't put the clock back, eh? I'd give anything for you to be back like you were.'

One of the nurses approached with a cup of cordial for Tom to drink through a straw.

'Would you like to help him with it?' she asked Mercy. She seemed stiff and formal, yet not unkind.

Mercy held the straw to Tom's dry lips. He knew what to do and there were soon loud slurping noises as he drained the cup. When he finished he said, 'Ahhh,' loudly. Mercy smiled.

'Was that nice?' She felt as if she were talking to Stevie. She put the cup down on the grass, took her hat off and laid it in her lap.

'See, if I don't talk to you, Tom, there's no one now. And I know you'd be kind to me and understand.' She drew closer and quietly poured out all her troubles to him.

'I've tried so hard with my life,' she finished. 'You know that, don't you? I can't make sense of it. Everything seems to happen before I'm ready for it . . .' She found she was suddenly weeping again, warm tears coursing out. She'd never cried so much in her life as in these few weeks. It was as if all her defences had been trampled down.

'I don't know what I'm going to do. I just don't know how I can bear it . . .'

Tom moved his head suddenly and let out an 'Er-r-r-r' sound which she found comforting, as if he'd heard and wanted somehow to reach her. She kissed his hand.

'You were always so kind and good. You don't deserve this, Tom, none of it.' There was nothing else she could say to him that she hadn't said over and over. 'I'm so sorry. I wish, I wish...' If only he could talk and yell out all the horror and injustice of being trapped in there forever, in his useless body. But he sat silent now, like an inscrutable puppet.

She said goodbye to him, promising she'd come back.

It was as she left the hospital that despair hit her fully, a great surge which washed through her. She leant against the wall outside and closed her eyes, the rough brick against her forehead, crumpled with agony inside.

Tom would sit there like that for the rest of his life. How long? Ten years, twenty, thirty, more? And Paul – she saw his eyes looking into hers with all his pained tenderness, his need of her. She loved him so much. However often she tried to convince herself that she could be strong, could move forward, it was not true.

'I don't want to spend my life alone ... I can't, I need someone. I need you, Paul. I can't bear it.'

But she'd told him there was nothing for him here. She was no better than a tart, a trollop, carrying the child of a bullying, selfish man. She was alone in the world, nothing to anyone, and that was what she had always been. She thought of the railway, of lying across the track, hearing the train thrumming faster and faster towards her, the singing, the thundering roar of it. Then blackness. No more. Her troubles would be over, and who would care? She could have peace, blessed peace ...

'You all right, missy?'

She turned, bewildered, and found herself looking into the watery eyes of an elderly gentleman with white hair tucked under a smart black Homburg. He was rather stooped, carried a stick, and his face wore a sad, gentle expression.

'Yes.' With an effort she straightened up. 'Thank you. I just came over a bit dizzy.'

'It's a warm day.' He looked at the sky for a moment, with a sideways swivel of his head. 'I saw you visiting one of the young men, didn't I?'

'Yes – my, er, friend. ' She remembered the old man now, from among the visitors. 'I'm just going for the bus.'

'Perhaps I could give you a lift somewhere, my dear? I've got my car. My sons say I shouldn't be driving any more at my age but I can't see the harm. I don't go at any great speed.'

'Oh – it'll be out of your way. I live right near the middle of Birmingham.'

'Not at all, my dear. Let me help you – look, just along here . . .'

The idea of being driven was very attractive. He opened the door of the motor car and Mercy saw the blue veins standing out on his hands. She sank gratefully into the leather passenger seat.

The gentleman's driving was perfectly in order, though he must, Mercy saw, have been nigh on eighty. Now and again he wiped his eyes with a handkerchief. They drove in silence for a few moments, until he burst out, 'That was my grandson in there. Was. Like a vegetable now.' She could hear all the grief pressed into his quavery voice.

'Only eighteen he was, when it happened.' He punched the air impotently with one hand and the car swerved. 'Arras. That's where it was, curse it! If only I could take his place—'

'I feel that too.'

'You?' He glanced round at her, eyes wide. 'Oh no – not you. You're much too young, my dear. It's us old, useless things – he should be out working, prime of his life ... And you – lovely girl like you. I don't know how you can even think such a thing.'

'The way things are, it'd be easier.'

'Now, now, now – nothing can be that bad, surely? Not compared with them in there. Young slip of a thing, life all in front of you. No war on now, nothing like that ...' He reached out and patted her hand. 'Only thing to do, you know – keep putting one foot in front of the other and you're sure to get there.'

Mercy managed a little smile. 'Yes. I s'pose so.'

She got him to pull up on the Moseley Road, saying she'd walk the rest of the way, and thanked him sincerely.

'I'll perhaps see you there again. What's your name, my dear?'

'Mercy Hanley.'

The old gentleman let go of the steering wheel and slapped his thighs in amazement.

'Extraordinary! Well, well, d'you know, my name's Hanley too? Joseph Hanley – delighted to make your acquaintance. No relation, I don't suppose!'

Mercy's heart started to thump harder. No, surely it couldn't be – he must be long dead ...

'You're not – surely – that Joseph Hanley – the Hanley Homes?'

'Yes, my dear. The very one – they're still going strong, I'm happy to say.'

'I can't believe it!' She clasped her hands to her cheeks. His face was much more shrunken now, softer, with an innate sympathy, and she could barely see that it was the same person. 'I grew up in the home in Aston,' she told him. 'They gave me your name because I had no one—'

'Did you, my dear?' Mr Hanley's face creased in wonder. 'Well I'm proud to know you! This is a great day for me, seeing how you've grown up into such a fine girl.'

Mercy swallowed. 'I, er – I was the one that bit you.'

Mr Hanley's forehead wrinkled. 'My, my – now you come to say it, I do remember that. Tiny little blonde thing – eyes like a cat. I had a mark on my hand for years after . . .' He glanced at his thumb, then back at her. 'It's gone now though!'

'I'm sorry, Mr Hanley. I wasn't cross with you, not really. You gave me a roof over my head. But they sent my friend Amy to Canada and I felt I was all alone . . .'

Mr Hanley shook his head, still astonished. 'Well well. I shall look forward to telling my family I've met you, Mercy. And I hope we shall run into each other again.'

Mercy climbed out of the car and looked in through the window, smiling. 'So do I,' she said.

Chapter Thirty-Nine

Dorothy Finch waited on the step outside the Adairs' house the next Saturday morning, a perplexed frown on her face. Emmie opened the door, and seeing her, clapped a hand over her mouth.

'Oh – sorry, Miss Finch – only we've been so worried about Mercy. D'you know where she's gone?'

'What d'you mean, "gone"? Ain't she here?'

Margaret Adair appeared, her face pale and tired. She immediately recognized the woman's rather old-fashioned clothes and her dark, soulful eyes.

'Thank goodness someone's come at last – we haven't known what to do. Please come in, won't you? Emmie, you can go now ... We're all rather at sixes and sevens without Mercy.'

In the sitting room, Dorothy could see the woman was quite distressed. She motioned Dorothy to sit but remained standing herself, moving restlessly round the room.

'I imagined she must have come to you. I just don't understand it. She had seemed just a little unwell, but – is she all right? Where is she?'

Dorothy felt dread spreading through her. She clenched her teeth for a moment to quell her anger. How could they have just lost her!

'It's news to me that she's not here, Mrs Adair. I expected to see 'er last Thursday. She comes to meet me about once a month as a rule, as you may know. I thought I'd come and see if she were awright like ... When did she go?'

'Nearly three weeks ago!' Margaret wailed. 'We all got up one morning and she'd gone – just bundled up some of her things and walked out in the night. For a terrible moment I thought she might have taken Stevie. That's what's so odd – she was so fond of him! What could have induced her? We thought of calling the police, but then it seemed she must have wanted to go, and the trouble is—' – Margaret sat down suddenly beside Dorothy – 'she talked occasionally about the home she'd grown up in, but I've been thinking about it and I don't ever once remember her saying the name of the street. There've been letters coming for her too, I think from that young man. He even telephoned ... I don't know if all this had anything to do with him, but if she'd gone with him he wouldn't need to write to her, would he? And I can't even send the letters on. I do feel so very worried about her. And rather let-down to tell you the truth. It's so out of character ...'

Dorothy stood up, stemming the flow of Margaret's agitated chatter.

'You should give me the letters, Mrs Adair. Don't worry,' she added grimly, tucking the envelopes into her pocket, 'I'll find her. Good day to you.'

'But ...' Margaret stood up after a moment. 'Where are you going to ...?'

Dorothy had already gone.

'So, miss – what d'you think you're doing back here?'

Dorothy's voice was harsh with worry. She'd come

straight from the Adairs' and caught Mercy an hour before she was due at work. But Josephine had come to visit with her three kids and there was nowhere for them to talk in private.

Mercy didn't look especially pleased to see her either. She seemed quite put out at her arrival. Dorothy saw how thin she was, gaunt and tight-lipped, a dull expression in her eyes. She'd last seen Mercy after her return from America, blooming with health and happiness. Whatever had got into her?

'I'm just off to work,' she said curtly, picking up her cardigan.

'I'll walk with you then.' Dorothy's tone brooked no argument.

'I'm in good time,' Mercy said. 'Let's go round Camp Hill way.'

She didn't speak as they passed through the streets of St Joseph's parish, wouldn't answer Dorothy's agitated questions until they reached the bustling thoroughfare at Camp Hill. Mercy was almost choked with nerves. She had to tell Dorothy, 'course she did. But it was the hardest thing yet. Dorothy had known her all these years, had tried to help her live a good life. She would expect better of her.

'I didn't think I'd see you,' she said lamely.

'And why not, pray?'

Mercy shrugged. Angel Street felt like a completely different existence that she'd slunk back into to hide, expecting everyone to just leave her alone to get on with it. She wanted to be left alone, to forget she'd ever had any hopes.

'What's going on, Mercy?'

They stopped by an ornate street lamp across the road

from the Ship Hotel. There were trams passing, bicycles, people bustling along. The bell of Holy Trinity struck one.

Mercy folded her arms tight, looked into Dorothy's eyes and told her. She expected disgust, scorn and anger. Instead, Dorothy's face lost all its colour and she had to lean against the lamp-post for support.

'Oh Mercy. Oh my Lord, you mean he . . .? Of course you couldn't tell Mrs Adair why you were going! Oh, Lord above.' She put her hand over her eyes. 'I knew summat terrible must've happened.' She turned, face hard for a moment. 'Tell me you didn't encourage 'im.'

'On my life.' Mercy's lower lip was trembling. 'You've got to believe me, Dorothy. I hardly knew what he was doing before it was too late, and I just couldn't think that he was going to . . . It was all so strange and horrible . . .'

Dorothy breathed in and out deeply, trying to steady herself. Mercy was moved by her emotion. Dorothy really did care about her, almost like family.

'What're you going to do, Mercy?'

'Have the babby. What else?'

'But there are places – well, like Hanley's – after, you know . . .'

'No!' she shouted, so enraged she didn't care who heard. She could hear blood throbbing in her ears. Lowering her voice a little she said, 'Are you saying I should just throw my babby away the way my mother did me? She didn't care, did she? She just did what suited her. But I'll never cast my child off!' She laid a hand on her belly. 'It's my babby – the first person I've ever had who's related to me by blood. Blood tells in this world – or it damn well should anyhow. I'll look after my own, not like some.'

The two women stood glaring at each other for a moment, then Dorothy reached into her pocket.

'You're not telling me everything, are you? Mrs Adair said—'

'You went to see her?' Mercy was filled with panic. 'You mustn't, Dorothy – don't tell her! She must never know. It'd destroy her and I don't want him knowing, making any claims, or—'

'He won't make claims!' Dorothy said scornfully. 'I'd've thought you could at least work that one out for yourself. He'd run a hundred mile rather than admit that babby's his, in his position. But if you was to tell just him, you might get some money out of him.'

Mercy stared back at her as if she were deranged. 'I don't want his filthy money! I don't want anything to do with him!'

'You might think different when it's born and going hungry.'

'Alf and Mabel won't let us go hungry.' Mercy pulled herself up straight, making a show of strength. 'And I'm going to provide for it too. I can survive. I've always had to, haven't I?'

A tram rumbled past on the street beside them. Dorothy pulled Paul's letters out from her pocket and held them out. Only then did Mercy's face crumple. Her eyes widened before filling with tears. She covered her face with her hands.

Mercy sat in the ticket booth at the cinema while the first showing was on. She could hear the music from inside. She slit open the envelopes containing Paul's letters, her hands trembling so much she could barely manage.

The first, two weeks old, contained the usual news from Cambridge. Paul's father was deteriorating, had had another slight stroke. Paul was caring for him continuously. The sight of his handwriting wrung her heart.

By the second letter he had received her last note, posted on her flight from the Adairs'. Mercy began reading, then looked up, unable for a moment to go on. In the dim light she could just see her pale face reflected in the glass. When she looked down again to read the letter, the pain and bewilderment contained in his few quiet words seemed to burn from the page.

My loved one,

I can feel – I hope – the distress of your last letter to me. I have read it over and over many times, trying to make sense of it. How could you imagine for a second that I could ever forget you? Or perhaps there is another reason, another person in your life, and that is why you want to forget me? What is it, my love? What could have made you write a letter like that all of a sudden, as if I could just stop feeling what I do for you and that everything between us was nothing? If only I could see you, I'm sure we could make ourselves understood so much better.

Until I hear from you again I shan't be able to believe you meant your letter. Please write and tell me it was a mistake, that the future is not just the bleak nothingness it feels to be now.

Yours ever,
Paul

*

'She says she's going to keep the child. Won't hear of anything else.'

Grace had gone to the window as Dorothy talked, standing in the shadows by the long curtains, looking, but seeing nothing of the street outside.

Dorothy waited, knowing Grace had heard everything she'd said. The carriage clock on the mantelpiece ticked, deafeningly, it seemed. The sound of time passing. Dorothy watched Grace's profile, her fashionable, jaw-length hair caught neatly behind her left ear. Standing like this she looked quite youthful, still slim, in her white pleated skirt and a soft blue blouse. But as soon as she turned towards Dorothy, every day of her years of suffering showed in her face. It was not the suffering of physical deprivation, of hunger or the grinding lack of money and warmth. But Grace had never known a day in the past twenty years without emotional pain.

'It's the worst.' She spoke barely above a whisper. Her face had suddenly taken on the creased look of an old woman's. 'I can't think of anything – if she dies it could scarcely be worse. To think of her having to endure the pain, the shame and hardship . . .'

'You did it – you survived it.' Dorothy wanted to reach out, to give comfort, but Grace was untouchable. 'She has people round her who are perhaps more forgiving than you did.'

'I ran away. But I always knew I could go back. He said I could always go back so long as there was no child. I was a coward. But she has so little to go back to – not wealth or comfort as I had.' After a moment she said in horrified wonder, 'James Adair . . . are you sure? My memory of him is of a rather kind, stuffy fellow.'

'I can only go by what she says, dear. But there is someone else – was. In America. But she said she'd had to put him off.'

'What did she say to you? What are her thoughts?'

Grace stepped forward, desperately. 'Oh, I feel I know her so well, and yet . . .'

'She said she'll never give up the child. Whatever happens she's sticking with it.'

Grace paced the room, unable to keep still. 'No one knows better than you what I've been through, my dearest Dorothy. You know never a day has gone by without my thinking of her, praying for her . . . But I've asked myself over and over again whether I was wrong, whether I should have faced every shame and denial that would have been handed out to me. I could have stayed in that room, with that Mrs Bartlett, while I still had a little money.' She shuddered. 'I suppose somehow I should have survived. But Dorothy, I was so young, so very frightened. I felt I'd sunk beneath the level of life itself when I was there, into an appalling hell . . . But Mercy has lived most of her life in such places. I condemned her to that. And she has strength – oh God, that I had had her courage! If they hadn't made me – if I hadn't let them make me . . . If he hadn't gone away – I should never have abandoned my own flesh and blood . . .'

As her distress mounted, Dorothy went to Grace and took her gently in her arms. If only she could take this pain from her! Grace sobbed brokenly against her shoulder.

'He would've been no good for you. Not in the end.'

'My life has been one long pretence – this parody of a marriage . . .' She looked up, wet-eyed, into Dorothy's face. 'D'you know, before Neville left – in the War – I prayed for him to die?'

'Yes, well – so did I.'

The two women looked at each other solemnly. Grace suddenly broke away and sat down.

'I have spent my life safeguarding all the wrong things.' Dorothy saw in her a moment of the steeliness that reminded her of Mercy. 'Even now, to protect my sons I am a stranger to my daughter. To protect this facade of a respectable marriage which suits my husband I tolerate him spending more time in common whorehouses than he ever does with his sons.'

She straightened her back, her chin jutting out. 'Mercy must know who her mother is. I owe her that, and so much more.'

'What about Neville – if he were to find out?'

'I think', Grace said calmly, 'I shall probably kill him.'

'Grace!'

'It's all right, Dorothy. I don't think I mean it. I don't wish to rot away in prison for the rest of my life. All I mean is, I have to be prepared to pay the price, whatever it may be. But now the boys are old enough, they see their father with clear eyes. I'm certain we can trust them to support us.'

'What's up with you, wench?' Neville said when he got home that evening. His voice, as ever, was sneering. 'Didn't the wind blow the way you wanted it to today?'

'I'm quite all right, thank you,' Grace said mechanically. She knew her eyes still showed signs of tears, and she evaded his brief, insolent glance.

Neville had returned from the War a much leaner man. Over the past year and a half though, he had bloated into middle age, with a complexion ruddy from over-indulgence. His cheeks were loose and flushed and merged with his thick chin with scarcely a hint of jawline present. His body was short and stocky and he walked, legs apart, with a swagger. Lately he grew more quickly short of breath. Over the years his catalogue of charming habits about the home had grown in number and intensity: bawling about the place, hawking phlegm in his throat, drinking regularly to excess, cursing, belching and passing wind with orchestral loudness. And despite Grace's barely concealed revulsion for him, he hadn't left off his intermittent, gross mauling of her in bed.

She had learned early in this loveless marriage that he could be two different men. Out of the home, or in company, he could be gregarious, charming, humorous. He had a generous side to his character and a loud, infectious laugh. This was how he had appeared to Grace's father when their marriage was arranged. They had not been married more than a few weeks when, with her, he became moody, foul-mouthed, out of control. Both of them were unhappy. Grace knew that nothing she could do ever seemed to give him satisfaction and never had, since the very earliest days, though she had tried and tried.

That night he flung his hat down in the hall and went, as usual, straight to the whisky decanter. He poured half a tumbler of the burning strong liquid, downing it in gulps. Grace usually avoided him, but tonight she stood at the threshold of the parlour, watching.

'I don't know why you've bothered to remain in this marriage.' She spoke with such cold objectivity that he turned, mouth swirling a gulp of whisky, startled to find her observing him. He narrowed his eyes and swallowed.

'It's the thing to have a wife. If I have to have one it might just as well be you. Out of my way.' He pushed past her and stumped heavily up the stairs.

*

'Boys, I have something important I want to talk to you about.'

She sat on Edward's bed. He, the younger of the two, was now ten. He sat up, grey eyes fixed solemnly on her face. Robert, twelve, was puppyish and full of often misdirected energy. He hurled himself across from his bed and landed on Edward's legs.

'Ouch!' Edward yelled. 'Get off, you great lump of a thing!'

'Boys, please just sit still,' Grace said, her voice sharp with nerves. 'I want to tell you something important.' For a moment she wished that Edward, the one most akin to her, was the older.

Once they were sitting quiet, sensing her seriousness, she told them what she had to say, her tears coming unbidden. She felt she was confessing to them, her own children, laying bare her shame.

'You see,' she finished, looking up at them bashfully, 'perhaps Mummy isn't quite the person you thought she was.'

'So—' – Robert was frowning, attempting to take in the implications of this – 'you mean we have a sister ... somewhere?'

'That's right. Her name is Mercy.'

'And she's much bigger than us and she's never going to live with us?'

'Yes, dear, both those things are true too.'

'Oh,' Robert said, beginning to lose interest. 'Well, that's all right then, I suppose.'

'Mummy,' Edward said, 'can I carry on reading *Treasure Island* now?'

Grace smiled. 'In a moment. There's something else, just as important, I need to say to you. I don't often ask you to keep a secret, though this is a very special secret that I thought you were old enough to know. But this is something I don't ever want you to breathe a word to Daddy about. Ever. It would make him very, very angry. Can you understand how important that is, my darlings?'

'Oh yes,' Edward said dismissively. 'Daddy never listens to anything we say anyway.'

Grace knew this was true. And even when the boys spoke to their father it was never a relaxed interchange. It was a risk she had taken, but it was unlikely anything would slip out in an unguarded moment of jollity, for such moments did not exist in their household.

'And Robert – listen to me now, very carefully.' She had a special task for Robert to perform, and he was going to have to be very grown up about it.

Chapter Forty

'Miss Hoity-toity's been 'ere again.'

Mabel stood across the table from Mercy who was ravenously eating bread and scrape. She'd just got in from work and was, as ever, nearly dropping from hunger. Rosalie was brewing a cuppa and Alf and Jack'd be in from the pub any minute. Soon as they arrived Mabel'd be sweet as pie to her, Mercy knew.

'Dorothy, you mean?'

'Left you this. In an envelope too.' Mabel held out the note. Obviously the sealed envelope rankled with her as she couldn't have a nose at it. Mercy examined the back of it to see if she'd tried to steam it open, but there was no sign. She took another mouthful of bread, longing for the comfort of food in her grumbling stomach.

'Aren't you going to open it?'

'In a tick. Give us a chance to eat. Ta, Rosalie.' She stirred sugar in her tea, feeling Mabel's eyes still boring into the letter.

Despite Mabel's grand speeches and her attempts to be kind, the two of them still only just managed to get along. Mercy knew Mabel wanted to show herself in a good light to Alf, her husband-to-be. Maybe she'd even meant it all, wanted to be kind, be liked. The fact was, they still rubbed each other up the wrong way.

She looked at Mabel who was stirring a pot of broth. Elsie's range, Elsie's room. The place was still full of ghosts: Elsie, Tom, Frank, Cathleen, Johnny . . . No wonder Jack wanted out and Rosalie's little face was so sad, so grown up before her time. No wonder Alf wanted a new start.

She stopped eating for a moment as a lump rose in her throat. Why was she worried about letting Margaret Adair down? She did miss her, it was true, and she'd been so kind. But Margaret could soon hire herself another servant. What these people – her people – here had endured was so much greater.

Alf and Jack came in then, both smelling of ale and heavy under the eyes with fatigue.

As Rosalie gave the men their bit of supper, Mercy sloped off upstairs and lit the candle in Rosalie's room. Dorothy's writing was a stiff, rather childish copperplate, but her spelling was good:

Mercy –
　　There's an urgent matter I need to talk to you
　　about in private. Meet me, Saturday 11 a.m. near the
　　gate in Highgate Park. Don't let me down.
　　Yours,
　　Dorothy Ann Finch

Mercy sighed and tore the letter into tiny pieces. It didn't say anything much but she wasn't going to give Mabel the satisfaction of a look at it. Truth to tell she felt irritated with Dorothy. What was she making such a to-do about?

I suppose I ought to be grateful to her, she thought, preparing herself for bed. She laid her skirt over the chair, smoothing her hand over the soft, wrinkled cotton. It was cream, sprigged with leaves and yellow flowers. A bit old-fashioned-looking though, that length, she thought. I'll hem it up a bit ... She stopped herself short.

What'm I going on about? For a second she almost laughed. What the hell's fashion going to matter when my belly's pushing everything out at the front and I can't get into it anyway?

She looked down at herself in her blouse and bloomers. Was there anything to see yet? She must be, what? Between three and four months gone? She moved her hands round her slim waist, then down over her belly, feeling the warmth of her skin. Wasn't it just a tiny bit rounder? She kept her hands there for a moment. There was nothing she could do – it was going to grow inside her, bigger and bigger until she had to let it out. She felt very solemn. So this was what it was to be a woman, to find your future lay in the hands of your child.

My mom must have looked at herself like this, she thought. Must have hated me for being in there, come to ruin her life. For a moment she felt a sad sympathy with her, that young, terrified woman, whoever she was. For the first time it occurred to her to wonder where her actual birth had taken place. Had she borne her child in the gutter? Was she alone, penniless, sick? Did she die in the throes of birthing and someone else take the child from her, carry her to safety where she could at least survive? Was anyone else present at her arrival? The old feeling of being lost, abandoned in the world, swept over her. It wasn't right, any of it. Everyone should have a chance to know where they came from.

What did Dorothy want? she wondered, pushing her thin arms through the sleeves of her nightdress. She felt very weary of it all suddenly, didn't want Dorothy planning for her, trying to rescue her. Not again. That would only lead to more trouble, more pain. She just wanted to be left alone to struggle with her life in her own way, come what may.

When she set out there was a light, mizzling rain, but the clouds had an insubstantial look to them and the sun was already trying to break through their swirling veil. Mercy had put her coat on but immediately felt too hot. She peered at the sky, unbuttoning the coat.

Just stop blasted raining, she thought. Then I can take it off.

There were plenty of people out Saturday shopping, going to get stuff out of pawn for Sunday, kids playing out along the pavements. She walked along Stanley Street, crossed Catherine Street, where a young man on a rough, wooden crutch was making his way along with terrible slowness, gripping a paper under his spare arm which ended at the elbow in a stump. He shuffled along on his one leg, unshaven face turned towards the ground. Mercy had seldom seen a face look more desolate. She wondered where Johnny was. Whether he'd found somewhere he could be at peace.

Before she reached the park the drizzle stopped and it grew even warmer. Mercy took her coat off, leaving her navy-blue cardigan over the white blouse and floral skirt.

The entrance to the park was opposite a row of big, posh houses on the Moseley Road. Mercy stepped inside, looking across the sloping grass. She wasn't sure of the time.

'Mercy.'

She jumped, hearing Dorothy's voice, and, as she turned, heard St Joseph's clock in the distance begin striking eleven.

Dorothy had a boy with her, a solid, rosy-cheeked lad dressed in good quality short trousers, a jacket and shiny black shoes. He was staring at her with a pointed curiosity which verged on insolence.

Mercy looked from one to the other of them. Dorothy appeared to be in a right state. She reached out to touch the boy's shoulder and Mercy saw her hand was trembling. She was breathing fast and for a moment seemed unable to speak.

'Who's this?' Mercy asked. 'One of your mistress's, is 'e?' Dorothy couldn't have anything much to say to her if she'd brought a child along as well.

The boy opened his mouth to speak when Dorothy put her fingers urgently to her lips and shushed him.

'Yes, this is Robert.' She spoke very quickly as if afraid for the words to linger in her mouth. 'And we've got summat to show you, haven't we, Robert? Mercy, I think you'd better come and sit down, dear.'

Mercy felt her heart thump harder. She was bewildered, and Dorothy's tone made her feel very nervous. Her hands began sweating and she had to wipe them on her skirt.

They went to a bench beside a flower bed of mixed pansies and sweet william. Dorothy sat the boy between the two of them. She took a deep breath and held it for a second.

'Now,' she said finally, on a rush of exhaled air, 'Robert is going to show you . . . Go on, Robert.'

Obviously aware of the solemnity of the occasion, Robert pulled a soft handful of something creamy-white from his pocket. Mercy frowned. As he opened it out it began to look familiar. She thought her heart was going to hammer its way out through her ribs. She gasped, clapping a hand over her mouth.

The boy opened out the handkerchief and laid it across his knees. Embroidered in one corner in a blue thread, with exquisite neatness, was the name ROBERT. He unfolded the second and in almost the same cornflower blue she read EDWARD. There was a third square of linen, older, more yellowed, just like hers, embroidered, just like hers, in a faded mauve: THOMAS. She stared and stared. She couldn't make sense of anything. Here were the very same linen squares, the same stitching as on the only small possession she had had since birth. The one tiny clue to her identity. And here this stranger, this young boy ...

With her hand still pressed to her lips she looked uncomprehendingly at Dorothy. Dorothy's eyes stared back at her, full of mingled fear and tenderness.

'If you'd been a boy,' her voice trembled, 'you'd have been called Thomas. She had it all ready for you, long before ...'

A winded, choking sound escaped from Mercy. She dragged her hand from her face and pressed it over her heart as if to contain the violence of its beating. Her whole body began to shake.

'What d'you mean, Dorothy? What in heaven's name are you telling me?'

The boy looked up at her. 'Mother says, and Dorothy says that you're my sister. Well, half-sister at any rate.'

Mercy felt her head had been filled with smoke, thicker than that billowing from any factory chimney. She couldn't see through it who the boy was, make sense of what he was saying, or why Dorothy was here with him. She felt dizzy and hot. The fog grew darker and darker, until only a few lights were flashing somewhere at the side of her vision, confusing her further, until the darkness began to fold in round her.

'Mercy? Mercy! 'Ere, get your head between your knees and you'll feel better.'

Dorothy's hands were pressing on her shoulders. The darkness cleared and she could hear blood pounding in her ears until the pressure of it was too much, her belly felt cramped and she had to sit up. She was sick and groggy.

'Stay here with 'er,' Dorothy instructed Robert, patting Mercy's shoulder. 'I'll go and ask up there for a drink of water.'

Mercy closed her eyes. This was all too much. She wanted to sleep, not hear any more. Go back to how things were. But she could never go back, she knew. Her life was tumbling round her and she was powerless to stop it.

'Are you all right?' Robert asked courteously.

She opened her eyes. 'I'm OK now. Thank you.' She examined his face as she might have done a mirror, looking for traces of herself, but she found nothing. Robert sensed this, had seen the same look in his mother's eyes.

'She says I'm the image of my father.'

Mercy noted that he didn't say 'Daddy'. Nothing that sounded affectionate.

'What's your mother's name?' she asked faintly.

He had to think for a second. 'Grace Elizabeth Weston.'

'Grace Weston.' Hearing her name, Mercy did recognize it, faintly. Dorothy had named her before. She turned the name round in her churning mind. Grace. Grace. What did this Grace have to do with her? Of course she had considered that her mother, a real flesh and blood person, might exist somewhere. But in her heart she had never believed it fully. No! Not a living, breathing person, who did ordinary, everyday things like anyone else.

Dorothy came back with a jam jar full of water and handed it to Mercy. 'They said we don't need to take it back. Big of 'em, eh?' Her dark eyes were full of anxiety. Mercy drank, then sat gripping the glass jar, head bowed.

'Tell me, Dorothy.' Her hands, legs, every part of her was still quivering.

Dorothy sank down on the bench.

'When your mother had you she wasn't wed. She comes from a respectable family. Religious, God-fearing sort of people. Her father was a lay preacher – Methodist – very strict man, he was. Any road, when she was forced to tell him he as good as washed his hands of her. Said she was to come home when she'd got rid of it, one way or other. He didn't want to know nothing about it. He'd've packed her off there and then if her mother hadn't persuaded him to let her stop at home 'til nearer the time it was due. They kept her in like, so no one'd know. Hid her.' Dorothy told the story in a flat voice as if she could hardly bear it.

'I was her maid then. We're of an age, see. When the time came near she went out and didn't come back. None of us knew where 'til after. It was her way of punishing herself, I think. Otherwise I might've gone with her.

'She went off, somewhere no one'd know her and soon after she had ... you. She knew if she kept you she'd have no roof over her head. Her mother, Mrs Bringley, had given her a bit of money to help her get by. There wasn't a lot else she could do. Mr Bringley was a stern man, had her right under his thumb. Grace would've been on the streets else, or in the workhouse. No home, soon no money, no way of earning a crust – nowt.

'She'd seen the Hanley Home. You were born somewhere around there. It was the only thing she could think of – you'd be taken care of. They might've sent you to Canada – they started that soon after you was taken in there.'

'Amy . . .' Mercy said faintly.

'Yes, like Amy. She thought it was the only way the both of you could survive. After two or three months she sent me over there asking for work. When a job came up they gave it to me as I wouldn't leave 'em alone. So there was always someone there, someone watching over you . . .'

The smoke cleared out of Mercy's mind as suddenly as if a tornado had swept through it. Her fists clenched tight.

'You mean . . . you're saying . . . all this time, ever since before I can even remember anything, I've had a mother? And you've always known who she was and where she was?' She gasped, memories flooding through her. 'And you brought me clothes – from her? And those jobs you got me – all her, and you?'

Dorothy nodded, her expression full of pain.

Mercy stood up as if propelled by an electric shock. Rage seemed to crackle through her, making her limbs turn rigid, her jaws stiff. She turned on Dorothy, eyes ablaze with outrage and fury.

'All this time, the pair of you kept it from me, my own beginnings, my family! All these years I've felt like . . . like nothing – thrown in the gutter because no one wanted me, and all the time . . .' She could barely speak, reeling under the violence of her hurt and anger.

'You and she have dressed me in the clothes she thought right, you nearly forced me to take that job and leave Susan, who was the only person who ever showed me any real love. You both treated me like a – a puppet, organizing my life, pushing me here and there as if you owned me . . . And she hid behind you and never had the guts to come out and own me as her child . . .'

She stopped abruptly, feeling she might be sick. She swallowed, panted. Robert stared at her, frightened.

'She abandoned me,' she said in a hard, quiet voice. 'And then she still wanted to run my life, giving me nothing of the things a mother should give a child. I had nothing. I was starving from lack of love and protection, and when did I ever see her eyes looking at me with worry or love—'

'But I saw them—' Dorothy interrupted, pleading.

'When did I ever feel her arms round me? Knowing this is worse . . .' She began to weep suddenly, weak and overwrought. 'It's far worse than thinking she might have been too poor or sick to keep me, or thinking she might be dead . . .'

Dorothy stood up, her face full of anguish, and reached her arms out, 'Oh, bab . . .'

Mercy backed away. 'Leave me, you deceiver,' she spat. 'You hid her. Why did you do that, all this time? What did you owe her that you don't owe me? You could have told me. You're just her servant, aren't you?'

Dorothy made as if to speak, then helplessly closed her mouth.

'I'm going,' Mercy said, holding out her hand as if to stop Dorothy in her tracks. 'I'm sorry, Robert.' She was suddenly aware of the child. 'I don't know what you thought – that I'd just come running? Leave me, Dorothy. I'm going home. I don't want to see you again. I may have a mother, but she's left it too late by a long way. I've got my own child to bring up now.' She started walking away.

'It's going to cost me, like being a mother should,' she

said, turning, walking backwards for a moment. 'Never cost her much, did it?'

'Oh, it did,' Dorothy implored her. 'Believe me – it did.'

But she was gone, a bright-haired, solitary figure, striding across the park.

Mercy cried all the way back to Angel Street. She couldn't help it. Loud, racking sobs she couldn't have prevented even if she'd wanted to. Her emotions were so mixed, so overwhelming, that she had not even the strength to fight for control. Anger, humiliation, a sense of betrayal, of huge loss and sadness were all mingled together. And the old, deep emptiness inside her. It felt as if her grief was bottomless and she would never be able to stop its flood. It was as if all her unshed tears of childhood were pouring from her now.

At home she couldn't stop either. Couldn't hide it. She had to tell them. Jack was off somewhere, but Alf, Mabel and Rosalie were all home. She had their absolute and rapt attention as she sat gulping out her story, and after, there was silence for a moment, all of them standing round.

'I always thought there was summat queer about that Dorothy Finch keeping on coming round, that I did,' Mabel said in a tone which suggested she'd known the truth all the time. 'In fact, it crossed my mind to wonder at times whether she wasn't yer mother 'erself – 'cept there was nothing in the looks, of course.'

Just what Paul had said, Mercy remembered.

'So you've got a little brother?' Rosalie said timidly.

Mercy's eyes welled again. 'Two. They said two ... How could she – all these years – deny I ever existed?'

'It's a disgrace,' Mabel said, arms folded self-righteously over bosoms. 'Abandoning a child like that.'

Alf cast her a look which plainly said, 'Shut yer great big trap, wench,' and Mabel subsided.

'You're not going away, are yer?' Rosalie asked.

'No, 'course not,' Mercy said fiercely. 'Why would I be?'

'But it does mean—' – Alf leant forward and Mercy could see the white stubble on his cheeks close up, the red veins in the curves of each nostril – 'somewhere you've got a family, Mercy. Blood ties of your own. That means summat, don't it? You can't just forget that.'

Mercy's eyes widened with dismay. 'D'you want me out – is that it?'

'No – no, wench.' Alf closed his hand awkwardly over hers for a second. 'It's just – well, she must've had 'er reasons like, for doing what she did. No one gives a babby up easy. And one day, when you've 'ad time for it all to sink in, you might want to know more about her and where you come from, that's all.'

'Where does she live, this mother o' yours?' Mabel asked.

'I don't know.' Mercy's brow wrinkled. 'Handsworth, I suppose – that's where Dorothy works – if she works for her now. I s'pose she does. I never asked.'

A week passed. Mercy gave up her job at the Futurist for something which didn't mean working evenings. She looked for work in a shop, and went back to Wrigley's Bakery to see if they might take her on again as she remembered it fondly. Mrs Wrigley recognized her at once but said she had a regular girl in now and couldn't let her go.

So she went from shop to shop along the Moseley Road, Ladypool Road. In the end she found a job with a Miss Martin who owned a draper's at the end of Camp Hill. Miss Martin's health wasn't any too bright and she needed help. Mercy was tempted to say, 'That makes two of us,' but wisely buttoned her lip. It'd be a nice quiet job, regular, with a half day on Mondays. And not hard: cutting from the bolts of cloth in the dimly-lit little shop, selling cottons, spools, zip fasteners, pins, buttons and all the other little cards of things Miss Martin had on her racks. Seeing them reminded her of all the evenings she and Susan had spent carding.

All that week as she walked the streets, her head was full of Dorothy's disclosures. Over and over, round and round it all went like the clothes in a maiding tub. The truth. Her truth. At first all she could feel was the raw hurt and an enormous, violent anger. She'd been treated like something of no worth, like a clockwork toy, expected to live her life according to her mother's desires and ideas. She wondered exactly what this woman had had planned for her before Mabel came along and mucked it all up, taking her off where they couldn't find her. Served her right!

As the week passed her anger gradually calmed and began to seep away. She found herself thinking as much about Dorothy as her mother. Maybe she'd been wrong to be so angry with Dorothy. After all, who else had ever shown her such devotion and care? Paul might have done – but she tried to push the thought of him away, the pain of it. She hadn't answered his last letter, felt completely unable to. Dorothy had been the one who protected her as a child, had displayed genuine emotion when she found her again, and genuinely cared for her.

The more Mercy thought of this, the more baffling it

was. Who was she, in the end, that Dorothy should bother with her? And what about this shadowy mother Dorothy was protecting? Grace Weston. Mother. She found herself repeating it over and over. Mother. My mother.

Gradually mingled with the hurt and bitterness came a surging curiosity which at first she could barely admit. When once she did voice it at home, 'I wonder what she's like . . .?', Rosalie said, 'Well aren't you going to go and see 'er? Swallow yer pride. I would. I miss my mom like anything. It's not too late for you, is it?'

'Oh no!' Mercy's voice was adamant. 'I'm not going barging into her posh little life. Not after all this time. She's never wanted me before, has she? Why should she now? I'm not giving her the chance to throw me out again. Oh no. Never.'

Chapter Forty-One

Mabel and Alf's wedding was a fortnight off and a woman down the street was making Mabel's trousseau. It wasn't being kept any great secret though.

'I had all that caper the first time,' Mabel said. 'All of them superstitions and none of them brought me much luck.'

'I should keep it plain and simple,' Alf had said, obviously worried how much she might be thinking of forking out.

'Don't fret, I will. But we'll make a good day of it all the same.'

Rosalie was to be her bridesmaid, and the same needle-woman was stitching a frock in pretty pink sateen for her.

The other women in the court, knowing there was a wedding afoot, were in and out of the house discussing, offering help. Mary Jones was out at work now her children had reached school age but she was round as soon as she'd fed them enough to keep them quiet.

Mercy, so many causes of distress tugging at her heart that she could scarcely think clearly about any of them, kept out of the way. Not that everyone wasn't kind. Her news spread round the yard like a blaze and there was no one who didn't know what had happened. All of them had soft, sympathetic words for her and questions. But she couldn't stand talking about it, not to anyone. It was still all too raw.

She went to see Tom again. He was outside, as before. Always as before, she thought. Nothing changing or moving on. That was the awfulness of it. She sat holding his hand and just once he gripped hers in return.

'I've got such a lot to tell you.' She spoke very quietly, pouring out everything that had happened. It surprised her how much better she felt after talking to him. He couldn't respond, but knowing he'd loved her once, that he likely still would if he were able, warmed her burdened heart.

After a time she saw Mr Hanley shuffle across the grass on his thin, bowed legs. He noticed her immediately and raised his hat, giving her a sweet, wistful smile. She waved back, full of unexpected excitement at seeing him. Her mind was still trying to marry this stooped old man with the fat fellow she'd felt so much aggression towards at the age of seven.

Mr Hanley drew himself up a chair beside that of another inmate about Tom's age. He had light brown hair and a round face. Mercy saw him turn his head for a second and thought ah, he's all right, he can recognize his grandfather. But the head lurched round again to face the other way, then back and forth in a convulsive motion and she could see the blankness in his eyes. She saw Mr Hanley take his hand as she had done Tom's, and begin gently to talk to him.

When later she got up to leave Tom, kissing him goodbye, Mr Hanley rose as well.

'Hello my dear.' His voice was thinner than she remembered. 'How nice to see you again.'

'How are you, Mr Hanley?'

'Oh – bars of iron, bars of iron.' But his eyes were sad and watery. 'May I have the privilege of transporting you home again?'

They walked down to the gate together.

'It's so hard coming here, isn't it?' Mercy said.

'Hardest thing I've ever done I think,' Mr Hanley agreed.

'Does anyone else come to see your grandson?'

'Oh yes, on other days. His mother, of course, and his sisters. I do Sundays – it's become a sort of routine. Now – just a moment, dear.' He stopped, fumbling in his jacket for a pipe and a pouch of tobacco and spent a little while obliging it to light. Eventually he managed and the sweet smell of the smoke reached Mercy. 'Ah, good. Now – how are you, my dear? Life treating you well?'

His Austin was parked not far from the gate and he opened the door for her. Mercy turned to him, feeling a great need to tell him. After all, he wasn't just anyone. He'd seen her as a child, too, and he was kind.

'Mr Hanley, d'you know what? I found out I've got a mother after all.'

Joseph Hanley nodded gently. 'Well, of course, my dear. Many of our unfortunate children aren't orphans in the strict sense of the word.'

'No, but I was,' she said fiercely. 'I was the one left on the doorstep. The one who didn't even have a name so they gave me yours. I had no one in the world . . .'

She poured the story out to him as they slowly made their way into Birmingham, and he listened intently. However many times she told the story it came out raw, angry, bewildered so that it seemed to her that she would always feel the same.

Mr Hanley stopped in the same spot on the Moseley Road. He reached over and took one of her young hands in his gnarled ones, turning to look into her eyes.

'I can see you're in distress, Mercy. Shocking for you, of course. Perhaps you'll be able to forgive your mother eventually for her difficulties. You know what they say, my dear, to know all is to forgive all. Whatever happens, I wish you all the luck and good fortune possible.'

He squeezed her hand for a second, then released it.

Another week passed. On Sunday afternoon Grace caught a bus into Birmingham, resolved to walk the rest of the distance. She had thought carefully about what to wear. So unimportant in one sense, yet it seemed vital for her first appearance. She was presenting – offering – herself. She dressed simply: the white mid-pleated skirt – white, to go to such a place! Yet she wanted to show her confidence, not arrive in some murky-coloured garment looking as if she were afraid of dirtying herself. On top, a white, lacy blouse covered by a soft wool cardigan in her favourite colour: cornflower blue. Her shoes were two-tone – white and navy, with an elegant heel.

Dorothy said goodbye to her, her face tense with worry.

'She's stubborn, you know. I don't know that she'll've calmed down yet. Don't be surprised if she . . .'

'Rejects me?' Grace looked back at her steadily. 'I'm certain I must do this. Mercy's right. I have risked nothing all these years. Always what Father wanted, then Neville. Believing they knew what was right for me. And yet my father married me to a man who is scarcely more than an animal. Now, I'm truly going to do the right thing.'

Dorothy seized Grace's shoulders and kissed her forehead. Grace raised her right hand and laid it over Dorothy's where it still rested on her shoulder.

'I'm so terrified, I can't tell you,' she said, eyes cast down.

Dorothy said nothing, squeezed her shoulders.

'But I must go.' Grace raised her head, the pale hair brushed immaculately round her face. Her eyes were wide and sad. 'Living with myself has been hard enough these twenty years. But now . . .' She pressed Dorothy's hand, then released it, stepping back. 'I've thought about it endlessly and I can't carry on – not like this.'

She was not accustomed to travelling on buses. Inside it was warm, stinking of smoke and old beer. She got off in town, hatless in the warm sunshine of early July, and walked across the Cathedral Square.

She felt a heavy-headness come over her. After her sleepless nights of turmoil when her mind seemed to protest, 'No more!', she was now filled with a fatalistic calm. What would be would be. She could only follow her conscience and her instincts. Her child, her flesh and blood, was in trouble and this sharpened her own memories of being alone, carrying a child, in desperation and shame. She wanted to make reparation. Give comfort. Make peace.

She walked briskly and purposefully through the centre of Birmingham, past the smart shops and banks towards New Street Station. Around Smithfield Market factories and workshops clustered in increasing numbers, hemmed in by the warrens of slum housing. The air was acrid with the smells of smoke and swarf, chemicals and grime.

The horror of it flooded back to her. Those days in Aston, where the same smells were mingled with that sickening, vinegary tang from the HP Factory. She knew, logically, that she had survived it, come safely through, but the terror and degradation her twenty-five-year-old self had suffered was engraved on her very soul.

Dorothy had described the route to her many times, and she had been here herself just once before. Just to look, to be able to picture it. Perhaps catch a glimpse of

. . . But she had not seen her. From her memory, nothing had changed: pubs, houses, everything timelessly the same. She knew that where she wanted was down on the right.

'Nine,' she muttered under her breath. A man pushed his cap further back on his head and stared at her.

'Oh God, give me strength!' Here it was, the dank, mossy walls of the entry. Nine Court, Angel Street. Her heart seemed almost to rise into her throat.

They were all there when she arrived, except Jack, who was always out if he could be, these days, Mercy, Mabel, Alf, Rosalie and Mary Jones, talking about food for the wedding. The door was open to let a breeze in, even though it meant they could smell the drains every time there was a fresh waft of fetid air.

They heard the footsteps, the light, ladylike clip of her heels, their hesitation as she approached the door and found it open. She didn't need to knock. She could see the ring of people inside, all quite still now, watching her, Alf and Mabel with their heads screwed round to look.

For a moment no one said a thing. Mercy could barely even breathe. She was paralysed, felt as if the room had begun to sway around her. There seemed to be a spell on them all. The moment went on and on. She saw the woman's elegance, her pale skin, gold hair, the deep grey eyes. Those eyes fastened immediately on her, and in them she saw the intensity of her sorrow, longing and fear.

Then Mabel said quietly, 'Oh Lor',' and stood up, scraping her chair. 'You'd best come in then.'

The woman stepped, with humble attitude, over the threshold and stood in front of them all. For a moment she couldn't seem to think what to do. Then, visibly gathering together every last ounce of courage she possessed, she stood tall, jutting her chin out a little.

'You know, don't you, who I am?' She spoke gently, entreatingly to Mercy.

Mercy just had the wits to give a small nod. Everyone else's eyes bored into them.

'I've come here because – because Dorothy said – you could feel nothing but anger and disgust towards me, and I . . .' For a moment she seemed about to lose control, her hands covering her face convulsively for a second. She removed them, clawing back her composure and returned them to her sides, gripped tight into fists. 'I knew that if we were ever to meet it was right that I should be the one to come to you.'

Alf stood up suddenly too. 'Come on,' he instructed the others. 'This ain't no time for us to be 'ere. Let's get out and leave 'em on their own.'

'Why should we get out?' Mabel griped. 'If 'er's got summat to say she can say it in front of us, and not before time neither.'

'You're Mabel?' Grace turned to her. 'You're the one that . . . took her?'

'Ar, I did.' Mabel folded her arms aggressively. 'And I gave 'er a home to grow up in and took 'er back when she came 'ere in trouble like. And I never deserted none of my kids, that's for sure.'

Mercy roused herself for a moment and turned her head. 'Oh, didn't you?'

Reminded of her absent months with Stan Jones, Mabel flushed an ugly red.

'Come on.' Alf jerked his head again. 'Out.'

They trooped to Mary's house leaving a sudden, engulfing silence between Mercy and Grace.

Mercy was still sitting, her hair loose and falling round her face. Grace stood, her eyes fixed with yearning on Mercy's bowed head, willing her to speak.

The silence went on, during which the conflict of Mercy's emotions was so acute she couldn't move or speak. She sat trying to summon up all her pain and anger, all the loneliness and hurt of the past years, but instead found herself overcome by helplessness, a sense of dream-like unreality. Her mother, the woman she had never been able to imagine was standing in front of her. Had come to find her. Flesh and blood. An unassailable tie which drew her like a magnet however hard she tried to resist. There Grace stood, looking at her with her own eyes, her hair the same straw gold. But she couldn't quite bear it. Not yet.

In a voice unmistakable in its hostility she said, 'So you're my mom then?'

'Yes.' Grace's voice began to break. 'Yes, Mercy. I am.'

Chapter Forty-Two

Grace pulled a chair out. 'May I?'

Mercy nodded, still not looking at her.

'So what d'you want off me then? Decided I exist after all, have you?'

Silence followed, for so long that she was compelled to look up. Grace's eyes were fixed on her, sorrow spilling in wet lines down her face.

'Oh Mercy, how callous and wicked you must think I am!' She wiped her eyes, though more tears came immediately. 'How can I explain to you that I did the cruellest thing a mother could do to her child, and yet I loved you so much – still love you – so that never a day has passed when I haven't ached to be able to have you properly in my life?'

Mercy felt a tightness take hold in her chest, a hard ache like a gigantic sob trying to escape. It was a sensation so overpowering it filled her with panic. Don't let her reach you! her mind screamed. Keep her at a distance . . .

'So why now?' She made her voice as bitter and sarcastic as she could. 'All of a sudden, out of the blue.'

'Because I know that you, my daughter—'

'Daughter!'

'That you are also carrying a child. And I couldn't live, knowing the suffering you would go through without . . . support. Family. I can't describe to you how it has been watching you from a distance all these years. Knowing all your difficulties. And then when we lost you ... When Mabel ...' She ran a hand over her face. 'My life has been tied to yours since the moment you came into the world.'

Mercy tore her eyes away from Grace's face, from her anguish. The tension inside her increased further. Her sense of being lost, rejected, worthless, tussled with her enormous, unsatisfied longing to mean something to someone else, for family bonds, to belong. But she mustn't let it surface, mustn't allow herself the prospect of being satisfied, and she moved her hands under the table to hide their trembling. She was shaken by all the hungry needs of a child, so many and so intense. She was the tiny, bereft creature in the cellar who could not help herself.

'I'd like to tell you,' Grace said, 'May I?'

Mercy nodded, swallowing hard. Her teeth were chattering again and she had begun to shake all over, so much that she couldn't hide it.

'Oh, my dear,' Grace said, seeing her. She moved to get up. 'I—'

'Just tell me,' Mercy interrupted savagely. 'Tell me and then go.'

Grace leant back in her chair again. She spoke in her soft voice, looking away from Mercy, giving her a chance to compose herself. From the corner of her eye she could see her shuddering attempts to do so.

She described the wretched house in Aston to which she'd resorted in desperation, the women who had birthed her, and her departure, still shaking from shock and exhaustion, in the middle of the night.

'When I reached the home, it was very late. Three o'clock – the clocks were chiming, I remember. The streets were so very dark and I was terrified. I'd never been out at that time before and I was afraid that someone might see me. A policeman perhaps. Then it would have all been impossible.

'It was so cold. There were icicles hanging on the railings. I'd wrapped you in everything I had, but I was worried it wouldn't be enough, that you wouldn't last the night. I thought I must just leave you, once I'd put you down on the steps. Leave you and run right away, or I'd never be able to give you up.

'But I found I couldn't. Simply couldn't physically leave. It was as if you were still attached to me. I went and sat on the steps of that school – your school – across the road, and all the time I was straining my ears to hear if you made any sound. Every so often I crept across and made sure you were still breathing. After a time you started crying. I was just on the point of getting up when I heard voices along the street. I couldn't imagine who it could be. I hid behind the wall with my cloak pulled over my face.

'There was a lamp outside the home, so there was a pool of light. When they came I saw there were five of them. Boys, no more than that. All rather oddly dressed – big boots, cravats and bowler hats with a peculiar pointed bit at the front.' She gestured, making the shape. 'I realized after a moment what they were. There were a few of them about in those days, boy gangs calling themselves "Peaky Blinders" – to do with the hats, I s'pose. I'd heard snippets about them because they were notorious for terrible, vicious fights ... Anyway, they were only young really, but their voices sounded so rough and threatening to me.

'They started arguing – it was because they heard you crying. "Here – what's that?" – "It's only a cat." – "No, it's a babby." – That sort of thing. One of them bounded up the steps. I was biting my hand so hard I drew blood. He said, "Eh – it is an' all! It's a babby!"

'I can't describe to you how I felt at that moment. These disgusting creatures in their filthy moleskin trousers and belts with vicious-looking buckles, going up close to you. Inside I was screaming at them, don't touch my baby!'

Grace laid her hand over her heart. 'My baby – oh, when I uttered those words to myself . . . One of them bent down and picked you up. Actually lifted you, cradling you in a mocking sort of way, and took you down the steps. "Ah," he said. "Don't cry there." The others were jeering in a horrible manner. I thought they were going to make off with you . . .' She shuddered.

'They crowded round, making horrible comments – I can't remember . . . But then one said, "Look – his face's got blood on it!" They assumed you were a boy, I don't know why. They said, "Ugh – d'you think it's only just been born?" They all made jeering and retching noises, bending over. One of them dropped his hat. I remember him stooping to pick it up.

'The lad holding you said, "Who wants it, eh?" He started to circle with you, swinging you as if he was going to throw you and you were screaming louder and louder. "'Ere – catch!"

'I screamed then. As I ran down the steps—' – Mercy saw her face contort with disgust – 'there was blood running down my legs. I shouted and shouted, "Give me my baby!" I must have looked like something from Bedlam. I felt like a madwoman. I was snarling – it was pure instinct, like an animal. I would have done anything, scratched their eyes out – killed them if necessary.

'"Is it yours then?" he said, and I shouted, "Give me

my baby" again. He pretended he was going to throw you at me, looking round at the others. Then, carelessly, he handed you over.' Grace's arms made the motions of holding a child.

'"Shouldn't leave 'im lying around next time!" one of them shouted. They went off laughing, shouting back more crude remarks.

'You were still crying so wretchedly. You were hungry, and I was shaking. I couldn't stop my teeth chattering, like someone with a fever.' She glanced at Mercy. She was sitting bent over the table, her arms wrapped round herself as if now, too, she was frozen, but her eyes were fixed on Grace's face.

'My legs could scarcely hold me up. I took you back to those icy school steps and sat down, soiled and damp as I was. And then I . . .' She broke off, tears rushing from her again, her voice high, cracking so that for a time she struggled to speak. 'I did the one thing I'd avoided doing up until then, the thing I knew would entangle my heart with you for ever. I unfastened my clothes and let you suckle. You had all those instincts ready and you sucked strongly while I cradled your head . . . And I cried. I don't know how long we sat there exactly. I must have slept a little, keeping you warm. When I woke my head was leaning against the wall and it was getting light. I was filled with panic. Someone might see us!

'I had to hurry and put you down. But still then I couldn't leave. I watched until I saw a lady carry you in. And then I knew you'd gone from me.' Her voice sank to a distraught whisper. 'For ever.'

A sound came from Mercy. A high, unstoppable whimper. Her head was in her hands, the backs of them resting on the table, for she was bent right over as if felled by grief, curled like a cowed little child.

'Mercy!' Grace stood up in alarm. 'Oh, my dear – my dear child!' Trembling, she went to stand behind her. The girl's shoulders were heaving, but some time passed before the sound of her weeping broke into the room, so far did it have to travel from the very depths of her.

'Oh . . .' Mercy gasped and broke into desperate sobbing.

For a long time Grace hesitated behind her, racked herself by the heartbreaking sound. Very cautiously she reached out her hand and laid it on her daughter's shoulder.

Later, when they were a little calmer, Grace offered to leave. 'You may want me out of here . . .'

But the thought of this woman – mother, her mother – leaving now with so much still to say was suddenly appalling to Mercy. She could feel her resistance falling away.

Grace gently requested tea, thinking the activity might steady her, and, in a daze, Mercy went out to the tap in the yard to fill the kettle. Hungrily, Grace watched her slim figure for echoes, resemblances, and they were only too easy to find.

'It'll be a few minutes,' Mercy said awkwardly, as she put it on to boil.

'Of course,' Grace smiled.

Mercy felt very strange. Exhausted and churned up. She had done her best to keep a barrier up between her own howling loneliness and this woman who had given her away. And she had failed, broken down completely. The story she had told of that filthy, leaking attic room she had inhabited, when all her life she had been used to the comforts of greater wealth, the anguish of the night of her birth as well as Grace's undeniable grief had made her begin to understand. Both had been helpless, the mother as much as the child. They had drawn a step closer. But now the moment of most acute emotion had passed, it was hard for them to know how to talk to each other again. They were silent, looking at each other awkwardly, and then away. Both began speaking at once, then faltered.

'No – you, please,' Grace said.

'It's just – your father. Dorothy said he was very strict.'

Grace sighed. She stood holding on to the back of a chair. Mercy saw how smooth and well kept her hands were.

'All my young life my father ruled everything. I suppose I let him. My mother did the same. Both of them are dead now. They were religious people in the worst sense – rigid, afraid ... After – after I'd had you, I mean, because everything was different from then on – he made me marry Neville, my husband. He thought Neville shared his views ...' She gave a harsh laugh. 'Well, there was a mistake. The one and only thing they had in common was that they were both bullies. But those were my alternatives at the time: destitution or Neville. Father said he'd cast me out if I didn't marry him. I'd disgraced myself; now I had to do precisely as I was told. D'you know, at the time it didn't seem to matter. I felt as if my life was over in any case.' She sighed. 'My agony was in having given you up. Perhaps when I had you I could have found some home for fallen women like myself. Even kept you. But the only choice I could see then was to get back into the safety of home or perish, alone and starving.'

She stopped talking. Mercy looked guardedly at her.

'It's all right, dear – but I've been talking so much that I've barely even heard your voice.'

'But you know about me.' Her tone was still accusing. 'You've been watching me all my life. What I want to know is: who is my father? If your life was so sheltered, how did it happen?'

She blushed at her own bluntness and saw the colour flame in Grace's cheeks as well. The kettle murmured loudly in the background.

'Oh—' She sank down at the table again with a long sigh. 'Of course you want to know. I was such a foolish, ignorant girl. Romantic, but with not the first idea . . .' She broke off for a moment and without looking directly at Mercy said, 'Was James Adair – forceful with you?'

The burning in Mercy's cheeks heightened until she thought she might catch fire.

'Dorothy told you that as well. Of course – Dorothy tells you everything. Like what sort of clothes I should wear so you could go out and decide for me. Buy me the clothes I should have.'

'Oh no – I didn't buy them! How could I have done? I have no money of my own. No, they were passed on – from friends who had girls. I made up charitable causes and so on that I was giving them to. I didn't choose them.'

Mercy digested this. Grace seemed to have had as little choice in her life as she had had herself.

'No,' she said eventually. 'He wasn't exactly – didn't knock me about. Not the first time. But he forced me all the same. I was afraid of what he'd do if I didn't . . . I didn't know what he'd do, or what I should do. Then he came back another night and he was rough, pushed me down, made me . . .' Once more she started to cry. She no longer seemed to have a guard on her emotions. The kettle gushed out steam behind her and she turned, hiding her face as she brewed the tea.

Grace had been drinking in her words, the sound of her soft voice. She was conscious of the gulf between their experiences, yet in this one, very fundamental one, they were the same: each being alone in the world with a child.

'I'm so, so sorry Mercy. If I'd had any idea he might behave so appallingly I wouldn't have dreamed of suggesting you go there. It astonishes me that he's of such weak character. He seems so . . . upright.'

'I know,' Mercy said, turning. 'That's why I couldn't believe it, even while it was happening.' She brought Grace her tea. 'Please – tell me about my father.'

'Oh dear.' Grace sighed again. 'I was in love with your father. I was young – well, not so young, of course – and very naive and innocent. I have only one younger sister, Ruth, so there was no one to show me the way. Our mother was a true Victorian. Never breathed a word about the physical aspects of life. Your father wasn't of our – of my – class . . .' She fiddled with the spoon in her saucer, abashed. What was Mercy's class, after all?

'He came to our house as a gardener and handyman. His name was Daniel. Danny. He was so beautiful. Dark brown, curly hair, brown eyes, a smile which just lit up his face. And he was ambitious. He wanted to move on – didn't want to stay in service and I used to encourage him. He liked to talk to me – we were much of an age. I fell in love with him.' She gave a sharp, ironic laugh. Mercy watched her with absolute attention. 'Helpless with it. I'd have done anything for him. Anything he asked. After some time we became lovers. You might ask how, since I was so ignorant of the meaning of it. But it was such a gradual thing. He had a little room at the back of the house. It wasn't difficult to be alone. He led me, little by little, not forcing, so that when we were – united – for the first time I hardly knew how I'd reached this point, but I knew it was something I couldn't undo. That it was wrong, morally. Yet I felt so safe with him. We learned together and the pleasure of it grew. It was exciting, illicit.' Mercy heard her tone soften as she spoke of it. 'We were like children really. I didn't even know that was how babies came.'

Her tone grew desolate and she looked across at Mercy. 'Of course in the end I fell pregnant and it all came out. My father dismissed him at once. I hoped he'd wait for me, that I could escape – we'd marry and have our child. He left Birmingham soon after. He wrote, before I'd even given birth to you, telling me he was going to America. To start afresh.'

Mercy thought how many people connected with her had crossed that ocean.

'He did go. He succeeded in that. Two years after he arrived he was killed. An accident on the railway. We never heard exactly what. Another man he'd teamed up with wrote and told us. Just a note, no more.'

Mercy looked perplexed. 'Told your father?'

Grace was about to say something, but checked herself, seemed to be looking at Mercy with a new kind of dread. She spoke very carefully, watching Mercy's face.

'No, not my father, Mercy. When Danny came to work in our house he came to join his sister. His name was Daniel Finch.'

Mercy seemed to stop breathing for a moment.

'Yes, my dear. Dorothy is your aunt.'

She leant across the table and dared to take Mercy's spare hand in her own. Mercy didn't resist.

'You have hands like his.' She looked searchingly into Mercy's eyes. 'He was a good man, your father. He didn't love me as I loved him, but he had a lot of love in him.

He and Dorothy came from a terribly unhappy family and they looked after each other.'

For a second she raised Mercy's hand and brushed it against her lips before releasing her.

'Dorothy – my aunt . . .?' Mercy was still dazed. 'So that's why – that's what kept her with you.'

'Dorothy would have stayed with me anyway. She came to us when she was fourteen. She loves me and I her,' Grace said matter of factly. 'But we shared these extra bonds – Danny, and you. We had you, from a distance. She was absolutely distraught when that Mabel Gaskin took you. She'd been ill, you see – you remember, perhaps? We were at our wits' end and Dorothy felt it was her fault. We'd hoped to get you adopted by a good family so you could have had a proper life and been better cared for.

'When Dorothy found you at Mabel's and we saw how it was, your attachment to Susan, we thought the only thing to do was wait until you were old enough to go to work and then we could help find you something worthwhile and safe. Oh, those years were terrible. Seeing you suffering with that woman, so poor and ill-treated! You have no idea how much time we spent talking about how we could change things and help you without Neville suspecting. By then I had the boys to consider . . . Your brothers.'

She stopped, seeing again how deep in shock Mercy was. The trembling had started again and she was very pale.

Mercy felt as if a landslide was happening inside her, everything tumbling, splintering, tilting, the person she had always thought herself to be torn apart. And yet, she knew a sudden, slow-awakening joy.

'My brothers,' she whispered. 'My mother . . . my aunt . . . Oh my God!' Her eyes were stretched wide. 'Oh, I can't take it all in.'

Suddenly she found Grace was kneeling close in front of her on the hard floor, her head bowed.

'Mercy – all I ask is that you'll let me see you sometimes and get to know you as I should. And one day – one day – I hope you'll be able to understand a little and begin to forgive me.'

Mercy couldn't speak. Very slowly she stood up. Grace looked up at her and Mercy held out her hand to help her to her feet. They stood facing each other, close in height, their hair precisely the same bright gold, both trembling. There was a second's hesitation, then Mercy held out her arms, sobbing as Grace embraced her tightly, her face washed with tears of love and relief.

'I've got a mom!' Mercy cried over and over. Her voice was broken, childlike. 'Oh, I've got a mom!'

'You have, my darling one.' Grace stroked her hair, held her close, trying to soothe her. 'You've always had a mother, and she's always loved you.'

This made Mercy sob even harder.

They stood for a few moments, the mother comforting her daughter, the daughter the mother. They could start, very gradually, to weave together the threads of all their lost years. It was a beginning.

Chapter Forty-Three

For someone who'd been married before and was now in any case living in sin, Mabel was surprisingly girlish and mithered the morning of the wedding.

She went down to the public baths on the Moseley Road and treated herself to a good soak before Mercy and Mary helped her into her wedding garb: a calf-length skirt and flared jacket which she belted tightly at the waist, all in navy pinstripe. Under the jacket she wore a cream blouse and rounded it off with navy shoes with straps, and a straw boater to which Mary pinned a posy of yellow roses.

'Look at me,' she said, holding out her arms as Mary tightened the belt round her. 'I'm all of a quiver! I'll never get through this blooming service, I'm a bag of nerves!'

'You look very nice,' Mary told her. 'Doesn't she, Mercy?'

'Yes,' Mercy agreed generously. 'You really do, Mabel. You should stop fretting.'

Mabel did in fact look splendid. The suit flattered her broad, curvaceous figure and the deep blue set off her dark colouring. Her hair was coiled low on her neck, and she looked a handsome, mature woman, despite sounding much more like a sixteen-year-old.

Mary was also spruce in a pale blue frock. She had lost her gauntness now her children were older and her face had taken on a rounder, almost sweet look.

'You look lovely too, Mercy,' she said wistfully. 'But then you always do.'

Mercy was wearing her white dress with the sailor-suit collar. It was mid-calf length and loose at the front. She'd plaited her hair and twisted it into a simple knot at the back, leaving a few soft, wispy curls round her face, which had more colour back in it now she was over her morning sickness. She helped Rosalie into her pink bridesmaid's dress.

'It's lovely!' Rosalie twirled round. 'Oh, thank you, Mabel! It's the prettiest frock I've ever had!'

'You deserve it,' Mabel said indulgently. 'You've been a real good kid, what with yer mother and all that's happened.'

Everyone made noises of agreement.

Food was laid out under a muslin cloth on the table and Alf emerged from the pantry where he had been getting himself scrubbed up over the sink. His best suit was a tight fit on him now.

'It'll have to do, though,' he said, patting his stomach. 'One thing about you, wench, you can at least cook.'

'Cheeky bleeder!' she retorted. 'I've got a bit more know-how than that, I should 'ope!' and she gave him a suggestive wink.

Mercy wrapped a bit of sacking over her dress to keep it clean and heated the kettle. She watched Alf combing his hair in his shirtsleeves, intently turning his head this way and that in front of the little mirror, looking like an anxious young lad on his first date. Mercy smiled wistfully at the sight of him. He and Mabel would be happy enough together. At least something good could come out of all the tragedy of the past years.

The women were to leave in half an hour, Alf going on a bit earlier.

'Here – a cuppa to keep you going,' she said when it was ready.

'Oh, ta,' he said as if she'd offered him a large slug of whisky. 'I could do with that, I can tell yer.'

She sat sipping her tea, hoping the little fruit cake she'd baked would be all right and the bread wouldn't curl and wanting everything to go well for them. The baby was kicking now, more and more. She could feel its insistent flutter. But she was still a very tidy size. In the loose dress no one who didn't know could have guessed.

She looked round at the others' faces, all quiet and solemn as the moment approached. The thing to do now, she thought, is to go on. Try and put away the past. I've got a future and it starts today. With a surge of excitement she reminded herself for the umpteenth time that she had family coming to the wedding. Real family. Grace had asked humbly whether she might be at the service.

'I shan't impose any more on your hospitality,' she'd said to Mabel on Sunday before she left. 'I'd just like to be there with Mercy – well, and you.' Grace had tried to swallow all rancour she felt towards Mabel. 'You brought her up, after all.'

Mabel appeared a bit bemused, before remembering to look self-righteous and aggressive. 'Well, if that's what Mercy wants,' she said, in the tone of someone who'd never had anything but Mercy's best interests at heart.

Mercy found both of them looking at her. She gave a tense smile, and nodded.

'Thank you,' Grace said. To both of them. 'Thank you so much.'

They made quite a procession down Catherine Street and along the Moseley Road. Neighbours from Angel Street turned out to wave and wish them well, and there were a few well-meaning whistles as Mabel strode majestically along, smiling her gap-toothed smile. She looked a happy woman.

Behind her walked Mary and family, the Ripleys and McGonegalls and some others who tagged along to see her wed.

Mercy heard Josie Ripley say to Mary, 'Ain't she got a husband already somewhere?'

Mary looked round indignantly at her. 'It's all regular. She told the vicar like – I mean 'e deserted 'er nearly ten year ago!'

The square tower of St Paul's loomed with impressive solidity in the sunlight, though its stones were blackened with soot. Mercy could hear small birds twittering in the trees round the church. Taking in a long, nervous breath, she leant her head back and felt warm sunlight on her face.

Mabel, Rosalie and Mary waited outside while the rest of them went in. None of the neighbours were church-goers. The McGonegalls occasionally went to St Anne's to Mass in a fit of guilt, but they all seemed to feel muted and out of place in the gloom of the church. As Mercy's eyes got used to it she saw how stately and beautiful it was inside, how you could see leaves rippling through the coloured glass. For a second she was back in the hall of the Hanley Home, dreaming her way through the long window.

Mercy soon heard the clip-clip of well-made heels, and felt her heart leap with shy expectation. That's the sound of my mother, she thought. Mother. She'd saved a third row pew. She turned, and in astonishment, saw not only Grace, but Dorothy and Robert, and another smaller boy with almost white-blonde hair. In a haze she stood up, feeling everyone's eyes on them.

Grace smiled at her, adoringly, defiantly. This was her daughter. She wanted everyone to know. Mercy moved to the far end, Grace and the boys following her, and Dorothy sat by the middle aisle. She leant foward and gave Mercy a long, meaningful look which said, I know you know everything. But there'll be time afterwards. Plenty of time.

Grace took her hand and squeezed it and Mercy smiled. She thought she might explode with the amazement and wonder of the past few days. None of it had fully sunk in yet. But she kept saying to herself, I'm not alone any more. I'm not alone in the world.

'This is Edward,' Grace whispered, as the organ began to play softly in the background. 'You're very alike.' Edward stared at her with naked curiosity and Mercy found herself doing much the same in return.

'Dorothy says you looked very like that – he's ten.'

'I suppose,' Mercy mused, her eyes not leaving the boy's face. 'But I don't remember any mirrors.' She reached out her hand nervously, not knowing what to do, and smiled. 'Hello – I'm Mercy.'

'Edward,' he said with grown-up solemnity. 'Pleased to meet you.'

Mercy laughed softly. 'I'm pleased to meet you, too.'

'She's coming!' someone hissed, and they all stood up as the wedding march struck up and Mabel appeared at the back of the church. Alf peered round at her from the front.

Mabel, having no living relatives to accompany her, had rather unusually asked Mary to walk her down the aisle. Mary was all smiles, Mabel more nervous and solemn, and Rosalie behind, with her little posy of pink and white carnations.

The church was only a quarter full, but everyone there wished them well. Mabel joined Alf at the front, the door closed at the back.

They all stood up and sang 'Praise My Soul the King of Heaven'. At the words, 'ransomed, healed, restored, forgiven,' Mercy felt Grace looking at her and their eyes met for a moment. Mercy was struck with admiration for her, coming here, laying herself bare to everyone. It had taken some guts, that had.

The service began. The heavy door at the back opened and closed a couple of times to let in latecomers. Mabel and Alf said their words with dignity. They looked small and humble standing side by side under that immensely high ceiling in their plain clothes, the only sort they could afford.

Mercy felt a great sadness rush through her as they finished their vows. However much she tried to forget, to count her blessings, it all surfaced unexpectedly. She was to have been married. She and Paul had made their promises to each other and she had rejected him. Missing him gnawed away at her inside. She looked down at her hands folded in her lap, tears in her eyes. The feeling had to go away sooner or later, this ache for him. The door must close, she thought. It just wasn't meant to be. And this was no time to be dismal. Hiding behind the pretence of wiping her nose, she surreptitiously dabbed the corners of her eyes. Grace kept looking round at her. Couldn't seem to stop looking at her. She tried to smile.

The ceremony was almost over and Alf, hat in hand, and Mabel were soon exchanging their first kiss as a married couple. Everyone was smiling. Mary Jones's eyes were wet.

They stood to sing 'Now Thank We All Our God.'

As soon as the first, rather ragged verse was underway, Mercy felt a tap on her shoulder and turned. One of the churchwardens had crept along the side aisle and whispered discreetly in her ear.

'Sorry miss – but there's someone outside requires your assistance.'

Who on earth? They'd asked for some ale to be delivered at the house, but surely to goodness he hadn't come here to see her about it? She put her hymn book down and with a baffled shrug said to Grace, 'I'll see you outside.' She followed the warden, very much on his dignity, to the back of the church.

'Didn't want to disturb you but it seemed urgent like,' he said stiffly, pulling the door open. 'There you go . . .'

There was no one in the porch, so she went out, bewildered and rather irritated. What was so urgent that it couldn't wait until they'd finished? She looked from side to side.

'Mercy.'

He stepped out from under the trees. His face was sallow, exhausted-looking, the suffering in it plain to see.

'Paul,' she said, at a loss. 'Oh heavens – Paul.'

They stood looking at each other, the hymn sounding thinly from inside the church.

'How did you get here?' she asked him, somehow calmer than he was. His agitation was obvious, his hands gripping the edges of his open jacket. His face was even thinner than she remembered, fatigued. The sight of it wrung her heart.

'You told me the name of the street. So I asked – in a

shop. They said you'd gone to a wedding, and I thought at first . . .' He shrugged helplessly.

'No – oh, no! It's Mabel – and Alf. My . . . my . . . the people I live with.'

He turned away a fraction. 'My father died last week. So I –'

'Oh Paul.'

'Mercy, why did you write that letter? What on earth happened? I haven't been able to sleep, to think straight. I had to ask myself, were you just playing with me – all the time? Is my judgement completely wrong? Was everything that happened just a . . . a . . .' He put his hand to his forehead. 'I knew you, or thought I did. You were so straight, so true. I can't make sense of anything. I thought you'd just write back and say everything was all right, that it was just a mistake, joke even . . .' He raked his hand through his hair.

She looked anxiously over her shoulder. 'They'll be out in a minute, come round here.'

They crept round the side of the church under the shade of the trees. A blackbird rose from one of them, chirruping in alarm. Mercy felt weak, trembling, but she still had a small pool of calm inside her. She longed to put her arms round him, to comfort, spread her love round him, but that would be wrong. She would tell him the worst, the truth, and then he could forget her as she had tried to forget him. He deserved to know. She would tell him straight, bluntly, the thing a man would least want to hear.

Standing apart from him she looked into his eyes. He watched her, arms folded as if to protect his heart, yet his eyes were so full of tenderness she was forced to look away again. Her own expression was brave, but infinitely sad.

'I'm expecting a babby.'

He was silent for a moment, then his hands hung loose at his sides. His tone was flat, defeated.

'Oh – I see.' He was struggling to take it in. 'So you're already married then.'

'No, Paul, I'm not.' She told him with a truthfulness that was almost brutal, about James Adair.

'It happened twice. I didn't know how I could stop him and I didn't want it. If you can believe anything I say, please believe that. I'd never have thought it of him then – and I was so frightened . . . didn't know. I just didn't know what to do.'

Her distress began to seep through, despite her efforts to remain calm. She put her hands over her burning face. This was the most horrible, the dirtiest moment of her life, facing all this again, having to tell him of all people.

When she looked up, he too had his face in his hands. It's over now, she thought. He knows the very worst of me.

After a moment he said brokenly, 'I came wanting to be angry with you . . .' He looked up at her. 'Did you love him?'

'Love him?' She was aghast. 'How can you ask me that? Paul, I was spending every waking moment I could with you. It was like a nightmare – every time I went back to that room. I couldn't tell you what was happening. I felt so ashamed, so used and dirty. I'd try and put it out of my mind in the day, almost as if it were happening to someone else. And with you – you were the one I loved with all my heart. I still . . .' Her control was slipping away from her. 'Oh Paul, I've wanted you so bad I can't even tell you. I was so scared and sick and ashamed when I got home – when I found out there was a babby and it wasn't all going to go away. I didn't want you to know because ... How could I tell you something so disgusting about me so that you'd despise me? I had to run away from the Adairs in the middle of the night and I wrote to you, and I thought, better just to ... to cut it off. Finish it.' She wiped her eyes and looked up, overcome to see tears in his.

'Mercy.' He stepped closer to her, cautiously. 'Do the Adairs know about this child?'

'No! They must never know! It would make her so unhappy and even more, I don't want him to know. I can survive without him. He lied to me,' she finished furiously. 'He used me like a dirty handkerchief and he said it wouldn't happen. I wouldn't have a babby – as if he knew! No – I may be alone, but I don't want him anywhere near.'

The door of the church opened and they heard whoops of laughter as Alf and Mabel came out to be showered with rice.

Paul grasped her hand and pulled her even closer to the wall, out of sight.

'Tell me something.' He spoke with immense intensity, his face close to hers, eyes still wet with tears. 'Tell me truthfully whether you could ... whether you still feel anything for me.'

She saw the anguish with which he waited for her answer. 'Oh Paul, of course I do,' she said gently. 'There's only one man I love with all my heart and that's you. I've never stopped loving you and I've missed you so much sometimes, I felt like coming to find you. Except I knew it was all impossible. That it's hopeless now. Sometimes I think I'm fated always to be on my own.'

'Why?'

'Why what?'

'Why should you be alone?'

'Paul,' she reminded him gently. 'I'm carrying another man's child. How could I expect you to forgive that, however much I didn't want it?'

Paul suddenly pressed his hands to her face, lifting her chin a little. His palms were hot on her cheeks.

'Say again that you love me.'

Tears ran down her face. 'I do. I love you.'

'And I love you. YOU. I told you before, whatever the past, whatever we are and what we've done, or what's been done to us, I want to spend the rest of my life with you. I can't live without you. Not properly.'

'But this isn't the past, Paul, it's now.'

He released her, but stayed close. 'Do you think, in the great scheme of things, that my bringing up a child that isn't mine is so very terrible? Mercy, I'm not looking to you for purity or perfection or any of that mumbo-jumbo. I'm so sorry for all you've suffered believing I was, but you were wrong. I've learned that surviving is about more than just staying alive. It's about holding on to the few worthwhile things there are, the things that make sense, that you can love.'

They stared into each other's eyes, both their faces wet with tears. He reached for her hand. 'Now, once more, my dearest love – please will you be my wife and share your life with me?'

'Yes,' she whispered, weeping. Then finding her voice, 'Yes. Yes!'

As if in response to their promises a cheer broke from the front of the church as their arms reached for each other, cheeks, then lips meeting, each clinging to the most precious thing in life.

*

Grace was standing rather at a loss with Dorothy at the front of the church while the rest of the party talked and celebrated in the sunshine. Mabel and Alf posed for a couple of photographs, solemnly side by side. There was food waiting at home, but no one was in a rush. It was a lovely day and a celebration, so what was the hurry?

Holding Paul's hand, Mercy led him shyly round to the jubilant little crowd. Grace looked relieved, then puzzled on seeing her.

Mercy stopped him for a moment. 'Paul, I've got summat else to tell you. This has been the strangest, most wonderful week of my life.' Her eyes radiated joy and excitement, but Grace could also see that Mercy's face was flushed from recent tears and her heart filled with anxiety for her.

'I want you to meet Grace Weston,' Mercy said, leading Paul over.

Each of them shook hands, smiling politely, a little baffled.

'Paul – Grace is my mother. My real mother. And mother – Mom,' she giggled, still unused to saying it, 'this is Paul Louth, the man I dearly love and am going to marry.'

Paul and Grace both dealt with these surprises with perfect courtesy and gladness. Mercy took huge delight in introducing him to the boys – 'my half-brothers' – and to Dorothy.

'Dorothy Finch is—'

'I remember you talking about Dorothy,' Paul said.

Dorothy's eyes were welling with emotion.

'Yes, but Dorothy is my auntie – oh Dorothy, come here!' Both very tearful they hugged and hugged each other.

'You don't know how often I've wanted to tell you,' Dorothy sobbed, 'only I couldn't.'

Mercy took Paul's arm. She felt she wanted to hold and hug everyone around her all day long. 'If you're all confused we'll explain on the way back,' she said. She looked round anxiously. 'You will come back, won't you?'

'Well,' Grace was uncertain. 'If Mabel doesn't mind.'

'She won't,' Mercy said firmly. Suddenly she broke away from Paul, and for the first time in her life, went to Mabel and kissed her cheek.

'You be happy now,' she said. 'You just make sure.'

Mabel looked startled, then grinned. 'I'll do me best.' She patted Mercy on the arm.

The wedding party made its unhurried, celebratory way back along the Moseley Road, Mercy, in the middle of it, arm and arm with her mother and her husband-to-be.

Grace looked round at her beautiful, indomitable daughter, who had in the last hour transformed into someone lit up by great happiness. Grace, too, was full of a calmness and joy she had not experienced for many, many years. A sense of rightness and completion. She was not anxious about her husband. She had kept Mercy from him for twenty years and she would continue to do so. The rest of them would not let her down. Neville was an irrelevance.

But there was one anxiety. Her eyes met Mercy's and then she glanced at Paul.

Does he know? her eyes queried. Does he know the truth?

Mercy's eyes shone back at her full of deep, unclouded joy.

He knows, hers responded. He knows. And he forgives.

Grace smiled and squeezed her arm. Bless you, that loving pressure said. Bless you, my darling. Be happy.

Epilogue

Margaret Adair picked up the letter from the table in the hall and frowned at the rather childish hand.

'What's that?' Stevie said, full of questions as ever.

Margaret patted his head rather absently. 'A letter. I don't know who from. You go on upstairs now, darling, and see how Nanny's getting on with the twins' breakfast. Then she'll take you all out.'

She took the letter into the sitting room and sat by the window, slitting open the envelope.

The address at the top provided no enlightenment. It was simply 'Birmingham, May 1923.'

Dear Mrs Adair,

I've been meaning to write to you for such a long time to apologize for leaving you and Stevie the sudden way I did. I was sorry to do it, especially with you having the baby on the way. There were some bad problems in my family and I had to go. I hope you can forgive me. I did miss you.

I expect Stevie is a big boy by now and has forgotten me long ago. But please give him a big kiss and cuddle from me.

You might like to know that I'm married. My husband is an engineer working at the Austin, and we have two children and another on the way. Our two little girls are called Susannah and Elizabeth and they are very healthy and full of energy.

We had a very special surprise last year. I had met, after many years, a Mr Joseph Hanley who founded the home where I started life and we had become friends. I'm sad to say he died last year, but he left me a tidy little sum of money which has been a great blessing for our family life.

We are all in good health and hope you are too. My warmest regards to you and your family. Perhaps one day we shall meet again.

Yours,

Mercy (née Hanley)

Margaret read the letter twice, with a mixture of emotions. She had been hurt and saddened by Mercy's mysterious flight from their house, had worried about her, and was delighted with news of her happiness. Yet something about the letter troubled her. Mercy's reasons for leaving them that way didn't seem quite right. Surely she had been on bad terms with her family such as it was? And why could she not have have talked her troubles over, not dashed off like that as if she were eloping?

'Who's that from?' James popped his head round the door before setting off for work.

Margaret looked up. 'It's the strangest thing. It's from Mercy – little Mercy Hanley – you remember?'

The immense pang which passed through James Adair's heart at the mention of her name did not register in his face. He stepped into the room, hands in trouser pockets.

'Our little fly-by-night? Ah yes – what news of her?'

'She sounds very well. She's married, two little girls already. But she doesn't say who to.' She turned the paper this way and that. 'No address or anything.'

'Hmm. Curious. Still, there we are. And you say she's well and happy?'

'Seems to be, yes. I'm glad for her. Odd business that, altogether.'

'Odd, yes . . .' James said dismissively. 'Anyway, must go. Give Stevie and the girls a kiss for me will you? I'm in a bit of a hurry.'

'All right, dear. Have a good day.'

James left, then on second thoughts came back and unexpectedly kissed her cheek, caressed her shoulder.

'Goodbye, my darling.'

She smiled up at him in happy surprise.

Some days later, the postman pushed a thin, cheap envelope through the letter box of a terraced house in Bournbrook which had a climbing honeysuckle lazing, sweetly scented, up its front wall.

Mercy picked it up in the hall as Paul came downstairs with the two girls. Susannah, determined to walk down by herself had a mass of blonde curly hair like a corona with the light from the landing window behind her, and striking dark brown eyes. The little one, Elizabeth, in Paul's arms, was unmistakably going to have his long, sensitive face and brown hair.

Paul sat Elizabeth down on the hall floor. 'There now, miss, you can crawl about – and keep off the stairs.'

He crept up behind Mercy and caught her by the waist, stroking her swollen stomach. The baby was due in four months.

'Your family coming round in droves today?'

Mercy laughed. Paul loved teasing her about her family, Grace's and Dorothy's eagerness to share her children, and the house was hardly ever quiet. Even after nearly three years of marriage she was still in a state of wonder at the richness of her life. The love of her family, and this house, their house, to which she could welcome them, with space and running water and a generous strip of garden for the girls out at the back. Paul had just built Susannah a swing from the pear tree.

'Oh, I dare say someone will be round!' she said.

Paul rested his head against the back of hers for a moment. Her hair was hanging loose and he lifted a hank of it to kiss the back of her neck.

'Look,' she said, squirming with pleasure. 'From America.'

They read it together, he over her shoulder.

'Yola and Tomek!' Mercy said. 'Oh – they've moved again, look – the address is new. Maybe now they'll have a bit more space for all these babbies of theirs.'

Yola already had three and was due with the fourth.

The letter was very short. Slowly, gradually they were learning to write English as well as speak it.

'*WE ARE ALL GOOD*,' Tomek had written carefully in capital letters. '*NEW PLACE IS GOOD. YOLA HAS A BABY BOY.*'

'Oh, lovely!' Mercy exclaimed.

'*EVERYTHING FINE. WE HAVE FOOD AND GOODS. WE ARE ALL FINE AND HOPE YOU TOO FINE. LIFE IS GOOD. TOMEK PETROWSKI.*'

'Life is good.' Mercy turned in Paul's arms, still holding the fragile letter. She felt her embrace returned with equal passion and gratitude.

'It is, isn't it?' she said. 'Very, very good.'

The Narrowboat Girl

For my daughter, Katie

ACKNOWLEDGEMENTS

Thanks are due in large measure to David Hearmon, owner of *Raven* for so generously sharing his time and expertise, and for his e-mail friendship; to my sister and brother-in-law Julia and Timothy Woodall for their hospitality and help, to Stoke Bruerne Canal Museum and to the staff of Banbury Museum.

I also owe a debt to canal enthusiasts Ray Shill, Wendy Freer and the Birmingham Canal Navigations Society for their publications. Above all, thank you to Sheila Stewart for her wonderful book about life on the cut – *Ramlin Rose*.

PART ONE

Part One

One

Ladywood, Birmingham, 1926

'Oi, Maryann – pack that in or your shoes'll be all scuffs. You'll 'ave our mom after yer!'

Sally Nelson sat primly on the step of the Garrett Arms, skirt pulled well down over her knees, thick blonde hair fastened back with a rag ribbon, and her baby brother clasped tight on her lap. There was a frown on her round, pretty face as her younger sister skipped impatiently up and down, aiming kicks at the grime-encrusted wall.

Maryann turned, sticking her tongue out as she sprang back and forth, an ice cream in one hand and ample signs of it in evidence round her top lip. She stopped for a moment and stared down the length of her skinny, scab-kneed legs to her feet, pushed into an old pair of cast-off shoes, their buckles dulled with wear.

'They're all scuffs any'ow, so what yer on about?' She licked urgently at the ice cream before beginning again on her hopping and twirling, her bobbed, black hair flying wildly round her face. 'Oh – where's our dad got to? 'E should be 'ere by now!'

Sally's big-sister bossiness couldn't rile her today. Maryann was as full of fizz as a bottle of Nanny Firkin's dandelion and burdock and just as close to exploding with excitement. It was 17 September, her twelfth birthday, the sun was still shining even though

3

the summer was over and they were back to school, and today was the day their dad had promised they'd go and fetch the kitten home from Nanny Firkin's. Even though she'd have to share it with Sal and Tony and babby Billy, really it was going to be *hers*.

After school that day she'd come dashing home well ahead of Sal, her excitement even overcoming her wariness of her mother. 'Mom! Mom! You there?' She tore up the entry, to find Flo Nelson in the yard still toiling away on the mangle outside the brewhouse. It was Monday, washday. Billy, with just a vest on, was stamping to and fro in a scummy puddle of washwater with his little peter out on show, the lot. Wet clothes strung on lines along the yard, flapped against Maryann's face.

'Course I'm 'ere. Where else would I be, sunning meself in the South of France?' Flo Nelson snapped, wiping her wet hands in an irritable gesture over her blonde hair to keep it out of her face. She was a broad-hipped, rather stately woman, once as beautiful as Sal would one day be, but sagging now. Her manner was petulant and long-suffering. 'And keep yer grubby 'ands off of there. I ain't been slaving away all day for you to come and bugger it all up. 'Ere—' She reached down the front of her blouse for a twist of cloth from which she took a sixpence.

Maryann's eyes widened with glee. Mom was never going to give 'er a whole tanner! Blimey, she knew it was her birthday, but Mom never handed out even a farthing without being *asked*! Flo Nelson bent and hoiked her youngest son to his feet.

'You and Sal go and find yerselves an ice cream – and get some drawers on 'im and take 'im with yer – 'e's running me ragged.'

4

A beam spread across Maryann's freckly face.

'Ice cream, oh *ta*, Mom. Come on, Billy – eh Mom, what about Tony?'

Her five-year-old brother would be whining round her if he saw her with an ice.

''E's round with Alec.' Flo jerked her head towards the wall adjoining the next-door yard. 'What 'e won't know won't hurt 'im. Make sure yer finish 'em before yer get back 'ere!' Her face surrendered to a rare moment of softness at the sight of her scallywag of a daughter. 'Go on with yer, birthday girl. This time twelve year ago I weren't enjoying meself any too much I can tell yer.'

Sal was just coming along the road.

''Ere Sal! Our Mom's being nice today – I've got a tanner!'

The girls found an Eldorado ice-cream cycle on the corner of Garrett Street and went back and settled by the door of the pub. Dad wouldn't be back yet, however much Maryann willed him to be. They'd long finished the ice creams, wiped Billy's face and were trying to stop him crawling in to play on the beery, sawdust strewn floor of the Garrett Arms when the men started coming out of the factories.

'Awright, Sal?' some of them said, coming into the Garrett for a pint or two after work. 'Waiting for yer dad, are yer? 'E'll be 'ere in a tick, Walpole's is out.'

Maryann noticed that when some of the men spoke to Sal, their voices altered, as if they were telling her a joke that Maryann didn't understand. And one or two of them would give her a wink. Sal favoured her mother's fair looks: the pale skin, gold hair, the white, rounded body. Quite the young lady she was and they treated her almost as if she was a grown-up woman.

They didn't do that to Maryann, a skinny whippet of a kid, with her black hair hacked off straight round her jaw and her face all freckles. She didn't care: she was a tearaway, a tomboy, besotted with animals and hungry for adventures.

She carried on skipping about. Walpole's were out! Walpole's, a firm making aluminium ware, was where her dad worked, the only man she cared about. After all these years he had a proper job and was earning a good wage and everything was getting better and better. Next year Sal would turn fourteen and there'd be two wages coming in. Then Mom'd never have to take in washing again.

Sally turned from bending over Billy to find Maryann shinning up the lamp-post on the corner by the pub.

'Oh get down before yer kill yerself,' she snapped. ''Ere, look – it's our dad. Yer that busy fooling about you've missed 'im coming.'

Maryann slithered down the pole and tore along the road, all sharp knees and skirt flying.

'Dad!'

Harry Nelson, a tall man with a lean, tired look, watched his daughter's wild progress along the street, followed more sedately by her older sister and baby brother. Harry stopped, throwing his coat over his shoulder, a grin spreading across his face. He held his arms out as Maryann catapulted herself at him.

''Eh – you're getting too big for that!' He laughed, fending her off.

'Dad, Dad – can we get the kitten now?'

'Well—' He eyed her, teasing. 'I had in mind a couple of pints with the lads first.'

'Oh *Dad*!'

He laughed. Harry Nelson had big, tombstone teeth

and needed only to part his lips to look as if he was smiling. 'There'll be no peace till we do, will there?'

'She's been keeping on and on,' Sal said, trying to sound superior, although in truth she was almost as thrilled about the kitten as Maryann.

Maryann dragged him by the hand. 'Come *on* then!'

Nanny Firkin lived in a back house on a yard off Ledsam Street, along from the Borax factory. It was a short way across Ladywood, the other side of the railway shunting yard and the cut in which lay the sluggish, scum-ridden water of the Birmingham Main-line Canal to Wolverhampton. The house where Mary-ann and the rest of the Nelsons lived was also a back house, with two tiny bedrooms on the first floor and an attic, but Nanny Firkin's house at the far end of the yard was more by way of a cottage: two up, two down, with a little patch of garden at the front, and Maryann loved going there. Nanny Firkin, a widow of some years, loved animals too and told Maryann she was a 'chip off the old block'.

When they reached Ledsam Street, Maryann ran on ahead, heart pounding with excitement, up the entry to Nan's and across the greyish-blue bricks of the yard. The door was open, as it nearly always was, and one of Nanny Firkin's cats, an exceptionally hairy ginger tabby, was curled, asleep on the front step. Maryann peered into the dark kitchen, which smelled of coal and onions and the sour odour of the parrot's cage.

'Nan? It's me, Maryann! Dad's brought us up for the kitten.'

'I didn't think it'd be long before you made an appearance.'

Nanny Firkin limped over to the door, a twinkle in her eye. She was a tiny lady, thin as a wisp, who lived on next to nothing and was always dressed stiffly in black, but with a little wizened face from which looked two eyes, watery and blue, and brimming with warmth and vivacity. She was full of affection for her grand-daughters and son-in-law. It was her own daughter Flo she found it less easy to rub along with, forever mith-ering and carrying on, although Nanny Firkin had done everything in her power to help Flo while Harry was away fighting – and the pair of them once he came back from France. Flo was a houseproud chit but lazy and self-pitying with it. Always hankering for a spick and span house but thinking it ought to get done by magic instead of knuckling down and doing the work herself. Flo Nelson called her own mother's house a 'bloody flea-ridden menagerie – yer go there alone and you come back with company.'

But Maryann had hardly ever caught a flea at her nan's. She'd be more likely to pick up company of that sort at her friend Nancy's house in another yard across Garrett Street, if the truth be told.

Nanny Firkin's kitchen was a cosy place. Her grand-mother had been chopping an onion at the table and the kettle was hissing on the hob over the black range. Beside it was squeezed the old chair with its horse-hair stuffing bulging out through holes in each of the arms. In one corner, balanced on a crate, was the cage where Walt her parrot lived, named after her late husband.

'Talks to me a darn sight more than Walter the flesh and blood man ever did,' Nanny Firkin often said.

''Ello, Walt!' Maryann called to him.

''Ello,' Walt said. ''Ello.' And added a metallic

sounding shriek for good measure, closely resembling the noise that came from one of the factories behind the yard.

When Harry Nelson appeared at the door with Sal and little Billy, Maryann was already bent over the black cat who was lying under the big chair with her litter. Out of the mass of warm, hairy bodies, Maryann saw a tiny face, tiger-striped grey and black, with shiny brown eyes gazing up at her.

'Oh look, Nan! Look at this one – the little tabby!'

She took the creature on her lap and it settled there, seeming quite content.

'Ain't they grown, Nan!' Sal exclaimed. 'No, Billy – yer must be gentle with 'em.' She restrained Billy's strong, pinching fingers.

'Oh Nan, can I 'ave this one!' Maryann looked into the animal's eyes and knew he wanted to be hers. 'Look at the way 'e's looking at me.' The kitten twisted playfully on to its back and pawed at her fingers.

'Don't I get a say then?' Sal stood over her, but she was smiling in spite of herself at the kitten's antics.

'It *is* madam's birthday,' Nanny Firkin said, brewing tea for Harry. She was always mothering him, trying to feed him up. 'Anyroad, I reckon 'er's picked the best of the bunch.'

While her dad gratefully drank his tea and ate Nanny Firkin's sticky ginger cake, and Sal and Billy played with the other kittens, Maryann sat with her new pal in her lap, laughing as his fur tickled her bare knees. She could scarcely believe it: a living creature, so tiny and perfect and beautiful, and he was all hers ... She stopped, looking carefully at him and turned to her grandmother who was sitting, as she always did, perched at the very edge of her chair as if in her long life she had never learned to take her rest and be comfortable.

'Is this one a boy or a girl, Nan?'

'Oh that's a lad, that one. Tigerface I call 'im.'

'Tigerface—' Maryann cocked her head at him. 'I think I'll just call 'im Tiger.' She nuzzled her cheek against him, brimful with delight. 'Thanks, Nan. 'E's the best ever.'

Maryann lay cuddled up close to Sal that night on the bed they shared in the attic. There was a strong whiff of damp, but they barely noticed, being used to it. They had an army blanket and a couple of old coats, and apart from that they had to keep each other warm. The nights were still quite mild now but it was perishing cold in the winter. Now she was older, Sal refused to have a 'bucket of wee' by the bed and, however cold the night, if she needed to go, she took the key and went off down the yard to the freezing toilets. Maryann wasn't so fussed and would go down and relieve herself in the bucket in Tony and Billy's room if needs be. Sal was getting far too particular, she thought.

'Move over,' Sal moaned. 'I'm half hanging off the edge of the bed over 'ere.'

'Sorry.' Maryann shuffled along the lumpy mattress. There was a pause. A mouse scuttled across the floor. 'Tiger's so lovely, ain't 'e?'

'Oh Gawd, not again. Yes, Maryann, 'e's lovely. 'E's the most perfect cat in the whole blinking world. Now will yer shurrup?'

There was silence for a moment, then Maryann poked her in the ribs and Sal rolled over, giggling. 'Oi, pack that in!' But she was only pretending to be cross.

The two of them snuggled up together. Despite being so different they were close. They'd had to be, the way their mom was.

There'd been great excitement when they carried Tiger home. Nancy Black and three of her brothers had invaded to look him over until Flo Nelson unceremoniously shooed them out again. Maryann had spent the whole evening holding him and playing with him and even Flo admitted he was 'awright, I s'pose'. Now he was asleep, exhausted, on a strip of rag by the range.

Maryann lay looking up at the dim rectangle of sky through the uncurtained attic window. The nights were drawing in now. 'I don't want to leave Tiger when I go to school,' she whispered. 'I wish 'e could come too.'

'Don't talk so daft,' Sal murmured. They lay together talking fondly about the kitten's antics until the downstairs door opened and they heard their father's tread on the stairs. Flo Nelson was always harassed and irritable in the evenings and hustled them straight from playing in the yard up to bed out of her way. She had Billy to settle down and didn't want any added trouble from them. But their dad always came up to say goodnight. Maryann squirmed with delight. It felt so cosy in bed, with Dad coming up to give them a kiss.

He had been a stranger to them when he came home from the war in 1919. Sal had been eight then, and Maryann five and it had taken them some time to get used to one another. Flo, exhausted after years of coping with two young daughters alone, of scrimping and queuing and struggling, had expected a man to come home who she could lean on, who would take over. Instead, for those first years, she had an unpredictable, helpless wreck on her hands. Often she exclaimed angrily that the men who came home may

11

have survived, but they were 'no bloody good to anyone, the state they were in'. The girls didn't understand what it was all about. They didn't understand the war, or the suffering of the soldiers, or that the man who had come home was one who had changed and couldn't fit in, wouldn't, for a long time, be able to hold down a job. But they did know they were loved. Harry Nelson was a man who felt incomplete away from his family. He adored his children, and that separation, added to the horror and degradation of the war, had increased his trauma further.

'How's the birthday girl?' he said, stooping his long body and sitting down on the bed.

Maryann giggled.

'That little Tiger of yours is asleep. Worn out.' Maryann felt him rub her back with his warm hand and he gave Sal a pat. 'Night night.' He leaned down and kissed them both. Maryann felt his lips press her cheek, the prickle of stubble on his top lip.

'Eh – 'ow about you sing to me, eh – our special song? Just the first bit. How'ds it go?'

The song was one Sal had sung at school while the war was on, a prayer for the soldiers and sailors. She had told her father about it when he came home and they had sung it many times. Now they both piped up:

> God bless our soldiers
> Guard them each day
> Make them victorious
> All the way.
> In the great conflict
> May they endure,
> And God bless our soldiers
> And make victory sure.

In the early months after he came home, he would ask for the song, and when they sang it he would sit on their bed, his shoulders beginning to shake until he was weeping uncontrollably. It had frightened them at first, but he was such a kind, gentle man that they used to sit beside him and put their arms around him. Flo had become resigned to his suffering and fractionally more understanding. They had had the two boys, who filled Harry with joy. It had taken years, but now, with the passing of time and the help of his family, in particular his children, Harry Nelson knew that the emotional wounds of the war were slowly healing.

Now he no longer wept when they sang to him. He sat quietly listening, then stood up as they finished.

'Nice voices, you wenches. Sleep tight.'

Maryann listened to him going slowly down the stairs to see the boys, the familiar creaks of each tread. She closed her eyes. She felt safe and warm and loved. Later, looking back at those cosy nights, she would wonder how she could have taken them for granted, when they were all too soon snatched away.

Two

It happened two months later, quickly, horribly, all in an afternoon.

Maryann was with her friend Nance. Nancy Black had been Maryann's best pal ever since they'd started school together. Maryann loved going to the Blacks' because there was always something going on. Even when Nance's dad came home tanked up he never took any notice of her – he and Mrs Black had a right lot of shouting matches, but he'd never done her any harm. As often as not when he arrived, Maryann and Nance'd shoot across the road to Maryann's house to keep out of the way until the trouble died down.

The Black family consisted almost entirely of boys: Nancy was sandwiched between three older and four younger brothers. Her dad, Joe Black, known as Blackie in the district, scratched what might have been a reasonable living as a cooper, going round the yards mending the maiding tubs, if he hadn't parked his barrow and drunk his earnings away most afternoons. Nancy's mom, Cathleen Black, had a head of salt and pepper curls, one crossed eye and a moany voice. Maryann's mom said Cathleen Black was a Catholic and 'not up to much' and having one eye crossed like that 'served her right'. Nancy said her mom was born like that so Maryann never understood how it could serve her right. Did God do things like that? Didn't

14

he like Catholics? And was that why she had to take in washing and cart other people's bundles off down the pawn shop on a Monday morning to make ends meet?

'Well, it's no good relying on that drunken bastard,' Cathleen said, placidly, of her husband. 'Or we'd all've starved to death by now.' But then, with a distant look in her eyes, she'd add, ''E was never like that before the war.'

Cathleen Black seemed to overlook the fact that Nancy was a girl most of the time and except for school, Nance wore her brothers' cast-off shorts and shoes, and her hair, black and curly as her mom's, was cropped short. Nance strutted about with her elbows stuck out and you didn't cross her. She was tough. Flo Nelson said it was a shame, her never looking like a proper girl, but she was damned if she was passing down her girls' clothes to people like that.

It was chilly that November afternoon, threatening rain, the air damp and rank with factory smells from all around and the stink of the yard privies. Both Maryann and Nancy had been ordered to keep an eye on their baby brothers, and Billy Nelson and Horace Black were at one end of the long, narrow yard, playing with a collection of marbles.

'Don't you go putting 'em in yer mouth, Horace,' Nancy shouted to him. 'They ain't rocks for sucking.'

Billy's fair head and Horace's dark one were close together and they kept picking up the marbles, throwing them at the wall, watching them bounce off and roaring with laughter.

'They're awright,' Nancy said, long-sufferingly. 'Let's leave 'em be.'

She strode over in her patched, baggy shorts to

where two of her older brothers, Jim, thirteen and Percy, ten, were trying to cobble together their own cart out of a wooden meat-crate they'd bought for tuppence – the proceeds of selling empty jam jars – and some old pram wheels.

'Get lost!' Perce scowled at her as he did something important with a piece of wire. 'You'll only muck it up.'

'Let's play hopscotch,' Maryann suggested. 'I gotta bit of chalk.'

For all her boyish ways, Nancy loved having another girl to play with. Blowing on their cold hands, they ran up the yard and started marking out a hopscotch grid. Nance started the game, throwing a pebble along the ground and jump-hopping back and forth. Mrs Black came out of the house with a scarf over her head and a cigarette jammed in one corner of her mouth and started hanging out a line of washing. She took the fag out and turned to them. 'Yer'd better not muck this lot up or I'll belt the pair of yer.'

The girls ignored her. One or other of their moms said this to them several times a week every week and had done ever since they could remember. It had the same effect as 'Don't get dirty', which also went straight in one ear and out the other.

'Is yer dad in yet?' Maryann whispered to Nancy as she took her turn on the hopscotch.

Nancy pulled her mouth down and shook her head. Not many minutes later though, they heard his voice in the entry, mumbling furiously to himself as he staggered along. He was a red-eyed, barrel-chested man, with such skinny legs to support his rotund girth that they looked as if they'd been pinched off someone else's body. He came lurching into the yard, cap in hand and swearing fit to blister paint.

'Oh, 'ere we go,' Cathleen Black said, vanishing inside her house to clear away the breakables.

Blackie stormed into the middle of the yard and bawled, 'Someone's nicked me fuckin' barrer!'

Nancy and Maryann looked at each other. Nancy's big brown eyes rolled expressively skywards.

Jim and Percy straightened up at the end of the yard. Other neighbours round the yard barely turned to look, this was such a usual occurrence. Blackie's favourite watering hole was the Beehive Inn in the next street. He'd bring his barrow, loaded with iron strips for mending the maiding tubs in which everyone did their washing, and leave it out at the front of the pub. By the time he came out it had almost invariably gone – moved for a lark by local lads who then watched Blackie's alcohol-befuddled indignation at its disappearance. Week after week he never seemed to remember that if he left the barrow outside the pub, the same thing would happen. That, Flo Nelson said, was because he was 'so bloody thick yer could stand a spoon up in 'im'.

'You sure, Dad?' Jim said, cautiously.

Blackie attempted to stride masterfully towards them, but ended up struggling to keep his balance.

''Course I'm bleedin' shewer! What d'yer take me . . .'

'It'll turn up, Dad,' Percy said. 'It always does, don't it?'

He and Jim weren't going to volunteer to go and get it and face the jeering ridicule of the lads in the next street.

17

'Someone's nicked my . . .' Blackie was just beginning all over again, when Sal came rushing up the entry, her face white as a china doll's.

'Maryann – oh Maryann!' she cried, then burst into hysterical sobbing. At the sight of her sister's emotion, a sick, cold feeling came over Maryann. For a moment they all stood numbly, waiting.

'Our dad's been in an accident,' Sal blurted out at last. 'A terrible accident.'

Cathleen Black left her sozzled husband to his own devices, picked up grime-streaked little Horace and marshalled all the children across the road to the Nelsons' house. Maryann immediately caught hold of Tiger and hugged him to her. Her chest felt tight, as if it was going to tear open. Nancy watched her with wide, concerned eyes.

'Our mom's up the h-hospital.' Sal sat down, still crying, at the table. 'This copper come and said our dad'd been hit by a c-car and 'e couldn't come home and Mom had to go with him. M-Mom told me to come over and get Maryann and stay 'ere with Tony and Billy till 'er gets 'ome.'

'Did the copper say 'ow yer dad is?' Cathleen stood over her. She couldn't stand Flo Nelson, always looking down her nose as if from a great height, but she was fond of the Nelson children, and she couldn't just leave the kids in a state like this.

Sal shook her head. Maryann started crying then. They'd taken her dad away and she'd never been inside a hospital and didn't know what it was like, only they looked big, frightening places, and he was hurt and she just wanted him home and everything to be back to normal. Her tears started Tony and Billy off crying too, and Horace looked at them all and began bawling as well.

The evening passed like a terrible, blurred dream. They tried to eat the mash and mushy cabbage Mrs Black cooked for them, but Maryann felt as if her throat had closed up and she could hardly swallow. The older ones went out into the yard after tea, but all Maryann wanted to do was play with Tiger and hold him tight.

Nancy tried to get her involved in a game, but Maryann just shook her head. Her dad, was all she could think of. She ached for him to come home, to pick up Tiger in his big hands and say, 'How's our little moggy then?' But the evening dragged on and still he didn't come, and neither did their mother. Everything felt strange and horrible.

It was after eleven when Flo Nelson finally walked in. Cathleen had got Tony and Billy to bed. Tony had cried and screamed and Maryann went up and sat with him, stroking his head until his eyes closed, his distraught little face relaxing finally into sleep. Sal and Maryann had been adamant that they would not go up until their mom came back. They sat silently at the table, Nancy with them, draped wearily over its surface, too tired to do anything and too worried to sleep. The younger Black boys had dozed off on the floor and Horace was fast asleep on his mother's lap with his thumb in his mouth. His nose was bunged up and his breathing was the loudest sound in the room.

Despite the fact that Cathleen Black barely ever set foot in her house normally, Flo Nelson showed no surprise at them all being there. As she came in through

19

the door, Maryann knew immediately that everything was different. Her mother's eyes wore the glazed, exhausted look they had had in the days after she had given birth to Billy, only then she had been cheerful, had carried him proudly about. Now her pained, defeated body looked as if she had been punched so hard she would never stand straight again. She closed the door and turned, seeming unable to raise her head and look at them all.

'How is 'e?' Cathleen said, softly. She struggled to her feet, still holding her sleeping son.

Flo Nelson shook her head. She couldn't speak. After a moment she put her hands over her face.

''E's not...?' Cathleen was deeply shocked. She hadn't thought it would be the very worst. Not this. 'Flo, 'e's not...?'

Flo nodded, hands still over her face. Slowly she pulled them away, staring at the table, not looking directly at anyone. 'Ten o'clock. 'E never came round – never knew what happened. 'E was in Icknield Port Road – it was a motor car knocked 'im down – his head...' She put a hand to her own head. At last she looked directly at her neighbour, eyes wide with shock and bewilderment.

'He was on the Somme, Cathleen. He came all through the Somme.'

Maryann and Sal lay clinging to one another in the cold darkness.

'We'll never see 'im again,' Sal sobbed.

The word 'never' stabbed through Maryann like a sharp sword. Never. Ever. No – it couldn't be true. Wasn't real. Tomorrow he would come back, she'd wait for him outside the pub, take Tiger for him to stroke with his long, rough fingers. Sundays they'd go down the cut or go over to Edgbaston reservoir with a fishing line and a jam jar. She'd hear him slowly, wearily climb the stairs to say goodnight, the same rhythm of his tread night after night . . . Never. Never again. She pressed her face against Sal and felt sobs jerk out from the very depths of her body. Everything felt frightening, and cold and utterly lonely.

Three

During the time between Harry's death and the funeral, his children stayed away from school. Flo couldn't cope with any of it and the girls had to take over their brothers completely. Sal minded Billy, while Maryann looked after Tony, helping him get dressed, trying to keep him occupied and out of Flo's way. For two days their mom scarcely moved from her bed, lying there with her pale hair matted round her head, face swollen with crying, and it was Nanny Firkin who came to take charge. She was not one for kisses or cuddles but she kept them fed and her busy presence in her rustling black dress was a great source of comfort. As she had all through the war, Flo leaned on her mother for help. Nanny Firkin came and cooked for them and stayed with the children while Flo hauled herself out of bed to go to the undertaker's on Monument Road, to make arrangements.

'Where's my dad?' Tony kept asking. He was five, and he didn't understand death. His dark-eyed little face was so solemn, so hurt, that Maryann could hardly stand looking at him.

''E's not coming 'ome again, Tony,' she said, gently at first.

'Why? Where's our dad gone?'

''E's – 'e's had an accident, Tony, and 'e ain't coming back.' She sat him on her lap, cuddling him, stroking his soft, squashy legs.

22

Night-time was the hardest, when he didn't come back from work. They couldn't hear his voice through the floorboards from downstairs, his loud yawn as he came up to see them. The house felt so quiet and empty. Their mom's sobbing was the only thing they heard, sometimes with Nanny Firkin's voice trying to comfort her.

'What 'm I going to do?' she kept saying over and over again. Every time she said it Maryann froze inside. Her mom was afraid they'd all starve! 'Four children and no 'usband! 'Ow're we going to get by? It were bad enough in the war, but then you 'ad to put your own troubles aside when they were over there fighting. But now there's four instead of two, and there'll be no end to it all . . .'

'You'll 'ave yer widow's pension,' Nanny Firkin said.

'But that's next to nowt! 'Ow'm I going to keep 'em fed and clothed?' She was tearful again. 'Life's cruel – so cruel. After all these years, these bloody 'ard, struggling years, Harry gets 'imself a decent job and then this 'as to go and 'appen!' She sank into a chair by the table and broke down. 'We'll not 'ave a stick of furniture – I'll 'ave to sell it all. Oh, I can't go through all that again – I want a bit of rest and comfort in my life, not scratching and scraping for every farthing till the end of my days!'

Nanny Firkin pursed her lips. It grieved her more than she could ever express that Harry had been killed. She'd loved the man like a son and her own heart was leaden with it and even more at the sight of her grandchildren's faces, especially little Maryann, so like him in looks and his favourite. The child was heartbroken, clinging to that kitten. They should have had a better life, Harry and Flo. Married at eighteen, then Sally had come along. Harry had an apprenticeship then and they looked set for a fair passage. He was going to work his way up to being a skilled worker, then emigrate with his family. There'd been big advertisements before the war, asking for people to go to Australia. That was Harry's dream, to start a fine new life away from the stink of Birmingham factories and the shabby, vermin-ridden houses of old Ladywood.

'I've got the energy of two men,' he used to say. 'You'll see, Mother Firkin. This family's going up in the world, up and out of 'ere and right the other side of the world. Flo and me'll live like kings – and we'll see to it you do as well. You can come and join us when we're all set up.'

And then the war came, and instead they faced the shadow of a man whom the fighting had spat out and sent home to them: used, then discarded, abandoned to eke out a future on ruined health and confidence, on shattered nerves. Whatever rays had broken through from that bright, possible future had faded and gone out and now all was darkness for Flo.

But Nanny Firkin had never been one to get carried away by dreams. You could dream, oh yes, dreams were what kept you going, kept you living one day after another. But stepping right into them and thinking life would pull itself round just to suit you – that was something else. Moonshine, that was. She watched her daughter's grief, day after day, and she saw things very clearly as they were.

'Well, Flo,' she said in her cracked little voice. 'You know I'll give yer all the help I can. It's no hardship to me spending time with my grandchildren – when I'm

24

allowed,' she added rather tartly. Flo looked up at her, her tear-stained face desperate. 'But as for you, you're gunna have to get yerself a job, one that pays enough to keep this family together. I can't do that for yer, Flo, I'm past all that. If I 'ad anything to give yer, yer could 'ave the teeth out of my head, but I ain't even got them now. You'd best get yerself into a factory on the best wages yer can find.'

In Loving Memory of
Harold Nelson
Who entered into rest 16th Nov 1926
Aged 33 years
Interred at Lodge Hill Cemetery

Funeral furnished by N. Griffin & Son,
Monument Road

Harry's funeral was held at St Mark's Church, next to St Mark's School, where Maryann and the others attended. Maryann sat next to Tony in the immense gloom of the church while grand words from the Book of Common Prayer whirled round her head. Her dad's coffin was draped with a Union Jack, the reward of respect given to a serviceman of the war.

At the cemetery they stood round in watery sunshine and a cold wind. Flo was distraught. She seemed to have no comfort to give to her family. She stood across the grave from them, being consoled by her younger brother Danny and his wife Margie. It was Nanny Firkin who stayed close to the children, arms stretched out, trying to spread her tiny frame behind them like a fan. Tony clung to Maryann. As they lowered the coffin into the grave, Tony turned and buried his face against her.

The undertaker, Norman Griffin, was a tall, respectable-looking, middle-aged gentleman, his broad shoulders encased in a smart black coat with a white wool muffler at the neck, black gloves and shoes gleaming with polish and elbow grease. She could see, from under his bowler hat, that his hair was a faded ginger, and his complexion also had the faded freckliness of the redheaded. His manner was tactful and deferential. When they had driven back to the house from Lodge Hill and Mr Griffin had dispatched the carriages, he lingered in the street with them for so long that eventually Flo felt obliged to say, 'Can we offer yer a cup of tea or summat for your trouble, Mr Griffin?'

'Well, I must say,' Mr Griffin said, rubbing his hands together, giving a practised, moderate, undertaker's smile, 'it's a right cold day – I won't stop for long, of course, but I'd be very grateful, I truly would.'

Flustered moments followed of building the fire and Nanny Firkin fetching water for the kettle while Mr Griffin sat by the hearth, looking round the room and lighting up a cigarette. Maryann watched him. He had sat himself, without a by your leave, in the chair that had been Harry's when he came home from work. Maryann gritted her teeth. She didn't like the smell of Mr Griffin's cigarette smoke (her dad had never taken to smoking), and even more she didn't like him parking his backside in her dad's chair, however much of a gentleman he was. Besides which, it was the most comfortable seat, so Nanny Firkin was left perched on a hard chair by the table.

Flo laid out their handful of best cups and saucers and poured the tea after the eternity it seemed to take to get ready, while none of them had anything to say. She spooned condensed milk into the cups, her fingers trembling.

'I'm afraid it's a bit on the weak side,' she apologized miserably, as if the tea was representative of their desolate state. 'Get Mr Griffin some sugar, Maryann,' she ordered, adding in a hissed whisper, 'and don't bring it in the packet.'

Maryann tipped the large grains of sugar on to a saucer, found a spoon and dutifully offered it to Norman Griffin, coughing as his blue smoke wafted up into her nostrils.

'Ah—' Mr Griffin turned to her and she felt herself turn red under his close examination. 'Thank you . . . er, my dear.' Close up to him, as well as the smoke, Maryann could smell sweat and some other funny chemical smell. Without meaning to she wrinkled her nose. Now he had taken his hat off she could see his hair was thinning on top and was smoothed back with soap or Brylcreem. He sat very straight, with an almost military bearing. As well as his smell, Maryann disliked his affected way of talking as if he was really posh, and the way he had ousted Tiger from by the fire with a rough shove of his shiny shoes, their soles muddy from the cemetery.

But they had to be polite and thankful to Mr Griffin. He had handled Harry's funeral at a discount: the hearse pulled by gleaming black horses, the wreath, the cards announcing the death. In the circumstances, Flo Nelson had genuine cause for gratitude.

'We couldn't 've managed it – not proper like – without yer being so kind,' she was saying, from a wooden chair opposite him, a tremor in her hands as she held her cup and saucer.

The children sat round, dumb with misery; Maryann squeezed on to a stool next to Tony, each of them with one leg on, one off. Sal was sitting holding Billy, asleep in the dim gaslight. Cathleen Black had looked after him for the day and he'd worn himself out playing with Horace. Mr Griffin seemed to take for ever to drink his cup of tea. Maryann could see the strain in her mother's face, her need to be left alone, not to have to be polite, to weep.

'Of course, I understand your feelings at this inauspicious time,' Mr Griffin was saying, clinking his half empty cup down on the saucer. His fingers were pale and stubby, the backs of his hands freckly and still red from the cold. 'My own dear wife passed away not two year ago.'

'Oh,' Flo Nelson said, with an effort. 'I'm sorry to 'ear that, Mr Griffin. I didn't know.'

''Course I've only the one son – worked for me in the business for a bit, till 'e decided to go his own way. I tried to persuade him to stay – 'e made a beautiful coffin when 'e put his mind to it . . .' As he spoke he looked round the room again. Sizing it up, Maryann thought.

'You've got yer 'ouse looking nice, Mrs Nelson. Daresay you'd move to a bigger place given the chance though, eh? Very cramped these yard 'ouses – with all the family you've got.'

''Er's always managed,' Nanny Firkin put in, sharply.

'We ain't got much chance of moving now,' Flo said. 'To tell yer the honest truth, Mr Griffin, I don't know 'ow we're going to manage with my Harry gone . . .'

Unable to hold back her emotion any longer, she burst into tears and Sal began sobbing as well. Maryann felt her own emotions swell inside her as if she might explode, but she wasn't going to cry with *him* here! She folded her arms tight across her bony ribcage, pressing herself in.

Mr Griffin leaned forwards, breathing loudly through his nose. 'Oh dear, oh dear, now, now. I am sorry for your trouble, my dear. I do know what a terrible time this is for you ... You know, I feel very sorry for you, a woman left to fend for 'erself with family. Now if you need any help – if there's anything I can do for you ...'

Maryann squeezed her eyes tightly shut. *Go away, you horrible smelly old man!* her mind screamed. *Get out of our dad's chair, and out of our house!*

At last he stood up, seeming to take up half the room, and put his hat and coat on. Suddenly he turned and enacted a little bow towards Sal and Maryann.

'Goodbye then, girls. You'll help look after yer mother, now won't yer?' They sat, mute, not even meeting his eyes.

'Thank you again, Mr Griffin,' Flo said meekly. 'I don't know what to say, yer've been that good to us.' She saw him to the door.

'Goodbye, m'dear.' Mr Griffin lingered for a moment. 'Now don't you go forgetting what I've said, will you?'

Flo stood on the step, staring thoughtfully after him as he disappeared into the smoky gloom.

Four

December 1927

'And where d'yer think you're going?'

Flo's question was flung furiously across the room, through the paper streamers which hung in sagging loops from yesterday's Christmas festivities, at Maryann, who was by the door, forcing her arms into the sleeves of her coat.

'Out.'

Flo advanced on her, hands still black from shovelling coal.

'Oh no you ain't, yer little madam. You get back 'ere and find a civil tongue for Norm – for Mr Griffin for once in yer life. 'E'll be 'ere any minute and yer can sit there and be polite. There's summat 'e wants to say to you all.'

But Maryann was already out and across the yard, still pulling the coat round her, the door rattling shut in Flo's face. It opened again.

'You get back 'ere, yer uppity little cow!'

Maryann disappeared at a run, down the entry to the street. She felt the cold come down on her like a weight, the raw air biting into her cheeks on this day of deep, silent midwinter. The cobbles were icy and the slates glazed with it: the sun hadn't broken through all day. She pushed her hands deep into her pockets, thrusting her chin down. She had on a pair of Sal's old stockings, held up with garters. Everything she had handed down from Sal was on the big side. She could feel the stockings wrinkling down her legs.

Flo's angry words seemed to propel Maryann along the road. 'I'm not staying in there – not to see *'im*,' she said out loud, her breath swirling away from her, thick and white.

She turned down towards Nanny Firkin's. In her left pocket she found a halfpenny, and gripped her hand round it, squeezing hard. She and her mom had never been what you'd call close, but nowadays all she ever seemed to be was on the wrong side of her. All year it had been like this, getting worse and worse. Since her dad had died and since Mr Griffin kept on coming round week after week bringing presents: joints of meat, cakes, thrusting bags of sweets under their noses, sitting himself by their fire on Sunday afternoons. He had even begun to take off his shoes and park them up against the fender as his socks steamed in the heat.

Maryann knew exactly what Mr Griffin wanted to say that afternoon. She was sick at the thought, because it had been coming all year. He was going to sit there in the chair, her *dad's* chair, with them waiting on him hand and foot. There'd be her mom's, 'Oh yes, Mr Griffin, no, Mr Griffin,' which had gradually turned into, 'Oh yes, *Norman*, no, Norman,' as Flo recognized a chance if ever she saw one. Mr Griffin was going to sit holding a cup of tea in those pudgy, freckled hands and tell them he was going to marry their mom. And he would say it in that wheedling, smarmy voice which made Maryann want to be sick all over his shiny shoes.

She knew this as clearly as anything, because as his visits had become more frequent, Norman Griffin had come making hints and promises.

'You're a good woman, Mrs Nelson, showing such

31

kindness to a poor old widower like me. You shouldn't 'ave to spend the rest of your days slaving away on yer own . . .' 'Nice little family you've got 'ere, Mrs Nelson – you need someone to take care of yer . . .' And gradually, 'You want to get yourself wed again, Flo – the factory's no place for a fine woman like you . . .'

Late in the summer, when a reasonable period of mourning was seen to have passed, and Flo had wept and worried and worked so hard in the brassware factory she had turned scrawny, she started going out for the odd walk with Mr Griffin on a Sunday afternoon, returning with flushed cheeks and a hard, determined look in her eyes.

When he came to the house Maryann tried to avoid even looking at him. She hated him being there and refused to speak to him unless forced to. Sal was more biddable. She missed her father but brushed out her long, pale hair on a Sunday, made tea and was polite. Maryann pulled hideous faces behind his back and dropped dust and dead ants in his tea, reduced to being childish by her powerlessness over the situation. She missed her dad with a terrible ache in her that never seemed to get any less.

She kicked at a rotten piece of wood on the pavement and it skittered into the gutter. She bent over and spat on it. 'Norman! Bloody sodding *Norman!*' She stamped and spat until tears ran down her cheeks.

Walking on, wiping her eyes, she crossed over the railway and went along to the spot where there was a hole in the fence and she could get down to the cut, scrambling down through scrubby bushes and alongside the wall of a warehouse on to the path. Down here it felt even more cold and utterly still. Fog hung thickly over the canal so that she could see only a few yards ahead: the factories, chimneys and warehouses were all shrouded in the saturated air. The place felt completely deserted. It was Christmas of course, and she saw the water of the canal was frozen over. Near where she was standing a stick poked up, frozen in at an angle, black against the grey ice. She walked along the path in the eerie whiteness, in towards the middle of Birmingham, over a little humpbacked bridge and past the Borax Works towards the wharves at Gas Street. Ahead of her she could just see the ghostly shapes of the wharf buildings and in front of them two rows of joeys, the boats which mainly did journeys of a day there and back. They were tethered shoulder to shoulder along the Worcester Bar. As she moved closer, she became aware of a sound coming to her intermittently through the fog. She wasn't alone down here then. Someone was coughing, a laboured sound which went on and on.

Then she saw him, on the path in front of her, close to a boat which was tied by the bank. He was bent over, coughing from drenched-sounding lungs and struggling for breath. At first she assumed he was an old man, but as she approached, intimidated, yet somehow fascinated as well, she saw this was not so. He was quite unaware that she was there because he had to submit completely to the process of coughing and this made him seem somehow vulnerable. Maryann was also drawn by the look of him. He had a thick head of curls and a beard, all deep auburn, which appeared to glow in the greyness of the fog like a sanctuary lamp in a church, and he was clad in thick, brown corduroy trousers and heavy boots, and a thick jumper with a worn, black worsted jacket over the top and a muffler at the neck. As he stooped, hands pressing on his thighs, one hand also held a black cap.

She saw that the boat by which he was standing was a horse-drawn family boat, and she noticed too that the man's hands, clasped so tightly on his thighs, were black with coal dust. Near him, on the ground, was a galvanized bucket.

At last the fit passed and he stayed in the same position for a moment, seeming exhausted by it, let out a low groan and shook his head quickly from side to side as if to shake the fit off. Then, still bent over, he raised his head and looked up along the path. Maryann felt her heart beat with panic, and she stayed quite still. For a moment the two of them looked at each other in silence. The man had a round face, though his cheek-bones jutted a little, adding a chiselled look to it. His eyes, from the distance at which Maryann stood, looked dark and his gaze was strong and unflinching. He stared at her without hostility. Just looked, taking her in. Then slowly, he straightened up and replaced the cap on his head.

''Ow long've you been stood there?' His voice was soft and quite gentle.

Maryann swallowed. She had been ready to run if he was angry or strange, but didn't feel the need now. The man didn't talk like Birmingham people, she noticed.

'Only a minute.'

'What're you doing out? It's Christmas, ent it?'

Maryann shifted her weight from one foot to the other. She felt conscious of her stockings, wrinkled round her ankles. 'Well, you're 'ere.'

'Well – yes, that's true.' She thought she heard him give a wheezy chuckle.

'Why?'

He indicated the boat. 'I live 'ere. We ent s'posed to be 'ere – brought a load of coal from Cannock to the

Borax Works – before Christmas that was. And got blooming iced in, dint we? They ent 'ad the icebreaker out to free us up. I've been smashing it up at the edge 'ere to give 'er a wash out.' He indicated the bucket. 'Got to get the coal washed out, see, before we can put a new load in.'

Maryann nodded and moved closer. The long hold of the boat was black with coal dust and the rope fenders were grubby with it too, but apart from that she looked in good trim. She was painted red and yellow, with castles painted in the panels of the cabin doors, roses round the edge, and on the side of the cabin was painted her name, *Esther Jane*. Maryann looked at her with great curiosity, at the painted water can on the roof, the brass trimmings on her chimney, from which drifted dense yellow smoke. She looked round.

'Where's yer horse?'

'Old Bessie? Stabled up. Having a rest.'

'Can I see inside?'

The man smiled. She saw he had big, square teeth. The smile creased up his face and gave him a comical, cheeky look. 'You'll get dirty.'

Maryann shrugged. 'Don't matter.'

'Come on then – just for a minute but mind where you put your 'ands.'

She thought he seemed pleased. He climbed aboard ahead of her and when she stumbled climbing down into the boat, he gripped her arm. He felt very big and burly and strong.

'Go easy!' Another low chuckle came from him. For some reason he seemed to find her rather amusing. 'You don't want to hurt yourself. Look – that's the tiller – what we steer the boat with. Now, come on in.'

35

He opened the cabin doors and Maryann found herself stepping down into a miniature house. The man, who was too tall to stand upright in the cabin, sat down on a bench along the side, and gestured for her to sit beside him.

'There you go – this is our 'ome in 'ere.'

She gazed round, astonished. It was like being in a magic story where everything had shrunk. In front of her was a little black-leaded range, which made the cabin so stifling hot that Maryann unbuttoned her coat and took it off. There was a brown and white teapot and a big brass kettle, well polished, on the hob, which gave off a lovely warm glow. To her right was what looked like a cupboard, which jutted out into the cabin, and further back, a little area where there was another bench, divided off by red and white check curtains, tied back at each side. On the near side of the cupboard and on shelves on the wall by the stove were pretty china plates, some with lattice edges with velvet ribbons threaded through and tied in a bow. The man watched her taking it all in with some amusement.

'We pull this down 'ere—' He opened a small cupboard in front of him and the flap folded outwards. 'That's our table. That cupboard you can see' – he pointed towards the back – 'folds down for a bed.'

'But it's so . . . *small*!'

'It's small all right.'

'Don't you 'ave a house to live in an' all?'

'Nope. I was brung up on 'ere – lived 'ere all me life. Only time I been on the bank was in the war.'

She gaped at him. 'I've never seen in one of these before.'

'I can see that!'

'Who lives on 'ere with you then?'

'My dad, my little sister, Ada – she'd be a bit younger 'un you I'd think – and Jep, that's our dog. They've gone off to get us some food and see about who's going to get the ice broke up. We can't stick around long, you see – 'ave to get moving. We was s'posed to be at Napton by Christmas but we got stuck 'ere. We ent starving yet though. 'Ere—' He reached to a little shelf at the side of the cabin. 'Want a bit of this?'

'Ooh yes!'

She took the two thick squares of Cadbury's chocolate, nibbled and sucked slowly, making them last. The man bit some off too, smiling at her enjoyment. He had such a kind face, she thought, somehow old and boyish at once.

'How old're you?' Maryann said.

'Me? Old as the hills.'

She frowned. ''Ow old's that?'

'I'm going on twenty-nine. What about you, since we're asking?'

'Thirteen. What's yer name?'

'Joel Bartholomew. And what's yours?' He was making a game of it. Maryann found the corners of her mouth turning up.

'Maryann Nelson. I'll *always* be Maryann Nelson.'

'Will you? Why?'

''Cause no one's going to make me be called anything else.'

'Well – that's settled then.' Joel watched her carefully, rubbing his huge hands on the legs of his trousers. Then he stirred himself. 'Best get on – the others'll be back soon and they won't take to me idling.'

They stepped back out on to the bank. It felt very cold outside after the snug little cabin. Joel showed no sign of being cold, but he saw her shivering.

37

'D'you live far, Maryann?'

'Garrett Street.'

This meant nothing to him. 'Shouldn't yer be at home?'

Maryann shrugged, miserable again at the thought of home. 'I wish I could come with yer.'

Joel smiled. 'Not this time o'year you don't.'

They stood by the bank and she felt shy again, as if she'd stayed too long. She put her coat back on.

'Better go then.'

Joel suddenly held out his hand in a teasing way and she took it. His was big and very rough.

'Nice to meet you, Maryann Nelson.'

'Can I come and see yer again?'

''Course you can – if you can ever find us. T'ent easy that, on the cut!'

She turned and left him, pulling her too-big coat in closer round her, face and hands aching with cold. Reaching the bridge she turned back and saw Joel watching her. She waved, and for a moment he raised an arm.

She went to Nanny Firkin's house next, although she didn't say a word to her grandmother about Mr Griffin and why she wasn't at home and her nan didn't ask. She could see the girl's unhappiness in every line of her. She'd had words with her daughter and would have more, but she wasn't going to inflict more on her granddaughter.

'Yer just making up to 'im for a meal ticket!' she'd accused Flo, and Flo whirled round, livid.

'Yes – I am! 'E's said 'e'll move us into a bigger 'ouse and I'll not need to stand in that stinking factory

38

turning out kettles all day long. I'll be able to live without being worried to death about where every meal's coming from. Harry's gone – 'e ain't coming back and a meal ticket's what I need, without any sodding lectures on the subject. I don't want to end up like you, living on nothing and surrounded by mangy flaming cats for company!'

Maryann stayed with Nanny Firkin, warming herself again by the fire and drinking a cup of tea. She sat stroking the cats and talking to Walt the parrot, in the musty familiarity of her grandmother's house and she waited long enough so that Mr Griffin would have gone through his usual rigmarole of wiping his mouth, putting on his jacket and shoes and standing, holding his hat in front of his stomach and thanking her mother, with a little bow, for the afternoon tea which, he always said, brightened his lonely life. She thought about Joel and the boat and hugged this to herself as a lovely, warming secret.

When she got home she pushed the door open cautiously, making absolutely sure she was not going to see Norman Griffin's head, with the pasty, balding patch at the back, still in place in the chair.

Sal was putting away cups and saucers on the shelf. She turned and raised her eyes to the ceiling, implying that Flo was upstairs, then shrugged, with an expression of sorrowful resignation. Tony ran to Maryann.

'Where've yer bin, Maryann? Our mom's ever so cross with yer and she's going to get wed to Mr Griffin. Don't say anyfing and make a row, will yer?'

They heard their mother's tread on the stairs. She had almost reached the bottom and stopped, staring across towards the door. Maryann waited for her temper to erupt, but she just stood there and they all gazed back at her. Maryann looked at Sal, then back to her mother.

''Ow can yer, Mom?' Maryann said quietly. ''Ow can yer do it?'

'I'll tell yer how I can do it.' Flo came down the last of the stairs and across to fix her younger daughter with the steely, determined expression that had become hers since her husband's death. 'By thinking about what life'll be like if I don't. Norman Griffin's got a business. 'E's got enough money to keep us, we're going to a new 'ouse and 'e's got a job lined up for Sal.'

'Do I 'ave to work with 'im, Mom?' Sal asked timidly. 'I like where I'm working now.' Sal's first job after school was with a local bakery.

'Yes. You do. We'll be all right now. We shan't 'ave to worry. I know 'e's not yer dad, but from now on 'e'll be the head of this family and you'll treat him with respect and a bit of gratitude. D'you 'ear?'

Five

1928

'There's someone at the door, Maryann!' Flo Nelson shouted.

Maryann went to the front door and found Nancy grinning in at her. 'So this is yer new 'ouse then!'

Maryann's solemn expression broke into a smile as well. 'Come on – I'll show yer.' Nancy went to St Peter's, the Catholic school, so the girls didn't see one another in the daytime.

Flo and Mr Griffin were married in the new year, and soon after he announced that there was a house waiting for them two roads away in Anderson Street and they were to move in immediately. He had it all planned. It was a little bit nearer his premises, where Sal had started work straight after Christmas, and was a two up, two down, with a tiny yard out at the back behind the kitchen and definitely a step up from a back-to-back.

You stepped straight in off the street into the front room. By the hearth was a peg rug, which Flo and Sal had botched together, and Harry Nelson's chair. Apart from that, the only piece of furniture which came from the Nelsons' old house was a small cupboard. The other two chairs and a low table were provided by Mr Griffin. He had a little china cabinet, a table and chairs and another comfortable chair (although he still preferred Harry's) and a heavy brass oil lamp which he liked to keep well polished and light in the evenings. It had been his father's, and his 'beloved mother' who lived in Handsworth, had passed it on to him.

Nance's eyes were wide, looking round.

'Ooh, it's nice, Maryann—' After the cramped squalor of her family's back house this seemed almost palatial.

Flo was in the kitchen cooking and there was a smell of ham knuckles boiling.

'Oh – 'ello, Nancy,' Flo said, rather snootily. Cathleen Black may have helped her out in her time of need, but that didn't make them equals in Flo's eyes. They had only moved two streets away, but it felt far enough to represent a new start. Flo was managing to pull herself up in the world and she was going to do it, no matter what the cost. There always was a price: that was just how it was. She hadn't anything in the way of feelings for Norman Griffin, except for gratitude that he'd come along and been prepared to take on her and her family. That was no small thing. But he was gentlemanly in his ways, and he'd shown her the gateway out of absolute poverty: she never, ever wanted to be faced with that again. She'd have to live with his mauling her about in bed of a night – she shuddered slightly at the thought of Norman's white, flaccid body, his thick lips and tongue. But that wasn't too high a price to pay, she thought: he wasn't one of these oversexed men, thank heaven. And he showed great consideration – never went all the way, so to speak. They'd agreed that there weren't to be any more children. Her own four were enough of a handful.

'Go on and show Nancy upstairs,' she said, irritated by the girls watching her.

'You ain't been round our 'ouse for ages,' Nancy complained as the two of them clattered up the stairs.

'I know. We've been busy. Moving and that.'

Upstairs were two rooms, one shared by the new Mr and Mrs Griffin, with Billy on a little bed on the floor, and the girls and Tony in the other. Maryann wrinkled her nose as they went in. She could smell urine from where Tony had wet the bed again that morning. He was forever asking if he could get in with her and Sal, but they said they weren't having him wetting them too. Tiger was curled up asleep in the middle of the bigger bed that Maryann shared with Sal. She and Nance sat down on it and Maryann reached for Tiger and stroked him. He arched his back, purring.

'D'yer wanna come and play out then?' Nancy said. She wasn't one for sitting still for long.

Maryann kissed the stripy top of her cat's head, between the ears. He was such a comfort, amid all the changes.

'Maybe – in a bit,' she said. She felt edgy, almost tearful, sitting there with Nance. Nance was her best pal, but there was a distance between them suddenly that Maryann didn't know how to overcome. Her emotions were all tangled up and confused and she couldn't find the words to tell Nance how she was feeling. She cuddled Tiger tightly. The day they moved their few possessions out of Garrett Street, Norman Griffin had stood in the living room and prodded Tiger with the toe of his boot.

'We don't need to take *that* with us, do we?' he said.

Flo looked at him, not understanding for a moment. 'You mean the cat?' Even she could hardly believe what he was suggesting.

'We don't want a cat in the new house, do we? Dirty animal, under yer feet all the time. I nearly tripped down the stairs over the thing the other day. Be a good time to get shot of it.'

Maryann stood behind him, so tensed with shock at what he'd said that for those moments she couldn't react. She saw her mother look across at her. Flo ran her hands over her pale hair, as if preparing herself, and stepped closer to her new husband.

'Norman – I really don't think we can leave the cat behind. The children . . . I mean, it's Maryann's. It'd break 'er heart.'

Norman turned and saw Maryann's piercing expression. For a moment he hesitated, then decided to smile. 'Oh, awright then. If we must, we'll take the thing. It'll most likely follow us over there anyhow.'

So Tiger had come. At least her mom had stood up for her over him. That was something.

''Ow's Sal getting on?' Nancy asked. 'What's she doing at Griffin's? Eh—' She dug Maryann in the ribs. 'She ain't building coffins?'

'No!' Maryann elbowed her back. 'Don't be daft. I dunno. She's in the office. Bits and bobs. Messages, taking down details for cards and that. She ain't really said a lot.' Sal never seemed to say a lot about anything nowadays.

'Sounds awright,' Nancy said. 'Soft job that.' With a giggle she added, 'If yer go for that sort of thing.'

Maryann managed a laugh, feeling Nance dragging her up out of her gloomy mood.

'Yer dad home yet?' she asked Nancy.

Nancy rolled her eyes. 'Sleeping it off. But we could go over the yard, take Billy – Tony as well, if you like?'

'Awright then.' Maryann stood up without much enthusiasm.

'We're going over Nance's!' Maryann called out, downstairs.

'Take Billy with yer then!' Flo predictably shouted back.

It was cold, but bright outside. The girls set off with Billy between them holding their hands, and Tony dragging his feet behind so they kept having to turn round and call, 'Come on, Tony – get a move on, will yer!'

Maryann took a deep breath of the freezing, acrid air and managed to grin at Nance. This is better, she thought. Away from that house, *his* house, she felt lighter, free again.

'I'm glad yer came over,' she said to Nance.

Norman Griffin had habits of almost clockwork precision. On certain nights of the week he locked up his premises, went down to his favourite pub, the Duke of Wellington, for a pint, then came home. Every evening he expected them all to polish their shoes and line them up against the fender ready for the next day. He inspected them every night, turning each one over, frowning if there was obvious wear in the sole. On Sundays they all had to go to church with him, and afterwards he spent the rest of the morning in Handsworth with his mother. But for once tonight he was late, and Flo was especially exasperated as it meant Sal was late too, and she had the dinner all ready.

Maryann was pleased. The later he came back the better so far as she was concerned. The place felt much more like home, their real family, when he wasn't there. It was quite cosy with the gas mantle popping away and the warmth from the range. Flo was dishing up stew and potatoes when they heard the door open out of the dark winter evening.

''Bout time,' Flo muttered, relieved. Norman didn't take too kindly to them starting without him.

'Summat smells good!' they heard him say. Sal, her face paler than ever in the gaslight, slid into the room and sat down quietly at the table.

Norman came through, smoking the butt end of a cigarette. Maryann didn't like it when he stood over them. He was so big it felt intimidating. She saw Tony shrink down in his seat.

'What's happened, Norman?' Flo asked, serving his food. 'You seem pleased with yerself.'

'Oh no, no – nothing much. Just glad to be 'ome with you, my dear,' he said, sitting himself at the table. As he did so, Tiger stirred from where he had been sitting under the table and brushed against his legs.

'Get that thing out while we're 'aving our tea!' Norman said, scraping back his chair. He stood up and kicked Tiger out through the door. The cat let out a screech of pain and Norman slammed the door. Maryann burst into tears.

'Never mind.' Flo, startled by this sudden outburst, tried to appease her. She watched Norman anxiously. He was breathing heavily. 'Shoosh now,' Flo snapped at her. 'T'ain't summat to blart about.'

But Maryann couldn't stop. The tears just kept on coming out of her eyes, though she tried as hard as she could not to make any noise. Norman kept eating, steadily. Tony and Billy were wide-eyed, but they ate up obediently. Sal kept her eyes on her plate. Eventu-

46

ally Maryann let out a loud sniff and Norman leapt to his feet.

'Go on – get out of 'ere! I'll not 'ave yer snivelling and blarting at my table. If you can't eat quietly you'll not eat at all.'

Maryann, keeping her head down, left the room and ran upstairs. She lay curled up, crying, the clogging taste of the stew still in her mouth. When she was calmer she lay looking up into the darkness. She thought about her father, about the dreams Nanny Firkin had told her about. That he'd said he was going to take them to Australia.

That's what I'm going to do, Maryann thought. The resolve burned through her. I'm going to get out of here, as soon as I can. She didn't know where to: her young life had given her experience of nothing further away than these few Ladywood Streets and an occasional rare trip to the Bull Ring. But there was more out there, there had to be, beyond these smoke-blackened houses and stinking streets.

Comforted by this, she was already almost asleep when Sal came in to put Tony to bed and get ready herself. She brought a candle with her, and Maryann watched as she bent over and roughly undressed her younger brother. Her expression was tight, wooden.

'Sal?' Maryann wondered if she was cross because it was usually her job, not Sal's, to look after Tony.

'What?' She didn't look round.

'D'yer want me to do our Tony?'

'I've done 'im now. And don't you go wetting the bed again!' She pushed his shoulder. 'D'you 'ear me?'

When Tony was settled she turned away and undressed. Maryann frowned, looking at Sal's curving shape in the candlelight. She was clearly in a mood over something, turning her back like that, when normally she just pulled off her clothes casually and flung on her nightdress. Tonight her movements were abrupt. She put her nightdress over her head and her arms through the sleeves. Suddenly she sat down on the edge of the bed and put her hands over her face.

''Ow's it with the job, Sal?' Maryann asked.

There was no reply.

Maryann sat up and moved nearer, laying a hand on her sister's shoulder. 'What's up?'

'Nothing!' Sal flung her off and stood up. She threw her clothes savagely into the corner of the room, then climbed into bed. She turned her back on Maryann, blew out the candle and wouldn't say another word.

The next day, when she came home from playing with the Black children, Maryann ran up to the bedroom looking for Tiger. He was always her first thought when she came home, and very often she found him curled up in the dip of hers and Sal's bed. But he wasn't there. She peeped into her mom's and Norman's room. No sign there, either, nor was he in any of the warm spots downstairs, by the range or the chimney breast.

''E must be out,' Maryann said, disappointed.

Not long after, Flo got in, tired and irritable from an extra afternoon of chores. Nanny Firkin was feeling poorly and Flo had felt obliged to go and help.

'You seen Tiger?' Maryann asked her.

Flo stoked the range. 'Course I bloody ain't – I ain't been 'ere all afternoon, 'ave I?'

'Is Nanna better?' Tony asked.

'Not as yer'd notice,' Flo said. ''Er's in bed and that ain't usual. But she said to leave 'er, she'd be awright.

48

I've rubbed 'er chest with goose grease and left 'er 'er tea.'

When their own meal was over, Norman stood up behind Sal, hands on his waist, looking round at them all with a satisfied expression on his face.

'We'll all 'ave a game of cards, eh?'

He did this, every so often. Decided they were all going to sit together, 'be a family' and play whatever he was in the mood for.

'After I've got our Billy to bed then,' Flo said, sounding pleased. 'That's nice of Norman, ain't it?'

'I don't want to play cards,' Maryann murmured. 'I want to go and look for Tiger.'

'Look for Tiger!' Norman snorted with laughter. 'Yer don't want to bother with that! Cats can look after themselves, that they can.'

'I'm tired,' Sal said quietly. 'I think I'll just go to bed, 'stead of playing.'

Norman laid his hand on the back of her chair. 'Oh, I don't think a game of cards'll hurt before yer turn in, Sal.' His voice was soft, but Maryann heard a firm edge to it which always meant Norman wasn't going to be crossed. 'Young girl your age shouldn't be tired this early. Come on – help yer mother clear up then we can get to it the sooner.'

They had no choice but to do as they were told, as was the case with all his 'treats'. His taking them to church every Sunday, visits to the pictures, walking down the street all together, usually to see something that was too old for Tony and Billy, who would sleep or fret through it all. Maryann did like the pictures, but she loathed sitting anywhere near Norman.

Before going in for the dreaded card game she opened the back door into the little yard.

'Tiger! Come on, puss – where've yer got to?'

Nothing. No sign of him. She was filled with unease. He'd never done this before. What if he'd got under a train – or a car like her dad. Or what if he'd fallen in the cut?

Sal stuck her head through the door from the front. 'Come on – 'urry up. Let's get it over.'

'Coming,' Maryann said reluctantly.

Norman had pulled out the little table and was sitting shuffling his dog-eared packs of cards.

'Come on, our Maryann,' he said in a jolly voice as she slipped into the room.

Maryann sat down next to Tony.

'We'll 'ave a game of rummy,' Norman said, licking his thumb and dealing the cards. He paused to light a cigarette.

'You play with me,' Maryann whispered to Tony. Flo sat yawning. She wasn't the least keen on card games, but if Norman said they were going to do something there was no arguing.

'I'm not used to being a family man,' he'd said to her. 'I'm out of practice, Flo. But I'm doing my best . . .'

He jollied them along through a couple of games, laughing loudly at the least thing except at one moment when Tony picked a card to play and he frowned and said, 'Stupid boy . . .' and Tony turned his dark eyes on Maryann, looking worried about what he'd done. He lived in constant nervousness of Norman and his exacting ways. His lisping voice and tense face only seemed to aggravate Norman further.

'S'awright,' she told him, loud enough to be heard. 'You ain't stupid, Tony.' She put her arm round his shoulders, avoiding looking at Norman. Apart from that, and Norman's efforts at thawing them out, they barely said a word, all waiting for the moment when they could go.

Finally, Norman sat back at the end of a game and said, 'Well – that's enough for one night, I'd say.'

Maryann jumped up. 'Come on, Tony!' she said, and they ran upstairs, anything to get away from him.

By the time they went to bed, Tiger had still not come back, although Maryann had been to the door several times to check if he was waiting out there.

'What if 'e comes back in the night and wants to come in, Mom?' she said. 'Can we leave the back door open for 'im?'

'You mad?' Flo said. 'It's perishing cold. 'E's a cat, Maryann – 'e knows 'ow to fend for hisself without you coddling 'im!'

But Maryann lay in bed that night, miserable without Tiger's warm shape at her feet.

Six

Sally Nelson sat behind the desk in the austere office of 'N. Griffin's, Undertaker's'. In front of her lay two open ledgers and a small pile of newly printed death cards, almost identical to the ones they had had for her father. On another pad on the desk were Norman's various tottings up of the prices of coffin, hearse and cards. It was Tuesday evening.

Sal's demeanour was anything but relaxed. She sat chewing hard on the end of her thumb. Every so often she got up and tip-toed over towards the staircase leading down to the double cellar which ran under the building, and stood, head cocked, listening. After waiting at the top of the staircase for a long time on one occasion, she crept halfway down and stopped. She could hear Norman Griffin's voice, talking to Fred, the lad who worked down there building coffins. The last boy had left not long back and Norman was training Fred up. On Tuesdays he sent Fred home early.

'Shall I put all these away now?' Sal heard Fred say.

Then Norman's voice. 'No – leave that to me. I keep that cupboard locked, with the chemicals and that about. You can get off now.' She heard the clink of a key. Fred was about to leave. Her heart beat even faster. She opened her mouth to speak but her throat had dried out and she had to swallow before she could get any words out.

'Mr Griffin?' she called downstairs. She knew it was futile, but she had to try it. She felt she was going to explode inside. 'I'll be off 'ome now – our Mom'll be needing some help.'

Norman Griffin's face appeared round the cellar door, pale and moonlike in the gloom as he looked up at her.

'No, Sal – yer not to go yet. There's a few things want finishing.' He spoke in the low, respectful tone Sal and Maryann called his 'Undertaker' voice.

'But—' She tried to protest.

He closed the cellar door behind him, and then came another of his voices. 'No, Sal.' Now the voice was soft, wheedling. 'Yer to stay a bit longer. Don't want yer going home yet – or you know what'll happen, don't yer?'

Sal returned to her chair upstairs, trembling from head to foot. She was in such as a state she felt as if her throat had closed up, that she couldn't swallow. Oh God! She could run out and down the road now. But she daren't. Couldn't. Sooner or later she'd have to go home. And when she got home he'd be there. And she couldn't tell anyone and she'd have to come back to work with him and then he'd . . . he'd . . . She dug her nails into the palms of her hands.

They were coming up the stairs, Fred clumping along in his boots. He was none too with it, Fred wasn't. Gangly, greasy brown hair, big feet, yes, Mr Griffin, no, Mr Griffin, everything Norman wanted.

'G'night then—' He nodded at Sal, and Norman Griffin stood at the door as he went out.

Norman pulled his watch up from his weskit and squinted at it.

'Ah yes – time to close up.' He locked the door,

pulled the blind down over the door and windows and turned to look at her.

'Don't do that again, will you?' He spoke casually, but she could hear the threat underneath.

'What?' She could only manage a whisper. The tension in her was like a crushing sensation in her chest.

'Don't talk back to me in front of my employees like that,' he said, as if he had a whole empire of workers, not just herself and Fred.

'I'm sorry.' She kept her gaze on the desk in front of her, hands clasped tightly together in her lap. Her heart was beating so hard it hurt.

Then the wheedling voice was back. 'Come on then, Sal. You know what *will* please me, don't yer?'

She didn't answer, just kept her head lowered, and she heard him moving towards her. Sal squeezed her eyes tight shut. When he reached down and took hold of her hands she cried out, startled.

'Oh, don't get in such a state,' he said impatiently. His voice became clipped and cold. 'You know what yer 'ave to do – and then it's over and yer can go home. Simple. It ain't asking much.'

Much, she thought, as he pulled her towards the stairs. Ever since that first time, the start of it, when he had come up behind her and pressed his hands over her breasts, hurting her, it had been much. Far too much.

The cellar was a double one, extending under the premises behind. At the back end, through a white door, was the chapel of rest. The walls in there were plastered and distempered and it was kept very neat and clean. It contained a long trestle table and a small side table on which were a Bible, a candle and an arrangement of dusty silk flowers. There was access to it from the street behind, and any visiting bereaved were escorted in through there and all hammering silenced while they were there. Tonight, on the long table in the Chapel of Rest, a Mr Alfred Johnson lay in his coffin. His family hadn't wanted him at home taking up the room. The front end, under the shop, was much more workmanlike: unplastered brick walls, cobwebs trailing under the grating through which only shreds of light filtered from the street so that it had to be lit by gas lamps all day long. At one end, abutting the wall of the Chapel of Rest, was Mr Griffin's cupboard, but most of the space was taken up by a workbench and a long table. On the workbench tonight sat the almost completed coffin which Fred was due to finish the next day.

Mr Griffin was breathing rather fast. He reached up and made some adjustment to the light so that it burned less brightly. 'Now then, Sal, my dear.'

'No,' she begged, starting to cry. 'No – please. Not today. I'll do it tomorrow, but not today – I feel a bit bad today and I can't . . .'

'Sal—' He was speaking in his soft, fluid voice. 'You're just not used to it, my dear. You're young – you have to learn to enjoy it.'

She was shaking her head, wretchedly, unable to stop the tears from pouring down her cheeks.

His mouth was right close to her, his hot breath wafting the words into her ear. 'And if you don't, you know what'll happen, don't you?' He pointed to the far end of the cellar. 'There's my cupboard.' He patted his pocket. 'And here is the key. And you know what's in my cupboard, don't you?'

Sal nodded, gasping.

'Right then.' There was nothing wheedling about his speech now. It was icy, clipped. It made Sal wither inside. He pulled at the buckle of his belt with one hand, reaching out with his other to grasp her by her long hair, yanking her close to him.

His other hand was under her skirt, tugging, tearing. 'Let's get on with it.'

When Maryann got home from school that day she ran straight in shouting, 'Mom – Mom! Is Tiger back? Has 'e come home?'

Flo Nelson shook her head. She hadn't given a thought to the flaming cat. 'No – I ain't seen 'im all day.' She saw the hope drain out of Maryann's face. Maryann had been so sure he'd gone wandering and would be back by now. Her lips quivered and her eyes filled with tears.

'Tell yer what.' Flo saw an opportunity for a few more minutes peace. 'Yer could go and ask up and down the road if anyone's seen 'im – the neighbours and that. Someone might of done. 'E might be asleep by the fire in someone's 'ouse just along the street, yer never know. Or maybe 'e's sloped back off to Garrett Street. And take our Tony with yer, eh?'

A little cheered by being able to do something, Maryann called Tony. They went to Garrett Street and called at the Blacks' house. Blackie came to the door and the usual stink of urine and soiled baby's napkins assailed their nostrils as it opened. He stood blearily in the doorway, not seeming to know who they were. His shirt was unbuttoned halfway down and she could see black, springy hairs on his chest.

''Allo, Mr Black,' Maryann said. 'It's me – Maryann Nelson.'

'Oh ar,' Blackie said. For a second Maryann felt

sorry for him. He looked such a wreck. But she had more urgent things on her mind.

''Ave yer seen my cat? 'E's a little tabby with a face like a tiger ...'

'Cat? No – I ain't seen no cat ...' He stood looking at them, as if thinking what to say next.

'Maryann, is that you?' Nance came running downstairs. 'What's up?'

'It's Tiger – 'e's gone missing.' Maryann felt a lump come up in her throat again. ''E never came in last night and I dunno where 'e is. Our Mom said to come looking over 'ere.'

'I'll 'elp yer,' Nance said. She'd changed out of her school clothes and put on a grubby pair of boy's trousers.

Maryann was pleased to have some more company for the search besides Tony who kept saying 'Where d'yer fink 'e's gone, Maryann?' until she wanted to scream at him. They asked round some of the backyards in Garrett Street, Maryann saying hello to some of their old neighbours who asked a bit sniffily how they were getting on. Flo hadn't been back to visit a single one of them. Then they went back to Anderson Street. As the afternoon wore on, Maryann grew more and more dispirited. No one had seen Tiger.

'Ow can 'e just've disappeared into thin air?' she said to Nance. 'Someone must've seen him.'

'Yer never know with cats, do yer?' Nance said. She grinned, showing her wonky teeth, trying to cheer Maryann up. 'Knowing 'im 'e'll be back large as life. P'raps 'e's gone and got 'imself a lady friend!'

Maryann tried to smile. 'I 'ope so. It's lonely at home without 'im. Come on, Tony – we'd best go back. D'yer wanna come round ours for a bit?'

'Will yer dad be there?'

''E ain't my dad.'

'No, I know. Sorry, Maryann. I daint mean anything by it.'

They went back to the house where Flo put out a plate of broken biscuits for them. 'Ooh!' Nance cried, her face lighting up. This was sheer luxury by her standards. She tucked in as hard as she could and sat at the table chatting away happily to Maryann and Tony. Then Tony went to the back door, trying to open it, clutching himself urgently at the front with his other hand.

'D'yer need a wee?' Maryann opened the door as Tony nodded emphatically and ran out to the privy in the yard and pulled the door squeaking shut.

A few moments passed, the back door swinging open into the darkening afternoon, then they heard Tony shouting, 'Maryann, Maryann! Come 'ere – 's a nasty fing!'

He was standing at the end of the yard, his eyes wide, fascinated, beckoning urgently.

'What's up, Tony?'

Maryann and Nance both went out and looked along to see what he was staring at. Between the privy and the low wall at the back was a gap of almost a yard, which had a load of rubbish chucked into it by the last occupants. It was smelly down there, the corner of the yard best avoided. But Tony's gaze was fixed on the pile of refuse. What had caught his eye was a little patch of white, the white of a small, furry throat.

It was Nance who went down the gap and very carefully picked up the cat's cold, rigid body. She kept her head down as she came back, and only when she was standing right in front of her did she look at Maryann.

'Tiger?' Maryann whispered. 'No – not Tiger!' She just stood and looked, dumb with horror. Then she shouted, 'What's happened to 'im? Oh, Tiger!'

Beside herself, sobbing, she took him from Nance, who also had tears in her eyes, and hugged him to her.

'Oh, Tiger – my poor little Tiger!'

She held him away from her, looking for signs of blood, of injury. There was nothing to see, but as she did so, his head flopped back all at the wrong angle.

'Oh my God – look! His head's all – oh look, Nance!'

Tony was crying as well then and Flo Nelson came out of the back door to see what the matter was with them all. As she did so, Nance said, 'Someone's broke 'is neck. They must've throttled 'im and broke 'is neck.'

Maryann started running then, still hugging the cat's body to her, through the house and out of the front door .

'Maryann – where're yer going? Wait for me!' By the time Nance reached the front step Maryann was off down the road, disappearing into the dusk.

Her eyes were blurry with tears so that she could barely see, but she knew the way well enough. Every so often she slowed and looked down at the precious friend she was carrying in her arms. For a second each time there was a flicker of hope. It was all a mistake. Tiger wasn't dead. He'd look into her face and purr at her and close his eyes as she stroked the side of his head, then he'd wriggle around because he wanted to be let down to play. But Tiger didn't raise his head. His fur was bunched into damp points from lying out in the wet. In the half-light, just for a second it seemed his eyes opened and she gasped. But of course it was a trick of the light and her own wishes. His eyes were two tight, pained lines and his face didn't look like him any more. All the cheeky, fiery life that was in him had gone. Maryann could hardly stand to look at him, with his poor, floppy neck. She ran along the street sobbing her heart out.

'Oh, Tiger, my little Tiger!' She didn't care who saw her. And mixed with her grief she could hear Nance's words in her head, 'someone's broke 'is neck . . . throttled 'im and broke 'is neck' and the terrible knowledge, as she ran along, that she knew who that someone was. Someone who kicked Tiger out of the way with his shiny boot every time the cat crossed his path, the someone who liked to have clean hands and clean nails, who had sat making them play cards with him when all the time he knew where Tiger was because *he* must have put him there. She thought she might burst with her rage and hatred of Norman Griffin.

She ran down Ledsam Street and tore across the yard to her Nan's cottage, pushing in urgently through the door.

'Nan, oh Nanny – look what that bastard's done to Tiger!'

But Nanny Firkin was not in the kitchen and the place was as cold as ice, no fire in the range. Maryann had been in such a state she hadn't noticed the unusual darkness of the windows. There was a rank smell of cat urine and as Maryann burst in the three cats all rushed at her, tails up, miaowing for food, their fur appearing to be standing on end in the gloom. Walt the parrot shifted silently on his perch. There was a dish on the table containing the dried-up remains of porridge.

'Nan?' Maryann wiped her eyes with the back of one hand, the eerie feel of the place breaking through her grief over Tiger. The other cats were rubbing against her legs. 'Nanny, where are yer?' It was unheard of for her Nan not to be in her kitchen. Then she remembered Nanny Firkin was ill, that she'd had a cough and her chest was bad. Hadn't her mother been in that day? The cats were acting as if they hadn't eaten for a week.

Maryann went to the stairs. 'Nanny? It's Maryann.'

But there was no reply. She laid Tiger on the floor and climbed up, somehow feeling she needed to tip-toe. Maybe Nanny Firkin was asleep.

The old lady was lying in her bed. Maryann saw the little bump where her little feet were sticking up under the cover. The room smelt stale. When Maryann went over to her she saw in the dimming light from the window that her grandmother's hair was down out of the pins and straggly round her face and her cheeks looked hollowed out. She was on her back with her eyes and mouth half open and she looked like a wizened doll. There was no movement from her, not a flicker.

'Nan?' Maryann whispered. She knew there would be no reply, that whatever it was that really made Nanny Firkin her Nan, was gone, but she couldn't take it in. Nanny Firkin was always there like the sky, she was supposed to live for ever. This wasn't really her any more, this body lying here. Maryann suddenly felt a prickle of terror pass through her, her whole body shuddered and she backed away, and ran back down the stairs. She left Tiger and ran all the way home again.

'Mom! Mom!'

Seven

The lamplighters were round lighting up as they all ran back to Ledsam Street, Flo still in her apron, with Maryann, Tony and Billy. Flo told the boys to stay out and play in 'Nanny's yard' and snapped at Tony when he tried to come into the house. A Mrs Price, one of Nanny Firkin's neighbours, on hearing what had happened, asked if the boys would like to come into her house. She said she was sorry she hadn't been in to see old Mrs Firkin, hadn't had any idea how ill she was.

At that, Flo poured out her own guilt.

'I never realized myself,' she said to the woman. 'She weren't so bad yesterday – just a bit of a cough like. I'd've come earlier, only with it being washday and that I've 'ardly 'ad a moment to spare.' Maryann watched her mom as she spoke. She was full of grim, pounding emotion. Was it true what her mom was saying? How could Nanny Firkin have not seemed ill if she was poorly enough to die?

She followed Flo back into the dark house. Flo lit a candle, her fingers trembling so much that she had difficulties handling the match, then, carrying the flickering light in front of them, they went up to Nanny Firkin's bedroom.

'Oh—' Flo's hand went up close to her mouth as she looked down at her mother. 'Oh my word – fancy 'er going like that. 'Er heart must've given out. I'd never've thought...' She looked across into Maryann's reproachful eyes. 'I ain't stopped all day! I can't be everywhere at once, yer know. I never knew she were this bad – anything like. She just 'ad a bit of a chest on 'er. I was only 'ere yesterday afternoon. You can't say I neglected her – my own mother!'

'I ain't said a word,' Maryann said stonily. 'Did yer feed the cats yesterday, when yer come over?'

She saw her mother's brows pucker in the candle-light. 'No – I never thought. I mean, she were in bed, but I thought she'd been up and about...'

Clearly Nanny Firkin had been putting a brave face on things when Flo was there.

'Anyroad – I've got more to worry about than sodding cats. Maryann – go and get the range lit and ask Mrs Price who's nearest to lay 'er out ... And Norman'll 'ave to come...'

Maryann found another candle downstairs. There was a small amount of coal and slack in the coal bucket and she stoked the range, as she had seen her mom and dad do on so many occasions, standing over it to check it was burning. Then she went across to Mrs Price's house. She felt numb and strange, suddenly, as if she were moving through a dream.

'Oh, it's Eve Leadbetter you need,' Mrs Price told her. She gave Maryann the address, directing her to another house further along Ledsam Street.

Mrs Leadbetter was a strong, jolly-looking woman.

'A death in the family, is it? Well, 'er won't be going nowhere – give me an 'alf-hour and I'll be over. Ask yer mom to 'ave some water ready.' She looked down into Maryann's solemn little face. 'Yer nan is it, bab? I'm sorry for yer, that I am. Tell yer mom I'll be over.'

As Maryann walked back across the old, familiar

yard, she saw the shape of the house she'd known as her nan's all her life. Maryann stopped, the biting cold and smokiness of the air hurting inside her nose. The moon was rising, half full, casting a white sheen on the slates. There was still a candle burning in the upstairs window, and another where she had left it on the table downstairs. It looked as if Nanny Firkin was in, going about her normal evening's jobs. But she wasn't in. Nanny wasn't there, despite the frail old body lying stiffly in the bed upstairs. She would never be there any more to go to for comfort, to tell her about school, about Tiger and his antics as he was growing up ... With a terrible jolt she remembered the earlier events of the day. Tiger was lying there in Nanny's house, at the bottom of the stairs! And soon Mrs Leadbetter would come, and Norman would come – she would be sent to fetch him. No – she couldn't stand any more.

The front door was ajar as she went quietly into the house. There was no sign of the cats, but the fusty, urine-soaked atmosphere in there persisted. Maryann picked up Tiger's body, cradling him in her arms once more.

'Mom,' she called up to Flo. 'There's a Mrs Leadbet-ter coming. She said she'd be about 'alf an hour.'

'Oh thank God yer back,' Flo called down the stairs. Maryann heard her coming closer and she shrank back. 'Now listen to me, wench – there's a few jobs I need yer to do.'

'What's them, Mom?' Maryann was creeping back through the downstairs room. As her mom descended the stairs, her feet loud on the boards, Maryann pushed the door open and slipped out. She was away and across the yard in seconds.

*

She was running as if her life depended on it, as if by doing so she could escape the terrible events of that day. She still had the feeling of being in a dream.

It's not true, she thought. None of it. Please let it not be true.

Clutching Tiger against her chest was making it hard to breathe and she stopped for a moment when she'd turned out of Ledsam Street and stood panting under a lamp. For the first time she tried to think where she might go. If she went home Norman would be there. Before, she'd have run to Sal to pour out everything that had happened, but Sal was so odd and shut off from her nowadays. And she could go to Nance's. They'd be kind to her, but she couldn't face being there tonight. The house was always so smelly and chaotic and you never knew what state Blackie might be in.

Running on, she climbed through the gap in the fence and down into the cut, near to the bridge where the road passed over the canal. Down on the path, she was suddenly forced to stop. It was so dark! It felt as if a blanket had been thrown over her head and she couldn't see where to take her next step on the muddy path. From under the bridge she could hear, magnified, the drip of water and behind her, in the distance, the clink of a horse's harness. Thank God, someone was coming along – she wasn't alone down here!

She waited a few moments as it came closer, seeing the dim light from the oil lamp on the boat growing stronger, and the shadowy movement of the horse along the bank. She pressed back to let it pass, not wanting to attract attention to herself, then followed on behind. The boat was a joey, a long open cargo boat with a tiny cabin at the back, and a man was standing up at the back, steering it in towards the bank. The carrying area was filled with a dark, gleaming cargo of coal on its way to fuel a factory boiler-house in Birmingham. The horse was walking slowly, wearily, but at a steady pace. As the prow of the boat slid alongside the bank, another man, who Maryann hadn't even noticed, jumped across on to the bank in front of her and reached for the horse's harness.

'Awright!' he called out. 'Come on,' he said to the animal. 'Let's just get 'ome now.'

Maryann was extremely glad of their presence. She knew that sooner or later something would have come along on this busy stretch of water, but the idea of walking along the path, edged by dark warehouses and wharves was very frightening. She soon realized, as the joey continued its journey in front of her, that another boat was following not far behind. She waited for it to pass and saw it was a horse-drawn family boat, also laden down with coal. She couldn't read what it said on the cabin in the darkness, but it looked the same sort of boat as the *Esther Jane* and she followed behind, holding Tiger, comforted by the leathery creak of the horse's harness. They passed under bridges and between such a density of high buildings that even in the daytime the canal at that point was forever in shadow, and the only thing visible was the tiny light from the oil lamps on the boats. The joey had vanished ahead, and she followed the boat to the basin where the cargo was to be unloaded. There were other boats underway with the task, the sounds of shovels digging into the coal or scraping at the boards of an emptier vessel to gather up the last pieces into the waiting barrows to be trundled into the boiler storehouses. Maryann could hear voices and the hard breathing of men exerting themselves, men who had already worked for sixteen or so hours that day. The horse stopped and they found a place to tie up. There were gas lamps here, and she saw the breath unfurling from the animal's nostrils. The lights of the basin jittered brokenly in the black water.

Maryann stood on the edge of this activity, looking along the row of boats, her eyes searching in the dim light. Could it be – please God could it be that the *Esther Jane* was here, and Joel? She crept along peering into the gloom. Many of the boats were joeys, with a few family boats among them. Looking down into one she saw it was nearly empty and the man shovelling up into the barrow on the bank was having to lift each shovelful almost five feet in the air to get it into the barrow. Every time he lifted one he gave a loud grunt at the effort required. Small pieces of coal rattled back into the boat. Noticing her watching, he straightened up, expelling air loudly from his mouth and pressing a hand to the small of his back. He rested on the shovel, wiping the back of his arm over his forehead.

'What're yer after?'

'I want to see a man called Joel Bartholomew,' Maryann said. She was still holding tight on to Tiger and felt small and silly. She wondered if the man could see what it was she was carrying.

'What 'd 'er say?' The figure who had just approached behind the barrow, waiting to empty it, spoke up and to her shock, Maryann realized it was a woman.

''Er's after some bloke, Joel what was it?'

'Bartholomew.'

The two of them were silent for a moment.

'I dunno 'im,' the man said. ''E work on the day boats, does 'e?'

'No – 'e's on a boat like that one—' She pointed. 'Called the *Esther Jane*.'

'Oh well—' The man bent over to start work again. 'Sounds like one of the Number Ones. 'E could be anywhere, bab, if 'e's a long distance ... Needle in a bleeding 'aystack.'

The woman stood braced by the barrow as the man started shovelling again.

'Tell yer what,' she shouted over the racket. 'We'll keep a look out for 'im, like. The *Esther Jane* did yer say?' She called over to another man who was passing. 'D'yer know the *Esther Jane*? One of the Number Ones I should think.'

The man shrugged, seeming almost too exhausted to speak. 'No. Can't say I do.'

'We'll ask around for yer,' the woman yelled across. 'And who shall we say was asking for 'im?'

'Maryann Nelson,' she said, without hope. She wasn't going to find him tonight and that was what mattered.

'Awright then. Cheer up. Word gets about fast.'

Maryann thanked her and turned back along the towpath. There were more joey boats, pulled by plodding horses and mules towards the city's canal loops and basins from the Black Country coalfields, so it was not completely dark, the edges of things picked out by the glow from their lamps. The disappointment that Joel had not been there was an ache in her that cut through her numbness. She hardly knew the man, but he was kindness and warmth; she knew instinctively that he was someone who could help her bear all the feelings that were welling up in her. Of course Joel wasn't just going to be there, like he had been the time before when she came down here by chance! How

68

could she have been so stupid, as if she could just will him to appear? The horror of that afternoon came flooding back to her. First Tiger, then Nanny Firkin. And Sal had gone all funny and wouldn't speak to her any more ... If only there was someone she could run to ...

'Oh Tiger!' She held him to her and brushed her cheek against his fur but it was wet and nasty and pent-up sobs began to shake her. She felt her way to the side of the path and laid Tiger in the undergrowth, covering his body as well as she could with grass and cold leaves, then she wiped her hands down the front of her coat.

'Goodbye, Tiger,' she sobbed. 'I loved yer, that I did.'

She walked back, still crying, beside the black water, towards home. Where else could she go? The cold sliced through her now, and under the bottomless winter sky she felt more alone and lost than ever in her life before.

69

Eight

May 1928

'Where're yer going? Oi come on – wait for me!' Nance trotted imploringly along beside Maryann.

'Down the cut.'

'Can I come with yer?'

'No.'

'Well, *sod* yer.' Nance stopped, hands clasped to her waist as Maryann strode off between the rows of terraced houses without even a glance back in her direction. Bloody charmed, I'm sure, Nance thought. What a pal she'd turned out to be. There was no getting near Maryann these days. Nance turned back towards home. She'd come out specially to see her friend after school. Now she'd be stuck playing with all her brothers again, if they'd have her.

'Still – better than that mardy little cow any'ow.' But she was hurt. She missed Maryann and the days when they'd been able to tell each other anything. Best pals they'd been, ever since they were knee high. But nowadays Maryann was just closed in on herself and they saw rather more of Sal at the house, hanging about, making eyes at Charlie. She'd never much taken to Sal though. She was older than Nance and she'd never been such a laugh as Maryann.

Nance stopped for a moment, almost changing her mind and following Maryann down to the cut. She'd had a few things to tell her about Charlie and Sal and what they were getting up to. But her pride got the better of her again. She'd keep it to herself. She wasn't going where she wasn't wanted. Maryann could stew if that was the mood she was in.

Kicking an old Woodbine packet irritably into the gutter, Nancy slouched back towards Garrett Street.

Maryann climbed through the fence and down through the scrubby trees at the edge of the cut. The leaves were bright green, crumpled and newborn-looking and even with all the various pongs in the air from the factories – metallic, chemical, getting in your throat – down here just in this scrubby little patch you saw some green and got a whiff of spring, which lifted her spirits. She spent all the time she could down here now, drawn to the back-to-front magic of the canal, the way it felt like another world when you were down there, closed in from the rest of the city, somewhere where, for her, the normal troubles of life no longer existed. You saw everything from the other way round down here: the rear ends of buildings, the low level of the path making you look up at things, the watery veins of the canals flowing round and through and under the heart of Birmingham like its secret circulation. It smelled of the murky, bitter water and of the trees, it smelled of a root to the country and of freedom.

'Did you know, children,' Maryann's teacher once told them, 'that Birmingham has more canals running through it than Venice? By length that is, I assume.' She had smiled. 'That's quite something, isn't it, when you consider that Venice is built only on canals instead of roads.'

'What's Venice, miss?' one of them asked.

71

'Well, I was hoping you'd ask . . .' She had grainy pictures of black and white poles edging canals in front of grey and black houses, gondolas tilting across expanses of dark water towards churches.

'Venice,' she said. '*Venezia*.'

'Bet our canals are a darn sight muckier,' one of the boys said and the others laughed.

'Well, perhaps. But they're very dirty in Venice too, when you consider that *everything* gets tipped into them.'

Everyone sniggered and made revolted noises. Venice didn't really sound like a real place. Real life was contained in these streets of Ladywood, collecting pails of horse muck and jam jars to sell for pennies. Maryann found herself smiling as she reached the path. Only two years ago that had been. Happy days. At school, and her dad and Nanny and Tiger all still alive. The smile fell from her lips and her face took on the scowl it wore habitually now. People had commented for a while: teachers, Cathleen Black – 'well, *she* don't look any too 'appy nowadays' – even her own mom. Now they'd just got used to it.

'I don't know what's come over you two girls,' Flo complained to them. 'There's Sal with a face like a wet Sunday and now you're even worse. And your behaviour to Norman, Maryann – I didn't know where to put myself.'

She'd come back from the canal that night, leaving Tiger's body with the cold companionship of the undergrowth and canal rats. They were all back by the time she got in. She had no idea how long she'd wandered in the cold but it must have been longer than she realized. She expected Flo to scream at her – the usual 'where've *you* been?' – but they barely seemed to notice when she walked in. They seemed only just to have got in themselves: Flo cooking, Norman Griffin sitting by the fire, feet up on the fender, his presence seeming to fill the room. Maryann slipped past and upstairs, where Sal was settling Tony and Billy. Tony was crying and without a word to each other the two sisters sat and tried to comfort him.

'It's awright, Tony,' Maryann told him, starting to cry again herself. 'Nanna's going to heaven to see God and Jesus and all the angels – and our dad an' all.'

'Bu-b-b- . . . I wanna . . . I wanna see 'er!' He was so bewildered, upset and tired.

'I'll see to 'im,' Maryann whispered, and Sal nodded and got up, sniffing. Maryann could see from her expression that she'd been crying too. The children had all been very fond of their Nanny Firkin. She'd always been good to them. Maryann expected Sal to go downstairs, but instead she went across and lay on their bed, the springs creaking as she sank down on it and put her hands over her face.

'And 'e took all Nanna's cats away, and Walt, and I dunno where 'e took 'em!'

'What're you saying?' Maryann turned to Sal.

Sal raised her stricken face. 'Norman took them outside and . . .' She made a wringing movement with her hands. Maryann went cold.

'Not Walt? Not *all* of them?'

Sal nodded, glancing anxiously at Tony.

Choking back her feelings, Maryann managed to sing a lullaby through her tears, stroking Tony's head until his breathing changed and she could tell he was drifting off to sleep. Sal lay on the bed, buried her head in her arms and shook with sobs. The smells of cooking floated upstairs: liver, potatoes, cabbage. The boys had

had slops and if it had just been the family there they'd have had the same, but Norman Griffin had to have his meat and two veg whatever the time of night. Maryann got up and went over to Sal, tapping her gently on the shoulder. It was like after their dad died when they'd cried together up here and Maryann expected her to sit up so they could put their arms round each other. But instead Sal seemed to shrink from her.

'Get off me!' Her voice came out muffled but the venom in it was unmistakable. 'Just don't bloody well touch me.'

'Please yerself,' Maryann said, feeling more tears well in her eyes. Why was Sal being like this? And today, of all days, when they'd lost their nan? The two of them had always been different and they'd always fallen out a lot, but in the end they had been close. But these last few months Sal seemed to have changed so much Maryann couldn't get near her, and tonight those changes felt unbearable. She was going to move away, but she looked back at Sal. She was curled on her side now, her hands over her face as if she couldn't bear to see anything. Now she was looking carefully at her sister she noticed the boniness of her fingers – Sal, bony! She'd always been the plump one. Maryann felt a sudden physical shock go through her. She knew her sister had been strange, moody lately. You couldn't miss the fact. But people said that was wenches for you when they began to get a bit older: she was just going through it, growing up. But now Maryann saw it was more than that.

In a soft, hesitant voice, she said, 'You don't look well. What's up with yer?'

Sal sat up with an abrupt movement and Maryann flinched, thinking for a second Sal was going to slap her. Her blonde hair was wild round her face and she spoke through clenched teeth. 'Why should there be anything up with me – eh? Just bloody well leave me be, stupid!'

Maryann stood up and backed away, leaving Sal glaring at her in the candlelight.

'I dunno what's 'appened to yer' – a sob caught in Maryann's throat – 'but you ain't like my sister any more. Yer 'orrible, I 'ate yer . . .'

'Oh who cares.' Sal lay down, indifferent. 'Just sod off, will yer?'

Maryann got halfway down the stairs and then sank on to one of the steps in the dark, hugging her knees, utterly miserable. She sat rocking for a moment, everything flashing through her mind, all the horrible things that had happened. Norman had done away not just with Tiger but all Nanny Firkin's animals! The swelling, explosive feeling built and built inside her until she could hardly breathe, she was so full of hatred and grief. At last she got up, not giving herself more time to think, and ran down to the front room where Norman Griffin was reading the *Mail*. She snatched the paper out of his hands, screwed it up and threw it into the grate before he had even taken in what was happening. The fire leapt into a great yellow blaze.

''Ere! What the . . .?'

Maryann saw his slitty eyes widen with astonishment and he sat forward as if to get up.

'You killed Tiger, didn't yer?' she shrieked at him. 'Who d'you think you are, killing my little cat and my nan's pets and throwing them out like bits of rubbish! I *hate* yer, you 'orrible man, coming 'ere thinking yer can take over from our dad. Well, yer can't because 'e was a good man and you're just a . . . a fat, murdering pig, that's what you are and I 'ope someone cuts yer bloody throat for yer!'

There were a few seconds of stunned quiet while the clock ticked and the fire crackled, then Flo's voice, 'Maryann!' at the door, her expression more appalled than Maryann could ever remember seeing it before. But she was past caring now, she was in a storm of crying, kneeling on the hearth rug, beside herself with grief and exhaustion.

'How could you've let him, Mom? 'E's a nasty, cruel man. 'E put his hands round Tiger's throat and squeezed the life out of 'im and that's the man you're married to, Mom . . . What'd Tiger ever done to 'im, poor little thing?'

The slapping Flo Griffin administered at that point almost floored Maryann, an almighty swipe across the side of the head.

'What d'you think you're on about, yer little bitch! Shut your mouth before I knock the living daylights out of yer!'

'Flo . . . Flo . . .' Norman Griffin's voice was calm, measured. 'That's enough now – calm down.'

The heat from the fire was intense on Maryann's back and her cheek was raw and burning. She looked out from behind her hands, keeping her gaze lowered, to see them both standing over her. Her eyes were at the level of their thighs. She knew without looking that her mother's face was contorted with rage. Next to her, Maryann looked down at Norman's stockinged feet planted wide apart. His shoes, well shined, were tilted up against the fender beside her. Slowly, she raised her eyes towards him. He seemed immense, looming over her, his face a great doughy ball on the end of his neck. She looked for the fury in his face, the eyes narrowed with loathing. But instead she saw something more puzzling. Norman Griffin looked relaxed, not smiling but as if a smile was waiting under the surface of his face. He seemed in some way triumphant. Maryann stared uncertainly at him, waiting, but then Flo started up.

'I'm so sorry, Norman, for Maryann carrying on like this. The girl's a disgrace, but what with losing my mother today and all . . .'

'Feed the girl and get her to bed,' Norman said. The expression on his face didn't alter and he spoke evenly, betraying no emotion. 'Today's not an ordinary day, is it? We don't want her going hungry.'

'Oh Norman.' Flo sounded quite awestruck. 'D'yer hear that, Maryann, after all the terrible things yer've said? Norman did the only thing that could be done with all yer nan's animals – we couldn't bring them 'ere, the filthy things. Now you get on yer feet and say yer sorry or you'll feel my hand across yer again, wench. Yer've got far better from Mr Griffin than yer deserve, that you have.'

Maryann stood up, her eyes fixed on the coloured splashes in the rug. She was astonished herself, but she couldn't say sorry. The word bulged like an egg stuck in her throat but it wouldn't come out. Sorry! She wasn't bloody well sorry. She wished she'd said far more. She wanted to get a red-hot poker and burn and burn him till he screamed.

'Maryann – say yer sorry!' Flo was almost shouting at her.

Maryann shook her head.

'Let it go,' Norman Griffin said quietly. 'We'll let it go. For now.'

Maryann lay in bed next to Sal. Sal hadn't come down, despite Flo calling her repeatedly. By the time they ate it was eleven o'clock and Maryann almost collapsed into bed and, exhausted and overwrought, fell asleep.

But she was wakened in the dead of night by Sal, moving restlessly at first, whimpering, then thrashing about more and more violently. Her arm came over and whacked Maryann across the chest.

'Eh – Sal!' Maryann pushed herself up on one elbow. 'Sal? You dreaming?'

Sal sat up suddenly and started gagging. Maryann's heart was going like a drum.

'Sal, Sal!' She tried to put her arm round Sal's shoulders, shaking her to wake her. Sal's whole body was heaving as if she was choking on something, her breath coming in sharp, desperate gasps.

'Sal, for God's sake stop it – say summat to me. What's the matter with yer?'

She gabbled on and on at her sister until Sal suddenly took a huge gasp as if something had come unblocked and her breath calmed a fraction. Maryann held her tight.

'Maryann?'

'Oh Sal. You frightened the living daylights out of me! I thought you was choking.'

For a moment Sal seemed to snuggle into her sister's skinny arms as if glad of the comfort. 'Help me, Maryann,' she said sleepily.

''Ow can I help yer?'

'Help me – I've got to get out.'

'Sal—' She wondered if her sister was asleep or awake. It was so dark she couldn't see if her eyes were open. She stroked Sal's shoulder and kissed her. 'I wish yer'd talk to me. Tell me what's up. Yer never talk to me these days, Sal. I want us to get on.'

There was silence then Sal said, 'Don't ever let 'er make you work for Mr Griffin.'

'I won't.' Whatever was she going on about? 'I wouldn't any'ow. Don't think 'e'd want me.'

Sal gripped her arm. 'Just don't. Promise me.'

'I promise.'

Nine

All that spring Maryann stayed away from home as much as she could and haunted the canal bank. The paths were not readily accessible – they were kept well walled and fenced off to stop thieving from the wharves – but she had her place where she could squeeze through. It was her secret escape route through which she could climb into this other world, different and hopeful. She was keeping out of everyone's way and it suited Flo Griffin to keep the cheeky little bint well out of her hair, except that she'd have liked her out of the way with her brothers in tow as well and Maryann had other ideas. Sometimes she took Tony with her, out down to play in the street or to the rezzer, but she never took him to the cut. That was her place. She tried to sneak out as quickly as she could every day, before Flo could tell her to mind her brothers, sometimes even slipping out the back, over the wall and away.

No one had got round to cutting her hair in months, and it hung in black trails each side of her thin face. When school was over she untied the strip of rag which held it back all day, put on her cotton frock in faded checks of dark and lighter blue and old rubber-soled pumps with no socks and she was off, the air on her bare arms, the sun pricking out freckles on her nose.

Ever since the morning a few weeks ago when Sal had sat up to find an ooze of blood between her legs, and Maryann learned that Sal had 'got her first monthly and become a woman' Maryann had decided she didn't want to be a woman very much herself. If it meant putting rags in your knickers and sitting about looking weighed down, groaning that your stomach hurt, they could keep it. And to have to marry horrible men like Mr Griffin so she could live in a half decent house and have meat every day of the week. She wanted to stay as she was for ever, light as wisp, to slip through the fence and run and run along the canal bank until there were fewer factories and more trees and she could lie looking up into leaves arched over her like a great green cathedral.

But she did have a companion to take on her wanderings. That week, after Mr Griffin murdered Tiger, Sal came home from work and, when they were alone, slipped something into Maryann's hand.

''Ere – saw this in the pawn shop. S'for you.'

To her delight, Maryann saw a little china cat, painted quite crudely in grey and black. It was lying down looking up with an alert expression. It didn't have a white throat, but in every other way it could have been Tiger.

'Oh Sal – ta!'

'S'awright,' Sal said.

It didn't make up for Tiger of course, and Sal soon sunk back into herself, but it meant such a lot that she'd thought to buy it. That Sal had reached out to her. Maryann loved the china cat. She called it 'Little Tiger' and carried it everywhere with her in the pocket of her frock.

At the weekends she went down to the cut and walked miles, closing her mind tight against her family, her life at home. She'd been down on the path out through Selly Oak, round the back of Bournville, her mouth watering with the smell of chocolate from the Cadbury factory as trains rumbled past close by, purple lupins amid the grass. Up Winson Green way, on a cold day, water outlets from factories making steam hiss up out of the icy canal, the routes winding and looping round the back of firms and out again, the path darkening under dripping bridges. And when she looked up and took notice she began to realize that Sal was sloping out every weekend too. Nance told her Sal was turning up round their place and she and Charlie were going off together. The park, they said. Never spelled out where. When Nance said it, Maryann shrugged.

'Good for them.'

'I don't know what's got into yer,' Nance said, offended. Before, they'd have gossiped and giggled about this development. Sal and Charlie – ooh, what was going on there!

'There ain't nothing wrong with me,' Maryann said. Nance got on her nerves nowadays. She seemed young and daft, wanting to play games all the time. Maryann just wanted to be away from it all, on her own.

But all the time, even though the canal had become a place of refuge in itself, she was on the lookout for that man, with his big smile and glowing red beard. Joel, who occupied her mind like a great burnished rock. The canals were busy with traffic day in, day out, mostly the joeys, day tripping, doing local deliveries round the factories, but among them were the family boats, the kings of the cut. Maryann narrowed her eyes when she saw one coming, looking for the right colours, the *Esther Jane*'s reds, yellows and greens, the scrolls, roses and castles painted on her doors. One day she thought she saw her, moving slowly along, a mile or so further out from where she had first met Joel. She ran towards the boat, full of excitement. But when she got closer she saw that it was wrong, everything was in a different place from what she remembered. The horse turned out to be a mule, not Bessie, and the boat was called the *Mariella*. A woman stood at the back holding a baby. Walking beside the mule, there was also a boy, about the same age as herself.

'D'yer know a boat called the *Esther Jane*?' Maryann asked him.

The boy hitched up the sleeves of a huge shirt.

'I dunno. *Mom!*' he bawled across towards the boat. At the same full volume he repeated Maryann's question, still plodding along as the mule towed the boat.

A man appeared. '*Esther Jane*? That'll be Darius Bartholomew's,' he called across.

'And Joel Bartholomew?' Maryann shouted.

'Ar – that's 'is son. You looking out for 'um?'

The boy's father gave the same promise as the coal-shovelling man had, those months ago, that he would pass word round. And why didn't she leave a message with the toll clerks?

So she had, a little note saying:

Dear Mr Bartholomew,
    When you pass this way again I'd like to see you, please keep an eye out for me. I'm on the path most afternoons.
        Yours,
            Maryann Nelson.

And one day she was suddenly there, a hazy afternoon when the cut seemed clogged with factory smoke and

83

no breeze to blow it away. She'd walked out almost as far as Smethwick Junction. The horse was skewbald, a solid little mare, and behind her Maryann saw the red, yellow and green of the boat and once more her pulse speeded as she ran closer. Before she could read the name she saw a man in a black hat standing holding the tiller, a huge white beard curling across his chest and, standing behind the small fore-cabin, staring out, a dark-haired girl of about ten years old. On the roof a brown mongrel dog was standing by the water carriers, wagging a long tail. Maryann's excitement drained away. No sign of Joel. It was the wrong boat again.

But as it drew alongside she saw the writing on the side of the cabin. *Esther Jane*. It was her! But where was Joel? Was the old man steering the boat his father?

She was too shy at first to call out to him. He looked rather grand standing there, face shaded by his hat, his back straight, beard billowing in the slight breeze, looking straight ahead of him along the canal. Maryann followed behind the horse towing the *Esther Jane*, and she kept glancing across to see if there was any sign of Joel. After a while, she saw the old man had noticed her and he raised his hand and saluted her. He reminded Maryann of a king in a fairy story, or what she'd been told God was supposed to look like. She waved back, uncertainly. She heard him say something into the cabin of the boat and in a moment she saw Joel's head appear out of the cabin. He waved as well and Maryann felt her cheeks turn pink with pleasure.

'Maryann Nelson!' he called across to her, and she giggled. She heard old Mr Bartholomew call to the girl at the bow of the *Esther Jane*. His voice was deep and growly and Maryann liked the sound of it. The girl began pulling on the tow rope, guiding the boat into the side. The old man moved the rudder and the *Esther Jane* glided up beside her. The girl leapt across the gap once she was able, and caught hold of the horse's bridle.

'Keep her moving, Ada,' Mr Bartholomew ordered. Maryann stood waiting nervously as the boat slid slowly along the bank. Now he was close to her, she could see that Darius Bartholomew had piercing grey eyes under the bushy white brows, and a forehead criss-crossed with lines like a railway junction. When he spoke he had several missing teeth. But best of all, she saw Joel smiling and reaching out his hand to her.

'Come on then, Maryann Nelson, hop in quick.'

She took Joel's hand with no hesitation and her own felt tiny, gripped in his palm, which was caloused and rough as a brick wall. She jumped across into the *Esther Jane* as it glided along, on to the tiny platform from where the boat was steered, and they pushed off again, Darius holding the long tiller while the girl stayed on the path guiding the horse.

''Ere,' Darius said to Joel. 'Tek over.' He stooped and disappeared into the cabin.

'Ent no locks to stop us along 'ere, see,' Joel said.

Maryann nodded. She was rather pleased with their little feat of getting her on board. And she liked the way he treated her as if it was quite natural that she should be there. The dog, who Joel said was called Jep, jumped down beside them, tail wagging frantically.

''Ello!' Maryann cried, patting him.

She stood with Jep beside Joel, looking round. The city began to close in on them more and more, factory walls blocking out the sky and from behind which she could hear clanging and shouting and the roar of machines. The boat moved smoothly along, her paint-work vivid against the blackened walls and leaden water. In places there was a pall of smoke across the cut. She had never felt so excited. There were plenty of other boats coming the other way; some empty, others filled with different cargoes: metal products from the foundries, boxes or barrels of provisions, heaps of refuse. As they passed other boats, Joel touched his cap and called 'How do!' and usually got a reply. Maryann was standing inches away from his elbow. His sleeves were rolled and she could see the red down of hair on his brawny left arm. She could hear his breathing, rather fast, his lungs seeming to make a rustling sound at each breath.

'So – you've been on the lookout for us?' he said eventually. She had been comfortable with his silence and was quite startled when he spoke.

'I wanted to see you again.'

'Bloke in the toll office said. Just tell 'im next time – 'e'll pass it on. Letters ain't no good to us.'

'Oh.' Maryann looked up at him. ''E don't like to be left letters to look after then?'

''E don't mind, but we don't read, us. Never 'ad much schooling. D'you want a go at this?' Joel indicated the tiller. Maryann nodded and Joel showed her where to put her hand, then laid his over the top of hers. 'It's busy down 'ere. Once we get round there we turn in and we can get unloaded.'

He guided her, tweaking the rudder, feeling his way.

'Is that your sister?' she asked, nodding over to the girl leading the horse, who kept looking round at her, curiously.

Joel nodded. 'That's our Ada.' Maryann was wondering how old the girl was, when Joel said, 'Ten years of age she is now. She could pretty well run the boat 'erself if she had to.'

She heard the pride in his voice. How she'd love that! To know how to look after a boat, steer it all herself, live in one of these cabins, away from the streets, from everything about home! Although Ada was younger than her she found herself looking at her with awe. She'd grown up on a boat and knew everything! She was a skinny girl, with dark brown hair and a pinched face, but in Maryann's eyes she looked very capable and grown up walking along at the side of the horse.

After a time of winding through the network of the city's canals they turned into one of the shadowy loops of water branching off it, where they brought the *Esther Jane* to a halt for unloading behind one of the factories. Joel told her they were carrying firebricks from 'up Staffor'shire'.

'Yer can get off of 'er for a bit now,' Joel said. Darius had emerged and was standing out on the side. Ada was strapping a painted can of feed under the horse's nose.

'I don't want to get off,' Maryann said and she heard Joel give his chuckle, like a wheeze in his chest.

'Awright – well, yer can stay on if yer want. But it'll take a good while.'

A little round man with glasses came bustling over, smiling.

'Yer early, ain't yer, pal – what're yer feeding that pony o' yours?'

It was more than two hours before all the firebricks were unloaded. After a time, as Joel, Darius and two other men shifted the cargo, hand over hand, working as a team, Maryann jumped out and went to see Ada and the horse. She was standing watching Bessie finish off her fodder, patting her brown and white neck. Jep was near by, sniffing round.

'She's called Bessie, ain't she?' Maryann asked.

Ada nodded.

'She yours?'

'Oh ar – she's our 'orse. She's a good'un, Bessie is.'

'Never seen an 'orse eat out of a bucket before.'

'That ent a bucket – that's a nosetin!' Ada laughed. Maryann liked her cheeky face. 'I got to fill up wi' water. You coming?'

'Awright.'

They each took one of the colourful metal water cans, both covered in painted flowers, and went to a tap round the side of the factory. The ground was a crunched up morass of broken brick, dust and mud.

'So you're Maryann Nelson,' Ada said, holding her can under the tap. 'You met our Joel.'

Maryann nodded.

'You writ a letter.'

'I wanted to see Joel again.' She looked over at him. Joel had stopped, was coughing.

'Why?'

''E was nice to me. And I like the boat.'

'She's called the *Esther Jane* . . .'

'I know,' Maryann said, rather impatiently. It was her turn to fill her can. She heard the water rising in it and supported it with both arms.

'That was our mom's name.'

'Where is she then?'

'She passed on when I was born. Our dad called 'er the *Esther Jane*. Joel says before that she were called *Elizabeth Ann*.'

They carried the water back to the boat. Once more, Maryann was able to go inside the cosy little cabin and she watched as Ada stoked up the range, stood a big pot on the heat and made cups of tea, handing them out to the men. She gave one to Maryann, with lots of sugar in, and the two of them sat out, balanced on the edge, each side of the stern. Ada told her that she and Joel had an older brother called Darius who worked what she called 'fly' on a Fellows, Morton and Clayton boat. This was the city's biggest carrying company, Ada explained seriously, and Maryann nodded: she had seen boats with their name on many times. Working fly meant having a shift of five or six men working day and night to cover the long distances.

''E goes down London,' Ada said. 'Works the Gran' Union.'

Ada asked a little bit about her family, but Maryann could tell as she talked that Ada didn't really understand what her life was like, just as Maryann didn't hers. Ada had never lived in a house that stayed still in one place, the same every day. She was a boat girl, born and bred. Maryann could feel the difference between them. The weather-beaten look of Ada's face, the confident way she dealt with the boat, the horse. Her strength, thin and small as she was, the way she thought and spoke differently.

When the butty was finally empty, Joel came over to them. He looked exhausted.

'Got the stew on, Ada?' he asked. 'And you'd better get yerself home, hadn't yer, little Maryann?'

'But I don't want to go 'ome!' Maryann protested. 'I don't ever want to go home!'

Ten

The light was fading now and the two Bartholomew men's faces were hollowed out with shadows as they stood looking at her. Jep was between them, looking up at their faces questioningly. Maryann presented them suddenly with a strange puzzle, an obstacle to be overcome. Darius, as if at a loss, moved stiffly away and the dog followed him.

'Well, you can't just stay 'ere, can you?' Joel suggested gently.

'Why not?' Her voice was fierce. 'I don't want to go 'ome. I'd rather stay with you.' She looked imploringly at Joel, who was standing with his arms folded. '*Please* – just for a bit.'

'Look – come up 'ere—' He reached his hand out and pulled her up on to the bank, going down on one knee in front of her. 'What's all this, Maryann? You've got a mom and a dad . . .'

'I ain't got a dad!'

'What about your mom?' Ada said. 'You can't just stay out, can yer?'

'She most likely won't even notice,' Maryann said mutinously. She gripped her hand round the little china cat in her pocket, felt her lip begin to tremble. More than anything she'd wanted ever, more even, she thought, than wanting Tiger, she longed not to have to go home that evening. Home meant Sal's terrible silences and Mr Griffin being horribly oily and nice to her. There was something wrong with that after the way she'd shouted and raved at him and she felt as if she was living on borrowed time, that he was cooking up some punishment for her, made all the worse because she didn't know what it was. And there'd be Tony with his big eyes, imploring someone, anyone, to take some notice of him.

'I'll run back in the morning,' she pleaded. 'I'll go to school. And I could sleep anywhere – outside if I 'ave to!' But saying this, she hugged herself, running her hands down her bare arms. It was chilly now the sun had gone down and all she had on was her cotton frock. She put her head on one side, looking with the full force of appeal into Joel's face. He was watching her with a mixture of amusement and concern.

'Sleep outside . . .' He shook his head and she heard him laugh, his chest making a rustling noise. 'Look, Maryann – this ent right. We'll be loading up at dawn and then we're off out of Birnigum again . . . You can come on the boat again – leave a message with the toll clerks. Let me walk you back to your house tonight and see you safe, eh?'

She looked down at her shoes and wanted to cry because it felt as if Joel was babying her, as if she was younger than Ada. She swallowed hard and looked him in the eyes, annoyed at the fact her own were swimming with tears.

'Please, Joel,' she whispered. 'Just once. I won't get in your way.'

'Go on, Joel – let 'er,' Ada said. She seemed excited by the idea. 'She can bunk up on the bench. I'll go on the floor.'

Joel sighed and pushed himself upright so he was

standing over her, hands on his waist and she stood looking up at him like one might at a mountain. She could see his beard silhouetted round his face. She knew he was exhausted, that they'd had a long, hard day's work and why would he relish the thought of having to walk her back home through unfamiliar streets, houses pressing in, to be greeted by her angry family?

Eventually he said, 'Best 'ave summat to eat, then.'

Maryann turned to Ada and saw her grin, her teeth gleaming, and she smiled back, hugging herself even tighter with excitement.

Joel lifted the lid off the stew pot and stirred the contents. Maryann went with Ada to stable Bessie for the night. On the way back Ada explained cheerfully that they had a bowl in the cabin and if she wanted to wee she'd have to go off and find somewhere. Maryann blushed.

'I'd best go now,' she said.

Ada handed her the bowl and Maryann slipped off in the dark and squatted down near the edge of the canal. She decided she liked weeing in the open even if it was a bit nerve-racking – anyone might come along. She saw that the moon had come out.

When she climbed down into the cabin of the *Esther Jane* over the coal box which was used as a step, she found a big smile spreading over her face. She was enchanted every time she stepped inside. However did they manage to live in a space this small? The house she'd grown up in in Garrett Street had been cramped enough, but here the whole living space was nine feet by seven.

'You sit 'ere—' Ada indicated the side bench, next to Joel. Maryann sat shyly beside him, smelling the delicious frying potatoes he was cooking. Jep came up and sniffed at her and she stroked his head until Joel said, 'G'won – out with you,' and he squeezed out past Ada on the step of the cabin.

Darius Bartholomew who was already sitting on the bench at the far end, dressing a wound on one of his fingers with a strip of rag, had given her a grunt of acknowledgement. She was shy of Darius, but sensed that he was gentle, even if he was not sure about her being there. Now he had taken off his hat Maryann saw he had a fine head of grizzled hair. An oil lamp fixed to the cupboard beside the range cast a cosy light round the small space, though she could see Darius was squinting to see properly. She looked round at the grainy ceiling, the pretty paintings of roses and castles on the cupboards, the strips of crochet work edging some of the shelves. It was warm in the cabin from the heat of the stove and the steam gushing out from the kettle. Maryann enjoyed every moment of it.

'You hungry?' Joel said.

Maryann nodded. Joel suddenly grinned at her. 'Nearly ready now. Table down.'

Joel swivelled the lamp round on its bracket so they could see better. Her eyes felt stretched very wide, taking everything in. Joel chuckled again at her amazement and she saw Darius smile as well, his bushy moustache making the smile appear even broader. They were enjoying seeing their own life through her eyes, this quaint little wench from off the bank, who saw things that they had always known and taken for granted as new and surprising.

They ate what tasted to Maryann like the best meal she had ever had. Mutton stew with big chunks of carrot, fried potatoes, bread, from pretty plates and a cup of sweet tea. No one said much and that suited her. Jep was peeping in through the door, nostrils working. She could feel the weariness of the men, although Joel said it had been not too hard a day for them. He was squeezed in on the bench next to her, her skinny legs dwarfed by his solid thighs. She could hear his jaws working as he chewed on huge bites of bread, and in the confined space, the wheezing sound of his lungs. During the meal he started coughing and had to go outside. She heard the coughing go on and on and he came back wiping his eyes.

'Where's she going to sleep, then?' Darius asked. Maryann saw that though he was the older man, the father, it was Joel who was in charge of the *Esther Jane*.

''Er can 'ave the bench,' Ada said again. 'I'll go down under for tonight.'

Joel nodded, patting the bench they were sitting on with his hand. 'This is your bed then, Maryann. How d'yer like that?'

'Ooh yes,' she said. 'Ta, Ada.'

Ada laughed. She seemed to find a lot of things Maryann said funny.

She watched, after they had cleared away the meal and folded back the table, as Darius pulled out the door of the bed cupboard and inside was a thin mattress and a couple of blankets. She thought for a moment he was going straight to bed, but it seemed the men were off to the pub.

'Back a bit later,' Joel said. 'You'll be all right with Ada 'ere.'

Ada grinned, shuffled herself down under the bed with another blanket, rested her head on her coat arm and, to Maryann's surprise, fell asleep straight away. Jep was allowed to come and curl up next to her.

'You can have this,' Joel said, handing her what felt like an army blanket. He indicated that Maryann should lie on the bench. Maryann settled herself down. The bench was hard, but she didn't care. The cabin felt so snug and warm. Joel took off his jacket and folded it roughly. 'Put this under yer head.'

The jacket was worn and the material scratchy, and it smelled of Joel.

'Ta,' she whispered.

Maryann dozed for a while in the light from the lamp, and was woken by the two men coming back in. Darius manoeuvred his way across the cabin and was very soon just as fast asleep as Ada.

'You awright, little 'un?' Joel asked. She caught a whiff of beer on his breath.

'Yes – ta,' she whispered.

'Oh – you won't wake them two – not once they've gone off.' But he still spoke in a soft voice. She watched as his huge shadow moved round the walls of the cabin.

'Joel?'

'What's that then?' He came and sat beside her, his feet up on the step.

''Ve yer always lived on 'ere?'

''Cept for the two year – nigh on – I were in France.'

'Our dad was in France. 'E was a soldier. Were you a soldier an' all?'

Joel nodded. There was silence before he spoke. His talk came in brief bursts, as though he had to get himself ready for it.

'Was 'e killed in the war?'

'No, by a motor car.'

Joel watched her face. 'You got to go back in the morning, little 'un. You shouldn't be 'ere, should you?'

'I know. I will. I just wanted . . . I just like it 'ere.'

For a second she felt his huge hand laid on her head. 'Sleep, that's a girl.'

''Night, Joel.'

He put the lamp out and the cabin was in complete darkness while she heard him move carefully across and settle himself on the bed beside his father.

She did not sleep well that night. The bench was very uncomfortable and she kept feeling she was going to fall off it. It was quite stuffy, and she could smell Jep's doggy smell and it was all strange being there, with no Sal beside her and no Tony across the room. She lay listening to the silence, thinking of the water under them, wondering if she was sleeping above any fish or frogs. After a time she realized it had started to rain, the drops drumming steadily on the roof, which made the cabin feel even more of a cosy refuge when the sky was only a thin shell away. Lulled by its rhythm she dozed, but later was woken by Darius Bartholomew snoring. Some time after that Joel was moving about, coughing, and once he got up and left the cabin. She listened to him straining for breath outside. The sound made her feel sorry for him; a big man's cough so loud, such a wrenching, painful noise.

When she heard him come back in, she said, 'Don't your cough ever get any better?'

He felt his way across, hands moving over her feet, and sat down on the edge of the bench. She heard him say 'Lie down!' to Jep.

'So you're still on the go, are you? Was it me woke you?'

'No.'

'Have yer heard of gas?'

''Course.'

'The sort they used in the war?'

'Did you get gassed?'

'Could've been a lot worse. But my chest's always bad. Worse in the winter.'

'Don't you 'ave a missis?' Maryann asked.

She heard another small seizure of laughter from Joel. 'No.'

'Don't yer want one?'

'Me?' There was a pause. 'Well – yes, course. But it ent happened yet. You don't meet up with people for long, working the cut. Here today, gone tomorrow. Don't s'pose I'm very easy to live with, neither.'

'I wouldn't mind living with yer,' Maryann said.

She heard Joel's laugh again. She liked the way he laughed when she said things, as if he found her surprising and funny.

'Don't know what yer mom'd say about that. She won't be very pleased with you in the morning, will she?'

'No. I s'pose not. But can I come and see yer again?'

'I told you you could. We work up and down this route. We can send word when the *Esther Jane*'s coming through.'

'Oh, *will* yer?'

Joel stood up. Once more she felt him pat her, this time her shoulder. 'You don't give up, do yer? Go on – off to sleep.'

They were up at dawn, the sky grey and rain still falling, the men with many hours of work ahead of them. Maryann said her goodbyes and thanked them.

'Look out for us!' Ada called to her.

'Oh – I'll be back!' She was shivering in her thin frock in the wet, but so happy she didn't care.

She watched as the *Esther Jane* began to slide along the wharf, off to collect her next load to be moved north, Jep standing on the cabin roof, Bessie plodding along, the white blotches of her coat standing out in the overcast morning. Joel waved at her.

'Go on now – I want to see you on your way!' he called, then coughed.

'Come back soon!' she shouted, watching until they were out of sight before she tore back round on to the towpath towards home. She had to get changed into her school clothes!

It was fully light when she got home, the lamps were out, people were setting off for work. When she opened the front door she could hear the sound of her mom shovelling coal. The cellar had flooded so they were keeping it out the back under a tarpaulin. She stood in the front for a breathless moment, hearing footsteps on the stairs, which came down into the corner of the front room. The stairs door opened and Sal appeared, face white as a sheet.

'Maryann! Oh my God, Maryann. Where were yer? I thought summat 'ad happened to yer! Our mom's going to 'ave yer for this!' To Maryann's astonishment, Sal flung her arms round her, sounding tearful.

Flo came and stood in the doorway, hair still plaited from bed.

'Well—' she began menacingly. 'Where in God's name 've you been?'

Maryann shrugged. She wasn't telling *them*. 'Out.'

'Out!' Flo was about to get herself worked up but then the effort seemed too great. She badly wanted a cup of tea and there was obviously no harm done. 'Well – you're back now, ain't yer? We'll 'ave to see what yer father 'as to say.'

Eleven

That evening Maryann was settled in the kitchen after tea, about to start on her bit of homework. She was still wondering with astonishment why no one had said anything. They'd all sat through the meal together and there'd been not a word. Had she got away with it? Then she heard Norman Griffin's voice from the front.

'Maryann – come through 'ere.'

Her heart started racing then, stomach tightening in dread but she kept her expression blank as she went through to the front room, clutching one of her books to her chest. Sal had stood up and was hovering behind Flo's chair. Maryann didn't look at her stepfather. She fixed her gaze on the grate: the poker with its brass handle was lying across the fender. The room stank of his cigarettes.

'I've not heard anything in the way of an explanation about you disappearing off for the night, Maryann, worrying yer mother half to death.'

Maryann hung her head.

'So where were yer?'

She said nothing. Nothing on God's earth was going to make her tell him, even if he took a stick to her. She'd slept on the *Esther Jane*! That was something they couldn't take away from her and she'd never forget it.

'Are yer going to tell me, or what?'

'What.'

Norman propelled his rotund bulk up out of the chair. 'Why, yer impudent little bugger!'

'Maryann!' Flo sat forward on the edge of her chair, eyeing her husband. 'I'll not 'ave yer speaking to Norman like that. Now come on – spit it out. Was you at Nance's, or what?'

'I ain't telling yer.' She looked up into Norman's face. Her legs had gone weak and trembly. Sal had a desperate expression in her eyes, her hand over her mouth.

Norman seemed at a loss for words. 'Go up to bed,' he said, his voice tightly controlled. 'But you needn't think I've finished with yer.'

'Don't do that, Maryann,' Sal said when they were upstairs, undressing in their candlelit room. 'Just tell 'im where yer went for God's sake, we was all worried. Where were yer?'

'I'm not telling you neither!' Maryann flung her cardigan on the chair. Her voice was a fierce hiss. 'And I bloody ain't telling 'im, Mr Smelly Pig!'

'Keep yer voice down – you'll wake Tony. You're a silly little cow, Maryann. You're just making trouble for everyone.'

'Not for everyone – just me. You ain't in no trouble, are yer?'

'That's what you think – you don't know what 'e's like, none of yer – you ain't got no idea . . .' Sal's voice started to crack. She put her hands over her face. 'Oh God, Maryann . . .'

'What the 'ell's the matter now?' Maryann managed a rough transition from being furious to sounding sympathetic. At least Sal was talking to her for once and not just telling her to shove off. She was really crying her heart out as well, shaking with it. 'Come on, Sal – I'm on your side, you know I am.'

'I can't ...' Sal was shaking all over, could hardly speak, teeth chattering. 'You don't know what 'e might do!'

'Don't talk daft – what's 'e going to do? 'E can't do nothing!'

But the emotion she could feel coming from Sal was so strong that she hugged her tightly with one arm, taking her hand with the other, trying to steady her. 'God, Sal, you're freezing! What's happened – you can tell me. I won't breathe a word, you know I won't. Cross my heart.'

'It's ... it's ... I can't ... It's too dirty ... I'm dirty ...'

'Sal!'

But they both froze then, eyes meeting each other's, as they heard the door open at the bottom of the stairs.

'Don't you worry, Flo love, I'll deal with it my way. You stay 'ere – it'll all be sorted out in a few minutes.'

Moving as one body the girls blew the candle out and flung themselves into the bed, half undressed as they were, the springs on the bed giving them away as they pulled the covers up over them, lying down and squeezing their eyes tight shut. Maryann could feel her heart thumping as if it might burst.

The heavy steps came closer. He was in the room, standing looking down at them. They could hear his breathing. Maryann felt Sal grip her arm, squeezing until her nails dug in.

'I know you're not asleep. I don't need a candle to know that.'

There was a long silence, so long that Maryann had an odd floating sensation as if she was dreaming, that he was not really there, but she couldn't open her eyes because it felt as if Norman Griffin could see everything, each flick of an eyelid, as if the room, for him, was full of light. It wasn't completely dark outside and you could just see the outlines of things in the room. She felt Sal give a gasping little breath. What was he waiting for? Why didn't he say anything? Then at last he moved closer along Maryann's side of the bed.

'So – secrets, eh?' Speaking more softly this time, almost singsong.

Another pause.

'Maryann?'

She said nothing, stopped breathing, remembering to do so again with a gasp.

Norman cleared his throat. 'We all have our little secrets, don't we, Sal? See, Maryann, Sal and I've come to a sort of agreement, haven't we, Sal? And I don't see why you shouldn't be part of that now as well. Sal's getting older and there are certain things older girls ain't no good for.'

Maryann felt him sitting himself down on her side of the bed and she squirmed further across towards Sal. What was he talking about? She didn't understand at all. It was no use carrying on pretending to be asleep. She forced her eyes open and, though fully aware that he was there, she jumped when she saw him leaning close, looking at her. Her heart was racing frantically. With an abrupt movement he pulled back the cover and laid his hand on her chest, fumbling round her tiny breasts. His hand felt hot and heavy, pinching and hurting her, and Maryann whimpered.

'Don't touch my sister!' Sal sat up, trying to find a thread of courage; then her own voice trailed pathetic-ally. 'Please Mr Griffin. Not 'er as well. 'Er's only a child. It ain't right.'

'Oh – jealous now, are we!' He laughed. Maryann had the same feeling she had the night she found Nanny Firkin dead, that this couldn't really be happening. It was a horrible dream.

'D'yer want it an' all, Sal?' He reached across and Maryann heard Sal cry out.

'Stop it – I'll call our mom, yer dirty man.'

'Call yer mom!' he mimicked her. 'D'yer think she'd believe a word you say, little Sally Griffin. She ain't gunna believe any of this in a month of Sundays. And you ain't so brave, are yer, not normally.' The voice was hard now, cold as steel, talking on and on, and they had no choice but to hear it.

'Just remember, Sal, what I'll do if I 'ave any trouble from you. Do I 'ave to remind you again, eh? You ain't no good to me now, and I need someone who is. And this one' – Maryann felt him prod her – 'she's still clean and she's got a bit of spirit to 'er an' all. You can leave school in a couple of months, can't you, Maryann? And then we'll see about a job for yer.' He ran his hand down the length of her body, hovering at the top of her thighs. 'Secrets, Maryann. Yer a good wench if yer can keep a secret. Because if you say a word . . .'

He left the threat hanging over them, unfinished, as he got up and went off downstairs.

Sal turned away, crying, curling herself up as tight as she could.

'Sal – oh Sal, don't! Talk to me!' Maryann felt horrible, having him touching her, but she didn't understand what it was all about, she just knew it was all wrong. 'Why was 'e doing that? Sal, tell me what 'e's been doing!'

'I can't.'

'Why not?'

'I just can't tell yer – couldn't say the words. Just, Maryann—' She rolled over, peering down intensely into Maryann's face. ''E's bad and dirty and I don't want 'im going anywhere near you. 'E does things 'e shouldn't.'

'What d'you mean?' Maryann asked in a small voice.

'Things you shouldn't even 'ave to know about. Look, Maryann – you're better at standing up to 'im than me – do anything yer can, even if you get into trouble. But don't let 'im make yer work in that place. Get yerself another job after you've finished school.'

'I will,' Maryann said. 'But why don't you leave an' all? You don't 'ave to stay there, do yer? Just walk out – 'e couldn't do nothing about it.'

'I can't,' was all Sal would say.

Maryann couldn't understand her. It was as if their stepfather had cast a spell over her and she couldn't resist anything he did, wouldn't stand up to him. She just couldn't get Sal to tell her more. She lay awake, full of disturbed feelings at the thought of Norman Griffin's hand moving over her. At the end of this school term she would reach the end of her education, of being a child. She was nearly fourteen. What had he meant when he said Sal wasn't clean any more? Was that to do with the bleeding? None of it made any sense. All she knew was that nothing at home felt safe any more. She thought with sudden longing of Nance. Nance had always been a good pal and she'd treated her badly. If only she could patch things up with her. She needed Nance now more than she'd ever needed her.

Twelve

''Ello there, stranger!'

Cathleen Black appeared when Maryann knocked on the half-open door.

'Well – we ain't seen you in a while, even though Sal seems to think she lives 'ere nowadays! Awright are yer, Maryann?'

'Oh yes, ta,' Maryann said, distracted from everything else by the sight of Cathleen Black's enormously swollen belly. It would have been impossible not to notice that she was expecting another child, she was so big she looked as if it might decide to pop out any moment.

'Look who's 'ere, Nance.' Cathleen waddled over to the range and picked up her cup of tea.

Nancy was doling out spud at the table to the four youngest, and a grubby lot they were, all grime and snot but cheerful. Perce was eleven now, William and George, nine and six, and Horace who was two and a half and kept sliding off his chair and running about. Nance tutted and banged the pan down.

''E won't keep still, Mom!' She picked Horace up and slammed him down on the chair again. 'Just park yerself and for God's sake stay there!'

'Ain't yer going to say 'ello to Maryann?' Cathleen said.

Nance's eyes were unmistakably hostile under her curly black fringe.

'So yer've turned up all of a sudden then. Don't I stink after all?'

Maryann blushed. Nance was in the right. She had been vile to her for ages. 'I know I've been a bit mean to you, like, Nance. Only I wanted to see you.'

'Go on with yer, Nance.' Cathleen put her cup down. 'Get yerself a plateful and yer can go and eat it on the step and cant with Maryann – I'll see to this shower in 'ere.'

'S'awright, Mom,' Nance said stiffly. 'I'll 'elp yer first.'

'Don't talk daft.' Cathleen waved a hand at her. 'You've been carrying on about 'ow yer ain't seen Maryann, so get off with yer. You'll 'ave plenty of 'elping to do when this babby comes, so yer might as well enjoy yerself while yer've got the chance.'

Nance doled the unappetizing food out on to a plate. Maryann watched with a pang of guilt. Her family had much better food than the Blacks – meat every day! 'What won't fatten will fill,' were words often on Cathleen Black's lips, and most of the Blacks' meals were in this vein. Then they both sat squeezed in side by side on the step. The yard was full of metal smells from the foundry at the back.

'Sorry I ain't been over,' Maryann said. 'Only things at 'ome 've been a bit . . . well, you know . . .'

'Is it yer old man?' Nance asked through a mouthful of tater.

Maryann hesitated, then nodded.

''E killed that cat, daint 'e?'

'Who else?' She wanted to pour everything out to Nance. Coming back here again felt nice. Mrs Black chatted to her children, asked them the odd question about school, was always on about one or the other of them's First Communion. She took an interest, unlike her mom. Being here was a taste of the old times and it made her long for everything to be as it was before, back on the old footing, without all the horrible things going on at home. But she didn't have words for all of it. How could she say what had happened last night, Norman Griffin pawing at her through her nightshirt? She couldn't tell Nance or anyone that, but she did want to joke and laugh like they used to, before her dad died and everything went bad.

'It's my birthday next week,' Nance said. 'I can walk out of that school and never go back – get myself a job of work. You can an' all soon, eh?'

Maryann shrugged. 'S'pose so. Where're you gunna go?'

Nance grinned. 'Kunzle's'd be nice. Eat cakes all day! I'll go round the firms, see who'll 'ave me. Eh—' She nudged Maryann. 'If you're looking too, why don't we go round together?'

'I've got a bit of time to go yet.' Maryann felt cheered. Nance was so warm-hearted and she already felt forgiven.

'Oh ah, that's a thought. Anyroad, I'll let yer know what it's like, wherever I end up.'

They chattered on a while while Nance scraped up the last of her food, and they had a bit of a giggle.

''Ere—' Nance grinned and budged up a bit closer. 'I saw your Sal and our Charlie at it kissing the other night. They was in the brew'us and they never knew I was 'aving a look in!'

'They never!' Maryann didn't know whether to feel glad or not. Sal had turned fifteen. She was growing up. But she'd never said a word about it. There were too many things about Sal she didn't know nowadays.

'She was all over 'im,' Nance went on with relish. 'She ain't backward, your Sal, and that's a fact!'

The two of them were tittering over it, but while Maryann was intrigued – Charlie Black was a handsome devil, there was no denying – she felt hurt and left out.

'She never breathes a word to me about it,' she complained to Nance.

'Well, what d'yer expect! – O-oh,' Nance said as they heard loud muttering and blaspheming approaching along the entry.

Blackie appeared in the yard, walking with a gorilla-like gait, arms swinging, cap on askew, his jacket hanging open.

'Dad,' Nance said. 'Over 'ere.' She and Maryann got up out of the way and Blackie looked and looked.

'The door!' He pointed a wavering finger. 'Shome-one moved . . . the fuckin' door.'

'Oh come on in, yer silly sod,' Cathleen shouted from inside.

Blackie stumbled in through the door and they heard a grunt as he fell into his chair, followed by a loud, grating belch.

'Well,' Nance said with a wry look. 'That's 'im finished for the day.'

Friday night was bath night. Maryann got home feeling much more light-hearted after her visit to Nancy's and found Flo filling up the tin bath which usually hung on a rusty hook on the wall of the privy outside.

'Glad you're back at last,' she said resentfully. 'Yer can come and bath the boys for me.'

Maryann agreed gladly. She enjoyed soaping the

boys in the warm water, the feel of Billy's soft little body. He was nearly five now, still small, with shoulder blades like little angels' wings.

While she was pouring in a last kettle of water, Norman arrived home, bustling through the front door. Maryann felt herself tense as if there were pins pricking her skin. He was not a man who could move quietly. He was always a noisy, disturbing presence about the place. She hated the way he came and looked in when they were bathing, especially after last night. Sal refused ever to have a bath in the house now: she went down to the public bathhouse.

He came and stood at the kitchen door, hat in hand. 'Oh-ho, bath night, eh?'

Well, it's not as if we only do it every hundred years, Maryann thought. She didn't look up at him or answer, but she could feel him staring at her.

'Your tea's nearly done, Norman,' Flo said. 'Yer might as well come and sit down.'

'I'll just wash my hands.' He came and leaned over the bath opposite Maryann, took the bar of soap and rubbed his stubby white hands, using the nails of one hand to dig out the grime from under the nails of the other. She watched, repulsed. For a moment he looked into her face and she could feel his breath on her cheek. Maryann got up abruptly and moved away to call Tony and Billy.

She bathed the two of them while Norman sat at the table eating his mutton stew, Flo sitting opposite him. He ate up quickly, then sat back and lit a cigarette, watching them lazily, his eyes narrowed a little.

'I can do myself,' Tony said, so Maryann concentrated on Billy, splashing about to make as much noise as she could and drown out the sounds Norman made when he was eating. Billy laughed, pouring water energetically over his fair hair.

'Go easy,' Flo snapped. 'You'll soak the whole floor else. Where's Sal got to, Norman?'

'She said she 'ad to go to the shop for yer.'

'For me? I never asked 'er.'

Maryann rubbed Billy dry on a strip of cloth and he put his clothes on again.

'You go in next,' Flo said. 'Use the water 'fore it gets cold.'

Maryann felt her body go stiff. Not with him sitting there, she thought. 'When tea's finished,' she said.

'Oh, that's awright – you can carry on,' Norman said.

Maryann looked at her mom mutinously. 'I'll wait till you've finished.' And she walked off upstairs, knowing Flo was too idle to follow. When she was certain Norman was ensconced in the front room with his paper, she crept down, closing the kitchen door. Flo was in there, tutting about how long Sal was going to be. Maryann could hear the boys playing out with some other lads at the back.

She slipped her brown skirt off and her cream blouse, wishing she had the room to herself, without even her mom there. She felt suddenly curious about her body and would have liked to be alone to have a good look. Lately she had sensed it changing, little swellings on her chest when it used to be quite flat. But there never seemed to be a place where you could be on your own without a brother or sister or *someone* gawping at you.

She dipped one foot in the water.

'Can I 'ave one more kettle, Mom?'

Flo sighed. 'Oh, go on then. As it's boiled.'

She topped up the bath with hot water and it felt lovely as she sank down into it, even though it was scummy from Tony and Billy going in it before. She couldn't quite lie down full stretch any more, she had to keep her legs a bit bent up and in the winter you could feel the cold nibbling round whichever bit of you was sticking out of the water. But today it was warm and she relaxed, then sat up and began soaping herself. She was just rubbing suds over her shoulders and arms when the door opened and Norman came in. Maryann instinctively crossed her arms over her chest and tucked her head down.

Get out! she felt her whole being scream. *Just get out of here and don't look at me.*

He had his hands pushed down in his trouser pockets. Maryann turned away, trying to block him out.

'That looks nice in there,' he said. ''Ere – let me put some of that soap on your back for you.'

'No!' she almost shouted. 'I can do it myself.'

'Oh, don't talk so silly, Maryann,' Flo said irritably. 'Norman won't bite yer – 'e's just trying to give yer a hand. You can't reach yer back, can you?'

He was kneeling down, rolling up his sleeves and grinning at her. She cringed away from him.

'There you go—' Round and round he rubbed the soap in his hands until they were frothy with it. Her back was rigid. She wanted to jump out of the bath and run away from him, but she couldn't move.

Flo went to the back door. 'Billy? Billy! Get in 'ere now. It's time you was getting to bed.'

He was kneeling on her left, she could smell him. Death, he smelled of. He began to soap her back, his right hand circling round and round, caressingly.

'There,' he said. 'Nowt wrong with that, is there?' The soap slid from his left hand into the bath with a plop. 'Oops. Now where's that gone then?'

He was pretending to look for the soap, but she saw his eyes were on her breasts, his hand still circling on her back.

'That's the trouble with soap . . .' His breathing was louder. 'Slippery blooming stuff . . .'

'Billy!' Flo was shouting, furiously.

Maryann couldn't believe at first what she was feeling: a hard poking between her legs which for a second she couldn't connect with anything but then knew it was Norman's finger or thumb, jabbing, forcing up into her.

'Youch!' she cried, pulling away with a splash. 'What the 'ell 're yer doing?'

'Ah – 'ere it is!' A quick sweep of the bath and he brought up his hand, triumphantly holding the soap. They looked into each other's eyes and his were as icy as pebbles. Maryann turned cold all over.

'Sorry – did I catch yer by mistake?'

Flo, oblivious to all this, was bringing Billy crossly in through the back door. 'Look at the state of yer – you'll need to go back in the bleedin' bath!'

'Language, love!' Norman stood up. 'There we go – another one all fresh as a daisy.'

'Out you get then, Maryann,' Flo said. 'Billy's dipping back in.'

Maryann sat quite still. She couldn't look at Norman, at any of them. Shame seemed to burn up from her chest to the top of her head. Was this what Sal meant, this, and more, things Maryann could not even imagine? After a moment, Norman went out again, closing the door.

'It's nice the way 'e tries to be a dad to yer,' Flo commented.

Two days later, when she went up to their room, Maryann found Sal sitting on the bed. Her left arm was held out, underside upwards in front of her. In her other fist was a kitchen knife with which she was stabbing at her outstretched arm, making jerky little digs into her flesh, some not breaking the skin, others harder. There was a thin trail of blood running down over her fingers.

For a second, Maryann couldn't believe the sight in front of her.

'Sal! What 're yer doing!' She seized the knife, stopped its jabbing motions which seemed to be happening almost independently of Sal's will. She opened her sister's fingers and prised the knife away from her. Sal looked round mildly as if woken from a dream.

'Blimey, Sal – what've yer done to yerself? Look, I'll go and get summat to wipe yer.'

She bound her sister's arm with a rag then sat beside her, half afraid to touch her. Sal looked so beautiful sitting there, pale and still, the evening light catching her hair.

'Is it *him*, Sal? What's 'e done to yer, eh?'

Sal just shook her head, seeming unable to speak.

'Is 'e . . . is 'e . . .' Maryann could barely say it, like when she had wanted to talk to Nance and no words would come, not for something like that, that couldn't really be going on, not in real life. She sensed that whatever had happened to Sal was much worse than anything he had done to her, but she didn't know about anything, couldn't imagine what it could be. 'Is Norman *dirty* with yer?'

To her enormous vexation Sal suddenly started laughing, head back, until the tears ran down her cheeks.

'Well, *what*?' Maryann said furiously. She was trying to help and this was what she got. 'What's so bloody funny then, eh?'

'Dirty! Oh, Maryann!' Still laughing away.

'Well, I meant like the other night – touching yer and stuff.' She couldn't go on.

Sal turned to her, solemn again. 'Don't let 'im near yer, Maryann, that's all.'

Thirteen

Cathleen Black had her new baby. Nance had been allowed to help out with the birth and there was great celebration when it turned out to be a girl.

'I tell yer, Maryann,' Nance said after, 'I never want to go through that in my life. Our mom says it's like passing a pig's bladder. She was on the go till right the last minute an' all. I kept telling 'er, "Mom, just go and 'ave yerself a lie down," but she says, "No, Nance – I've got to see the lads 'ave 'ad their tea. Any'ow, the longer I'm on my feet, the quicker the babby'll come."'

Maryann had her first peek at baby Lizzie when she was only one day old, with her mop of black hair, scrumpled up face, closed eyes and tight little fists. She was allowed to go up into Cathleen and Blackie's room where Cathleen lay in a motley mess of bedding consisting of what looked like rags and coats. The room was bare except for the metal bedstead and a chamber pot, and though the window was open there was a sickening miasma of sweat and blood. Cathleen looked hollow-cheeked but she raised a smile when Maryann said, 'Oh, ain't she lovely!'

'Makes a change from all them lads, don't she?' Cathleen said. ''Bout time we 'ad a wench to finish off with, 'cos I'm buggered if I want to go through all that again.'

Billy was also captivated by Lizzie, by her sheer

smallness. He stood for ages stroking her waxy hands, trying to get her to straighten her fingers.

'Why don't our mom 'ave any babbies?' he asked.

'Well, you was a babby not so long ago,' Cathleen said, adding as an aside, 'She's got more bloody sense, that's why.'

Outside, when the boys had gone off, Maryann asked Nance, 'What's yer dad been like over 'er?'

'Oh, 'e's soft as anything with 'er. 'E's always wanted another girl. Said she were 'is life's work or summat – and that were before 'e'd been down the pub!'

'Nance—'

'What?'

'How do – I mean, how does the babby get in there – d'yer know?'

'All I know is it's got summat to do with a man's – yer know – thing. 'Is willy.'

'Oh.' Maryann's brow puckered. 'Has it? You sure?'

''Course,' Nance said, all worldly-wise, though she wasn't really sure at all.

Maryann had never seen a man naked, except for her brothers. When she was younger she'd wondered whether their little willies grew with them when they got bigger, or did they stay the same size?

But she knew the answer to that now, for certain. On Sunday afternoon, Sal had gone out, and Flo was with her brother Danny and her sister-in-law Margie who had come on with her babby and she'd promised to help if she could. Norman was in the front room. Maryann was just about to call the boys to go up to the Blacks'.

'Maryann—' She heard his voice calling softly through to the kitchen where she was clearing up.

'What?' She stuck her head round the door.

'Come 'ere a minute, pet.' His voice was wheedling. It didn't quite sound like him.

She went and stood beside the chair. He was lolling back, feet up on a stool, and his face was flushed even though there was no fire in the grate.

'Fancy going to the pictures?'

'What, now? All of us?' She had had other plans, but she did love the pictures. There were the talkies now, too, people really speaking instead of just the piano banging away while you tried to read the words off the screen.

'I'll give yer a shilling and you and that Nance can go with the lads. Treat yerselves.'

'Oh – ta,' Maryann said awkwardly. Was this him 'trying to act like a dad' again? Anyway, if he was in a good mood she might as well make the most of it.

'C'm'ere first.' He beckoned her closer. 'Part of the treat for yer. There's a couple of tanners in 'ere – you come and get 'em.'

He held his pocket open, shifting in his seat.

'Go on, Maryann, I won't bite!' He was grinning, showing his yellow teeth, sweat on his forehead.

She slid her hand into the open pocket, expecting her fingers to find the two sixpences tucked in the soft material. But as soon as her hand was in there Norman slapped his own hand over it and pulled hers over, pressing it down on to his hard willy, waiting down there. She yanked away, managing to pull free and run to the door.

'Tony! Billy! Come on, quick – I'm going now.'

He was laughing. 'Don't you want your shilling then, eh?'

He wouldn't leave her alone these days. Watching

her all the time, so the feel of his eyes on her made her feel dirty. Once or twice, when he got the chance, he'd rub against her, or feel her round her chest. She could never relax when he was about and she stayed out all the time she could. Outside, at school or with Nance it was all right. She could shrug it off because these disgusting things weren't happening away from the house. It wasn't real out there, and she could forget. She dreaded being at home. Sometimes Maryann thought about trying to tell her mom. But any little thing she criticized about Norman and Flo was down on her like a ton of bricks. She'd never believe Maryann. She was always on his side. He seem to infect everything. Even when he wasn't in there were reminders of his presence: the oily dent in the chair where his head went, the paper thrown on the floor where he left it, the smell of his fags hanging about the place. Always there. Always.

It was well into June and the weather was warm now. Thin shafts of evening sunlight had found their way in through the back windows, dust motes swirling in them. Maryann smiled, remembering how Tiger used to jump up and biff at them when he was a kitten.

Sal had come in with Norman from work, had eaten her tea and the last Maryann had heard from her was the slam of the front door as she took off out again. Huh, Maryann thought, covering Tony up in bed. But she couldn't really blame Sal. She really seemed to be sweet on Charlie Black and if Maryann could have thought of a place to go she'd have gone out as well. She was beginning to get the hang of when the *Esther Jane* might be likely to be in town from the run to

Stoke. She left messages at the toll offices and ran down to ask. But she didn't hang around the cut any more, waiting. She'd seen Joel, Darius and Ada once since her night on the boat, but they'd been held up along the cut and were pressed for time, so Maryann just walked along a bit of the way with Ada and Bessie and Jep, and left them to get on. They all seemed pleased to see her though, and Joel waved.

'See yer next time!' she yelled as they headed into the gloomiest part of the cut.

She'd sung Billy a lullaby and was coming downstairs again when she heard a knock at the front door, then Flo's voice, 'Danny – what're you doing 'ere? Oh my God, what's up?' Danny's wife Margie had also given birth to a little girl, Cissie, who was now four days old.

Maryann heard her uncle panting. He must have run all the way over.

'It's the babby, Flo, 'er's bad and Margie's in a right state over 'er. Can yer come over and 'elp us, right quick? 'Er breathing's terrible.'

'Well, I don't know as there's much I can do,' Flo was saying. 'You'd be better fetching the doctor out.'

'We 'ave, but she wants you there – please, Flo —' Maryann came down into the front room and saw her Uncle Danny looking as if he was going to burst into tears. 'We'd feel better if you was there. You know what to do with babbies – we don't know 'ow to go on!'

'You go, Flo,' Norman said. 'Yer brother needs yer – there'll be summat you can do, with all your know-'ow, I'm sure.'

'Awright,' Flo agreed reluctantly.

Maryann watched her mother disappearing out

through the front door, and it was only then it dawned on her. If Flo went out she'd be all alone in the house with Norman, except for the boys sleeping upstairs. She tore out behind her mom as if she was on springs.

'I'm coming with yer! I might be able to 'elp.'

'Oh, don't be daft, Maryann!' Flo was all flustered. 'Go on in with yer. Danny and Margie've got enough on their plate without you getting under all our feet.'

'Please, Mom, let me come!'

'Maryann, go back inside.' Danny spoke roughly in his anxiety. 'Do as yer mom says. We need 'er for now.'

Maryann knew she couldn't argue. She stood on the step watching them disappear along Anderson Street. The sun was sinking now. Martins' huckster's shop was still open of course, along the way. She felt like going and standing in there, amid all the mixed smells of rubber and soap and sweets until her mom got back, but she had no money and whatever could she say to Mrs Martin?

'Come in and shut that door, Maryann,' Norman Griffin ordered her.

Her heart was thudding. The idea of being left alone with Norman Griffin now alarmed her so much that the hairs on the back of her neck were standing up and her hands shook as she closed the door. But how could she refuse?

There he was, sat in his chair as normal, she told herself, clasping her hands together so that he should not see the tremor in them. What was there to worry about? He was just sitting, looking across at her. And she knew better than ever to put her hand in his pocket again.

'So, then,' he said.

'I think—' Maryann swallowed. She was straining to keep her voice casual. 'I'll go up to bed now.'

'Oh, it's too early for that, ain't it? Why don't yer come over 'ere and sit with me for a bit?'

'No, I, er...' In her awkwardness she rubbed one shoe against the back of her other leg like a much younger child. 'No, thanks.'

Mr Griffin leaned forward with a grunt and eased himself up out of the chair. Blood started to pound in her ears. But Norman went over and drew the curtains, even though it was still light outside, so that the room turned dim and green. He lit the gas mantle and the pop-pop sound started up. Then he stood with his hands straight down by his sides, looking at her. Maryann ran her tongue over her lips and looked down at the floor. Slowly, knowing in her heart that he was not going to let her go, that there was something he wanted badly from her, she began to edge across the room towards the door to the stairs.

'No, don't go!' His voice had a hard edge. 'I said stay 'ere with me.'

He walked over to her.

'I like you better than your sister, I must say.' He picked at a lock of her dark hair and stroked it. She drew her head back. 'D'you know why, Maryann?'

Still not looking at him, she shook her head.

'You ain't like her. You've got more fire about yer and I like that in a woman.'

Woman? Maryann thought. *But I'm a girl, not a woman. I'm still at school.*

'Sal were good to me for a bit. Helped me out and did what I told 'er. See, we men are different from you women.' He spoke in a very reasonable voice. 'We need – satisfying – now and then. That's what comes natural

121

to us, see, that's all. And you girls have a way of getting me ... excited.' He was taking his jacket off. She heard him throw it on to the chair.

His hands came down on her shoulders and she cried out.

'No need for that. I'll show yer what to do. This is what wenches're made for. I'm just teaching yer, that's all. Now – you just do as I say and we'll 'ave a nice time.'

His arms came round her and she felt herself lifted off the ground and carried to the peg rug by the hearth. When he pushed her down she banged her head on the floor and gave a moan of pain, which seemed to arouse him. She heard his hard, ragged breathing.

'What're you doing?' Her voice had gone squeaky. 'You shouldn't be doing this.'

'Who says so?' His voice had lost its wheedling tone and was as cold as the frozen east wind. 'Who's gunna stop me now? You, yer little bitch, eh?'

His hands forced up her skirt and she felt him tearing her underclothes down.

'No!' She lashed out, trying to kick him. 'Stop it ... stop it! Get off me.'

'Shut yer mouth.'

Everything went darker as he leaned over her, blocking out the light and his weight came down on her so she was struggling then only to be able to breathe, gasping. Her legs were being forced apart and that hard prodding started like in the bath until she was sobbing it hurt so much, with him pushing and jabbing, burning his way up inside her, panting in her face, filthy words dropping from his lips.

When he climbed off her she was like a rag doll, dizzy, her back sore and smarting. She went very cold, starting to shiver until her teeth chattered, wet stuff oozing out down her legs as she stood up.

Mr Griffin went out to the kitchen and she heard the splash of water. He came back, buttoning his fly.

'Now. That's it then. Sal could keep a secret and I know you can. Anyhow – your mother wouldn't believe a word if you started on about this – you know that, don't you? You can go to bed now.' He turned away. 'I've finished with yer.'

She could barely remember getting to bed, struggling to wash first, shaking so much she could scarcely attend to herself. All the water in the sea could not wash Norman Griffin off her. She lay alone in the bed, hugging herself tightly with her arms, sobbing and shaking. She felt frightened and sick and bereaved, as if there was something enormous that she had lost, and she wept for all the losses she could think of: her lovely dad, her nan, her little cat. All those she had loved and would never again be able to hold in her arms.

Fourteen

She slept for a time in fits and starts, crying at first, dozing, dreaming dark, broken dreams, and still feeling, even in sleep, the ache between her legs. Then she jolted awake as she heard Norman Griffin coming up to bed. The light of his candle and his shadow moved past the crack in the door, and for those moments she stopped breathing. Was he coming to her room . . .? Not with Tony here, surely? She gripped the cover close to her throat.

But she heard him go to his and her mother's room across the tiny landing. She knew from the solitariness of his sounds that Flo was not here, had not come home. There must be something dreadfully wrong with baby Cissie that she'd had to stay out at Uncle Danny's house so long. But even more worrying was that Sal was not lying beside her, and that had never happened before. Where in heaven could she have got to? She lay there, hearing him moving, fear and anxiety growing in her until she could hardly breathe.

She wasn't going to be able to sleep. She got out of bed, tiptoed over to pull the door open and listen. She could hear Norman's loud, stertorous breathing from the front bedroom. Pig, she thought. She pulled on layers of clothes and crept downstairs to the front. The fire was dead in the grate so, as quietly as she could manage, she scraped the ash out, leaving it in a metal pail by the back door, then built up a new fire. She'd always liked putting a fire in the grate, even though it was dirty work. It made the room cosy, and she was a little comforted by the sight of her twists of newspaper as they jumped, flaming into life at the touch of her spill. The flames filled the room with warm, twitching light. She sat on the rug with her knees close to her chest, pulling her baggy cardigan down over them, and watched the fire, sometimes leaning down to blow on it, or adding a few more bits of coal to keep it going properly. Behind her the room was very dark, but the fire in front of her felt like her warm protector.

She tried to shut out any thoughts of Norman Griffin, even though this was the very spot where he'd forced her down on the floor. If she hadn't been so sore still it wouldn't seem real now. But she wouldn't let her mind dwell on it.

Where are you, Sal? she wondered again and again. With each half-hour she grew more worried. The fire was glowing a deeper orange now. After some time there was a tiny rattle of the mechanism from the clock on the mantle before it struck its gentle bong-bong-bong, then it went quiet again and there was only the sound of the fire.

She woke to the sound of Norman Griffin's feet on the stairs and found herself lying cold and cramped by the grey ash of a dead fire. Her heart pumped violently at the sound of him approaching and she sat up. The clock said half past seven. When Norman appeared he was already dressed.

'Where is everybody?'

'Mom must still be at Uncle Danny's.' Maryann sat hugging her legs again, shivering.

'Sal still abed?'

Slowly Maryann shook her head, though with a sense of unreality. Perhaps Sal *was* in bed after all? Maybe she'd been there all the time, or slipped in after Maryann had fallen asleep?

'Well, where is she?'

He turned impatiently and went back upstairs, looked in girls' room, then was back down. 'Where's 'er gone?'

'She never come in,' Maryann said, looking down at her knees, the loose-knit mesh of her blue cardi stretched over them. She knew then for certain that something had happened.

'No bloody breakfast on the go neither, I s'pose.' There was a coarseness to Norman this morning, usually hidden under his oily smoothness when Flo was about. 'Get the kettle going, wench – at least yer can make a cuppa tea.'

Maryann did as she was ordered, then went up to wake Tony and Billy. She sorted out breakfast for Norman and the boys, blanking out all other thoughts.

'Tony, you'll 'ave to go to school with Alec,' she told him. 'I'll have to stop here till our mom gets home.'

'Oh Maryann!' Tony complained.

'Do as your sister tells yer!' Norman said, with such savagery that Tony cowered.

'You'll be awright,' Maryann said to him. 'Only I've got to stay – who's going to mind Billy, else?'

Tony nodded, dumbly.

'Tell that Sal to get 'erself down the shop when 'er turns up,' Norman said, putting his hat on by the front door. 'I'll 'ave a few things to say to 'er, that I shall.'

'Come on, Billy – we've gotta go out.' Maryann impatiently shoved her little brother's shoes on. 'Push yer feet in, will you!'

'Where we going, our Maryann?'

'You'll see when we get there.' She dragged him out and along Anderson Street, then softened. 'You can come and play with Horace.'

'Oh!' Billy moaned. 'Horace is a babby, I don't wanna play with 'im!'

'Well, 'ard luck 'cos yer gonna 'ave to.'

Pulling Billy along so he had to run, Maryann went as fast as she could to Garrett Street. They were about to run down the entry but found it blocked by Blackie Black and his barrow coming the other way, loaded with his tools and metal hoops. He wasn't looking any too good but he managed a wan smile.

'Awright, Mr Black?' Maryann said.

'Awright,' he murmured amiably. Maryann turned to watch him, saw how his walk had become a shambling, dragging gait. But he didn't seem to have noticed anything was amiss, anyroad.

Everyone was out except Cathleen and Horace and the baby Lizzie. The room was in a right state, spilt tea and crumbs all over the table, and on the floor, dirty clothes, a pile of nappies, the lot.

Cathleen was at the table, Lizzie tucked in on her lap, feeding. She pulled her blouse together a little, but not before Maryann had seen the white, mottled skin of her breast. 'What're yer doing 'ere, Maryann? No school?'

'Mom's at Uncle Danny's – the babby's took bad,' Maryann said. She felt tears come into her eyes. All the fear and worry of the night welled up. 'And our Sal's disappeared. She daint come home last night so I come to see if she was 'ere last night, sleeping over?'

Cathleen gave a laugh which dislodged the baby from her breast. 'Sleeping over – 'ere? Where d'yer think 'er'd sleep – in the coal scuttle? Sorry, Lizzie – 'ere yer go.' She pushed her nipple back between the baby's gums.

'But she was with Charlie last night, wasn't she?' Maryann was frustrated by Cathleen's lack of concern.

'They went off together in the evening. I never saw 'em – Charlie must've come in late last night. I were that tired what with this one up and down, I got me 'ead down when I could, and Blackie were too kalied to notice, or 'e'd've been giving out to 'im.'

'So Charlie was here this morning?' Maryann struggled to be patient.

'Well, I s'pose 'e was – I never saw 'im though, come to think of it. 'E must've come down and gone off to work, like.'

Clearly Cathleen had no real idea whether either of them had ever come back the night before.

'They'll turn up,' Cathleen said serenely. 'I s'pect they're both at work by now. Don't get mithered.'

Loath as she was to go anywhere near Norman Griffin, Maryann called in at Griffin's Undertakers. There was no sign of Sal.

'I'll tan 'er bloody hide when I find 'er,' Norman ranted. 'We've got a lot on today.'

*

Maryann spent the rest of the morning worrying and trying to occupy Billy. She could see why he drove her mom mad with his non-stop chattering.

At last, just as Maryann was thinking she ought to get something for his dinner, she heard the front door open and she rushed through from the back, leaving Billy in the yard. Flo came in, exhaustion showing in every line of her. When she turned from closing the door, Maryann saw that her eyes were red and her face was different, somehow, tighter.

'How's little Cissie, Mom?' she whispered.

Flo shook her head, taking off her hat. 'She daint make it, Maryann. The doctor came, but she breathed 'er last this morning, poor little mite. I stayed for a bit to be with Margie.'

'Oh Mom!' Maryann was so tired and worried that she was not far from tears as it was, and the thought of babby Cissie dying brought them on fast. Poor little thing, what had she ever done to anyone!

Flo sat down, filling up herself. 'Oh, it's a terrible thing to see a babby die, Maryann. Thank God I never had any more of yer to worry about.' Unguardedly she added, 'I've been lucky marrying a man who's not that way inclined, that I have!'

'Mom—' Maryann wiped her eyes, though the tears just wouldn't seem to stop coming. 'It's – I know yer've got enough to worry about, but – it's Sal . . .'

'What?' Flo's tone was sharp. 'What about 'er?'

'She never came 'ome last night, she ain't at work and Mrs Black don't know where she is neither.'

'Mrs Black? Why the hell should she know where our Sal is?'

'Because—' Maryann stopped. Sal didn't want

anyone to know, that was obvious, or she'd have told them herself.

'Because what? Come on, get on with it.'

'Well, Sal's been knocking about with Charlie Black – and Mrs Black ain't quite sure 'e came home last night neither.'

Flo stared at her as if none of the sense of this was getting through to her brain. 'You mean they might've took off together?'

'I dunno,' Maryann said miserably.

Flo sank down on the chair behind her. 'They can't've done. What would Sal want to do that for? She's comfortable enough 'ere. Got no worries. Anyone checked where Charlie works?'

Maryann shook her head.

'Go on. See if 'e's there.'

It was quite a walk to the place where Charlie had his current employment, a dark workshop in a side street where they turned out copper rods and wire. Charlie Black? No, he hadn't been in. And if he missed another day there were plenty of others who could do his job.

By the time Maryann got home Flo was asleep and she slept for the rest of the afternoon. The evening wore on and there was no sign of Sal. Norman came home in a bad humour because he had been without his general dogsbody all day. After tea, Flo ordered Maryann upstairs, took her into their room at the back and closed the door.

'Now look – what's going on?'

'I told yer – Sal's gone. Charlie Black weren't at work today. I think Sal's sweet on 'im. They must've gone off together. And she . . .'

'She what?' Flo hissed.

'She – I'm ever so worried about 'er. She ain't right in 'erself and . . . and . . .'

'Ain't right – what're you on about?'

''E touches us. Mr Griffin. Where 'e oughtn't – and 'e – 'e's a dirty man, Mom . . .'

Flo had been soft and emotional over babby Cissie: they'd almost felt close in those few moments. Surely her mom would take her word on this? Maryann started sobbing all over again.

'What *are* you saying to me, yer foul-mouthed little bitch?' Flo sprang at her and slapped her face so hard that Maryann cried out at the pain. 'How dare you say such a filthy thing! I've a good mind to put carbolic on your tongue for that. Where d'you get such disgusting ideas from?'

'From 'im!' Maryann sobbed. 'Where else would I know 'em from?'

She received a matching slap, this time on the other cheek. Flo swelled with self-righteous fury. 'How *dare* you? Norman's a good, clean-living man. Almost a gentleman, that 'e is, and I ain't having that talk in my house from my own daughter!'

Holding her burning cheek, Maryann went up close to her mother, speaking right into her face.

'You don't see what's in front of your nose, Mom, do yer? You think more of that disgusting man than you ever do of yer children 'cause 'e buys you dresses and keeps you comfortable. But 'e ain't what you think. 'E's evil, but it don't suit yer to see it, does it?'

Flo stood before her, speechless, and Maryann fell sobbing, distraught, on to her bed.

Fifteen

Days passed, and still Sal didn't come home. Charlie Black didn't make an appearance either, and it was obvious they really had done a bunk together. Maryann couldn't stop thinking about them: where had they gone, and was Sal all right? Sometimes she was angry with Sal for leaving her alone. Mostly though, she was just worried.

Norman was all concern.

'I just don't know what can've come over the girl, Flo,' he said, shaking his head. 'I'm only sorry she's causing yer all this worry. That's young 'uns for you – selfish, never give a thought for anyone else. Don't you get upset, my dear – the pair of 'em'll be back with their tails between their legs sooner or later.'

'You 'adn't 'ad words with 'er had you, Norman?' Flo asked cautiously. 'Not done anything to upset 'er?'

'Oh no!' He laughed. 'Not our Sal. That Maryann's the minx I'm most likely to 'ave words with, as yer know. But not Sal – a good girl that one. I've been very pleased with 'er.'

Flo was appeased by the fatherly tone in which he spoke. He was right – Maryann *was* a minx, running off here, there and everywhere, making up terrible stories, like about Norman killing that kitten – and now, all that filthy language she'd come out with. She needed watching, taking in hand, that she did.

Flo went reluctantly to Cathleen Black, picking her way grandly across the yard and smoothing her hair as if she was too superior ever to have set foot in such a place before. Cathleen, who was holding the baby, looked very worried.

'Sal's been coming 'ere ever such a lot of course,' she said, laying Lizzie down on a blanket on the chair. She felt her own poor drabness beside Flo's relative glamour. The woman was wearing lipstick and powder. 'Look – won't yer 'ave a seat and a cuppa with me now yer 'ere?'

'No ta,' Flo said, wrinkling her nose at the frowstiness of the house. 'I'll not be stopping long.' Heaven only knew what you might sit on if you accepted a chair in this house, and as for drinking from one of their cracked, grimy cups, oh dear no! She wanted to be angry with Cathleen, to lay blame on her and her son, but she felt at a great disadvantage as a mother who had known nothing of her daughter's whereabouts for what had apparently been quite a long time. It made her look very bad.

'So,' she probed, 'Sal and Charlie've been knocking about for quite a time?'

'Ooh yes – din't yer know, Flo?'

'Well, of course I *knew*.' She could hardly let Cathleen Black realize she'd had no idea Sal could prefer spending her evenings in this slovenly household. 'What I daint know was she was hanging round with some idle good-for-nothing who'd make off with 'er to Christ only knows where!'

Cathleen rounded on her. 'Don't you come 'ere carrying on about my son like that! Your Sal wouldn't've gone off with 'im if she weren't a little trollop – you obviously ain't seen the way 'er's been carrying on lately or yer wouldn't be as surprised as you are. You want to pay a bit of attention instead of preening yerself, Flo Griffin, with yer frocks and yer warpaint. Looking down yer nose at my family – we may be rough and ready but we rub along. You want to look at what's going on under yer nose, 'cause one thing's for certain – your Sal never wanted to go back 'ome when she were 'ere, and that's a fact.'

'Don't you talk to me like that, yer filthy slut!' Flo yelled back. 'Yer the lowest of the low you are – look at this place! I'm surprised that babby of yours 'as survived in this filth. You ain't any place to carry on at me with yer drunken husband and yer bloody idle sons. I just 'ope our Sal comes to her senses before long and gets 'erself back 'ere because what sort of life's she gunna 'ave with one of your lot, eh?'

Flo stormed out of the Blacks' house and across the yard, all too aware that her old neighbours had probably heard all that loud and clear.

Life for Maryann at home had become one of constant fear and dread. Every time she stepped into the house she began to feel sick. The very walls were tainted with Norman Griffin. Once she heard him come home she could never relax for a moment. His eyes seemed to be on her so much of the time, watching, waiting. Her mom showed no sign of having believed what she'd told her. There was no one she could trust or rely on. She missed Sal dreadfully. School was the one thing that got her out of the house: it was somewhere to go.

One morning, though, as they were all having breakfast, Norman said to Flo, 'Our Maryann's almost finished with school now. When can she leave?'

'She's got to see out till the end of term,' Flo said. 'She ain't fourteen till September.'

'Well—' Norman sat back at the table. Maryann watched him link his hands over his belly. 'No need to see out the last stretch, is there? Dragging it out, that's all, when 'er's fit and ready for work. Let's 'ave 'er take over where Sal left off – I'm short-handed and I could do with it. Start 'er straight away.'

Even Flo was not oblivious to the pleading look of horror on Maryann's face, and Cathleen Black's remarks hadn't entirely passed her by.

'But, Norman – if Maryann leaves early she won't get her bit of paper from the school and that – for getting work.'

'Well, she won't need it if she's coming to work with me, will she? I'd see 'er awright, Flo, you know that. I say start 'er today – soon as possible.'

'No, Mom.' Maryann's tone was desperate. 'I 'ave to stay – Miss Bentley said. I *do* 'ave to!'

'It's only another couple of weeks, Norman,' Flo reasoned. 'Then she'll be ready for yer.'

Norman pushed his chair back and leaned over to kiss the top of Flo's head. Maryann looked away.

'Awright then, my sweet. Whatever you say. You can twist me round yer little finger, can't you?'

Maryann looked back in time to see Flo glancing at her. She experienced a rare moment of gratitude towards her mother.

'I do think it's for the best, Norman. I'm thinking of Maryann's future.'

*

After school every day she haunted the cut. She left message after message at the toll houses and was becoming a familiar figure to the workers there.

'Look,' one of them said to her that week. 'I think they'll be through in the next couple of days if they're on the normal run. I'll make sure they get yer message.'

The next couple of days! Maryann could think of nothing else. But suppose she missed them? What if they came through when she was at school? She *had* to see them, to see Joel above all, hear his lovely country accent. The very thought of him was comforting. She didn't know what she could say to him, she couldn't tell him what was happening to her, that she would not, could not work for Norman Griffin, not for anything ever. But she did know he was the one person with whom she felt safe and happy. And she liked Ada, with her raucous voice and cheeky face as well. She longed to see the *Esther Jane* come gliding along the cut with Bessie plodding alongside.

The next day she was so keyed up with nerves she could hardly stand it. She set off to school with Tony and his pal Alec. She waved them off at the boys' entrance.

'See yer later, Tony!' But he hardly took any notice, he was so thick with Alec. Maryann smiled with relief. She was glad Tony had such a good pal. She didn't feel able to give him any attention herself.

She looked round, making sure none of her own classmates was in sight, and darted off again down the road, looping round the back and along to where she knew she could get down to the cut. In each of her pockets was tucked a piece of bread she had sneaked from the kitchen. That'd keep her going. This could be the day they came and she couldn't miss it – just couldn't!

They came in the late afternoon, when the sun was sinking behind strips of candyfloss cloud. She saw them as they drew into view near Soho Loop. Peering into the smoky gloom she wasn't sure at first. There was the horse, all her white splotches standing out, no one walking with her on the bank. Maryann ran forward to meet her. A train clattered over the iron bridge across the loop, but Bessie barely even twitched her ears. It *was* her, and there was Joel, she could see now, standing majestically at the tiller. The boat was clothed up, tarpaulins tied over to cover the cargo, so she couldn't see what was in there. They must've come through rain.

'Joel! Joel!' Maryann bounced up and down, waving, saw him turn his head, then the slow arc of his wave back to her. Could she see his smile, or did she imagine that? After a moment she saw Darius's head appear out of the cabin and he waved as well.

'Shall I walk along with Bessie?' Maryann shouted.

Joel nodded. 'We'll need yer!'

'Where's Ada?'

His voice floated over to her. 'Gone.'

Gone? It was too far to talk properly. She'd have to ask when they stopped. Where could Ada have 'gone'? And where was Jep? She patted Bessie's neck, feeling the dried sweat on it.

'Have you had a hard day, Bessie? Poor old girl – you'll soon be there and have yer nostern.'

She felt proud, knowing a word of the canal dialect. It was different, the way they spoke. Birmingham was

Birnigum. She'd heard Darius call Rugby 'Ruckby', and Ada had run together the names 'Fellows, Morton and Clayton' as if she had no idea where each began and ended. Reading and writing was a mystery to her. She had no pictures of words in her head to know the edges of them.

The city closed in on them and every so often there was a horse bridge where Bessie had to be led over. It grew darker and darker, the blackened walls and filthy overhead enclosure of roads, railways, mills and foundries. The canal had been so built over that in parts it was so dark the gas lamps burned day and night. The water was horrible here, choked with scum and oil and refuse. No wonder Joel said Birmingham was always the grimmest part of their journey. Once she saw a man's sleeping body slumped by the wall at the side, which she mistook at first for a pile of rags. She shuddered. The place felt gloomy and hostile and she was glad Joel was not far away.

Eventually he shouted to her that they were to turn into the private wharf to unload. As the *Esther Jane* pulled in, Joel stepped across on to the bank, ruffled Maryann's hair in greeting and handed her the nostern containing Bessie's feed just as if she was Ada. Maryann grinned and tried not to show she was struggling as she fastened it on.

She knew the next couple of hours would be spent unloading. She left Bessie for a moment and went timidly up to Joel.

'Shall I make you and Mr Bartholomew a cuppa tea?'

'That'd be grand.' Joel's brow wrinkled. 'Think you can manage it?'

Maryann grinned. 'Just 'cos I'm off the bank don't mean I don't know 'ow to do nothing.'

'Go on with you then.'

He walked off, smiling. He seemed well and cheerful.

She was dying to ask where Ada was, and Jep, but she knew they were preoccupied. In the meantime she stoked the little range in the cabin, filled the kettle from the water can, which was always in place on the cabin roof, and put it on the heat. When it was ready she took the tea out to them, Joel winking at her in thanks. She made herself busy then, looking for a spot where the water didn't look too mired up to pull bucketfuls out to do some cleaning. However did Joel and Mr Bartholomew manage to keep things clean without Ada?

She found they weren't managing all that perfectly and the cabin was well in need of a scrub. To the grunts and shouts of the men unloading the firebricks outside, she wiped down the shelves and surfaces in the cabin, moving things off carefully and replacing them. She eyed the crochet pieces along the shelves, the precious work of the real Esther Jane. It was grimy grey in colour.

'I'd give *you* a wash given the chance,' Maryann said, stroking a hand over it. 'But there ain't no time for that now.'

She swept and scrubbed and kept the range going and eventually all the unloading was done and she stood up on the steering platform, watching as Joel and his father finished off with the factory men and finally turned back to the boat.

Joel climbed aboard, followed by Darius, who gave her a nod.

'I'm going for water, Joel,' he said, and went off with the can.

Joel and Maryann went into the cabin and he sat on the bench, looking at her with amusement in his eyes.

'So, little Maryann Nelson. Can't keep away from the cut then?'

She beamed. 'No, I can't. D'yer like what I've done?'

Joel looked vaguely round the cabin.

'I've been cleaning for yer.'

'Ta. She could do with it.'

'Where's Ada gone?'

'Oh, working another boat, the *Lucy* – another of the Number Ones. Their little 'uns're all grown now and they needed some 'elp.'

'But to send 'er off without you!'

'It's done on the cut. Times are hard, Maryann – more boats than cargoes these days and we're all chasing the work. You don't keep moving, you don't eat. Ada's a good little crew – she'll earn 'er keep on there. They let her take Jep with her.'

'But don't you need her?'

'We could do with 'er, but needs must. Good job you came today to find us. We're starting a new route tomorrow. Going south, Oxford way, back to where us came from. Any'ow—' He rubbed his hand wearily over his face. 'I'd best start on cooking.' He pulled a paper bag with some bacon in it off the shelf and put a pan on the stove.

'How's our Maryann then?'

The question was asked lightly but it brought tears flooding to her eyes. Oh Joel, she wanted to cry out, help me! Please help me!

'I'm awright.'

Joel turned to look at her. 'Don't sound too happy to me.'

Maryann didn't say anything. She shrugged and sat

140

watching Joel as he went back to work. He cut thick chunks of bread. She wanted to touch him, feel close to someone. Most of all she wanted to curl up in his arms for comfort, like a child.

'Joel—' she burst out at last. She wanted to speak to him before Darius got back because she was more shy of talking in front of him.

'What's that?'

'Please let me come with yer! I could help – do all the things Ada ain't 'ere to do, like cleaning and stabling Bessie and ... and everything. And I wouldn't get in yer way and I don't eat much, honest I don't!'

'No, I shouldn't think yer do, the look of yer.' Joel sat back and gently put his arm round her. She leaned against him, feeling the great warmth he gave off. 'Maryann – what's wrong with being at 'ome with yer own folk, eh?'

'I just – nothing. Only I know they won't miss me, not at all. There's nowt happening now – it's the summer holiday and it'd be awright, I promise.'

She knew Joel would have no idea when school terms began and ended. 'I ain't fourteen until the autumn and then I'll 'ave to start work, but I could come with yer till then – my mom'll be glad to get me out of the way!'

She felt Joel looking at her, his face close to hers.

'Well – I dunno,' he said eventually, sitting back. 'It's one thing having an extra from another boat, but one off the bank is different.'

'I'll learn. I'll do anything!' Maryann begged excitedly. She touched Joel's hand. '*Please*. I don't know how else to tell yer 'ow much I want to come with yer!'

'Oh, yer not doing too badly,' Joel said wryly. 'But

I don't want it causing no trouble, them turning up saying we've taken yer off or anything.'

'No – I'll go 'ome and tell them. I'll get some things. Oh Joel!' She was jigging up and down with longing to hear the word 'yes' come out from Joel's lips.

'Well—' he said again, ruminatively. Then looked round at her. 'Go 'ome and see. If it's awright, meet us back here with your things tomorrow – not too much mind. We'll be gone before daybreak so make it early.'

'Oh!' Maryann's face was alight. 'Oh Joel, you're the best!'

Sixteen

She was back at the wharf by five in the morning in a light mizzling rain, her coat pulled round her and a bundle of belongings in her arms.

On her bed she had left a note:

> Dear Mom,
>   I am going away for a bit. Don't worry I'll be safe, no need to look for me.
>   Maryann.

She had crept downstairs, weak-kneed with anxiety, and once she reached the street she tore along until she'd turned a corner, convinced she was going to hear a shout or running feet behind her and equally anxious in case the *Esther Jane* had already left without her.

The men were up and having breakfast when she arrived, frantic and panting, and she climbed on to the steering platform helped by Joel's outstretched hand.

'Morning, nipper.' He gave his slow smile. His cap was shiny with minute droplets of rain.

Maryann grinned, overjoyed. She was here – at last!

Joel sat her down inside and handed her a cup of tea and a thick, man-size wedge of bread.

'I don't know as I can eat all that,' she said.

'I should get it down you. You'll need it.'

Darius Bartholomew had not said a word in greeting,

so Maryann turned to him. 'Morning, Mr Bartholomew.'

In reply she received a reluctant-sounding grunt from behind the magnificent white beard, but Darius didn't meet her eye. After a few moments, chewing on the last of the bread, he got up, bending over as usual in the low cabin, stuck his hat on and ducked out through the door.

The joy had faded on Maryann's face. ''E don't want me 'ere, does 'e, Joel?'

Joel finished his mouthful, ruminatively. You couldn't hurry these men into speech.

''E's glad of an extra pair of hands. It's only that, well, living on a boat's quite a close life, intimate like. It'll take a bit of getting used to, someone about who ent family. But we'll manage. Plenty of others do.'

'I'll do whatever you want,' Maryann said desperately. 'I'll do yer washing, cooking – anything, only let me come. Don't send me back 'ome!'

Joel ruffled her hair again. 'I know yer will. We'll manage for a round trip. Don't you fret.'

When Darius came back, Joel went out and spoke to him, the two of them standing over by the stack of firebricks, and when they came back in, Darius nodded at Maryann.

'Mornin'.'

'Morning, Mr Bartholomew. I shan't be any trouble, I promise.'

Darius nodded. 'Let's get on then.'

Warmed by her breakfast and by Darius at least acknowledging her, Maryann went with Joel to fetch Bessie from the stable and watched with great attention as he harnessed her up.

They moved round to a new wharf to load up. Maryann stood watching with Bessie munching beside her as a crane lowered the cargo of iron pipes, load by load, down into the *Esther Jane* with much clanking and banging in the morning air. As she waited there it stopped raining and grew lighter though the rising sun was obscured by cloud and the smoke and smuts in the air. Joel went off to pay the toll and Darius went to fill up with water once more. Maryann offered to go, but he seemed not to hear her. She watched his slightly stooped back moving away from her.

At last they set off: Bessie straining hard against the harness to get the *Esther Jane* on the move, her hooves sliding and scraping, easing the boat forwards until it would begin to drift off and gather its own momentum. Joel led the horse, telling Maryann to stay on board with Darius.

She felt her eyes stretching wide to take everything in, thrilled at the boat beginning to start off slowly under her, and so caught up in the sight of the wharves and chimneys and canal cottages sliding past that she forgot to feel anxious standing beside Darius Bartholomew. She felt bubbly with excitement. They were really going, and she could leave it all behind her: home and school and Sal's disappearance and most of all, Norman Griffin. He'd be livid that she'd given him the slip – there he was commanding her to go and work for him without even giving her a say, and she wouldn't be there in two weeks after school ended, she'd make sure of that. Miss Bentley was a kind teacher and she'd persuade her somehow to give her her school leaving certificate. She'd cross that bridge when she came to it. But for now, in this one precious week, she was going to learn to work the cut and see something of outside Birmingham for the first time in her life. Up until now she'd hardly set foot outside Ladywood!

She held on to the cabin of the *Esther Jane*, a smile on her lips as she watched Joel stepping along the bank. She took in a great lungful of air. Stinking and smoky as it was, just then it felt like the breath of freedom.

The days that followed she would always remember as the closest heaven ever came to earth. It was the newness of it all, how right it felt – her being on the boat and life opening out in front of her like a picture in a storybook. For the first time in such a long while, she felt safe.

That morning, as they moved south, Maryann watched carefully, drinking in every detail as Joel and Darius manoeuvred the boat through Camp Hill Locks. Gradually the dark city began to fall away, the sun burned through the clouds. They left Birmingham with a cap of cloud over it, but outside the haze cleared and at last the sky was a rich summer blue.

'Is this the Oxford Canal then?' Maryann asked, excited.

'Oh no – we don't get on the h'Oxford till after Wigram's Turn – down at Napton. This is the Warwick and Birnigum. We're headed for a cleaner part of the cut now, you'll see,' Joel told her. They referred to 'Birnigum – that stinking 'ole' and as they progressed out into the Warwickshire countryside, Maryann could see why. She kept gazing round her, enchanted by the space, the wide, rolling country with its green pastures, black and white cows, its cornfields and snug-looking cottages, amazed at being able to see so *far*, further than she'd ever been able to see in her life before.

She could have sat and stared around quite happily all day, but she was anxious that Darius shouldn't regard her as a 'good-for-nothing' while she was aboard. Also the place felt rather lonely without Ada and Jep and she wanted to keep busy. She asked Joel what she should do.

'Well, you could give the brightwork a polish,' he said, pointing to the brass fittings on the chimney, kettle, horse brasses and handles inside the cabin. Since Ada left they hadn't had the time for 'prettifying' the place and the brasses were tarnished. Gladly Maryann set to work until they were smooth and gleaming and she could see a distorted version of her face looking back at her in them. Then she cleaned the cabin, wiping out all the smuts and dust and sweeping the floor. She was small and agile, kneeling to poke right into the corners in a way she could see was hard for big, muscular men. The cabin was so small, yet so prettily decorated inside with its scumbled paintwork, its roses and castles and scrolls, and its shelves of china, that Maryann felt as if she was playing houses. She had to remind herself that this really was their house and that Joel, and certainly Darius, had never known any other home.

In the middle of the afternoon, with Joel's help, she pulled a bucket of water out of the cut, and with a chunk of soap set to and washed the cabin's crochet work until she had it looking, not gleaming white, for it was already yellowed with age, but at least a good deal better.

'Can I hang them out to dry?' she asked Joel. She

always went to him instead of his father, although the two of them were both there in the stern. Bessie knew the routine and plodded along for a lot of the journey without being led.

'Oh – can't rig up a line any too easy with a load on,' Joel said, dismissively. 'We do that when the boat's empty, see.' But he caught the crestfallen look on Maryann's face. She had so wanted to do something to help!

'Awright then – I'll see what I can do. Those little bits don't need to hang down far, do they?'

Maryann felt Darius's eyes on her and wondered what he was thinking. She watched nervously as Joel climbed forward over the cabin and made his way along the planks which were laid over the cargo. He was holding a line attached to the cabin and unravelling it. He stretched it across to the low mast at the front and tied it, creating a washing line.

'There y'are!' he called to her, scrambling back across the planks.

It was obviously her turn to climb over. Joel handed her some pegs which she put in the bucket. She was glad it was a calm day without wind, and that the boat didn't have its tarpaulin sheeting on – the planks would be positioned higher, over the top of it, if they had to cover the load. The only time she felt really wobbly was when she straightened up after bending over to pick one of the cloths out of the bucket, almost losing her balance and falling off the planks. It wasn't far to fall but she was determined not to lose her dignity. Soon, not far above the cargo, the line of crochet work was fluttering like bunting. How pretty it was! Fancy being able to make things like that, Maryann thought. She saw Darius exchange a quiet smile with Joel as she came back to them. Suddenly Darius said, 'Why don't you 'ave a sit up there and look round. You've bin working enough I reckon.'

She realized he meant she should sit up on the cabin. He said he could see past her.

'Ooh,' she said, climbing up. 'It's hot up 'ere again!' The roof of the cabin was baking to the touch in the sunshine. Joel handed her the soaking mop. Periodically, in the heat, they swabbed down the roof of the cabin to stop the heat shrinking the timbers and cracking the paint. Maryann laid her coat on the damp roof and sat feeling the sun blazing down on her skin, screwing her eyes up against the bright sunlight on the water. Life on the cut was so quiet and peaceful compared with home, where there were always factory sounds, the whirring, whining, clanging of machinery, trams and buses and people shouting over all the other racket. Out here there were just the gentle noises of Bessie's hooves, mostly muffled by mud now they were out in the fields; the boat passing through the rippling water; the creak of the tiller and the men's occasional speech. Maryann began to attune herself to new sounds: birdsong from across the fields and in the trees, the occasional lowing of a cow, waterbirds quacking away from the boat and the breeze in the grass. There was nothing to look at that was grimy or ugly, just fields, trees and sky, farm cottages and church spires, and the bright paintwork of the boat winding along the ribbon of water. As they glided along, she thought the cut was the most beautiful place on earth.

Every so often another boat would appear, coming from the opposite direction, and the boats would pass one another a few inches apart in the middle of the channel, the boatmen exchanging a 'How do!' or more if they were better acquainted, as they often seemed to be. A couple greeted Darius and Joel with, 'We ent seen you for a bit!'

She was still sitting dreamily on the cabin roof that afternoon when there came another, incongruous sound advancing towards them, a ceaseless 'phut-phut' getting louder and louder, until round a bend in the cut they saw a vessel coming along with smoke streaming out from it.

'See that?' Joel shouted up to her. 'That's one of they moty boats!'

As it drew closer Maryann saw it was towing a butty, both of them clothed up with tarpaulins over the cargo so she couldn't see what it was. The noise it made seemed extraordinarily loud after all the quiet. The family aboard all waved and shouted greetings, trying to make themselves heard over the engine. Maryann turned to watch it disappear behind them and saw that Joel and Darius were doing the same. Darius was shaking his head as if in disapproval at this noisy 'moty boat'.

Joel leaned over to her. 'You don't get many of them down the h'Oxford,' he said. 'The locks're wider down 'ere to London.' On there, he explained, the boat could tow a butty through all in one go, whereas on here they had to pull them through the narrower locks one by one and it all took time. Maryann was learning that the one overwhelming command on the cut was 'keep moving!'

That night they tied up near a pub called the Cape outside Warwick, a little distance after the long flight of locks at Hatton which Joel told her were called the 'Steps to Heaven'. There were three other boats tied up there too. Once Bessie was fed and stabled, Joel, Darius and the other men caught up with the gossip in the pub. Maryann sat out on the bank and played with two little children from the other boat and their mother seemed grateful to have them occupied while she got on. Joel and Darius came back with groceries they'd bought from the pub.

Maryann bedded down on the side bench again that night, as she had before when she slept on the *Esther Jane*, and watched Joel ready himself for bed. She was lulled by the reassurance of his presence, his huge shadow moving round the cabin. Neither of the men undressed much for bed. They left their boots by the door and took off their jackets, undid their belts which they fastened at the back to keep the buckles from digging in when they bent over, and unfastened a few buttons. Both of them lay to sleep in shirts and their thick, corduroy trousers.

Before he lay down, Joel stepped over to her. 'You tired after your first day, Maryann?'

'Ummm.' She smiled sleepily up at him. His face was in shadow. 'It's been *bostin* – the best day ever.'

He patted her shoulder and she could hear the smile in his voice.

'Night – young nipper.'

The bed creaked as he lay down beside his father.

Maryann wanted to lie awake, to hear the sounds of the countryside at night, but she could scarcely manage it, she was so exhausted after all the new sights and a day in the fresh air. Everything smelled different. There was always the smell of the canal all round them. The sounds of family life from the boat moored behind them were dying out. Her mind passed over the day they'd had, what she'd seen, how she'd learned the way a boat manoeuvred through a lock. Something screeched outside. She imagined the *Esther Jane* from the outside, under the stars, resting on the black water. And then she was asleep.

Seventeen

Soon after the *Esther Jane* set off again the next morning, they passed through Warwick and later that morning, the stately, calm town of Leamington Spa. As they approached each town, buildings and roads grew up along the cut, shutting out the view, and with more people about there was a sudden sense of bustle.

When they reached the lock at Radford Semele, Joel said, ''Ere – you give me a hand this time.'

The day before he had told her to stay on the boat at most of the locks, but today he took her with him and showed her how to attach the windlass and turn it to open and close the gates. Maryann watched with intense attention, all her senses alert to learning to do everything as quickly and as well as possible.

He brought her round in front of him and she took the handle of the windlass which was warm from his grip on it. Each of the men had a favourite one or two of these implements for turning the locks, and the handle of Joel's was smoothed with use. His rough hand tightened over hers, concealing it completely and together they turned on the windlass, opening the gate to let the *Esther Jane* through now that the water was level. Maryann felt the immense strength of Joel's arm.

Just before they reached Wigram's Turn where Joel had told her they would join the Oxford Canal, Maryann was in the cabin and heard Joel and Darius suddenly start shouting and calling outside. She was astonished to hear them so voluble and excited and she poked her head out to see them both waving like mad at a boat approaching from the other direction.

The man at the other tiller was waving back.

'Who's that?' she asked.

'That's our Darius,' Joel said.

As they drew nearer, Maryann saw a large, muscular man with black hair curling out from under his cap, dark eyes and strong, chiselled features. He wore a rather solemn, austere expression. He reminded her of Ada except he didn't have her cheeky grin. She wondered if old Mr Bartholomew had looked like that as a young man. The younger Darius was one of the crew on a Fellows, Morton and Clayton boat which was lying low in the water, its hold heaped high with packing cases.

There was a lot of 'how do'ing and exchanges of greeting as the boats passed.

'You're low in the water,' Joel called out. 'You'll 'ave sparrows drinking from yer gunwhales!'

The young Darius grinned back and what had looked rather a forbidding face lit up suddenly and Maryann decided he looked nice after all. Joel called out that he should keep an eye out for Ada with Josiah Morley and there were shouts of 'see yer at Christmas time if not before!' and then they were past. That was the nearest they were going to get to a family reunion. The boats had to keep moving. Maryann wanted to ask Joel more about his family but she was shy in front of the elder Darius.

She helped Joel as they went up the flight of locks south of Napton, carefully doing everything she was told. The day became blisteringly hot as they set off down the Oxford Canal, so much so that Maryann found that at times she could barely touch anything on the outside of the cabin without scorching herself. She busied herself with the mop. The sun glared off the water, blinding to the eyes, and she felt her nose and cheeks turning red and sore. There were trees in a few places close to the canal, but mostly it ran through remote, open fields, and the need to keep the towpaths clear meant discouraging anything inclined to hang down over the cut. So there was little shade either for the boat or for Bessie.

For a time, Maryann walked beside Bessie along the path, enjoying the feel of stretching her legs, the smells of the fields and the hot horse beside her. Bessie wore little crocheted sleeves on her ears to keep the flies off and she seemed to plod more slowly in the intense heat. The route wound and twisted along, nestling against the contours of hills. Sometimes there were villages and little wharves tucked right beside the canal but much of the time there were just the fields stretching into the distance, trees outlined against the skyline, and it felt as if they might not see anyone else ever again. The only sounds were the rustling reeds and the twittering of invisible birds. Once she saw a huge bird lift from the bank ahead of her, its legs trailing, flying off with a heavy, cumbersome flapping of its wings.

Later, back on board, Joel told her it was a heron. She went into the cabin. It was stifling hot in there and a heavy bluebottle was batting against the windows. Maryann felt like lying down and going to sleep, but she knew she mustn't. The last thing she wanted was to be seen being lazy.

Joel's head appeared at the door. ''Ent you got a bonnet with you?''

She shook her head. 'I ran off in such a hurry – I forgot it.'

He hesitated for a moment, then seemed to decide something. He came into the cabin, squatted down and rummaged right at the back of the cupboard he called the 'monkey 'ole'. He brought out a large, squashed paper bag and from it he drew an old-fashioned boat-woman's bonnet with a peak at the front and layers of black frills which went right over the top of the head and ended up hanging down at the back.

Maryann stared at it. It looked old and dusty, like a dead raven.

'It were my mother's,' Joel told her gruffly. 'She 'ad it made special in black when the old Queen died. These 'ere bits' – he pulled at the long material at the back – 'them's your curtains – 'll keep the sun off yer neck.'

Was he expecting her to wear it? The hat looked so worn and old-fashioned. It was a heavy, *ugly* thing and she wished she had her little straw bonnet with her.

'I can't put that on. Not if it was your mom's.' This was a rather awesome thought.

'I'd like to see yer in it.' Joel held it out to her. 'It's ten year since it were worn. She passed on before I came home.'

'Why daint Ada wear it?'

'Oh – she had her own bonnet.'

Seeing she didn't take it, he put it on her head himself. Maryann felt strange, seeing the fond look in his eyes. The bonnet felt much too loose.

'Bit big on you, ent it? But it'll do just for a bit while it's so hot. We don't want you getting caught by the sun.'

Joel was the last person Maryann would ever want

to offend so she smiled uncertainly at him. She felt like a granny in the bonnet. She had seen a few older women wearing them along the cut.

She followed him up out of the cabin. As she straightened up she saw Darius's eyes fasten on her. He actually started at the sight of her and a look of utter outrage came over his face.

'What's 'er doing in that?' he demanded.

'I thought she could wear it for a bit,' Joel said. 'She ent brought a bonnet with 'er. And it's nice to see it wore again.'

Joel had made a terrible mistake. Maryann could see just how terrible by the look in Darius Bartholomew's eyes.

'That's my Esther's bonnet – moy best mate. Not one else ever wears that bonnet. Get it off yer, lass!'

Maryann was already tearing the hat from her head, her hands trembling at the emotion in the old man's voice. Joel took it from her.

'Sorry, Dad – only I thought yer'd like to see it on again, the way I did.'

Darius was breathing heavily. 'Put it away.'

Joel ducked back into the cabin with the bonnet. Maryann couldn't look up. Her cheeks were burning and she had a horrible feeling inside as if she'd committed a crime. She had offended Mr Bartholomew so badly when what she wanted more than anything was for him to accept her. It was unbearable that he would think her uppity enough to take his dead wife's bonnet and wear it.

'I'm ever so sorry, Mr Bartholomew,' she managed to say, her voice quavering.

'It weren't your idea I don't s'pose,' Darius said abruptly.

Though she knew this was true, his rough words scarcely made her feel any better. Joel came back out and laid a hand on her shoulder for a moment.

'My mistake, not yours,' he said.

But it was not until much later that day that the feeling of discomfort this incident had brought Maryann began to ease off and she could feel a little more comfortable with Darius Bartholomew again. After that she doubled her efforts to show him she could work hard and try to please him.

That night, after fourteen hours on the go, they tied up at Fenny Compton, where there was a small wharf and a pub. A couple of other boats were tied up there and the men went out to the pub as usual after they'd eaten. Maryann didn't mind being left behind. She rather liked the novelty of having the cabin to herself.

As it was so warm, she didn't feel like slaving away cleaning the cabin. She was hot and tired and she went out and sat on the bank in the evening air. She could smell smoke and food cooking and she breathed in deeply, a great feeling of well-being coming over her.

Glancing towards the pub, she suddenly noticed that Joel was on the bridge and there was a young woman with him. Maryann screwed up her eyes to see better. She was short and rounded looking, with a wide, healthy face and curly brown hair. She and Joel were standing quite close together, relaxed, each leaning on the bridge, and now and then their laughter floated over to her. Maryann was immediately curious. Was she someone Joel was very close to? She found herself full of mixed feelings. Joel had told her he had been courting a girl before the war changed everything. Of course he'd want to get married like other men, but she had had in her mind a future stretching ahead in which she could live on the *Esther Jane* and everything would stay the same.

After a time, the two of them left the bridge and walked round the wall of the pub, out of sight. Maryann sat on, feeling suddenly desolate. She wasn't really part of all this, however much she wanted to be.

When Joel came back in she was already lying down. 'Who was that lady you was talking to?'

He frowned for a second.

'On the bridge.'

'Oh – that's Rose.' He laughed, then coughed to clear his chest. 'Ent seen 'er in a good long while. We've been catching up.'

'She's pretty,' Maryann said. She knew she sounded sulky.

'S'pose she is. Known 'er all my life.'

'Are you going to marry her?'

To her surprise, both men started laughing.

'Marry Rose? Bit late for that – she's got a chap and three kiddies, Rose 'as!'

Maryann went off to sleep feeling much happier. However much she told herself she was stupid to think she could have Joel all to herself, the thought of him being in love with that pretty Rose had made her feel jealous and left out.

The next day was just as long, and in the evening they pulled into Thrupp where the canal was edged by little terraces of canal workers' cottages. Joel told her they were now only about three hours away from Oxford.

She helped to get the range going and cook the food.

Joel had also made her responsible for unharnessing Bessie, feeding and stabling her. On these scorching days she also had to wipe out Bessie's eyes with a rag dipped in paraffin, to keep them free from flies and parasites. Mostly, as they went about their evening chores, even Maryann was too tired to speak. Darius went off and kept himself separate, collecting water, or coal if they needed it, and at Thrupp he asked around for return loads to take back north after they had delivered the pipes in Oxford. She and Joel did their chores, often in silence, but always at ease. Sometimes he looked at her and smiled and she'd grin back.

She was more than ready for bed every night after all the physical activity and fresh air of the daytime. As they drew further south away from Birmingham, home seemed more and more unreal, like a bad dream. In the daytime she was so caught up in all the details needed to keep the *Esther Jane* on the move that she barely had time to think, and that suited her very well. She wanted to forget all of it: Sal, Norman Griffin. When she did allow herself time to think, she was filled with anxiety. Where had Sal gone? Was she with Charlie Black and were they both all right? And what about Tony and Billy, left at home? Most of all she felt badly for Tony, about her going off and leaving him. But nothing would have made her give up these days on the cut. Nothing.

By ten the next morning they were pulling into Juxon Street wharf in Oxford amid a collection of boats waiting to unload. The wharf was very busy. Maryann stabled Bessie, gave her a feed and cleaned her harness. She wound her way back to the *Esther Jane* through the stacks of cargo standing on the wharf waiting to be collected: coal and stone, barrels, packing cases, sacks. The hard work of loading and unloading was going on all round and she could have stood all morning watching, but instead she hurried back and got the stove going to make cups of tea. The *Esther Jane* was due a big clean-out while they were tied up. In the meantime she heated more water, got the tin tub and dolly from off the roof and did some washing, scrubbing at the men's thick corduroy trousers, struggling to lift them when they were saturated with water.

'They're *filthy*,' she said to Joel, pummelling them wearily with the dolly. Her shoulders were aching like mad.

'You should see 'em after a hold full of coal.' Joel grinned. '*That's* filthy!'

The afternoon passed loading the *Esther Jane*, the long iron pipes swinging high in the air above her head before being deposited with a loud clanking on the bank. Joel and Darius were preoccupied with securing a return load to take north again. The country wharves sometimes wanted loads of grain taken up for grinding in the Birmingham mills, but it was close to a new harvest now and the stores were low. They needed to find something in Oxford. Joel went off to some of the other wharves, and by late afternoon he had secured a load of timber to be taken to Birmingham. In the meantime, Maryann strung the washing along the boat and helped Darius to swill her out with water. She was ill at ease being left to work with him, but she did everything he said to the letter and by the end of the afternoon she felt that even if she did not have his approval in great measure, at least he had accepted the help she was offering and she had not let herself down.

Eighteen

That evening though, for the first time, she felt lonely. With the work done and the cargo to be loaded in the morning, Joel and his father went to see Joel's auntie, Darius's sister, and then for a few pints at the pubs round Jericho, the area near the wharf. Maryann, as ever, was left alone.

She cleared up the tea things, put everything away. The men brought food in daily if they could, as nothing would keep in the heat, so there was only a bit of bread and bacon on board for next morning. The place was tidy, and as she had been washing and cleaning most of the day she could think of nothing she needed to busy herself with. Now they had achieved the journey down to Oxford the urgency had gone out of things. Before, she hadn't minded being left here, had rather relished having the cabin to herself, but tonight, with nothing to do, she felt suddenly bereft. She sat by the table for a time, biting her nails, and unwelcome thoughts of home and Norman Griffin began to crowd into her mind. She knew if she started on that it would just keep on going round in her head. No – she must think about anything but him.

She got up and folded back the table so she could make up her bed on the side bench with the little flock mattress and the blanket she slept under. She lay down and concentrated on the rosy light of the lamp reflected in the brass fittings. It was such a snug place and it felt like home now. Maryann found herself smiling, snuggling down cosily and growing more sleepy. Every so often she heard the sound of the water lapping gently against the wharf. She was coming to love the sounds of the cut at night. If only she could stay here! There were a few lonely moments, but nothing like the isolation she felt at home where there was no one she could turn to. There was no threat here, not with these big, quiet men. She felt safe with Joel, safe and reassured, as if he was a strong, fairytale brother who'd come to rescue her.

The thought of home filled her with dread. She would have to go back – for Tony if no one else. But why did she have to stay at home? Why could she not just live on the cut with the Bartholomews? Joel had said it was hard enough working the *Esther Jane* three-handed, let alone two, and Darius wasn't a young man any more. But what would Joel say if she asked him? And Darius? Had she proved her worth enough during these last few days?

By the time the men came in she was dozing. She woke again as the cabin door squeaked open, letting in the night air. Darius, walking unsteadily, immediately went and let down the bed at the back, gave out a loud, beery belch, then readied himself for the night. Joel, however, seemed restless. Seeing Maryann looking sleepily up at him he came and sat on the end of the bench. She slid her legs out of the way for him. For a time he just sat there holding his cap while she watched him. His wiry beard and wavy hair were a lovely bronze colour in the pink, subdued light. She looked at his gentle face and huge, worn hands and felt she couldn't imagine a time when she had not known him.

Why was he just sitting there instead of going to bed, she wondered. But she liked it, didn't want him to move, wanting instead to ask him if she could stay with them, but Darius was there and she didn't have the courage.

He looked across at his father now and then, and when Darius was obviously asleep he turned to her and said, half whispering, 'Well – it's been a soft day for us today. I don't know about you, but I ent ready to settle yet. I fancy a walk. How about you, young nipper?'

'Ooh, yes!' She sat up, immediately cheerful. Anything Joel suggested seemed good. An adventure!

She put her shoes back on and her cardigan and they climbed back out into the starry night. The moon was almost full and the wharf buildings were sharp edged, the colour of pewter under its light.

They set out along Juxon Street. Maryann found it strange to be back on a road, with buildings hemming you in on either side, after the cut. She tried to imagine how it would feel never to have lived on the bank.

'D'yer think you'll ever live in a house?' she asked, looking up at Joel.

'Oh – you can never tell, can you? There are folks moving off the cut all the time. It ent easy, with the moty boats and lorries taking over the cargoes. We'll hang on as long as we can though. It's what we know.'

'But you wouldn't give up the *Esther Jane*, would yer?'

Joel shrugged. 'I hope not. But we had to sell the butty – we had a pair before, but we had to part with one of 'em. That's how it goes these days.'

Maryann felt sobered by this. The thought of the Bartholomews living like other people was inconceivable. They turned into another street, then another, in silence, except for the sound of their feet on the road. Silence was easy with Joel. It never felt uncomfortable.

'But—' she said eventually. 'You were born on the cut, weren't you?'

'I was s'posed to be born 'ere at h'Oxford. My mother was coming to town to 'ave me and I was in too much of a hurry – arrived just south of Banbury!'

'On the *Esther Jane*?'

'She weren't called the *Esther Jane* then.'

'No, I know. Joel – will you tell me about your brothers and sisters?'

They turned on to a wider road where there were a few more people about, coming out of the pubs.

'You're a proper chatterchops, ent you?'

'I ain't!'

She liked Joel calling her a chatterchops, but in fact it was hardly justified. There'd been very little time to talk much on the way down. They were always busy, or the men were in the pub or too tired.

'When'll you see Ada again?'

'Well, if we don't run into 'er on the cut, it'll be Christmas. We all try and 'ave a rally at Christmas time, tie up at Braunston or Hawkesbury for a couple of days. See young Darius and Ada.'

'Won't she miss you?'

'She will. But a lot of young 'uns work away from their families. It's the only way to do it – someone always needs a pair o' hands.'

'What about the others?'

'Darius is the oldest. There was Daniel who fell sick and passed on as a little 'un. I never knew 'im. Then there was Esther – she drownded when she was not more than fifteen. Then Ezra – 'e died in the war, and so did Sam, then there was me, then Sarah and we lost 'er to the h'influenza and our mother lost a pair of babies in between – she was very poorly after them – and then there was Ada and through her we lost our mother.'

'Oh Joel, your poor mom!'

'Yep—' he said gruffly. 'She were a good'un, our mother.'

'Did Darius go away to the war?'

'No. Someone 'ad to stay. We younger ones went and I was the one come back. Anyhow – that's how it went. How many's in your family?'

She told Joel all about Tony and Billy, and Sal running off and her dad dying and Mom marrying Mr Griffin, but she didn't want to say much about him. She could feel Joel listening beside her.

'Is your stepfather good to you?'

'No,' she said abruptly. 'Well – I mean, we eat enough and that. But . . . I don't want to talk about 'im, Joel. Don't let's spoil it – it's lovely out 'ere.'

As she began to take an interest in the town unfolding round her, she saw that it was indeed beautiful. There were a few lamps, but mainly the buildings were lit by the moon. Maryann looked up at the spires and towers, the grand, dark fronts of the colleges all around them.

'This is h'Oxford University,' Joel told her. 'They do a lot of book learning 'ere, that's what.'

To Maryann it seemed like fairy land, like nowhere else she'd ever been before.

'I'll show you summat lovely,' Joel said. 'Come along 'ere.'

He led her down a side street, then another, and into a square. All along the sides were castellated buildings, no factories or houses at all. There was a huge, rounded building in the middle. It was covered in little stone arches and columns and stone balustrades, and its roof was domed. Its windows reflected back the moonlight.

'Oh!' She looked round in wonder. 'What is it?'

'They say it's full of books,' Joel said, with a slight air of disbelief. 'Let's go down by the river, shall we?'

Maryann could tell that, while awed, he was not comfortable between all these walls. He led her out the other side of the square and across another road hemmed in by buildings that seemed like palaces to Maryann.

'D'you wish you could read?' she asked him. 'If you wanted to learn I could 'elp yer.'

She heard Joel's wheezy laugh come to her through the darkness. 'Reckon I've got this far without. There ent much call for it on the cut.'

She walked with him, down to where the river flowed past the backs of the colleges. For a moment they stood looking back. It was a beautiful sight, the old stone lit by soft moonlight.

'S'funny how many different ways there are for folk to live, ent it?' Joel said. She felt him reach down and take her hand in his, and she nuzzled against his arm, happy. 'Bet you've never seen nothing like this before.'

Maryann shook her head. 'Joel?' Her heart began thumping fast.

'What's that?'

'I don't want to go home. I want to stay with you and your dad and work the cut.'

There was silence as Joel stared down into the water, that flowed past quite briskly, not like the still, sluggish canal water.

'I don't know about that. You've been a good'un,

learning how to work the boat, no doubt about it. And I can't says I won't miss you, specially with Ada gone. But you can't just stay on without your family giving their by-your-leave. That ent right.'

'Oh *please*, Joel. I can't go home. It's not . . . I can't say why. But it's horrible at home and they won't care if I'm there or not . . .'

'Now, now—' He turned to face her. 'That can't be true now, can it? You got family – people who need you.'

'But Ada just went off to live with someone else, daint she? Why shouldn't I do it too?' She knew she sounded desperate, almost tearful.

'That's what life is on the cut. We boat people do that. But it ent the same where you come from, is it? I ent saying we don't need you – a pair of hands is like gold to us. But you should go back and make things right with your family first. I can't feel right about you just running off and them not knowing where you are, Maryann. You can see that, can't you?'

'I know.' Her voice sounded high and young. 'But I just want to stay with you, Joel.'

'Oh – now—' He pulled her towards his big, burly body and she felt herself pressed against his scratchy weskit, her little budding breasts tender against him, his strong arms tight round her. She put her arms as far round him as she could reach, laughing. She hadn't felt so warmed or happy since she was a little girl, held in her dad's arms after he came home and she nestled against him, loving the feel and smell of him. Joel could save her, he could take her away from that life at home that she so dreaded, she knew he could. He could do anything.

'Don't you get all upset,' Joel was saying, tenderly

stroking her hair. His hand felt enormous on her head. 'We'll see what can be done.'

She looked up into his face and saw his eyes twinkling down at her affectionately in the moonlight.

Nineteen

During the small hours of the next morning, the weather broke. Maryann woke in the night to hear thunder and, soon after, the sound of rain drumming on the cabin roof. The next morning it was still raining. She went out with her coat on and the water was soon running off her hair and down her cheeks.

They moved the *Esther Jane* down to Isis Lock – Joel and Darius called it 'Louse Lock'. To load up, Joel explained, they had to move from the narrow Oxford Canal on to the wider Thames, the adjacent 'Mill Stream', to where the imported timber was brought from London on lighters, towed by tugs, which were too wide for the Oxford Cut.

'When they come up 'ere' – Joel pointed after they had come through Isis Lock – 'they got to get past the railway, see? There's a bridge there, cranks up by 'and, lets 'em through.'

'But what if there's a train coming?' she said.

Joel laughed at her foolishness. 'You don't do it when there's a train coming!'

Maryann did not see any of the lighters coming through, but on the wharf waiting for them was a stack of timber sawed into all sorts of different lengths and thicknesses.

'It's one of the awkwardest bloomin' loads we ever carry,' Joel said, taking off his wet jacket. 'We've to load each bit by hand, or it won't fit in. You can help.'

Maryann soon found out what he meant. Darius, with his lifetime's experience of settling a load into a boat just the right way, stood in the hull as Joel, another worker and Maryann passed him down each plank, piece by piece. Darius said which bit he wanted next and laid them all in, fitting them like a patchwork quilt. The wood was very rough and splintery, not planed smooth. Some of the pieces were so heavy that Maryann couldn't lift them, but she worked hard taking over whatever she could. She wore a thick, hessian apron over her dress. Sometimes she squatted, resting a plank across her knees for Darius to take it from her. The rough wood burned her hands, splinters jabbing into her like needles, and she was soaking wet. The men never seemed to stop and rest: the boat and load always came first. By mid-morning, when the load was almost on board and the rain was still falling, she was close to tears she was so wet and tired, and her hands were bleeding and swollen. But she was determined not to show Darius how close she was to getting up and running off. She gritted her teeth and passed him another plank, wishing he'd at least notice how difficult she was finding it. But after they had secured the last pieces and the *Esther Jane* was now riding low in the water, Darius patted her shoulder briefly as he passed her.

'That were a good job,' he said.

Maryann beamed back at him, elated yet with a lump in her throat. She had truly done something right and won his approval! She skipped along to help Joel harness Bessie, who was quite frisky after her extra half-day's rest. Once she was harnessed up, tolls paid, coal and water aboard, they were off.

Maryann was thrilled to be on the move again. The cut stretched out ahead of them as they slid slowly out of Oxford, the spires and towers receded into the distance and they were in the country again.

'This is the proper life,' she said.

Joel grinned at her. 'If you say so, missy.'

They only travelled as far as Thrupp that day and the sun never broke through. The second morning, they woke to rain and the wind was getting up. Their clothes from the day before were still not dry even though they'd hung them in the warm cabin while they were in bed, but it was obvious that if they put their spare set on they would soon be soaked through as well. Once Joel and Darius had gone out she pulled her damp dress over her head with a shudder. It was slightly warm from being close to the stove, but it soon cooled on her and she was shivering before she had even gone outside. For the first time she started to have misgivings about this life. If this was what it could be like in the middle of summer, what must it be like living here in the freezing winter wind and rain?

They warmed themselves with a cup of tea as they went along. But the day started out as a hard, maddening one. The wind was the real enemy on the cut, pushing even a well-loaded boat about like a plywood toy from side to side. Joel stood at the tiller working it with all his strength to keep it from being blown into the bank, and the shallows where often there were reeds, and other plants with big leaves that looked like rhubarb. Maryann annoyed him by asking, before she realized, 'Will you teach me to steer today, Joel?' and he snapped back, 'Not today – can't yer see what it's like?'

As the wind got up further, Darius took to the bank

to help keep Bessie steady. Every so often the boat was caught by a gust and blown into the side. The water was the colour of milky cocoa. Joel abruptly ordered Maryann off to help pull them off. The first time, the stern of the boat was forced right into the side. Joel yelled at her, telling her how he wanted her to pull. She hauled on the rope with all her strength, the rope yanking away and burning through her agonized hands until she couldn't help crying with the pain. They'd no sooner get straightened up again than another gust would send the *Esther Jane* off at some other angle. As well as keeping the boat on course, round Banbury there were all the lift bridges over the cut to be raised and lowered again as they passed. The morning seemed endless; cold and hard and wet. Maryann was already near to exhaustion and everyone was tense and bad-tempered. Darius kept yelling at her to pull harder, Joel was cursing on board the boat. Maryann almost wished she was at home. She had a sudden longing to see Tony and Billy – someone younger who looked up to her and loved her and didn't order her about.

But the worst was to come on the afternoon. Worse than Maryann could ever have imagined. They'd passed Banbury and reached Slat Mill Lock. As they struggled into the lower pound – Joel striving to keep the boat straight, another boat following close behind, which added to the pressure on them – he shouted to Maryann, 'D'you think you can do it?'

'Yes!' she called back proudly. ''Course.'

Darius was already out on the bank too. 'You take the 'orse,' he said.

'No, please,' she said. 'I can do it. I know how.'

With obvious reluctance he handed her his windlass, which he carried tucked in his belt, and stayed holding

Bessie. Maryann fitted the windlass on to the lock mechanism and started turning. One of the men from the boat behind pushed on the gate beam to swing it open and Maryann stood out of the way, feeling pleased with herself. Joel had spelled out many times the danger of standing in the wrong place and getting swept into the cut. None of them could swim and even if they had been able to, the men especially would have been weighed down by their heavy trousers, boots and overcoats. Maryann stood with her hands behind her back, the windlass clutched between them as the two boats moved into the lock chamber and the men closed the lower gates, trying to look as if she had lived on the cut all her life and knew just what she was doing. But she noticed that on the boat behind there was a boy with only one leg, and it was a sobering sight. People with missing limbs were not uncommon on the cut. What accident had befallen him in this dangerous life?

When the lower gates were closed and the boats were secured, waiting for the water to rise, she struggled along, leaning into the wind, to the upper gates, hearing Joel shout something to her as she went. The wind whisked his words away.

'S'awright!' she called back. 'I can do it!'

She started turning. Though she'd done it a number of times with Joel, it was hard by herself but she was determined to manage. The muscles on her arms strained and eventually it was so difficult that she was leaning her whole weight on the windlass to turn it and haul it back round at the bottom. The paddles were opening and the water started to gush in with a great roar.

And then it all went wrong. She was leaning back, bringing it round, when she lost her balance. Her hands slipped off the windlass and it snapped back the other way, flying round and round, and Maryann fell over backwards. Frantic and mortified, she scrambled to her feet just as the windlass flew off the spindle. There was a metallic clink, then a splosh. She stood there, paralysed. No – it couldn't have done! Darius's precious, favourite windlass, the one Esther Jane had given to him, his wife, his best mate, had disappeared down into the cut.

Everyone was shouting: Joel, Darius, the other men in the boat. Tears welled up in her eyes. She didn't know what to do.

Darius was suddenly beside her. 'Take care of th 'orse,' he shouted at her.

She saw him go to the shaft where the windlass should have been. He looked round on the ground, then down into the water. He went to Joel, shouting to him for his spare windlass. Maryann slunk back to Bessie with the most leaden heart she had ever had. She was sick with shame. She wanted to hide her face in the horse's hot, wet neck and give in to crying, but she knew this would put her in even more disgrace.

'Your windlass taken a look in the cut, eh?' one of the men on the wharf called out to her. 'Oh dear, oh dear!'

The teasing was not unkind, but it made her feel even worse; young and stupid and incompetent. Worst of all, it made her feel an outsider again, just as she thought she was beginning to get the hang of it. Waiting to finish getting through that lock felt the longest few minutes she could ever remember. When they were through, she went to Darius, looking down at her muddy shoes, unable to face him.

'I'm ever so sorry, Mr Bartholomew.' The tears ran

down her burning cheeks. 'I never meant to lose your windlass. I wish I could go down and get it. I feel ever so bad.'

Darius Bartholomew could not seem to speak. Maryann looked up to see him trying to gather himself. He was breathing deeply and she could see he was furious, but seemingly unable to find the words to yell at her as she knew she deserved. He looked at her for a moment, then strode past. Once they were through the lock Maryann climbed back into the boat, wishing she could just disappear.

'The windlass – I lost Mr Bartholomew's favourite windlass. I don't know what to do, Joel – he's so angry with me.'

'Well, of course 'e is!' She had never heard Joel raise his voice to her in anger before. 'I told you to wait for 'im. You have to do what you're told, not just mess about! What d'you expect him to do? He'd had that windlass more'n half his life.'

'I daint hear you. I promise I daint, Joel!' Maryann was really sobbing now. It was no good thinking she could come here and be one of them and start a new life. She was hopeless, even at the first test and now Joel was fed up with her as well. She wanted to get off the boat, get away from them and from feeling so small and ashamed.

'Oh, there's no need for all that,' Joel said crossly.

Maryann stood looking out, wiping her eyes as Joel wrestled with the tiller, struggling to keep the boat moving straight. He took some time to gain control again. After what seemed a cold, miserable age, he turned to her.

'Eh – cheer up. You weren't the first and you won't

be the last.' He patted her shoulder. 'We'll make a boatwoman of you – don't you worry.'

But to her it still seemed a huge and awful thing she had done and she didn't know how she was going to face the rest of the journey with Joel's father.

Later she apologized again to Darius Bartholomew and he said gruffly, 'These things happen. It taught you, I hope.'

Maryann felt almost forgiven by the men, but she was finding it very hard indeed to forgive herself.

For the rest of the journey she was quiet and subdued. She listened with great care to what she was asked to do and did it with all her concentration, trying as hard as she could to make amends. Darius treated her much as he had before, but he did not reach out to her with any words of reassurance and she couldn't feel forgiven, even though Joel tried to jolly her along.

The last night, when the men were asleep, she gave into her feelings and lay sobbing, trying to be as quiet as she could. After a time, though, she heard the cross bed creaking as Joel sat up, then came over to her.

'What's up, chatterchops? You ent been yourself these last days. Eh – come on now, you don't want to worry so much. There ent nothing wrong.'

He sat down beside her and took her hand in his.

'Oh Joel!' She pressed his hand against her cheek. 'I feel so bad about eveything – I can't stay 'ere 'cause I'm no good to yer, but I don't want to go 'ome. I just can't go back there!'

'Now, now—' She became aware that he was stroking her hair with his other hand and it gave her such a warm, reassuring feeling. 'Don't go saying you're no good to us. You've been a good little boatwoman.

Everyone loses a windlass some time – that's life on the cut.'

'But Mr Bartholomew's best mate's windlass!'

'Well, that were a pity, but what's done's done. In the past now. You want to forget about it.'

But Maryann's heart was so heavy she couldn't feel consoled yet. She couldn't stop crying.

'What is it, eh?'

'Can I stay with yer, Joel? Just come and live 'ere?' she pleaded again.

'We said all this already.' His voice was gentle but firm. 'You must go back and tell 'em where you've bin. It's no good. If they're happy about it . . .' His voice trailed off.

'What? Tell me, Joel!'

'Truth is, I can't say I won't miss you. I've got used to you, sort of thing.'

'Oh please—' Maryann sat up eagerly. 'Say I can stay!'

He took her in his arms and rocked her, and she clung to him. In wonder, she felt him kiss the top of her head.

'You go 'ome and sort things out. Then we'll see. 'Ow about that, eh?'

Birmingham grew up around them, dark and rank with factory smells and the grim stenches of slum living. Buildings blocked out the light.

'I never knew 'ow much it stank 'ere till I got out of it,' Maryann said, standing on the steering platform. Darius was on the bank with Bessie. 'It's so dirty and dismal, ain't it?'

Joel laughed. 'Don't say that about your 'ome!'

As they moved further into the town, the noise increased: the cut busy with laden joey boats, the boatmen in a rush and shouting and swearing at each other to get ahead, trains clattering overhead dropping smuts, the air laden with factory smoke. Maryann's spirits dropped again. She had to get out of here. The narrow streets, the meanness of everything – and worse, much worse than that, Mr Griffin . . . Winter on the cut, however cold and hard, could not be worse than this.

When they pulled into the wharf under the laby-rinths of factories to offload the wood, Joel said to her, 'You'd best get off now, 'adn't yer – be getting back to your own people.'

'I'll be back,' she said. 'I will, Joel – I'll leave word for yer!'

She saw his slow smile. 'Well – we'll see, won't we. We'll try and stay on the h'Oxford. I know my dad's happier going down that way.' He leaned over and rumpled her hair. 'Cheerio for now, young nipper.'

She politely said goodbye to Darius Batholomew. He said, 'G'bye, lass,' in a kindly way and his leathery face creased into a smile, even though they were in a rush to get unloaded, and that made her feel better. Waving at Joel, she left with her little bundle of clothes and set off towards Ladywood.

Twenty

'Well.' Flo's face was distorted with anger and her arms tightly folded across her chest. 'What've yer got to say for yerself then?'

Maryann had made sure she didn't arrive until after Norman Griffin had left, and when she got in only Flo was at home with Billy, who ran through from the kitchen calling, 'Maryann!'

''Allo, Billy love.' She put down her bundle and squatted down to cuddle him.

'Norman's been going mad!'

Maryann's expression darkened. She scowled at Flo over Billy's blond head. 'Ain't that typical, eh? I go away for a week and all yer can say is "Norman's been going mad!"' She mimicked her mother's tone. 'That's all you cowing well care about, ain't it?'

Flo stood glaring at her, then suddenly kneeled down so her face was level with Maryann's.

'That's always the way with you, ain't it? Never a thought for no one else. Do you know why I married Norman? Do yer?'

''Cause yer wanted his money.'

'Yes – 'cause I wanted his money! And d'yer know why I wanted 'is money? So I could feed my family and keep it together. So you could 'ave the clothes you're wearing on yer back, Maryann. So's I daint 'ave to hand over Tony and Billy to Barnado's when I couldn't afford to keep them!'

'No, Mom, that's the excuse you've always had but I don't believe yer. We wouldn't've starved the way you'd like us to believe. You 'ad a job – in a couple of years Sal was out at work – then I'd've been. Other people do it – look at Mrs Winters.' Mrs Winters was a widow with five children who they'd known in the Garrett Street days.

'Huh,' Flo said contemptuously. 'Yer needn't think taking in washing was the only way *that* one was making ends meet! She had men in and out of there like rats in a nest. And look at the state of 'er – 'er looks sixty if 'er looks a day and she ain't no older than I am. I weren't living like that – I struggled and scrimped all through the war, and then with yer dad coming home in the state 'e was–' She leaned closer, spitting the words into Maryann's face. 'You was too young to know what it was like. You don't feel it all when yer a babby, all the worrying and going without – you just 'ave the bread put in your mouth and that's all you know. It's the mother feels it. I'd 'ad enough, Maryann. Norman ain't yer dad – course I know that. I loved my Harry, that I did, even when 'e come home half the man 'e'd been. But when 'e'd gone I couldn't face no more. You needn't think it's easy for me. You don't know what it's like to lie every night next to a man yer've no feeling for.'

An expression of revulsion came over Maryann's face. 'Don't I? And Sal – don't she?'

'Don't start on them lies again.' Flo turned away in disgust. 'I don't want to hear 'em.'

'No – you don't, do yer?' There was great bitterness in Maryann's voice. 'That's the one way I can rely on you – not to want to hear the things that don't suit yer.'

'Norman's given us a good home and a good life – and you girls just can't see it. We could get on awright but you go running off – you're nothing but trouble. First Sal, and then you . . .'

To Maryann's vexation, her mother put her hands over her face and burst into tears.

'That's it – go on and cry then.' She walked away across the room. 'Twist everything round so everyone has to feel sorry for you. That's always your way, Mom, ain't it? You never want to hear what anyone else's got to say.'

She stamped her way upstairs, full of bitterness. The bedroom felt damp, and very cold and empty. After a moment she heard her mom following her up. Flo came and stood at the door with Billy who was watching them both, wide-eyed with alarm.

''Ve yer heard from Sal?' Maryann asked, her back to Flo.

'Not a word.' Flo wiped her eyes on her apron. 'I've been worried to death. And then you take off as well – fancy leaving a note on your bed like that. You can be a cruel, selfish little bint, can't yer? And I can smell you from 'ere. Yer stink as if yer've been living in a ditch. Where've you been?'

'I ain't telling yer.' Maryann turned, hands clasping her upper arms and her jaw thrust out. 'You can ask me till you're blue in the face. I've been somewhere where I can 'ave a better life than I ever do around 'ere with you and that dirty husband of yours. But of course you don't want to hear about that, do yer?'

Flo was breathing hard. She narrowed her eyes. 'Tell me the truth, Maryann, or I swear to God I'll take my hand to yer. You've been with Sal, ain't yer? You know where she is!' She was shouting, moving closer. 'And I bet that Cathleen Black knows an' all!'

'I am telling you the truth. I ain't seen Sal. I wish I had but I don't know where she is, on my life.' She backed away from her mother. 'But I ain't telling you where I've been. One thing is – I'm going again, soon as I can. I ain't staying round 'ere for a second longer than I 'ave to!'

'So – you're back.'

Flo was in the kitchen with the boys when he came in. For the few moments Maryann was alone with him in the front room, Norman Griffin looked older and flabbier than she remembered, such a contrast to the muscular strength of the Bartholomews. He was looking at her with undisguised lasciviousness, as if his eyes were fingering her through her clothes, and her skin prickled with revulsion.

He moved closer, speaking very softly to prevent her mother hearing, in his low, wheedling tone. 'I'm not going to ask where yer've been, so long as you're back now.' His hand reached out and stroked her left breast. 'To stay.'

Maryann's lip curled with disgust and she stepped backwards, folding her arms tightly across herself. She stared past him, at his brass lamp on the table by the wall.

'I do believe you're growing up.' He was smirking at her, undeterred. 'Quite a young lady all of a sudden.'

'Norman?'

He turned as Flo came in. She looked at them both for a moment, as if puzzled, then continued. 'Oh –

you've seen she's home?' She kept her voice light and persuasive, as if Maryann was forever just disappearing for a week at a time.

'Yes. And ready to start work.'

Maryann stared hard at Flo, willing her to speak. When things had calmed down a bit earlier in the day, Flo had said to Maryann, 'The wag man was round earlier in the week. I told 'im you was ill and lucky for you 'e didn't come in to make sure. But yer'd better get back to school next week.'

Maryann agreed readily. She could collect her leaving certificate, even if she might never need it, and it would keep her away from Norman for a week. By the time she was supposed to start work for him, it would be about the time Joel and his dad would be back from another run if they worked the Oxford Cut again. And she'd be off and away for good ... She felt calmer facing them all because she knew that. There was nothing for her here.

'So I've told Maryann she'd best get back to school next week,' Flo was saying.

Norman put on his most amenable tone. 'All right, m'dear. Whatever you think. So long as she's ready to start a week on Monday.'

It felt odd to be home. Maryann felt as if she'd been away far longer than a week. As if in those few days she had grown up and changed so much that she just didn't fit. But the changes were not just in her. She was most anxious about her brothers, how they had been while she was away. Billy seemed much as usual. Tony, though, didn't come home until it was almost time for tea and when he did he didn't seem at all pleased to see her. He slouched to the tea table and sat down without looking at any of them.

'You been out with yer pals, Tony?' she asked him.

She received barely a grunt in reply. She watched him, hurt. Tony was eight now, tall for his age and thinning out. He had a tight, closed expression on his face and was shovelling his stew down as if he wanted to get away from them all as soon as possible. Maryann looked at Flo, who shrugged.

Upstairs, when Tony was in bed, Maryann went and sat on his mattress and tried to get him to speak to her. He lay on his side facing the wall with his back to her, tucked down under the bedclothes so that she could only see dark tufts of his hair.

'Tony – turn over and look at me.'

He didn't move.

'Tony – please. I'm sorry I went away without saying goodbye and that, but . . .' She couldn't tell him where she'd been or that she was going back. A pang went through her. He felt abandoned, she knew, but it was her and Sal who were the ones at the mercy of Norman's disgusting habits. She couldn't tell Tony that, couldn't tell him why . . .

'Look, I'm back now, Tony. Can't you speak to me? Let me make it up to yer?'

But there was still no reply. She wondered if he was asleep and not just pretending, but she sensed that he wasn't. With a sigh she got up. 'All right then – let's 'ave a talk another time.'

Lying in bed, she heard Flo come up and settle herself down. She waited for Norman to come up too: the terrible, familiar sounds of him breathing heavily on the landing from climbing the stairs, his cough, all of which made her lie so tensely that she was scarcely breathing, then his murmured words to her mother as he bedded down beside her. But there was nothing. He had not come to bed. She waited for what seemed hours and she was so tired. Eventually, thinking about Joel and missing him, wondering where the *Esther Jane* was tonight, and were they missing her, she fell asleep.

It wasn't the squeak of the door which woke her. She was conscious a second before that, perhaps from his furtive tread on the stairs, or some second sense which alerted her. Before she had come to properly, his hand was over her mouth and nose and she was fighting for breath, panicking and struggling out of the bed-clothes, tearing at his arm.

'Ssssh.' He moved his hand so that it was only over her mouth and she took fierce, gasping breaths, feeling her nostrils flaring in the darkness. He was sitting on her bed, his face close to hers.

'Don't you dare make a sound, yer little bitch, or I'll do to you what I did to that cat.'

He was manoeuvring himself in the darkness, with difficulty, she could tell, hearing his loud breathing, his hand still over her mouth, though less tightly. She was paralysed with fear and horror at the thought of what he was going to do, unable to move. She heard a small whimpering sound escape from her and felt his fingers claw at her face.

'I said not a sound . . .' His voice was tight, strained. 'I've been waiting for you – I don't like waiting. I'm going to 'ave you. I've waited long enough.'

It did not take him long. When he had gone she crept downstairs and out into the yard in the thin moonlight. Dizzily she leaned over the low wall, resting her head wretchedly in her hands. After a few moments her body revolted against what had happened. She bent over and was violently sick.

Twenty-One

Maryann's teacher, Miss Bentley, didn't seem perturbed by her absence and asked if she was feeling better.

'Yes thanks.' Maryann couldn't manage a smile. She quite liked Miss Bentley, and in some ways it was nice to be back at school and see all her pals. But she felt cut off from them now. She couldn't ever tell them what went on at home. But she also felt rather superior to them all. After all, she'd been working the cut all last week, learning all that she'd learned about real life while they were still all sitting here in rows! But now she had joined them again and was back in her school frock looking round at the tiled walls with pictures hanging on them, and at all the other girls round her, there was a poignancy about those few days. Many of the children had been at school together since they were infants and by the end of this week quite a number of them would be signed off from education for ever, into the adult world of work. Some of them were talking about what jobs they were going to.

But I, Maryann thought, will be off: gone for good. She wanted to tell them, but thought they'd laugh. Children off the cut were the butt of jokes because they couldn't read or write and were regarded as dirty and ignorant. So she wasn't going to say anything. This was her secret. Only a few days now and she'd be away . . .

But on the last Thursday something happened which

she could not have foreseen. They were at home after school when someone hammered on the front door.

'Go and see who's making that racket, Maryann!' Flo shouted from upstairs.

Nancy was on the doorstep, still in her school dress. She looked astonished to see Maryann.

'Well, where've you been?' she demanded, panting. 'Your mom said you'd gone off!'

'Never mind that,' Maryann interrupted. She wasn't going to say anything, not even to Nance. 'I just went away for a bit, that's all. What's up with you, nearly banging the door down?'

'It's Charlie . . .'

'What's all this?' Flo appeared downstairs.

'Mom sent me. Our Charlie – 'e's come 'ome – just now.'

Maryann and Flo both started talking at once. 'Where's Sal then? Where's 'e been?'

Nancy was shaking her head. ''E won't say.'

'Won't say! Well, bugger that. Billy – get in 'ere! We're going out.' Flo was already heading for the door. 'I'll soon get it out of 'im!'

Hoiking Billy by the arm, she marched off down Anderson Street like the wrath of God, with Maryann and Nancy following. When they reached the old yard in Garrett Street it was full of the Black youngsters who'd obviously been sent out of the house. When Flo marched in without a by-your-leave, only Charlie was in, with Cathleen and Lizzie.

'So – where is she then?'

Charlie was in the chair by the grate, hunched forwards, arms resting on his thighs. He clearly hadn't had a haircut during the weeks he'd been away and he looked haggard and very tired. Seeing Flo, he seemed to shrink further into himself.

'I said where is she? Where's our Sal?' Flo stood by the table, grasping the back of a chair so tightly her knuckles whitened. Maryann and Nancy stayed watching by the door. Maryann couldn't take her eyes off Charlie. In just a month he seemed different. Older, and dulled. Cathleen, standing with Lizzie on one arm, looked agitated.

''E won't say,' she told Flo. 'I can't get out of 'im where they've been or what's been going on.' She advanced on her son. 'You'd better tell Flo where Sal is, Charlie my lad. You've caused nothing but trouble and worry – there's her on my back and we'll 'ave Father Maguire round again and you just sitting there – you're a disgrace, Charlie.' She was shrieking. 'You tell us where she is – now!'

''Er doesn't want yer to know,' Charlie said to the floor.

Cathleen and Flo exchanged looks of utter exasperation. Flo went to Charlie and poked at his shoulder with her finger. 'Well, why don't she? Eh? What's up with 'er? Why ain't she come with yer?'

Charlie shrugged. 'I wanted to come back 'ome and she daint, that's all.'

'Yer needn't think I ain't asked him all this before you come in,' Cathleen said. 'It's like talking to a block of wood. Will I get Father Maguire round 'ere now, eh? Will that get yer to open yer mouth?'

Flo's expression darkened further and she leaned even closer to Charlie. 'What's to hide, eh? What's ailing 'er? Have you got 'er in the family way and now she can't come back and face us? Is that it? You'd better start talking, Charlie, 'cause I ain't going away till yer do. Why d'yer just take off and leave 'er, eh?'

Charlie stood up with a fierce movement and slammed his hands flat on the table. 'Because 'er ain't right in the head, that's why.' He lifted a finger to his temple and swivelled it round. 'I don't know what's up with 'er – 'er never used to be like it. It got so's I never knew what was going to happen next with 'er, and I weren't sticking around no more to find out!'

'What d'yer mean, Sal ain't right in the head? What's 'e done to 'er?' Flo yelled at Cathleen Black. 'There weren't nothing wrong with 'er when she left.'

'You sure about that?' Cathleen said.

'What do you mean?' Flo snarled at her.

'Sal ain't been 'erself for a good long while. You only 'ad to look at the girl.'

Flo drew herself up, ablaze with defensive indignation. 'There ain't nothing wrong with my wench – or there weren't till she got in with that lout of a son of yours. What's 'e done to 'er?'

Maryann and Nancy jumped out of the way as Charlie seemed set to slam out of the house. But Flo was too quick for him. She nipped round and barred his way.

'Where d'yer think you're going, you no good little bastard? You needn't think yer can just run off. You're not leaving and neither am I. You're gunna tell me if I 'ave to beat it out of yer!'

He pushed his way to the door. 'Oh awright. Yer welcome to 'er, the silly cow.' He gave them an address in the Jewellery Quarter.

*

Maryann sat nervously on the tram over to Hockley, beside Flo, who had Billy on her lap. She was desperate to see Sal. Now she knew they would see her she realized just how much she'd missed her sister and was full of worry on her behalf after what Charlie said about her. *She*'d known Sal wasn't herself, and now she knew exactly why. She would have given anything to put the clock back, to feel young and innocent herself, not living in terror of what her stepfather would do next. And to have Sal back as she was – her bossy big sister, who had been full of herself and her budding young womanhood. She felt like crying at the thought of it.

'Mom – don't be too angry with 'er, will yer?' she begged.

Flo seemed thoughtful. She looked round at her. 'We might be able to talk some sense into her between the pair of us. Not that you've got much yourself. I don't know what's come over this family, that I don't. Where *did* you take off to last week?'

She kept asking this every so often. This time, though, she didn't sound angry. Her voice was soft, persuasive. 'I ain't going to keep on at yer, Maryann. I want to get this sorted out. First Sal, then you. I want to know where a girl your age goes off to if she ain't with 'er pals or 'er sister.'

Maryann almost yielded to the concerned tone in her mother's voice. What a relief it would be to be able to talk about all the confused and turbulent feelings inside her. To tell her properly about Norman without it turning into a shouting match, for her to make it stop, and about Joel and how he was like family to her, like a big, loving brother, and about working the cut.

To be able to stop having these burdensome secrets. She looked into her mother's pale eyes. She came so very close to pouring it all out. But then she remembered the last time she had tried.

'I *am* your mom,' Flo was saying. 'I was worried about yer. And Norman was. I said to him, there's summat wrong with both my daughters taking off at once. Is there summat the matter, Maryann?'

I've told you! a voice seemed to scream in Maryann's head. *I've told you and you wouldn't listen. You wouldn't believe me.*

'No, Mom.' She turned away. What was the point in trying? 'I was just . . . with some pals.'

'But who?'

'Just pals, that's all.'

'Well, next time yer decide to go gallivanting off,' she sounded indignant now, 'don't go bloody doing it without telling us. Anyway' – she shifted Billy on her lap – 'you'll be working for Norman soon, so we won't be having any of that. D'you 'ear?'

Maryann didn't reply. She stared out of the window at the streets outside.

They found Sal's lodgings in a street off Constitution Hill: a terrace with an attic. The landlady, a sharp-faced individual, looked at them suspiciously.

'I've come to see my daughter,' Flo said, pushing Billy in front of her as if he was a certificate proving her motherhood.

''Er ain't 'ere,' the woman said. ''Er's at work.'

'Well, we'll wait then,' Flo said haughtily. 'We've come a distance and I ain't stopping out on the street.'

The woman hesitated, then shrugged as if she

couldn't be bothered to argue. 'You'll 'ave to wait up in 'er room,' she said in a snooty voice. 'I'm expecting company down 'ere.'

They all climbed up to Sal's room. The first flight of stairs was covered by a threadbare runner of grubby carpet, its original colour impossible to tell. The attic stairs were bare and their feet made a racket as they went up. The room at the top was a good size, but the boards were rough and stained and the distemper on the walls was in a terrible state, flaking off and discoloured. Cobwebs hung in the corners, and the ceiling near the front end of the house was bulging with damp, right over the head of the bed. The bed was three-quarter size, and against the opposite wall stood a rickety table and chair. There was a small grate, full of dust, with no sign of a fire in it. One of Sal's dresses was hanging on a hook behind the door, her nightdress was on the pillow, and there were a few of her belongings in the room: a pair of shoes, a cup and a bar of soap on the table, a candle stuck on a grubby white saucer and, beside it, hair pins and two little pots. Maryann opened them and looked inside. One contained rouge, the other face powder.

'Well, this is a cheerless bleeding 'ole,' Flo said, peering out through the filthy, curtainless window at the houses opposite. She seemed sobered by the sight of it. 'What the 'ell does she want to stop 'ere for?'

Maryann sat on the bed in the chilly room and made Billy sit beside her. There was one threadbare blanket folded on the mattress. The idea of Sal here on her own made her want to cry. She tried to imagine Sal coming here with Charlie. They must've told the landlady they were married though, heaven knew, they looked too young.

It wasn't long before they heard voices down below, then feet on the stairs. Maryann braced herself for seeing Sal. Flo turned, standing with her back to the window, silhouetted in its meagre light, and sharply shushing Billy who'd got up and started clattering about on the bare boards.

The landlady had told her they were waiting there so Sal was prepared. She flung the door open and stood looking brazenly across at her mother. Maryann gasped. She might have walked past Sal in the street and not recognized her! She'd put her hair up like a grown-up lady's, all piled and pinned round her head, and she was all made up lipstick, the lot. There was something else queer about her face. Maryann saw that Sal had plucked out all her fair eyebrows and painted them in instead, with dark, thin lines. She looked ten years older than she really was.

Flo fixed her with a stare which took in all of Sal's altered appearance, and her mouth twisted with distaste. At last, in a bitter voice, she said, 'Well – I hope yer proud of yourself. You look like a proper tart in all that warpaint.'

Sal stayed in the doorway, as if ready to run. 'I ain't coming back if that's what yer 'ere for.'

'Look, Sal—' Flo moved towards her, realizing she'd started off on the wrong foot. 'I only wanted to see yer – see 'ow you are. After all, yer just took off, never a word or a thought for the rest of us. We've all been ever so worried about you. Look – if there's any trouble we'll get it sorted out, but you can't just stay 'ere on your own. You're only young, running off with that no-good Charlie Black . . .'

' 'E's a darn sight better than some I could mention,' Sal spat at her. 'Don't you come 'ere lecturing me, mother. I ain't coming home whatever you say. I've got a job and I can look after myself.'

'But Charlie's left you!' Flo had been trying to be appeasing, to control her temper, but it all came spilling out again. ''E 'ad more sense than to stick around 'ere in this dump. What the 'ell's got into yer, taking off and going about looking like a trollop! You'll be in trouble soon, my girl, that you will, if you go about looking like that.'

'Charlie Black ain't the only fish in the sea,' Sal retorted smugly. 'I don't notice no shortage around 'ere. And you're a fine one to lecture me – you're no more than a slut yourself, taking up with Norman for 'is money.'

Flo whipped her hand out to slap Sal's face, but she stepped back out of the way.

'Don't, Mom!' Maryann cried. There were tears running down her face. 'Don't hurt her! 'Er'll never come 'ome if yer treat 'er like that.'

'That's awright with me!' Flo blazed back. 'You can stay 'ere and rot, you ungrateful little bitch. If you can keep yerself then all the better for the rest of us. But don't come whining round me when yer in the family way and thrown out on the streets! I've warned yer, and I wash my hands of you. Come on, Maryann, Billy – leave 'er. She don't want 'er family.'

'No—' Maryann sobbed. 'I want to stay. You go on home.'

Flo stopped by the door. 'If that's what you want.' She looked hard at Sal. 'You used to be a good girl – you were the easy one. I don't know what's got into yer, that I don't. I've done my best – whatever 'appens now, you can't blame me for it.'

They heard her clomp noisily away down the stairs with Billy, leaving the sisters alone.

'Oh Sal,' Maryann cried. 'Are you awright? I know why yer don't want to come 'ome, but . . .'

'What do you know?' Sal snapped.

'About . . . about . . . you know, *him*, what 'e done to yer.'

'Don't talk about him!' Sal came over and got her by the shoulders. 'I don't want to talk about him. I've got away from him and I'm making my own life now – and you've got to do the same, Maryann. Don't work for 'im – don't let 'im near yer. Don't let 'im get you in that cellar down there . . .' She sank down suddenly and Maryann thought for a second that she was choking, her chest heaving, but she was crying, gasping. Maryann was about to embrace her when she stood up and began banging her head against the wall, hard, sobbing and crying.

'Sal! Sal, don't!'

Maryann pulled her away, trying to take her in her arms. Sal tore away. 'Don't touch me!'

'Sal – what's the matter with yer? I know what's 'e's done, what e's like, but why're yer doing that to yourself?'

Sal stepped back and collapsed limply on to the bed. She stared ahead of her so strangely that Maryann was even more frightened. At last she whispered, 'Maryann – don't leave me. I don't know what else to do.'

Sal broke down and cried and cried, at last allowing Maryann to put her arms round her and hold her tight.

'I'm losing my mind,' she sobbed. 'Oh Maryann, I don't know what's happening to me – I keep thinking such terrible things I'm frightened to be 'ere alone. It's not so bad when I'm out at work, but when I get back 'ere . . .'

'Can't yer come home?' Maryann pleaded. 'You don't 'ave to work for Norman no more . . .'

'No!' Sal clutched at Maryann's wrist so hard her fingers were digging in. 'I'm never going back there. Never! I'm never going anywhere near 'im again – you don't know what 'e can be like, Maryann. You've got to get out too . . .'

'I will, Sal – I was going to. But I can't leave you – not like this!' She could hardly bear to look at Sal. She used to be so pretty and now, with that paint on her eyebrows, she looked cheap and horrible. 'Why did yer go and do that to yourself?' she asked.

Sal shrugged, not replying.

'Oh Sal!' She put her arms round her sister again and held her close. She wanted to say, let's go somewhere together, just you and me. Somewhere where they can't find us and we can start again. But she didn't want to live in some slum with Sal. She wanted to be out on the cut with Joel, with Bessie plodding alongside. It wrung her heart to see Sal in this state, but it also frightened her. Sal was supposed to be her big sister, but now she was different, not the same Sal. How could she live with her in this state?

'Look, Sal – I'll 'ave to get 'ome. But I'll come and see you tomorrow – and every day I can now I know where you are, awright? And Tony and Billy can come an' all. And Mom – I'll talk 'er round . . .'

Sal's eyes widened. 'Not him! Oh God, Maryann – what if she tells 'im where I am! What if 'e comes 'ere? What if 'e starts following me about?'

''E won't,' Maryann tried to assure her. 'Course 'e won't. You can tell the landlady not to let 'im in. Anyhow – he thinks he's got me now.'

Maryann stayed on until it was almost dark and then

she made her way home in a turmoil of emotions. This was the afternoon she had been going to leave a message for the *Esther Jane* when she came back through some time in the next few days. But how could she leave now with Sal like this? She'd felt badly enough about leaving because of Tony and Billy when she thought at least Sal was happy with Charlie. But now she was the oldest one at home: she couldn't just desert them all.

Twenty-Two

On Sunday she left a written message for Joel, hoping one of the toll workers would read it for him. 'I can't come yet because I've got to look after my sister but I'll be back again soon. Love Maryann Nelson.'

She started work for Norman on the Monday, promising herself that if it was too bad she'd go somewhere else. She didn't want to cause a family row. Flo was in a good mood, and she watched with approval as the two of them set out together.

Maryann walked beside him along Monument Road. He wore his hat and top coat although it was high summer. He had a rolling, stately walk, said good morning to people with a gentlemanly lifting of his hat and was always greeted with respect: a pillar of the community walking out with one of his stepdaughters. The shops were opening up, awnings rattling open over the pavement, cars, carts and bicycles weaving along the busy street at the heart of Ladywood. They passed all the shops with their smells: cooked meat from the butcher's, strawberries outside the greengrocer's, bread from the bakery, then the Palais de Danse on the corner. At last they reached Griffin's, with its shrouded frontage and sober gold lettering, and Norman pulled out his bunch of keys and opened up.

Inside, he pulled up the little blind that covered the

glass in the door, turned the sign round, and Griffin's was open for business.

'Right then,' Norman said, hanging up his coat. 'You sit down at the desk. You're a quick-witted young thing – you'll soon pick it up.'

Maryann did as she was told, looking at the ledgers, cards, pens and blotter. She kept eyeing the door of the shop. If only Fred, the lad who made the coffins, would come in so that she wasn't alone with Norman.

'I'll come and show you what you need to know.' Norman walked round behind the desk and her skin felt suddenly as if it had been scrubbed with sandpaper. He leaned over at one side of her and his smell of sweat and smoke seemed to envelope her. She found herself breathing through her mouth so as not to smell him.

'This is a quiet time of year compared with the winter, but then of course you're going to have people coming to their natural end any time of year,' he said whimsically. 'When someone comes in, the golden rule is you treat 'em with courtesy and respect. Our job is to be invisible. If you do it well they don't remember much about you, but set a foot wrong and you're out of business. No laughing or joking in the presence of the bereaved, *ever* . . .'

Maryann nodded, listening as Norman outlined procedures concerning dates for interments, churches, death cards, hearses and coffins. All the while she was on edge because she thought he might touch her like he did when they were alone at home, pawing at her breasts or trying to pull her against him. But he made no attempt at this. This was work. Gradually she began to relax. And after a few minutes Fred arrived, crashing in through the front and saying 'Mornin', Mr Griffin!'

in his clogged, adenoidal voice. At last, she wasn't alone!

Later, Norman went out and Maryann was left sitting expectantly in the chair which Sal had occupied all those months. Norman had told her she was responsible for keeping the shop clean but it already looked immaculate and the desk was tidy. She was soon bored. She could hear Fred sawing away at some wood in the cellar.

'Don't let 'im get yer down in that cellar . . .' Sal's words came to her. What had she meant? Was that where Norman had always forced his vileness on her? Or was it more than that?

Maryann tiptoed to the top of the stairs and looked down. She could scarcely see the bottom of the staircase, it was so gloomy down there and the sight of the place brought her up in goose pimples. That was where they took the dead bodies. Surely he hadn't been down there with Sal when there were dead bodies . . . It was too horrible to imagine. Looking down there, she thought, *I can't stand being here*. She'd have to bring Flo's and Norman's anger down on her head and say she wouldn't work for him . . .

She climbed down, jumping as the treads creaked, but Fred was making such a noise he couldn't have heard her, and she wasn't bothered about him. Maybe, she thought suddenly, if she could make friends with Fred, it wouldn't be so bad working here. She could get him to stay on until she went home each day, so she wasn't left alone with Norman . . . Sal had described Fred as being 'as thick as horse shite' but Maryann was hoping she'd been exaggerating.

Peering round the door, she saw into the poorly lit

cellar. The door to the chapel of rest was closed. In the far corner she saw the cupboard, almost like a smaller room built into the cellar, with brick walls, about six foot by four, extending halfway along the far wall. The long bench on which Fred was working was at the front end under the grating.

Fred was a pale boy of eighteen, with a gaunt face and prominent lips, his eyes set far apart, and thin brown hair.

'Hello!' Maryann called out.

He looked up, bewildered, and stopped sawing so abruptly that the quiet was startling.

'I'm Maryann. Sal's sister.'

'Oh ... ar – I saw yer. Upstairs.'

He stared at her. Maryann, with a sinking heart, began to see that Sal's assessment of Fred might have erred on the side of generosity. He stood watching her as she explored the cellar, walking over first to see what he was doing. He had sawdust all over his boots. She liked the smell of the bruised wood. She went to the cupboard and tried the door, which was locked.

'What's in 'ere?'

'That's Mr Griffin's cupboard.' He didn't leave the workbench, just turned to watch her.

'Yes. So what's inside?'

He shrugged. 'I dunno. Chemicals and suchlike for that em ... emb ...'

'Embalming?'

'Ar – that's it. 'E don't let anyone go in.'

''Ve you been in there?' Maryann grinned conspiratorially.

'No!' Fred looked alarmed. 'I don't want the sack – I'd never go in there! No call to.'

'It's awright, don't get all worked up. I was only asking.'

She tried the door once more. Sal knew what was in there. There was something down here that had frightened her badly. Something that had seemed to make her lose her will.

'I'll leave at half past five when Fred goes, shall I?'

Maryann was watching the clock, both out of boredom and anxiety. Norman had come back at dinner time and Maryann told him she'd had one woman in who needed to bury her mother. Maryann had felt sorry for her, had taken down her details and thought she'd handled it all right. The woman had been calm and unemotional. Norman had been in all afternoon as various people came and went, and all the time he had on his sombre, upright citizen face. But when she asked him about leaving he turned, scowling. 'You'll leave when I tell you and not before. Now get this floor swept – there's dust and bits all over it.'

Maryann obeyed, sweeping the brown linoleum of the dirt Norman seemed to imagine he could see there. She worked slowly, still glancing continually at the clock. Whatever happened she was going as soon as she could. She had to get over and see Sal. And she could sense a change in Norman as time wore on. He was at the desk, thumbing through the ledgers, not looking up at her, but all the time she could hear his breathing. As she swept beneath the chair the pace of his breaths increased a fraction. She had heard it before, when he made her put her hand in his pocket, and when he touched her. It was the barometer of his excitement.

Her own heart beat faster with dread and she was all nerves. Any second she expected him to reach out and grab her. She couldn't do this. Not stay and work here. Until now she had held on to herself, kept her mind aloof from it: although he'd done things to her that sickened and disgusted her, she still had her spirit. But she could not endure more of it. It wasn't going to work. She knew that much more of it and she would lose herself, like Sal, and wither away inside. As she turned, pushing the few bits of dust and fluff away with her broom, Norman's hand fastened on her thigh, pushing her skirt between her legs and she jumped, letting out a little scream and moving quickly away.

He stood up, cleared his throat and crossed the room to the stairs.

'Time Fred was off.' She saw his wide shoulders disappear through the door, heard him going downstairs.

Oh Lord, Maryann thought, *why did I come here?* Why hadn't she just stood up to them and said she wouldn't work for him? She looked wildly round the room. It was five and twenty minutes past five. She left the broom against the wall, grabbed her hat and cardigan and ran to the door, cursing the loud, tinkling bell, and fled out on to the street.

He arrived home soon after her, not taking the trouble to conceal his fury.

'What d'yer think yer doing running off before I tell yer to go? Eh?'

He became aware that Flo was watching from the kitchen door. She could see a sheen of sweat on his pale, freckly face. 'Don't you *ever* do that again,' he snarled. 'D'you hear?'

Maryann kept her gaze turned down to the floor so he should not see the defiance in her eyes.

'No, Mr Griffin. I certainly won't.'

She hurried over to Hockley that evening, but the landlady said Sal wasn't in.

'Can I wait for a bit?' Maryann asked. 'I don't s'pose she'll be much longer.'

'I shouldn't bet on it.' The woman was even less friendly than last time and sounded very disapproving. 'To tell yer the truth I'm thinking of looking for a new lodger. That feller who came with 'er weren't 'er 'usband at all, was 'e?'

Maryann didn't answer. She felt an ugly blush creep up her cheeks.

'Thought not,' the landlady said, sounding self-satisfied. She stood back, folding her arms. 'Go on up then.'

Maryann sat in Sal's dismal room, picking at the loose threads in her frock and reduced to twiddling her thumbs, until it was almost dark outside. She got up from time to time and stood on tiptoes to look out of the window, though she could not see the street properly from up here. Gradually the night came on, lamps were lit outside, and still her sister didn't come. Maryann grew more and more anxious. Where had Sal got to? Her landlady would never put up with her if she carried on like this.

Eventually she had to give up and go home, and by the time she got there Flo had already gone to bed.

Maryann realized her mistake as soon as she walked in through the front door and found herself looking into Norman's eyes as he sat waiting by the fire.

'I'm going to bed,' she said, hurrying across the room.

'Oh no – not yet.'

He sprang out of his chair and grabbed her just as she reached the door to the stairs. He clamped his hand over her mouth.

'Thought you'd avoid me today, then, did yer? I'm not 'aving that.' He ran his hands over her chest. His eyes were terrible; cold, full of hatred. 'You're turning into quite a young lady nowadays, aren't yer, eh? And I'm going to make the most of it while yer still a child. Yer no good to me once yer've got yer monthly . . .'

Maryann tried to speak, shaking her head and making a strangled noise.

'What's that?'

'I 'ave – come on. Just last week,' she babbled as he released her. She yanked herself away from him. 'You touch me again and I'll scream. I'll get my mom down 'ere and then she might believe what an evil, filthy bastard you are.' She had her hand on the door to the stairs. 'You're never touching me again.'

Norman lunged at her and Maryann opened her mouth and managed to force out a scream.

'Shut it!' He was ablaze with fury and frustrated lust. 'Shut up that racket, yer little bitch.'

He went to put his hand back over her mouth but she yanked the door open and screamed again. There came the sound of a door opening upstairs.

'Norman?' Flo Griffin's voice was full of sleep. 'What's the noise? What's going on?'

Maryann fled up the stairs, not meeting her mother's eye.

'Nothing, love – just Maryann being silly. Now she's gone and woken yer.'

'I'm not working for you no more.'

He was eating breakfast. She stood by the table, in front of all the family.

'What're you talking about?' Flo turned on her at once. 'You've only been there one day!'

'I ain't staying.' She screwed up every ounce of self-possession and courage and looked into Norman's eyes. *I'm not scared of you*, her expression said. She was, she was terrified, her hands were shaking, but she pressed them together. She wasn't going to let him see. 'I'm going to look for another job today.'

'How *dare* you talk like that!' Flo erupted. But Norman raised a hand to silence her.

'I can't say I'm not disappointed in yer, Maryann. It'll cause me a lot of trouble 'aving to get someone else. But if yer not happy – I know some people don't take to working with the dead. I don't want anyone saying I'm not a reasonable man. And if you go in one of the factories you should get a decent wage.'

'But, Norman!' Flo protested. 'You're surely not just going to let 'er get away with this, the little minx?'

'It's awright, Flo. 'Er's more hot-headed than our Sal. Let 'er go 'er own way. As long as you work out the rest of the week, Maryann, that's all I ask.'

'There,' Flo cried. 'See 'ow nice yer father's being after all the trouble you've caused!'

There was a long silence. Maryann felt Tony's eyes

on her face. She looked away across at the range where the kettle was starting to boil.

She spoke quietly. 'I'm finishing today.'

'You'll work the week out.' She couldn't look at him any more, couldn't face the cold hatred in his eyes. She knew that beneath the calm exterior, Norman Griffin was seething with rage at being thwarted.

'No,' she said. 'Today.'

She found a job at a jam factory, where she had to be in as the hooter went at ten to eight. Another went off at eight and work began. The girls all wore clogs, which were hard and blistered her feet. Fruit and sugar were brought on carts and the jam stirred in huge vats, its smell sweet and cloying. Maryann was in the labelling department, not an arduous job, but even if it had been, anything would have been better than working with Norman Griffin. She had some laughs with the other girls, biding her time. This wasn't where she was going to be for ever. As soon as Sal got herself sorted out a bit she'd be off. She spent as little time as she could at home and at night she took to ramming her bed close up against the door so it couldn't open. She wasn't going to let him get at her, never again. When she heard him come up to bed the first time, and push at her door, she lay seething with hatred of him and fierce satisfaction.

That's stopped your game, she thought.

As the summer passed and turned into autumn, she knew Norman, too, was biding his time. But she was at work all day, and she managed carefully to avoid being alone with him at any time. Her main worry was Sal. She couldn't keep going over every day, especially as Sal often wasn't there. She did try and go at least once a week. But after that time of closeness when Sal had cried in her arms and admitted how wretched she felt, she never let Maryann see her true state of mind again.

Twice when Maryann went in August, Sal came home late and clearly the worse for drink.

'What the hell's kept yer?' Maryann raged at her the first time, as Sal came staggering in after dark. She'd been waiting ages, cursing Sal, worrying about her. She felt as if things had reversed and she was the older sister now, having to keep an eye on Sal all the time. 'You're in a disgusting state. You're going to have to pull yourself together or you'll get thrown out – she's already said she don't like the way you carry on.'

Sal lurched over to the bed. Her cheeks were grimy with sweat and face powder, she was dishevelled, hair all in a mess and she stank of drink.

'I'm in a disgusting state!' she repeated. She rocked back and forth as if thinking about this, then started laughing, a drunken, foolish laugh that made Maryann feel like slapping her. Instead she stood over her and shook her by the shoulders.

'Who've yer been with? Who is it's buying yer all this booze?'

'Oh, mind your own bloody business,' Sal sneered. Her face was grotesque in the candlelight, with its pencilled-in eyebrows. 'I've got my own pals now, ta very much. I've got my big strong friend Bill, looks after me. Oh yes 'e does – 'e's a big'un now, 'e is . . .'

'You're horrible—' Maryann pushed her away. 'You're nearly as bad as Norman. Look at yourself, Sal. What's going to become of you?' She went to the door.

'I'm not staying with you like this. There ain't no point in talking to you.'

'If you don't want Norman on you,' Sal called after her, 'just tell 'im you've come on.'

'I did,' Maryann snapped back at her. 'I ain't stupid and nor's he. He daint believe me. Don't you worry about me – not that you were. I've got my own way of dealing with him.'

A week later Sal was caught trying to smuggle a man up to her room and the landlady threw her out. She moved to another grim attic in a nearby street.

Maryann felt desperate about her. She tried to talk to Flo about Sal again, but all Flo said was, 'What can I do about 'er? 'Er's the one walked out on us. If 'er's going to the bad there ain't nothing I can do about it. I washed my hands of 'er. Sal can go to hell 'er own way, that's my way of looking at it.'

Sal was the only thing keeping Maryann at home now. And she was dangerously close to giving up on Sal herself.

Twenty-Three

Another month had passed. It was October, the nights drawing in, leaves in the gutters and foggy mornings. Maryann had been loyally visiting Sal so far as she could manage it. Sometimes Sal was in when she got there; more often she wasn't, and Maryann was fed up with waiting, anxious and hungry, in those dismal lodgings for her to come back. She kept thinking one day Sal would walk in and be the sister she had been before, bossy and hoity-toity, but kind and good for a laugh. But when she did come back, Sal was often rude and offhand.

Maryann had confided about it to Nancy only the previous weekend, she had felt so heavy-hearted. The two of them sat at the table in the Blacks' downstairs room, sipping lemon pop out of jam jars. Her mom and her dad were out and Nance was holding Lizzie on her lap and minding some of the younger ones who were running in and out. Nance hadn't got her dream job at Kunzle's and was working in a laundry, but she seemed cheerful enough about it.

'Last time I went to see 'er,' Maryann complained, 'she come in – in the end – and says to me, "What're *you* doing 'ere?" As if I was vermin or summat. She's drinking ever such a lot, Nance. And the other night I was sat there and I 'eard 'er come in. There was giggling and shushing on the stairs – I could tell there was someone else with 'er. In they come – 'er and this bloke.

Oh Nance, I swear to God 'e was the 'orriblest looking man I've ever seen, broken nose, the lot, and 'e was ever so much older than 'er.

'"Who's this then?" 'e says, swaggering about like one of them cowboys. Sal 'ad to shut 'im up talking so loud 'cause 'e weren't meant to be there. "That's just my baby sister," she says. "And 'er's just leaving, ain't yer, Maryann?" She was all nasty and superior – didn't care about me at all and that I'd been there waiting for 'er.'

'Ooh,' Nance said. She was biting at the nails of her right hand, which already looked red and work-worn. 'Fancy your Sal carrying on like that. I mean our Charlie would've married 'er, you know, when they was old enough, if things'd've been different. He was ever so sweet on 'er. And when yer think what 'er used to be like!'

'I was that upset – well, I was furious with 'er! But I could see they'd 'ad a few and I wasn't going to start a shouting match or I'd've got 'er thrown out again. But, oh Nance, it made me feel so bad seeing 'er with that great *ape* of a bloke . . .'

'So what did yer do?'

'I went 'ome and left 'em to it.'

Nance shook her head in a way that reminded Maryann of Cathleen. 'What's up with 'er then? I mean there's you and 'er – had everything the same and there's 'er going right off the rails.'

Maryann quickly looked down. She couldn't tell Nance. Blackie Black may have been a broken man and a drunk but he didn't do those things, did he? Not like Norman Griffin, who had shut them off from everyone, alone with their sense of disgust.

*

She'd delayed going back to Sal's place in Hockley, putting it off after the way Sal had treated her. Why should I keep running after her if that's how she goes on? Maryann thought, I'd be on the *Esther Jane* with Joel if it wasn't for her. She dreaded going, wondering who she might find Sal with. She knew deep down that this wasn't the real Sal, that her sister was broken and desperate inside, and it wrung her heart to see her behaving the way she was and not know what to do about it.

That day, after work, she forced herself to go. When she got off the tram her heart started pounding and her legs turned shaky with misgiving.

Don't be so daft, she told herself. Sal won't even be in yet – not this time of day.

When she reached the house, the front door was half open. The usual fusty smells greeted her. She walked straight in and tiptoed up the stairs, holding her breath. When she reached the top, Maryann stood uncertainly outside. Should she knock? Just supposing Sal was in there with some man, she'd be livid with her and the last thing she wanted was to witness such a scene. Sal had never told her anything, not directly, but Maryann knew what Sal let those men do to her. She could see it in her sister's eyes, she had seen the lust on the ape bloke's face when he looked at Sal, drunken and lecherous.

But surely it was too early for that. She leaned close to the door. Not a sound. The door opened with a squeak. She could tell immediately that the room wasn't deserted after all. It had the feel of a person in it. It smelled stale. The bedclothes, such as they were, were pulled up over the hunched shape of a body lying face to the wall.

'Sal?' Maryann cried, alarmed. 'What's up? Are you bad?' She yanked the blanket down. Sal seemed to be in a very deep sleep. Maryann nudged at her, pulled her so that she flopped over on to her back and at last Sal managed to prise her eyes open.

'Sal! 'Ve you been lying there all day like this? What's up?'

Sal winced, laying an arm over her eyes to shut out the light.

'Ooh,' she groaned. 'My *head*! What time is it?'

''Bout half past five, or later. Ain't you been to work today?'

'Nah.' There was a silence, then, 'They let me go – Monday. Said I weren't no good to 'em.'

'They didn't! How're you going to get by? You bin out to find summat else?'

Sal pulled her arm away and attempted a smile, which emerged as a sly grimace. 'There's easier ways to earn money.'

'Sal . . .' Maryann stared at her. 'Yer don't mean . . .?'

'Oh, pack in carrying on at me, will yer? My 'ead's fit to split. Go down and see if yer can get a cuppa tea out of that skinflinty old cow down there, will yer? I gotta 'ave summat to ease it.'

'Awright,' Maryann agreed reluctantly. 'But I can't see 'er handing over a cuppa tea.'

She went down the dim kitchen at the back of the house where a hairy Scots terrier, as corpulent as its mistress, was lying by the range. Without bothering to shift itself, it started up a shrill barking as soon as Maryann appeared. The lady of the house was slumped in a greasy old armchair close by, everything about her seeming to be drawn inexorably down towards the floor: her sludge-coloured hair, cheeks, chins, sagging

214

breasts. She was drinking out of a cup and there was a jug on the table. Maryann could tell from the smell that it was ale.

'Stop that yapping, will yer!' the woman bawled at the dog. Looking round she spotted Maryann. 'What're you doing barging in 'ere, eh? Made me bloody jump.'

'Can my sister 'ave a cuppa tea?' Maryann asked as politely as she could. 'Only she ain't feeling well today.'

The woman took a mouthful from her cup, which left froth on her top lip. 'Kettle ain't on,' she said, turning away indifferently. 'And it won't be neither.'

In the end, Maryann ran down the street to find a coffee house where she bought Sal a glass of tea and paid an extra penny to retrieve when she took the glass back. Sal was still lying staring at the ceiling. The light was going and the sight of her made Maryann feel so sad she almost started crying. Her emotion made her speak sharply.

'Come on – get this down yer, sis, and pull yerself together.'

Sal hauled herself, wincing, up to a sitting position and leaned forward, cradling her head in her hands. She still had her black dress on from the night before, rucked up round her waist.

'Oh God, Maryann, I feel that bad, I do.'

'Drink up,' Maryann said, more gently. 'It's getting cold. I got it down the road – there's plenty of sugar in it.'

'Ta.' But Sal still couldn't seem to move. Her blonde hair was loose and hanging lank round her face. Maryann pulled it back over her shoulders and held the cup to Sal's lips.

''Ere—' Her voice was tender now. ''Ave a sip, Sal.'

Sal leaned towards the glass and sipped. The sisters

sat quietly together as Sal managed to get almost half the tall glass of tea down her. Maryann stroked her back.

'You can't go on with all this boozing,' she said.

But Sal stopped drinking and began to whimper. 'I'm going to be sick, Maryann!'

Maryann rushed across the room, ducked under the table for an old yellowed newspaper that was lying there and opened it in Sal's lap just in time. A gush of tea and bile pooled in the newspaper. Sal retched miserably, and when she'd finished, Maryann folded the ends of the dripping paper into a bundle and dumped it by the door. Sal panted and then her gulping from being sick turned into gulping from her tears.

'You don't want to keep on like this, do yer?' Maryann said, wrapping her arms round her. 'Oh, sis, I hate to see you like this.'

Sal cried even more, shaking her head. 'I'm scared, Maryann. I'm so scared.'

'What're you scared of? You're just feeling poorly, that's all.' But Maryann was scared too. 'You need to get some food inside you and you'll feel better. Shall I go out and see if I can get yer a couple of cobs from somewhere?'

'No!' Sal shook her head, then groaned and pressed her hands to each side of it to still the pain. 'It ain't only that, Maryann. It's . . . I think I'm expecting.'

'Expecting?'

'A babby.'

Maryann drew back, gaping at her. The thought had never crossed her mind. 'Oh no – oh Sal! Whose babby?'

Sal wouldn't look at her. 'I don't know. God 'elp me, I don't even know.'

She just couldn't tell her mom when she got home, not out with it, cold like that. It didn't seem real to her. She only had the vaguest knowledge of the connection between what men and women did together and how babies came out of it. She knew her mom'd be livid and most likely go over there and give Sal a beating.

'Well, what's ailing 'er?' Flo was demanding, standing over Maryann as she tried to force down some of a mutton chop and congealed gravy.

Maryann looked up at her. 'I've never seen 'er so bad, Mom. She ain't 'erself, and she's poorly. Will yer go and see 'er? Be a bit nice to 'er, like?'

Flo put her hands to her waist in a defensive posture. 'I don't know why Sal can't get 'erself over 'ere to see us. I mean, I've got quite enough going on, what with Billy and the house...' She saw Maryann's face. 'Awright – I'll try and get over to see 'er some time. She don't deserve it though, everyone running at 'er beck and call, that she don't!'

Maryann knew she had to go over and see Sal the next day. Poor Sal would have been there all day on her own, with only her thoughts for company and hardly the strength or will to get herself any food to eat.

She changed into her shoes and left the factory at the end of her shift, absent-mindedly calling goodbyes to her workmates as they all streamed out to the street, eager to get home. The light was fading and the air, foggy and full of smoke, stung her nostrils.

The lamps were lit by the time she got to Sal's lodgings and the pubs were already doing a brisk trade. This time she had to knock and it seemed ages before she heard the woman shuffling along the hall to open the door. The landlady peered out, suspiciously.

'Ow, it's you. I ain't 'eard nothing out of 'er today.'

Well, that ain't any surprise, Maryann thought. When you've got your nose in a jug of ale all day long. She didn't say anything, just went on up the stairs.

'Sal?' She tapped the door and went in. To her surprise the room was dark, and she felt a sudden rush of hope. Maybe Sal had been mistaken, had just had a fancy that there was a babby on the way because she was poorly. Maybe today she was feeling better and had gone out. Even Sal's old habits seemed better at the moment than the plight of being in the family way.

Cautiously Maryann stepped across the dark room.

'Blimey, it's cold in 'ere today!' she muttered. It was bad enough normally, but this was worse than ever. She stepped closer to the dormer window and heard glass crunch under her feet. From the faint light from the street she saw that one of the panes was broken. 'No wonder Sal's gone out. I wonder 'ow that 'appened? P'raps a bird hit the window.'

She decided to wait, at least for a time. If Sal was all that long she'd go out and treat herself to some faggots and peas instead of buying them for Sal. She felt more cheerful. Maybe soon she'd be off on the *Esther Jane* after all! She felt her way to the table where Sal kept a candle and a box of matches. There was only a stub of candle left. Never mind, she thought, generous in her sense of relief. She'd go out and get her some, and other things she needed. Maryann lit the candle, which was stuck on the lid of a treacle tin, and took it closer to the window again to look, but the flame began to gutter in the draft so she turned away, treading carefully over the sharp slivers of glass.

And then she jumped so hard she almost dropped the candle. The light of the flame was caught, reflected in Sal's open eyes.

'Oh my God, Sal—' She could make out Sal's shape lying along the bed. 'Why didn't you say you was in?' Maryann pressed her hand over her heart. 'Flamin' 'ell. You nearly frightened the life out of me! Sal?'

She leaned closer and smelled it, the heavy, sickening stench of blood.

'Oh Sal . . . oh Christ no, Sal. What've yer done?'

It was everywhere. Holding the candle high, Maryann saw that most of the middle part of the mattress was dyed with it and it was dripping from Sal's left arm, which hung over the edge of the bed, to a black pool on the floor. Maryann seized her arm, memories rushing back to her of Sal, that day, sitting jabbing, cutting at her arm.

Maryann heard herself whimpering, making strange, unbidden sounds. She knew now what had happened to the glass in the window, knew it all. Howling, she threw herself down on her knees beside her sister's bed, regardless of the pool of blood, kissing her poor cold face, stroking her hair again and again, beside herself.

'Oh Sal, my Sal – why did yer do it? I'd've taken care of you – I would. Oh Sal, don't die, you're my sis. We can look after each other!'

But she knew it was over, that there was no point in running to any doctor for help. Sal must have lain for hours like this. Maryann knelt with her arms round her sister, holding and rocking her, rage and sorrow possessing her like no emotions she had ever felt before. Sal was released from her agony now. Her heart was not beating. But she had not killed herself: she had been murdered slowly, brutally, over these long months, and the person who had killed her was Norman Griffin.

Twenty-Four

The day they buried Sal was wet and cold. The carriages
followed the hearse to Lodge Hill Cemetery, and the
horses' hooves sounded louder in the damp weather,
their warm breath swirling round them in the damp.
They were decked out in black feathers and smartly
polished harnesses.

It was an extravagant funeral, beyond anything they
could normally have afforded.

'We'll make sure she has the best,' Norman had told
Flo. 'We can't bring her back – Lord knows what
possessed her – but we can give her a good send-off.'

'It's more than 'er deserves really,' Flo had sobbed.
'Taking 'er own life like that – it ain't right. But it's all
we can do for her now.'

They stood at the graveside as rain fell all round
them, pattering on the leaves banked up at the sides of
gravestones, dripping off the brims of their hats and
gathering in little pools on the lid of the coffin. The
priest looked thinly clad and unwell, and the only
sound apart from the rain and his voice nasally intoning
the burial rite was that of Flo's weeping.

As the first handfuls of earth were thrown down on
to the coffin, she burst into uncontrollable sobbing.

'My little girl,' she moaned into her handkerchief. 'My
baby – oh my little baby . . .' Maryann saw Norman lay
his hand on her shoulder for a moment to quiet her.

Tony was crying silently, his hand in Maryann's, and she squeezed it and kept Billy close to her. There were no tears in her eyes. She watched Norman across the yawning slit in the ground into which Sal had been lowered, fixing him with an unwavering, icy stare. As she stood watching him across the grave she knew she would not weep here, at the funeral he had provided. Never, in front of him. Not after what he'd done.

'. . . blessed are the dead which die in the Lord,' the vicar was saying, '. . . for they rest from their labours.'

Maryann raised her eyes past Norman at the skeletal trees behind him. The wind was blowing rain sideways across the graves. In a few moments it would be over, the final prayer was being said and then they would leave the gravediggers to finish shovelling in the earth. She looked back at the coffin once more in a final farewell.

I won't let him get away with it, Sal. I'll make him pay, that I will. But you rest now, sis. You rest.

Holding the boys' hands, she followed the others back across the cemetery to where the horses were waiting. She looked at Norman's back, long and tall in his black coat, and she knew with sudden certainty what she was going to do.

She lay beside Tony that night, waiting for him and the rest of the household to settle for the night.

Flo came up first, followed by Norman, and Maryann relaxed a little, breathing more easily. He wasn't waiting up the way he did when he was going to try and come to her room. Gradually it all settled down, the padding of feet, the wrench of bedsprings, then quiet at last. The rain seemed to have stopped now but it was still windy.

She had thought she was far too pent up to sleep, but some time later she found had been dozing and woke very suddenly and sat up, her heart hammering. It came flooding back to her: Sal was dead. She had to do it, to go tonight. Now. Getting out of bed with enormous care, she lit the candle and looked anxiously across at Tony – at his thin face, his straight, dark eyebrows, so relaxed as he slept – and for a moment all her resolve withered.

How can I just go away and leave him and Billy? she thought. But then she thought of Sal, of Joel and, fortified, put the candle down on the floor and crept round the bed to gather up her few things: her shoes, bits of clothes, and the little china cat which she laid lovingly on the pile.

When it was all ready she tiptoed round to Tony's side of the bed and knelt down by him. I mustn't touch him, she thought, or I'll wake him and mess it all up.

'I've got to go away, Tony,' she whispered. 'I'm sorry to leave yer, that I am. I know I'm not much of a sister to you, but you've still got our mom and Billy and your pals. You look after our Billy now, eh?' Tears came into her eyes at the thought of the two of them, little blond Billy and dark-eyed Tony, hand in hand as if alone in the world without her.

'Only – I've got to go tonight, 'cause if I don't, I'm gunna be in trouble, Tony. I don't *want* to leave you, Tony, honest I don't. 'Ere—' She got up again and went over to her little pile of things, took out the china cat and brought it to him, laying it on his pillow, close to his sleeping face. 'You 'ave little Tiger so yer know I'll be thinking of yer.' She couldn't quite bear to go without touching him, and she reached out and stroked her hand over his head. 'T'ra, Tony.' He didn't stir.

Taking deep breaths to calm herself, she lifted the chair away from the door and blew out the candle. Every sound she made seemed deafening. The door opened almost soundlessly, but when she went to cross the small landing, one of the boards gave a loud, unexpected crack. Maryann froze, panic-stricken. The house was full of boards like that, which might suddenly betray her!

All you've got to do, she told herself, is get into that room. He sleeps nearest the door, so you can just reach across . . .

Clenching her teeth over her bottom lip, she pushed the door of her mother and stepfather's room. To her amazement it swung open without a sound. She could hear Norman's breathing, a rasping sound which helped her get her bearings as she stepped through the door. She could tell where the head of the bed was all right, with him making that racket. She stepped behind the door and, holding on to the wall, slid along the gap between it and the bed until she got to the chair. As she reached out for it her mother sighed and shifted in the bed, and she froze again, waiting. But all was well. Her hand met the scratchy tweed of Norman's jacket which was flung over the back of the chair and she felt along it, searching for that pocket he pushed his hand into when he was walking along . . . The cold weight of the keys seemed to fall into her palm as if they had been waiting for her and she clenched her fingers tight to stop them jangling together.

'Got yer,' she mouthed in the darkness.

Moments later, shoes on and holding her belongings, keys in the pocket of her coat, she slid out through the front door.

The street was deserted but it was warmer than she expected, the sky busy with puffy clouds moving across a thin crescent moon. There was still lamplight to guide her, reflected in the puddles along the pavement.

She couldn't believe she'd managed it, that he wasn't behind, following her as she walked along to Monument Road. Even though hers were the only steps she could hear on the street, she kept turning to glance behind, expecting to see him. Pulling up her collar, she shrank down into her coat.

When she reached the door of the shop a cold feeling overcame her, a creeping sense of horror. She should forget this thing she had come for, the obligation she felt towards Sal, and just go, get right away from here for good. What was it Norman had said to Sal, or shown her, that afterwards, together with those dirty things he had made her do, had meant she was never free of him? She had steeled herself to do this and she couldn't just walk away.

'Don't let 'im get yer in that cellar . . .' Sal's warning rang in her mind. She took out the keys and as she did so, she noticed in the faint light that one of them seemed to be a darker colour than the others. As she examined them, a sound came from along the street. Quickly she unlocked the door and shut herself inside. She waited, but heard nothing further.

Norman kept matches for the lamps in one of the

desk drawers. Groping her way over to the desk she talked to herself in her mind, trying to fight her irrational terror of darkness.

Once she'd lit the lamp she started to feel a little better. The blinds were all down so no one could see in. The office looked exactly as she remembered: a small, bare, workaday place, much as it would have looked had she been left alone there on a winter's evening. Now she just had to go downstairs, she told herself. That was all. Just have a look. Pretend Fred was down there, hammering away . . .

She lit a candle to take with her and, keys in the other hand, climbed quickly down the yawning darkness of the stairs, knowing that if she hesitated she might seize up with panic and run back out into the road. She had to unlock the cellar door – she had not known Norman kept it locked at night – and, with a huge effort of will, she went inside. She knew she must check inside the chapel of rest to see if there was anyone laid out in there. If so, she would have to rethink what she was planning to do. It took her a few minutes to find the courage. First of all she lit the gas lamps in the cellar and though the light was reassuring, she was trembling so much she could scarcely manage to insert the key in the lock and open the door of the chapel of rest. Every fibre of her was poised ready to run away should there be the slightest sound or movement.

Gritting her teeth, she swung the door open suddenly and held the candle high in the doorway. The long table was empty, with just a sheet folded on it. She let out a long, relieved breath. Thank goodness!

The place suddenly felt much more normal and unthreatening. She noticed then, though, that it was unusually messy: the floor covered in rings of wood shaving, which gave off a sweet smell, sawdust and offcuts of wood all over the place, hammer, chisels and other tools left out on the bench. Norman was so obsessed with tidiness and precision and chivvied Fred to leave the cellar looking tidy. Getting ready for Sal's funeral had evidently been a rush.

She turned then to Norman's cupboard. 'Right, mister – let's see what yer got in 'ere . . .'

Holding up the bunch of keys, she eyed the keyhole of the metal door and saw instantly the one which must fit. The keyhole had been smeared with black paint. Her heart beating painfully hard, she inserted the black key into the lock.

''Ere goes . . .'

Peering inside, holding the candle out, she could see nothing very much to start with. Her eyes grew more used to the deeper darkness in there and she saw that running along each wall were two shelves, one above the other, neatly arranged with an assortment of objects. There was a sense of order and fussiness characteristic of Norman. On one side seemed to be stored old ledgers, and a musty odour of aged paper mingled with the chemical smells. On a low shelf lay what looked like old tools – hammer, chisel, fretsaw, awl – each rather rusty, laid out straight, one by one. On the higher shelf to the left were arranged dark glass bottles and jars and beside them, an assortment of books. Stepping inside she pulled one down. It had a soft leather cover and worn gold letters on the spine. *Whiteacres' Manual for the Practice of Embalming the Human Body.* Quickly she put it back, not wanting to look inside. Her toe kicked against something and she looked down to see a can of paraffin for the stove they used in the cellar on the coldest winter days. Maryann smiled grimly. *Good.*

Turning to look at the back of the cupboard, she saw to her surprise that in the small space at the back, right in the middle, was a chair. It looked like an ordinary kitchen chair. Maryann moved closer, frowning, holding the candle higher. It took a moment for her to make out any details, but when she did the very blood seemed to freeze throughout her body. Her free hand went to her mouth.

Details jumped out at her one after another in the flickering light. The chair was straight-backed, with two struts across the back and a flat wooden seat. Fastened round the uprights of the chair back were two iron brackets which were screwed into the wall. Resting on the seat was a carefully coiled length of chain, curled round itself like a Swiss roll and glinting in the candle-light. With it was a pair of manacles – another pair was positioned on the floor by the chair legs – and a second length of chain dangled from the back in a snakelike loop to the floor. Over the back of the chair, folded very neatly, was a square of white cloth, perhaps a scarf. Maryann took in the sight, unable to move, the implications of it sinking into her mind. Had he threat-ened to tie it round and round Sal's mouth? Had he actually done it? Left Sal chained and gagged here – for how long? What else had he done? Was this the threat that he had held over Sal, month after month, until he had invaded her with fear, emptying her of her very self?

The restraining cords with which Maryann had held back her emotions that week burst open. She strode out of the cupboard and put the candle on the workbench. Moving with increasing frenzy, she began to gather up the mess that was strewn on the floor: the sawdust and wood shavings, the ends of wood, the sheet from the chapel of rest. Anyone who had seen her just then might have said she'd lost her mind. Going to the cupboard, she pulled out the armful of ledgers, tearing at their pages and throwing them down, their remaining pages splayed, then the books on embalming the dead. She tore into the cupboard and yanked with all her strength at the chair, trying to wrench it apart, levering it against the hold of the iron brackets, but it was strong and she couldn't release it. In the end she brought the other chair from the cellar and added it to the pyre. Going back into the cupboard, she picked up the tin of paraffin and poured it over the mess. Finally she rested the candle, with almost reverential care, on its side in the middle of it all. She stood the tin carefully by the door.

Flames immediately began to work on the dry curls of wood with a tiny crackle. Maryann stood for a moment, arms tightly folded, watching it all begin to burn.

'Burn, burn!' she hissed, her eyes gleaming. 'You evil, murdering bastard, burn!'

She seemed to do everything automatically, laughing, crying, as she did so, looking round for more things to stoke the fire. There was too much brick down here, too many hard surfaces. But she hadn't started on upstairs yet . . .

The smoke was beginning to build up, the flames reaching up towards the chair. She'd have to get out of here, but she needed to drag the trestle table out from the chapel of rest to make sure it carried on burning, or on the stone floor it might go out. She was coughing now, the cellar filling with smoke.

'Burn, go on, burn!' she urged, laying the trestles on their side amid the flames.

She heard a sound that penetrated her concentration. A bang from upstairs.

Norman. She was paralysed. It must be – he was here. Had followed her!

She stood listening, trying not to cough, but it was impossible. The smoke was getting too much. But he mustn't get her down here! If she was to encounter Norman it must be upstairs, where she stood a chance.

Halfway up the stairs, she stopped and listened, taking in deep breaths. Nothing. Was he waiting, in that spot just by the door? She could see no shadow. The smoke was winding up the stairs with her and the coughing was impossible to control. Suddenly, unable to bear it, she tore up the stairs into the office, just as there came another *bang*! The front door slammed shut. The office was empty, but the door was not properly closed, had gusted open. Maryann found she was so unsteady with shaking that she had to sit down at the desk. For a few moments she put her hands over her face and wept, distraught.

'I've got to try and forget this.' She knew even then, without time to reflect. 'Or I'll lose my mind thinking of it. Sal's gone – I'll be gone. No more girls for 'im.' She stood up, fiercely wiping her eyes. 'And this place'll be gone. I'm gunna make sure of that.'

Trying to hold her breath for as long as she could, she felt her way down the dark cellar steps once more. At the bottom she could feel the heat through the door and she picked up the paraffin can and ran up again, gasping frantically for breath as she reached the top. She splashed some paraffin over everything she could manage: ledgers, the padded seats of the chairs, the blinds over the windows, the contents of the desk drawers which she unlocked and took out. On opening the bottom one she paused, looking inside. In this, the deepest drawer, Norman kept his petty cash box. She quickly searched the bunch of keys for the little one which unlocked it. There it was. She tipped all the money into her pockets.

Striking match after match, she went round the room. The blinds were already ablaze as, picking up her things, she ran out into the street and tore away along Monument Road.

Twenty-Five

Running along the cobbles which gleamed wet in the gaslight, she headed instinctively towards Garrett Street and the old yard where she'd grown up, past all those childhood places, the Garrett Arms, dark entries into the back yards, the huckster's shop on the corner near her house: all so familiar, and yet tonight everything felt changed. Because she was changed. Nothing now could ever be the same again. She had to go now, to run away. She had no choice.

In the entry she slowed, treading softly. Though it was pitch dark she could remember every lump and bump in the bricks, the big hole three-quarters of the way down on the left where you could turn your ankle and break it. In a moment she was standing under the lamp in the yard, panting, but feeling suddenly much safer.

There was no hint of dawn, the houses black against the dark sky. She had no idea what the time was. She wondered whether she should wait out the rest of the night in the brewhouse along the yard where they kept the copper for washing clothes, but there was no telling who might come in and find her there first thing in the morning and there might be chickens and all sorts in there. No, she'd have to knock up the Blacks and get them to take her in until she could find Joel.

She knocked cautiously on their door. When she'd

paused and tried a second time the door opened and a tousled head and indignant face appeared. It was Alf Black, holding a candle. He and Charlie, now seventeen and eighteen, slept downstairs.

'It's me, Maryann,' she whispered, going up close to him. 'Don't make a racket, Alf, will you? I don't want no one to know I'm 'ere.'

'What's going on?' Alf demanded.

'Sssssh – for 'eaven's sakes. Can I come in?'

'Yer do know what time it is, don't yer?'

'No.'

'The middle of the fucking night, that's what.' All the same he stood back. 'Lucky I got up for a piss or I'd never've 'eard yer – and 'e'd never've neither.' Charlie was snoring on the old lumpy sofa. Maryann looked down at him with very mixed emotions. He must have lain beside Sal like that, handsome, his dark hair curling at the nape of his neck, long dark lashes. He had loved Sal, Charlie had, or so Nance said. If he hadn't gone off and left her, maybe she'd be alive . . . Alf stood at a loss for a minute. 'I'll get Nance, shall I?'

Nancy appeared a few minutes later with a candle.

'Maryann? What's going on? Flamin' 'ell, you stink like Smoky Joe. What've yer been doing?'

'Can I stop 'ere for a bit?' Maryann heard her voice turning tearful. 'I don't want them to know where I am. I've done summat terrible, Nance.'

Nance eyed her brother. 'Come up and yer can bunk down with me. You go back to bed, Alf, and keep yer trap shut about this, awright?'

Nance shared one of the two upstairs rooms with Percy, William, George and Horace. Maryann snuggled down with Nance on her single mattress on the floor.

'Come on then,' Nance whispered. 'Out with it.'

'Cross yer heart and hope to die yer won't tell no one?'

'Cross my heart.' Maryann felt Nance going through the motions of crossing herself in the dark.

'I set fire to Norman's offices – I 'ope I've burned the 'ole bloody lot down!'

'You *what*? What did yer do that for?'

'Because 'e...'e...' Maryann felt a sudden lurching inside her, as if she might be sick and she sat up, gulping. She was still shaking.

'You awright?' Nance sprang up again as well.

Maryann fought back the feeling. She felt so strange. All the time since she'd found Sal she'd felt peculiar, as if disconnected from everything around her, from her own feelings. She didn't know she was in shock. She just felt as if she was living behind a glass wall which she couldn't reach through.

'I can't tell you, Nance. I just can't. But Norman Griffin's not like what 'e seems at all, you know, kind and a gentleman. It's all lies. 'E killed our Sal, Nance – 'e did...'

'Maryann! What're you saying? You've 'ad a terrible time with Sal... dying and that. But that can't be right, can it? Yer stepdad daint *kill* 'er – she...' Nance paused. 'She ended 'er own life, Maryann.'

Maryann was shaking her head. 'I 'ad to do it. I 'ad to get 'im somehow. 'E killed our Sal...' She was gulping again. Nance's arms came round her, warm and comforting.

'Oh now, Maryann, there, there. I know yer in a state – and yer can stop 'ere with us for a bit if it'll make you feel better. Our mom won't mind...'

'I'm going away—'

'Are yer?' She could tell Nance was humouring her

and didn't really believe her. She was stroking her arm. 'Where're yer going then?'

'I can't tell yer.'

'Awright then, Maryann. Look – you lie down 'ere with me, eh? We'll get some kip and see 'ow things look in the morning.'

'They mustn't know I'm 'ere!' Maryann was still rigid, resisting lying down. 'The coppers'll be after me.'

'Awright, awright . . .'

'I *mean* it! I need 'elp, Nance. This ain't pretend, you know. If them lot see me' – she jerked her head towards the sleeping boys – 'they'll be gabbing away to everyone.'

'No they won't – we'll just say yer've come to stay for a bit. They ain't interested. Come on – lie down.'

Maryann tried to sleep, but felt by the morning that she hadn't had a wink. The bed was cramped, there were mice scuttling round the room and she was too churned up with emotion. She got up to face the mayhem that was the Blacks' household.

Nance told the boys Maryann had just come round to 'stop for a day or two' after which they lost interest. Maryann met Blackie on the stairs, clad in a greyish singlet and trousers, who said vaguely, 'Awright? What're yer doing 'ere then?' but he didn't stop long enough to wait for an answer.

Cathleen noticed she was there sure enough. In the midst of all her sons guzzling down bits of bread, she sat feeding Lizzie who was kicking her legs enthusiastically as she suckled. Cathleen had a cold and a hacking cough and kept wiping her red nose on an old rag. When Maryann and Nance came down she squinted with her lopsided eyes, the rag halfway to her nose, then let out a huge sneeze.

'Oh – oh . . . atchoo! Jesus, Mary and Joseph – where did you spring from in the night?'

'Maryann just wanted to stop 'ere for a bit,' Nance said, making faces that indicated she'd tell more when her brothers were out of the way.

She sat Maryann down and gave her a jam jar of weak tea and a slice of dry bread, which made Maryann feel a bit better. She had scarcely eaten all week.

Cathleen stirred herself from her chair to chase her husband and children out to work and school. As soon as she moved she began coughing again, doubled up with it.

'Oh—' she groaned. 'I got through four pair of bloomers coughing last night – I'll be washing all morning . . .'

'Is it awright if I stay for a night or two?' Maryann said, hesitantly. 'I can give yer some money . . .'

'Don't be daft, course yer can,' Cathleen said, shooing the youngest ones out of the door. 'So long as your mother don't mind.'

'They mustn't know I'm 'ere.'

Cathleen turned, Lizzie under one arm. 'Ah now – I'm not so sure about that. Why's that then?'

'Please,' Maryann begged. She searched round for a reason. 'Mom and me 'ad a bit of a ding-dong. It's only for a while.'

Cathleen gave a wan smile. 'Ah well. Can't say I ever liked yer mother, she's a stuck-up bit o' stuff if ever I saw one. So she won't get nothing out of me.'

Nance grinned. 'Thanks, Mom.'

'Thanks, Mrs Black,' Maryann said. 'I'd best get off to work now.'

*

The light was fading as Maryann waited at Camp Hill Locks, later that week, her bundle of possessions in her arms. She was waiting close to the cut, as she had waited now for most of the time since she had run away. The Blacks thought she was at work. Each morning she left the house after breakfast and went to the cut. That first day she said goodbye to Nance when she turned off to go to the laundry and hurried to the toll house where she thought the *Esther Jane* was most likely to come through.

'You back again, are yer?' the man said. 'Darius Bartholomew? S'far as I know they're still working down the Oxford, tekking what comes. I'd say they'd be through 'ere soon if they'm coming. I ain't seen 'em in a while.'

She spent the days walking to keep warm. She had enough money to buy food and cups of tea to keep a bit warmer. The coins in Norman's cash box had added up to four pounds, eleven and sixpence and she felt great satisfaction in spending it on her own comfort. She was afraid of missing the *Esther Jane* but knew she could ask at the toll house. Most of the day she walked along the bank, sometimes sitting down for a while or leaning against a bridge to watch the activity on the cut, but it was too cold to rest for long. These were cold, brittle days. You could see your breath on the air all day long. Under her coat she had on a warm dress and woolly jumper and stockings, though her heels were through them like potatoes and her shoes were too small and pinched her feet. On the second day she went up into Small Heath and looked round the pawn shops for another pair, but she could find nothing but battered old shoes that were all too big. In the end she decided to spend fifteen shillings of

Norman's money on a new pair of brown boots with sturdy soles.

These'll be good for on the cut, she thought, walking along, breaking them in. She kept looking proudly down at her feet. She felt no guilt whatever at having stolen Norman's money. The boots were like the sign of a new life. But she was very, very lonely. The ache in her to see Joel was almost overwhelming. Joel, who was the only person left who felt like family, who had shown her real affection and tenderness. If only they'd come and she could climb on board with them and feel safe and warm at last!

That evening, as the sun was setting, the night growing even colder, she was standing at Camp Hill Locks, where a conglomeration of bridges crossed over the cut as the road, railway and canal all met. She was hungry, her hands and feet were frozen and she felt low and desperate. The sun was setting and the cold becoming more intense, the air sharp and smoky. A line of joey boats was queueing to get through the locks and into basins for the night, all in a hurry to get tied up, and Maryann watched as a fight broke out between two men when one tried to barge in ahead. The loud, cursing voices and snarling expressions jarred right through her, making her feel all the more lonely and desolate as if they were attacking her. It seemed to stand for all the anger and meanness in the world and she turned and walked away, her arms folded across her chest, her head down and despair in her heart.

She longed to go back to the warm, fuggy atmosphere of the Blacks' house, but it was only about six o'clock. If the Bartholomews were putting in a long hard day it could be ten o'clock before they came into

Birmingham. She walked on, past the dark backs of warehouses.

She had walked up and down for another half-hour when a family boat came out of the darkness, its dim headlight moving steadily towards her. Her heart began to race. Surely she could make out the faint glow of white patches on the horse! She tried to keep her hope at bay – she couldn't bear the disappointment if it wasn't them.

'Bessie!' she whispered, peering through the gloom. Cautiously she started to run. Surely that was Bessie, couldn't that be the light of the *Esther Jane*?

As she came close she saw someone was leading the horse, someone big, solid. The one person in the world she longed and longed to see . . .

'Joel! Joel – it's me, Maryann!'

She heard the low rumble of his laughter out of the darkness, then its lapse into coughing for a moment. Then his arm came round her and she was safe.

'How do, our young nipper! Where've you bin then?'

Twenty-Six

She was woken very early the next morning by the delicious smell of bacon frying. Someone was sitting pressed up to her feet. Opening her eyes she saw Joel, bent forward towards the range, outlined against the light from the open cabin door. He was pouring dark, steaming tea from the brown and white teapot.

'Why didn't you wake me?' She sat up. Usually the faintest sound disturbed her. The men must have got up and moved in and out doing morning chores and she hadn't heard a thing. It was the first really sound night's sleep she'd had since Sal died.

Joel turned and grinned at her. His gingery beard glowed in the white dawn light. 'You was sleeping like a baby. Seemed a pity to wake you.'

Maryann smiled back, drinking in the sight of him. Now she had seen Joel and was back on the *Esther Jane* everything felt so much better and full of promise. Even Darius had seemed quite pleased to see her last night. 'I feel as if I've come 'ome, Joel.'

He nodded. 'Reckon so. We're finding it hard two-'anded – 'arder than it's ever been. My father ain't getting any younger and we're chasing loads wherever we go. Another pair o' hands'll be a godsend. All right with your folks now, is it?'

'Oh yes.' She spoke lightly. 'S'awright with them.'

'Good. Well, that's that then.' Maryann felt his blue

eyes on her, as if really examining her for a moment, and she hugged her knees. It was a special sort of look he was giving her and she didn't know what was he was thinking, but it felt nice, him looking at her like that.

He handed her a plate on which there was a thick wodge of bread topped with crispy bacon.

''Ere you go. Get that down you.'

They loaded up that morning, their cargo sacks of bolts and screws bound for Banbury, and by midday they were well underway. Maryann worked as hard as she could, pulling on ropes with all her strength, turning lock gates with the windlass. Both men knew they didn't need to tell her to be careful. She had learned that lesson back in the summer. But she still felt nervous in front of old Darius.

'I'll try not to do anything wrong,' she told him. 'And I'll work ever so 'ard for yer.'

'That's all right, lass,' he said. 'Everyone makes a mistake now and then. I can see you're stroving 'ard as you can.'

His leathery face stretched briefly into a smile. Maryann thought he seemed tired through and through. She had seen that both his hands and Joel's were rough and cracked, the tips of their fingers split from the wet and cold, and Joel was wheezing and coughing badly.

'Your fingers look sore,' she said to him. Joel held out his enormous hands, turning them this way and that.

'Not very pretty, are they?' he said.

Maryann was proud to think she might be of help, but she knew she was about to find out about the harshness of life on the cut in winter. The day was another bright, frosty one and she was very glad she'd bought the new boots. But she was ready for it all.

For that first morning she was filled with an almost insane sense of relief and excitement. She'd got away, she'd found the *Esther Jane*, she was safe, and no one would ever come and find her here! She ran along the bank, a ball of energy, taking the windlass and running at the locks until Joel said, 'Eh, steady on there. There's a long way to go yet!'

But she couldn't seem to help it. As the day wore on, though, her energy began to flag and the cold, strange feeling that had possessed her came back. They had left Birmingham behind, and she shrank into herself and quietened. For a time she climbed up and sat, huddled in her coat, on the roof of the cabin as she had in the summer, and she looked out at the beauty of winter on the cut in Warwickshire. The fields spread out around her, grass hard and sparkling with frost in the low sunshine, the reflection of which rippled along the water. Where there were hedgerows close enough she could see blood-red berries, and the grating cry of crows echoed across from the hoary trees in the distance. The sights were magical, but the further they went, the more the awful numbness seemed to possess her. She was back behind the glass screen where nothing around her felt quite real. She looked down at her hand with its bitten nails, stroking it along the *Esther Jane*'s wooden roof. Even her own hand seemed distant and unreal. She was frightened by it.

''Er's steadied down a bit,' she heard Darius say to Joel. They were at the tiller and didn't seem to expect her to hear although she was not far away. 'Like a barrowload of monkeys she was, this morning.'

Joel must've nodded or made some other sign because she didn't hear him reply. Maryann sat listening, head lowered so that her long hair fell forward. She heard Darius say, 'That child's grown up into a proper lass since we last see'd 'er. She's a proper 'and to us now, Joel, and that's a godsend.'

Maryann felt a blush rise up through her cheeks, filled with a contradictory mix of pride and self-consciousness. It was true, she had grown, suddenly, her body filling out, but it felt odd to hear them talking about her like that. Darius was pleased with her and wanted her on board! She really had found a new life where she was wanted, away from all the disgust and fear and sorrow of her life in Ladywood. Tears blurred her eyes as she looked along the cut. If only she could start to feel back to her normal self, everything would be truly fine.

They were back in the rhythm of the cut, working hard, not speaking much throughout the jouney. Maryann fell exhausted into bed the first night while the men were still in the pub. She was too tired to feel lonely. The second evening they reached Fenny Compton. It was the first of November and very cold, though not quite severe enough to freeze over the cut. By the time Bessie was stabled and Maryann had prepared the evening meal, the frost was setting in. The sun set over the fields in a glow of orange fire and the spare shapes of the trees were silhouetted against the eggshell-blue sky higher up. She saw Joel looking at her as she wiped unexpected tears from her eyes. She never seemed to know what her mood was going to be from one moment to the next.

They ate the stew round the tiny table without saying much, but she felt Joel's eyes turning to her often, his face anxious, and to her frustration her own eyes kept filling with tears which she had to wipe away. All that afternoon, however hard she had tried to force them away, memories of Sal kept pushing into her mind, not as she had last seen her, in despair and death, but as she had been when they were young, so lively and pretty with her long blonde hair, running and laughing in the park or leading Tony by the hand. Sal had loved having a baby brother. Maryann could hardly swallow down any of the food, however much she tried not to think of it. After a while she gave up. She went out and climbed on to the bank, trying to calm herself, looking out across the stern of the *Esther Jane* along the darkening water, her vision blurred by tears.

''Ere – you'll need this.'

Joel was holding out her coat and she put it on, glad of it.

'Come on with me, this way. We'll 'ave a bit of a walk.'

He led her away from the cut and the pub, along a footpath into the fields. There wasn't much light and she had to concentrate on walking on the frozen mud track. For a while Joel led her in silence, along the edge of the field until they came to a gateway, which opened out into another field where black and white cows were just visible in the dying light, standing huddled together not far away.

Joel leaned over the gate for a moment. Maryann looked up at him. He seemed so familiar standing there, his face, the shape of him, his big, work-roughened hands on the gate – it was as if she had known him all her life. He turned to her, one elbow still leaning on the gate.

'You ent yourself since you've come back with us, Maryann.'

'I'm ... I'm awright.' Once more the rush of tears. She wanted to stamp: stop it, stop it, I'm all right! Don't make me talk or remember. I'm where I want to be, just leave me alone!

He stepped away from the gate and put his hands on her shoulders, turning her towards him. She had grown a little, she realized. Her head now came up to his chest.

'Look, little 'un—' Despite his affectionate names for her, she sensed he was treating her differently, like someone older. There was vulnerablilty as well as kindness in his expression. 'I can see there's summat amiss. I don't know what's driven you away from your family, but I do know what a sunny face you 'ad before, Maryann, and I don't see it now. The Maryann that left us is 'ardly the same 'un that's come back.'

Maryann kept her eyes on the ground, shoulders heaving as the great swell of her grief struggled to the surface.

'Speak to me, girl,' Joel said gently. 'It can't do no harm.'

'M-my sister...' she managed to say, eventually. 'She ki ... ki ... took 'er own life. We only buried 'er in the week.'

'Oh no – oh—' she heard Joel say. 'My poor little bird.'

He took her in his arms and she felt herself held tight against his chest as his deep, growling voice made ceaseless, comforting noises. Over and over again he stroked her hair as she wept, beginning to let out some of the reservoir of horror and pain inside her.

He held her, murmuring his comfort to her for as long as she needed it, not asking questions, just letting her weep until she began to grow quieter. She went limp, leaning against him, gulping and sighing.

'Oh Joel,' she said eventually in tired despair.

'Poor little thing.' There was great tenderness in his voice.

'I thought I'd be awright back with you, and look 'ow I'm carrying on.'

'You will be awright. In a while.' There was a pause, then he said gruffly, 'We didn't half miss you. *I* missed you.' He squeezed her shoulders. 'You ent 'alf growing up, Maryann. I can't help seeing you a bit different. I've not 'ad soft feelings for many lasses, but you – you're coming to be special to me. Silly old fool, ent I?'

Maryann felt the affection and warmth of his words go through her. She gave a tiny laugh. 'No you're not, Joel. You're just you and I want to be with yer.'

He leaned down and carefully planted kisses, first on one cheek, then the other, and she giggled as his whiskers tickled her. His face was still close to hers and he was looking into her eyes.

'You're so sweet,' he said longingly. 'Just so sweet, lass.'

His holding her, the desire in his voice, aroused a flicker of excitement in her. He brought his lips close to hers and gave her a soft peck of a kiss. When she didn't pull away, he embraced her properly, closed his eyes and kissed her more passionately, hungrily. For those first seconds as he had looked at her, kissed her, she had been deeply touched by his gentleness, his desire for her. Then she felt his tongue between her lips, his hands pressing her now more ardently, and in her hurt state, her confusion, something hard and cold slammed down in her like a shutter. What was he doing? He was supposed to be her friend, her brother! And he was starting on this dirty stuff, *invading* her like Norman Griffin had done! But this was Joel. Joel didn't do things like that . . .

'No! Stop it!' She pulled away with such vehemence that he released her immediately, confused. 'Get off me! Don't you ever touch me. I hate anyone touching me!' She was crying again, distraught, starting to run from him, but she had only gone a few paces before her ankle turned on a hummock in the frozen ground and she fell over.

Joel reached down to help her up but she slapped his hand away. 'Don't you ever touch me, yer dirty bastard. I hate yer!' She scrambled up.

'Maryann, don't – what've I done to you?' He seized her arm and made her stop. 'I'm sorry. I just thought you'd . . . You seem so grown up and I've such feelings for you, but I wouldn't hurt you for the world. Please – don't be like this. I'd never do a thing to harm you . . .'

'Take me back to the boat,' she snapped, yanking her arm away. 'Don't touch me. Just take me back.'

Joel stood, hands on hips, staring at her, completely bewildered. 'We'll get back then.' He sounded confused, irritated even.

They walked back in silence. Maryann's mind was in turmoil. How could he have done something like that? He was a grown-up man and she was just a girl! This was supposed to be her safe place, the refuge she had run to for help. But it wasn't safe. He was just like

Norman, he'd made her feel foul and loathsome, and nothing on the *Esther Jane* would ever feel right again.

She refused to speak to Joel again that night, despite him trying to make up with her. She lay down on the side bench and turned away from him. She barely slept at all, listening to the sound of the men a short distance from her, repelled by both of them, wanting now to be anywhere else but here.

The next day they docked at Banbury and work began on unloading the cargo. Darius was busy overseeing that, and Joel had gone in search of another load to take on south or back up to Birmingham. Maryann would have expected to use the time to clean up the cabin, do some washing and put a sparkle on the brasses. Instead, once the men were out of the way, she wrapped up her few things again, pocketed the last of the money she had taken from Norman and climbed ashore, looking round her to make certain both the Bartholomews were out of sight. She walked briskly through the busy wharf area and slipped away, unnoticed, into the bustling town of Banbury.

PART TWO

Twenty-Seven

1934

Maryann carried the tray along the gold carpet of the landing, at pains not to slop tea from the large cup into the saucer. Beside the cup, arranged on delicate china plates, were two boiled eggs, one in the cup, one tucked beside it in a cosy, three slices of buttered toast, a pot of Chivers marmalade and a starched linen napkin in a silver ring. When she reached the last door along the landing, she set the tray down on the floor and knocked.

'Come!'

Each day she carried his breakfast to him, after she had already been up for four hours and had had her own meal in the servants' hall. Roland Musson liked to lie late in bed and eat his breakfast late, and it had been long agreed by the rest of the family that he should because this was what was good and right for him.

'On the table as usual please, Nelson.' He was sitting, tousle-haired, on the edge of his bed, his sturdy frame wrapped in a tartan wool dressing gown although it was May and quite warm. As usual, the room was fuggy with cigarette smoke.

'How do you come to look so hot and rosy-cheeked,' he complained petulantly, arms folded tightly across his chest. 'I feel quite shivery this morning.'

Maryann smiled. 'I keep warm working – it's non-stop this time of day.'

Roland Musson didn't reply, but sat looking sunk in gloom. He had the solid Musson looks, large blue eyes and a shock of thick fair hair, but his complexion was growing ruddy from too much drink. When she first arrived at Charnwood House Maryann had found him bad-tempered, demanding and unlikeable. She asked the other housemaids why this young man, a robust twenty-seven-year-old, as he had been then, spent his life confined in the parental home, and much of the time lounged about without purpose in his room.

'It were the war,' Letty, the first housemaid, told her. 'Shot 'is nerves to bits. 'E's better now, Mrs Letcombe says.' The housekeeper could remember the five Musson children as babies. ''E were ever so bad when 'e came 'ome. Crying, nightmares and everything. Wouldn't 'ardly go out of 'is room for months on end.'

'Why doesn't 'e go and get a job?' Maryann asked, thinking this a rum way to go on.

Letty laughed. ''E don't really need to, living 'ere, does 'e? 'E's comfortable enough, and to tell you the truth—' She lowered her voice to a whisper, as the two of them were polishing the dining-room floor and anyone might be within earshot, 'I don't think *she* wants 'im out of 'er sight, what with John being gone and that.'

John, the eldest Musson, an officer in an Oxfordshire Regiment, had been killed in 1917 and Mrs Lydia Musson, an elegant, though rather vague woman with a wreath of thick, wavy hair coiled round her head, seemed to encourage her second son's invalidity. She referred to him as 'poor, dear Roland' and he remained, at once petulant and pitiable, neither challenged to leave, nor seeming to have the will or incentive to do so.

It was getting on for six years since Maryann had come to Charnwood House, four miles out of Banbury, and in that time Roland Musson did seem to get out more. He worked in the grounds in the afternoon with Sid and Wally, the two gardeners, and he had a motorcycle on which he roared dangerously along country roads and across the fields. He had a few friends locally and they sat for hours at a time in village pubs. Maryann, though, couldn't help but compare his plight with that of her father, also scarred by the war, trying to adjust back to family and civilian life and having somehow to struggle on and get jobs, keep afloat, without the cushion of wealth that Roland Musson had beneath him. And Nance's father, Blackie Black, too, and Joel ... But no – she wasn't going to think of Joel. Whenever her mind strayed down any path which would lead her to think about home she blocked out such thoughts. She had found a life that was free of pain and trouble and she wanted to keep it that way. And over the years her dislike for Roland Musson had faded as she grew to understand him better, turning instead to a mixture of tenderness and pity.

Sometimes when she carried Roland's breakfast tray in he was quite jovial and chatty; other times down and sunken into himself. That morning, Maryann stirred two lumps of sugar into his tea and handed it to him, thinking today was one of his depressed days, but he suddenly looked up at her.

'How old are you, Nelson?'

'Nineteen, sir. Twenty come September.'

'You look *different*,' he said taking the cup. 'What is it about you?'

'I really don't know.' She hadn't changed her hair, her morning dress was as usual. She wasn't aware that

Roland ever *saw* her anyway. She was a servant, and they had to stand to one side in the corridors when a family member passed, trying to make themselves invisible.

'You look *yourself* – as if that's how you're meant to look. Chap in my unit – that's what it makes me think of.' Roland spoke musingly into his teacup. 'Went out on a night patrol – one of those bloody woods on the Somme. Can't think what it was all for now but anyhow, they were successful. We'd heard the shots – didn't know who was getting it at the time. But they came back, all of them, full of it.' Roland spoke in his odd, clipped way. 'Anyway, this fellow was one of them. When I saw him the next morning, he looked, well, *altered*. That's it. That's what you made me think of. As if he'd grown into himself overnight.' He took a long drink of the cooling tea and Maryann, puzzled, thought he'd finished and began to turn away. But he carried on.

'Day after that the chap stood up for a few seconds and bang – killed by a sniper. So what was that all about? Man grows up, becomes himself overnight, then—' He snapped his fingers. 'Like a bloody butterfly.'

A moment later he looked up at her again. 'All right. I don't expect you to have an *answer*. Off you go.'

She went back down the stairs, pausing on the landing to look out over the garden, where Wally, the elder of the two gardeners, was bent weeding the long border which edged the drive. It was at its most beautiful at this time of year, the lawn wide and green, the beds bright with flowers, trellises of climbing roses up the outbuildings and the mock orange and laburnum in blossom. The mingled scents drifted in through the open window. From close to the house, out of sight, she could hear the Mussons' two dogs barking: Freddie, a wild young fox terrier with his insistent yap, and the deeper bark of their spaniel, Lily Langtree, who was beginning to run to fat. Freddie suddenly launched himself, a black and white flash across the lawn, with Lily lumbering after him.

Different? What had Roland Musson been on about? Maryann looked down at herself. She may be different, but it certainly hadn't happened overnight. She had grown, of course, and filled out on the plentiful and stodgy servants' food at Charnwood House. When she first arrived she had had no appetite and even Mrs Letcombe cajoled her to eat.

'Come on, girl – you'll have no energy for the work if you eat like a sparrer.'

Gradually, she settled into the rhythm of the house. As she got to know the characters of the other servants and appreciated that she had a good employer and a comfortable life, she felt secure and happy. She liked the predictable routine, the steady days and years. She was under-housemaid to Letty and Alice, and once she'd got used to the place, resolved that she would try hard and work her way up through the pecking order of servants. Two years later, Letty, who was then twenty-one, had married and moved on and Maryann became second housemaid. That was a start, but the job she had her eye on was not to be a housemaid at all. The job she wanted was Ruth's. Ruth, who was in her mid-twenties when Maryann arrived, was lady's maid to Mrs Musson, and to the Misses Diana and Pamela Musson when they were at home, which Pamela still was. Ruth was a quiet, dark-haired, neat young woman, whose job seemed to be regarded in realms high above that of housemaid. As she looked dreamily out at the spring garden that morning,

Maryann was speculating excitedly about the fact that Ruth was now courting with a young baker from the nearest village. If they were to marry, surely Ruth would leave and then perhaps . . .? But would they give the post to Alice, the first housemaid? Surely not! Alice was a good, hard worker, but she was a rough diamond. Was she, Maryann, neat and respectable enough for the job? She had done her darndest to make herself so. Every morning she brushed out her long, black hair and pinned it immaculately in a bun behind her head. She kept her nails short and her uniform mended. Smoothing her hand over her apron and trying to walk with Ruth's cool serenity, she went on down the stairs. Could that have been what Master Roland meant, she thought hopefully, that she looked like someone who wasn't meant to be a housemaid? Was she really destined to be a *lady*'s maid?

''Urry *up*!' Alice snapped when Maryann appeared down in the kitchen. 'You should be half done with the bedrooms by now!'

Evan, who worked under the butler, Mr Thomas, winked at her over Alice's shoulder as he passed with a tray of steaming cutlery ready for drying. Maryann ignored him. Suddenly, after a few months of banter with Evan, he was becoming too friendly. He had started creeping up on her in the pantry and putting his arm round her. 'Gerroff!' she'd say to him. 'What're yer playing at?' It made her feel horrible and prickly.

'Master Roland was talking to me,' she retorted to Alice. 'I couldn't just walk out, could I?'

'Well, you'd better get on with it double quick now's all I can say,' Alice ordered.

Maryann made a face behind Alice's back. Since she'd been first housemaid Alice had gone power mad.

She began on Pamela Musson's room. Pamela,

voluptuous, blonde and loud, was only two years older than Maryann and was the youngest of the Musson children. The room was pretty, decorated in pale blue and white, with a soft, silky bedspread, curtains the colour of bluebells and a thick blue carpet. As usual, Pamela had left her nightclothes strewn across the floor and the bedding tipped off right over the side. Her dressing table was a litter of powder puffs and perfume, there was face powder spilt on the floor, stockings dangling languidly over the edge of one drawer and coat-hangers and underslips dropped on the floor by the cupboard. Maryann sighed. When she had arrived she found it almost impossible to take in that Pamela was the same age Sal had been. She was both a child and a young woman, both so much more sophisticated and knowing than Sal, yet so much more sheltered and childlike in other ways. She and Diana had gone about in their 'flapper' outfits, or their fashionable lounging clothes in bright colours with wide flowery bandeaux round their hair and hanging jauntily down at the back. Maryann had been astonished by their energy, their colourful freedom and confidence as they danced and giggled their way through life. Diana was married now and had stopped giggling some time soon after the ceremony. Pamela, who had done secretarial training, did her 'bit of work, to show willing' and otherwise existed in a round of social visits and Young Farmers' dos and 'hops' in Banbury and kept talking about 'getting a little job in London'. Pamela was rather hoping someone would marry her quite soon too and she sometimes told Maryann about her beaux.

Maryann gathered up and folded Pamela's fine stockings. If she was a lady's maid she would deal with their pretty clothes all the time and help them do their hair instead of cleaning out grates before the sun had risen of a morning and polishing floors with beeswax and turps! She pictured herself. Maryann Nelson: lady's maid. And then her hope withered. They most likely wouldn't even think of her for the post. They'd stopped wincing now every time she opened her mouth, but she'd never forgotten Diana Musson's mirth the first time she heard Maryann speak.

'Where on earth,' she screamed, between red-lipstick lips, 'did she get that *terrible* accent?'

'Birmingham, my dear – I gather,' Mrs Musson told her, and Diana looked closely at Maryann as if she was a rather exotic wild animal.

'How perfectly extraordinary! Is the child quite well? She looks so dreadfully *thin*.'

Maryann shook out the crumpled underslips and put them out for Ruth to iron. Then she stood and looked at herself for a moment in Pamela's long mirror. A dark-eyed, serious face stared back at her. She was no longer 'dreadfully *thin*', that was one thing for certain. Slender, but curving, and rounder in the face than she had ever been.

I'm a woman now, she thought, looking herself up and down in surprise. Women were supposed to marry and have babies. Maryann had spent so much time not thinking of herself, of her body, of her past, it came as a shock to her to notice she had grown up so much.

Will I ever be able to be normal? she thought. Questions, feelings, which she had closed off in herself, were beginning to nudge their way to the surface.

She pushed the cupboard door shut, closing off her view of herself. She didn't want to look. It was too frightening.

Twenty-Eight

Charnwood House had been a haven to her, a place where she had enjoyed a long period of calm, like an animal in hibernation. Her fondest memory of arriving to work at Charnwood, after the nerve-racking interview with Mrs Letcombe (for which she prepared herself in the local baths with a good wash and change of clothes), was that first Christmas. By then she had been in the Mussons' employ just a few weeks, having arrived at Banbury in early November, and she was still thin and withdrawn, closed in on herself. Looking back on it now, she could see that she had been really beside herself, in shock at Sal's death, at her own cruel treatment by their stepfather, and by her feelings that Joel had betrayed her.

That Christmas she began to close the door on the past. By the time the celebrations began she was already getting used to the day-to-day work of Charnwood House. She liked Letty and Alice wasn't too bad, if rather petty. Letty was fair-minded and made sure everyone did their share, and life in the servants' quarters was orderly and amiable. Mrs Letcombe was a motherly person – indeed she was a widow and mother of four grown-up children. Cook was blunt and strange and there were rumours that she had been crossed in love. Her dearest pleasure was to moan and mither, but most of it was just talk, and the butler Mr Thomas was touchy and pompous, but a kind man at heart. All of them assured her she had landed on her feet, and she soon found it to be so.

The week before Christmas, Sid and Wally, overseen by Mr Thomas, dragged a huge Christmas tree in through the front door and it was set up in a gleaming brass pot in the front drawing room where there was a fire blazing for the holiday season. Maryann and some of the others were allowed to watch Mrs Musson dressing the tree, accompanied by Diana and Pamela; Hugh, the third boy, whose age fell between that of the two girls, was not yet home from boarding school. Maryann stood warming herself in the lovely room, with its comfortable chintz-covered chairs and long, sweeping curtains and watched, rapt, as the girls trimmed the tree with baubles and red and gold ribbons and a beautiful angel with gauzy wings which was pinned to the very top by Diana, on tiptoe on a chair.

'There—' She stood back afterwards and admired their work. 'How do you like that?'

She turned to Maryann, who mumbled back nervously, 'It's very nice.'

Diana burst out laughing, looked at her sister and said, 'Noice – oh isn't she a scream!'

Maryann blushed, but they laughed so much and without malice that she joined in in the end.

'Don't mind us,' Pamela said sweetly. 'It's just we've never met anyone from Birmingham before.'

Diana suddenly peered closely at her. 'You're very young, aren't you? Why have you come down here?'

Maryann's throat went dry. 'Erm – I was looking for work.'

'But however did you *get* here?' Pamela asked.

'Down the cut.'

The two girls found this hugely funny.

'Down the *what*?'

'She means the canal, I believe,' Mrs Musson said, selecting sprigs from a pile of holly and laurel leaves from the garden. 'Did you now, dear – that *is* an unconventional way to travel, I must say.'

Maryann was very relieved when they left her alone. But she couldn't stop looking at the tree, which was the biggest and most beautiful she had ever seen, and the fire beside it, stacked with apple wood which made a delicious smell as it burned.

They had had a very busy time preparing the house. Maryann drew pleasure from simply moving about in such a lovely home, with its shining wood floors smelling of beeswax, the wide staircase with its red carpet and smooth wooden banister, the long windows and beautiful curtains. So much space, such sumptuous furniture. Compared with this, the houses in Ladywood seemed so dwarfed and mean.

On Christmas Eve, the Mussons' relatives started to arrive and the house was full of cries of greeting, doors opening and shutting, luggage being carted up to the rooms and the frantic barking of the two dogs. Mrs Musson's sister came with her daughters, and Pamela and Diana ensconced themselves in their rooms in the evening with their cousins – giggling, exchanging clothes and making themselves up for dinner.

In the days before Christmas, Diana had called the three housemaids together in the hall, lined them up with an indulgent grin on her face, and said, 'Now – we always give our people a little gift for Christmas. I'd like you to think of something you'd like. Nelson – what about you?'

Maryann, standing to attention with her arms by her

sides, felt her hands begin to sweat and her heart was thumping hard. Whatever was she supposed to say?

'I ... er ... I dunno, miss,' she gasped. She looked desperately at Alice and Letty but they were both staring straight ahead of them.

'There must be some little thing you could do with, surely?' Diana Musson quizzed her.

'Well – I could do with a comb,' Maryann dared to say.

Diana gave her loud laugh. 'A comb? Oh my dear, how sweet! I think we can manage a comb, don't you worry.'

Maryann was relieved to find that Alice and Letty's requirements were barely less modest than her own. Alice asked for a roll of ribbon and Letty wanted some needles and sewing thread. Diana went away, laughing cheerfully.

On Christmas morning the family walked out along the frosty lane to the village church and came back gusting in on the cold air and still singing scraps of carols. Mr Musson had evidently been asked to read from the Old Testament. His loud, declamatory voice boomed up to her as she passed along the landing upstairs.

'The Lord has forsaken me; my God has forgotten me! Can a woman forget the infant at her breast—' There was a pause as he seemed to be struggling, with a grunt, out of his coat and there was laughter downstairs. '—or a loving mother the child of her womb?'

Maryann had slowed, listening. The words brought back the smell of St Mark's Church in Ladywood, the dark, hushed space inside. And they pierced her heart. 'A loving mother ...' A great pang of homesickness passed through her. She could picture the house in Anderson Street, Christmas Day: Tony and Billy waking to find one of Mom's old stockings on the foot of the bed with a penny and and orange, maybe a knob of sugar and a little notebook and pencil or toy inside. Her mom'd never been bad at that sort of thing. It was the thing to do and she'd always been all right at 'the thing to do'. It was anything requiring more emotional effort she couldn't seem to manage. Maryann's eyes filled at the thought of Tony and Billy. Half the family gone, no sisters to give them any love.

She wrote notes home to Tony and Nance every now and then, wanting them to know she was still thinking of them. She couldn't bear to think of Tony believing she had completely deserted him without a thought. In all this time though, she had never had letters back, as she had not disclosed her address to them. She didn't want anyone knowing where she was. But sometimes she felt so desolate, never hearing from any of them. Had Tony still got the china cat she'd given him that looked like Tiger? Did he ever think of her, she wondered. He and Billy must be quite grown up by now. Her throat ached with tears. She was just on the point of breaking down and crying when she heard footsteps coming towards her. It was Letty.

'Maryann – you all right? Mrs M wants us all down in the games room.'

When they went to the games room at the back of the house, Maryann found the servants all beginning to line up, and on the billiard table, a row of little wrapped parcels. Mrs Musson was there, and her daughters and their female cousins. Mrs Musson's greying hair was pulled back into a more elegantly styled bun than usual, and she wore a dress of rich red velvet trimmed with gold brocade, which Maryann thought the loveliest she had ever seen.

As she and Letty joined the end of the line, Mrs Musson was already calling the names of the servants one by one. Each parcel had a label in the shape of a leaf. Maryann saw Mrs Musson shaking hands with Mr Thomas and wishing him 'the good health and joy of the season'. Then Mrs Letcombe, followed by Cook. When Mrs Letcombe opened her parcel, which was rather larger than most of the others, the layers of flimsy paper revealed a batch of balls of soft, lilac-coloured wool. Mrs Letcombe did a great deal of knitting and she gasped with pleasure.

'Oh Mrs Musson, Miss Diana, *thank you*.' She laughed. 'Oh that's beautiful, that really is.'

'Now you make sure you knit something for yourself and not just all those grandchildren of yours!' Diana teased her. 'It's for *you* to have something nice.'

When Maryann's turn came, she felt her hand taken into Mrs Musson's cool, smooth palm and she glanced up at her shyly before lowering her eyes in confusion to the floor.

'A happy Christmas to you, my dear,' Mrs Musson said. 'I do hope you're settling in well with us. Mrs Letcombe says you're a credit.'

'Thank you,' Maryann mumbled, unsure where to put herself. 'It's very nice 'ere – thank you, Mrs Musson.' She glanced up again at Diana, whose red-lipped grin was bearing down on her as usual.

'Here's a gift for you, Nelson.'

'Thank you, miss.' She gave an awkward sort of curtsy as she accepted the parcel excitedly. Whatever it was, it wasn't just a little comb!

Tearing the paper off carefully, she found a brush and comb set, with a mirror included. The comb was tortoiseshell and the brush had a smooth wooden handle. She felt a big smile spreading over her face. 'Oh these're lovely, oh they are!'

Letty had been given a beautiful little embroidered sewing pouch with needles and coloured threads, a silver thimble and a tiny pair of scissors, and Alice had three rolls of satiny ribbon in green, purple and royal blue. They were all delighted.

'Back to work now,' Letty said. 'No rest for the wicked.'

The day was indeed hard work, feeding the Mussons and their visitors, clearing up and tending to all the rooms, but Maryann loved the atmosphere of the house, the comings and goings, the laughter and loud air of festivity. Christmas was her favourite time at Charnwood, even though every year since she had been there she had to fight back poignant thoughts of home.

The years gradually took on a routine. In the summer the Mussons went to the sea for several weeks, living in a cliff house they owned that looked out over the Salcombe estuary in Devon. Roland never went with them, however much Mrs Musson entreated him, saying the change and sea air would do him good. It was as if any such change to his habits had become impossible for him. But Maryann was allowed to go some years and every time plans were being made she hoped and prayed she'd be taken along. That first time, in 1929, was the first time she had ever seen the sea. They arrived, snaking slowly down the coast road on a dazzling July day, seeing the blue spread out until it faded into a blur at the horizon, and Maryann thought she had never felt so happy and excited. The month she passed there with Letty and the family was not arduously hard work and the two girls were allowed to go paddling in the sea, walk on the cliffs smelling the yellow gorse and sit on the beach licking ice creams. Maryann thought she was in heaven.

'I don't ever want to go 'ome!' she said to Letty. 'I never knew there was places like this in all the world!'

Letty laughed, wiggling her back into a comfortable position on the sand. 'Well, if you play your cards right you'll come back next year.'

And so the seasons went, and so she grew up: Christmas, spring cleaning, summer holidays, autumn coming round again; living through the events of the family: Miss Diana's wedding, Pamela's ups and downs with 'chaps', Hugh leaving school and joining Mr Musson at the bank, and Roland, who was always, disquietingly, at home. The three girls followed the lives of their employers like characters in a storybook or a play. The Mussons' events were often their events. And this suited Maryann more than she even realized. Living through their lives saved her from having to live her own.

And then Evan came and began to prise her feelings open again.

Twenty-Nine

Maryann stood in the kitchen, waiting as the toast for Roland Musson's breakfast tray browned on the griddle. The back door was open as it was a warm morning of blue sky and puffy clouds, and a breeze blew into the kitchen, dispersing the smells of egg, soap and disinfectant that lingered there. Cook was at the table laying chump chops in a row ready for lunch and murmuring about needing to 'get on and steam that pudding'.

Maryann snatched the toast from the griddle and on to a plate before it could burn and went to the pantry to fetch the butter. Out of the corner of her eye she saw Evan come into the kitchen and did her best to ignore him. She removed the eggs from the pan with a spoon and arranged them as usual on the tray. But as she was buttering the toast she sensed Evan sliding round beside her. For a second his hand rested on her buttocks.

She twisted away from him furiously, hoping Cook would notice and tick him off, but it was her turn to disappear into the pantry.

'*Don't*, Evan!'

His dark eyes looked laughingly into hers. 'You're a proper tease you are, aren't you, girl? Never mind – there'll be time for us to have some fun later on.'

Maryann looked into his round face with its habitual jaunty expression, his plump little neck squeezed into the collar of his uniform. He winked at her, as usual, and she turned her back on him again. Whatever she said to Evan, however many times she asked him to leave her alone, it seemed to make no difference.

'I dunno why you're so nasty to 'im,' Alice said to her sometimes, jealous that no one was fixing their attention on her. ''E's handsome and 'e'll get on – 'e's a good worker.' Maryann and Evan were the same age, and in the months Evan had been there he had pursued Maryann with increasing determination. She realized she represented a challenge, even if he didn't like her very much.

Maryann would shrug. How could she explain what she felt to Alice, how much the sight of Evan filled her with panic. He revolted her and she was enraged by his assumption that she didn't know her own mind, that if he kept on and on at her she'd fall willingly into his arms.

'Go on – come for a walk with me this afternoon, eh? You and I could 'ave a lot of fun. Spring fever and that, eh?' He nudged her with his elbow and gave a wink. It was her afternoon off every Wednesday and by hideous coincidence it was also Evan's.

'No,' she said abruptly. 'I don't want to walk out with yer, Evan. I don't know how else to get it through your thick head. I ain't coming with you and I never will. Now get out of my way – I've got to take up Master Roland's breakfast and you're holding me up.'

'Evan,' Cook commanded. 'Get on with your work or you won't be going anywhere this afternoon.'

Evan backed away, making gestures behind Cook's back and grinning in a way that made Maryann want to punch him. She put the teapot on the tray and set off upstairs. She felt horribly unsettled. Evan had only been in the house a matter of months, but gradually he had begun to transform it from her haven of safety and certainty to a place where she was always on her guard if he was about. She would creep softly to the door of the kitchen to check that she was not likely to be alone with him in there. She very seldom was, as Cook was almost always at her post. She checked round corners now, to see if he was coming. When he came near her the feeling of panic that rose in her set her pulse racing uncomfortably. He was so single-minded, so cunning and yet so stupid, and the combination was completely unnerving.

As she put the tray down and knocked on Roland Musson's door, the thought came to her that not once, in all the time she had been at Charnwood House, had Roland ever felt dangerous to her in this way.

'Come!'

The door swung open. He had actually got up off the bed and opened it for her. Maryann stood in the doorway, astonished.

'Thank you.' She bent for the tray but he said, 'Allow me,' and swooped down beside her, looking like a tousled-haired little boy.

'Another delicious breakfast,' he said, sniffing at the toast. 'I'm well ready for it today.'

'You won't be needing me then.'

'Oh yes, do come in. Come and do some of your tidying up or something.'

'But—' Usually she worked on his room later, once he'd gone out.

'Don't argue. I don't mind you doing your work with me in the room.' He closed the door behind them. 'In fact, you're one of the few things that breaks the monotony round here.'

He sat on the bed, pulling the small table close to

put the tray on, and began to eat. Uncertain for a moment, Maryann looked round the room, then began to pick up Roland Musson's clothes which were thrown on the floor all round the chair. As she was folding his shirt, trying not to watch him eating as it seemed rude, he said, 'How long have you been here now, Nelson?'

'Five years last November, sir.'

'Extraordinary. Is it really that long? God, what an appalling thought.'

'What's that?'

'Well, here're you, five years later, grown-up, opening up like a bud and a lovely one at that. Moving on, you know. And here am I, thirty-three years old, stuck here like an old fossil in a lump of rock.'

Maryann hesitated and looked across into his eyes. She felt she had to be very careful what she said. 'You had to go through the war, sir.'

'So did plenty of others. I'm not the only chap in England who's terrified of sleep, you know. Did you lose anyone in the war?'

'Yes, sir. My father. At least – no, well he didn't die in the war . . .'

Roland paused, a spoonful of egg in mid-air. 'What d'you mean?'

'He didn't die in the war. It just felt as if 'e did – in a way.'

'Yes.' He pointed the spoon at her. 'Yes, that's it exactly. You're a sharp girl, Nelson.'

After a moment he said, 'I suppose you find me a useless piece of goods. The way I've never picked up.'

'No, sir.' Not useless. What was more puzzling to her was that there was no *necessity* for him to work. It went against everything she had grown up used to.

'Don't pretend to me, Nelson, please. I have buried

myself alive here. Buried in the safety of mother love and a full belly. But d'you know what?'

He waited for her to speak.

'What – sir?'

'I almost think that one day I shall leave here. I shall do it. Resurrect myself. Live.'

Maryann said nothing, not knowing what to say. She picked up his shoes and laid them straight on the gold carpet. They were very big, moulded touchingly into the shape of his feet.

'D'you think I could manage it? I shall go to ... to, let's say, Algeciras. Yes. What about that?'

'I – I don't know where that is.'

'It's somewhere Johnny always wanted to go, you know. Don't know why now. Its name seemed to have a magic for him. Algeciras...' He drifted off into silence. Often he couldn't finish a conversation, lost the thread of it somewhere.

'Yes,' he said eventually. 'It's all a great pity.'

That afternoon when Maryann had finished her lunch-time duties she went up to change. Hers was a small attic room, with a rug on the bare floorboards, but with a high window facing over the drive and she had grown very fond of it. She had few possessions, but over the years had accumulated things to decorate the walls; pictures from magazines of soft-faced, smiling ladies with silken clothes. She loved to look at them and imagine dressing up like that herself. And now spring was here she had gathered a little posy of flowers from the garden. Last time she had been out, as she some-times did in the evening, she had come across Roland, walking up from the lower end pushing a wheelbarrow.

Usually if she wanted flowers she asked Sid or Wally. This time though, she had not even had to ask. Roland had lowered the handles of the barrow, stepped over and picked several sprigs of orange flower which he presented to her with a shy gallantry.

'There you are. I expect you'd like those. All women like flowers, don't they?'

She'd thanked him, startled. The flowers were still sitting in the jar in her room and the scent of them came to her powerfully every time she went in. Poor Master Roland, she thought, smiling at them. His awkwardness had touched her. What would become of him?

She changed out of the grey dress and white cap and apron which made up her morning uniform and put on her one summer frock, a cotton dress in a pretty blue floral print which Pamela Musson had handed on to her, and put some money in her purse. She now earned ten shillings a week at Charnwood House, but apart from a few small necessities found little to spend her money on, and she had savings of almost thirty pounds which she kept in her room, wrapped in an old handkerchief. She had long grown out of her boots bought for working on the cut, so she kept her black work shoes on, picked up her cardigan and set off downstairs. She planned to walk into Banbury and post another note she had written to Tony. Of course, the family could have moved house by now for all she knew, but every couple of months she dropped him a few lines, and included messages for Billy. It was hard to believe that Billy must be nearly ten by now – and Tony was old enough to start work. Billy had most likely forgotten who she was, but even if that was true, she wanted her brothers to know she still thought of them and cared for them.

Carrying the letter she crept down the attic stairs, then the back stairs to the kitchen, where she found Cook dozing on an upright chair by the window, her head sagging on to her chest. Sensing someone standing close to her she woke with a start and looked, for a few seconds, quite demented.

'Oh! Maryann you didn' 'alf make me jump. Ooh my word!' she grumbled, clutching her chest. 'What're you creeping about like that for? I thought you was off out.'

'Where's Evan?' Maryann whispered.

'Oh 'e's gorn – 'alf 'n hour back I should think.'

'Oh good. That's awright.' She felt she was breathing more easily. 'I'll be off myself then.'

She walked down the drive of Charnwood House, along the scented border of flowers, between the tall elms, all pushing out fresh green leaves, and on to the side lane that, after about half a mile, joined the main road to Banbury. At the road she stopped for a moment, emerging from the shade of the trees, put her head back and closed her eyes, enjoying the feel of the sun on her face and arms. It was a warm, calm afternoon and she breathed in deeply, luxuriating in a few hours of freedom.

She walked quite briskly along the road, bordered on each side by hedges, hawthorn and blackthorn and buttercups, bindweed and blue field madder in the grass beside them. Young blackbirds and thrushes twittered from the hedges. After a few moments she stopped, moved close to the hedge and looked across to the field beyond. It was a rough pasture and a short distance away she could see the white tails of rabbits as they bucked nervously around a warren, so far oblivious to her presence. Maryann smiled, watching them. A gentle breeze ruffled the grass, but otherwise it was very quiet, not a sound except for the birds. Somewhere over there must be the cut, winding through the fields. She looked down, suddenly aware of herself, standing here alone, with time to think. It seemed very *odd* suddenly that she was here in this life so divorced from her childhood.

How did I get here? she thought. Here am I, nearly twenty – I could be here doing this for the rest of my life. She turned the envelope in her hands and looked at her brother's name. 'Master Tony Nelson'. He was supposed to be Tony Griffin, but she would never, never call him that. This was her family now: two boys who she might never see again. She didn't count her mom. A great feeling of loneliness came over her. Would she never have anyone to call her own? Would her whole life be spent here? She might become a lady's maid, but then wouldn't she just be a dried-up, middle-aged woman, living through all the events of the Mussons' life instead of having any real happiness of her own? The bleakness of this outlook brought tears to her eyes. Until now, Charnwood had offered the haven she needed. It had brought her a sense of calm. But now it suddenly didn't seem to be nearly enough.

She walked on, wiping her eyes, deep in thought, no longer noticing the beauty around her, and turned on to the main road. For the first time in a very long while, she allowed herself to think about the events that had driven her to this place. Sal's death, the fire, Joel ... Joel's betrayal of her, the disgust she had felt. She relived that journey down to Banbury on the cut, the night he had taken her out to the fields, trying to see his face in her mind. The lust in it, the disgusting, frightening emotions that drove men ... Joel's face swam into her mind, lit by the silver light of that winter night.

'I've such feelings for you...' He'd said that. She hadn't heard, she'd only panicked and fought him off. That face had been full of Joel's tenderness and shame and bewilderment.

I was only a child, she thought, clinging bitterly to her anger. He shouldn't've done that to me.

But now the memories came to her of the feeling of being held by him, the comfort and power of him, the sense of safety he had always given her. Had she made a mistake? Had she got it all wrong and twisted because she was young and in a terrible state? She stopped, looking up the road. Joel was long gone now, of course – she couldn't say any of this to him. But she needed to admit it to herself. There was a gateway up ahead and she decided to go and rest on it, to let herself think for a little while, however much it hurt.

On her usual visits to Banbury what Maryann normally liked to do was to spend a couple of hours strolling round the town, along the Horsefair, past the famous Banbury Cross, looking in the windows of shops, perhaps buying a few small things, sometimes more notepaper to write to Tony. She would often treat herself to a cup of tea and a Banbury cake in one of the teashops. Today she bought a stamp and posted Tony's letter, first kissing the envelope.

'Hope yer get this, Tony,' she murmered, slipping it into the posting box. Her hand was shaking as she held it out. 'I hope yer awright, you and Billy. God bless yer both.'

She began her usual wandering, peering in the window of a china shop at the beautiful Wedgwood cups and saucers, the pretty ornaments, little vases and painted animals. Further along was a dressmaker's and haberdashery store. Should she buy a length of poplin to make a skirt? But her heart wasn't in it. She wasn't very good at sewing, even with all the help and guidance Mrs Letcombe had given her, and today she couldn't seem to keep her mind on anything. She found herself wandering purposelessly among the Banbury streets, across the Market Place amid the clamour of the busy vendors and shoppers and smells of food.

Before she realized it she found warehouses growing up around her, the scents of bread and fruit fading to be replaced by more grimy smells of coal and dust, wharf buildings growing up around her and the sudden sight and smell of the cut. She had only once been back to the cut before, further along, when she wandered there by mistake a few years earlier. Since then she had kept away deliberately.

The sight of it flooded in on her. A pair of narrowboats were gliding towards her, towed by a stringy mule, his reflection shimmering in the grey, murky water. A great rush of memories flooded into her mind. The cabin of the *Esther Jane*, the beauty of the Oxford Canal when she had seen it in glorious summertime and with the white frost of winter. And the steady, tranquil glide of the boat, with Joel at the tiller, his great strong arm guiding her. In her mind she heard his laugh, the way she had heard it that first time she met him, then later, when she ran to him in the dark by the lock. She found tears welling in her eyes again at the thought of him, at the love she had for him that she had rejected, that she had run from and turned her back on.

'Oh Joel,' she whispered. 'Wherever you are – I shouldn't have run away from you like that!'

Thirty

She went back to Charnwood House to start work that evening. When she walked into the kitchen Evan was there, leaning nonchalantly against the table talking to Alice.

"Ello, Maryann,' Alice said. 'D'you 'ave a nice afternoon?'

'Yes, ta,' Maryann said abruptly, walking past them both. 'I'll take the water upstairs,' she added.

One of her tasks in the evening was to carry up the heavy brass cans of hot water which the family used for their evening wash before dinner, draping them with a towel to keep the heat in before the water was poured into the porcelain basins. Polishing the cans was also one of her daily duties. Once they were down having their dinner, she and Janet, the third housemaid, had to scurry round tidying rooms, picking up dropped clothes, plumping cushions and, in winter, brushing round the grate and refuelling the fire. In the summer the workload was lighter.

She took Pamela Musson's water to her room and found her lolling on her bed. 'Oh my – is it that time already?' she said languorously. Next, Maryann went down and fetched Roland's water. Once the cans were full they were quite arduous to carry. She felt herself starting to sweat. She hoped Roland wouldn't be in his room as he always seemed to want to delay her these days. But when she knocked he called, 'Come!'

'Your water, sir.'

'Ah – it's the lovely Nelson again.' He'd clearly just come in from the garden and was still dressed in his working clothes. There was a glass of whiskey on the table and she could smell it in the air. 'Very civil of you, Nelson,' Roland said. 'Pour it in – usual place.' He held out his arm expansively.

Maryann obeyed, thinking, someone's been pouring something stronger down him by the look of him.

'I don't know why – I feel in a damn good mood today,' Roland said, flinging himself down on the bed.

'That'll be a bit of sunshine, sir.'

'Yes, perhaps you're right.'

She went to the door.

'Nelson?'

'Yes, sir?'

'I—' He opened his mouth, then closed it again, brow wrinkling. 'I was on the verge of saying something tremendously important just then, but I'm damned if I can think what it is. God – d'you think I'm really past it, Nelson? Is this the first sign?'

'I think it may be the whiskey,' Maryann suggested.

Roland Musson lay back and roared with laughter. ''Course it is! Course it is! Why didn't I think of that?'

She slid out of the door and downstairs. As she reached the bottom, Evan came out of the kitchen on his way to the dining room.

'Aha!' he hissed. ''Ere she is then. 'Ello, beautiful!' He came up close to her so that she had to press herself against the wall with Evan's face close to hers. She was immediately filled with panic. Every encounter like this brought back Norman Griffin, him forcing her against her will. Head back against the wall, trying to get as far away from Evan as possible, she managed to look into his eyes, praying her own would not betray her fear. He was smirking at her. This was just a game to him. He breathed into her face.

'I'm still waiting for that kiss.'

It went on and on. She avoided Evan at all possible times, but it got so that everywhere she went she seemed to see his round, leering face, even if he was nowhere near. She even dreamed about him, thinking he had come into her room at night and she woke sweating with fear. All her old ghosts came out to haunt her. The horror of being pursued, trapped by a man for his own dirty purposes, rose in her until she was beginning to live on her nerves and couldn't sleep at night.

Both of them were busy most of the time. Evan was under Mr Thomas's wing and Maryann had plenty of work. But eating meals together in the servants' dining room next to the kitchen became a torment. His eyes scarcely seemed to leave her face. Every time she looked up, there he was, ogling at her until she was put right off her food. Once she found herself on the point of bursting into tears and had to hurry out to compose herself. He was always looking for opportunities to get her on her own. Usually she could dodge him, but the time that was most difficult was Wednesday afternoon: the time they both had off together.

'Alice,' Maryann asked one day. 'D'you think we could change – you 'ave Wednesday off and I'd 'ave the Thursday instead?'

Alice frowned. 'Ooh no – I don't think so.' She had

no good reason for wanting Thursday as her day off. She just wasn't one to oblige other people. 'No – I'll keep my Thursday.'

Maryann got so she was too scared to walk into Banbury in case Evan followed her. Even staying round the house she felt very uneasy. In the summer months she liked to go into the garden. To one side, near the bottom end, was a walled rose garden, bright with blooms at this time of year, sheltered to sit in and deliciously scented by the rose petals. The servants were allowed to sit there during their leisure time, provided none of the family wished to use it.

So, one Wednesday in July, a baking hot afternoon, Maryann went out of the house, looking round her as she seemed to do all the time at present. The garden was warm and peaceful. She could see no sign even of Sid or Wally, and Roland only worked when it suited him. Taking her cardigan to sit on she walked down under the trees – a mature old oak, a young monkey-puzzle tree, maples with beautiful coloured leaves – and into the rose garden. Peering through the gap in the wall she saw no one was there, and immediately she was within the walls she relaxed.

The rose garden was square and immaculately main-tained, with beds all round the edge, a path running round inside them, and two large beds of roses in the middle. Between them was a long lozenge-shaped patch of grass. Though the two benches along the side received the most sun, Maryann spread her cardigan on the grass and lay down. She was tired and longed to lie in the sun, have a snooze and relax after all the hard work of the week.

It was very hot. Lying back with her eyes closed she felt immediately drowsy. Somewhere in the far distance she could hear a tapping noise, a mallet on a wooden post, which seemed to echo on the air, and closer by there were the sounds of birds and buzzing insects. The sun's rays beat down on her face and she began to fall asleep straight away.

It took her a few moments to notice that the sun had gone in and a shadow had fallen across her. She put a hand up to shield her face and open one eye, then sat up with a horrible start. Evan was standing, straddling the place where her feet had been, hands on his waist, staring down at her.

Maryann wrapped her arms tight round herself in protection.

'What're yer doing creeping up on me?' She tried to sound angry and commanding but her voice had gone squeaky.

Evan lolled down on the grass beside her, shuffling up close so that Maryann had to lean away from him.

'I saw you come down here. Don't seem to be able to find you on your own these days, Maryann.'

'What d'yer want?' As if she didn't know. She edged away from him.

'You're a funny one you, aren't you?' He sat back, leaning on his hands and looking at her. He sounded reasonable.

'Am I?'

He leaned towards her again and she felt his hot breath on her cheek. 'Look, there's not much time around 'ere, is there? Why can't you stop being so prim and proper and enjoy yourself while it's on offer?'

Maryann was all knotted up inside and her limbs had gone weak. She pulled her chin down on to her knees. 'I don't want it, Evan.'

'Come on—' He budged closer and started to play with her hair. 'You just need to get started.'

A moment later his other hand slid in behind her knees, feeling for her breast, and she felt his lips on her ear.

'Come on, girl – I've got something for you in 'ere—' He pressed his body hard against her, pinching her breast as he did so. 'Why don't we go up to your room and I'll show you? No one'll see.'

'Oh, get *off*!' Maryann launched herself to her feet, catching Evan off balance and leaving him sprawled on his side. 'Get yer dirty 'ands off of me. I don't want yer touching me.'

She saw a really ugly look come over Evan's face that chilled her. 'You're not normal, you, you know that? Not a proper girl at all.' His top lip curled in a snarl of disgust.

'Leave me alone—' She was growing distraught. 'Whatever I am, just leave me alone. I don't want yer anywhere near me. Go and make up to Alice – she'll 'ave yer like a shot. But if you come near me again I'll go to Mrs Letcombe and I'll get you sent away from 'ere.'

'She won't listen to you!'

It was Maryann's turn to stand over him. 'Oh, you're wrong there, Evan. I've been 'ere a hell of a sight longer than you have and Mrs Letcombe's been good to me. So you keep yer filthy hands to yourself from now on.'

She snatched up her cardigan, determined not to let Evan see that her legs and hands were trembling, and strode back to the house.

As the summer passed in the usual way, events in the wider world seemed very distant from Charnwood

House and its inhabitants. Mrs Lydia Musson sat every afternoon with a shawl round her shoulders and her feet up on a stool reading a newspaper, so the hunger marches from the north of England and the rise of Fascist groups constituted some of the drawing-room conversation. But they were not a highly political family. And Maryann was barely aware of the world outside Charnwood and its small domestic dramas.

Evan continued to smirk at her and make snide remarks, but he had not made any more attempts to touch her or kiss her and gradually Maryann could relax again a little. But the inner calm that she had possessed for the last years had deserted her. She felt restless and lonely. Ruth was to be married in a few weeks, but no one had said a word about who was to replace her as lady's maid. A year ago Maryann would have been on pins with anxiety about this, she had wanted the post so badly for so long. But now she began to find Charnwood confining. She loved her afternoon off and made sure every week now that she went out, into the town to the shops and for a wander along the cut to see the boats being loaded and unloaded. She liked the bustle, the smells and sounds, and the way the canal made her feel connected to things again, instead of buried alive at Charnwood. For that was how it was coming to feel.

The turmoil inside her that she had avoided for so long was returning to her like an old family chest being opened. Norman, Sal, Joel and her brothers. Round and round in her head. And her own future. Was there happiness waiting for her somewhere else? Would she be capable, after all, of love?

*

Ruth was married on a Saturday at the church in the nearest village and the staff were allowed leave to attend the service before coming back to Charnwood for a celebratory meal. Ruth, as ever, looked calm and serene; her long, dark hair was knotted beautifully and she wore a simple cream dress. Her husband, tall and blond, kept looking at her as if he couldn't believe his luck. The two of them left for Banbury in a horse and trap decorated with garlands of flowers, to begin their married life. Both the servants and those of the family who were at home came to wave them off. Maryann saw Roland shake hands rather awkwardly with Ruth. Pamela flung her arms round her tearfully and Mrs Musson slipped a little package into her hand. Maryann kissed her and wished her every happiness.

'I hope some of you'll come and see us,' Ruth said, kissing and hugging everyone. 'We're not far away, but I'll miss you.'

It had been announced that Ruth was to be replaced by a young woman called Eve. As Mrs Letcombe told them, Maryann experienced a pang of envy and disappointment, closely followed by relief and a surprising sense of freedom. If she'd been given the job, somehow in her mind it would have tied her to Charnwood, when in her heart she could feel the stirrings of change.

Thirty-One

That week, when Maryann walked into Banbury, she didn't even get as far as the shops. Slipping along the side streets, she found herself heading for the cut. More and more now, she found herself thinking about the past.

She went past the Strugglers Arms and down to the cut, walking on the towpath for a time. There were horse boats and motor boats on the go. She stood aside every now and then to let a horse go past pulling one of the boats. The smells of the water, the hot horse scent, the water splashing on the sides of the cut and the sunlight glaring on the ripples all filled her with a great sense of nostalgia and excitement. When she'd walked a way along, tied up on her side of the cut she saw a family boat called *Miss Dolly,* a rather scruffy vessel with chipped red and yellow paint. From the back on the steering platform peered three young children and Maryann heard a woman's voice shouting crossly to them from inside the cabin. Several others were playing along the bank and there was a string of threadbare clothes, stained grey with coal dust, strung on a washing line along the boat.

Maryann smiled at the children in the boat and said, ''Ello there, awright?'

''Ow do!' one of then chirruped back. The older ones were throwing stones into the cut with little plopping noises. She saw they were aiming at something floating in the middle of the channel. It was sodden and feathery: a dead pigeon turning gently in the water. She stood watching for a moment, then turned back, still smiling.

It was hard living on the cut, she remembered that very well. She knew how they rushed and competed for the loads, how the Number Ones were up against the company-owned boats, how it was work work work for long hours every day. Yet there was a freedom in it too. She stood looking north along the long, thin strand of water, following its course in her mind. On it went, out through those remote fields where you scarcely saw anyone about, only trees and birds and the sky overhead and the sun glinting in the brasses. What a life that was!

After a time she came towards the dry dock called Tooley's Yard where boats were taken in for repairs. She remembered Joel telling her about the place. Every so often the boats had to be taken there for recaulking. 'So they don't go letting no water in,' Joel had said. 'They seal up the seams and blacken 'er bottom to keep 'er watertight.'

She'd never been in the place and she thought she'd slip in and have a look. Just as she was about to go into the yard, two men came out, talking earnestly. One was a portly, middle-aged man with a red face looking out from under his trilby hat. The other, in contrast, was much taller, dark and strong-featured, with black curly hair and a large, slightly beaked nose. The tall dark man's face looked furrowed with some strong emotion, worry or anger. They passed her, talking earnestly together, and turned off away from the cut.

It was only as Maryann turned into the yard that she

realized she recognized the tall, dark man. She stopped for a moment. Where had she seen him before? If she could only think! She looked across Tooley's Yard and could just see the hull of a boat in the dry dock. Those lovely yellows and greens. And then it came to her, where she knew him from. A boat passing, Joel calling out as they slid beside each other, smiling, happy to see each other . . . the man with dark curly hair was Darius Bartholomew the younger: she was certain of it! Heart racing, she turned and ran in the direction they had gone, but they had disappeared. In any case, what could she say to Darius? He didn't know who she was, did he?

But she couldn't resist a look round the yard. It wasn't a large place – there was a brick shed and the dry dock, which would take one boat at a time, was a long, rather ramshackle building by the cut. She saw a couple of the Tooley's workers eyeing her up admiringly. She felt as if her skin was prickling. She knew she looked pretty in her blue dress, slim and shapely, black hair tucked under a little navy straw hat with a down turned brim. But she so disliked the feeling of being stared at, sized up in that way.

'Was you looking for someone?' One of the men approached her, looming over her.

'I – I just wanted to see—' She spoke timidly, but then found the courage to say, 'That man who just went out, was that Darius Bartholomew?'

The man took his cap off and rubbed sweat from his forehead with his arm. 'That 'un? Darius the younger. That's 'is boat, the *Esther Jane* down there. We'll be working on 'er next.'

'That's the *Esther Jane* – over there?' She couldn't keep the excitement out of her voice. Along from the dry dock she could just see the prow of another boat. 'Oh – can I go and see?'

The man shrugged. 'Don't see why not. Ain't no one aboard 'er though.'

He left her to walk over by herself, picking her way over the muddy ground. The boat was tied up by the bank, waiting for her turn in the dry dock, where she'd be strapped up while the water was drained out of the dock so that the men could work underneath her. It was with a feeling almost of disbelief that Maryann approached her. There she was, the *Esther Jane*! And on the roof, curled asleep, a little brown and white dog.

'Jep?' She could hardly believe it! He looked up on hearing his name and, jumping down on to the bank, came and licked her hand. 'Oh Jep – it *is* you!' He was a little grey round his sandy muzzle, but still full of life. 'Oh – is Ada back on board with you now then?' She was full of happiness and excitement. How could she have left them? How could she have stayed away so long? Still squatting, petting Jep, who was all awriggle with pleasure, she looked over the boat.

'Hello there,' she found herself saying softly. 'So 'ow're you then, old girl?'

While the boat made no reply, the state of her seemed to speak for itself. The last time Maryann had seen her she was in good repair, freshly painted and spick and span, brasses polished, her hold washed out as often as they could manage between loads. But now what she saw filled her with dismay. She looked a sad, worn-out old lady. The paint was cracking off her, it looked a long time since her brasses had had a rag anywhere near them and she was covered in grime all over. Chances were she was in the same state inside – dirty and heaving with bugs if they hadn't had time to stove her. In her dismay Maryann immediately felt like jumping aboard and setting to work but she knew she mustn't. It was clear the *Esther Jane* had fallen on hard times. Her mind was jumping with questions. What had happened? Why was Darius back running the boat? Where was his father and, above all, where was Joel?

With Jep following her she went back to look for the man who she found in the dry dock, working on another boat called the *Venus*.

'D'you know if Mr Bartholomew's coming back soon?'

The man looked at her over his shoulder. 'Oh, I should think so. That was one of Essy Barlow's men 'e went off with. Don't s'pose 'e'll stay with 'im long.'

'Samuel Barlow?' S.E. Barlow owned one of the carrying companies and she'd often seen his pairs of boats on the cut. ''E ain't selling the *Esther Jane*?'

'Seems like 'e might be,' the man said. ''E could do worse. Times're tough, everyone chasing about for not enough loads. If 'e sold out to Barlow 'e wouldn't 'ave to chase the loads 'imself, would 'e?'

Maryann was appalled. She knew how hard old Darius and Joel had always worked to stay independent, to be Number Ones like they'd always been, not tied to a boss, a company. How would Joel feel about this?

'Can I wait till Mr Bartholomew gets back? I'd like to speak to 'im.'

'Stay as long as you like.' The man winked at her. 'Don't see anyone complaining, do you? So long as you don't get under anyone's feet.'

She went over to the side of the yard. From somewhere near by she could hear the sounds of a forge: a horse being shod. She hoped Darius Bartholomew wasn't going to be too long. In a couple of hours she would need to set off for Charnwood House, but the way she felt just then she would have waited for ever and damn everything else. Having seen the *Esther Jane* it was almost as if the past six years had not existed. She was back on the cut with the boat and the people she loved and she was desperate to know what had befallen them. Suddenly it was all that seemed to matter.

Almost an hour later Darius Bartholomew came back. She saw him the second he strode, grim-faced, into the yard. He was a large, striking presence. He looked puzzled and not especially pleased to see someone standing by his boat.

'Mr Bartholomew?' she said, even before he reached her.

She found him rather forbidding, in the same way she had often found his father. Those strong, chiselled features seemed to scowl down at her.

'My name's Maryann Nelson. I—' How did she explain? 'A few years back I lived on your boat – with yer dad and Joel – and Jep here – until Ada went off. . . .'

For a moment he stared blankly at her, then his face softened a fraction. 'Did you? I remember they 'ad a lass on board for a bit.'

He seemed about to turn away, sinking back into his own thoughts again, so Maryann asked quickly, 'Only – I wanted to ask after everyone. Your father and Ada – and Joel.'

Darius Bartholomew climbed over into the *Esther Jane* and stood on the steering platform looking back at her. He shook his head. 'You won't be seeing our Ada no more. She were drownded four year ago, God rest 'er.'

'Ada?' Maryann gaped at him. 'Oh no ... No!' Not cheeky, vivacious Ada.

'They was working the Grand Union – right down to the Thames. It's all wider and faster there, with currents and that. Our Ada was knocked overboard – got swept away. Took 'em days before they found 'er.' Seeing the tears in Maryann's eyes he looked down with a sigh. 'She were a good'un.'

Maryann swallowed, wiping her eyes. 'And your father?' She could hardly bear to ask about Joel.

'I left 'im down at h'Oxford with 'is sister what lives on the bank. What with Joel and the boat in this state I said I'd bring 'er up 'ere one 'anded. He ent a young man. He's finding the life harder and harder and 'e's been poorly.'

'And Joel?' she breathed.

Darius started shaking his head in that grim fashion again and Maryann felt as if a great pressure was bearing down on her chest. Not him as well. He couldn't be drownded as well, oh please God, no!

'Bad,' Darius said. He seemed almost glad to have someone to whom he could pour out all his troubles. 'He's took real sick. He's been heading for it since the winter, what with 'is chest, but this time it went from bad to worse. I had to get him took away to the 'orspital at Birnigum even though 'e begged me not to leave 'im on the bank. But he was that burning up with fever I couldn't look after 'im and see to the boat and the loads ... And with fighting for regler loads and back loads—' He wiped one of his huge, dark hands over his face. 'It looks as if we're giving in – going to Essy Barlow. S'the only way now.'

'Oh dear.' Maryann wiped her eyes again. 'I'm ever so sorry you've had such troubles, Mr Bartholomew.

I truly am. I know how Joel and your father felt about selling up.'

'Times move on – what with the roads taking over ... Some of 'em're acting like they've never heard of the cut these days. I don't know what can be done, that I don't.' He pushed open the cabin door. 'I'm going to get the stove going and brew up. You stopping for some tea?'

'Yes please.' She was desperate to know more about Joel. She had to know how he was, where he was ...

'Come aboard – that's if you don't mind?' He eyed her pretty frock. 'It ain't spick and span like it oughta be.'

Stepping into the *Esther Jane* again after all this time was a wonderful feeling and despite her anxiety, Mary-ann found herself smiling as the memories poured back. She sat by the tiny table, looking round, itching to get to work and clean the place up: the plates and copper kettle and Esther's brown and white teapot. The crochet work was filthy, the whole cabin dull and dirty compared with how it had been before when either she or Ada had kept it nice. She watched Darius stoking the range and suddenly found herself aching for it to be Joel here beside her so that she could see him again. She remembered her younger self, confused and frightened, lying alone at night in this cosy cabin, this place of refuge as it had been.

'Where have they taken Joel?' she asked as the kettle was heating.

'I told you – to the 'orspital up Birnigum.'

'Yes, but which one? D'you know?'

Darius looked round at her, stooped over, scraping old leaves out of the teapot. 'I never 'ad the chance to see 'im. Our father weren't well neither and what with chasing the loads I don't know 'ow Joel is even. 'E'll not like being on the bank for long. That's if 'e even . . .' He trailed off, but she knew he was going to say 'lives'. 'Never been right really, 'e ent – not since that war.'

Every moment she sat there, she was filling more and more with an urgent determination. Joel was sick, maybe dying, and she had to see him. He'd been so good to her and she'd repaid him unkindly. Now it was her chance to do something for him. She didn't need to ask if there was anyone else in Joel's life. No one had been mentioned and Joel would only have married someone who could live on the cut, who would be his 'mate' aboard the *Esther Jane*. If there was any such woman in his life, where was she?

'Is 'e all alone there?' she asked. 'No one who can visit?'

Darius shook his head, ashamed. 'There ain't no one.'

'Can't you think which 'ospital it *might* be? Daint they say when they took him?'

Darius's brow wrinkled. 'I think it might be the one near the chocolate fact'ry.'

'The chocolate factory? Bournville. Would it be the Infirmary at Selly Oak?'

'Might be,' he said hopelessly. 'Ain't no good me knowing when I can't 'ope to get there, is there?'

'But I could go.'

Darius stopped in the middle of handing her her cup of tea. 'You?'

She reached out and took the cup and the absolute resolve in her face was plain to see. 'Yes. Me.'

Thirty-Two

'I'm sorry, Mrs Letcombe, but I really do 'ave to go – it's someone in my family.' How else could she describe Joel? 'He's very ill, maybe dying.'

'But when will you be coming back?'

'I don't know. I'm ever so sorry.'

And she was sorry. Almost heartbroken. Throughout the train journey to Birmingham the tears kept rising up in her eyes. She could go back, Mrs Letcombe said. They'd give her a week or two. But she knew that she wouldn't be returning, that everything had changed and that she could only look forward. Deep in her heart she had known that one day she would have to go back to Birmingham and face her family and now that day had arrived. And it was Joel who had brought her there. He seemed closer to her now than he had in all the years she had been away. The thought of him, and her worry about him and his weak lungs, was with her all the time. Now she knew she had to see him she was in a desperate hurry to get there. Darius had said he would try and get to Birmingham when the *Esther Jane* was ready. But she had to get there more quickly. Throughout the journey she wanted to command the train to go faster, faster!

She looked out as it chugged slowly into Birmingham. It was a hot but overcast day and a grey pall hung over the city: all the smoke from the factory chimneys and no breeze to blow it away. A blackness lay over everything and along the tracks the buildings seemed to be closing in, the workshops and warehouses, with what windows they had poky and filthy, their walls covered in soot and grime. The sight of it shocked her. What a grim, stifling place it looked! She had been away so long, had become used to the space and clean air of the country, the warm-coloured stone of the houses, and felt almost panic-stricken at the thought of being enclosed behind these dark, cramping walls again. But down there, under it all, she told herself, was the cut, slipping through and between and under. Another world, sealed off from the rest of the city, and the thought gave her hope and a way out, a sense of freedom.

When the train lurched to a standstill her pulse began to race even harder. This was really it now. She was back. People were jostling to get out of the train and she pulled her little case down from the luggage rack.

'Time to face the music,' she thought. 'But not before I've seen Joel.'

Changing platforms, she waited for a local train to Selly Oak, and it wasn't long before she was stepping out of the station. It was dinner time, a bit early to go and visit, so she went along the Bristol Road to find a place to sit and have a cup of tea and a sandwich and try to steady her nerves. She found a workmen's café and sat listening to the voices round her, remembering how much Diana Musson had laughed when she had first heard her talk at Charnwood. That place which had at first felt so strange and foreign had become a second home to her. It felt very odd to be back in this big, clanging, rackety city. Once again the thought of Charnwood brought tears to her eyes.

She had said her goodbyes the evening before. It was no hardship to part with Evan, but even the crustier characters like Sid and Wally and Cook had shown surprising affection for her. Cook had flung her arms round her and gone all dewy round the eyes. Parting with Mrs Letcombe had been very emotional even though the housekeeper herself was rather unconcerned, because she was sure Maryann would soon come running back, and kept saying, 'There there, m'dear, I don't know what you're crying about.' Even saying goodbye to Alice had brought tears to her eyes: though she'd never had very warm feelings towards her, they had spent a lot of time working together.

To her surprise, though, it had been Roland Musson who had aroused the most emotion in her. When she went up last night to prepare his room during dinner he had come in as she was turning down the bed for him.

'Oh—' he said, taken aback. 'I forgot you'd er, be ... Just popped up to er ...' She saw him go to his decanter of whiskey, pour himself a generous couple of fingers and gulp them down. He turned to her, shame-faced, still holding the glass. 'Ah – that's better. Mother doesn't like to see me – you know. Says I drink too much.'

'Er—' Maryann delayed him, nervously. 'As you're 'ere, sir, I'd just like to say, I'll be leaving the 'ouse first thing in the morning. I don't know if I'll be coming back.'

Roland just stood staring at her.

Maryann blushed. 'I'm sorry, sir ... I know it don't matter to you one way or another who makes your bed and that, but I just thought it'd be polite to say goodbye.'

'But, Nelson – you're not really *going*, are you? You don't mean it?'

'I 'ave to, sir.'

'This is appalling news. I mean, you can't! You're just *always* here – in fact you're the one really cheering person about the place. I rely on you, Nelson!'

She looked at the carpet, not knowing what to say.

'Well – damn it. I can't just shake your hand, not after all you've done for me over the years. Come here, girl.'

And he wrapped his arms round her in a rather clumsy but, she could tell, heartfelt embrace, and for a moment she allowed her arms to rest round him as well. She felt him kiss the top of her head.

'You're a damn fine girl, Nelson,' he said thickly. 'Damned fine.'

'Thank you, sir. And good luck to yer.'

When he'd left the room she kneeled down for a few minutes by the bed and wept silently with her hands over her face. Sitting thinking of it now, a lump rose in her throat.

Pulling her thoughts back to the present, she wiped her eyes and stood up to pay for her tea. The café proprietor stared at her curiously but she was too preoccupied to notice. Pressing her hat down she went out into the street. It was threatening to rain and she walked on quickly, carrying her case, towards the hospital.

When she enquired inside, she was told she was too early and would have to wait another half-hour. So she went out and strolled up and down Raddlebarn Road feeling more and more nervous.

What was Joel going to think of her turning up all of a sudden? Would he even remember who she was?

She felt ashamed when she thought of him, and worried. How ill was he? Was Darius exaggerating when he said he didn't know if Joel would come through? He must be seriously ill if they'd got him to move away from the cut and his beloved boat, especially at such a worrying time. Maryann's thoughts spun round and round. She turned at the bottom of the road again. It must be nearly time for them to let her in. Oh God, her heart was beating so hard! She pressed her hand over it. It felt as if all her future depended on the next half-hour. All her feelings, wounded and battered as they had been, were now reaching out to Joel with great longing. How would she find him, and what would his reaction be to seeing her again?

She approached the door of the ward with great timidity, her stomach clenching uneasily. Hospitals frightened her. They had ever since her dad had been taken away to one and never come home. The nurses in their stiff uniforms, their starchy white veils and starchy manner also intimidated her and there were those smells: bodily stenches, disinfectant.

An older nurse, with a cross face and muscly arms and legs, walked briskly up to her. 'Yes? Who is it you've come to see?'

Maryann cleared her throat. 'A Mr Joel Bartholomew . . . please.'

'Bartholomew? Chest case. Oh no – I don't think so.'

'P-Pardon?'

'No visitors. Too ill to see anyone. And you're not a relative, I assume?'

'I'm . . . no, a friend, but . . .'

'Relatives only, I'm afraid.' The woman started to turn away.

'But they can't come – any of them!' Maryann burst into tears in vexation. 'They all work on the cut and they can't leave the boat. His dad's poorly too and his brother's stuck in Banbury and there ain't anyone else and I *know* he'd want to see someone. *Please* let me – just for a few minutes. I've come all the way from Banbury myself today!'

The woman stood, considering. Maryann was afraid she'd be snooty and spiteful because she knew Joel was off the cut. But she said, reluctantly, 'Very well. A couple of minutes. But he is very ill. And don't go cluttering up the ward with *that*. Leave it with me.' She took Maryann's case and walked off with it, saying over her shoulder, 'He's just down on the right.'

She found him halfway down, a physical jolt of shock going through her when she first saw him and took in that it was him. If it had not been for his blaze of hair against the pillow she would not have recognized him. For the big, burly Joel she had known was now much thinner, his cheekbones pushing out the flesh of his face, and they had shaved off his beard. His frame, as he lay prone under the sheet, was shrunken and weak and his eyes were closed. She could see that each breath he took was a painful struggle to him.

Her instinct was to stand there for a long time staring at him, trying to take in his changed state, but she was afraid the bossy nurse would come back, and she slipped alongside the bed and sat on the chair, trying to shrink down and make herself as invisible as possible. She could feel the man in the bed opposite staring at her.

Close up, she could see a film of perspiration on Joel's face and hear the rasp of his lungs. His face wore a frown, as if of pain and concentration. Watching him she felt as if the years since she had last seen him were very short, like a dream which takes only moments yet in which you can experience half a lifetime. She felt as if her heart would melt with sorrow and tenderness. She sat torn between fear of disturbing him and the unbearable thought that she might be ordered to leave before he knew she was there. Slowly, trembling, she reached out her hand and laid it over his.

'Joel?'

For a moment she thought he had not heard, but then his head moved a fraction and she saw him struggle to open his eyes, as if even the effort to prise his lids apart was enormous. He looked round, eyes unfocused for a moment, then slowly rolled his head, sensing someone next to him. She felt his eyes on her.

'Joel,' she whispered, leaning towards him, finding there were tears streaming down her face. 'It's me – Maryann. I saw Darius and he told me you was here and how poorly you are.'

There was a moment while he took her in, staring at her as if he couldn't make sense of her presence and she watched his reaction fearfully. He swallowed, frowned slightly. His hand lifted, then laid over hers.

'You came . . . My little . . . nipper . . .'

This made her all the more emotional. 'Oh Joel,' she sobbed. 'It's so lovely to see you. I'm so sorry, Joel – I've wanted to say to you for ever so long that I'm sorry for running off the way I did when yer'd been so good to me. I was in a state. So many terrible things'd happened and I daint know what I was doing and I know you daint mean anything bad. You were the one person I could always go to and I can't stand to see yer looking so poorly like this.' She took his hand and kissed it again and again. She could hear his breathing becoming more agitated and she looked anxiously into his face. There were tears running down into his hair and she wiped them gently away with her fingers, knowing how unmanly it must seem to him to weep. He was trying to speak and she leaned close, barely able to hear his whisper.

'I did wrong—' He had to rest between the words to gather enough breath. 'You was ... only a young 'un ...' He closed his eyes as if condemning himself. 'My fault.' The final words cost him a huge effort. 'You seemed older ... I felt for you. It weren't ... just lust ... Truly ...'

'You were lovely, Joel – you were. I know that now and I'm sorry. Only I *was* young and I was in a mess ... I've grown up a bit since then. I've thought about you – when I let myself. And I missed you ever such a lot.'

He gave a nod which seemed to encompass and elaborate everything she'd said, and he clutched her hand.

'I'll be here now – till you get better.'

Joel laid his spare hand over his chest, gasping for breath. 'I knew they'd get ... me ... in the end ...'

She knew he meant his damaged lungs and a chill went through her.

'Don't say that, Joel! You're in your thirties – that's not old! You just feel it because yer sick at the moment. You can get better – you can! I'm going to come and see yer every day. Please don't give up – say you won't give up, you'll try for me, won't you!'

Slowly he brought his other hand across and cradled her hand in both of his.

'Oh Joel—' She leaned forward and kissed his cheek, barely knowing what she was saying. 'I love you *so*

much.' She was laughing and crying together, but
quietened herself to hear the words he whispered, still
clasping her hand.

'My little . . . love, you . . . came back.'

Thirty-Three

When the tram reached Ladywood, Maryann stepped down a couple of stops early so that she could walk along Monument Road and try to get used to being back. Glancing down Waterworks Road she looked for Perrott's Folly, the old brick tower which loomed over the houses, and she passed some of the old familiar shops, St John's Church, the Dispensary, all looking the same as when she left and it gave her a strange feeling. She prepared herself for the fact that while buildings change little in six years, people do, and that she might even walk past one of her own brothers without recognizing him.

Turning down Anderson Street she was filled with a dread so strong it forced her to stop and stand nervously near the corner, trying to find the courage to go on. Again, the place looked much the same. School was out and there were kids playing on the pavement, skimming marbles along the blue bricks as they always had. She might have run along the road with Norman Griffin's keys in her hand only weeks ago. For a moment she could smell the choking smoke from the fire in her nostrils. She was going to have to see *him* again. However much she knew she was now a grown woman, that she could leave at any time, that he had no power to do anything to her, she could only feel herself as a child in relation to him. A powerless child who he could use for his own cruel, disgusting appetites as he had used her sister and then destroyed her. The old anger in her rose up again until she was trembling with it.

Oh I can't, she thought. I can't go back there. I ain't got the strength. She put her case down and stood facing the wall of a house, composing herself, clenching her teeth, trying to get her shaking under control. I will not, she told herself, let him do this to me. I *won't*. Furiously she snatched up the case and marched along the road. But she still couldn't go straight to the house and walk in. She had to know how things stood.

The Martins' huckster's shop still looked just the same, the windows plastered in labels: Oxo, Cadbury's, Woodbines, the same little 'ting' of the bell as she pushed the door open. The smells hit her: soap, camphor, rubber, cough candy. For a second she saw Tony in her mind's eye as she remembered him, standing on tiptoe to peer over the counter.

'Penn'orth of rocks yer got there, bab?' Mrs Martin would say.

Maryann imagined Tony's wide-eyed nod.

Mrs Martin, her hair now white instead of metal grey, came through from the back, wiping her hands on her apron.

'Can I 'elp yer?'

''Er – Mrs Martin, it's me – Maryann Nelson.'

The woman stared at her, bewildered. 'Who?'

'Maryann – Flo Griffin's daughter. Tony and Billy's sister.'

Mrs Martin's mouth sagged open. '*No!*' she exclaimed eventually. 'Little Maryann? Ooh – I can see now, them blue eyes. Ooh my word!'

'I've been working down south and I've come back

for a visit, only I just wondered – you know, 'ow things are . . .' She jerked her head over in the direction of the house.

'Oh no – you won't find 'em over there. Daint yer know?' Her brow furrowed at Maryann's extraordinary ignorance of her own family. 'Your mother went to live back over in Sheepcote Lane when 'e left 'er. Couldn't pay the rent no more, could 'er? In a right state 'er was. But that were a good while back – five year or more. We don't see 'er round 'ere no more. Daint you know, bab?'

Maryann shook her head, her pulse racing. 'You mean Mr Griffin ain't living with them no more?'

'Ooh no – 'e took off after 'is premises went up. There was a fire, like. Gutted the 'ole damn place. You must remember that, daint yer? They've only just got it put back up now and Steven's the drapers're setting up. But your mother, Flo – well 'er version of events was 'e was never the same again after it and 'e took off and left 'er. Oh, Flo was in a right state I can tell yer.'

Maryann could tell from the way Mrs Martin was squinting at her with her head a bit to one side that any moment she was going to start interrogating her. She backed away towards the door, almost falling over a pile of galvanized buckets.

'So you say Mom's gone to Sheepcote Lane?'

'Sheepcote. Ar, that's it, bab.'

Maryann pulled the door open again. *Ting!*

'You're a right grown-up wench now, ain't yer?'

Maryann smiled. 'Ta very much, Mrs Martin.'

She passed the old house, peering closely at it. There were pale lilac curtains inside the lower window, and a black dog was lying asleep beside the step. She could sense it had all changed, would look very different inside from how she remembered, yet the thought of walking in through the front door made her flesh creep. Too many memories. Too many ghosts of the tormented little girls she and Sal had been in that house. She held on to the thought of Joel, to the love she had seen in his eyes which made her strong. Knowing she had Joel again she could face anything. Much better to keep walking and see what the present held than to linger here dwelling on the past.

The only way she could think of finding her mom in Sheepcote Lane was to ask, yard by yard, even house by house down the poor end. Poverty would have driven her to a smaller house – what fierce resentment that must've bred in her! But maybe, when Norman left her, she had been able to see him as he really was: a conman who had married her for his own vile motives: for the fact that she had two young daughters and would look after him in comfort in exchange for his money. God knows, she thought, he wasn't *rich* – not really. It was just that Mom was desperate. Maybe at last she'd be able to face the truth.

She did not need to look far. In the second back court she went into she was confronted by the sight of a woman, her back to Maryann. Her legs were thin and stringy, and her hair which had once been thick and blonde was now faded to grey, twisted and pinned up savagely behind her head. She was reaching up to unpeg a sheet from a crowded line of washing which billowed in the damp air. Maryann knew her immediately. She felt a surge of pity. Flo's bitterness and exhaustion was clear in every movement she made. Even during the war she had been quite a voluptuous woman, but now she was very thin. She kept reaching up to the line, unpegging and yanking sheets, bloomers, an apron down from it, shaking them angrily when the breeze tried to force them the wrong way. Maryann hadn't the courage to go to her in the yard. She hovered in the entry until Flo had picked up her enormous basket of washing and struggled into the end house.

It was about five o'clock. Her mom'd be cooking soon. Best go over there and get it over with. She was just stepping out across the narrow yard when two boys ran out laughing from another house. They were both about ten years old, one dark, one blond. Seeing the fairer of the two, Maryann stopped. Something about him, the way he moved, his colouring told her immediately that this was Billy. He and the other boy were tearing up and down the yard chasing one another and laughing. They saw her looking and took no notice. Both of them were in shorts cut down from longer trousers and grubby shirts hanging loose at the back. As they came closer, Maryann called, 'Billy?'

He slowed, peering at her, and came closer. His face was grubby and red from running and she saw he had a trail of freckles across his nose. From the big blue eyes, the way he held his head, she knew that he was her brother.

'Billy – it's me, Maryann. I'm your big sister.' Tears came as she said it. All those years of his life she'd missed. A little, soft thing he'd been when she left, who'd sit on her lap for a love and let her bath him. Now he was a long, skinny lad, almost grown up!

'Are yer?' She could see him searching his memory. Surely he'd been old enough when she left for him to remember her? But then she'd changed too. A sad look came over his face for a second, and she thought he was going to say something else. But then he seemed to remember the other boy with him and he wasn't going to go all soft in front of him. 'Our mom's indoors,' he said with a toss of his head. 'See yer.' And the two of them careered off again.

Gripping the handle of her case, Maryann walked along the yard. If it had been a house she'd ever lived in herself, she'd have just walked in but here she felt she must knock. She saw one of the front panes was broken and covered with cardboard, and the green paint on the door was flaking and dirty. She rapped it with her knuckles.

'Oo is it?' Even her mother's voice sounded different, thinner, somehow cracked.

Maryann pushed the door open. It was gloomy inside and it took a few seconds for her eyes to adjust. She immediately recognized the table and chairs which stood to one side of the little room as the ones they had had in the last house, bought by Norman Griffin after they left Garrett Street. Her mother was standing between the table and the range, gutting herrings which were stinking the place out. She had looked up without stopping what she was doing until she saw Maryann. Flo straightened up, holding out blood-smeared hands in front of her.

''Ello, Mom.'

The expression on Flo's face, already harsh and unsmiling, grew more taut. Maryann was shocked by just how much she had changed, as if in six years she had fallen into old age. Her face was pallid, almost yellow, the skin had lost its elasticity so that it sagged over her cheekbones. She looked hard and shrewish.

'Is that you, Maryann?'

Maryann nodded. 'I've been in service. Not in Brum.' Even now she couldn't bring herself to give away where she'd been.

Flo became suddenly aware of the mess her hands were in and picked up a damp rag from the table to wipe them. There was an ominous silence as she did it and Maryann could tell she was gathering her thoughts.

'Where's Mr Griffin?'

Flo slapped the rag back down on the table before walking round and advancing on Maryann, staring at her with her eyes full of loathing.

'Where's Mr Griffin?' she mimicked. For a few seconds she couldn't seem to find any more words. Maryann shrank back as her mother came right up close.

'Mom! What're yer doing!'

'You did it, daint yer? You set that fire at Griffin's before yer buggered off. Norman knew it was you, you evil little bitch. You destroyed my life, d'yer know that? D'you even care what yer did? You ought to be banged up in Winson Green, that's where. You ruined everything we 'ad. He walked out and left and I 'ad nowt and two boys to bring up. I've been slaving in factories ever since, thanks to you. And d'you know why 'e left? 'Cause 'e said 'e weren't staying in a family of bloody lunatics who'd taken away his livelihood. And it was all your fault, Maryann.' The words rained down, sharp and hateful. 'You ruined your own family – so 'ow d'you feel about that, eh?'

Maryann thought Flo was going to go for her throat with her fishy hands and she twisted away from her and backed across the room. She had such strong emotion rising in her she felt she might burst. The injustice of everything her mother thought and felt, the way she'd never listen or see the truth – never had. She'd never taken their side, hers and Sal's. She was beyond tears: her feelings were too raw and harsh.

'You're a sad, blind woman, ain't yer, Mother?' She stood clutching the back of one of the chairs as if to contain the violence that raged inside her. Her voice was low and trembling with emotion. 'Yes – I set fire to Norman Griffin's offices and I 'oped they'd burn to the ground so there was nothing left for him. But that ain't why he left you and you know it. 'E left because *we*'d gone, me and Sal, and there was nothing left for him that he wanted. 'Cause 'e didn't like grown-up women, did he? He liked little girls he could bully and do his dirty business with and turn them into ... rag dolls, with no feelings or life left of their own.' She in turn advanced on her mother. 'D'yer know what it was he did to our Sal so she lost 'er mind and he'd've done to me too if 'e'd 'ad the chance? D'yer want to know what I found in the cellar of those offices the night I went down there? Do yer?' She was shouting at the top of her voice, distraught.

'No, *no*, shut up, you lying, wicked girl...' Flo laid her arm across her face as if to protect herself.

'No – you don't want to hear that anything might be *your* fault, *your* greed, putting money and dresses and your comfort over and above your children.' Now she'd begun to open the floodgates she couldn't stop. She was growing hysterical. 'You don't want to hear about Norman, the oh-so respectable Mr Griffin chaining our Sal to a chair and doing God knows what to 'er and most likely promising to leave her down there with a corpse for company all night. Because that's something that wouldn't be my fault or Sal's, would it? You'd have to face that you didn't see and you wouldn't see because all you could think of was saving your own skin. You daint see her stabbing at her own arms with a knife because she couldn't live with herself. And it weren't you that found her with her wrists slit open, was it? You never even went to look at her after ... Was the mess too much for you, Mother? Too real for you that, was it?'

She couldn't go on. She bent over the chair with her hands over her face as sobs choked her, the long-buried grief welling up from deep inside her. After a few moments she glanced up to see her mother looking at her with a terrible, twisted expression on her face.

'Get out of my 'ouse.' Her voice lashed across the room. 'You've done enough damage to us. We've lived without yer all these years. We don't need you back 'ere now. Tek yerself and yer poison away from 'ere. I don't want yer coming 'ere again.'

Maryann wiped her eyes, chilled by the hateful finality of her mother's words. 'I want to see my brothers.'

'You ain't seeing no one. Get out!' Flo shouted. 'Get out now and don't ever come back. Never!'

Thirty-Four

Maryann walked back out of the yard in Sheepcote Lane so blinded by tears that she could barely see where she was going. Her mother's rejection of her was so total, so final it had cut her to the bone. They had never been close as mother and daughter but she had hoped that somehow, after all that had happened and with Norman Griffin gone, there could have been a reconcilation. Now she had lost that hope for ever.

If only Nanny Firkin was still 'ere, Maryann thought. I could've gone to her – she was proper family. She'd've been glad to see me and it would've felt like home. The thought of this made her cry even more.

As it was, the only person she could hope to turn to now was Nance. She found her feet turning almost automatically to the familiar territory of Garrett Street. Somehow she didn't doubt that the Blacks would be living in the same place. Before she went into the yard she tried to compose herself and dried her eyes. She was pleased at the thought of seeing them and even smiled slightly as a familiar sight met her eyes in the old yard: Blackie Black's 'fuckin' barrer' leaning as drunkenly as she had frequently seen its owner do, against the wall of the brewhouse.

The Blacks' door was open and Maryann peeped her head round. The family was at the table having tea.

Cathleen's squiffy eyes, Blackie's bloodshot ones and those of the six children round the table all peered at her.

'Oo're yer looking for, wench?' Cathleen said. – 'Eh, 'ang on a minute, I know you, don't I? It's . . . It can't be Maryann?' She pushed back her chair and stood up.

'It is,' Maryann said shyly.

''Eh, Blackie, it's little Maryann, our Nance's pal!' Blackie squinted at her but there was a vacant look in his eyes. He made a sound between a grunt and a whine.

'Come on in, bab!' Cathleen came and stood gazing at her. 'Don't mind Blackie – 'e ain't none too well these days. Well – look at you! Our Nance'll be ever so pleased to see yer. You ain't been round to see 'er, 'ave you?'

'No – I've only just got 'ere.' Maryann put her case down gratefully, trying to keep the tears from welling up yet again. It meant so much to be greeted kindly by people who were pleased to see her.

''Ere – 'ave a cuppa tea – it's just brewed. You seen yer mom?'

Maryann nodded.

'Well – what'd 'er say?' Cathleen was stirring the teapot vigorously.

'She daint offer me a cuppa tea, I'll tell yer that much.'

'Ooh dear – like that, was it?'

Maryann nodded, conscious that the family were all staring at her. Good heavens, – that oldest one was Perce – he was eighteen now! And young Horace who'd still been sucking his thumb and peeing his pants was a lad of nine now! There was Lizzie who'd only been a babby. And who was that? There was another little girl sitting at the table between William and George, who were now also a good deal more grown up.

'You 'ad another daughter then?' Maryann smiled at the child.

'Ar – that's our Mary,' Cathleen said. 'She were the last. Four year ago that were. I 'ad to 'ave all my – you know – taken away after. It were a blessing really, God forgive me, but I've 'ad my ten and that were enough for anyone.' She watched anxiously as Blackie pulled himself up from the table and lurched over to his old chair with the fag burns and settled into it with a loud groan. She leaned forward shaking her head and whispered, ''E ain't 'imself.'

'What's up?' Maryann whispered back.

'Oh, they don't really know. They think 'e might 'ave 'ad a bit of a turn. 'E can 'ardly speak. Not that 'e was a great talker before. I dunno.' She sighed, looking across at him worriedly. Maryann felt sorry for her, poor, worn-out woman. Cathleen and Blackie had both aged considerably.

'Any'ow, enough of our problems – where've yer been, Maryann?'

She told them a bit about Charnwood, then asked after the rest of the family.

'Where's Nance – and Charlie?'

'Oh, our Charlie's been wed a good while now – three kiddies they've got. All girls, would yer believe it! Alf and Jimmy've got one apiece. Alf was wed two year ago and Jimmy last year. They're all good wenches they've found themselves, all Catholics 'cept Jimmy's wife Lena, but she ain't no trouble.

'And our Nance married Mick just a few months

back – in the spring. She 'ad 'er nuptial mass in April. It were lovely, weren't it?'

'Me and Mary was bridesmaids,' Lizzie chipped in.

She reminded Maryann a little bit of Nancy when she was younger, with her head of black curls, although she had a softer, more feminine look about her.

'Nance'd've asked yer to the wedding only she daint know where yer were,' Cathleen said. ''Er missed yer, yer know, after yer went.'

'I know,' Maryann said. 'I missed 'er too. But I 'ad to get away.'

Cathleen nodded sympathetically.

'Where's Nance living? And what's 'er name now she's married?'

'Oh, Mrs Mallone. Mick Mallone's 'er 'usband. They only live over the back in Alexander Street. Yer can pop round and see 'er when yer've 'ad yer tea.'

'Any babbies on the way yet?' Maryann said smiling.

Cathleen shook her head. 'No – but they've only been wed a few month. It'll give 'er time to settle.' But Maryann thought she seemed rather lacking in warmth on the subject of Nance's marriage, however nice the wedding had been. She glanced at Blackie and saw that he appeared to have fallen asleep, his head lolling down on his chest.

''Ere – if you're going round to see our Nance, take the girls with yer and get 'em out of my hair for a bit, will yer? They like going round there.'

Nance was living in a front house which opened on to the street. The door was open and the two girls ran straight in.

'We've got Maryann!' she heard Lizzie shouting excitedly.

Immediately, as Maryann reached the house, Nance's face appeared at the open door, looking out with a combination of wariness and disbelief. For a second Maryann was shocked by Nance's thinness and the dull sullenness of her expression under her mop of black curls, until she registered that it really was Maryann and burst into delighted laughter.

'Oh my God – well I never! It really is – Maryann!'

Laughing and tearful at the same time, the two of them flung their arms round each other.

'Why didn't yer tell me where you was living?' Nance reproached her. 'I wouldn't've let on to anyone and I couldn't drop yer a line back or invite yer to the wedding or nothing! 'Ere – come in. It ain't much but we've got it to ourselves.' She drew Maryann inside and shut the door. 'Let me get that kettle on – or d'yer want a nip of summat stronger, eh?'

'No – tea'd be nice, Nance.'

The two little girls seemed to have disappeared upstairs. 'I've got a couple of old dollies and a few bit of clothes up there for when they come round,' Nance said. She rested the kettle on the hob, then stood back to look at Maryann.

'You ain't changed – not really. You look ever so well.'

Maryann smiled. Hadn't changed? How could Nance say that? She felt like a different person. And Nance looked different, too, in a middle-aged woman's dress and her apron. She was beginning to look just like her mom!

'I'm awright,' she said. 'Got lots to tell yer. But what about you, Nance. Look at you – a married woman!

What's your 'usband like?' She had noticed uneasily the cut healing on Nance's left cheekbone, a yellowed bruise round it. Nance seemed to feel her looking and put her hand to her cheek.

'I could tell yer everything's perfect, Maryann. Wedded bliss and that. But I've never lied to yer. 'E's a boozer like me dad only not so soft-hearted. 'E's down the pub now. 'E ain't too bad when 'e's sober but with a skinful inside 'im 'e gets all maudlin and sorry for 'isself.'

'Why's 'e sorry for 'imself?' Maryann asked.

'Oh Christ alone knows,' Nance said impatiently. ''E's one of them 'as a few and 'e 'as to wallow. 'E ain't got me expecting yet – 'e 'as a wallow about that.'

'But yer've only been wed, what a few months?'

'Three months – nearly four.'

'Well then.'

Nance shrugged. 'To tell yer the truth I'm bloody glad of it. I only married 'im to get out of 'ome. There's kids and mess and noise everywhere and now our dad's bad 'e's sat there like a dummy even when 'e ain't been on the bottle. I thought, I've got to get out of 'ere or I'm going straight round the bend. And Mick came along and 'e was willing and a Catholic so I married 'im and we kept our mom 'appy doing it proper like. And I got me own 'ouse. That's worth 'aving to put up with Mick, I can tell yer. If 'e stays down the boozer, good riddance.'

It sounded to Maryann as if there was a fair bit of bravado in what Nance was saying, making the most of a bad situation, but at least her spirit was far from being broken.

'If I don't get a bun in the oven for a year or two it'd suit me, I tell yer,' she said rattling cups. 'It's not all on one side, yer know – I give 'im one back sometimes, the mardy bugger.'

While Nance finished making the tea Maryann sat down at the table in the sparsely furnished little room. There was nothing but the range, a couple of shelves for keeping their few crocks on and the table and three chairs. On the table in a jam jar was a bunch of buttercups. Maryann smiled at the sight of Nance's homemaking. She thought of the luxuriant vases of flowers at Charnwood.

'Right then—' Nance sat down with a grunt. 'You tell me all about it. For a start, where the 'ell've yer been all this time?'

With the luxury of knowing that there was little of her past Nance was ignorant of, Maryann told her: Joel, the *Esther Jane*, Charnwood, Evan and Roland Musson. And finally meeting Darius and Joel again, and what had happened when she went to see her mom – only Nance kept chipping in.

'You were never on the cut all that time, were yer? They're a rough lot, them canal workers – they're like gypos!'

She oohed and aahed when Maryann told her about Joel and Roland Musson and listened spellbound when she got to the bit about seeing Flo again. Maryann poured out everything, how she felt about Joel and how sick he was and how Darius was going to be forced to sell the *Esther Jane*.

When there was a gap in the flow, Nance put her head on one side and said, 'You're in love with 'im – really in love, ain't yer?'

Maryann smiled bashfully. 'Am I?' she said in wonder. 'Yes – I do love 'im. I *do*. I'm going to spend every minute I can with 'im and try and 'elp 'im get better.

I've missed spending so much time with him – all those years, and 'e could've married someone else but 'e daint.'

'In love . . .' Nance said wistfully. 'Well, yer one up on me there, Maryann.'

'Nance – I know this is a cheek with me coming breezing back in after all this time – but could I stop 'ere with you a while? Only I ain't got nowhere else to go and I've got to be near Joel. I've got money saved – I can pay my way and that.'

Nance looked hesitant for a moment. Then her face cleared. ''Course yer can. I'd love to 'ave the company with ole misery guts coming 'ome kalied every night. Don't take no notice of Mick if 'e says anything. You can stay and that's that.'

'Ta, Nance – oh, it is good to see you!'

Nance grinned. 'Seems like yer never left.'

Maryann couldn't help feeling it didn't seem quite like that to her. 'Did you 'ear anything about where 'e went – Mr Griffin?'

Nance shook her head. 'No, but by all accounts 'e left only a week or two after the fire. Our mom went to see yours but she wouldn't even open the door to 'er. It weren't long before she 'ad to move back over Sheepcote Lane but she still 'ad a smell under 'er nose – sorry to say it, Maryann, but Flo always thought she was above us. We ain't 'ardly seen 'er: she don't want nothing to do with my family.'

'I know,' Maryann said apologetically. She was frowning. 'Norman Griffin can't've gone that far, yer know. I wonder if 'is mom's still alive – he was all over 'er.'

Nance shrugged. 'Good riddance to 'im I'd've said. Any'ow, you don't want to go asking questions about where 'e is, do yer? What about what you did to 'is business?'

'No, I s'pose ... But, Nance – what about Tony? I've got to see 'im. I've written to 'im and Billy ever since I left. How is 'e? D'you ever see 'im?'

'Oh – Tony's awright. 'E's got a job carrying hods for Paddy Murphy. Going to be a brickie. 'E's a strong lad and 'e's doing awright. I've seen him about now and then.'

'Does 'e ever say anything about me?'

'Said 'e'd heard from yer – nowt else.'

Maryann sighed, holding out her cup as Nance offered more tea. 'I saw Billy. 'E barely knew who I was.'

'Well, yer been gone a good while. You can't expect them to be all over yer from the word go.'

'No, I s'pose not ...' Maryann was saying, when the door burst open, kicked by a heavy workman's boot which set the latch rattling.

'Oh, 'ere we go,' Nance said. 'Oh my God, Maryann!' She gasped, panic-stricken. 'I've forgotten all about making tea! Oh Jesus, I'll be for it now!'

She stood up as a stocky, dark-haired man stumped into the room. He had ruddy skin and a weatherbeaten complexion with lines under his eyes that were almost creases. Maryann's first thought was, but he's so *old*! She realized then that he was no older than Joel, but she had expected Nance's husband to be much closer to her own age. Mick Mallone must have been nearer to forty than thirty and looked rough with it. He was swaying from the drink and stood looking at the pair of them. Maryann stood up as well.

''Oo the 'ell's this?' Mick demanded.

'No, Mick – don't start,' Nance said. 'This is my pal

Maryann – I told you about 'er. I've said 'er can stop 'ere with us for a bit, 'cause 'er ain't got nowhere else to go.'

He gave Maryann a mere glance. 'Where's my dinner?'

'I'm going out to get us fish and chips,' Maryann said quickly. 'And I'll take Lizzie and Mary home. Give us a few minutes and I'll be back.'

As she went to the door, Nance shot her a powerful look of gratitude.

Thirty-Five

Carrying the fish and chips back down the road, warm and delicious smelling in their newspaper, Maryann realized how hungry she was. What a long, long day it had been! But she felt relieved after pouring her heart out to Nance. She tried to keep the thought of her mother out of her mind and instead recalled the look in Joel's eyes when she had told him she loved him. This made her so happy that she grinned at a group of children out playing, remembering how she used to play out just round the corner, waiting for her dad to come home.

Back at Nance's she found Mick slumped asleep over the table. She could hear Nance moving about upstairs and, leaving the bundles beside Mick's head, she crept up the creaky stairs to find her.

'That you, Maryann?'

'Yes – I've got the fish and chips. Mick's asleep I think.'

Nance rolled her eyes. 'Best thing. We'll wake 'im up for 'is tea. I was just making up the bed for yer.'

Once again Maryann was struck by how middle-aged Nance seemed. 'Ta, Nance – I dunno what I'd do without yer.'

'Well – pals, eh?' Nance said quite bashfully. Suddenly for a moment they were little girls again. 'Never found another pal quite like you.'

Maryann grinned. 'No – nor me.'

They woke Mick up and he sat blearily with them as they all ate out of the newspaper. The fish and chips tasted to Maryann like some of the best food she'd ever had.

'D'you get work from Marron again?' Nance asked Mick cautiously. He nodded, mouth full of chips. 'What about tomorrer?'

'Maybe.'

Maryann watched him out of the corner of her eye. Nance had told her he could only find work as a casual labourer, bits here, bits there, hanging about early morning with groups of men all looking to be taken on. Long, gruelling days in builder's yards or toiling on roads, and no security. She thought of Evan with his soft cheeks and his soft job at Charnwood, his certainty of 'getting on', and she pitied Mick Mallone. He took no notice of her at all and behaved as if she wasn't there, but she didn't really mind.

Later, when they'd all gone up to bed, Mick and Nance were arguing next door. Every word of it floated through to her as she lay on the lumpy mattress in the back bedroom.

'Yer've never got a word to say to me when yer get in – they get more out of yer down the pub than I ever do. You just expect me to be 'ere like a skivvy – tea on the table the minute you set foot in the door . . .'

'Yes – I do!' Mick yelled, his Kerry accent thickened by drink. 'And I don't think that's too much to expect you to manage when you're here all day. You've got no one else but yourself to think about, now have you?'

'Well, if I ain't got a babby coming whose fault's that then, eh?'

'Shut your blathering mouth, woman!' There was a sound of struggling.

'Stop it, Mick! Yer cowing filthy navvy, don't yer touch me!' Then a cry of pain. ''Ow – you bastard!'

'Fuckin' barren bitch!'

On and on they went, the shouting getting louder. Maryann sat up, all tensed up. Was this what always happened at night? Or did Nance need her help? There was another sharp yell of pain from Nancy and Maryann pushed back the bedclothes, her heart pounding, ready to rush in next door. Maybe her visit had provoked Mick beyond what was normal.

Suddenly all went quiet. She sat on the edge of the bed listening. Gradually another sound rose from the next-door room. Listening in disbelief she realized it was weeping she could hear. Mick Mallone's weeping.

Drunken bastard! she thought. He's knocked Nance about and now 'e's gone all maudlin and sorry for 'imself!

But she heard Nance's voice, soft now but with an edge of impatience, saying 'there there' and 'it's awright' until Maryann heard them climbing into bed, and at last there was quiet until Mick started snoring.

'I'm sorry about the row last night,' Nance said next morning. She was downstairs before Maryann. Mick had already gone. Her lip was cut and very swollen. She handed Maryann a cup of tea.

'Oh Nance – you shouldn't 'ave to put up with that! Have you bathed your lip? That looks ever so sore.'

'I'm awright.'

'Does that happen often?'

Nance gave a bitter laugh. 'Not every night, if that's

what yer mean. Look—' She turned, holding her teacup cradled next to her chest. 'You 'ave to understand – about me and Mick. I married 'im to get out of 'ome. 'E married me 'cause 'e wanted someone – *anyone*. 'E 'ad a wife before me – Theresa O'Sullivan she was before she married 'im. Mick doted on 'er. She was nice so far as I remember – sweet natured, gentle like. Died three year ago. They never 'ad any kids. Broke Mick's heart. 'E thought they never caught for a babby 'cause of 'er. Thought she weren't the type. Too weak and frail. But it ain't 'appening with me neither and 'e's starting to think it's 'im – probably is 'im I reckon and that ain't easy for a man to come to terms with. 'E don't love me – not really and I don't love 'im. But I feel for 'im. 'E used to be a fine man.'

'But 'e knocks you about, Nance!'

'I can stand up for myself,' she said with a sigh. 'You don't really know what the last few years've been like shut away out in the country, do yer? There've been that many out of work and the Means Test. It's been bitter 'ard for the men.' She put her cup down. 'I took what I could, Maryann. Couldn't see much else on offer . . .' Her hands went over her face suddenly.

'Oh Nance—' Maryann went to comfort her as her shoulders began to shake.

'And now I don't think 'e'll even give me a babby either. I try not to mind, but I don't know 'ow I'm going to face being married to Mick if it's just 'im and me and no one else for the rest of our lives!'

Maryann spent the morning with Nance, helping her out round the house and listening to her pour her heart out. Whatever brave face Nance was putting on about her marriage, however much she tried to laugh it off, Maryann could see how unhappy she was. She was thinking about Nance as she travelled to the hospital that afternoon to see Joel.

I'll slip Nance a bit of extra money to treat herself, Maryann thought. She had her savings and she wasn't going to go scrounging off Nance and Mick – she'd pay her board. But she could try and cheer Nance up a bit too.

She stepped off the tram and walked along Oak Tree Lane, hurrying anxiously to get to Joel. How would she find him today? She hoped he'd be just a bit better – better for seeing her perhaps?

But when she said, 'I've come to see Mr Joel Bartholomew,' to the plump, red-headed sister, the woman's expression turned very grave.

Maryann's blood seemed to freeze with dread. 'What's the matter?'

'I'm afraid Mr Bartholomew took a turn for the worse in the night.'

'Oh no ... Is 'e—? 'E's still ...'ere?' She looked wildly down the long Nightingale ward to see if she could see him.

'He's here,' the woman said stiffly. 'But perhaps not for much longer without a miracle. Are you the girl who came to see him yesterday?'

Maryann nodded, her eyes full of tears. Oh this couldn't be true, Joel couldn't die, not when they'd found each other again and they had so much between them! How could she face the future again without Joel? She wanted to give so much love to him, to make up for all their lost, lonely years.

'I really don't think ...' the woman began, but seeing Maryann begin to weep in front of her she hesitated.

'Please,' Maryann sobbed. 'I told the nurse yesterday – 'e ain't got no one else.'

The sister relented. 'You better calm down before you go to him.'

Maryann nodded, unable to speak. She wiped her face, pulled her shoulders back and walked along the ward, feeling the eyes of the other male patients on her.

Joel looked very bad. For a moment as she approached the bed she thought he wasn't breathing and his face was sunken and pale, head turned to one side like someone trying to catch the sunlight. Her tears started to fall again in spite of herself as she looked at him. He seemed so weak and defeated.

Kneeling in the narrow gap by the bed, she took his hand and brought it to her cheek.

'Oh Joel,' she whispered. 'Stay with me. Please don't go – don't die. Can you 'ear me? Joel, please open your eyes – please still be 'ere.'

Watching his face, she saw, rather than heard, his shallow breathing and waited, staring intensely at him, for a flicker of movement, some sign that he was not leaving her. For a second his lashes flickered and she thought he was going to open his eyes.

'Joel?'

But the movement stopped and left her feeling more desolate than before. He couldn't hear her. He was slipping away. She talked to him frantically in a low voice, begging him, talking about all the things they'd do when he was better, saying over and over again how she loved him, clinging to his hot hand. But there was nothing. Eventually the sister came and approached the bed.

'I think it's time to leave him now, dear.' Her

kindness terrified Maryann more than brusqueness would have done. It seemed to indicate that she was sure Joel was going to die.

'If only I could stay with 'im—' She found it unbearable to tear herself away from his hand. 'D'yer think – will 'e last the night?'

Her gaze not meeting Maryann's, the sister said, 'I'm afraid I couldn't tell you that.'

She stepped out of the ward as if into another world. It was late afternoon and sultry, the air full of acidic smells from the battery factory near by. She turned away from the city and walked numbly towards Lodge Hill Cemetery, stepping in through its gates to the tranquillity of flowerbeds and trees and gravestones. She made her way to the two graves which belonged to her, not side by side but not far apart, each with a modest headstone.

'HAROLD NELSON – 1892–1926' she read, and then, 'SALLY ANNE GRIFFIN – 1913–1928'.

The sight of Sal's gravestone brought all her rage and hurt to boiling point. Griffin! Her mom had buried Sal under that bastard's name – the one who'd all but killed her himself.

'How could she have done it?' She found herself kicking at the stone, screaming out her pain and fury. 'How could she, how *could* she?'

Not even looking to see if anyone was about, past caring, she sank to her knees and rested her head on Sal's grave, sobbing. 'Oh Sal . . . oh God . . . sis . . . sis . . .' The memory of that night she had found Sal filled her mind, of the day her dad died, and then Joel, lying there, hardly seeming to be alive even now.

Would she be visting him here too, having no one to talk to but the graves of all the people she loved? She curled up tight by Sal's grave, smelling the earth close to her face, and cried until she could cry no more.

Thirty-Six

Nance only had to look at Maryann's face when she got back.

'Oh Maryann – 'e's not . . .?'

She came to greet her, anxiously wringing a cloth in her hands. The bruising had spread round Nance's lip but the sight of her friend pulled her mind right away from her own troubles. Maryann sank down at the table.

'No. But I don't think—' She looked up at Nance, her eyes filling again even though she thought she'd cried all the tears she was capable of. 'They don't think 'e'll last the week – maybe not even the night. 'E hardly seems to be breathing. I can't bear it, Nance . . .'

'Oh Maryann, no!'

Nance pulled the other chair round and perched on it beside her, clasping Maryann's hands in her rough ones as her friend poured out her feelings.

'I was hoping 'e'd be better today, but he couldn't even open his eyes and look at me. It almost seemed he was dead already. Oh and 'e's got no one with 'im – I wish they'd've let me stay with 'im!'

'What about 'is family? Ain't there anyone round about for 'im?'

'No – there's only Darius, his brother and 'e's—' She got abruptly to her feet. 'Darius! I must let 'im know 'ow bad things are. I don't know if 'e can make it but I'll 'ave to give 'im the chance to try. Have you got a bit of paper I could write 'im a note on?'

Nancy managed to find a scrap of paper and left Maryann with it at the table while she went out to see if she could beg an envelope off one of the neighbours. She soon came back with one and Maryann addressed it to Tooley's Yard in Banbury and ran out to post it. Someone would have to read it to Darius – if he was still there. She told him in the note that she'd leave her address for him at the toll office at Farmer's Bridge. She slipped it into the box, praying Joel would hang on. The thought made her cry all over again.

She went to the hospital the next day, sick with dread. But she found Joel in much the same state as he had been in the day before. She sat beside him, willing him with all her strength and love to hold on to life.

'I'll be here, Joel, waiting for you, praying for you. Just don't leave me – I love you.'

She could hardly bear to let go of his hand and go away, she was so afraid that she might not see him alive again. She was living from moment to moment. Thinking about the future was impossible. She couldn't face it now without Joel.

That evening she went to find Tony, waiting at the end of Sheepcote Lane, hoping she could intercept him before he reached home. She stood watching both ends of the street, afraid she would not be able to recognize him and full of misgiving that if she did see him he would reject her just as angrily as her mother had.

At last when he appeared she knew immediately who he was. He turned into the road, walking briskly, whistling, a small canvas bag slung over one shoulder, his jacket slung back over the other. His boots and clothes were pale with dust and smears of cement, his cap was pushed far back on his head, showing a dark-eyed face which was also covered in muck. He was much bigger, just about her own height, quite grown up into a wiry, muscular lad. When he drew nearer and caught sight of her, he stopped in mid-whistle.

''Ello, Tony.'

He came nearer. She couldn't read his expression, except that it didn't hold surprise. Her mom must have told him she'd been back. 'Maryann?'

She was full of emotion, remembering the little boy she had left sleeping the night she ran away. 'I s'pose you thought I was never coming back.'

'Well – I dunno. I mean it's been—' He shrugged, looking down at the ground, awkward, and embarrassed by her emotion. 'Mom said you'd been to see 'er.'

'It's a wonder she could bring 'erself to mention my name,' Maryann said bitterly. 'What did 'er say?'

'Not much. Said yer wouldn't be coming again.'

Maryann wiped her eyes and looked into his face. 'What about you, Tony? You angry with me too?'

She saw a flicker of hostility, then sorrow in his dark eyes. She could sense his confused loyalties. 'Dunno. No. Not really.'

'And *he* left then? Norman?'

Tony nodded, raising his head. 'Mom said it were your fault.' He sounded angry, despite his denial. 'We had to come back down 'ere—' He jerked his head to indicate the lane. 'Why did yer do it, Maryann? I know 'e weren't our dad but 'e weren't all that bad. What did yer 'ave to go and ruin everyfing for?'

It was Maryann's turn to look away, shame rising in

her, the blood rushing to her cheeks. Her tears started to fall. How could she tell Tony what Norman Griffin had done to her and Sal – above all to Sal? How could she speak like that to her little brother? Little Tony who spoke in a gruff man-boy voice, who still couldn't say his 'th's properly?

'I'm sorry, Tony . . .' She couldn't help crying however hard she tried, and she stood in front of him weeping there in the street. 'I'm sorry – I had to go. *I had to do it* . . . I can't explain it to yer.'

'Why not? Don't yer think I'm grown up enough to be told what's going on, eh? I feel like a right bloody mug I do. I'm old enough to keep food on the table but I ain't old enough to be told anyfing. 'Ow about letting me in on a few fings, eh?'

'Ssh – oh Tony, please be quiet!' Maryann seized his arm. 'Don't – not in the street. I don't want people staring and gossiping. Look – come for a walk with me, away from 'ere.'

'I'll come,' Tony said, on his dignity. 'But you'd better be straight with me, Maryann. So far as Mom's concerned you were the ruin of the family. It ain't how I remember yer or think of you, but you'd better 'ave summat to say to me.' Suddenly he seemed near tears himself. She wanted to put her arms round him as she had done when he was little, but knew she mustn't.

'Oh Tony – I will tell you. Only you have to promise me you'll believe what I say. Mom never would – that's why I had to go in the end. I couldn't stand telling you if you start saying I'm a liar.'

She led him, as if automatically, to the place where they could squeeze through down to the cut, and they walked side by side away from town, breathing in the murky smell of the canal, reflections shifting on the water's surface. She found it very difficult to talk. What had happened in the past had been buried in her for so long that at first she skirted round and round what she needed to say and at last she blurted it out clumsily, knowing she owed Tony the truth.

'You daint know – you were too little. I know Mr Griffin took us to the pictures and we always had enough and didn't go short, but there was another side to him, Tony. A filthy, wicked side. And it was Sal had the worst of it. He was ... he was ...' Oh God, how could she say it?

She forced herself to glance round at her brother. He was watching his feet, a slight frown on his face. Maryann took in a huge, ragged breath and forced herself to go on, telling him, explaining, indirectly at first, then, uncertain if he knew what she meant, in more detail. The memories came back, raw and sickening. She stopped walking and sobbed out to him how she'd found Sal that day.

'He destroyed her. Week by week. He killed her from inside, Tony. That's what happened to your sister. She took her own life because she couldn't stand living no more after him and what it did to her. She thought she was expecting a babby as well, Tony – you won't've known that. And I ... d'you know, that night I went down there I daint 'ave a plan. I knew I was going to do summat, I was so full of grief and anger for Sal but I daint know what. And then when I saw what I saw down there – I went mad. I was ready to do him in – destroy him and everything that was his. That was when I started the fire, and then I had to go—' Tears on her cheeks, she begged her brother, 'Don't say you don't believe me, Tony. Please don't. It's the truth – I swear to you on my life!'

She could see just how much she'd got through to him. Tony's thin face looked stunned. Eventually he said, 'Did Mom know?'

'I told 'er. I kept trying to say, but she daint want to 'ear it. All she wanted to see was the respectable side of him. I s'pose she shut it out of her mind. She was scared to frighten him off. In the end I did it for 'er.'

They stood in the dusk on the canal bank. Maryann found she could not look into his eyes. She felt dreadful after what she had had to tell him. Tony was silent for a time and she ached to know what he was thinking. At least he hadn't rejected her story straight away and told her she was a filthy liar. She sensed he was thinking hard.

'I fink I remember,' he said eventually. 'Yes – I do.'

'What?'

'Him – Griffin – coming in – of a night. When you and Sal was in the bed. It feels like a dream – but I know 'e was in there sometimes – on your bed. I remember the creaking and his voice in there.'

'Oh Tony! D'you really – you remember that?'

'I remember the bed squeaking – and 'im breathing and saying fings to yer.'

'Oh thank God!' Maryann cried. It was then, at last, she went and put her arms round him. 'Someone who knows I'm not making it up – oh Tony ... I'm so happy to see you again. I've missed you so much – you and Billy, but especially you. I've been so lonely without you.'

He was awkward in her embrace at first. But then he dropped his jacket and bag on to the dry ground and his arms came round her as she cried.

'Did you get my letters?'

'Yes.'

'And the little cat I left on yer pillow?'

'Yes—' He sounded embarrassed. He was crying too.

''Ve you still got it somewhere?'

She pulled back and looked at him. Tony nodded, quickly wiping his eyes on the back of his hands.

'See – I was always thinking of you. Tony?'

'What?'

'What d'you call yourself – Nelson or Griffin?'

'Griffin.' He looked at her, ashamed, then said quietly, 'But not any more, Maryann. Never. Not after what you've told me.'

They walked on through the half-light, talking much more easily now. Maryann told Tony about Charn-wood House, about the *Esther Jane* and Darius, and that he was so desperate he might have to sell her, and about Joel and how worried she was. And Tony told her something of how it had been after she left.

'When 'e saw what'd happened – with the fire, he came 'ome and knocked our mom across the kitchen. I copped 'old of Billy and took 'im outside, out the way of mean old man Griffin – 'e was like someone else that day. Frightened us.'

'He *is* someone else,' Maryann said grimly. 'That's who is really is underneath. Cruel and scheming. I wonder where 'e went to after.'

'Oh – we know where 'e is,' Tony told her, almost casually.

'*Do* you? What – somewhere near by? In Birming-ham?'

'Oh yes – course. Near 'is mom.'

'Oh my God – she ain't still alive?'

'I dunno – she was a while back. 'Er must've been nearly ninety then. 'E's set 'imself up again, over on the Soho Road. The other place was insured, yer know – 'e ain't no fool.'

'No,' Maryann agreed. 'So our mom knows where 'e is?'

'Oh ar – I mean when it first happened 'e went and lived with old Mrs Griffin. Mom went over to 'ers a number of times begging 'im to come back but 'e weren't 'aving it. Said 'e'd had enough and that was that.'

Nothing there for him, Maryann thought grimly. Not without me and Sal. 'What, so Mom just gave up?'

'Had to. She wanted money off of 'im but 'e said the family'd already caused him quite enough trouble and she weren't 'aving a farthing. She come back ever so upset every time but there was nothing 'er could do. She 'ad to come to terms with it – 'e'd gone and that was that. She 'ad to make the best of it and fend for 'erself. So we moved up the old end and got on with it.'

'But she ain't going to forgive me, is she?'

'Not in a hurry, no.'

By now they'd reached the part of the bank in Ladywood where they had to scramble up and climb through the broken fence.

'It's him should be paying for all the grief he's caused – not Mom. Not us either,' Maryann said, once they were up on the road again. 'If I could just see 'im, I'd . . .' But her voice trailed off, hopelessly. What could she do? What did it matter now? The only things that mattered were that Joel was lying in hospital fighting to stay alive, and that she had seen her brother and he forgave her.

'Meet me again, will yer?' she said to him. 'And bring Billy with yer.'

Tony nodded, his eyes very dark in his pale face.

'You'd best get 'ome. You must be hungry.'

'I could go and 'ave a look – over round 'is place,' Tony said suddenly.

'Well – if you can stand the sight of 'im.' Maryann touched his arm, smiling. 'T'ra, Tony. See yer soon.'

When she got back to Nance and Mick's, Nance started up from the table as she walked in, trying to pretend she hadn't been sitting crying, and quickly wiped her eyes.

'Oh Nance – what's wrong?' Maryann wasn't fooled for a moment. 'I do wish you was happier, that I do.'

'I'm awright—' Nance hurried over to put the kettle on. 'It's just I wish Mick'd stay in a night or two sometimes. 'E never seems to be 'ere lately. But never mind, eh? How's Joel?'

'No better.' Maryann sank down at the table. ''E just seemed the same as yesterday. Oh Nance – I wish there was something I could do.'

Thirty-Seven

Maryann spent the following days in an agony of waiting. Though she was pleased to have had such a good meeting with Tony, and enjoyed Nance's company, her mind was never far from Joel. She was sick with worry. Her appetite had disappeared almost completely and she had trouble sleeping, thinking of him lying there as she saw him every day, hanging between life and death, not quite belonging to either. She often cried out her desperation in bed at night, trying to keep quiet so Nance and Mick wouldn't hear her next door.

On the other hand, they often weren't quiet themselves and Maryann realized her own presence was making things worse.

'How much longer've we got *her* hanging about for?' she heard Mick demanding one night.

Another time he made some comment about her living off them.

'She ain't 'ad a penny off of us,' Nance snapped back at him. 'So yer needn't start on like that. Maryann's got money of 'er own and she ain't mean with it neither.'

But this only seemed to increase Mick's resentment, and the added conflict she was causing between Nance and her husband made Maryann feel even more desperate. If only she could leave them in peace, but where else did she have to go?

On the third day after she had seen Tony she woke

after a broken, wretched night and lay in bed, unable to sleep but too limp and tired to get out of bed. She heard the door bang as Mick went off to work, and closed her eyes. She always felt relieved knowing he was out of the house.

She was still dozing when there came more banging. Nance was downstairs and Maryann heard voices, then Nance calling up the stairs, 'Maryann – someone to see yer!'

Bewildered, she hastily pulled her dress on and ran down without combing her hair, her mind full of irrational questions. Was it news about Joel? Had he passed away in the night? But no, of course not – no one came out to tell you. And it still felt very early.

Downstairs, she found a man with dark curly hair, looking enormous in the little room, his head almost touching the ceiling. He looked exhausted and was twisting his cap between his hands, obviously most uneasy to be in this strange place. It took her a moment to realize who he was.

'Darius – you got my letter then!' She felt so pleased to see him, as if he was a member of her own family. 'How did you get 'ere?'

'I come almost non-stop,' he said. 'After I 'eard from you. Bessie's all in. Pulled into Birnigum as it was getting light. So—' He stepped closer, urgently. 'What about Joel – have I got 'ere in time?'

'Oh Darius . . .' Tears came so readily to her eyes at the moment. 'You have if 'e's the same as yesterday. I've been waiting and watching every day and 'e's been lain there, not knowing what's going on around him and his breathing's that bad. Every day when I go I don't know . . .'

'Well 'ow about us go now – where is it? Is it far?'

Maryann managed a wan smile through her tears. 'We 'ave to go in the afternoon – they won't let us in now.'

''Ere–' Nance gestured shyly at the table. ''Ave a seat, Mr Bartholomew, and I'll make us some breakfast. I've even got some eggs today, thanks to Maryann.' Maryann noticed that Nance seemed quite over-whelmed by his presence.

Darius sat down rather reluctantly, as he had been all primed to spring into action straight away. Maryann sat with him and they drank tea as Nancy cooked, quietly listening and turning often from the range to look curiously at Maryann and this great, rugged visitor.

'So you came in the *Esther Jane*?' Maryann quizzed him.

''Course. What else? You got to me just in time. They'd just finished 'er up at Tooley's Yard and I was off to load up when your letter came.'

'So, you ain't sold 'er yet – to Mr Barlow?'

Darius shook his head slowly, swallowing a mouth-ful of tea. Maryann saw the muscles move in his thick neck. She waited for him to speak. The Bartholomews never hurried anything they wanted to say.

'Not yet. I couldn't sell 'er out from under the nose of my father without 'im being there. Nor Joel. Mr Barlow said 'e could wait.'

'So ... you didn't come the whole way single-handed?'

'No. There's a nipper come up with me this time. The Higgins family loaned me young Ernie. I left 'im asleep–' For the first time something like a smile came to Darius's weathered face. Maryann saw Nance watching him, intrigued. 'That's a trip 'e won't forget in a hurry!'

'How's old Mr Bartholomew?' Maryann asked.

Darius shook his head. 'Mending – slow though. Oh, ta – very good of you.' He nodded appreciatively at Nance as she set before him a plate piled with bread and butter and *three* fried eggs. Maryann's plate held one and Nance appeared to be having only bread. Maryann raised an eyebrow at her.

''E's 'ad a long night,' Nance said, blushing. ''E deserves a good feed.'

They ate in silence for a time. Darius seemed ravenous and emptied his plate quickly, wiping up every last drop of yolk with the bread. Nance's knife and fork looked like toys in his big hands. She nibbled at her bread, seeming fascinated by Darius. Maryann also found her eyes drawn to his face as she ate. Having him here was wonderful to her, like having part of Joel. Though they looked different, there was something about the way they both moved and in the tone of their voices that was similar. She felt proud that he had appeared. But she was longing to ask him, keep on at him – you can't really sell the *Esther Jane*? You're not really going to? And her heart ached. She knew how much this would mean to Joel, how much he would struggle with every ounce of strength he had to stop it happening if he were able. But now perhaps Darius would be left alone for ever. Perhaps Joel would never . . .

Feeling tears welling in her eyes again she tore her thoughts away and looked up at Darius. He'd drunk his tea and his eyes were drooping, his whole body sagging with weariness.

'You need a sleep,' she told him. 'Would it be awright if 'e went up on my bed for a bit, Nance?'

For a second Nance looked put out, and Maryann knew she was calculating what Mick would have to say about this. But Darius would be gone long before Mick appeared.

''Course 'e can.' She smiled warmly. 'You show 'im up there, Maryann.'

Darius was dead to the world all morning. Maryann helped Nance around the house, glad to have plenty to do to while away the morning. She scrubbed the front step and helped with a load of washing, mangling it and pegging it out in the hazy sunshine, a shaft of which penetrated into the yard round the back where they were working.

'On the cut they hang the washing out along the boats,' she told Nance, shaking out a dress of her own before she pegged it on the line. It smelled rather harshly of soap.

Nance looked up, bent over the mangle. 'Do they? Fancy—' She frowned. 'I always thought them people on the cut were just a bunch of gypos. But that Darius seems a nice man.'

'They ain't gypos,' Maryann said hotly. 'And they ain't *all* rough. They just live a bit different, that's all.'

Nance looked doubtful. '*Very* different, going by what I've 'eard. Still – some of 'em are awright I s'pose.'

'Yes.' Maryann still sounded cross. ''Course they are. You want to see for yerself before you start canting on about things you don't know.'

''Eh – there's no need to bite my 'ead off—' Nance

began mangling again furiously. 'Bet you'd've said the same if yer didn't know.'

Maryann took Mick's spare trousers as they rolled through the mangle. 'S'pose so,' she conceded. 'Sorry, Nance.'

'That's awright. I know you're on edge.'

After a few moments, without looking up from the mangle, Nance said, ''E's got a wife, I s'pose?'

'No.' Maryann was stretching up to the line.

Nance looked over at her. ''E ain't married? Your Joel ain't married. I mean they're getting on, the pair of 'em. What's the matter with 'em?'

'There's nothing the matter with them!' Maryann snapped again, irritated by the way Nance said it. 'Joel 'ad a sweetheart when 'e was young and she married someone else by the end of the War. I don't know about Darius – they're working almost every hour of the day and it ain't that easy to meet up with anyone on the cut. You just don't know what it's like, Nance.'

'No. So yer keep saying. I'm just surprised a man with 'is looks ain't wed by now, that's all. 'E looks a bit of awright to me.'

'Does 'e now?' Maryann teased. 'Well – you'd better watch yerself then. Old married woman like you.'

She didn't fail to notice the blush that rushed through Nance's cheeks.

They had to wake Darius after midday. He emerged from sleep utterly bewildered as he looked round, then seeing Maryann, he sat up in a panic.

'Is it time – are we too late?'

'No – yer awright. Nance's done us a bit of dinner, and then we'll go.' She gave her hair a hasty going over with her treasured brush she had had that Christmas at Charnwood. 'Don't worry – we'll be in good time.'

Don't worry! she thought later as she sat beside Darius on the tram along the Bristol Road. Well, there was a daft thing to say. The whole of her life was consumed with worry. She looked round at Darius. He didn't look any too happy on the tram. It was quite full and she could sense how uneasy and out of place he felt.

Inside the hospital was even worse. He walked along the corridor beside her, tense and silent, looking about him. Maryann felt the usual sense of panic and dread engulf her as they approached the ward but she fought against it, determined not to show Darius how bad she was feeling.

At the door she forced herself to look along, her gaze racing to the spot where Joel had been lying all that week. For a moment she couldn't take it in, could not make sense of anything, and then she saw properly as the room came into focus.

'Oh—' she gulped. 'Oh, it's awright, Darius – 'e's still there! Come on.' She found herself taking his arm, leading him down to Joel's bed.

She had grown used to the sight of how Joel had become through illness and that his beard had gone, and she had not thought to warn Darius. The shock registered in his face. Plainly Joel looked a lot worse than when Darius had last seen him.

They went to the side of the bed and Maryann searched hungrily for any sign of change. Joel still lay with his eyes closed, his breathing shallow and laboured. Each time she saw him his body seemed more slight and the sight of him filled her with pain. He was disappearing. Slowly, inexorably, day by day, the man she loved was slipping away. Darius sat on the chair, cap in hand, staring at his brother in appalled silence.

Maryann kneeled down and took Joel's hand, kissing it as she always did.

'Joel? It's me again – Maryann. And Darius – your brother – he's here with me. He's come all the way up from Banbury to see you – brought the *Esther Jane* out of Tooley's Yard and she's 'ere—' On her own she often broke down talking to him, receiving as much reply as she would from a stone, but today she wanted to be strong for Darius's sake. She looked round at him. 'D'yer want to say anything to him?'

Darius leaned forward. 'Joel. It's Darius—' He looked round the room distractedly, as if searching for the right words. 'I 'ope you're going to get better, Joel – on your feet soon, eh?' He sat back, clearly at a loss, but his gaze never left Joel's face.

'D'you 'ear that, Joel? What Darius says? Please get better and come back to us. We all need yer – Darius and me and your dad and the *Esther Jane* . . . .' More softly, she added, 'And I love you, Joel – I do love you so much.'

It was then she felt it. Just for a second. She turned with a gasp to Darius. 'He moved his hand! I felt it. 'E sort of squeezed mine – there, 'e did it again!'

'Don't 'e do that normally?'

'No – no! I've not had anything out of him. Oh Joel – can you hear us?'

Again, a pressure round her hand. Then a faint fluttering of his eyelashes. She and Darius stood waiting, absolutely still. There was nothing more, though they waited on and on.

'Nurse!' Maryann was too emotional to be frightened of the nurse. The woman came over to her, her face grave, obviously steeling herself.

'What is it?' Her voice was sharp.

''E just squeezed my hand – a few times. He squeezed my hand!'

The woman's face relaxed, looking relieved, then pleased. 'Did he, now?'

Maryann left the hospital with Darius feeling like a different person. It had been a small thing, that tiny movement that told her Joel knew he was still with them, but it changed everything. They had hope, hope which lit the day brighter than the brightest summer sun.

'I'm so glad it happened with you 'ere,' she told Darius, who seemed to be grasping just how much this meant. 'Oh – I feel so happy!' She felt like shouting and singing. 'Are you coming back to Nance's?'

'No – reckon I'll get back to the boat.'

'I tell you what, let's take Nance to see 'er. We've got to go back that way any'ow and it's not far. How about that?'

'Awright. If that's what you want.' He smiled. 'Reckon young Ernie'll just be awake by now and starving 'ungry!'

Nance was all of a tizz when they got back and asked her to come out with them. 'But I can't – I mean I've got to do the dinner, and . . .'

'Oh come on, Nance!' Maryann chivvied her, untying her apron. 'No arguments – you're coming.'

'Maryann!' Nance laughed. She could see the change in Maryann immediately.

'We'll get some liver or summat on the way back – that's nice and quick. It's a lovely day today – you don't want to spend it stuck in 'ere, do you?'

'Well – if Mr – if Darius don't mind?'

Darius shrugged. 'I can stay 'ere a bit longer. If you want to come that's all right with me.'

They walked out into the bright, hot afternoon. Darius told them he had tied up not far from Farmer's Bridge and Maryann led the way through the streets of buses and trams and hurrying people, which seemed to be as foreign as a jungle to Darius.

'Did you bring her up empty?' Maryann asked him.

'Oh no – I got a load on grain into 'er – unloaded that this morning.'

'There she is!' Maryann cried as they reached the spot. The boat sat high in the water. 'Ooh, she's looking nice, Darius – much better than when I saw 'er before.'

'She's 'ad a good going over,' he agreed. 'And a lick of paint. She was in a bad state before. Only we 'ad to keep getting ahead – there was never time.'

Young Ernie Higgins was sitting out on the bank beside the boat chewing on an apple. Darius helped Nance on board and Maryann followed.

'Oh my – it's tiny in 'ere!' Nance said, peering into the cabin. Astonished, she turned to Darius and Maryann. 'D'you live in 'ere – all year round?'

'Got nowhere else,' Darius said. 'That's it – home to us.' He smiled, obviously enjoying her amazement.

'And you lived on 'ere an' all?' she said to Maryann. 'Where on earth did yer sleep?'

Maryann took great pride in showing her the cabin, where they slept and cooked and old Mrs Bartholomew's crochet work, almost as if she'd been born to the life and wasn't a newcomer 'off the bank' herself. Nance sat at the tiny table.

'It's like playing doll's 'ouses!' She laughed. She was more light-hearted than Maryann had yet seen her. 'I've never seen anything so tiny. And it's ever so clean – not like them dirty old joey boats. Ooh – ain't it nice?'

'There's nothing like it,' Maryann said, taking a seat beside her. She looked round contentedly. Darius had had time to polish the brasses while he was at Tooley's Yard, and the cabin was fairly clean too. Her eye still picked out a lot of things that needed doing. It felt like *her* home.

'Oh Nance—' She squeezed her friend's hand. 'Joel's going to get better. I know 'e is! This feels like the happiest day of my life!'

'I'm glad for yer,' Nance said sincerely.

Darius poked his head through the door of the cabin and smiled. 'I'll brew up a cuppa tea, shall I?'

He seemed to enjoy their company and was far more relaxed now he was back on the cut, having come through the ordeal of going to the hospital. They sat drinking tea – Darius and Nance perched at the stern, Maryann sat half twisted round on the cabin step. Darius told Nance about the life and how they worked. Maryann could see she admired Darius and he was at ease with her, seemed to like her. She made him laugh. And Nance basked in the sun, her pale, thin body seeming to relax and become more youthful away from home. Maryann saw Darius looking at her often. If only things were different, she thought, I do believe these two might've had something. But it was no good thinking of that. She thought bitterly about Mick. Shame you could never see what was just round the corner.

'Now I've seen Joel,' Darius was saying, 'I'll go looking for a load tonight – get off in the morning. I'd thought I might 'ave to be here longer, if . . . but I'll get ahead for a bit. Keep 'er going. There's nothing I can do 'ere for now.'

'Oh – I wish I was coming with you,' Maryann said.

'I almost wish I was from what you've told me.' Nance laughed. Maryann hadn't heard her laugh like that in ages.

'Ah well.' Darius smiled. 'God knows, you'd both be welcome. I could do with more hands on board. I s'pose we'll manage though.' He nodded his head towards Ernie. 'For now.'

Thirty-Eight

'Don't tell 'im where we've been, for God's sake,' Nance implored later as they got the tea ready fast and furiously. They'd stayed too long down on the cut and had had to run back, via the butcher's. The prospect of Mick's fury if everything wasn't ready when he got home set the pair of them off and the cooking became a joke. Maryann was chopping onions frantically at the table. Nance was so dithery she dropped the liver on the floor so it had to be washed and then she got the giggles.

'Oh, look at that! What'd Mick say if 'e saw me throwing 'is tea on the floor!' Her laughter almost got the better of her as she mimicked her husband's indignation, swaggering and waving a piece of liver around in her hand like a weapon. ' "Sure I don't see my dinner ready. What sort of a wife is it who can't even put a meal on the table when a man walks through the door!" Oh my Lord!' she spluttered. 'I don't know what's got into me!'

Maryann was laughing just as much, her eyes also streaming from the onions. She was bubbly with relief and hope over Joel, and really happy to see what difference a little break had made to Nance, who looked younger again suddenly, face pink from the sun and full of mirth under her mop of black curls. They were both laughing so much that for a few minutes they were incapable of cooking anything at all and the liver and onions lay untouched on the table.

A rattle at the door sobered them instantly.

Nance gasped, horrified. ''E can't be back already!'

But the door didn't open.

'Must be someone else,' Nance hissed and crept over to open it. 'Oh – 'ello, Tony love.' She started giggling again with relief. ''Ow're you? Come on in. Don't mind me.'

'S'Maryann there?'

Maryann experienced a flutter of pleasure that he had come to find her. *My brother.* He had clearly just got off work again and was as grubby as the last time she saw him.

'Awright, Tony – ain't yer coming in?'

He looked awkward and anxious at the same time. 'Can yer come out – just for a bit?'

Maryann looked doubtful. 'Can you manage, Nance?'

'Yes, go on – I'll get on quicker without you setting me off.'

She walked with Tony down to the end of the street, passing men on their way home from work, a few kids playing out. Smells of cooking drifted from the houses as they walked along.

'I thought you were going to bring Billy to see me,' she reproached him.

'Not this time.' Tony seemed tense.

'What's up?'

'I know where 'e's living.'

Maryann didn't need to ask who. 'You went to see him?'

'*No.* Course not. I followed 'im home. 'E does just what 'e did when 'e was with Mom. Leaves and locks up just the same time, quick pint and 'ome. 'E lives up behind the park in Handsworth.'

'And has a shop on the Soho Road? An undertaker's?'

'It's an undertaker's, but it ain't under the name of Griffin. 'E set 'imself up under a new name: Arthur Lambert. 'E's made 'isself a new life awright.'

'The slimy . . .' Maryann began, but Tony interrupted.

'T'ain't the main fing though. After I followed 'im home I waited for a bit to see if I could see anyfing. I daint see much, but when it was getting dark this woman come and shut the curtains at the front.'

'Woman – what, you mean . . .? Could be a landlady, couldn't it?'

'Could be. I dunno. But then, when I was getting fed up, nuffing to see – I s'pose they'd been 'aving some tea – the door come open and two girls came out and went off down the road.'

'Girls?' Maryann stopped, full of foreboding. 'How old?'

'Couldn't see for sure. Younger'un me.'

Maryann felt herself swell inside with suspicion and fury. 'Oh no – oh Tony, d'yer think . . .?'

Tony shrugged. 'Dunno – couldn't make out anyfing else.'

'No. Course yer couldn't.' She felt sorry he was involved. He was still only a kid, even if he was tall and muscular and doing a man's work. He shouldn't even have to know any of this. 'Look – thanks, Tony. For doing that.'

'What're yer going to do, sis?'

It warmed her heart to hear him call her that – already, when she'd been away so long. Made her feel she belonged. This search for Norman Griffin was bringing them together. Once again she thanked God that Tony believed her, was on her side. She couldn't have faced this alone.

'I don't know, Tony. I really don't. What *can* I do? It makes me feel bad just thinking about it.' She wouldn't say more to him, didn't want to fill his head with disturbing details.

''E wants a good 'iding, 'e does,' Tony said fiercely.

Maryann almost smiled. A 'good hiding' sounded so innocent, like something a child might be threatened with. It was the least of what she had in mind. ''E does that, Tony. And I'm going to think about how he's going to get it an' all.'

When she got back, Mick was home, eating in silence. Nance winked at her over his head but Maryann could tell the atmosphere between them was very sour. Nance was back to the cowed, weary-looking woman she had been before and Maryann felt Mick's resentment of her as soon as she walked in. She ate up her own tea quickly and said she was going to bed.

Soon after she'd gone up she heard them start downstairs, arguing, voices getting louder, savage in tone. She undressed, full of tension. It was horrible to hear.

'Don't you start carrying on like that!' she heard Nance shout. 'I 'ate it when you show yer face through the door these days, yer miserable sod. I don't know why yer bother coming 'ome the way yer keep on when you're 'ere!'

'This is my house and you'll not talk to me like that.

If I'd known what sort of a wife you'd make I'd never've married you, so I wouldn't . . .'

'Not like the blessed Saint Theresa yer mean!' Nance shrieked harshly. 'Well, 'er was never so bloody perfect as yer make out – and you never managed to get 'er a bun in the oven neither, did yer?'

It always came back to that. Maryann screwed up her eyes, hearing Nance's howl of pain and then a crash as something fell and smashed on the floor. There was more shouting, followed by a roar which almost made Maryann's heart stop.

'You bitch! You evil fecking bitch – look what you've done!'

She ran down and stopped at the bottom of the stairs, appalled. Suddenly everything was quiet. Mick was standing clutching his left forearm, blood oozing out round his fingers. Nance, mouth open in horror, was still holding the knife she'd used to slice up the pig's liver.

'Oh . . . Mick!' Nance gasped. 'What've I done?' She seized a cloth and went to him to staunch the wound but he snatched it and backed away from her.

'Don't you come near me, you mad bitch!' he snarled. 'Look what you've done to me! You're not right up top – you're not fit to be a wife to anyone.' Clutching the cloth to his arm he backed out of the door, kicked it shut so the house shook and then they heard his feet going down the path.

Nance looked stunned. Maryann went and took the bloodstained knife from her quivering hand and laid it on the table.

'He punched me.' Nance's mouth was trembling, the tears starting to come. 'It 'urt so much . . . I daint know what I was doing.' She laid her hand over her right breast. 'Punched me just 'ere.' She sat down and started to cry. Maryann poured her a nip of whiskey and put it down beside her. ''E should've never punched me there – it 'urt too much. Oh Maryann – what've I done?'

''E'll be awright. It's only a cut.'

But she knew Nance didn't just mean Mick's arm. She meant everything.

Maryann scarcely slept that night. She lay awake, awaiting the sound of Mick coming home again. Her thoughts swirled round. She was so upset for Nance, and in the night's darkness she felt full of doubt about everything and very afraid. She had felt Joel squeeze her hand and had been so hopeful, but he was still so ill. It didn't mean he was going to get better, did it? Perhaps even now he was slipping away and she'd never see him again ... She pushed this thought away but it was replaced by all the things Tony had told her about Norman Griffin.

I'm free of him, she thought. I need never have anything else to do with him. I should just give all my strength to Joel and go away and never think about any of it again. He probably has a landlady with children – or they were just visiting ... She tried as hard as she could to persuade herself that this was what was right. It was nothing to do with her. But she could not stop thinking about Sal and herself when Norman was living with them, of the trap of fear and disgust he had built round them. What if he was doing it all again and those two girls were having to live through the same hell that he had put Sal through?

She twisted back and forth in the bed, then lay on her back, hands behind her head looking at the window. There was a full moon and its light was shining through the gap between Nance's thin curtains.

'Tell me what to do,' she whispered. 'I don't want anything to do with this. Let it all just go away.' She ached for the morning to come.

She had left the hospital full of happiness yesterday, but going back today she approached it with terrible misgiving. She was weighed down by the grim thoughts brought on by lack of sleep and what had happened the night before. Mick had not come home all night.

'Oh – 'e'll've gone to 'is mom's to get fussed over,' Nance said. She was trying to take it lightly but she was pale and drawn and Maryann could tell she had not slept either.

This didn't feel like a day for anything good to happen. Her head aching, eyes watering in the sunlight from sleeplessness, she walked to the hospital.

She arrived to find Joel with his eyes open. All her dread drained away, seeing his gaze follow her hungrily towards his bed as if she was the one thing he had been waiting for. There was a little cup on the chair so she sank down on her knees by the bed and for a moment they just gazed at one another in silence. Joel tried to squeeze her hand and she could tell how weak he was.

'You're back,' she said. And burst into tears.

Joel tried to speak but the attempt produced instead a fit of coughing. He reached out for the cup and she passed it to him. He coughed painfully into it, then covered it with his hand. A nurse came and whisked it away and returned it empty a few moments later. Maryann wiped her eyes and got up to perch on the edge of the seat. Joel lay back, panting from the exertion.

'You poor thing,' she said.

Joel patted his chest. Maryann leaned over to hear him whisper, 'I think I've got half the cut in there from what's coming out.'

'But you're going to get better. I know you are. Oh Joel – I've been that worried about you. You've no idea.'

He looked very tenderly at her and she smiled tearfully and buried her head for a moment in the bedding beside him, still holding his hand and drinking in the feeling of being close to him. Then she sat up and examined him again.

'D'you feel better in yourself?'

He nodded. 'Seeing you.'

'I've been in here every day. Did you know? Did you know Darius came?'

Joel looked confused. 'Darius – in here?'

'No – I don't s'pose you remember. He stopped off to see you and then 'e went back to chase another load . . .' She remembered with a pang that perhaps Darius had seen Samuel Barlow again – perhaps had sold the *Esther Jane* already. She didn't know if Joel knew anything about it and she didn't want to have to tell him – not now especially. 'Anyway – your dad's on the mend. 'E's still down at your auntie's in Oxford but Darius said 'e should be back aboard soon. Darius had a young lad with 'im – Ernie Higgins I think 'is name was.'

She saw Joel nod faintly, and she could tell he was drinking in everything she was telling him. The boat was his life and she could see the hunger for it in his eyes. She leaned forward to catch his words.

'Want to get back aboard . . . soon.'

'Oh Joel – I don't think you'll be ready for a while yet.'

'Soon as I can . . .'

'All right—' She appeased him. How long would it be before he could even walk, let alone work the cut! But she didn't want to upset him.

'Maryann—' He pulled her closer.

'What, love?'

He gazed, very seriously, into her eyes. 'When I get back to 'er – will you be there this time – with me?'

He was coughing again and once more she had to wait for the seizure to pass. It exhausted him, but still he pulled her to him, full of urgency.

'Please . . . will you and me get wed?'

'Oh Joel, love—' She laid her hand against his cheek, stroking it, gently cradling his head. 'You're everything to me. Of course we will.'

He closed his eyes for a moment, quite spent, but with a smile of great joy on his face.

Thirty-Nine

The summer was slipping past. The schools closed and the streets, back yards and parks were full of the sounds of children playing.

Maryann had settled into being Nance and Mick's lodger and for the time being things were better. Mick had stayed away for three days and nights and came home with his arm bandaged and the look of a man who has been severely lectured by his mother. Mrs Mallone the elder, a staunch Catholic, wouldn't countenance the shame of a broken marriage in her family and had told him so in no uncertain terms. He arrived home at the end of a day's work and Maryann got out of the way to let him and Nance sort things out. They arrived at a truce.

'We've decided to stop arguing about us 'aving a babby,' Nance said bravely. 'We'll just 'ave to see what 'appens. And 'e said 'e should never've hit me the way 'e did and 'e don't really mind you being 'ere.'

Maryann thought that remained to be seen, but she was relieved as well. She just hoped Mick could put up with her until Joel was better.

Each day Maryann saw an improvement in Joel. He became a little stronger, bit by bit. Although he was still terribly thin his skin started to lose its deathly yellow colour, and he was able to talk more without being crippled by the agonizing cough. They talked a great deal on every visit, catching up with some of the time they had missed over the intervening years.

Sometimes Joel looked longingly at her. 'I wish we weren't sat here on full view of everyone – then I could give you a proper kiss.'

Just for a moment Maryann experienced her old surge of dread at the thought of any man touching her, and she had to reason with herself. Not every man was Norman Griffin. And this was Joel – her beloved Joel. She laughed happily. 'You *are* getting better, ain't yer?'

'Every day. I'll soon be strong enough to pick you up and carry you out of 'ere.'

She knew he'd give anything to be away from the alien place which the hospital was to him. 'Not long now,' she told him. 'Your chest'll be clear as a bell soon.'

'Oh – I don't think it'll ever be that!'

But she thought with misgiving about Joel going back to the cut. Was he going to find that his home of a lifetime no longer belonged to him? It didn't matter so much to her. It would still be the same boat, even if it did have Samuel Barlow's name painted on the side. And Darius had said there were a lot of advantages to working for someone else. They chased the loads and you got regular pay and insurance. But she still knew Joel would want to fight it.

She hadn't seen Darius since he'd visited Joel in hospital, although she left messages for him regularly. She wondered what was going on. She was almost as impatient as Joel for this time of waiting to be over so she could get away from Nancy and Mick's house and she and Joel could be together and plan their wedding.

Wedding! She was overcome with excitement and disbelief every time she thought about it. It felt so right, as if from the first time she had met Joel they had been picked out for each other and he had been just waiting for her to grow up. The two of them could go away. She imagined herself gliding off along the golden water of the cut at sunset, into a new life.

It was early one morning when she went to Handsworth and walked past Norman Griffin's new premises, reading the sign, 'Arthur Lambert'. She saw her own reflection, her tight-lipped expression, in the shop's dark window. The place wasn't open yet. She knew Norman Griffin horribly well and recalled the time of his methodical comings and goings. Oh, he was always organized, all right. You had to give him that. She waited in a shade-filled doorway on the other side of the road from his house so that he would not have to pass her. It wasn't that she didn't believe or trust Tony, only that she had to see him for herself.

He came, as she knew he would, a few minutes before nine o'clock: a black, square-shouldered figure, topped by a Homburg hat and moving at a stately pace along the street towards her. She could barely make out his face and didn't dare move closer. She clenched her fingers, digging in with her nails. He looked like any other respectable, middle-aged man who was running to fat a little. How could he look so ordinary, so harmless?

He took the keys from his pocket and unlocked the shop, then stepped inside out of sight. Maryann found she was sweating, her pulse racing. Six years had passed. She was a woman now, but the effect he had on her was just the same. She wanted to run away and never set eyes on him again.

But those little girls ... She had to know, somehow, whether they were suffering as she and Sal had suffered. If they weren't, then she could feel free to leave, never to go anywhere near Norman Griffin ever again. With slow, reluctant steps she set off towards the address Tony had given her, feeling very nervous and foolish. What on earth did she think she was going to do? A strange woman turning up, trying to talk to two girls who'd never seen her before, who'd be bound to tell their mom and then she'd tell Norman ... They wouldn't know who she was, but he almost certainly would.

I've got to find a way, she thought grimly. I just have to. When she reached the street of small terraced houses, she discovered with relief that almost opposite the address Tony had given her, number twenty-two Beechwood Road, was a side road leading into the next street and it was deep in shadow this morning, while the sun was shining brightly on the opposite side. At least she could walk less conspicuously up and down.

A half-hour passed. Some people moved up and down the pavement. A couple of women looked curiously at her as they passed. Another half-hour. A clock struck ten in the distance. Maryann was beginning to feel very bored and worried that people were watching her.

I'll come back tomorrow, she was thinking, when she saw the door open and someone coming out! She stood in the shade and watched. First she saw one girl appear with long auburn hair and carrying a shopping basket. Maryann guessed her age to be about twelve. She was followed by another, smaller girl, very similar looking though her hair was curlier and not as long as her older sister's. They were dressed in buttery yellow frocks, like a pair of pretty dolls. They obviously weren't living in the depths of poverty. But then they wouldn't be, would they? Maryann thought bitterly.

Then she saw their mother appear on the step, her own auburn hair coiled up at the back and a pleasant, though tense-looking face. She was leaning forwards, supporting herself on two sticks, and it was clear she had great difficulty in negotiating her way down. She handed one stick to the younger child and was helped down the front step by her older daughter. Taking up with both sticks again she waited while the older girl shut the front door, and then they began to make their way along the road. Maryann realized that there was going to be no danger of losing them. In fact, it was going to be hard to follow and not be seen because she was having to walk so slowly. The woman was apparently able-bodied in every other respect than in her right leg, which left her body at the hip at such an awkward angle that her walking on it was greatly hampered and twisted her from side to side as she did so.

She followed the grindingly slow progress of this family as they made their way round the shops fetching their groceries. Maryann saw that the girls were quite used to this routine and helped carry everything, or sometimes went into shops for their mother who called instructions to them if the entrance was particularly awkward for her. They seemed close and amiable together. She learned that the older girl was called Amy.

When they finally reached home, Maryann waited, and at last saw the two of them emerge from the house alone and set off towards Handsworth Park. Amy was carrying a hoop and they were skipping along quite fast. With a pang she saw herself and Sal, before, when their real dad was alive and they'd gone off to play like that with Tony in tow, scurrying off to the rezzer on hot summer afternoons. Maryann had to hurry now to keep up with them.

Once they reached the park they started throwing the hoop. There were other children playing in the park and Maryann relaxed, feeling she could stroll round them, keeping an eye on them. They kept busy with their hoop amid the yells and laughter of the other children. Maryann watched them carefully and in a very short time noticed something that made them stand out from the other children around them. They played with great intensity and never once did she see them laugh or even smile. They seemed only to notice each other, as if they were sealed in, away from everyone outside. Maryann knew that feeling. She saw the younger one surreptitiously touch herself, just for a second, between her legs, wincing. It was a gesture that probably no one else would have noticed. But Maryann began to know then, really know. She had to be absolutely sure though.

Moving round, she positioned herself in the path of the hoop that the older one was holding behind her head ready to lob overarm. It bounced and skittered across the grass. The younger girl ran but Maryann got there first, catching it as it spun past her.

'Oh – caught it for yer!' She smiled as the girl ran urgently towards her. 'Here you are, love.' She held it out but when the girl took it, Maryann held on so she couldn't just run off.

The girl tugged at it, frowning furiously when Maryann didn't immediately let go.

'It's awright – I'm not taking it away. It was just coming at me so fast I caught it.' Out of the corner of her eye she saw the older girl running towards them. 'It's a nice one, ain't it? Who bought you that then?'

There was no reply.

The older sister arrived, looking very wary.

'I just caught your hoop – you threw it so hard,' Maryann said.

'Sorry,' she said, dully.

'No – it's awright.' Maryann gently released the hoop, asking as she did so, 'You must have a mom who's good at sewing – did she make your lovely dresses?'

Amy nodded. She seemed to see that Maryann was being friendly. While she still looked solemn, the hostility drained out of her expression. She stood holding the hoop against her legs, with her weight on one foot, the other leg bent back, the toe of her black rubber pump resting on the ground.

'Well, she's better at sewing than I am.' She fought desperately for a reason to keep them with her and fumbled in her pocket. 'Look – I've got some toffees. D'yer fancy one?'

The girls looked at each other, then nodded in unison.

'Here y'are.' Maryann sat down hoping they would do the same, but they stood above her, the toffees bulging in their cheeks. They each had freckles, the older one just across the bridge of her nose, while the younger one had them scattered, golden, all over her face.

Maryann wanted to be gentle with them, befriend them, but she was also worried they'd run off before she could ask them anything, so she came straight to her questions. 'So – your mom or dad not out with you?'

Amy shook her head.

'Your dad's at work I expect?'

The two girls seemed to draw physically close, together as their eyes lost contact with hers and looked down at the ground. The fierce tone of the older girl's voice as she half spoke, half whispered, brought Maryann's flesh up in goose pimples.

''E ain't our dad.'

The emotions were there for anyone who knew how to read them the fear, the disgust and loathing. And for Maryann it was like listening to herself speak, as if her own soul had addressed her from out of the young girl's mouth.

She kept them with her for as long as she could. They accepted another toffee but still wouldn't sit down.

'What's your name?' she asked the older one. Of the two she had the longer face, was rather pretty with her autumn looks. But her gaze slid distractedly away when Maryann spoke to her. She might meet her eyes for a fraction of a second, then she would stare away across the park towards the trees or look down at her feet.

'I'm Amy. This is Margaret.'

Margaret's gaze didn't leave the ground. She was standing with her weight on the outside of her feet, concentratedly chewing her toffee. Hers was the rounder face, hair more carroty, expression closed tight as a trap.

'How old're you then, Margaret?'

'She's nine,' Amy said. 'I'm twelve.'

Maryann longed to ply them with questions but she did not want to frighten them. Margaret had still not said a word to her. 'You'd better get back to your game then,' she said. 'D'you come to the park every day?'

Amy nodded in her vague way, eyes sweeping the park. Margaret put her head on one side and looked sulky.

'Might see you again then.' Maryann got up. 'T'ra for now. Have a nice game.'

They returned immediately to their hoop as if she had never existed.

She found them the next day sitting on the grass not far from the park entrance, the hoop lying on the ground beside them, each wearing turquoise dresses and a white bow in their hair. They were turned slightly towards each other, their heads bowed, and Maryann thought that from the way they were sitting they must be busy playing or making daisy chains. As she came closer, though, she saw they were not doing anything.

'Amy? Margaret? Hello there – thought I might see you again.'

Margaret, as ever, kept her head down, but Amy glanced up and her mouth almost twitched into a smile. Maryann sat down on the grass beside them. What she said next had taken some careful thought.

'I never said what my name was when I saw yer yesterday. I'm Esther. Esther Bartholomew.' She didn't want to tell them fibs. But nor did she want to ask them to keep her meeting them a secret from their mother. If she told them her real name though, and they mentioned it in front of Norman ... She went cold at the very thought. ''Ere – I brought some bull's-eyes today – d'yer fancy one? I never go anywhere without a bag of rocks.'

When the girls were both sucking their sweets, she

took the plunge. 'So you live with your mom and stepdad, do you?'

She got no reaction from little Margaret, but Amy nodded, tugging furiously with her thumb and forefinger at the short, dry grass.

'What happened to your real father?'

'He went away.' Amy spoke so quietly Maryann could barely hear.

'Oh dear, did he? How old were you when he went away?'

'Nine.'

'And has your stepdad been with you a long time?'

Amy nodded. A long time could mean anything, Maryann realized. Most likely it seemed like an eternity to them.

'I had a stepdad when I was your age,' she told them. 'My own father died in an accident and our mom got married again.' She took a deep breath. 'I daint like 'im. In fact I hated 'im.'

Amy looked at her, her expression betraying nothing more than mild curiosity. She was tapping her foot up and down on the grass.

'Is your stepfather nice to yer?'

''E's awright. Takes us to the pictures, and that, sometimes.'

'D'you like going to the pictures, Margaret?'

The girl's head seemed to sink further down, her hair hanging over her face. There was a long silence.

'You're a quiet one,' Maryann said gently.

'She don't speak,' Amy said.

'Not to anyone?'

'Only me. Sometimes.'

'I s'pose you'll be back at school soon.'

Amy nodded. 'Next week.'

'D'yer like school?'

'S'awright.'

She could think of nothing to say which might lift their apparent dull acceptance of life. It was as if there was a wall round the two of them. How could she, a stranger, break through it? She didn't want to frighten the girls. Mostly she wanted to put her arms round them and comfort them.

She left them that day, feeling desperate, as if she had let both them and herself down.

That afternoon when she went to see Joel again, she didn't mention Amy and Margaret. She hadn't told Nancy either. She couldn't bring herself to speak of it. And if it was hard for her, she knew that it was well nigh impossible for those little girls to put into words what was happening to them. She couldn't go barging into their family and confront Norman. After all, who would believe her? Her own mother hadn't. It seemed hopeless, the seal of privacy around respectable family life behind which a man's tormenting habits could hide and grow monstrous. Whatever could she really do to help them and stop Norman Griffin's vileness – for good?

Forty

'What're yer wearing that long face for?' Nance asked the next morning. She was clearing away the remains of Mick's breakfast – a bloater and bread and butter – screwing up her nose at the fishy smell. Maryann leaned over to wipe the table, glad that her hair swung forward to hide her face.

'*Have* I got a long face on?'

'Yes, you 'ave. I thought everything was awright – you said Joel was looking much better yesterday.'

'Oh – 'e is – I was just thinking, that's all.' Maryann quickly rearranged her expression along less perplexed lines and stood straight, shaking back her hair. The strain of the past weeks showed in her face, even though she tried to look calm.

She couldn't tell Nance just how much those two little girls were possessing her. She lay awake at night thinking of them. One minute she was telling herself she was imagining it all. They were well dressed and cared for, they played in the park like any other children. She should stop thinking she had any place in their lives. But it was the tiny signs which she understood so intimately that gave them away. Margaret's silence, the shame that made Amy's eyes slide away from anyone's gaze, the very way they held their bodies, never quite at ease. They were suffering and only she could imagine how. What could she do? She felt furious at her helplessness. That night she had resolved before she went to sleep that she would go and see the girls' mother and speak to her. At least tell her what she suspected, alert her to what might be going on in her home. Now, this morning, this seemed preposterous. Maryann ran the cloth over the table, mopping up rings of tea and crumbs. She must talk to Amy and Margaret again first, see if she could get them to trust her, open up to her.

'How long d'yer think it's going to be before Joel can go out of the hospital?' Nance was saying, scraping off Mick's plate into a piece of newspaper.

'Wish I knew, Nance. 'E's so weak it's hard to watch 'im sometimes. 'E can barely stand out of bed. Sometimes I want to just pick him up and carry him he looks that thin.' She went and rinsed out the cloth in the pail of water Nance kept out the back. 'I just want 'im out, Nance. All this time I've been away and now 'e's stuck in there. It feels as if we'll never be able to be together.'

'Oh – you will.' Nance turned and looked through the door at her, wistfully. 'You're ever so lucky. You know – starting out right with someone.'

Maryann came back in from the scullery. 'But you and Mick're getting on better. I mean you ain't been fighting and carrying on like you did before . . .'

'No – I know.' Nance pushed her hands down behind the belt of her apron. She looked miserable. 'But there's no *feeling* between us. Never was really – we both sort of went along with it. I'd never 'ad those feelings, see. So I daint know I was missing anything. But I know there's summat more and you've got it – you and Joel. It's made me see . . . And now I'm stuck with 'im for ever . . .' She stopped, looking down miserably. 'I've always tried to be good, you know, Maryann. Listened to what the priests said and done what I was told. But I don't 'alf 'ave some bad thoughts lately. I don't even dare go to confession and say what's been going through my mind.'

'Oh Nance . . .' Maryann, who'd never had to go to confession in her life, struggled to find the right words, but failed and just stood looking at her, full of pity.

Nance put her hands over her face for a moment, then drew them away and turned round. 'Well – this won't get nowt done. I'd better get cleared away and off up the shops.'

'I'll finish clearing up,' Maryann said. 'You go on out. It'll make you feel better.'

When Nance had gone she washed and dried the breakfast things as usual, swept the room and got ready to go out, feeling nervous and unsettled. Should she talk more to the girls today? Tell them the truth: that their stepfather had also been hers? Would that be the best thing? But her heart was heavy. What did she think she was trying to do – break up a family? Thrust them out of one kind of suffering into another – the insecurity and poverty into which she had condemned her own mother?

It was raining gently outside, through a heavy, late summer warmth. She took her coat and started off down the road. But before she had got very far she saw a tall figure turn in at the end of the street, walking towards her through the drizzle with an unmistakable gait. Her pulse quickened.

'Darius!' Overjoyed, cheeks flushing a healthier pink, she ran down the road to meet him. He smiled, seeing her dashing along the street, impatiently pushing strands of her black hair out of her face. 'When did yer get in? I daint know when we'd see yer again!'

'I'm glad to see *you*,' he said. 'I wasn't sure I'd find the right place again.'

'You just caught me – I was off out. Come on down to the 'ouse. Nance is out shopping but she'll be back soon. Oh Darius, you should see Joel – 'e's looking so much better than last time you was 'ere.'

'Oh—' Darius seemed to sag with relief. 'Thank 'eavens for that. I've been thinking, round and round, what we're gunna do. My father's still not right and I've 'ad to keep Ernie on. I couldn't think 'ow I could manage – even selling out. Joel looked that bad – I thought 'e might not come through after all. Is 'e going to be in there much longer?'

'I don't know – he's ever so keen to get going. You know Joel. He'd be out of there by now if he had the strength to move hisself.'

Darius chuckled. Once more he seemed very tired, but more relaxed now he had heard the good news. He sat at the table in Nance's house and Maryann stoked the fire and put the kettle on again.

'You'd like some breakfast, wouldn't yer?'

'Wouldn't mind – if you've enough. Been going most of the night again.'

'We ain't got much in till Nance gets back, but 'er won't be long.'

'Oh – a cuppa'd do me.'

'You can 'ave that for a start – our Nance'll feed you up like a turkey cock.'

She made tea for them both, scraping out the last of the condensed milk, and sat down, beaming at him. 'I've got summat to tell you.' She couldn't wait any longer. It already felt as if he was her brother. 'Me and Joel, we ... well, 'e asked me if we'd get wed.'

Darius stared at her, swallowing a mouthful of tea.

A smile spread slowly across his face. 'What – and yer'd come and . . .?'

'Live on the *Esther Jane* – course we would. Where else d'yer think Joel'd ever live?' She was full of excitement. 'I'm so glad you've come now because I was afraid you'd already've sold her and you don't need to – we can all work her together and stay as Number Ones . . .'

Darius held up one of his huge, callused hands. 'Now – 'old your 'orses a minute. You don't know the life, Maryann – not 'ow things've got now. For a start, we could all keep the *Esther Jane* going, but you and Joel ain't gunna want me about for long if you're wed, with a family coming along. That's one thing. Now I'd go back and work a Fellows' boat down London like I done before and leave you to it once Joel's got 'is strength back if that were just it. But it's all changing. We just ain't keeping ahead and getting the loads we need. Now – I've thought long and hard about this, and tomorrow Essy Barlow's gunna be 'ere and 'e's taking on the *Esther Jane* – and what's more—' He held his hand up again to prevent Maryann from interrupting. 'There're going to be changes. 'E's promised to put a motor in 'er and we'll work a pair again. When you and Joel are ready to work 'er together you can 'ave 'er for your home with my blessing, but that's 'ow it'll 'ave to be. I don't like it neither, but we're going to 'ave to 'just to it. That's the only way we're gunna keep up.'

'A motor? You mean – no more Bessie?'

'No more Bessie, and a lot of noise and stink besides. But it's the only way forward. There's more and more moty boats now and they shift the loads. We ent keeping up – simple as that.'

Maryann was digesting this when the door opened and Nancy appeared, panting with two heavy bags of shopping, her coat shiny with rain.

'Oh—' She had expected the house to be empty and was really taken aback. ''Ello ... Darius.' She seemed very flustered and turned away to put the bags down, but not before Maryann saw how much she was blushing.

'Can I get Darius a bit of breakfast? 'E's been on the go a long while again.'

'No – let me get it,' Nance said at once.

'Very good of you, Nancy,' Darius said gruffly.

'No – it's – I'm glad to. I wish I'd've known you was coming – I'd've got a bit of bacon in ...'

While Nance fussed about cooking eggs and sawing doorsteps off a loaf of bread, Maryann reported to her what Darius had said. Nance presented him with a moutainous breakfast of eggs and fried bread and bread and butter, then sat down with some satisfaction to watch him eat it.

'You come to visit yer brother again then, 'ave yer?' she asked.

Darius nodded, his strong jaws working away. 'Thought I'd see Joel. And deal with Mr Barlow tomorrow ...' He paused, then added, 'I just wondered. Today's the last day she'll be our boat, proper. D'you want to come out on 'er for a bit – see 'ow she really goes before they stick a moty on 'er?'

Maryann was just about to answer when she realized his question had been addressed to Nance. After all, she was no stranger to the *Esther Jane*!

'Ooh, well ... today? What, now like?' Nance seemed to swell with excitement.

'The day'll be over, else. See, a bloke at Gas Street

said if we go down the Worcester and Birnigum Cut it goes past the back of the chocolate fact'ry and we can turn down by Selly Oak Wharf – and you said that's near Joel's 'ospital.'

'Yes, it is,' Maryann said. 'We could go and see him from there. We'll 'ave to stop 'im breaking out of the 'ospital to come and see 'er! Oh go on, Nance – it'll be lovely, look – the rain's going off already.'

Nance was all smiles. 'Oh – go on then. I'd like that, Darius – I really would.'

Maryann could tell from her expression that this was something of an understatement.

'Poor old Bessie – she's tired,' Maryann said as they slid out away from Gas Street amid a busy to-ing and fro-ing of joeys, some empty and riding high, others laden and low in the water. The sky was hazy with cloud and smoke, but the rain had gone off and it was clearing up.

'Well – we'll go gently. Tomorrow she can 'ave a long rest,' Darius said.

Young Ernie, who'd worked his way up with Darius, was quite happy to spend a day away on the bank. Nance had stepped aboard saying, 'Just think, Maryann – this'll be your home soon. How on earth are you going to manage?'

Maryann laughed, patting Jep, who had greeted them wagging not just his tail but the whole of his body. She felt she could manage anything so long as Joel was going to get better and be beside her. 'I'll 'ave to get good strong arms, that's all! It's a killer on yer shoulders working on 'ere.'

'Bet I could manage,' Nance said, prodding her

muscles. Nancy had always had a robust frame and now she was thinner she looked wiry and strong, like a greyhound.

Maryann saw Darius watching Nance appraisingly. 'Reckon you could,' he said.

They wound along between the smoking factories, the wharves and warehouses, down the Worcester Canal, moving south. As they glided out through the Edgbaston tunnel to Bournbrook then Selly Oak, the route became greener. Trains chugged past to their right and occasionally the sun broke through the cloud and transformed the dull, scummy ripples to silver. After a short time Maryann had taken up her favourite position on the cabin roof, her hand stroking Jep who sat panting beside her. Coots and moorhens scooted away from the bow of the boat. Butterflies shimmered round flowers in the grass. She took deep, contented breaths. However hard this life, whatever the struggle, this was what she wanted: this was her place and these were her people. Somehow it seemed to have chosen her.

Nance stayed with Darius at the stern and Maryann could hear him instructing her how to work the tiller. Often she heard Nancy's laughter and smiled. It was so good to hear Nancy enjoying herself. She felt herself swelling with happiness, everything else forgotten except that she was here and Joel was getting better. She throbbed with love and longing for him. If only he could be here today, it would be perfect!

They tied up at Selly Oak. Jep pottered off to explore the towpath while they ate bread and cheese that Nancy had brought. Darius had some plums on board, the skins a beautiful reddish orange that seemed to contain the very sunshine that had ripened them. They were sweet and delicious, and they spat the stones overboard.

'So're we gunna turn round 'ere then?' Nance asked.

Darius laughed. 'You can't just turn 'er anywhere. The cut's narrower than the boat – look.'

'Oh yes—' Nance chuckled. 'So it is. I never thought about that before!'

'You 'ave to find a winding 'ole where you can turn – it's just keep going otherwise.'

All morning he had been explaining things to her. Maryann had never heard him speak anything like as much before. She watched them as they perched together at the stern, eating their lunch. It was only then it truly dawned on her. It was so clear in their eyes, the way Darius looked at Nance, her radiance in his presence. However much they tried to hide it, to behave normally, she could see the two of them were falling deeply in love, and she was filled with dread and sorrow.

Maryann turned away from them. What Nance had said this morning, *But now I know there's summat more . . .* Had she just been talking about what Maryann and Joel had? She hadn't, had she? She had been saying so much more. She could hear their voices behind her, and it only increased her sense of disquiet. She thought of Mick and pitied him. But she pitied Nance just as much, and Darius for his lonely, hardworking existence.

There came another peal of laughter from Nance; a youthful, carefree sound.

God, Nance, Maryann thought, just keep yourself under control.

Whatever happened, if they gave rein to their feelings, someone was going to end up broken-hearted.

*

'Look who I've brought!'

Joel was just waking as they arrived and Maryann leaned down and kissed him tenderly. He returned the kiss, clasping her hand, then caught sight of his brother.

'Darius!' He made a couple of attempts and finally managed to haul himself up. 'Damn it – I keep forgetting I'm weak as a kitten!'

'This is my friend Nance – she's putting me up for the time being.'

'Putting up with 'er more like.' Nance laughed. 'Nice to meet yer at last.'

'We'll go out for now,' Maryann said, taking Nance's arm firmly. She had words to say to her. 'Let you two 'ave a chat.' She knew Darius was going to have to tell Joel about Mr Barlow.

'What's going on, Nance?' she demanded in a fierce whisper, once they were out in the corridor. There was a constant flow of people up and down, nurses and visitors, so no one took much notice of them.

'What're you on about?'

'You – making up to Darius, that's what.' Maryann found she was furious and boiling over with frustration. Of course Darius and Nance were right together! It stood out a mile. When she was with him, Nance was the happy, laughing person she had been before her marriage. She should be able to be with him and spend her life with him. But it couldn't be like that because Nance was Mrs Mallone and Mrs Mallone she would have to stay.

Nance looked crestfallen. 'Oh Lor', Maryann – does it show that much? I never meant it – I know 'ow wrong it is. Only whenever I'm near 'im I just can't help myself. I know 'e likes me – you can tell, can't yer? I just feel so *right* when 'e's here. Oh, I'd give anything. . . .' She looked appealingly at Maryann. 'Look – I know why yer going on at me. But Darius'll be gone soon and once you're away I'll never see 'im again. I'll just 'ave to swallow the fact. Let me enjoy today, that's all.' With tears in her voice she finished, 'Then I'll 'ave to get back to my proper life.'

They pulled back into the Gas Street wharves in the cool late afternoon.

Maryann had been leading Bessie for the last part of the journey, patting her and talking to her to encourage her. Despite the horse's obvious weariness she seemed happy enough to plod along. There were few flies to bother her and it wasn't too hot.

'I'm going to miss you, Bessie,' she murmured, kissing her hot, smooth neck. 'What's going to become of you, eh?'

When she had gone back in to see Joel, Maryann looked anxiously to see how he was taking the news about the *Esther Jane*, but he looked calm enough.

'You've told 'im then?' she asked Darius.

'We'll still have our home.' Joel looked at her and she swelled inside with happiness. 'After all this I'm happy knowing I'm going to be alive. Everything else comes after that.'

As the afternoon wore on, she felt increasingly that she should leave Darius and Nance alone together and give them a chance to say anything that needed to be said.

She was walking ahead of the *Esther Jane* with Bessie, but once when she looked back she saw that Darius had an arm round Nance's shoulders, their faces were close as they talked with obvious intensity. The

shortage of time together had speeded up events. Maryann looked away, full of sorrow.

When they had tied up and stabled Bessie and it was
time to say goodbye, Nance could contain herself no
longer. Maryann had come back from the stables, tearful at parting with Bessie, to find her and Darius in
each other's arms. Seeing it was time to go home, Nance
also burst into tears.

'Oh, I can't leave yer, Darius. I can't – it ain't right.
Today's been the best day of my life – I just want to
stay with you!'

'I know,' he said, gently trying to loose her from
him, though Maryann could see how little he really
wanted to. 'But you can't just come with me, Nancy.
You're married – it'd be wrong.'

'Why's it wrong when I don't love 'im? I love *you*.
Oh, I've said it now—' She stood sobbing, distraught,
beside the *Esther Jane*. 'But that's how it is. I've never
loved 'im and now I'm stuck with 'im and it ain't
right!'

'Oh Nancy . . .' Darius put his hand on her shoulder,
casting a desperate look at Maryann. 'You don't know
what I'd give for things to be different . . . I'd like you
as my wife, and that's the truth of it . . .'

Still weeping, Nance thrashed her hands back and
forth through the air in furious frustration. 'It ain't fair.
Why do things 'ave to be as they are – eh? Why did I
go and say I'd marry Mick? It was so stupid – *stupid*
. . . as if 'e was the only man who was ever going to
come along!'

'Come on, Nance—' Maryann said gently. 'We're
going to 'ave to get home . . .'

'Go on—' Darius said, his voice cracking. 'Please –
go now.'

They held each other one last time before Darius pulled away and stepped down into the *Esther Jane*. He ducked into the cabin as if he could not bear to watch them both walk away.

Forty-One

On Monday morning Maryann set off to find Amy and Margaret again. It was a cool, overcast morning with a definite nip of autumn and she was worried that the girls might not come to the park. If they didn't come out she would be forced to go to the house. She knew she had to see them.

It had been a difficult weekend. Nance was as low as Maryann had ever seen her and she had spent as much time with her as possible, trying to console her and keep her mind away from Darius. Maryann had gone to Mass with her and Mick, and Nance kept filling up with tears all the way through.

'What the hell's the matter with you?' Mick demanded when they stepped outside the church.

'Nothing *you*'d ever understand,' Nance snarled at him which sent Mick swearing off into the distance in a temper.

'I feel as if my life's over,' Nance sobbed to Maryann.

All weekend she had been casting hateful looks at Mick. Maryann felt terrible for her, but they both knew Nance was going to have to settle down and forget Darius.

On Sunday when Maryann went to see Joel he was sitting up waiting for her.

'They've said another week or so and I can be off

out of here!' He beamed. 'Oh – I've almost forgotten what it's like to breathe in fresh air. Just the idea of being able to go out and walk round outside seems – well, I can hardly take it in!'

'Oh Joel – I can't wait until we can be together,' Maryann said. She was desperate to leave Nance's house with all its unhappiness. Although she felt guilty about leaving Nance there was nothing she could do about her situation. She longed to get on with her life with Joel after all the waiting.

'We'll 'ave to start fixing up a wedding day.' Joel looked into her eyes with a sense of wonder. 'Little Maryann – and you're going to be my wife.'

She smiled back, face alight with happiness. 'Soon as we can manage,' she said.

He stroked a finger gently down her cheek. 'We can share everything that comes – best mates, eh?'

She thought about this as she walked to Handsworth. Joel had said they could get married in Oxford, near to where his auntie lived and where old Darius Bartholomew was recuperating.

'But if you want to get wed here – so your family can come,' he said. 'We could think of that instead?'

'No,' she said firmly. 'My mom won't come wherever my wedding is. I might be able to get our Tony down for it, but your family's my family now, Joel. Oxford's lovely and it'll suit me fine.'

She felt strong and joyful inside, as if nothing could ever harm her again, Joel's love warming and strengthening her. Her only anxiety was his leaving hospital so soon. Where were they going to go if Darius didn't get back? But even this didn't seem insurmountable. She still had some money left. If necessary they'd have to rent somewhere until the *Esther Jane* was ready. She wouldn't stay with Nance any longer than she had to. She felt she'd already brought enough trouble into her life.

Turning into the park she looked round for the girls. It was much quieter today, an end of summer quiet. School was due to begin the next day. With a sinking feeling of dread she thought for a moment that they weren't there. It was almost midday – this was when she had found them before.

After a moment strolling round she spotted them over by the pond, both kneeling, peering down into the water. Her heart went out to them.

'Hello, girls,' she said softly.

Still kneeling side by side, they swivelled round together so that the tops of their heads were almost touching. Their eyes held the usual closed blankness, though she thought she saw a flicker of welcome in the older girl's expression. Amy stood up slowly.

'Hello.'

Margaret turned away.

'I thought I'd come and see you – school tomorrow, ain't it?'

Amy nodded.

'I've er . . . I've got some nice peanut toffee – d'yer want some?' She felt like a wicked witch in a fairy story, luring them with sweets, but she had to get them to come and sit with her somehow. Margaret just shook her head and carried on facing the other way.

'I'll 'ave a bit,' Amy said. 'Please,' she added.

''Ere – I'll sit down next to yer,' Maryann said, tucking the skirt under her on the grass, sitting quite close to Margaret. Even if she couldn't get her to come and sit with them she wanted to be sure she heard what she was going to say. Amy sat on her left, chewing the toffee, her legs bent, leaning sideways on one arm.

There was no point in dilly-dallying. She had to say something.

'Look, Amy – you must've thought it was a bit strange me coming and seeing yer in the park. I mean it's been nice for me getting to know you a bit – but there's another reason why I've been coming.'

Amy's hair was hanging half across her face and she didn't look up but Maryann could tell she was listening.

'I've seen your stepfather – going to his shop and that. I know he calls himself Arthur Lambert, but the truth is, that ain't his name. Or at least that ain't always been his name.' Her heart was beating terribly hard. Was she wrong to do this, was she? She forced herself on. 'The thing is – I used to know 'im under another name. He was called Norman Griffin and he was my stepfather an' all – when my sister and me were not much older than you are now. And . . .'

She swallowed, almost unable to go on. Amy cast her a quick glance, then looked down again. Margaret was sitting by the water, absolutely still.

'The thing is – when 'e was living with us, he daint treat us like . . . like a dad ought've done. He was . . . bad. 'E . . .' She took a deep, shuddering breath. 'Oh God help me for saying this to yer!' She spoke with her gaze fixed on Amy's face, watching for her reaction to her words. She didn't want to leave them in any doubt as to what she was admitting to them, but she was trembling as she spoke.

'He was wicked, the way he was with us. At night he came to our rooms and . . . and made us do things –

things children ain't s'posed to do – and he made us feel dirty and different to everyone else . . .'

She couldn't go on. Her voice was choked with tears. Looking at Amy she saw that the girl had turned her head and it was tilted so that her hair completely hid her face. She had brought her hand up and pressed it tightly over her lips. The gesture spoke more loudly than any words.

Maryann wiped her eyes, trying to control herself. Very slowly and gently she reached out her hand and pushed the girl's hair aside.

'Amy? I was so frightened of speaking out of turn and getting it wrong. Is it . . . is he still the same?'

She released Amy's hair and watched her. There was a long pause during which Maryann almost despaired of an answer. But then the coppery hair began to quiver and she saw the girl was nodding. A quick, frightened nod.

'Oh God,' Maryann gasped. 'You're saying yes, ain't you, Amy?'

This time the nod was more definite.

'You poor things . . .' She wanted to reach out and take the child in her arms, but she restrained herself. Half whispering she said, 'What about . . . Margaret?'

Again the nod, more vigorously this time.

'Your mom – does she know anything about it?'

This time a shake of the head.

They all sat in silence for a minute. Margaret had still not turned round.

Maryann sat thinking furiously. Her own mother had not believed her. Why should theirs be any different? She had her life to protect, her security. And Norman was so smooth and respectable. Why would the woman listen to a complete stranger?

'There's one more thing I want to tell you, Amy. My name's not Esther Bartholomew like I told you. I daint want to tell you my real name in case you mentioned it at home in front of him. I'm Maryann Nelson – you can call me Maryann. Look, I can't promise you anything, Amy. I don't know if I can make it stop – if I was to see your mom. She won't want to hear it. But d'you want me to try?'

Amy's head swung round and for the first time she looked into Maryann's eyes. Her own were full of tears. Never had Maryann seen a more desperate, yearning face.

'Please,' she whispered. 'Make it stop.'

'Come on then.' Maryann stood up and Amy did the same. 'It's now or never, Amy.'

She looked warily at the younger girl. Amy went to her.

'Margaret – come on. We're going 'ome. This lady's coming with us.'

Margaret slowly, almost mechanically it seemed, got to her feet and turned to come with them. As she did so the blank expression in her young eyes chilled Maryann to the bone.

Maryann brought her hand up to knock at the door. Amy had been about to open it but she said, 'No – wait. I can't just go walking into your mom's house. I'll knock first.'

She was terrified, her knees like jelly, yet somewhere in her she was also triumphant. No longer did she have to feel wicked, to be told she was imagining things. She was not alone. She and these girls could stand together.

389

'She'll be cross,' Amy said uncomfortably as Mary-ann knocked. 'Takes 'er a while to get to the door.'

They heard her moving painfully along the hall. When the door opened Maryann suddenly found herself looking into the face of the auburn-haired woman. There were lines across her forehead and at the corners of her mouth which indicated that she suffered pain. She had pale skin, lightly freckled, wide eyes of a deep blue and a gentle, patient expression. Maryann was reassured. Her face was not the tight, bitter mask her mother had taken on through her hardships.

'Oh—' the woman said, eyeing her daughters. 'Is summat the matter? I hope they haven't done anything wrong?'

'No—' Maryann smiled nervously. 'Nothing like that. Only – I've met your daughters over in the park a few times recently and we've got a bit friendly like. There's a reason why I was looking out for them ... D'you think I could come in and talk to you for a minute or two? There's summat I'd like to say to you.' She glanced at Amy and Margaret but their faces were blank once more.

'Well – awright then,' the woman said doubtfully. 'I 'ope it won't take long though. I've got the dinner on.'

She led them into the nearest room, which was the front parlour. Maryann was not in a state to take in much detail except that the room was very clean and neatly arrayed, with polished brasses by the grate and moss green curtains.

'Sit down, won't you?' the woman said, easing herself into a chair. They were positioned either side of the fire and there was a rag rug between them in bright colours. Maryann could smell lavender. Nervously she took off her straw hat and sat holding it on her lap.

'Why don't you run along, girls?' Janet Richards said.

'Oh – no, please,' Maryann said quickly. 'They need to stay.'

'But I thought you said – I mean they're not in trouble . . . ?' She frowned anxiously.

'No – at least, not the way you mean. Oh dear, this is so . . .' She clasped her hands under her hat to try and stop them shaking. 'I don't know where to start.'

Janet was beginning to look as if she doubted her own wisdom in letting this stranger into the house, so Maryann plunged in and began talking quickly, explaining, trying not to put things too harshly nor to skirt round the truth. The girls stood close by.

'See – as soon as I saw him again I knew it was him,' she explained. ''E weren't called Arthur Lambert when 'e lived with our mom – Norman Griffin was his name. But it was him, and when I saw your daughters, the way they were, I just knew. It's hard to explain unless you've suffered it yourself. No one'd believe me when I was their age. My mother turned against me – she still won't see me. And today I asked Amy whether 'e was . . . well, doing the same to her and Margaret and when she said 'e was I just couldn't let it rest. I know this'll be a shock to you and you must think I'm terrible to interfere, but I had to come and say something rather than let them go through the same . . .' She ran out of steam at last.

The woman's expression was frozen. Shock, fear, disbelief all competed and for a time she couldn't speak.

'Amy—' she gasped eventually. 'Amy? What's she saying – who is she? And what've you been telling her?'

'Oh, don't be angry with them!' Maryann implored

her. She all but got down on her knees in front of the woman to plead with her. The girls stood listening, hanging their heads. She wanted them to speak up and plead with their mother, but she knew they couldn't do it. 'They shouldn't get in any trouble for telling me. They've been through enough – it's him you want to ask questions of. He's the one who takes over people's families, wrecks their lives. I know 'e looks like a gentleman and 'e's polite and well dressed and everything but underneath 'e's summat else – there's a side to 'im only a few of us have seen.'

The woman's eyes narrowed into slits, the look of sweetness quite gone from her face. She struggled to her feet, raising her walking stick as if she was going to hit Maryann, who hastily stood up as well.

'Who *are* you?' she hissed. 'What d'you think you're about, coming into my house and coming out with this *filth* in front of my two young girls? What've you been saying to them – poisoning their minds and filling them with these dirty lies. What do you want? You must be wrong in the head. Why didn't you say this woman'd been hanging around yer, Amy? What's she been saying to yer? Did she tell yer to come and make up stories about your father?'

Maryann's hand went to her throat as she watched Amy. For a second, which seemed eternal, the girl stood motionless. Then she raised her head a little and her face was burning red. Eyes still looking at the floor, she said, 'She daint make me, Mom. It's true. It's what 'e does – to Margaret and me. 'E does . . .' Her mother was shaking her head in horror. ''E *does*, Mom – upstairs, at bedtime.'

They all froze then, because there came the sound of the front door opening and a man's heavy tread entering the house. The front door was closed, loudly, and his footsteps moved through to the back.

'Janet!' They heard a moment later, 'Janet?'

She looked round at her daughters and at Maryann with utter contempt. Maryann, feeling her legs give way, sank down on to the chair.

'He's come home for his dinner.' Janet's mouth twisted bitterly. 'Now we'll see, won't we? Arthur!' she called. 'We're in the front.'

The door opened and Maryann found herself face to face with Norman Griffin.

Forty-Two

He looked so wide, filling the doorframe, standing there in his black coat. There was a long silence. In a corner of her mind, Maryann could hear the clock ticking and a horse's hooves passing in the street. His glance swept round the room, rested on her for a fleeting moment during which her pulse seemed to stop, then passed over to his family.

He had shown not a flicker of recognition. Have I changed that much? Maryann thought. Looking at him she was stunned once more by his familiarity, as if even now when he was fatter and his hair thinned she could remember every pore of the skin on his face, every quiver of expression. Her body, seeming in his presence to remember even more, his loathsome touch, felt turned to water. If she had not already been sitting down she would have collapsed.

'My dear? What's going on?'

Janet Lambert was standing, leaning on her stick, the girls near to her. 'Oh Arthur,' she said and then burst into tears. He was beside her immediately.

'Whatever's the matter, love? What's been going on? Who's your visitor?' His words dripped concern like syrup.

'She came in with the girls – she's been saying the most terrible things, Arthur . . . And now Amy's saying

them too – the same lies ... I can't even bring myself
to tell you ...'

He turned, looked at Amy and Margaret, then Maryann felt his eyes boring into her.

'What's going on in my 'ouse? Who're you?'

She thought her anger might choke her. She managed
to stand up, clutching folds of her skirt in her hands to
steady herself. 'You know perfectly well who I am, Mr
Griffin,' she spat at him. 'I'm Maryann Nelson. Remember – your stepdaughter? And under the law you're still
married to my mother, Mrs Florence Griffin.'

She heard Janet Lambert gasp. 'Arthur no! She must
have the wrong person. What's she saying?'

Norman Griffin gave a bewildered shrug that could
have won him a part in a troop of actors. 'I've no idea,
my dear – where on earth did you pick 'er up from?
Has she got loose from the asylum or summat?' He
even managed a chuckle. 'Never heard anything like it.
Why did you let her in?'

'You know who I am!' Maryann shouted at him. She
could feel herself becoming hysterical. There was such
a pressure rising inside her that she felt as if she might
explode.

'D'you think I'd ever forget the man who did things
to me that shouldn't be done to an animal, you vile,
filthy pig?' She faced Janet Lambert. 'He's the one who
came to our room night after night and interfered with
us so's we prayed every day that night would never
come. D'you think anyone'd ever forget that? And
now' – she turned on Janet Lambert – 'you've got two
daughters praying the same thing. Because from the
day you let that *animal* into the house they lost their
childhood. They were never safe again. Tell her Amy—'
She stepped over to the girl and held her shoulder.

Speaking softly she said, 'You know what you told me – say it to your mom. Tell her the truth or he'll just go on and on and you'll never get away from it.'

Amy's shoulders were shaking. She put her hands over her face. Her mother watched, appalled, her eyes stretched wide. Maryann squeezed her shoulder.

'Come on then, Amy.' Norman's voice was soft, mocking. 'Let's hear it then. All the terrible things I do to yer – buying you nice frocks and taking you both to the pictures. Tell us all about that. Oh – and we're going to the zoo next weekend, aren't we – better get that off yer chest as well.'

'Amy?' her mom said quietly. 'Have you got anything to say or was it just this woman talked you into it – got you to make up a story?'

As Amy sobbed, Margaret remained in stony silence. Her gaze never left the floor.

Norman turned to the girls' mother. 'I don't know who this woman is or what she wants, but the last thing I'd ever want is for you to think badly of me or have any suspicions about me. Is there anything else you want to ask her before I put her out of our house?'

Janet looked round desperately at all four of them: her daughters, silent except for Amy's weeping, at Norman who was looking at her in wide-eyed appeal, and at Maryann who was staring pleadingly at Amy, her own face wet with tears. She stepped towards Maryann, a hateful expression in her eyes.

'How could you come and say such terrible things to us. What's wrong with you?'

'But they're true – every one of them! Look at your daughters! They're too frightened of him to speak. When did Margaret last speak at all? And that's what he's done to them – you've got to believe me. Why else would I come to you – you're strangers to me. But I saw your daughters and I saw myself in them ...' Her weeping took her over then. 'Oh why doesn't anyone ever believe us?'

'That's quite enough of that.' Norman suddenly laid both his hands on Maryann's shoulders and began to propel her fowards. 'Get out of my house, away from my wife and daughters with your filthy lies ...'

'If she's your wife then you're a bigamist!' Maryann shrieked helplessly. She twisted round. 'Amy – Amy, I wanted to 'elp you. I did – I wanted to be there with you.'

Amy looked across at her, her face blotchy with tears. Suddenly they heard her voice raised in a howl. 'But you *won't* be here, will you?'

That was Maryann's last sight of her as Norman propelled her to the front door. In the few seconds before Janet managed to limp out into the hall he spun Maryann round and forced her up against the front door, one hand against her throat. This time there was no doubt as to whether he recognized her. His eyes were malicious slits.

'Don't you *ever* come near me again, or you'll regret it. You know I mean what I say, don't you, Maryann?' He pulled her back and opening the door, handed her out into the street.

'I know you!' she yelled, spinning round. 'I know who you are even if they don't!'

The door slammed, sealing the family in behind its solid green exterior.

For a moment she stared at it, stunned, then took off along the road.

*

She slid down into a deep black hole that afternoon, wandering the streets with no thought as to where she was going. Seeing Norman Griffin again at such close quarters, his physical presence, his denial of her had stripped her in just a few moments of the calmness and sense of identity she had painfully erected for herself over the years. She had come crashing back down into her childhood emotions. The child who had lain in her bed looking up into the empty darkness, helpless against the progress of Norman's feet up the stairs. Never again, she had said, never again will I let him have power over me – yet just a few minutes with him and she felt close to disintegration. She walked and walked, in such a state she saw nothing of the people, houses, factories, parks around her.

At some point in the afternoon she found herself walking along the boundary of a cemetery and when she reached the gate she went in and sat down in a quiet spot on the damp grass, looking out across the graves, scattered and tilted like old men's teeth. The sky was hazy and it was still warm. She gave no thought to whether she was warm or cold, hungry or tired. She tried to think clearly but only terrible, negative things came to her.

I can't stand up to this. Sal couldn't and I can't. Sal's dead and I'd be better off dead, peaceful like these people in here. I can't face anyone again. I can't marry Joel. Can't do anything . . . There's nothing left . . . And she had let those girls down so badly. She had utterly betrayed them. She kept hearing Amy's last despairing cry, 'But you *won't* be there . . .' What would Norman do to them now?

She lay on her side on the grass, wishing there was something that could cover her: a blanket, a mantle of leaves or a thick fall of snow, or that she could burrow into the earth like an animal, anything so that she could hide her grief and self-disgust away. Curled up tightly, she could smell the grass, the earth. Birds chirruped in the trees. Eventually, overwrought and exhausted, she fell asleep.

It was dusk by the time she turned into Nance's road, the light going and the air full of smoke, trapped in the breezeless space between the houses. She was trembling with weariness and lack of food and couldn't put on a brave face to hide her leaden despair.

Nance was sitting at the table darning a sock with sharp, angry movements but she got to her feet immediately. 'What's 'appened? You look terrible!'

Maryann sank down at the table and began to weep wretchedly. 'Oh Nance . . .'

'What is it? It's not Joel, is it?'

Maryann shook her head. 'I ain't seen Joel today. It's *him* . . . I've seen him, his family. . . .' Nance sat back down again as it all came pouring out. Norman Griffin, Amy and Margaret, everything.

'I wanted to save Amy and Margaret and all I've done is let them down and make everything much worse for them and I can't do a thing now. I can't marry Joel – I can't even face seeing him. I feel like I did that time I ran away from him before – I thought it was all better, but it ain't. I ain't normal, Nance. I'd be better off finishing myself off, that I would.'

'What *are* you going on about?' Nance blazed at her. 'You love Joel and 'e loves you! What the 'ell's got into yer? You can't let that bastard wreck yer life for you the way 'e did Sal's! You and Joel are made for each other. How can yer even think about saying that? If I had even a tiny bit of a chance to marry Darius I'd be off like a shot and there's nothing standing in your way, Maryann. You're lucky – just you remember that!'

Maryann put her face in her hands, shaking her head. Through her fingers she said, 'I don't feel lucky. I feel dirty and disgusting. You can't be happy, Nance – so why do I deserve to be?' Face wet with tears, she looked up at her friend.

'Oh Maryann,' Nance said sadly, her anger gone. 'I know I don't know 'ow it feels to 've 'ad all that going on with him and Sal and that. Only – there must be a way of making things right. If you let 'im wreck yer chances with Joel he'll've spoiled all yer life . . . Look – you ain't in a state to think about anything. Let me get you a bite to eat and a cuppa tea and then you can 'ave a sleep. You'll see everything straighter in the morning. I saved yer a helping of stew – soon get it heated up. And there's apple and custard.'

'Ta, Nance,' Maryann said dully, wiping her eyes on her sleeves, grateful for Nance's mothering. 'Don't know what I'd do without you.'

Nance gave a crooked smile. 'You don't 'alf look a sight, you do.'

Maryann looked down at herself. She knew her hair was all hanging down. Her hands were grubby and there was mud on her grey skirt and shoes. She got up to wash her hands in the scullery.

'Where's Mick?'

She saw Nance's expression tighten. 'Not been 'ome yet.'

'What – not for 'is tea? That ain't like him.'

'Nope.' Nance stirred the stew fiercely.

Maryann went to her. 'You don't think summat's happened to him – an accident?'

Nance shrugged. 'If it 'as, no one's been to tell me about it.'

Maryann sat to eat her tea and did feel a little less wretched after it. She and Nance sat drinking tea together and still there was no sign of Mick. The hands of the clock moved past ten o'clock and Maryann found she could no longer keep awake.

'I'll have to go up,' she said. 'I'll doze off down 'ere else.'

'I was just thinking,' Nance said. 'Them little girls – you could at least tell them where you live – you know, just in case like.'

Maryann got to her feet. 'But this is your address.'

'Well – if it'd make yer feel any better, I don't mind them knowing that. For the time being.'

'Awright, thanks, Nance.' Maryann was grateful but felt suddenly hopeless again. How could she even get it to them?

'You go on up,' Nance said. 'A good sleep'll sort you out.'

But a good sleep was not what she was destined to have that night.

Forty-Three

Before Nance had come up to bed the front door opened with a bang that shook the house. Within moments the shouting and screaming had begun and Maryann was jerked out of a deep sleep. She soon realized that Mick and Nancy were fighting with a ferocity beyond anything that had gone before, and she climbed out of bed, disorientated from being woken so suddenly. She hated interfering between them, but it sounded as if someone would have to. As she put on her shoes and slipped a cardigan over her nightdress, she heard crashing and the splintering sound of china breaking and she ran downstairs.

Mick was so drunk he couldn't stand without swaying perilously. He still had his work jacket on, covered in muck, his face was puffy and florid and he was standing by the humble little shelf they had in the living room to keep their few crocks on, picking them up one by one and hurling them across towards the far end of the room.

'Stop it!' Nance shouted, pushing at him. 'You'll break the whole lot, yer kalied bastard!' He swung round and smacked her in the mouth and Nance groaned, reeling back away from him, too stunned to have a go at him. He reached round for another cup, lurched to one side and seized hold of the shelf to save himself. It came off the wall with a crunch

402

and everything crashed down, plates, cups, saucers, Mick falling with it, ending up in a pile of broken china. He hit his head on the wall and there was a split second's quiet.

'Look what yer've done, yer drunken Irish navvy!' Nance had recovered enough to run at him, so beside herself with fury that she kneeled down, oblivious to the shards of white china all over the place, and began raining blows down on her insensible husband. There was blood trickling from the left side of her mouth and another shiny mark on her cheek.

'I hate you!' she yelled, hitting and slapping. 'Hate you, hate you, yer fucking useless bastard. Yer not even a proper man, are yer? Yer useless to anyone ... I bloody hate yer ...' She was sobbing hysterically.

'Nance!' Maryann could barely get near her. 'Nance – stop hitting 'im – I think 'e's knocked himself out – look!'

'Good! I 'ope 'e bloody kills hisself!'

'*Nance!*' She succeeded in grabbing both of Nance's arms at once and held on, gritting her teeth while Nance fought like a rabbit in a sack before suddenly going limp. Maryann let go of her and gingerly went over to Mick, afraid for a moment that the bang on the head had really done him in.

'Is 'e awright?' Nance suddenly sounded frightened.

Maryann prodded Mick and he stirred, groaning.

'Oh, 'e's awright,' Nancy said, disgusted. 'Can't even knock 'isself out properly, the silly bugger.'

'What the hell was all that about?'

Nance's face crumpled. 'His brother Paddy – 'e's gone and got Marie in the family way *again*. That'll be their fifth, popping them out like peas every year and God can't spare us even one – just one little babby—'

Her voice cracked and she let out a howl of distress. 'Oh Maryann – if we could at least 'ave a babby I could think of staying with 'im without wanting to cut my own throat.'

'Oh Nance . . .' Maryann kneeled down with her amid the wreckage and held her tight. 'Poor old Nance . . .'

'What 'm I going to do, Maryann? I'm going to go round the bend living like this.'

Maryann rocked her, feeling desperately sorry. There was nothing she felt she could say.

'I feel as if there must be summat I did when I was younger to deserve punishing like this.'

'Oh, yer didn't do anything. Course yer didn't.'

'I'd better go and see Father Maguire and make a clean breast of everything that's been going through me 'ead,' she said. 'I might be able to stand it better then.'

There came another moan from beside them and suddenly Mick sat slowly up, rubbing his head. 'Christ Almighty.'

'Don't blaspheme, yer bleedin' navvy,' Nance snarled at him.

He stared blearily at the chaos of breakage round him, saw Nance and Maryann staring at him in disgust and groaned, 'Oh God save us.' Slowly, like a great ox, he lumbered to his feet and disappeared up the stairs.

'Well,' Nance said dully. 'Now yer can go back to sleep.'

'Not before we've cleared up.'

'Maryann—' Nance took hold of her wrist as she squatted, about to get up.

'What?'

'Go and see Joel tomorrow.'

Maryann hung her head, not meeting Nance's eyes.

She barely slept at all after that, hearing Nancy crying next door, Mick snoring, and all their troubles churning round in her head. She couldn't stop thinking about Amy and Margaret as well, full of frustration, anger and pity. In the morning she woke early from an uneasy doze, her head aching. But she got up, dressed silently and slipped out of the house. There was at least one small thing she could do.

There was a mist and the streets looked ghostly but she was glad of its grey obscurity in which to hide herself. When she got to Handsworth she waited in the side street where she had stood before. As time passed the streets took on a purposeful atmosphere. Children started coming out of the houses in their school clothes and scurrying down the road. Soon, the door of the Lamberts' house opened and she saw Amy and Margaret come out. Maryann shrank back. Janet stood for a few moments with her arms folded, her hair a bright flame in the pale morning, face turned to watch her girls. Then at last she stepped back and the door closed. Maryann slipped round quickly after them.

They were almost at the school gates when she caught up with them. She watched them tenderly from behind. They stood out amid the rag-taggle bunch of children as among the best dressed and neatest. Amy's hair had been plaited immaculately and each plait tied with a blue ribbon and Margaret's was put up in bunches, big bows tied with the same ribbon. As ever she was walking with her head jutting forwards, eyes fixed on the ground.

'Amy—' Maryann spoke softly, but her urgency was clear. Amy turned and gasped, seeing her. They stopped for a moment, letting the other children stream past them.

'What d'*you* want? Mom'll kill us if she sees yer!'

'Don't worry – I won't get you into trouble. You awright?'

Amy's gaze slid away. She swallowed. Nodded.

'I'm sorry, Amy. I'm so sorry,' Maryann said helplessly. She felt a huge lump rise in her throat. 'I was hoping yer mom'd listen – but then she daint know me from Adam, does she? I don't know what else to – 'cept I brought you this—' She slipped a scrap of paper into Amy's hand with Nancy's address on. 'That's where I live just now. It's my friend's house. I won't always be there but if you need help, go to her. She's kind, and she can get in touch with me . . .'

'Where'll you be then?' Amy asked.

'I don't know where I'll be—' It was her turn to look away. 'Look – yer'd better go now. I can't do any more for yer, not the way things are. But remember – if you want to get away, go to Nancy. I know she'll 'elp yer. Don't let yer mom see that though.'

She saw Amy look down at the piece of paper and nod.

'Tara then—'

And they were gone, two little figures amid the tide of other children.

*

Nance looked terrible. Her face was all in a mess, she was exhausted and in a foul temper. Mick had woken with a splitting head, said he wasn't effing well going to work and rolled over back to sleep. When he woke later in the morning he was contrite and gave Nance the money to buy some more crockery as they scarcely had enough left for a cup of tea between them. Maryann had wondered about buying some on the way home but resisted the thought. It wouldn't do Mick's pride any good having her chipping in again. Nance went out and came back with a few cheap willow-pattern crocks and an even more raging temper.

'If 'e ain't pouring 'is wages down 'is throat 'e's up to these sort of tricks,' she said, slamming the parcel down on the table so hard Maryann wondered if anything inside was left intact. 'Moan, moan, moan about not 'aving enough and now we 'ave to go and spend it on summat we 'ad already. 'E can 'ave bread and lard for 'is dinner and like it 'cause we ain't got enough for anything else.'

'Well, Nance – I could give yer . . .' Maryann began.

'No! Yer bloody couldn't! You've done quite enough. Let 'im put up with it. That'll teach 'im where 'is boozing and carrying on gets us!'

Whatever Maryann did to try and help, she got her head snapped off. She'd have to leave this house soon, she knew, however much Nance kept begging her to stay. She was only making everything worse.

After they'd had their bit of dinner and Mick had slouched off out somewhere, Nance turned on her. 'Now – you get yerself down to that 'ospital.'

Maryann was washing up the new plates. She didn't answer.

'Maryann?'

She hung her head over the sink. 'I can't, Nance. Not today. I'm not myself today. I just can't tell yer 'ow bad I feel . . . I can't face 'im.'

'Well, what're yer going to do?'

'I'm going to bed. 'Ave a sleep. I can't do it, Nance – not today . . .' She felt her voice crack with tears.

'Right—' Nance pulled her apron off and flicked it so hard down on a chair that the cloth made a snapping noise in the air. 'I've 'ad enough. If you're too bloody stubborn to go, I'll go meself.'

'Nance!'

But she was already out of the front door and off down the road.

'Nance – what the 'ell're yer playing at?' She was already a good way down the street, striding furiously along. She turned for a second, gave Maryann a look of complete exasperation, then carried on at the same breakneck pace.

'Oh Nance . . .' Maryann stood biting her nails, helplessly watching her friend disappear. She wasn't sure which she felt most, anxiety or gratitude.

'Maryann . . .'

There was a persistent tapping on her arm. Nance was standing over her and the light in the room had changed. She must have slept for hours.

'Nance – what time is it?' She sat up at once. 'Did yer see him? What did you say to him?'

'Plenty,' Nance said non-committally. The bruising on her face looked worse in the shadowy light. 'Come down – I've got the kettle on.'

Maryann scrambled guiltily off the bed. 'I never thought I'd sleep that long . . .'

'Come on,' Nance said grimly. 'Get yerself downstairs.'

Maryann frowned at her tone. Whatever had happened? Full of misgiving she followed Nance down the stairs, clothes all rumpled. Nance reached the bottom and stood back to watch her. Maryann got halfway down, then gasped.

'Oh my . . . what're *you* doing here? How did . . .?' She looked back and forth between them.

'Couldn't stop 'im,' Nance said, beginning to smile. 'Any'ow – I'm popping round to spend a penny – back in a few minutes.'

He was sitting in the chair by the fire. His cropped hair had grown a little, he had not been shaved for a few days and he was just beginning to look more like the old Joel. He looked across at her, a gentle, loving smile of anticipation on his face and started trying to get up.

'No—' She was across to him immediately. 'You mustn't . . . You must be worn out! How did you get here?'

'Trams.' He reached out and took her hand, holding it between his two enormous ones. 'She said you was in trouble . . . family troubles like and you was upset. So I came – wasn't staying in there a moment longer than I 'ad to. You awright, little 'un?'

She was overcome by tears at the sight of him, at his loving tone. 'Yes . . . no. Oh Joel, I don't know – I'm sorry . . .'

He pulled her closer. ''Cause I know you when you get all in a state – running off like a rabbit. Couldn't

409

'ave that, could I? Come 'ere, my lovely – come and sit with me.'

Her resistance broke like a dam as he pulled her on to his lap and she sat crying, her head tucked close to his neck as his hand smoothed her hair. Her worry poured out of her, her shame that she could have doubted her feelings for him.

''Eh now – there's no need for all this, is there?'

'Oh Joel,' she sobbed. 'I'm sorry.'

'Sorry – what for? There's nothing to be sorry about – you got me out of there, dint you?'

'Are you all right? Aren't you too weak?' She wiped her eyes and sat back to look at him.

'It was hard going – still wheezing like anything, but it's getting better. Bit by bit, every day.' He smiled at her joyfully, and reached up to wipe a tear off her cheek. She tried to smile back.

'Now what's up?'

'I'll tell you,' she said wearily. 'But not now. I saw my stepfather . . .'

His face darkened. 'Oh. I see.'

'It'll keep. Now I've seen you.'

He pulled her closer again. 'Your Nance'll be back in a minute. You got a kiss for me before she does?'

'Oh Joel, course I 'ave.'

They held each other close and she kissed him, full of love and gratitude, and felt the strength of his passion for her in the kiss he gave her back.

'We'll start again away from 'ere,' he told her. 'You need never see 'im again.'

Maryann looked into his face. 'I do love you such a lot.'

Nance came in to find her still sitting on Joel's knee

410

with a watery smile on her face and steam gushing in great clouds out of the kettle.

'God in heaven,' Nance said, rushing to lift it off the heat. 'Don't crush the life out of 'im, will yer?'

Forty-Four

They had waited in dread that night for Mick to come home. But he was back in good time, sober and contrite.

'This is Joel Bartholomew, Mick,' Nancy said nervously as he walked in. 'Maryann's intended.' Joel stood up with an effort which made him cough and held out his hand.

'How do, Mick. Your wife said I could stop 'ere for a few days until our boat's ready.' Seeing Mick frown, he explained, 'I'm a boatman – on the cut.'

'Oh – right then.' Mick nodded.

'If you don't like it, we'll move on somewhere else. It's your home . . .'

'Joel's just come out of the 'ospital,' Nance explained.

Mick nodded again. 'Ah – right. Well – sit down.' Nance immediately laid Mick's plate of tea in front of him and winked at Maryann as if to say, 'So far so good.'

They ate in silence but the atmosphere was not hostile, and when Maryann got up to clear the dishes away she heard Joel say, 'D'you fancy a pint then, Mick?'

'Joel!' Maryann said. 'You've 'ardly got the strength to stand up let alone get to the pub!'

'It ain't far!' Joel grinned. 'Anyway – 'ow'm I going

to get my strength back without a few pints inside me? I can tell you, Mick, it's been a good long while since I've 'ad anything but tea and slops.'

Mick looked warily at Nancy.

'Just don't let 'im overdo it,' she said to Joel. 'And you look after 'im, Mick. The poor feller's only out of 'is sickbed.'

'I'll do that,' Mick said. He looked relieved. 'You don't look too well,' he said to Joel. 'We'll take it easy now.'

Nance raised her eyebrows at Maryann. When the men had gone the two of them looked at each other and laughed.

'Jesus,' Nance said. 'They'd be dragging themselves off their deathbeds if it meant getting a drink inside them.'

But she looked pleased too. It was the most harmonious evening they'd had in ages.

The week passed quite peacefully, though it was a time of mixed feelings for Maryann. She was so happy Joel was out of hospital and they spent hours talking. She unburdened herself to him about Amy and Margaret and he agreed there was not much else she could do. But it was unsettling being here. They both wanted now to be off, to start their new life. Every day one of them – usually Maryann – went to see if there was any message from Darius, but so far they'd heard nothing. The weekend came and went. Tony and Billy came to see them. Billy was a young bruiser of a lad, and though they got on all right, Maryann knew it was going to be hard to see much of her brothers once she and Joel were working the cut, and this was a cause of sadness. All she could do was do her best to keep in touch.

Nancy had gone to confession on Saturday night and came back looking stern after a lecture from Father Maguire.

''E said I've got to put anything else out of my mind and sort out my marriage. And 'e told me God sometimes doesn't give people children for a reason.' She looked bleakly at Maryann. 'I mean I know 'e's right really, about my marriage and that. And Mick's really trying hard at the moment. But if God's got 'is reasons for not giving me a babby I wish 'e'd bloody well let me know what they are! – Ooh, Lord forgive me . . .'

She went to Mass with Mick on the Sunday, leaving Maryann and Joel a blissful couple of hours alone. Joel was asleep at first. Maryann had insisted he have her bed upstairs and wouldn't listen to any argument.

'You're the one that needs to get better and the sooner you do, the sooner we can go.'

He slept a huge amount. 'This is the first time I've had any peace at night,' he said. 'In there there was always someone coughing or summat going on. I haven't slept so well in months.'

He slept late that Sunday. At last, before Nance and Mick came back, Maryann took a cup of tea up for him and for a few moments watched him sleeping. His hair was longer, he was gradually letting his beard grow back and, slowly, her Joel was reappearing. He looked so pale and thin, though, and his coughing was still terrible at times. She sat by him thinking what a fool she'd been. He was so steadfast in his love for her. Through all the bad things that had gone on – were still going on – he had always been there, strong and gentle. He had been the one really good thing in her life.

She leaned over and tenderly kissed his face, pressing little kisses on his eyelids, cheeks, forehead until he stirred and woke to look at her. A smile spread across his face. 'Well – that's a nice way to wake up.'

'I brought you some tea. Nance and Mick've gone to Mass. I should've let you sleep but I wanted to see you before they get back.'

Joel pushed himself up. 'You should've woke me earlier.'

'No – I want you better.' She handed him the tea and he downed it in several big gulps, then put the cup down. He shuffled over in the bed, patting the space beside him.

'Come on in and sit with me. You'll 'ave to get used to a narrow bed on the *Esther Jane*.'

Maryann hesitated, blushing.

'It's all right, little bird – I just mean sit with me.' He held his arm out to embrace her. 'Come on – I won't bite. Promise.'

She slipped her shoes off and climbed in beside him, resting back against his warm arm. Blushing even more, without looking round at him, she said, 'I do ... I mean ... Oh dear, I don't know how to say this.' How could she tell him she wanted him, that she wanted to be held and touched, that when they were married she wanted to be his the way married people were supposed to – only she was afraid of herself, of finding she couldn't bear to do it when her only experiences of it had meant pain and fear?

'I do want – you know – to be properly married, Joel.'

He squeezed her gently. 'I know, love. And I'm not him, you know. I'm not your stepfather. I wouldn't want to hurt you, ever – you know that now, don't you?'

She rested her head against him. 'Yes,' she whispered. 'Course I do.' She leaned round and her lips reached for his, wanting to show him, to give all her love to him and he kissed her back, his arms pulling her close.

They stayed there snuggled close together, looking round at the bare room with its whitewashed walls and the little window behind them.

'I've scarcely ever been in a house before,' Joel said. 'I mean it's all right – a lot more space, of course. But I couldn't live like this. Not in one place all the time. Don't think I could breathe proper. D'you think you can live on the move all the time?'

'Think so. That feels the right way to live to me. So long as you're there.'

'It's a tough life, Maryann.'

She nodded. 'It's what I want though. That life – with you. I wish Darius'd get here, don't you?'

'Well – we've waited this long – a few more days don't make a lot of difference.'

'Poor Darius.' Maryann sighed. She'd told Joel about Nance and his brother. 'There's so much unhappiness we're leaving behind and nothing I can do. I just wish we could go now.'

'I know—' Longingly, he pulled her closer into his arms. 'I don't 'alf feel like the lucky one.'

'Joel! He's coming! There's a message from Darius – he should be up 'ere some time on Thursday!' Maryann came panting into the house two days later to find Joel sitting talking to Nancy as she worked.

Even in her excitement she noticed Nancy taking special care to control her expression. Maryann bit her lip. It seemed awful even to mention Darius's name if it upset her, but he was Joel's brother – what else could she do?

''E's got the moty in then,' Joel said. 'I wonder how 'e's managing?'

''E said it'd be easier,' Nancy said, attempting to join in the conversation brightly.

'Should be in the long run,' Joel said. 'But it'll all take getting used to.'

From then on, while they were waiting for Darius, everything changed. Joel and Maryann were full of expectation. Nancy, though, however hard she tried, became more and more glum as the time passed. By Wednesday afternoon, she was finding it impossible to remain cheerful at all. Maryann felt terribly awkward. It had been a peaceful week with Joel and Mick hitting it off well enough and Nance having company, and Maryann knew the parting was going to be hard.

On the Wednesday night Joel and Mick went out for a farewell drink while Maryann and Nance stayed in. Maryann tried to keep her talking, but Nance stared desolately into the fire. For a time they sat in silence. The clock struck ten with its mellow chime and roused Maryann from her thoughts.

'It'll be better when we've gone.' She sat forward in her chair, leaning closer to her friend. 'It's only making everything worse, us being here and talking about Darius – it's rubbing salt in the wound.'

Nance's face in the firelight looked hard in her

unhappiness. Maryann thought about her prettiness when she was with Darius on the cut.

'You and Mick,' Maryann persisted gently. 'I mean – things seem a bit better . . .'

Nance's lips began to tremble as she spoke. 'I s'pose they are. I think it's 'aving Joel 'ere – just knowing 'e can come 'ome and . . .' She lost control of her voice and the tears broke through. '. . . and not just find me 'ere . . . Oh God, Maryann, I know I married 'im in the sight of God and I know what the right thing to do is, but it's breaking my heart, it's so hard! I want to see Darius again more than anything else in the world, but I don't know as I can manage to see him. I don't think I could bear it.' She kept wiping her eyes furiously as if it was disloyal even to weep.

Maryann was just about to suggest that she try and keep Darius away from the house when she met him the next day, when they heard a knocking sound.

Nance frowned. 'Was that ours?' She looked round at the door.

The noise came again, and another sound of someone crying outside. Both of them got up and went cautiously to the door.

'Anyone in there?'

Nance opened the door, and in the dim light they saw a young, rather startled-looking policeman, and beside him a mane of red hair and a terrified, tear-stained face looking up at them. At the sight of Maryann she began sobbing uncontrollably.

'Amy?' Maryann went to her immediately and put her arm round her. She took in that the child was wearing a coat over her nightdress, her bare legs pushed into her boots. 'Are you awright? What's happened?'

The policeman was parking his bike up against the

wall. 'I found 'er, wandering about – over Winson Green way. In a right state she was – all she'd say was she 'ad to get over 'ere. You know 'er then?'

'Yes—' Maryann guided Amy into the room as she gulped and trembled. 'This is one of them,' she said to Nance over her shoulder. 'I wonder what in God's name's happened?'

'Oh my word,' Nance said, full of pity.

'Wouldn't say nowt to me,' the constable complained from the doorway. 'Thought the best thing to do was bring 'er here on my bike.'

Maryann put her hands firmly on the young girl's shoulders, trying to calm her. 'Amy – it's awright. You're safe here, love. You can talk to us – no one can hurt you here . . .' Seeing the distraught state of the girl brought Maryann close to tears herself. What had he done? What terrible harm had that cruel, self-obsessed man inflicted now?

Amy could scarcely get the words out. 'Sh-sh-sh . . .'

'It's awright—' Maryann caressed her shoulders. 'Slowly now.'

Amy took a great gulp of air and burst out, 'It's Margaret – I think sh-she's killed him.'

Forty-Five

That evening had, outwardly, begun like any other.
Amy and Margaret came home from school, spent their
few blissful hours alone at home with their mother
before their stepfather arrived home. Janet had cooked
mince for tea with potatoes and gravy and they had all
sat to eat together. Margaret said nothing, as usual.
Their stepfather asked polite, jovial questions about
how school had been and about their mother's day. The
conversation was strained. Afterwards, as it grew dark,
they had put on the gas lamps in the front room, and
Norman lit the wick in his brass oil lamp and placed it
with its glowing light on the little table in the corner.
He'd sat down to read the *Mail*, for the duration of
that dreadful pause between tea and his stretching in
the chair and saying, 'It's time you wenches were up
in bed.'

To anyone watching it would have seemed a normal
evening.

Yet the girls were living in constant fear and dread.
Since Maryann's visit, nothing had been the same.
Before, he had used them, abused them, convinced them
of their subservience. But now it had become something
much worse.

The night after Maryann had been, he had come up
for the usual 'bedtime story'. Amy and Margaret got
ready for bed, as ever, with feverish haste because if he

was upstairs when they were still changing his hands were everywhere, pinching, poking. He stood in the doorway for a moment, smoking a cigarette, leaning on the frame with a nonchalant air, taking his time.

'So,' he said softly. 'You thought you could get away with squealing on me, did yer?' He gave a low laugh, then took a drag on the cigarette. Its tip flared orange for a second. 'Did you really?' Smoke curled from his nostrils. 'Poor little things – that was silly. Wasn't it? Very silly. I don't like that. I think I need to show you how much I don't like it.'

He yanked the thin pillow out from under Margaret's head and with both hands pushed it down over her face. Amy heard herself whimper and saw Margaret's hand clawing at him, her young body fighting against suffocation. He forced it down over her for what seemed an age, his expression a cruel grimace. Amy felt she was going to burst. She could bear it no longer.

'Get off her!'

She sprang off her bed and flung herself at him. He was perched at an angle on the edge and her weight threw him aside. Amy dragged the pillow away from Margaret's face and Margaret sat up, panting, frantic.

'You could've killed her!'

He was half sprawled across Margaret's bed and the look he gave her chilled her to her very core. Inside him, where most people had a heart and soul, was a place of hard, emotionless cruelty. She backed away from him.

'So – you're getting uppity now an' all, are yer?'

He advanced on her slowly.

'No!' Amy moaned. She curled herself at the top of her bed, her knees brought up to her chest. 'No – don't touch me ... don't, please ... I'll do anything, but don't ...'

But it was no use. It made no difference. Whatever she said or did would never make any difference, she could see that now.

This evening he had come up, his plume of loathsome blue smoke trailing after him. Once again he stood, as he liked to do, in the doorway, like a man looking down a menu, choosing, relishing. He strolled over to Margaret and sat down. With the cigarette jutting at the corner of his mouth he whipped back her bedclothes. Amy jumped violently. She saw him yank Margaret over on to her back and pull up her nightdress. Then, clamping his left hand over her mouth, he took the cigarette out of his mouth and stubbed it hard into her stomach. Amy's hands went over her own mouth. Margaret's body lifted off the bed, writhing. A thin, terrible noise was coming from her. He held his hand there until Margaret quietened, then removed it.

'Now—' He wagged his finger at her. 'Don't do it again.'

Do what? Amy thought wildly, biting on her fist to stop herself shouting out. What had she done?

'I've put my mark on you, wench. You show anyone and there'll be worse. I can do much worse than that.'

Margaret was gasping, crying in agony. Amy slid down the bed and blocked her ears. She knew he wouldn't have finished, that cruelty always led to something else, it excited him. She closed her eyes, pressed her hands over her ears while he raped her sister. Then he buttoned himself up tidily and went downstairs. Margaret lay, absolutely silent.

Amy went over to her. 'D'you want me to put summat on it for you?'

She stroked her sister's shoulder but Margaret was quite still, eyes closed, like a dead person. She must've have been in great pain but she made not a sound. Not knowing what else to do, Amy waited for a long time until she thought Margaret must really be asleep. At last, she crept back to bed.

It was almost an hour later when she heard Margaret moving about. She got up and just stood for a moment as if she was in a trance.

Amy turned over. 'Margaret?'

She waited a moment longer, like a little ghost in her bare feet, then went out of the room. Amy sat up, wondering if Margaret was sleepwalking. She heard her going down the stairs and through the open door, the faint sound of her mother clinking cups in the kitchen. Uneasily, Amy got out of bed and stood shivering at the top of the stairs, waiting to hear her mother's voice ordering Margaret back to bed. Was she going to show her the burn? It must hurt so badly. Amy trembled at the thought. He'd said she mustn't! What if she did – what would he do then?

She heard nothing and crept further downstairs. Her mother was still in the kitchen. Where had Margaret gone? Amy stood on the bottom step. And it was then she heard the crash, the sound of glass breaking from the front room, a shout from her stepfather, 'What've yer done, yer little vixen?' then high, agonized screaming which grew louder and more panic-stricken. Amy knew it was not Margaret who was screaming.

'Arthur?' Janet hobbled from the kitchen. 'Amy, whatever's going on?'

Amy reached the front room first. For a split second she thought the room was on fire but saw an instant later that the blaze was confined to her stepfather. Flames were leaping all over the top half of him, shooting out from his hair, his clothing, and he was leaping a wild jig around the room, shrieking in agony as the fire took hold of his hair and clothes. As she came to the room he flung himself down on the floor, rolling back and forth trying to douse the flames but they refused to be put out and leaped back into life in the places where his body left the floor and met the air again. Not far away, Margaret stood with her arms folded, her expression blank. Near him on the floor lay his brass lamp, its glass shattered. His head must have been doused with paraffin.

'Oh—' Janet Lambert gasped. 'Margaret – oh Margaret, what've you done? Help him, one of you – get the rug round him!' She pulled herself frantically across the room on her sticks. 'Help him I said!' she cried. 'Don't just stand there.'

But her daughters offered no help at all. Margaret stood quite still as if she hadn't heard. Amy slipped upstairs, running as if possessed, and fetched her boots. Throwing her coat over her nightdress she slid past the front parlour, past the sobbing screams, past her mother beating helplessly at the flames and out into the night, running, running to the one person who she knew would help and understand.

The story she managed, in her distress, to sob out to Maryann and the policeman was a brief, disjointed summary of this.

'What'll happen to her? She must've smashed the lamp right over 'is head. What if Margaret's killed him? Will she go to prison? They mustn't put her in prison, it ain't right – it was him, he drove her to it! He burned her with his cigarette.'

The young policeman appeared rather out of his depth. 'Look – I don't s'pose it's as bad as you think,' he said.

'Of course it's as bad as she thinks,' Maryann stormed at him. 'Ain't you heard what she just said? The man's an evil bloody maniac!'

'I see,' the policeman said uneasily. 'Look – you keep 'er here for tonight and look after her. I'll get over there now and see what's happening and tell her mother where she is. The address is . . .?'

'Blimey – that's a good distance away, that is . . .' He was just writing it down laboriously in his notebook when Joel and Mick rolled in from the pub.

'What's all this then?' Mick started aggressively. Joel looked at Maryann, her arm round Amy's shoulders and guessed who the girl was.

'Now, Mick—' Nance stepped in. 'Don't you go getting on yer 'igh 'orse. The wench is in trouble and 'er'll be stopping 'ere tonight. You just keep quiet.'

Amy looked fearfully at Mick's red, rough-looking face.

'It's awright,' Maryann whispered to her. 'He won't hurt you. This is Joel – the man I'm going to marry—'

''Ow do.' Joel smiled kindly at her. 'You'll be all right here. We'll look after you.'

They saw the policeman out.

'You can sleep down here with me,' Maryann reassured Amy.

'Oh no you don't,' Joel said. 'You're having the bed, you two, and no arguments.'

It took Amy a long time to calm down enough to fall asleep. Even after she had gone off, her body twitched in a disturbed way. Maryann lay with her arm wrapped round the child, making soothing noises, trying to comfort her. But her own mind was spinning round. She would have to take her back the next day to her mother. What sort of reaction was she going to get? And what would happen to Margaret? Was Norman really dead as Amy feared? It was a long time before she got any sleep herself.

The next morning Maryann, Nance and Amy went straight to Handsworth.

'I'm glad you're with me,' Maryann said to Nance on the tram. She felt horribly nervous at the thought of facing Amy's mother.

The house had a very quiet feel about it when they got there and Maryann wondered if anyone was in. But after she knocked on the door, they heard Janet Lambert pulling herself along the hall to open it. Maryann gripped Amy's hand as the door swung open.

All her remorse and worry was evident in Janet Lambert's sleepless, tear-stained face. 'Oh – Amy!' she cried and Amy, also crying, ran into her arms. 'Oh love – are you awright?' Janet sobbed. 'I'm sorry – I'm so, so sorry, Amy ... Oh my God, as long as you're awright ...'

Maryann and Nance watched as the two of them cried in each other's arms.

'Oh my girls – how could he've done it – all this time?'

Maryann felt her own overwrought emotions surfacing and it was all she could do to stop herself crying as well. To see Amy was at last believed by her mother and accepted back tore at her heart.

Janet looked over Amy's head at her, her eyes full of shame. 'Come in,' she said.

Once more they sat in the little parlour room, Amy on the arm of her mother's chair, leaning close to her.

'This is Nancy – my friend,' Maryann said. 'I'm living with her at the moment so it's her house Amy stayed at last night.'

'Good of yer,' Janet said absent-mindedly. Nance nodded, sympathetically.

'Where's Margaret?' Amy asked.

'They took her away.' The woman was distraught, tears running down her face as she spoke. 'The ambulance came for him. He was burnt terrible. They took her as well. I don't know what I'm going to do . . .'

'Did she show you?' Amy whispered.

They all knew she meant the burn that Norman Griffin had inflicted on her, the bruises.

Janet lowered her head, nodding. 'They want to make that better – only they think there's other things the matter with 'er – her mind. Oh . . . my little girl. What've I done? Why couldn't I see it? He was always so kind, such a gentleman with me! I just couldn't believe he could ever . . . I mean he was never even demanding that way, you know, with me . . .'

'He was just the same with us,' Maryann told her. Now she saw how sorry the woman was, how she wanted to do right by her daughters, she felt great sympathy for her. 'My sister took her own life because of him.'

Janet's head jerked up. She looked deeply shocked. 'Did she? You never said . . .'

'You wouldn't've believed me.'

'No.' She shook her head. 'I wouldn't. It's like having two whole different lives, different *worlds* going on in your house at the same time. You look at him, the way he is, and you can't believe ... I mean you can't believe *anyone* could do things like that, can you? I still can't ...' She shook her head as if to reassemble her thoughts. 'Still can't ...'

'I know,' Maryann said gently. 'He's the one with summat wrong in his mind. He's like a devil. He's going to live then?'

'They think so.'

There was silence for a moment. Janet pulled Amy on to her lap and held her.

'Whatever happens, we'll be together now – we'll manage somehow. I'll never let him near you.'

Forty-Six

Maryann cried all the way home, as if releasing years of pent-up sadness and however much Nance tried to comfort her she was unable to stop. And Nance was feeling so miserable that she was tearful herself.

'If only my mom'd been like that.' Maryann sobbed. She knew people were having a good look at her but she was past caring. 'I mean I know Janet daint believe them to begin with – but seeing 'em like that, her cuddling Amy ... She wants the best for her girls at heart. But that poor Margaret – what ever's going to happen to her?'

'I s'pect 'er'll be awright,' Nance said doubtfully, adding, 'the poor little mites.'

Maryann was even less hopeful. Nance hadn't seen what Margaret was like. 'I feel terrible leaving with all this going on. But we'll come and see them – and you, as often as we can.'

Nance nodded, staring bleakly ahead of her.

When they got back home, Joel saw what state she was in and came and took her in his arms. Nance began bustling about to hide her own emotion. There was no one to embrace her.

'She believes them now,' Maryann said into Joel's chest. 'Whatever else happens, she's on their side.'

'Thank 'eavens,' Joel said. 'That poor little nipper. What about him?'

'Oh – he'll live, they say.' Her voice was savage. 'I'm glad for Margaret's sake anyway.'

When they'd told him what had happened Maryann whispered to Joel, 'No sign of Darius yet then?' They were almost certain he was due in that day.

'Thought 'e might've got 'ere by now,' Joel said, shaking his head. 'Still . . .'

'We could go down there and wait for him,' Mary-ann suggested.

'What's all the whispering about?' Nance demanded sharply.

Maryann looked into the dregs of her teacup. 'We was just saying – maybe it'd be better – for you, like – if we was to go and wait down by the cut for when Darius gets in.'

Nance came and stood by the table, hands on hips. 'No need for that – I think me and Darius both know how to behave,' she said tartly. 'And Joel don't look as if he could walk another step at the moment. He wants to save 'is strength for later, that 'e does. I don't know how 'e's going to manage on that boat.'

'Darius'll be there – and me. We can make sure he takes it easy.'

Maryann was tensed with anticipation. After the events of last night and now this waiting she felt very churned up and unsettled. And she was dreading having to say goodbye to Nance. If only they could just go, be there on the *Esther Jane* without all this to-do!

The afternoon crawled by. Nance declared she wasn't going to lift a finger that day to do anything in the house. There'd be plenty of time for that when they'd all gone. Maryann thought of Nance's days stretching ahead, full of work, just her and Mick, and she pitied her terribly. Nance had a home and a husband all right, but her life seemed so empty.

They sat reminiscing that afternoon, each trying to take each other's mind off the coming departure, laughing about their antics and Blackie Black with his barrow.

'Poor old Dad,' Nance said. 'Never managed much with 'is life neither, did 'e? 'E was always on about how 'e was going to get us out of Ladywood to somewhere better – soon as 'e had a shilling on him 'e was off down the pub.' She shook her head. 'The old sod. I can 'ardly stand to go and see 'im. 'E ain't going anywhere now.' Blackie's health was failing week by week. 'It's a good job our mom's got all the boys to bring in some money.' She looked across at Maryann. 'You not going to go and see yer mom again before yer go?'

Maryann bit her lip. 'I can't, Nance. Mom's made it clear what her attitude is to me. Tony said she's never said a word about seeing me and I ain't crawling to her again if she don't want me.'

'But what about Amy and Margaret – if you told 'er what's happened to Mr Griffin?'

'It makes no difference now. It's too late, Nance. She daint believe anything I said when it really mattered. Joel's my family now – 'e was always the one who was good to me in any case. Me and Mom were never close.'

Nance stared at her, smiling gently, her old friend with her wayward black hair and face that was still rather impish even now, in her twenties.

'You – a bargee – I can't believe it.'

'We ain't bargees.' Maryann sat up straighter. 'We're

431

Number Ones. Well – we were. I'll miss yer, Nance – but I'll be back. We always were best pals, eh?'

Late in the afternoon, when the waiting was becoming almost unbearable, at last there came a tap at the door. Maryann saw Nance's face tense up as Joel opened the door and they all saw Darius's stern features lifted into a rather flustered smile.

'At last!' Joel cried. 'I thought them moty boats was s'posed to be quicker.'

Darius stepped in, acknowledging everyone with a nod. 'The trouble I've 'ad with the bloody thing – there's been many a time today I'd've said we'd be better off going back to 'aving a horse any day. Once she got going though, she did put on a bit of speed. Takes getting used to I can tell you – she vibrates fit to shake your teeth out! Anyway – I've got a load on so we're all set. You ready then, are you?'

'Can I get you a cup of tea, Darius?' Nance asked softly.

'Nancy.' He nodded again, not meeting her eyes. 'Er – no ta. I think we'll be getting on.'

Nance nodded. Maryann could tell how much it hurt her that Darius was being so distant with her, but what choice did he have?

'Come on—' she said briskly. The less drawn-out the farewells the better, she thought. 'Let's get moving. You got everything, Joel?'

She had her case with her things in and Joel had a small bundle. They had few possessions and even if they had had more, there was little space for anything on the *Esther Jane*.

When they had gathered themselves together, Nance

suddenly untied her apron and said, 'Look – I don't want to say goodbye 'ere. I'll come down with yer—'

'You sure that's a good idea?' Maryann asked anxiously. It just seemed like prolonging the agony.

'It's awright,' Nance said staunchly. 'I just want to see yer off properly.'

Darius said he'd brought the boat through to Gas Street as it was nearer, and he'd already picked up a load of brass fittings to take south the next day. There was only about half a mile to walk. They took it slowly for Joel's sake. Maryann was concerned about how very easily he tired. She walked ahead with him, and Nancy and Darius followed at a distance which increased gradually as they went along. Maryann could just hear their voices, lowered, talking urgently. By the time they reached the cut, Nance was in tears. Maryann saw that while Darius was talking earnestly to her, trying to comfort her, he refrained from putting his arm round her shoulders.

The sun was beginning to set, glinting on windows, casting gold on the dark water and turning the chimney stacks and warehouses round them into black silhouettes. They had to step across a couple of other boats to reach the *Esther Jane*, turning their faces away, as was the custom, from the private living quarters of their occupants. When Joel stepped down into the *Esther Jane* his legs almost gave way. Maryann caught him.

'No work for you,' she said. 'You've got a lot of resting to do.'

But he sat beside the tiller, panting a little, and looked round in sheer delight. The boat was sitting quite low in the water, filled with sacks of brassware.

'Home – at last. It's felt like an eternity – 'specially in that 'ospital.'

'Saved your life though,' Darius said.

Joel nodded. 'They did. But I reckon it was someone else 'ere coming back to me really did it.' He laid his arm round Maryann's shoulder. She nestled into his embrace, though painfully aware of Nance's presence. They were all squeezed in at the back together. 'You'll 'ave to show me what they done to 'er.' Joel eyed the new chimney of the Bolinder motor jutting out of the *Esther Jane*'s cabin roof. 'When I've got my breath back.'

There was an awkward silence. A sliver of cloud crossed the setting sun and for a moment a chill darkness passed over everything, the gold leeching out of the ripples.

'Well,' Nance said, with a huge effort at cheerfulness. 'I'd best be getting back then. Get Mick's tea or there'll be trouble.'

'You've been very good to us,' Joel said. 'I'm ever so grateful to you, Nance.'

'Oh – that's awright,' she said, struggling not to cry.

She and Maryann flung their arms round one another.

'Thanks, Nance – for everything. We'll be back to see yer – often as we can.'

'You'd better—' Her voice was choked. 'Hark at me – I must go.' Hastily she held out her hand. 'Goodbye – Darius.'

'Tara.' He spoke very quietly, painfully reluctant to let go of her hand.

She turned and climbed back over on to the bank. 'Don't go falling in, any of yer!' she called, and Maryann could hear her tearfulness. She watched Darius as Nance gave a final wave and slipped away into the dusk which lay in thick folds along the wharves. His eyes didn't leave her until she was out of sight.

Though they spent the evening busily, somehow Nance was still with them. Darius and Joel spent some time peering into the engine as Darius explained how it worked and how they had to maintain it, while Maryann fried up their evening meal and then they sat in the tiny cabin together: Darius on the step, his plate held in his enormous hands; Maryann and Joel at the table under the little lamp bracket. It was as cosy as she remembered and she felt herself glowing with happiness. Here she was, on the *Esther Jane* with her two favourite people in all the world.

'Soon as Joel's up to scratch,' Darius announced, 'I'll go back and work for Fellows, Morton and Clayton. That way we'll 'ave another wage coming in. I don't think our dad's going to be up to coming back on the cut. You two can make this your 'ome. Essy Barlow'll give us another butty to tow so you can get a decent load.' Putting the motor in had taken up some of the space previously occupied by cargo.

Joel nodded. He knew how sore Darius was about Nance, but they would not put this into words. And on the cut necessity meant getting work and keeping moving at all costs. 'Thanks,' he said. 'You've held everything together, Darius. I 'ope it won't be long now – this blessed chest of mine.'

'Keep her in the family any'ow,' Darius went on. 'You'll 'ave another family growing up on 'ere.'

As soon as they'd eaten, Joel said he had to lie down and Darius pulled down the cross bench for him. Blushing, Maryann wondered where she was going to sleep. She'd have the bench, she decided – until she was married. The two brothers could sleep together.

As soon as Joel was settled, Darius said, 'I'll be off out for a couple of pints,' and out he went.

Maryann finished the washing-up. Joel was quiet, sleeping, she thought. She tried to put the plates away quietly, not clatter them and wake him. She eyed the cabin. She'd get the place spick and span again. She wasn't having any of the other boatwomen saying she couldn't keep it nice. The crochet work was looking worn and grey. She was going to learn how to do it and make her own, all fresh! When they were tied up somewhere she'd get one of the women to teach her.

Turning, she saw Joel was watching her.

'Ooh – you made me jump!' She laughed. 'I thought you was asleep!'

'Come and get in 'ere with me.'

'Joel! We ain't married!'

'We will be soon enough. Go on. Just a cuddle.'

She went and sat beside him. 'I thought you were tired?'

'Not that tired.'

'What if Darius comes back?'

'He won't. Why d'you think 'e went out?'

She unfastened her frock and lay down beside him in her slip. They lay very close together on the narrow bed, looking at one another in the rosy light of the cabin. She saw the speckled colour of his lashes and his loving expression.

'Back home.' He smiled. 'Maryann – my lovely Maryann.'

She stroked his face. After a week at Nance's his cheeks were covered by a down of gingery hair. 'Your beard's coming back. You're starting to look right again.'

He laughed. 'That's nice to know.' His arm pulled

her even closer and they kissed. Their bodies were pressed together and in panic she realized how aroused he was. 'That's not the only thing that's coming back,' he murmured.

She stiffened and he sensed it immediately.

'It's all right.' He kissed her flushed cheek, drawing back a little, and stroked her hair. 'It's awright, little 'un. I ent going to force myself on you without your say so. It just shows how much I love you, that's all.' He kissed her face in between talking to her. 'You're my little bird and I don't want you flying away. Just let me love you a bit tonight – bit by bit. I want you to love me too – not to find me horrible.'

She felt herself relax at his assurances. This was Joel – she had always been able to trust him.

'Oh Joel – I could never find you horrible. And I know how long you've waited. It's just – we ain't married and I'm – I'm a bit frightened of it . . .'

'I know . . . I know. But don't be frightened, lovely one . . . You're meant to like it.'

Gently, slowly, he began to love her body into life. She was moved by his desire for her as he stroked her.

'Your hands are softer these days,' she said.

'Oh – that won't last long on 'ere!'

She began to relax as he ran his hands under her slip and touched her breasts. Gradually he pulled the slip down and kissed her and the sensation made her gasp. Excitement rose in her, sudden and strange. For a moment her mind rebelled – no, no, it was wrong to feel this, it was horrible! And she tensed, but when he continued to touch her and she saw the pent-up pleasure and need in his face she tried to relax. No, it wasn't wrong. It had to be right. She and Joel could make it right.

437

She clung to him, stroking him. 'Oh Joel . . . oh . . .'

'It's all right—' He moved his hand between her legs and she flinched, then forced herself to relax. All the vile poking and prodding that Norman Griffin had done flashed back to her for those moments and she moaned, forcing her eyes open.

'It's all right, my love,' he kept saying. 'I don't want to hurt you – just to love you . . . love you, little bird . . .'

After a time he leaned close, his breathing very quick. 'Can I – please?'

She knew she couldn't refuse him. She loved him too much to refuse him anything and she gave a tiny nod. She must do it for him.

That first moment, feeling the weight of him and his moving inside her she almost screamed, but she watched him, seeing the love in his face, the way he didn't abandon her for his own pleasure but stayed with her, looking into her eyes. 'My love . . . my love,' he gasped. 'Oh my little love . . .' When he had reached his climax he kissed her again and again, and they lay holding one another tenderly.

Maryann was full of wonder, of relief. They'd done it! She knew it was something every married woman had to get over with. And it was going to be all right. With Joel it could be. She could be married in every sense, and not have to dread any part of it.

She woke next morning before dawn, cramped and stiff, and lay looking round, for a few moments, beside Joel's warm back. There was very little to see, but she could just make out the dark shape of the range and hear Darius breathing loudly on the other bench. She was here, on the *Esther Jane*! It was really going to be her home. How long would it be before she could stop pinching herself and really believe it?

And last night – Oh Lor', she thought. Did I really . . .? The thought that they'd fallen asleep and Darius must have come back and found them both side by side and dead to the world was mortifying. But this was outweighed by her happiness. She smiled, sleepily. It'll be all right, I can love him – I can be a normal woman! It was really too late to worry about Darius now. The next night she'd suggest sleeping on the other bed. But she found herself hoping Darius would refuse to let her.

She kissed Joel's warm back, then eased herself off the bed, pulled her clothes on in the dark and crept out, taking the bowl to relieve herself, thankful that there was little sound from anywhere around. Then she went back in and lit the lamp and got the range going to put a kettle on and by the time she'd done that, Darius was up and she heard others around them beginning to stir.

'We need to be on our way,' Darius said. 'I'm going to get her going.'

Maryann got a huge shock when Darius started the engine. It felt all wrong without old Bessie hauling away on the bank. He had said the boat vibrated, but when all the china in the cabin started rattling and she felt as if she was being shaken up inside a salt cellar, she realized life was going to be very different from when the *Esther Jane* had Bessie pulling them serenely through the water. Soon she could also smell the acrid fumes from the funnel as well as the constant phut-phutting sound of the engine. It woke Joel.

'It's *horrible*,' she said, dismayed. 'How on earth're we s'posed to get used to this?'

Joel didn't look too happy either. 'Darius says you

do get used to it after a bit. Thing is, Maryann – it's this or selling her altogether. At least we've got our home, eh?'

'I s'pose so,' she conceded, handing him a cup of tea. She smiled shyly, kissing him. 'Our home. That sounds nice, don't it?'

Darius swung in through the door. 'We'll untie and be off now—'

The boat seemed to make a lot of noise starting off, but when they were moving, she settled down to a more regular sound. They eased away from the other moored boats. Joel stood at the stern, watching in amazement in the pale dawn light.

They were just straightening up to move off when they all heard a cry from on the bank, a voice shouting with all its strength, '*Maryann! Darius!*'

'My God—' Maryann peered through the door out into the dim light. 'That sounds like Nancy!'

'*Wait! Don't go – wait, wait!*'

Darius instantly steered the *Esther Jane* towards the bank where Nancy was frantically shouting and running to keep up with them. He brought her in rather awkwardly and they bumped the side, almost causing Maryann to fall over.

Nance was panting so hard she could scarcely speak. Darius held out his hand and she jumped in.

'Nance – what the hell're yer playing at?' Maryann was quite annoyed. She'd said her goodbyes – that was that. Why spin it out even longer? She saw, though, that Nance had a fresh shiner on her left eye, which was only half open.

In any case, it was not Maryann Nance wanted to speak to. All her attention was fixed on Darius. 'I 'aven't slept a wink!' she panted. 'It's no good – I'm coming with yer! 'E gave me this as a present last night—' She pointed at her eye. 'I ain't never going back, Darius – it's you I want to be with – for ever!'

Darius's face took on a look of wonder and disbelief. 'But . . .' he stuttered. 'Nance – you, I mean . . .'

'Nance – what're you saying?' Maryann asked her. 'What about Mick – I mean, you said you'd never . . .?'

'I know what I said. I married 'im, I took vows in church and I can't divorce 'im and I'm most likely damned into the bargain. But it's you I love, Darius. I've never felt the way I feel when I'm with you – *ever* before. I've only got one life and I can't spend it with 'im when I can hardly stand the sight of 'im and 'e knocks me about and there'll be no babbies neither. It ain't a marriage, it's a prison sentence. If you'd not come along, Darius, I might never've known I could fall in love. I know we can't make it legal and regular but out 'ere it don't seem to matter. It's you I want to spend my life with – if you'll 'ave me.'

'If I'll have *you*?' Darius said. He could scarcely believe what he was hearing. He handed the tiller to Joel and pulled Nance into his arms. 'How can you even ask, girl?' He was laughing with sheer joy.

'Flamin 'ell, Nance!' Maryann was only just beginning to take in what had happened. 'Joel – this family's getting bigger every minute.'

Nance, laughing and crying at once, hugged each of them in turn. 'I can't believe I'm doing this! I'm going to wake up any moment!'

'Well,' Darius took command of the *Esther Jane* once more, 'let's get going before you do.'

With the water churning behind them, they weaved their way through the shadowy Birmingham Cut and out towards the fresher country air.

Forty-Seven

December 1934

The day of their wedding, Maryann woke in the little house where she and Joel were staying with old Darius's sister in Oxford. Joel's father was still in poor health and was staying on the bank for the forseeable future.

Maryann had been given a bed upstairs and Joel was sleeping on an old sofa down in the tiny back room. She could see that the sun was shining brightly behind the curtains and she climbed out of bed, shivering as she pulled her woolly on and then going to draw back the curtain. The sight that met her eyes made her laugh with pleasure. It was a diamond-hard, cold day, creaking with ice and from the roof hung huge icicles glinting in the bright sunlight. The rooftops were white and the tree she could see a little way along the street looked as if it had been dipped in icing sugar. She couldn't have asked for better than this sparkling white perfection.

Old Mrs Simons, Joel's aunt, had married away from the cut and spent her wedded life in Oxford, where her late husband had a grocer's shop. She was a diminutive lady with scrubbed pink cheeks, little spectacles and she wore black, old-fashioned bombazine dresses with white lace collars. She was delighted that Joel and Maryann had decided to be married at St Barnabas Church, just a couple of streets away, and where she attended regularly.

'Now, moy dear,' she said to Maryann later in the morning when they were ensconced together upstairs away from the men and she was helping Maryann dress. 'Just you stand still so's I don't nick you with this.' She bent over with a needle and thread in one hand, finishing a seam in the woollen dress Maryann had chosen. It was second-hand but in good condition and a lovely violet-blue colour. 'Looks very nice with your pretty hair.' Maryann's hair was fastened back in a shiny, raven twist behind her head, and with her rosy cheeks and bright, happy eyes she looked very beautiful.

Mrs Simons stood back and clasped her hands in front of her breast, her china thimble still on one finger, beaming with excitement. 'We haven't had a wedding in this family for such a time – what with all poor Esther's boys ... the War, you know. I began to think Joel and Darius'd never settle. ...' She drifted off sadly, then regained her state of glee. 'But it always makes me feel young again, a wedding! Now just you remember, moy dear – they're good men in this family, good sound men. But sometimes you do have to take a firm hand with them.'

'Do you?' Maryann asked, surprised.

'Oh yes.' Mrs Simons neatly packed away her needles and thread. 'Give 'em half the chance and they treat you like a man – like a *packhorse*, moy dear, to tell the truth – have you toiling day and night. Just remember to get Joel to treat you proper, however much strovin' there is to be done. You 'ave to pull your weight of course, on the cut, but don't let 'im forget you're a woman for a moment, that's my advice – specially when you're carrying a child. Nothing worse for child-bearing than toiling like an animal day in day out. Saw my mother's life come to an end through it, so I should know.'

'I'll try.' Maryann smiled.

She had a smart, royal blue hat with a white feather in it to top off her outfit, and blue shoes with an elegant heel.

'I suppose this is the last time I'll feel this smart in many a year.' She laughed.

'Well, you're realistic, I'll give you that,' Mrs Simons said. She squeezed Maryann's hand and stood on tiptoe to kiss her. 'Joel's a good boy – always has been. I hope you'll be very happy, moy dear, and have a big, healthy family.

It was unconventional, she knew, but as she had no one there in the way of family, Maryann asked old Mr Bartholomew to walk up the aisle with her and present her to his son. She did feel rather wistful that morning. Even Tony wasn't going to travel all the way down from Birmingham, although he had written her a letter. She knew there was no question of her mother coming. But Nancy and Darius were there, Nancy acting as her 'assistant'.

'I don't know whether I'm a bridesmaid or a matron of honour!' Nance joked.

She and Darius were working another of Samuel Barlow's boats and had managed to reach Oxford that morning by the skin of their teeth in time for the wedding.

And old Darius Bartholomew seemed delighted that Maryann was marrying Joel. 'I'd 'ardly've known you,' he said, looking her up and down when he first saw her. 'You was only a child when last I saw you.'

She would have known him anywhere. He was certainly shrunken and more stooped in stature compared with how she had first seen him, but his beard and bushy white eyebrows and his tanned, leathery features were unmistakable. He was rather splendidly dressed in an ancient suit which shone with wear, a red cravat in the neck of his shirt. She remembered how intimidating she had found him in the past. Now she felt only respect and fondness. It felt absolutely right when he took her arm and led her along the aisle while the organ was playing the wedding march, and she saw Joel dressed up – for the first time ever probably – in a black suit, his beard trimmed, waiting for her before the altar. Mr Bartholomew gallantly handed her to his waiting son with an expression of great solemnity. Maryann was surprised to find that her legs were trembling so much she could barely stand.

When they came out, their few well-wishers sprinkled them with rice and Joel kissed her in the doorway of the church as the others watched and cheered. A man took their photograph.

Nance kissed her enthusiastically, almost knocking both their hats off in the process. Nance's was perched precariously on her curls.

'I'm ever so 'appy for yer, Maryann! You look really lovely.'

'Ta, Nance – you do an' all.' Maryann linked arms with Joel on one side and Nancy on the other as they all walked along to the pub where they went afterwards to celebrate. It was lovely outside but so cold that they were anxious to get into the warmth and they walked briskly, watched by a few curious passers-by in the little Oxford back street with its rows of neat terraces.

Nance looked a picture of health. In the three

months since she'd been with Darius she seemed to have filled out and her eyes were alive with happiness.

'I've got muscles on me like bed-knobs!' She laughed. 'Eh Darius – bring the bride a drink, will yer!'

They were a small wedding party, but they settled down very happily together. Old Mrs Simons became quite merry drinking glasses of ginger wine. Maryann sat between Nancy and Joel.

'Well – there's not many of us, but we wish you well,' Mrs Simons said, raising her glass. 'You're a lovely girl and I know you'll make our Joel very happy.'

They all drank to Joel and Maryann's health. Nance nudged Maryann.

'My wedding to Mick was quite a big do and look where that got me,' she said quietly. 'You be happy, my girl.'

'I'll do my best,' Maryann said. She thought to herself that if she'd had the finest wedding in the land she couldn't be happier. She laid her hand over Joel's under the table and he smiled and leaned close to kiss her.

Maryann and Nance had a good old chinwag about adjusting to life on the cut, catching up on the past couple of months. After a month apart, when Darius had gone off to earn some money with Fellows, Morton and Clayton and Nance had stayed on the *Esther Jane*, the two of them had got their own Barlow boat and Joel had said he felt strong enough to cope – especially now the boat had an engine.

'I tell yer, Maryann,' Nance said. 'Some nights I'm so tired I'm near falling asleep standing up and I'm dreaming the engine's still going at night even when it ain't.' Maryann nodded her agreement. 'I never knew what work was till I went off with Darius. 'E's 'ad a right go at me a few times when I get things wrong. Still, I learned a lot off Joel when I was still with you so it could be worse. And I tell yer summat, I wouldn't swap it for the world – when yer get up in the morning and look out on the fields all white with frost and the sun coming up – never seen anything like that in my life before.'

'You don't miss the old life then?' Maryann asked.

'Sometimes, when I'm trying to do a wash and get it hung out and moving about in that cabin I curse it and wish I 'ad a house to live in. But then when I think back – when I did 'ave, I've never felt so miserable in all my life.' She looked sober for a moment. 'No. I couldn't go back. I mean I'll 'ave to go back *some time* soon – I've writ me mom, trying to explain. I know I've done Mick wrong and sometimes it weighs heavy on me. But we love each other, me and Darius. I 'ope Mick finds some way of getting on without me – but I wanted a life, Maryann . . .'

Her brown eyes earnestly sought Maryann's, needing reassurance. Maryann patted her hand. ''Course you did.'

'You been back to Brum?'

'I was there only last week. Went to see if Tony and Billy could come down for the wedding but Tony daint seem to think 'e could. And I went to see Amy and her mom.'

'Oh – how are they? What's 'appened to *him*?'

'*He*,' Maryann said, 'is still in hospital. Janet said his face and the top of him's burnt so bad you can scarcely recognize him. She was sort of shuddering as she told me. Said 'e's a terrible sight – it all got infected and it's taking time to heal.'

'Serves the bastard right.'

'She said she daint think he'll find any more young widows with families to charm his way into. Said they'd run away at the sight of him.'

'What about those poor girls of 'ers?'

'She and Amy are just living quietly together. She's taking in some sewing – it's very hard for 'er to get by but they're managing. She says she don't care what she has to do just so long as she can keep Amy safe. Amy seems awright – much more cheerful, though heaven knows – the scars run deep, Nance . . .'

'Poor child. What about Margaret though?'

'Well—' Maryann's face clouded. 'They've still got 'er in the asylum. She ain't right. God alone knows what he did to her. Her mom's worried to death and she visits, but she's that busy trying to make ends meet. She says they can still barely get the kid to say a word.'

Nance made a hissing sound through her teeth and was interrupted before she could say anything by Joel leaning over.

'My dad wants to say summat.'

They all looked at old Darius Bartholomew. Slowly he got to his feet and his stooped figure loomed above them.

'It's a very happy day for us all today,' he began ponderously, then stopped and cleared his throat. 'Turns out I've known the lass what's marrying our Joel since she were a nipper, and a fine young woman she's turned out to be.' He paused and Maryann smiled, blushing with surprise. 'It's a pity today couldn't be the wedding of both my living sons. My Esther Jane, God rest 'er, would've taken both daughters-in-law to 'er heart, even if they was off the bank.' It was Nancy's turn to go red. Darius said no more about her situation. It was a difficult one, but they could all see how she and Darius were together and Nancy, who was sturdy and a good worker on the boat, had been accepted.

'I don't have no finery to give you both on your wedding day, 'cept my blessing. But there is things I'd like to give to you. My working days on the cut're over now and it's no use in thinking they ain't. So . . .' He indicated to his sister to pass up a cloth bag from beside the chair and dipped his hand into it. 'This 'un's for you, Joel.' It was his second windlass, the one he'd had to use all the time after Maryann so shamefully lost the first.

Joel soberly nodded his thanks. Both of them knew what it meant: old Darius was handing over the *Esther Jane* after a lifetime's work.

'And there's summat for you too, missy.' From the bag he drew something black and crumpled, and as he opened it out with his twisted hands, Maryann gasped, seeing the honour that was being conferred on her. It was Esther Jane's black bonnet.

'Oh—' She hesitated then, seeing Joel smiling, took it gingerly from the old man's outstretched hand. 'I – I don't think I deserve this . . .'

'Well—' Darius sank into his seat and picked up his glass. 'Time'll tell. But you're a boatwoman now. A Bartholomew. My Esther was my best mate on the cut through good days and bad. Now it's your turn and Joel's. You look after each other, eh – and you two an' all—' He nodded at Darius and Nance who had tears in her eyes.

They all raised their glasses and Joel turned to Maryann, his face full of love.

'Best mates.'

She clinked her glass against his and kissed him. 'Best mates.'

Joel and Maryann had said their farewells for the moment to the family. Darius and Nance were going straight back to pick up a load and get ahead. Darius said they'd be likely to work the Grand Union next.

'Might not see yer for a bit,' Nance said as she and Maryann hugged each other goodbye. 'We'll get back on the Oxford soon as we can.'

'Try and get to Napton for Christmas!' Joel said.

That evening they moved the *Esther Jane* out away from the town and tied up in a beautiful, isolated spot where fields stretched out all around them and the only thing filling the middle distance were the sharp outlines of winter trees against a white half-moon. They left old Jep snoozing in the cabin and stepped out on to the bank in the moonlight. The cold was so intense it seemed to come down on them like a weight, but the sky was full of stars and they wanted to enjoy the sight of it. Joel put his arm round Maryann and they stood close together in silence for a few moments, looking across the silver fields, hearing the gentle slap of the water against the bank. A bird screeched somewhere in the distance, a high, lonely sound. Maryann shivered and snuggled closer to Joel.

'It's so beautiful,' she said. 'Feels as if there's no one around for miles.'

'Probably ain't.'

She looked up at him, the pale sheen of moonlight on his face. He was filling out gradually and beginning to look like his strong, burly self. She could hear, though, the loud wheezing of his lungs, an utterly comforting sound because it had always been one which accompanied him, but also a worrying sign of his vulnerability. She knew how close to death he had been, the risk that any illnesses meant to him in the damp atmosphere of the cut. She stood on tiptoe and kissed his face, overflowing with love and gratitude. She would treasure every day with him.

He took her in his arms. 'So – what happened to the girl who said she would always be called Maryann Nelson?'

She laughed. 'Fancy you remembering that!'

'You were very strong on it at the time. Funny, scrawny little thing you were.'

'I know – well, thanks for changing my mind. Maryann Bartholomew'll do me well. 'S a funny thing – being married does feel different. Even though we've been living on here – I just feel properly married now, 'stead of "living in sin"!'

'Can't 'ave you living in sin, can we?'

'Even if Nance is.'

'Ah well – what else can they do, eh?'

'And they're happy,' she said.

'And you?'

She hesitated. 'Happier than you know . . . Joel?'

'Umm?'

'I think, in fact I'm sure – I'm expecting.'

'A baby – a little 'un?'

She could hear his excitement and she nodded solemnly.

'Oh,' he said, awed. 'My Maryann. That's lovely, that is.' Suddenly, laughing, he lifted her off the ground. 'Oh love – a little 'un!'

They held each other close.

'Come the summer,' Joel said, kissing her nose, 'we could lie out in the fields of a night . . . no one about.'

'By summer,' she laughed, 'I'll have a belly on me like a barrel!'

'Well – tonight . . .'

'Not tonight, no,' Maryann said firmly, pulling on his hand. 'I'm turning rigid with cold already. Come on – let's go in.'

They took one last look at the star-flecked sky, the friendly land spreading out around them, then, still holding hands, they stepped back into the cosy little cabin.

Epilogue

August 1936

'If it's a girl,' Maryann was saying, 'let's call her Ada.'

'Or Sally,' Joel said. 'After your sister.'

'We'd better have two girls then.' Maryann laughed.

She and Joel were walking out along the road away from Banbury towards Charnwood House, on a boiling August afternoon, ripe wheat stretching away on either side of them, swaying and rustling in the languorous breeze. On Joel's shoulders, his legs jutting forward each side of his father's face was their little son Joel, who had had his first birthday the month before. Maryann, who was four months into another pregnancy, was still looking trim.

'Margaret's a nice name,' she mused. 'Only it feels unlucky – poor little Margaret.'

'And Margaret's – well, she's not dead like our Ada and your Sally, is she?' Joel said carefully.

'Might just as well be, where she is.' Her voice was so hard and bitter, Joel reached out and touched her shoulder and little Joel gave a squeak of panic as his father loosed one of his legs.

Margaret, like Sal, was someone Maryann tried hard never to think about. Such thoughts had great power to make her feel sick with rage and sorrow and as there was nothing she could do, she pushed them away.

There had been plenty else to think about over the past couple of years. Most of her first year on the cut had been spent pregnant and she found it completely exhausting, with the added worry that if she was able to do less Joel would be forced to work even harder and could fall sick again, so however tired or heavy she was feeling she pushed herself on. Little Joel was born slightly early, on the *Esther Jane* with a nurse present, and Maryann had then been faced with the challenge of bringing up a child in the confined space of the boat. It was all right when he was a tiny baby, but as he grew and began to move about she worried constantly for his safety. More and more she heard stories about infants losing their lives on the cut through accidents or sickness and she became acutely protective of him. But he was a steady, sensible little fellow, even as a young toddler, and he had come well through his first year. She longed now for a daughter who would be a companion for him as he grew up.

Every so often they saw Nancy and Darius. Blackie Black had died of a seizure back in the winter of 1935 and Nance had gone home to visit. While she was there she was afraid she'd have to face Mick. Cathleen told her that a few months after Nancy went, Mick had left too, taken off and no one knew where. Cathleen, in her usual placid way, had not made an issue of her daughter's actions and was more concerned that they remain on good terms.

Nance and Darius had had a baby son, who in the family tradition they had called Darius and who must, Maryann calculated, have been conceived on about the first night the two of them were together, a fact which gave Nance enormous satisfaction after the agonies of living with Mick.

Every time they passed through Banbury, Maryann had thought fondly of Charnwood and she said to Joel she'd like to go back and visit. She often remembered them all, especially Mrs Letcombe, and she wondered whether Roland Musson had found the courage to leave and make a life for himself, and whether Miss Pamela was married now. She even wondered about Evan. Up until now though, they'd always been passing through or too busy or tired to make the effort. Today, however, it was the *Esther Jane*'s turn to revisit Tooley's Yard, and the beautiful, sultry day seemed to be calling them out across the fields.

When they turned in at the gate of Charnwood she said, 'Oh – this does feel peculiar. It all looks just the same as it did – only the trees've come on a bit more.'

As they neared the house Joel said, 'My goodness – this is a smart place. Can't think why you ever wanted to leave!'

'I daint, for a long time. But I met Darius, remember? And he told me that *someone* was very poorly in hospital . . .'

'Ah yes.' Joel laughed.

'We'll have to go in the servants' entrance,' Maryann said. They went round the back of the house, with the wistaria sprawling across the back. As she glanced across the garden, Maryann's eye was caught by a figure sitting in a sunny spot near the wall of the rose garden. There was a new bench that had not been there before, and on it sat a figure dressed completely in black.

'That looks like Mrs Musson,' Maryann whispered, frowning. 'The lady of the house. She looks to be in mourning, wouldn't you say? That hat's got net on and everything. I wonder – it could be the anniversary of John's death. That was her oldest son, killed in the war. Or I wonder if Mr Musson . . .'

Someone must have opened the front door as she

spoke because there was a sudden frenzied barking and Freddie the fox terrier tore round towards them, followed at a waddling pace by Lily Langtree, the spaniel who had been quite fat when Maryann was working there and had now expanded into a dog of truly corpulent proportions. Little Joel laughed and pointed at them, but other than sniffing at the visitors' legs and barking loudly the dogs did nothing else except run back round the end of the house.

'Well, they ain't changed.'

Inside, they found that not a huge amount had changed among the servants either. She found Mrs Letcombe, looking exactly the same, seated in her little room, dozing over her knitting in the warm afternoon.

'My dear, it's very nice to see you,' she said, kissing Maryann and greeting both Joels warmly. She loved small children, and took little Joel on to her lap immediately. 'Oh – and this little fellow must have a piece of Cook's best seed cake. Come on now – we'll all have a nice cup of tea. Oh, I am glad things have turned out well for you, Maryann. You left in such a hurry, I was rather afraid that Evan drove you away – he was always more forward than he ought to be.'

They filled in the news of the past two years. Evan and Alice had got married, but were still living and working at Charnwood. Sid the gardener had died unexpectedly – 'His heart, they think,' Mrs Letcombe said as they all sat at the kitchen table with the tea and cake and little Joel tottering around practising his new walking skills. 'Otherwise down here, things are really much the same. It's a settled sort of house. But upstairs—' She rolled her eyes. 'Oh dear me.'

'What's happened?' Maryann said. 'I saw Mrs Musson – all in black.'

'Terrible. Only last month. It was Master Roland. Went off to that war in Spain. Upped and went. Said war was the only thing he knew and if he couldn't make a life here he might as well go back to that. So he went and fought for Franco. He lasted just three weeks.' She shook her head sorrowfully. 'That poor, poor boy.'

'No!' Maryann let the news sink in. She wanted to weep. The image of him roaring through the quiet countryside on his motorcycle came to her, as if nothing of stillness or quietness could satisfy his troubled mind. 'How terrible,' she said. 'Poor Mrs Musson.'

'Nothing'll console her. Two sons gone – there's only Master Hugh left and somehow she doesn't seem to have the same affinity with him. Miss Pamela's married now of course. To a farmer chappie, over near Thame and she seems happy enough.' She turned to Joel. 'And what is it you do for a living?'

When he told her, Mrs Letcombe seemed quite taken aback at first, then she laughed. 'I thought you were looking very brown and sturdy,' she said to Maryann. 'Well – I'd never've put you down as doing that but you look as if it's suiting you.'

'Oh – it is.' She laughed. 'Most days, any'ow!'

They spent a very friendly hour in the kitchen and she kissed Maryann again when they left. 'Come and see us again, won't you? With all your lovely children as they arrive.' She chucked little Joel's cheek as Maryann held him. 'Sorry you didn't see anyone else.'

But Maryann was glad. She hadn't wanted to see Evan or the others especially. As they left she looked down the garden and saw that the bench where Mrs Musson had been sitting was empty, and she was filled with a great sense of poignancy. Handing Joel their son to lift back on to his shoulders she slipped her arm through his. Among so many sad things, so much pain and unhappiness, her own joy seemed miraculous: a hard-won, precariously existing miracle.

'I'm glad I came to see them,' she said as they set off along the road. 'But I don't think I'll want to come again.' She felt oddly lost now, out in the country, without that sinuous line of water to guide her, to show her where she belonged.

'Today is today,' she said to Joel suddenly. He looked down at her, not quite sure what she meant. 'No one can take today away, whatever else happens.'

He did understand. 'No. Let's try and make a good tomorrow too.'

'Come on.' She squeezed his arm affectionately. 'Let's get back to the cut. Let's go home.'